ROCKED BY LOVE

TEREESA L. TUFF

CONTENTS

With tears pooled in the corners of my eyes, I welcome the smile I feel inching across my face as endless memories of you crash to the forefront of my mind. Hands down you were the strongest person I knew, a true epitome of strength.

I am blessed to call you uncle and claim you as my fav. Thank you for showing me what strength looks like and how to fight past my fears.

This one is for you, Joseph "Cadillac" Mosely.

Rest easy Old Man.

~ Your Fav

2015

CHAPTER ONE

*L*ooking at my phone for the third time since I sat down, I debated if I should respond to Emery's message. It had been approximately thirty minutes since the notification flashed across my screen, and I'd done everything but read his text. I checked my email, browsed my social media accounts, I even looked online at my upcoming class schedule. All unnecessary nuances just to avoid reading and replying to his text.

Finally relenting I firmly pressed my thumb against the small circle at the bottom of my phone and watched as my apps filled the screen. Deciding I had nothing better to do, I clicked on my message app and scrolled through my message list. A few seconds ticked by before I clicked on his name. I half-ass read over his long drawn out text while still trying to decide if I had the energy to entertain him. Just as I was about to type in our thread, my phone rang. I glanced at the caller ID. The call wasn't from someone in my contact list but definitely from a number I'd seen before. Curiosity got the best of me, and I decided to answer.

"Hello."

A deep raspy baritone greeted me, "Hey Rocky."

That got my attention. I sat up straight, lifting my back off the

1

cushions of the couch. His voice sounded familiar but not enough for me to recognize who I was speaking with. "Who is this?"

He let out a gruff chortle. "So now you don't know who I am Rocky? I'm offended," he teased.

I still couldn't place his voice, but I knew he sounded sexy as hell. His deep raspy tenor was relaxing and arousing. "Keep talking I'll figure it out."

Again, he released another deep snicker. The kind that sounded like it came from the pit of his stomach and traveled through his system, accidentally escaping from his mouth. Either way it amused me that he found my confusion funny.

"Okay, I'll play along since you're cute." There was a hint of seriousness behind his humorous tone.

This was not how I planned on spending my Friday night but since I've been in college, sometimes it seemed like I forgot what fun felt like. And although I wouldn't necessarily classify this as fun, I was definitely entertained by the mystery caller on the other end of my line.

Since it didn't appear Mr. Raspy planned on just telling me who he was, I continued playing along. "Okay, so you have a set of working eyes, but do you have a name?"

"I have a set of working ears too, and I see you still have a smart-ass mouth." His quick retort was delivered in the same deep tenor, sending a thrill down my spine.

I smacked my lips and couldn't help the giggle that escaped from my mouth. "Welp, some things never change they just get better with time."

I just knew I would be able to pick up on who he was at this point, but I was just as confused now as I was when I answered the phone. However, I had a sense of familiarity with him. Otherwise I would've ended the call a long time ago.

"I can't believe you still don't know who I am." I could hear the smile in his voice. "I'll give you one more clue, so you betta get this shit right."

I couldn't help myself as I continued to sass him. "Or what?"

He didn't take the bait. Instead, I heard him take a deep breath before speaking again. "You ready for your clue, Raquel?"

Hearing him call me by my government name jarred me. Suddenly, recognition set in. "Oh shit! Dre? Or should I say Andre since we're calling people by their government names now."

He laughed, his husky chuckle sounding more familiar now that I knew it was him. "I knew that would jog your memory."

He was right. However, I couldn't believe I didn't catch his voice sooner. Although Dre and I didn't talk on a regular basis, we were more than acquainted with one another. Hell, we practically grew up together. Dre lived on the same street as my identical twin brothers. Frequent visits and countless overnight stays provided me just as much access to Dre as he had with my brothers. Needless to say, the three of them were inseparable growing up. The trio was still tight, but because my brothers were attending school in Atlanta and Dre was here in Cincinnati, they didn't see each other that often. Nevertheless, the distance didn't seem to affect their bond. I was glad, because Lord knew my brothers needed positive male influences in their lives. And from what I knew of Dre growing up, dude was as solid as they came.

Since Dre and I both attended The University of Cincinnati, we would see one another on campus or at local events from time to time, but we didn't hang out. He was my brothers' friend, and we merely knew one other through that association. Dre and the twins are five years my junior so although they were always together when we were growing up, I didn't exactly hang out with them. Outside of my brothers, Dre and I didn't know each other.

I wasn't sure how Dre got my number, but I was curious as hell to know why he was calling. "What's up Dre?"

"I just got off the phone with the twins, and they passed me your number. Royce said you didn't go home for summer break."

I wasn't really sure what that had to do with him but didn't know how to say that without sounding like a bitch, so I attempted humor. "And what, you just thought you would check up on a sistah?"

Dre snickered. "Yeah, something like that. I was tellin the twins how I just got back in town and would be here the remainder of the summer, and they asked me to check up on you. They said somethin about you bein here solo since Carmen went home for break and Egypt — well you know she's the soft one out of the three of y'all."

I laughed to myself at Dre's summation of my two best friends. He was right though. Out of the three of us, Carmen and I were most alike: two carefree, outspoken, hot-tempered self-proclaimed divas ready to pop off whenever needed. Egypt, on the other hand, was as green as they came. She was sweet and the peacemaker of the crew, so I understood my brothers' concern. However, I was a grown ass woman and I didn't need a babysitter, especially not one five years younger than me. It was enough that my dad made me get this damn dog, now the twins were putting Dre on my ass. I swear being the only girl of the family definitely came with some headaches, in my case three of them by the names of Jonathan, Royce, and Ryker Banks.

It wasn't Dre's fault my father and brothers were overprotective of me, so I played nice. "So, what, you gonna babysit me until fall semester when Carm comes back?" My tone was light and playful; however, I was annoyed with the twins for getting in my business.

"C'mon Rocky, I know you're grown and don't need a babysitter, but I did tell my boys I would keep an eye out. So, if you need anything, I don't want you to hesitate to call."

Now ain't that sweet.

"Thanks Dre, I'll keep that in mind, but I think I'll be good." I hoped my annoyance wasn't evident.

"Coo that's all I ask. Lock my number in so we don't have to go through the bull next time I call."

Surprised, I asked, "Wait so this is gonna be a regular occurrence?"

Dre appeared amused. I heard the smile in his voice. "Like I said, I told the twins I would look out for you. So yes, that means me callin or textin to check on you periodically. Besides classes don't start for another week and a half. Let me know if you wanna hang out durin that time."

Whoa, I'm pretty sure that went beyond checking on me, but I didn't say that out loud. Besides, I was so ready to end this conversation so I could cuss the twins out.

4

"Okay."

I think Dre could sense that I was annoyed either that, or he was also over this dry ass conversation as well. "Alright Rocky, talk to you later."

"Bye Dre." I quickly disconnected the call. Slowly dragging the phone away from my ear, I stared at it like it was a foreign object.

What the hell just happened?

Deciding I was too exhausted to deal with my brothers, I opted to call my best friend instead. While waiting for Carmen to answer the phone I hopped off the couch and walked into my small dining area to peer through my wine collection. I selected one of my favorite wines, Cooper's Hawk *Barbera*. Holding my phone against my face with one hand and the bottle of wine in the other, I strolled into the kitchen and placed the bottle on top of the counter before digging through one of my utensil drawers for a wine opener.

I really need to stop being cheap and buy a damn automatic opener.

I paused when I heard my best friend's cheery voice streaming from the other line. "Hey chica, what's good?"

I hit the speaker button and sat the phone on the counter, going back to my search. "Hey boo, you busy?"

"I'm never too busy for my bff. Whatcha doin?"

Finally locating the wine opener, I opened the bottle and poured myself a nice tall glass. With my wine and cellphone in hand I walked back into the living room and plopped down on the sofa, kicking my feet up I rested my heels on the edge of the coffee table. "I ain't doing shit, but you're not gonna believe who I just got off the phone with."

Excitedly she asked, "Who?"

I paused dramatically before answering her. "Dre."

I heard the curiosity in her tone. "Dre who? Don't tell me you're talkin bout the twin's fine ass boy from back home?"

I snickered to myself at Carmen's quick assessment of Dre. "Yes, that Dre."

Carmen gasped. "Do tell. What his fine ass want? Wait, how'd he get your number?"

"He said he got it from the twins. Said somethin about them askin him to check on me since you left me here by myself for the summer," I teased.

Carmen smacked her lips. "Didn't nobody tell your nerdy ass to take summer classes. Besides, you're not alone—E is there."

I giggled at her playful jab. "I'm teasin you, boo. I know E is here, and I also know you're just a phone call away. I guess that's not enough for the twins tho. So now, I have Dre on my ass."

"If I had to have someone on my ass, I would definitely choose fine ass Andre Cameron," she sang.

Carmen was right. Dre was fine as hell, but she was missing the point. I didn't need nobody watching me. "Carm, I don't need a babysitter. I can look out for myself. Hell, I've been doin it for a while now."

"Excuse me?" she implored defensively.

Now it was my turn to smack my lips. "You know what I mean, Carm."

Her lighthearted chuckle filled the air. "I'm messin with you, chica but seriously, it doesn't sound like a big deal. Dre can check on my ass anytime."

Carmen was crazy, but she wasn't alone in her reverence of Dre's good looks. Almost all the chicks on campus were fans of Andre Cameron. I'm sure it didn't hurt that Dre was the star wide receiver on our football team. However, football or not, Dre had a thing about him. Yes, Dre was easy on the eye, but more than that, there was something about the way he carried himself. Like moths to flame, chicks constantly flocked to his ass. I can recall on more than one occasion being approached by some thirst bucket after being seen talking with him. So, in retrospect, I could have far worse problems.

I decided to stop complaining about my brothers putting Dre on babysitting duty and switched topics. "What was yo hot ass doin before I called?"

Carmen cleared her throat. "Since you asked, I was gettin ready to meet my cousins and Naomi for drinks. What you up to?"

"Girl, not a damn thing. I'm bored and I miss you," I whined.

"I know you cleared most of your startin lineup before school ended, but damn girl, you ain't got nobody to entertain yo ass?"

My mind drifted to Emery's text and I rolled my eyes. "Emery texted before Dre called, but I don't know if I feel like being bothered with him." I knew that probably sounded mean, but it was the truth.

"Now that's a name I haven't heard you mention in a while."

"That's because ain't shit to mention." I took a sip of my wine and sat the glass back on the table. "Seriously Carm, I'm so lame. What twenty-seven-year-old you know sits home alone on a Friday night?" I was whining again.

"Girl you're home alone by choice."

"Not helpin Carm."

"What you want me to say, it's the truth. You stay talkin shit about Emery, but you keep his ass on your team—ridin the pine, but he's still on the team. Hell, if you don't want to be bothered with him, you could always call Dre."

Picking up my glass, I took a big swig of my spirit, relishing the balmy sensation as it traveled down my throat. "I see you got jokes." I chuckled. "Emery is cool, so I can't cut him off completely, but you know we got history."

"I know I hear you talkin, but I ain't listenin. You keep that boy tucked in your back pocket for a reason," she stated plainly.

"Whateva heffa." I snickered at Carmen's no-nonsense breakdown of my perceived problem. "Alright girl, imma let you go. Just wanted to share and I needed the distraction."

"Love you chica. Call me if you need me."

"Thanks boo. Have fun and be safe. I love you too." I made a kissy sound with my mouth before disconnecting our call.

Dropping my phone on the couch beside me, I looked at Creed, my beefy pocket American bully, and shook my head. My conversations with Carmen and Dre had my mind spinning. Not really sure what to do about either, I slowly withdrew my feet from the coffee table and peeled myself off the couch. Creed responded to my movements, lifting himself off the floor while peering up at me he wiggled his tail excitedly. That was my cue. With my glass tucked close to my chest, I walked over to my patio door and let my furry friend outside so he could handle his business. Leaning against the doorframe, I looked off into the distance while carefully pulling my glass from my bosom. I felt a sense of nervous energy I couldn't shake as I took a hearty sip of my wine and rolled my eyes up in my head.

I really need to get a life.

The sound of Creed's collar drew my attention back to the door where he sat on the other side resting on his hind legs, letting me know he was finished. I took my time backing out of the way as he lazily ambled by. Tilting his head back, he looked at me like I was in his way as he continued trekking back into the living room with me following behind on his beefy heels.

I plopped down on the couch and switched my glass for my phone. After unlocking it, I went into my call history and stared down at the last call. My fingers hovered above the number before finally programming Dre into my contacts. Resting my body against the back of the couch, I sank into the soft cushions and contemplated my next move. Through squinted lids, I stared at the newly programmed name in my phone as Carmen's words played in the back of mind. Immediately, I leaned forward again, snatching my glass off the table I put it to my mouth only to realize it was empty. Irritation coursed through my body as I tossed my phone on the couch and walked into the kitchen to refill my empty glass. I sat the decorative goblet on the kitchen counter and reached for the wine bottle when I heard my phone chirp.

Placing the bottle of wine back on the counter, I walked into the living room and retrieved my phone. On the home screen I saw I had a text notification from Dre. Surprised, I immediately unlocked my phone and went into my text app and clicked on his message.

Dre: Hey Rocky, I hope I didn't mess up your night with my call. I gave the twins my word and just wanted to make sure you were good. I promise not to be a bugaboo.

How cute, he's concerned.

Me: It's no biggie Dre. My problem ain't with you, it's with my meddling ass brothers. We good. Thx for chk'n tho <winking face emoji>.

Not really sure if that was the end of our conversation, I kept my phone in my hand as I strolled back into the kitchen and resumed my place at the counter. I was quick about my business—placing my phone down then plucking my glass from the counter, I picked up the open bottle of wine and started refilling my glass. Halfway into my generous pour, my phone chirped again. Balancing my glass in one hand, I carefully rested the bottle in the crook of my arm then slid my phone toward me. A quick glance at the screen showed a text notification from Dre. I quickly pressed my thumb on the home button and waited, my phone opened to our message thread.

Dre: Damn girl, I wasn't expecting such a speedy response. I figured you would be busy on this beautiful Friday evening.

If only he knew.

I giggled to myself as I sat my glass down and picked my phone up from the counter. Careful not to tip the bottle resting in my arm I responded to Dre's text.

Me: If you thought I was busy then why you text <winking face with tongue out emoji>? I'm teasing. My ass is home bored out of mind right now. What, no hot date for UC's star wide receiver?

I tucked my phone inside the cuff of my bra before picking up my glass and taking a nice gulp of my libation. *Umm.* Gently pulling my glass away from my mouth, I carefully removed the bottle from the crook of my arm and topped off my drink before placing the bottle back on the counter and corking the top. Turning on my heels, I exited the kitchen and leisurely strolled back into the living room. Before I could sit my glass on the table, my notification chirped again. I was judicious with my movements, ensuring I didn't spill a single drop of my cocktail as I sat on the couch with both legs folded underneath me. Leaning forward, I placed my glass on the table and retrieved my phone from my bra. Tickled, but not really surprised, I clicked on Dre's message.

Dre: Such a smart ass. Lol. Nah, no plans for me tonight. Normally Jamison & I would hit some night spot, but he took the summer off. He's back in Kentucky until autumn semester starts.

Me: Oh, okay but I was referring to company of the female persuasion.

Dre: I'm not sure what you've heard about me, but I don't entertain just anybody. A man of my caliber must be selective you know <winking face emoji>.

Me: Is that right? And what caliber is that sir? For the record, I haven't heard anything. I make it my business not to get into other people's business.

Dre: Yeah okay.

I picked up my glass and sipped my wine, savoring its delicious flavor. Red wine was truly my favorite. I loved a good full-bodied, dry, crisp wine with a spicy finish. I sat my glass down and picked up my phone. I was just about to reply to Dre when my phone chirped.

Dre: I can show you better than I can tell you.

Whoa!! What the hell was that supposed to mean?

There was no silly emoji, no lol, or lmao, just a matter-of-fact statement.

Me: <Big eye emoji>

Dre: How else do you show someone something Rocky? I let you get to know me. I know we know each other but we don't KNOW each other.

A sudden unexplained feeling of disappointment washed over me, but I quickly dismissed it and reached for my glass when my phone chirped in my hand. I took a hurried nip of my cocktail and sat my glass back down.

Dre: We can start tonight. Wanna hang out?

I damn near choked on my drink. I definitely wasn't expecting that. Dropping my phone in my lap, I bumped my fist against my chest until I was able to catch my breath. Slowly, I gathered my phone from between my legs and hit Dre back.

Me: Sure, what you got in mind?

Dre: You shoot pool or bowl?

I wasn't really sure why I was entertaining this. Maybe it was the fact that I was bored or because I knew Dre was good people. Either way, I ignored everything in my head telling me to sit my hot ass down while snickering as my fingers busied themselves on the tiny keyboard.

Me: I do both, but I must warn you, I'm competitive and don't like sore losers.

I picked up my glass and polished off the reminder of my wine.

Dre: That's coo because I don't plan on losing. Don't think I'll go easy on you just b/c you're my boys' sister. Bowling or pool?

Me: Surprise me. I'm decent at both.

Dre: Coo. How long do you need to get ready?

Shit, I didn't consider my appearance when I agreed to hang out or whatever this was. I quickly hopped off the couch and sprinted down the hall with my phone in hand. I headed straight for the full-length mirror in my bedroom. Shaking my head at the pitiful image starting back at me, I surmised I needed about thirty minutes to make myself presentable. I hit the home button on my phone and waited for the apps to load. A few seconds later I was staring at our message thread.

Me: Umm, like 30mins. Is that cool?

Dre: That means 45mins to an hour, lol. Text me your address and I'll pick you up in an hour.

Generally, as a rule I never let dudes I didn't know, know where I laid my head, but Dre wasn't exactly a stranger. With a little hesitation I texted him my address, sat my phone on the dresser, and proceeded to get ready.

Forty minutes later, I was back in front of my full-length mirror examining myself. My hair was pulled on top of my head in an unruly curly bun. Since this wasn't an actual date, I dressed casually in a pair of crisp black distressed denim jeans tapered at the ends paired with a black Victoria Secret bling UC sweatshirt and a pair of black low top Chucks. I wore minimum makeup, just a hint of shimmer blush, black eyeliner, and my favorite matte red lipstick.

I continued staring at my reflection, debating whether to pull my septum piercing down and if I should switch out my nose ring. I decided to leave the hoop nose ring in but pulled my septum down. It felt appropriate for the look I was rocking. Backing away from the mirror, I glanced at a small clock on my nightstand as I passed. At just a little under an hour, I'd managed to pull together a comfy but cute look.

"Not too bad, Miss Banks," I praised out loud, while grabbing my phone off the dresser before confidently sauntering out my bedroom.

I returned to the living room just in time to hear the doorbell sound, sending my protective canine into a barking frenzy as he charged toward the door. I instructed Creed to be quiet while making my way to the door as I pushed past his burly frame. "Who is it?"

"It's Dre." The bass in his raspy tenor made my spine tingle.

I swear that man's voice could talk the panties off a nun.

I opened the door and dropped my hand. Aiming my palm toward Creed, I held it slightly out from my side, letting him know to stay. Creed didn't move and neither did Dre. My eyes shifted away from Creed toward the door where Dre stood on the other side bouncing his gaze between me and my intimidating looking pet.

I giggled while looking back at Creed to ensure he hadn't moved. "He's not as scary as he looks," I reasoned, bringing my eyes back to Dre.

Dre looked uneasy, but his face held a tight smile. "Easy killer. I'm not here to hurt your mommy."

I stepped away from the door so Dre could enter. Instinctively my eyes slid down to Creed. True to his protective nature, he was planted at my feet, his large head aimed toward Dre as he growled incessantly. I dropped down on my haunches and rubbed his head. It only took a few seconds for him to quiet and melt underneath my caressing touch. Sliding my hand down his massive skull, I grabbed him by the collar and looked up at Dre.

"Come closer, let him smell you."

Dre didn't move. Barely inside the doorway, he looked again from Creed back to me. "Smell me?"

I chuckled at his attempt to be cool when it was clearly evident, he was uncomfortable. "Yes, smell you. I promise I won't let him bite you."

Diffidently, Dre eased over to Creed. Reflexively he responded to Dre's movements, Creed bucked against his collar, forcing me to tighten my grip. When he stilled his movements, I used my free hand to gently brush his fur.

"Good boy. This is Dre, he's mommy's friend." I remained posted at Creed's side, stroking his head while he sniffed Dre.

After a few intrusive whiffs of Dre's lower limbs, Creed swung his head in my direction. He was done. He no longer considered Dre a threat. Comfortable with the shift in his disposition, I released Creed's collar and stood to my feet while instructing him to go lay down.

I watched as my gargantuan dog ambled into the living room and dramatically plopped down on his bed before casting my eyes back on Dre. "You good?" I had to ask because he still looked a little spooked.

"Yeah I'm good, but you could've warned a nigga before I got here.

"My bad, I wasn't thinkin. He's harmless unless you comin to hurt me. I'm surprised the twins didn't tell you about him seein as he was my dad and their idea."

Dre rubbed the back of his neck. "Nah, they never mentioned you had a killer for a roommate. What in the hell possessed you to get a pitbull for a pet anyway? I thought chicks liked lil foo foo ass dogs."

I smacked my lips. "Creed is not a pitbull, he's a pocket-size American bully. And trust me he wasn't exactly my idea. However, he was part of the agreement."

Dre hiked a brow. "Agreement?"

"Yeah, when I finally moved off campus, my daddy wanted to get me a gun, but I refused. So, he said if I wouldn't get a gun, I had to get a dog and not a . . ." Hoisting my hands in the air, I made air quotes with my index and pointer fingers, ". . . punk ass dog but one that would protect his baby girl. So, the twins helped me pick him out. We've been thick as thieves ever since."

I couldn't help the chuckle that escaped from my lips when I looked at the expression on Dre's face as he stared at Creed. I thought my explanation went over his head until his eyes shifted back to me. "I guess that makes sense."

"It was a compromise." I didn't have much else to offer, I was too busy trying to keep from laughing. Just that quick, Dre's attention was back on Creed.

"Un hun. Aye, you ready? Dude is over there lookin at me like I'm a fuckin pork chop." A nervous chortle spilled from his mouth as he ran his hand across the back of his neck again.

"Yeah let me grab my stuff."

About two weeks shy of May, the weather hadn't quite evened out. However, I felt pretty comfortable in my sweater, so I opted not to wear a jacket. I stepped to the right of Dre and grabbed my wristlet and keys off the console table next to the door before looking back at Creed. "Be a good boy."

I followed Dre out of my apartment, pulling the door shut behind us. I secured the deadbolt my father had installed after I moved in then hooked my keys onto my wristlet. I turned toward Dre, observing his attire for the first time since his arrival. Dre was also dressed casually in a pair of fitted black jeans with two big holes in the knees, a black UC hoodie, and a pair of black and red Nike Air Max 95's.

Damn he looks good and I be damn, we match.

Not sure if he peeped our matching outfits, I decided to tease him about it. "What part of the game is this? We look like twins."

Dre smirked at me as his eyes roved over my body. I watched as his amused gaze landed on my feet and slowly traveled up my body, stopping once he reached my face. "Twins? Nah, baby girl we look like a fly ass couple."

A wide grin tugged at the corners of my lips as I watched Dre pull his cell phone from his pants pocket. He opened his camera app and stepped to the left of me. Although we weren't touching, he was close enough for us to get a good shot and not look like strangers.

Stretching one of his long arms in the air he tilted his head toward me before speaking again. "We have to capture this shit. Say cheese."

Dre snapped about seven different pictures while we assumed various faces and positions for each one. Once we finished our mini photoshoot, he placed his phone back in his pocket and looked down at me, "You ready Short Stuff?"

Not bothering to hide the colossal size smile splayed across my face, I shook my head. Dre and I walked silently out of the building with me trailing behind him. Once we entered the parking lot, he directed me to his vehicle, a black Ford F-150.

Should've figured, a big ass truck for a big ass man.

Dre pulled his keys from his pocket and unlocked the doors with his keyless remote. I reached for the passenger door but stopped when I felt Dre's hand on mine. I looked over my right shoulder to find Dre shaking his head at me.

"Aye, what are you doing?" he asked, his bushy brows furrowed, and a slight grimace was set on his handsome face.

I dropped my hand from the door handle and turned my entire body toward him. "I thought I was gettin in the car."

Dre placed his big hands on my waist and gently moved me to the side. "I'm not sure what clowns you typically go out with, but whenever you're with me know that I will always open your door."

I nodded my understanding as Dre flung the door open and stood off to the side so I could climb inside.

Cute and chivalrous . . . I'm impressed.

Dre's truck was huge and not equipped with the foot railing I was accustomed to seeing on trucks this size. I placed my right hand on the inside of the passenger door, hiked my left leg and quickly put it back down. *Shit, how am I'm going to get in this truck without looking stupid?* I raised my left leg again, placing it on the inside of the truck I attempted to boost myself up but got nowhere. I heard Dre chuckle behind me as I struggled to lift myself into the passenger seat. On my second unsuccessful attempt, I felt Dre's hands on my waist again. Without saying a word, he hoisted me into the truck with little effort then stood by the door. He waited for me to bring both my legs inside then softly pushed the door closed.

I watched as Dre walked around the front of the truck and approached the driver's side of the vehicle. After easing inside and pulling his door shut, he turned toward me. "You ready Short Stuff?"

I nodded my head. Dre mimicked my head gesture while sweeping his head forward and buckling his seatbelt as he started the engine. A loud roaring sound emitted from the back of the truck. Startled, I damn near jumped out of my seat.

With a smirk on his face, Dre placed his right hand on my knee. "Relax Rocky, it's just the exhaust."

I shrugged my shoulders in embarrassment as I sank back against the seat. "Does it do that every time you start it?"

Dre put the car in gear and turned to look at me. "It better, I paid for it." I could hear the mirth in his voice.

"Why?"

"I thought it sounded coo. You don't like it?"

"It's cool, I guess. I just wasn't expecting it."

Facing forward again, Dre nodded his head. "You'll get used to it. What kind of music you wanna hear?"

"Ummm, rap is fine."

Dre hit some buttons on the center console, and a popular Drake song began blasting throughout the truck. Focused on the road, Dre coasted us out of the parking lot while I bobbed my head to the beat and listened as he rapped along to the lyrics. I was surprised when the hook began, and Dre sang alone.

Damn, dude has pipes. Who knew? I guess I shouldn't be surprised. With a speaking voice like his, it was no wonder he could sing.

I reached over and tapped Dre on his meaty thigh. He gave me a quick glance before reaching up and turning the music down. "What's up, Short Stuff?"

"I didn't know you could sing." My surprise was evident by my elevated tone.

A rosy hue tinted his sun-kissed skin. "Thank you. There's a lot you don't know about me, but we'll fix that."

I bit down on my bottom lip as I absorbed the meaning behind his words while purposely staring out the front window. In my peripheral, I saw a semblance of a smile on Dre's face as he reached onto the console and cut the music back up. We'd just made it out of my neighborhood when the track switched. The song was a slower tempo, but Dre didn't miss a beat. Just like before, he sang and rapped each verse. Captivated by his sultry tenor, I slowly turned my head, sneaking a peek at the man I had a feeling was going to do more than just check in on me from time to time.

Dre must have felt my gaze. Paying me a quick glance, a sly grin eased across his face. "What's up Short Stuff? You good?"

Quickly snapping my head forward, I released my lip from between my teeth. "Yeah I'm good," I mumbled, embarrassed he caught me gawking at him.

The reverberation of Dre's chuckle resounded over the music. The corners of my mouth settled into a soft grin as I pulled my left leg off the floor of the truck and tucked it underneath me. I relaxed in my seat as Dre merged onto 75 N. The expressway was slightly crowded, atypical for a Friday evening. *I wonder if there's an event tonight that my corny ass don't know about.* Slightly annoyed with my lack of knowledge regarding social events, I shook my head to myself as Dre navigated effortlessly through the semi-congested traffic.

Coasting the large truck into the left lane, I felt when he accelerated his speed. I nervously dug my nails into the leather cushion of my seat as I tried not to think about how fast he was going. Cars disappeared behind us, appearing smaller in the distance as Dre sped passed them. Between the music and him concentrating on the road, Dre was completely oblivious to my anxious state. Dre looked the opposite of what I was feeling. His posture was relaxed, leaned back in his seat with one hand gripping the steering wheel his head moved rhythmically to the beat of the music as the lyrics to each song flowed from his mouth. *I swear I could get lost just listening to him talk. His voice is sexy as hell.* Completely enamored by the sound of his voice, I allowed myself to loosen up. Forty minutes later, we arrived at our destination, Dave and Buster's.

*D*re and I had a blast at Dave and Buster's. We played like two big ass kids. I found out he is just as competitive as I was and tons of fun. He beat me in some arcade games, skeeball, basketball, and two rounds of bowling. But I spanked his ass in two games of pool, one game of bowling and a few arcade games as well. To my surprise he took each loss on the chin. However, that didn't keep him from talking cash money shit the entire time. I was glad I agreed to hang out with him tonight. It definitely beat what I was doing before his invitation.

At damn near two in the morning, Dre and I were finally heading back to my apartment. Once again, we found ourselves riding in silence while letting the vibrations of the radio fill the truck. Burnt out on the loud bass of another rap song, I slid my head in Dre's direction and placed a hand on his leg.

"What's wrong?" One of his full brows stretched high on his forehead.

I shook my head. "Nothing is wrong. I just wanted to know if you had any R&B?"

Dre relaxed his face. "Current or old school?"

"Surprise me."

Without missing a beat, he reached onto the center console and quickly changed the station. I was surprised when I heard Jagged Edge crooning through the speakers. And to my absolute delight, Dre started singing along.

"Now I know how you get all the ladies. With a voice like that I bet the panties just melt right off your fans." My tone was teasing, but part of me was dead ass serious.

Dre looked over at me with a smile in his eyes before returning his attention back to the road. "Actually, most women I entertain have no idea I can sing."

"What, you're kidding right?" I asked, totally surprised.

An amused chortle spilled from his slightly parted lips. "Facts. I'm not shy, but I'm protective of my gifts and who I expose them to." Dre glanced in my direction and winked at me.

"Damn, that was deep." My voice was low, barely above a whisper.

Dre had definitely impressed me tonight. Not that I thought he was trying.

Dre didn't respond. Instead, he acknowledged my comment with a coy grin while hitting a high note, matching the harmony of the R&B

quartet like he was a part of the group. I couldn't help but smile as I allowed my eyes to drift shut while resting my head against the seat rest. Amazed by Dre's unique vocal range, my shoulders relaxed in my seat while his velvety chords nearly serenaded me to sleep.

I wasn't sure how long we'd been driving when I realized we were no longer moving. Curious to know why we stopped I fluttered my lids open just as Dre was exiting the truck. I watched as he gently closed the door and s*hit, shit, shit!* A set of beautifully colored eyes peered at me as he propped an elbow up against the door. Embarrassed he caught me staring again, I slid my eyes down his face, stopping at his full lips. Slithering his tongue out of his mouth, he swiped it across his lips before pulling one side of his bottom lip in between his perfectly aligned teeth.

Damn, his young ass is fine as hell.

Unsure of what to make of his flirtatious gesture, I kept my expression neutral while allowing my eyes to drift back up to his. I noticed when he released his lip from between his teeth. A wide smile spread across his face, and a soft snicker spilled out of his mouth. Reflexively the corners of my lips twitched into a mimicking smirk as I fought to maintain eye contact.

A few seconds ticked by without either of us speaking before he pushed off the ledge of the door. Lazily peeling his eyes away from mine he slowly turning away from the window and headed toward the back of the truck. In one swift motion, I stretched my neck toward the rear of the truck and stared out the back passenger side window. Dre stood with his back to me, facing the gas pump. I used his position to my advantage. My eyes swept down his rugged frame, admiring the way his clothes clung to his muscular body. Trapezius, infraspinatus, and rhomboid muscles poked through the material of his cotton shirt while his beefy thighs looked like they were going to rip his fitted jeans. I allowed myself a few minutes of ogling before swinging my neck forward and staring out the front window.

Consumed with my thoughts, I damn near jumped out of my skin at the three loud raps against the glass. I rolled down the window and turned to face an amused Dre. "Yes?"

19

"You need anything from inside before we pull off?"

I nodded my head then watched Dre causally stroll back to the driver's side of the truck. A copious grin was splayed across his face as he settled inside and placed the truck in gear before pulling off. Quickly resuming what had now become our ritual, Dre immediately started singing along to the music while I listened in awe. He was in his own world concentrating on the road, and I was completely entranced by his voice.

Feeling the effects of the cocktails I consumed while gaming earlier, I stared at him, admiring his handsome features. My attention was directed at the source of my enjoyment in the moment: his mouth. I licked my lips as I concentrated on his thick, moist lips.

Ummm, I wonder what his lips would feel like on mine.

I shook my head while quickly dismissing that thought as I continued studying his handsome face. Dre's skin was smooth and blemish-free. A full mustache rested above a simple goatee that aligned perfectly around his beautiful lips. Below his bottom lip was a small, neat, dark patch of hair. His bushy eyebrows were the same color as his facial hair and sat smoothly on his diamond-shaped face emphasized by his defined jawline. His hair was the color of coal, cut low in a Caesar haircut. Although he always wore his hair low, there was no hiding its thick, curly texture, indicative of his mixed race. His sun-kissed skin tone was accentuated by his exotic eyes, hazel with specks of green. Low, oval-shaped eyes sat perfectly symmetrical to his small nose.

As if he could feel me staring, Dre turned and looked at me. An impassive expression was crest upon his face but there was a hint of a smile that reached his eyes. Flashing my dimples, I let a soft grin settle on my lips before quickly shifting my head forward. *Damn, I really hope he didn't catch me staring again.* Dre didn't utter a word. Instead the corners of his full lips twisted into a knowing smile as he focused his attention back on the road, filling the silence between us with a throaty rendition of an old Usher track. Relishing in the beauty of his voice, I concentrated hard as hell not to resume staring at him.

Consumed with my thoughts—mostly about the muscular, high

yellow man with the voice of an angel sitting next to me—I hadn't realized we were parked in front of my apartment building until Dre cut the engine and the music, along with his velvety voice, no longer resonated throughout the truck. Fluttering my lashes more times than necessary, I shook off my haze before unbuckling my seatbelt and shifting my weight to one side while allowing my gaze to land on Dre.

"Alright Short Stuff let's get you in the house so you can get your beauty rest. I've kept you out long enough." He winked at me while snatching his keys out the ignition and cupping them in his large hand.

I acknowledged his words with a simple head nod while read-justing myself in the seat and reaching for the door handle. From my peripheral I caught a glimpse of his flustered gaze. Instantly Dre's words sounded in my head, prompting me to pull my hand back and rest it in my lap. I could see an appreciative smirk settle on his face before a dry chortle spilled from his mouth as he exited the truck.

Just like at the gas station, I followed Dre with my eyes, watching his casual steps through my lashes until he rounded the bumper. A few moments later, my door swung open and the cool mid-spring breeze dusted over my skin, sending a light shiver down my spine. I shook off the chill. I turned to look at Dre, accepting his outstretched hand I allowed him to help me climb out the oversized truck.

"Thank you." I fluttered my lashes and let the smile I was trying to mask ease onto my face while shifting my gaze toward the ground.

Over my head I heard Dre snicker. "You're welcome Short Stuff but you don't have to thank me for something I'm supposed to do."

I guess chivalry isn't dead. I could get used to this.

The subtle sound of a chirp caught my attention. I looked up to find Dre dropping the key fob inside the pocket of his jeans then reach for my hand. I didn't move. Instead I looked from his hand to mine as he intertwined his fingers with mine. No words were spoken between us as he gently nudged my hand, prompting me to walk. That was my cue. Silently willing my feet to move I ignored the slight tingle coursing throughout my entire body. There was little space between us, Dre held our arms out in front of us while keeping me tucked close at his side as we took our time walking the short distance to my apartment.

I was dog tired, but I wasn't ready for the night to end. I tried to recall the last time I had this much fun hanging out with someone of the opposite sex but kept coming up blank. Carmen was right, I had cleared my starting lineup, so it had been a while since I'd been on a date. Granted this wasn't exactly a date, but I couldn't shake the feeling that it was more than old acquaintances getting to know one another.

Dre and I approached my door. I was slow to disconnect our hands before unhooking my keys from my wristlet and turning to face him. "I guess this is goodnight, Mr. Cameron. Thanks for tonight. I had a blast."

With his eyes locked on mine, Dre swiped his tongue across his lips. "Goodnight Short Stuff. Thanks for allowing me to take you out. I had a good time as well even though you beat my ass in more games than I expected."

Smiling, I tore my eyes away from his mouth, lazily skirting them up to his. His beautifully colored irises were lower than usual and his gaze intense. Decisively, he slid his exotic hazels down to my lips. A cunning smile rested on his handsome face as his eyes returned to mine. I tried deciphering the look in his eyes as he stood peering down at me. Dre took a step forward closing what little space there was between us, leaning his body into mine he placed a feather soft kiss on my forehead.

Dre shuffled back. Just barely out of my personal space, he looked down at me. "Go inside, Short Stuff. I'll leave once I hear the deadbolt click."

I did as he said, languorously turning toward the door I unlocked it and walked inside my dimly lit apartment. "Good night." I'd spun back around to face Dre, holding the door open with my hip while allowing my arms to drape at my side.

A soft smile was splayed across his face. "Good night Short Stuff." He took a step back and saluted me with a gentle nod of his head.

I paid him a final hurried glance then slowly eased the door closed and locked both locks. My head fell forward, resting against the door. My heavy lids drifted shut as images of Dre flashed through my mind.

I envisioned every detail of his face I'd studied earlier. I thought about his soft colored orbs, sultry penetrative gaze, and defined jawline. Grinning I could see his beautiful cinematic smile while my tongue drifted across my lips as I pictured his athletic physique. Andre Cameron was definitely fine and tonight I learned there was more to him than just his looks.

Shaking off the vivid images of the man who unexpectedly blew into my secluded world, I fluttered my lids open and peeled my head off the door. I spun around on my heels and kicked off my shoes—exhaustion hit me all of a sudden. I didn't even bother untying my sneakers. I just shuffled out of them and kicked them off to the side before stepping away from the door.

A thousand thoughts ran through my tired brain as I tried making sense of what I was feeling. I walked lazily into the living room to let my dog outside. Thankfully Creed was expeditious in handling his business, trotting back up to the door just minutes after I'd let him out. I waited until he was inside before securing the lock and heading down the hall toward my bedroom. Again, my thoughts turned to Dre. He had been a fortuitous surprise, and I didn't know what to think about his sudden presence in my life, especially since something told me tonight was a first of many more to come.

Goddamn twins and their meddling asses.

Walking into my dimly lit room, I pulled my cellphone out of my wristlet, tossed the small bag onto the dresser, then sauntered over to my bed. I plopped down on top of my comforter and fingered around my nightstand, feeling for my remote. Picking up the small device, I clicked on the TV and dropped the remote somewhere on the bed. I had no intentions of watching TV but needed the noise to fall asleep.

Sitting my phone beside me, I quickly removed my clothes and chucked them on the floor, leaving me in nothing but my panties and bra. I rolled down the straps of my bra, setting my arms free. Twisting the back so that it laid across my belly I quickly unhooked the clasps and tossed it on the floor with the rest of my discarded items. I didn't have much in way of the breast department, but if felt amazing to let my small A cups free. Comfortable and beyond fatigued, I scrambled underneath the covers and snatched my phone off the mattress. Pressing my thumb against the home key I waited for my apps to load before going into my messaging app. I scrolled down to my best friend's name and sent Carmen a message.

Me: I want to fuck him.

CHAPTER TWO

*I*t had been a week since Rocky and I hung out, and I'd be lying if I said I wasn't a little disappointed I hadn't heard from her since then. I could've called or texted her, but true to my word I refused to be a bugaboo. Besides, I knew my initial call took her by surprise just like I was sure my invitation to hang out threw her for a loop. Facts not lost on me as I twiddled with my phone, contemplating if I should call her or continue to wait it out. I choose the latter.

Instead of continuing to brood over it, I decided to return Payton's call to see what she was into. As expected, Payton gave me shit for taking so long to call her back, but she was more than excited to hear from me. Something made clear during the first fifteen minutes as we played catch up before making plans to hook up in an hour at Bengals, a nightclub owned by Terence Francis of the Cincinnati Bengals. Thirty minutes later after ending our call, I was dressed and headed out the door.

Inside my truck, I started the engine and immediately began laughing. Images of Rocky jumping out of her seat at the roar of the exhaust flashed through my mind. A startled expression adorned her pretty face, that is, until she discovered my eyes on her. I'd almost forgotten how tough she was but was quickly reminded when she wasted no time fixing her face. Damn, I couldn't stop thinking about her little ass.

I wonder what she's doing tonight.

That thought had me reaching in my pocket and pulling out my phone. Fiddling with it inside my hand, I found myself contemplating whether to call or shoot her a text. Both options made me feel like a bitch, but I couldn't stop thinking about her. Against my better judgment, I sent her a text.

Me: Hey Short Stuff, just wanted 2 say hi. Hope you're enjoying your evening.

My head shook atop my shoulders as I sat my phone inside one of the cupholders and shifted my truck in gear. Twenty minutes later I pulled up to Bengals and it was packed. Bengals was a relatively new night spot in downtown Cincinnati and was highly popular, so I wasn't surprised it was crowded.

I circled the block three times before finding a parking space large enough to accommodate my truck. Shutting off the engine, I snatched my phone out of the cupholder and eased out the truck. I pressed the wireless remote to lock my doors then looked down at my phone for any missed calls or text notifications; there were none. Dropping my keys and phone inside the pocket of my jeans I started the lengthy walk to the club.

As I neared the door, I could see the line had died down. Grateful that I didn't have a long wait, I entered the club and headed straight to the bar. It was congested as hell, so I decided to hang back and text Payton to see if she had arrived. In the midst of pulling my phone out of my pocket, I felt a light touch on my shoulder. I turned around and stood damn near face-to-face with a tall light-skinned woman. A gargantuan smile stretched up to her eyes adorning her pretty face as she swayed lightly to the beat of the music while staring at me. Her energy was contagious, causing my cheeks to hike up my face and expose my teeth.

"Damn Dre, can I get a hug or are you gonna just stand there smilin at me?" I read from her lips because I could hardly hear her over the music.

"My bad." Sliding my phone back into my pocket, I pulled Payton into a tight hug.

Payton and I met a year ago at a local barbershop I patronized while in school. Payton was the only female barber at Bladez, and baby girl was slick with her clippers. Her chair sat across from my barber, Tony, and every time I was in getting cleaned up, she flirted with me. One day when I was leaving the shop, she followed me out to my truck and told me she was interested in me. I liked her vibe, so we exchanged numbers. Payton was cute. She had a good sense of humor and was all around cool people. So, from time to time we hung out. I knew she wanted more from me, but I was honest from the gate when I told her I wasn't looking for anything more than casual friendship. My main focus was school and football. My life didn't allow for much more than that and Payton understood; albeit disappointed, she respected my position.

Payton was still giggling when I released her, causing a chuckle to spill from my own lips before I lowered my mouth to her ear. "You want a drink?"

Payton still hadn't stopped smiling but managed to reply with a simple nod of her head.

"Let me guess, your skinny girl drink?" My face contorted into a half scowl just thinking about that nasty shit.

"Stop makin that face. You can't knock what you ain't tried Dre."

"Yeah okay. I'll just have to take your word for it cuz I'll never drink that shit."

"You don't know what you're missin," she teased, playfully sticking her tongue out at me.

I waved a hand at her dismissively while snickering at the goofy grin on her face. "Tito's with club soda and a lime, right?"

I didn't bother waiting on her response, I knew what she drank. I stepped away from her, carefully maneuvering my way up to the front of the bar as the group of ladies in front of me walked off. I made eye contact with one of the female bartenders and waited for her to approach before shouting off my order. Minutes later, I was walking back toward Payton with our drinks in hand. I handed Payton her cocktail and took a big gulp of mine, enjoying the warm sensation as the alcohol traveled down my throat.

"Thank you." Payton held her glass out in front of her face.

I winked at her while taking another swig of my spirit.

"Wanna try and find somewhere to sit?"

I looked up from my glass and shook my head. Flashing me another smile, Payton turned on her heels and started what I considered an impossible task of finding us somewhere to sit. I didn't move right away, instead I allowed my eyes to descend to her ass. I watched her cheeks jiggle underneath the flimsy material of her summer dress while she finessed her way through the crowd of clubgoers. I allowed myself a few minutes of ogling before moving my feet and catching up to her.

By some miracle Payton found an empty barstool at one of the high-top tables aligning the windows of the club. After asking an overly friendly sistah sitting on the other side of the table if she was holding the seat for someone, Payton sat down and the two of them sparked up a conversation. I tuned them out, zoning out to the music I made myself comfortable next to Payton's outstretched legs.

Halfway through Drake's song "Energy" I felt my phone buzz in my pocket. I had half a mind to ignore it, but since Payton was still fully engaged in her conversation with the woman sitting across from her, I sat my drink on the table and pulled my phone out. I was surprised as hell to see a text notification from Rocky sliding across the home screen. Glancing at Payton from the corner of my eye, I shifted my body to the side before holding my phone in front of my face and positioning it at an angle I knew she couldn't see. Once my phone was unlocked, I opened my messaging app and clicked on Rocky's text.

Rocky: Hey 2 u 2. I'm doing the same thing you're doing <winking face emoji>.

What da fuck?

My face screwed up in confusion as I responded to her message.

Me: How do u know what I'm doing?

Rocky: b/c I'm looking right at you.

My hand fell to my side as I started looking around in search of her. I scanned to my right then my left but didn't see her. I stretched my neck and looked past the bar at the cramped dance floor—still no Rocky. Dragging my phone back up to my face I went to our message thread and sent her another text.

Me: U at Bengals?

After five minutes of repeatedly checking my phone and not receiving a response, I stepped up to the table and picked up my glass, quickly throwing back the remainder of my drink. A thousand thoughts ran through my mind as I replayed my text conversation with Rocky over in my head. But one in particular screamed at me, *How would she feel seeing me with Payton? Shit!* Flustered that Rocky had ghosted me, I slammed my empty glass on the table and ran my free hand down my face. I looked up to find Payton peeking at me over her shoulder.

"You good?" She held my gaze as one arched brow hiked up her forehead and unspoken questions danced in her big ambers.

I forced a smile on my face. "Always."

"You sure?" She glanced down at my hand still gripping the empty tumbler.

"I guess I don't know my own strength," I joked, while removing my hand from the glass. "As you can see, I'm empty. You want another one?" I looked down at her half-finished cocktail before sliding my eyes back up to her face.

Payton smiled at me and shook her head.

"Coo, I'll be right back." I checked my phone one more time. Still no message from Rocky. I tried like hell to get over it as I stuffed my phone back inside my pocket and took off for the bar.

I was halfway to the bar when my eyes landed on her. Stopping in mid stride, I froze as I gazed at her. She was standing with her back to me by a small cluster of tables set up near the bar. I took my time drinking her in, starting at her head and working my way down to her feet. Rocky was sexy as hell, and tonight was no different. The iridescent lighting radiated off her silky milk chocolate skin. Her hair was wild in its natural state. Untamed big curls framed her face and draped down her sable shoulders. Her thick thighs filled out the black skinny jeans she wore, paired with a black v-cut halter top, exposing her entire back. Rocky was definitely killing them tonight. The

29

sexiest part of her ensemble was the all black peep toe Christian Louboutin she wore, making her short five-foot-three-inch frame appear taller.

Shaking my head, I pulled myself from the trance her mere presence had trapped me in. I straightened my spine, held my head high, and stalked in her direction. Slowly Rocky turned toward me. The first thing I noticed was her immaculately made up face. Coral eye shadow adorned her slanted eyes, plum blush accentuated her high cheekbones while black eyeliner emphasized her mahogany eyes, and a deep wine-colored lipstick set off her plush pouty lips. I didn't see her septum piercing tonight but noticed she exchanged her hoop nose ring for a tiny diamond stud.

Fuck, this woman is absolutely gorgeous.

Our eyes connected, and a current jolted down my spine as she flashed me a bright smile. Her perfectly aligned achromic teeth were slightly parted and her deep dimples buried themselves in her cheeks. Entranced once again, I watched as she casually swept her eyes down my face before leisurely turning back toward Egypt. Assiduously I approached her and couldn't help the gargantuan ass smile etched across my face.

Leaning into her small frame I dropped my mouth next to her ear. "Hey Short Stuff."

Rocky turned to face me, still rocking a capacious grin. "Hey yourself."

Damn, she smells delicious.

I couldn't help myself as I invaded her personal space. I closed the tiny gap between us, bending down I scooped her off her feet and hugged her tightly against my chest. Reflexively Rocky wrapped her arms around my neck, her tiny fingers brushing across my skin as she melted into my frame.

"Boy if you don't put me down. People are staring at us," she breathed against my neck, but didn't make any attempts to leave my snug embrace.

"So." I squeezed her tighter, relishing how comfortable she fit inside my arms.

"Dreeee." Her usual soft timbre was replaced by a high pitch whine.

Reluctantly I lowered her to her feet, earning me an animated squeal as she stepped back and peered up at me. "If I didn't know any better, I would think you missed me."

I did miss her, but I wasn't going to tell her that. Instead, I bit my bottom lip before shifting my neck to the side and looking over at Egypt. "Hey E, how are you?"

Egypt chuckled before responding. "What, no Kool-Aid sized grin or bear hug for me?"

I snickered as I stepped around Rocky and gingerly tugged at Egypt's wrist, pulling her off her stool. Egypt continued feigning disappointment. She tilted her head to one side and poked her bottom lip out at me. Just a few feet away Rocky stood peering at us. An insidious grin tugging at the corners of her lips as her amused ambers bounced between me and her friend.

"Stop it," I demanded through a chortle, while tearing my eyes away from Rocky and focusing on Egypt. I wrapped my arms around her and pulled her into a quick hug. After releasing her, I made sure to find her eyes. "Better?"

"I guess," she ribbed, while stepping back over to the stool I pulled her from and sitting back down.

I winked at her then swiveled my head forward. My attention quickly shifted back to the woman I couldn't stop thinking about. Enjoying the view from the front as much as I did from the back, I took my time drinking her in. I scanned her body from head to toe.

"Damn Dre, you just gonna look a sistah up and down like that?" Her expression was neutral, but humor danced in her darkening pupils.

I smirked, drawing my bottom lip in between my teeth and quickly releasing it. "My bad Short Stuff, you look really nice."

Her deep dimples were on full display as she tried not to blush from my compliment. "Thanks, so do you." She did a speedy head to toe sweep of my lengthy frame before returning her gaze to my face.

I wasn't sure how long we stood there, only that I felt cheated when our silent stare down was disrupted by the buzzing of my phone.

Annoyed by the unsolicited interruption and eager to get back to whatever it was we were doing, I plucked my phone from my pocket and glanced at the dimmed screen. Payton's name flashed in the notification bar.

Damn, I forgot all about her ass.

Not bothering to check my text, I dropped my phone back inside the pocket of my jeans. "Do you and Egypt want something to drink?"

Rocky looked from my empty hand to my pocket before looking back up at me. "Nah, it's cool. I don't want to keep you from your date."

Although I wasn't sure why, hearing Rocky refer to Payton as my date bothered me. "I'm not on a date, just hangin out with a friend. Do you want a drink? I'm headed to the bar either way."

Rocky smirked at me, like she didn't believe a word I'd just said. "Sure, I'll take Rémy with a splash of cran, and you can get E an apple beer please. Thanks Dre."

I responded with a wink before walking off. The distance from Rocky's section to the bar was shorter than I thought. What I didn't anticipate was the large horde of people gathered around the L-shape counter, all vying for the bartender's attention. I managed to maneuver through the crowd where I found a spot one row away from the congested bar.

Posted up, I pulled my phone from my pocket and checked Payton's message while waiting. As I expected, she was checking to see what was taking me so long. I didn't trip, I had definitely been gone longer than I anticipated. I quickly responded, letting her know I would be back shortly then returned my phone to my pocket.

Tired of waiting, I decided to use my height to my advantage. I got as close to the bar as the crowd would allow. Stepping on the tips of my toes I extended my six-foot-three-inch frame and looked for the barmaid who served me earlier. It didn't take long to find her; she was at other end of the bar finishing a transaction with another customer. Keeping my eyes focused on her, I watched as she made her way across the bar, headed in my direction. I waited until she approached the end of the bar near where I was standing and contended for her attention. I extended my oversized arm in the air and called out to her. A bright smile stretched across her face as her eyes landed on mine.

I saw the switch in her narrow hips as she sauntered to the edge of the counter and couldn't miss the lust in her eyes as she leaned forward to take my order. Although I was accustomed to women reacting to me in the same manner as she did, it still took me by surprise when it occurred. I was fully aware of my physical attributes and how they appealed to women. That didn't bother me. Hell, I was grateful women found me attractive, but it was what women were willing to do for my attention that didn't sit right with me.

Quickly dismissing those thoughts, I placed a smile on my face and pulled my arm out of the air while leaning in between the two women who were standing directly in front of me. Neither objected to my invasion of their personal space. In fact, one whispered a salacious comment that I pretended not to hear. Flashing each of them a coy smile, I apologized for the imposition then shouted off my order.

Five minutes later I stood looking down at the assortment of drinks resting on the counter in front of me. *How da hell am I gonna carry all this shit?* It took less than a minute for me to come up with a plan. I bundled the three glasses together on top of the bar and placed Egypt's beer in the crook of my left arm, then wrapped my big ass hands around all three glasses and carefully lifted them off the counter. Miraculously I traveled the short distance back to Rocky's section without spilling a single drop. As I approached the table, Egypt hopped off her bar stool, charging toward me to grab two of the drinks from my hand. Egypt's sudden movements must have alarmed Rocky because she turned toward me with a concerned expression etched across her face. Masking a surreptitious grin, I placed the remaining drinks on the table.

"Dre, why didn't you call or text? I would've met you at the bar to help," she spoke over the music, while stepping directly in front of me.

I shrugged her off as turned toward the table and picked up my drink. "It's a small thing to a giant, Short Stuff," I supplied, turning back around to face her.

A fatuous smirk spilled onto her lips as she playfully rolled her eyes at me. I responded with a light chortle as I chucked the small straw inside my glass to the side and took a sip of my cocktail while keeping my eyes fastened on her. The small slits of Rocky's eyes narrowed, cascading down to my lips. Dropping the tumbler from my mouth I gave her a better view, roguishly flashing her a knowing smile. Her eyes grew wide before slowly sliding back up to mine. Neither of us spoke. She knew I'd caught her lingering perusal, but I wouldn't embarrass her by mentioning it. Instead, I tuned out the thunderous crowd and roaring music, following her with my eyes as she sashayed by me and back up to the table.

Lil Wayne's "6 Foot 7 Foot" blared through the speakers and the crowd went wild, including Rocky and Egypt. Egypt's little ass hopped out of her seat and started a cute two-step around the table. Rocky was a little more subtle. After pulling her arms out of the air, she bobbed her head to the beat. Her wild mane bouncing freely each time she dipped her head. Fixated on the woman dancing just a few feet away from me I felt my own head begin to move, damn near in sync with hers.

It was crazy. I stood in a club full of people, and the only thing I could do was stare at her. I had tunnel vision. Focused solely on Rocky, I took advantage of her having her back to me. I allowed my eyes to rove down her curvaceous body, stopping at her bountiful ass as she swayed to the beat of the music. Her jeans fit snuggly against her curves, prohibiting a jiggle, only giving way for a slight bounce as she danced in place. I couldn't take my eyes off her. I was completely caught off guard when I felt someone tug on my arm. Annoyance was etched on my face as I turned to see who was responsible for inter-rupting my private musing. My irritated expression landed on a set of angry ambers.

Oh shit! Payton.

I quickly adjusted my attitude as I replaced the grimace on my face with a spurious grin. "My bad Payton, it took longer than I expected to get our drinks. I just dropped off drinks to my home girls and was about to head your way."

It wasn't a complete lie, but I also knew it damn sure wasn't the whole truth. Bending slightly at the knees I aligned my face with hers and looked directly into her eyes. I searched her blazing orbs for forgiveness while she explored mine for sincerity. When she stopped scowling at me, I took that as a sign.

"C'mere, I'll introduce you." Not giving her a chance to respond, I grabbed Payton's hand and stepped up to Rocky and Egypt's table.

I could sense Payton's hesitation, so I handed her her drink and made sure to keep the introductions swift. I also made a conscious effort to keep my face neutral and my eyes to myself. Although Payton and I were just friends, I would never disrespect her or knowingly do anything to make her feel uncomfortable. I hoped by introducing her to the girls it would help alleviate some of her discomfort. I was wrong.

Posted up, damn near in the same spot I'd been in before Payton approached me, I stood silently sipping from my glass. I watched Payton size Rocky up. A tight smile was fixed on her face while her dark eyes discreetly searched Rocky's face before sweeping down her entire frame and slowly snaking their way back up. To the naked eye, Payton appeared calm and unbothered, but I knew her well enough to know that although she accepted my apology, she was anything but.

Oblivious to Payton's reticent bitterness toward her, Rocky attempted to engage her in conversation—conversation that Payton returned with one word and clipped answers. Seeing enough, I decided it was time to nip the shit in the bud before it got out of control. I approached the table, purposely standing in between Rocky and Payton I smiled at an observant Egypt. Just as I had been doing, Egypt had been quietly watching Rocky and Payton's interaction. And if the leer on Egypt's face was any indicator, she definitely knew what was up. Yeah, it was time to go.

I leaned into Rocky and placed my mouth next to her ear, "Imma let you get back to enjoyin your night, Short Stuff. Text me and let me know when you make it home." I slid my empty glass on top of the table and stood to my full height. "It was good seein you tonight."

Without saying a word, Rocky turned slightly in my direction and nodded her head in agreement. That shit threw me off. Payton had barely been here twenty minutes, and things had shifted that quickly. I tried checking my temper as I placed my hand on the small of Payton's back and guided her away from the table. I was pissed, but I couldn't figure out what I was more mad about: Payton's attitude toward Rocky or the way Rocky blew me off when I said goodbye.

I needed a drink or else I was highly likely to walk past the bar and out the damn door, Payton be damned. Dropping my hand from Payton's body, I stepped in front of her and headed straight to the bar as Payton trailed behind me. A quick glance over my shoulder I saw her head dipped low and eyes aimed at the floor. She'd clearly picked up on my sour mood, but I didn't give a shit. She was out of line and she knew it. I wasn't with the shits. I replayed Payton's interaction with Rocky over in my head while debating if I had the energy to address it. I decided against it, hoping a drink—nah fuck that, I would need a shot to help calm me down.

I was seething, and the more I reflected on it the madder I got. I understood Payton being annoyed. Hell, I expected it. But what I didn't expect was her attitude toward Rocky. Although it wasn't my intention to leave her waiting on me, and yes it was rude, but that shit wasn't Rocky's fault. However, like most women, instead of addressing the real source of her anger which happened to be me, she decided to take her attitude out on Rocky and that shit wasn't cool.

Lucky for me the bar wasn't as congested as it was on my last two trips. I found an open spot at the front of the bar and waited for a bartender to approach near where I was standing. In my peripheral, I saw Payton lift her hand to touch me then place it back at her side.

I turned to face her, trying hard as hell to remove the scowl from my face. "What's up P Body?" I called her by the silly nickname I used for her in an attempt to lighten the mood.

Payton bit her bottom lip, looked toward the floor then returned her eyes to mine. "I'm sorry." Those words came rushing out her mouth like she was holding fire between her lips. "I shouldn't have been rude to your friends, especially Rocky. I was irritated with you and took it out on her. Again, I'm sorry Dre."

I allowed the corners of my mouth to curl into a smile as I looked at her, appreciative that she recognized her behavior wasn't cool. I was never one to hold grudges, and since I decided to continue the night with her, I needed to let the shit go.

"It's all good. I'm sorry too. I didn't mean to leave for so long, that shit was rude."

Her light brown eyes lit up while a soft smile eased across her face. Extending her arm toward me, she held up a balled fist. "Truce?"

"Truce." I bumped her fist with mine then snatched her by the wrist and pulled her into a speedy hug. "You still drinkin?"

Payton was still drinking which meant she wasn't ready to call it a night. But more importantly it meant she was willing to put my fuck up behind us, so I decided to extend her the same courtesy. I turned my attention back to the bar just in time to see the bartender who previously waited on me sit a drink down in front of me. I hiked a brow as I looked her. "This mine?"

"Yep. Henny light ice with a splash of coke, right?"

Nodding my head, I couldn't help the errant grin that eased onto my face nor could I ignore the avidity in her eyes. I acknowledged her attentiveness with a dip of my head as a sign of my appreciation. I was flattered baby girl remembered my drink order, but I wasn't ignorant. I knew she was attracted to me. She made that clear in her subtle attempts to gain my attention. The long gazes, the fervor in her eyes every time she looked at me, the sizeable smile always on display, and the lingering touches when she handed me my drinks or took my money. I understood in this profession a certain amount of friendliness was expected, but I didn't see her extending the same gazes or longing smile when she waited on other customers.

I lowered my eyes while trying to collect my thoughts. Maybe I was reading too much into it. However, any doubt I had was washed away when I looked up and found her still staring at me. Without saying a word, her eyes asked a question I was unwilling to answer. Maybe under different circumstances I would've entertained her flirting but tonight it wasn't an option. I was here with Payton, and I would never disrespect her by entertaining another woman while we were out together.

Payton cleared her throat, making her presence known and ending my silent stare down with the overly friendly barmaid. Masking a smirk, I looked over at Payton and winked before turning my attention back toward the bartender. "Can I also get a Tito's with club soda and a lime please?"

She looked from me to Payton then back at me before scurrying off. Returning shortly with Payton's drink in hand she sat the fruity cocktail on the bar and informed me both drinks were on her. She also informed me if I needed anything else to ask for her and she'd take care of me. I flashed her an appreciative smile and thanked her for the drinks, purposely leaving her open invitation floating in the air.

For some reason, I got the impression that *anything else* extended beyond drinks. I pinched the bridge of my nose and shook my head to myself as I watched Payton pick up her drink and turn toward me. I picked up my own cocktail and took a huge gulp while deliberately ignoring the interrogation dancing in her eyes. Honestly, I didn't know how to take her right now. I wasn't used to this Payton. Payton and I hung out a fair amount of times since exchanging numbers, and I'd never seen her so possessive of me. The shit with Rocky I got. I didn't like it, but I understood why she reacted the way she did. But this shit right here, I couldn't figure it out. It's not like this was the first time a woman had hit on me in front of her. She'd definitely witnessed way bolder acts in the past.

In order to avoid any further drama, I decided it was time to move away from the bar. I chucked down the remainder of my drink and placed the empty tumbler on the counter. In need of some space I told Payton I needed to use the restroom and suggested she look for a place for us to chill, promising to meet her when I got back. Payton looked at me incredulously before turning toward where we sat when we first came in. I watched her walk off before making my way toward the restroom. I needed a minute to myself, away from her and Tianna. At least I think that's what baby girl said her name was; I was almost positive that's what she said. At this point the shit really didn't matter since I was done drinking.

Man, Jamison ain't gonna believe this shit.

I stood outside the restroom fixing my shirt. My eyes darted around the crowded club, landing on the dance floor. It didn't take long for me to recognize the beautiful chocolate goddess with big hair and killer body. I took a moment to enjoy the show, watching as Rocky danced with some lame who kept trying to grind on her ass. An amused chuckle fell from my mouth when I witnessed her smooth exit. She surreptitiously danced away from his thirsty ass, leaving him standing alone looking clueless.

Fuckin lame. That's what he gets.

I could've stayed there, just watching her for the rest of the night. But seeing how that didn't work out too well the last time, I set out to find Payton. Walking in the direction I last saw her, I maneuvered my way through the brimming crowd. Luckily my pursuit didn't take as long as I expected. Payton was standing near the same group of tables where we sat earlier. As I neared, I noticed her hiked shoulders fall to a relaxed state and her face soften. A relieved expression slowly spread across her face as her eyes landed on me. I wasn't sure if she was happy to see me because some lame had pressed up on her while I was gone or because she thought I was going to keep her waiting again. Whatever the reason, I was just glad to see the smile had returned to her eyes.

Although the night started off capriciously, Payton and I managed to have a good time. To my surprise Payton insisted on apologizing to Rocky and once she did, we spent the majority of the night with her and Egypt. I swear women were so unpredictable. I was grateful we were able to salvage the night, but once it was over and I'd walked all three women to their cars, all I could think about was my bed. I just needed to lay so I could stretch out.

Tired, I sat in my truck a few beats while trying to find the energy to start the twenty-minute drive back to the crib. Being on my feet most of the night had my dogs throbbing, not to mention we danced practically nonstop until last call. The girls alternated as they took turns dragging me out on the dance floor every time one of their *songs* came on. I didn't mind—we had fun, and it allowed me the opportunity to be close to Rocky.

Hell, after identifying the pattern, I found myself silently but eagerly waiting for Rocky to pull me out on the dance floor. Every dance, every brush up against me, every whiff of her intoxicating scent, and every touch of her tiny hands on my body silently drove me crazy. I found myself constantly reminding myself I was there with Payton and not Rocky. It took every ounce of self-control I could muster not to get caught up in her. She was that fucking alluring.

A smile flashed across my face as bright lights flickered in front of me, pulling me from my reverie. *Damn, I wish I had taken an Uber.* I needed to get this drive over with and quick. Starting the engine, I turned on some music to ride out to, and headed home. I was halfway to my apartment when my phone buzzed in my pocket. Carefully digging inside of my pocket, I pulled out my phone and glanced at the home screen. The notification bar alerted me that I had two messages. I assumed one was from Rocky and the other from Payton, letting me know they made it home safely. Being so close to the crib, I decided to wait before checking them. Dropping my phone in my lap, I continued the drive home.

I pulled up to my apartment complex a little after two-thirty in the morning, so I was surprised to see two of my neighbors sitting outside in front of our apartment building. Too tired to give it much thought, I parked my truck and grabbed my cellphone from my lap. I dropped the small device in my pocket and peeled my fatigued frame from my truck. Immediately I knew why Dale and Keith were perched up on the steps of our apartment building. The smell of skunk permeated the air while music from one of their cell phones serenaded the otherwise quiet night.

As I neared, I saw the source of the effluvious smell as Dale passed Keith a blunt. Two sets of eyes stared up at me as I stopped in front of them. I greeted them with a quick head nod. "Bianca inside huh?"

Dale burst out laughing, doubling over he held his round belly. Keith playfully shoved him in the shoulder then looked back up at me, "Yeah her funky ass is in there. Where you comin from bro?"

"Bengals."

Dale stopped laughing and looked up at me excitedly. "Word. How was it? I haven't been yet, but I heard it be lit."

Keith chimed in, "Man, I've been once, and that place was packed with a bunch of baddies."

"You better keep your voice down before Bianca come out here and beat yo ass," I teased.

Keith waved at hand at me dismissively, "Man, Bianca don't run shit but her mouth."

I smirked, knowing he was full of shit. "Yeah okay. So, you just wanna to be out here on the steps smokin instead of inside your own apartment?"

I watched as Dale tried to laugh but started choking on the blunt Keith just passed him. Slowly Dale regained his composure. "Bro, that nigga stay talkin shit, but he knows he whipped."

Keith sucked his teeth. "Fuck both y'all. I'm not whipped I'm considerate."

"Considerate my ass, bro you whipped," Dale continued to tease.

"Quit playin bro, you know Bianca doesn't like the smell of ganja in her weave. So, whenever she's over I blow outside," Keith justified.

Dale and I stared at one another then busted out laughing.

Keith snatched the blunt from Dale. "Fuck y'all."

Shaking my head, I gave Dale dap and slapped Keith on his shoulder as I walked by them. "Nah nigga, you need to put that blunt down and go inside and fuck Bianca. I'm going to bed. Check you niggas later."

I heard Dale laughing as I walked inside our apartment building and headed for my unit. Once inside, I immediately kicked off my shoes, leaving them by the door as I walked in the kitchen and grabbed a bottle of water out the refrigerator. I damn near chugged the whole bottle before closing the fridge. Satiated and beyond tired, I ambled out of the kitchen, sluggishly trekking toward my bedroom. I paused my steps when my phone buzzed in my pocket again. Cradling the half empty water bottle in the crook of my arm, I pulled my phone out of my pocket before continuing the stroll down the hall while opening my text app.

I had three messages: two from Payton and one from Rocky. I decided to open Payton's messages first to make sure everything was okay since she texted twice. As expected, the first message was her letting me know she'd made it home safely. The second one surprised me—she apologized again and asked if we were good. I responded to both with a quick message, letting her know we were cool and telling her I was glad she'd made it home safely. I ended it with a good night and a smiley face emoji.

I stepped inside the dark room and flipped on the light before tossing my phone and water on the dresser and clicking on the TV. Afterwards, I started undressing. My shirt was the first to go, followed by my pants then my basketball shorts as I walked to my closet. Stripped down to nothing but my boxers I dumped the discarded items in the hamper then used what little strength I had left to saunter back into my room.

Turning off the light I snatched my phone and the remote off the dresser then made a beeline for my bed. Instantly, relief set in as I stretched out across the firm oversized mattress. I laid there for a few minutes just staring at the ceiling before propping up on my elbows and bolstering two pillows behind my head. *Damn, it feels good to finally lay.* With my phone in hand I dropped the remote on the bed and pressed my thumb on the small circular button. When my apps loaded, I went straight to Rocky's message.

Rocky: Hey you, sorry for the late text. I'm home and so is E. 4got to text when I 1ˢᵗ got home. I headed straight for the shower. I'm sure you're prolly sleep but wanted to text b/c I said I would. Night.

The mere thought of Rocky in the shower had my manhood rising. The effect this woman had on me was crazy. And the wildest part was, she had no idea. I rubbed a hand down my semi-inflated dick and thought about rubbing one out as images of her from earlier tonight flashed through my mind. *Nigga, you trippin.* Removing my hand from my johnson I replied to her text.

Me: Nope, I'm woke. Glad you made it home safely.

Rocky: Oh wow. Really wasn't expecting a response tonight. What you still doing up? Wait, am I being nosy?

I smirked as the light from the TV illuminated throughout my room. *That was cute, but her ass knew what she was doing.* A silly grin remained on my face as I swiped my hand over the comforter. Grabbing the remote I turned to ESPN, lowered the volume, and dumped the remote on the bed again. The sound was barely audible but enough to drown out the silence of the night. Comfortable and happy as hell to have a piece of her time, I decided to assuage Rocky's concern, even though I thought she was full of shit.

Me: Nah, not nosy. I just got in & now I'm finally in bed. I chopped it up with my neighbors for a quick minute when I first got home.

Rocky: Oh okay, cool. Was hoping I wasn't interrupting u & Payton. I didn't want to piss her off again.

Recalling how petty Payton acted toward Rocky earlier had me on ten all over again, and the fact that she mentioned it didn't sit well with me. Because truth be told, if I had to make a choice, I would choose Rocky.

Me: I know Payton apologized already but I feel like I owe you an apology as well.

Rocky: That's sweet but no apology necessary <winking face emoji>.

Me: U sure?

Rocky: Positive. She was cool tho & I'm glad there is no bad blood. Hell, I mighta reacted the same way if my boo left me and was posted up w/some chick I didn't know.

Me: Payton is not my boo. I told you we're just friends.

Rocky: Umm, okay. What you young ppl call it now days, fuck buddies or is it friends with benefits?

That shit caught me off guard. I sat up in the bed, moving the pillows down toward the middle of my back I adjusted them to sit comfortably behind me.

Me: Young ppl????? Girl I'm a grown ass man. You better ask about me <winking face emoji>. And Payton and I aren't fucking, never have.

Rocky: I shouldn't have said that. It's none of my business either way. Sorry.

Me: Don't say sorry 4 what u mean. Besides, we developing our friendship so u can ask me anything.

Rocky: Anything <inquisitive face emoji>?

Me: Yep, shoot.

I wasn't sure where this conversation was headed but I was willing to entertain it with the hopes of establishing a trust between us and the opportunity to know her better. Plus, I was curious to know what she wanted to learn about me. At this point I was willing to show her my hand for just a peek at hers.

Rocky: I'm teasing Dre. I mean, I know the basics.

Me: <inquisitive face emoji> what u think u know?

Rocky: Well…. I know how old u are, where ur from, what school u graduated from, who u took to prom, I know your parents & that ur more than a cute athlete. I know ur pretty damn smart and graduated high school with honors. Oh yeah, I also know ur a lady's man. Is that enough?

I wasn't sure why women insisted that I was a ladies' man, I was simply a single man with friends. Yeah, I dated but I wasn't out here hitting everything in a damn skirt. I was definitely selective with who I put my dick in. Deciding to drop it in favor of keeping the conversation light and flowing I responded with humor.

Me: U 4got buff, funny, and charismatic but ur list was cool & accurate.

Rocky: My bad ur right, ur body is dope and ur definitely funny as hell. I dunno if I've seen u be charming but I believe u <winking face emoji>.

Me: Aaah shit! U just wait and see, imma charm the shit outcha little ass <smiling face emoji>.

Rocky: I'm looking forward 2 it <winking kissy face emoji>.

Fuckin flirt, she just doesn't know who she's fuckin wit.

Curious about something I'd heard a while ago I decided to ask my own set of questions. I just hoped she was game. I sent a one-word text to gauge her mood.

Me: Question.

Rocky: Shoot.

Me: Is it true you've never had a boyfriend?

When she didn't reply right away, I thought maybe I crossed the line, but I had to ask. I was curious as hell. I couldn't think of any twenty-seven-year-old woman that I knew who never had a man. Maybe the twins were just talking shit when they shared that piece of information with me. My phone buzzed and I was relieved when I saw she responded.

Rocky: Sorry, had to let Creed out one final time so he won't bother me early in the morning since somebody has me texting at this ungodly hour <smiling face emoji>. Nope, never had a boyfriend. Not one with a title anyway but I've dated/date.

Thank God, she wasn't pissed. Overall Rocky was a very carefree person, but I knew baby girl had a temper, just like her damn brothers.

Me: REALLY? I thought the twins were just talking shit. WHY? I mean, you're fine as hell, smart, ambitious than a mutha-fucka, sweet, funny/fun, and have a body women out here dying or paying for.

Rocky: 1st off, why are u and the twins discussing my business? 2nd, u know my family dynamics prolly better than anyone. Seeing that shit your whole life will make you look at relationships differently. And thanks for the compliments.

Damn, that was some deep shit. I mean, Rocky's family dynamics were wild but she was so lighthearted I never would've guessed that shit left her jaded.

Me: Damn Rocky.

Rocky: LOL, it's cool. It's no biggie to me. U don't miss what u never had. My shit works for me. U know?

Me: No, I don't know. I couldn't imagine never experiencing love or that type of closeness with another person.

Rocky: Okay, so I'll add sentimental to your list. Lol. I love my family and friends and I'm close to them. But romantic love, that shit is overrated Dre.

What the fuck? I knew the twins had a love/hate type of thing going on with their father and understandably so, but I never saw Rocky let it affect her relationship with them or her relationship with

JB. I guess I never thought how his lifestyle affected her in other ways. Honestly, growing up I thought Rocky's dad was the man. But now that I was a man, I would never want to make someone's daughter feel the way Rocky just expressed she felt. Fuck, this shit had me loathing JB right now. What has he done to his daughter?

Me: U have no idea Rocky. Love from the right person can be everything.

Rocky: Dre u are barely grown what u know bout love <winking face emoji>?

Me: More than u. I know how to do more than lay pipe Rocky.

Rocky: Well u will always know more than me when it comes to love b/c I will never fall for that shit. Who said u know how to lay pipe <inquisitive face emoji>?

Rocky had no idea how bad I wanted to show her both. I wanted to wrap her in my love just as much as I wanted to bury myself deep inside of her. Wow! This shit was deep, I still couldn't believe it. I mean, a girl's first love was her father. Her father sets the standard for which all other men were measured. He was supposed to show her what love looked and felt like. A father was supposed to show her how a man was supposed to love and treat her. Instead, JB's ass had Rocky running from the shit. My heart ached for her.

Before I could reply Rocky sent me another text. Fucked up about her transparent revelation I was hesitant to look at her message.

Rocky: Don't overthink it Dre. It is what it is. I'm going to sleep. Goodnight.

I guess that was her way of deading the conversation. I would give her that for now, but we would definitely talk about it again. I wasn't sure if she'd see my message, but I sent one anyway.

Me: Good night, Short Stuff.

CHAPTER THREE

*T*oday marked the fourth week of the summer semester, and I was already over it. Any ideas I had about my classes being easy were squashed the first day of class. My syllabus was loaded with extensive reading assignments, multiple papers, and two major projects. I released an exaggerated breath while placing my syllabus back inside the folder I'd pulled it from before stuffing it inside my book bag. *It is going to be a long ass twelve weeks.* I couldn't wait to be finished with this chapter in my life. Then again, I'd been a student for so long I wasn't sure I would know what to do once I wasn't.

Snickering to myself I recalled Dre's reaction when I shared that with him the other day. He told me I sounded crazy but assured me I would be just as amazing in my career as I was as a student. I appreciated his encouragement because although I was fully committed to my educational journey, there were times I found myself questioning my decision and my ability to really fulfill my dream.

I still couldn't believe I'd be entering the third year of my doctoral program next semester. That thought alone was scary and at times overwhelming, but I knew I was blessed to be on this journey, and I was determined to see it through. With the support of my family and friends, the first two years flew past. I just hoped I could say the same for the next three and a half. Ultimately, I knew in the end it would all be worth it. So what I didn't have a real social life right now. It was a small sacrifice to achieve my goals. And I was no stranger to sacrifices. Hell, the only reason I stayed in the city for the summer was to take a few extra classes to ensure I stayed on track.

Pulled from my musing by a clamorous thud, I rolled my neck in that direction. My eyes connected with a busty brunette hunched over a stack of books splayed haphazardly on the floor in front of her. She mouthed her apologizes then returned her attention to the mess gathered at her feet. Whipping my head forward, I stared at the open book resting on the table. My plan was to resume studying, but that task proved harder than it did when I first sat down two hours ago. My concentration was shot; the smallest noises managed to steal my attention. I tried like hell to reel it in, but when the words on the pages started meshing together, I gave up. Slamming my book shut, I dumped it inside my book bag, pulled the zipper close, and gathered the remainder of my things.

With my cellphone and keys in one hand, I stood from the table I'd been occupying, hoisted my backpack over my left shoulder, then grabbed my old Starbucks cup with the other and stepped away from the desk. Carefully maneuvering around the collection of tables gathered on that side of the library, I headed for the door, pitching my cup in the trash as I passed by before casually strolling outside. Instantly I was cloaked in the humid June air. We were still a couple weeks away from the official first day of summer, but the temperature had finally evened out, consistently ranging between the high seventies and low eighties. Today I felt every bit of the eighty-three degrees my phone had predicted when I left the house this morning.

Shit! It's going to be a hot ass summer.

I felt every ray of the bright ass sun beaming down on me as I started the short trek to my SUV. By time I reached my meter, sweat had gathered in the creases of my scrunched-up forehead and slowly started trickling down the sides of my face. Annoyed, I used the back of my hand to dab at my dank flesh to prevent the tiny beads of perspiration from dripping into my eyes. I was strongly reconsidering the run

I had planned once I got home but the way my thighs rubbed together during the short walk, I knew I'd push myself through it. Hopefully the car ride home would provide the temporary relief I needed to refuel my motivation.

Dropping my hand from my face I hit the button on my key fob to unlock the doors then practically dove inside. Bad idea. The sun had turned my leather seats into a bed of fire. The heated upholstery scorched the back of my bare legs, triggering a string of expletives to spill from my parted lips. My backpack weighed me down which hindered my ability to move my legs. Tossing the loaded sack in the passenger seat, I laid my phone on the armrest and attempted to alleviate the sting by jiggling my meaty thighs while reaching into the backseat for a towel. Quickly maneuvering the plush cloth underneath my legs, I created a barrier between my skin and the hot ass seat.

Finally, feeling a small semblance of comfort, I started the engine and immediately turned the air conditioner on full blast. Hot air smacked me dead in the face as the air worked double time to reach its maximum capacity. I didn't give a shit. Heat be damned, I refused to roll the windows down, opting to thug it out while waiting for cool air to fill my truck.

I pulled out of my parking space and cursed myself for not utilizing my automatic car starter. My discomfort could've been avoided, but clearly, I'd underestimated the heat. I hated being hot, the only time I didn't mind sweating was during exercise or sex. And since neither were the reason for the current puddles dripping from my body, I was over it. Exasperated, a warm stream of air toppled out of my nostrils and dusted over my top lip as I carefully navigated into the light flow of traffic.

Let it go, Raquel.

Heeding the words in my head I decided to focus on the drive home, trying my damnedest to zone out to the radio streaming from my Bluetooth. When the music switched from an up-tempo girl-themed R&B track to an old Teddy Pendergrass song my thoughts instantly shifted to Dre. Although I'd never heard him sing this particular song before, memories of our first time hanging out flooded my mind. I could still see the carefree expression on his handsome face as he effortlessly belted out every note to each song that played. Dre was no Teddy P, but his silky tenor definitely had a way of penetrating your core and evidently, burning vivid memories in your head.

Surprisingly, Dre and I had communicated via texts or phone calls damn near every day since Bengals. Unexpectedly, I found that Dre and I had a natural chemistry. It was weird the way we seemed to just click. I couldn't explain it, but I knew I had never experienced this kind of connection with any other man. We would spend hours talking or texting about everything and other times we would talk or text about nothing. Either way, the conversation always seemed to flow organically.

Stopped at a red light I picked up my phone and turned my ringer back on. My eyes darted across the small device, checking for any missed calls or texts. Per usual, there were none. My phone was as dry as the hot ass weather outside. I couldn't help but shake my head as I acknowledged my own thirst. It had been less than twenty-four hours since our last conversation and here I was checking my phone to see if Dre had called or sent a text.

F'it. Ain't no law sayin I can't be the first one to reach out.

I opened my messaging app and scrolled through the short list of names then selected our message thread. My intention was to send him a text when the driver behind me blew their horn, alerting me the light was now green. I stilled my fingers and placed a hand back on the steering wheel while cautiously proceeding through the light.

The grin that took residence on my face the moment I clicked on his name morphed into a full-blown smile. Flashes of our conversation the night after the club danced around my head. Although Dre hadn't mentioned it again, I knew the revelation about me never being somebody's girlfriend threw him for a loop. I could honestly say, his comments about love certainly jarred me. I mean, what could a twenty-two-year-old really know about love? Granted Dre was far from your average millennial but still, dude was twenty-two and a fresh twenty-two at that. However, talking to Dre over these past weeks had certainly shown me there was more to him than looks and athleticism. And I'd be a lie if I said I didn't like what I was discovering.

I was pulled from my thoughts when the car behind me precipitously sped to the right of my truck. Quickly reacting to their impetuous and erratic driving I steered toward the left to avoid running smack dab into the back of their bumper as they cut me off to pass by. Headed for the curb, I slammed on breaks to try and avoid hitting it. No such luck. Immediately my truck stopped as my front driver's side tire bumped up against the concrete barrier. Shaking my head, I watched as the inconsiderate asshole who ran me off the road sped off.

Anxious now more than ever to get home, I steered off the curb and slowly merged back into traffic. Instantly, I noticed something didn't feel right. But I refused to pull over. I continued my drive hoping I was just being paranoid while praying the wobbling that wasn't present before, would stop. However, less than a quarter of a mile from where the incident occurred, I couldn't ignore it anymore. Pulling over, I turned on my hazard lights and exited my vehicle.

You gotta be fuckin kiddin me.

Pissed, I ran a hand down the front of my face as I identified the source of the problem. A fucking flat tire. Bending down in front of my driver's side tire, I surveyed the damage, checking to make sure the rim wasn't bent. Satisfied there was no further damage I stood upright then made a wide circle around my SUV, inspecting the other three tires before walking to my trunk.

Completely defeated, I leaned against the back of the trunk and closed my eyes. I attempted to calm my nerves by pulling in lengthy breaths of air while silently counting backwards from fifty. It was hot and I was tired, but waiting on AAA was not an option, well at least not one I was willing to explore. Releasing a long drawn out embittered breath I slowly fluttered my lids open and pushed off the trunk. I was damn near pouting as I marched back to the driver's side of the vehicle and yanked the door open. I reached inside and popped the trunk before snatching up my cell phone and pushing start to cut the engine.

Thank God daddy insisted I learn how to change a tire once I learned how to drive.

Moving as fast as my short legs would carry me, I gaited back to the trunk and opened the lower tailgate. *Shit! I can't catch a damn break.* I released a heavy sigh and shook my head as I looked at all the shoes scattered on the cargo floor. Quickly tossing the dozen or so shoes into the backseat I lifted the cargo floor and secured it in place. Once that was done, I laid the tire lift on top of the spare and closed the tailgate. Grabbing the tailgate brace, I sat it to the side and prepared to remove the tire when I damn near jumped out of my skin at the sound of someone blowing their horn behind me. Startled, I slowly turned around to find Dre walking toward me with a perplexed expression cast on his face.

"What the hell you doing, Raquel?"

Slightly annoyed, I sneered at him as he stopped directly in front of me. "I'm about to change my tire Andre. What does it look like I'm doing?"

Dre didn't respond, instead he gently moved me to the side as he leaned into my trunk and pulled the lift assembly out and placed the bracket into the latch slot on the tailgate. Focused on the task at hand, Dre opened the tailgate and secured the brace so he could remove the spare tire. I silently watched him in total disbelief. I was surprised he was here and absolutely astounded he took over changing my tire.

With very little effort Dre removed the spare then turned toward me. "Which tire is it?"

"Front driver's side," I mumbled.

Giving me a quick once-over, he balanced my tire in one hand while stuffing the other inside the pocket of his basketball shorts. He pulled out his keys and handed them to me. "Here, go wait in my whip while I finish changin your tire."

Without saying another word, Dre left me standing frozen in place as he walked to the front of my SUV. My eyes remained glued to him as he leisurely bent down and placed the tire on the ground, leaning it against the front of the truck. His bushy brows furrowed in the middle of his head, causing his eyes to lower to a squint as he examined the damaged tire. After several moments of inspection, he slowly pushed off his knees and stood to his feet. Shoulders square, chest puffed out, Dre took long measured strides back in my direction. And I be damned if I didn't feel like I was watching one of those cheesy commercials. The kind whose target audience was women, so they used handsome actors or models to push their products. The only thing missing was the perfectly timed slow-motion reel as the camera panned in on said actor or model's face before slowly dragging the shot down the star's body.

I chuckled to myself, my goofy ass really made up a whole damn scenario in my head. But damn, that's how it felt watching Dre glide his fine ass back over to where I was standing. I had to force the silly ass smirk off my face when he finally reached the trunk. Thankfully he wasn't paying me no mind, too focused on getting my tired fixed. Well at least that's what I thought until he poked his head out of the trunk and glanced over his shoulder at me.

"What?"

His exotic orbs bounced around my face while his head slowly shook on his shoulders. That was his response. No words, just a nod of his head and an expression I couldn't read before he turned his attention back to the inside of my truck.

I continued watching him as he dug inside the trunk and removed the jack and tire iron. Tools in hand, Dre turned around and faced me, pinning me with his bright hazels he smirked. I reciprocated his gesture. I flashed him a quick smile while following him with my eyes.

Stepping into my personal space he closed the small gap between us. "Take yo hardheaded ass to the car and wait for me to finish."

There was finality in his words. Not bothering to wait for a response, he paid me one final glance before walking past me and heading back toward the front of my truck. I didn't move at first, partly because I was caught off guard by his authoritative tone but mostly because I enjoyed watching him. Dude was fine as hell. His large stature, athletic physique, and roguishly pretty boy appearance made it hard to take my eyes off him. Even dressed casually, sporting a crisp white tee and a pair of loosely fitted basketball shorts he still looked like he could grace the cover of any popular sports magazine.

An annoying vibration against my leg snatched me out of my reverie. Pulling my phone from my pocket, I silenced the buzzing while turning away from Dre and heading toward his truck. Carmen could wait. I needed relief from the blazing sun, not to mention I knew Dre would have my ass if he knew I was still standing where he left me. Phone in one hand and Dre's keys in the other I hit the fob as I neared the truck only to pause when I reached the door.

As if he could sense my hesitation, Dre turned in my direction. A sardonic grin tugged at his lips while his head shook softly. Embarrassed and slightly annoyed, I slid my eyes to the ground before quickly shuffling them back up to Dre's face. Standing to his feet, he wiped his hands down the front of his shorts while casually strolling toward me.

Amused, he stared down at me as he placed his hands on each side of my hips. "C'mon Short Stuff. I got you."

I planted my left foot on the floor of the truck and allowed Dre to hoist me up. He stood waiting by the door as I shifted in the seat, trying to get comfortable. After I stopped moving, he removed his keys from my hand, leaned into the truck and started the engine. An impish smile was displayed on his face as he turned and looked at me, I was sure recalling how I almost jumped out of my seat the first time I heard his engine roar. I smacked my lips and playfully punched him in the arm.

Damn he smells amazing. How is that possible? I know his ass had to be sweating out in that sun.

Laughing he stretched his arm and pushed a button on the center console. Instantly, cool air came blasting through the vents. Grateful for the comfort of the frosty breeze caressing my skin I relaxed in my seat as Dre slowly eased his colossal frame out of the truck and my personal space. As he turned to walk away, I remembered my manners and called after him. Turning back around to face me, he looked down into my eyes.

"Thank you. For everything, I really appreciate it."

His smile disappeared, glaring at me, the specks of green overshadowed the natural hue of his hazel eyes. "No thanks necessary. We'll talk later about why you were out here about to change your tire yourself instead of callin me in the first place. Let me finish so I can get you home." Without saying another word, he closed the door and jogged back to my vehicle.

Shit!

Eyes trained on the man who'd captured my attention from the moment he showed up like a knight in shining armor, I returned my best friend's call. I placed the phone on speaker and sat it in my lap while closing my eyes and leaning my head against the headrest. After the third ring Carmen's cheery voice came blaring through the phone.

"Why the hell you ain't answer my call heffa? Please tell me it's because you were climbin Dre's tree."

I smiled to myself at her snarky comment. "Girl bye, you know damn well I ain't climbin shit."

"But yo scary ass want to," she teased.

I knew I would regret sending her that damn text. Fluttering my eyes open, I stared out the front window at the subject of our current conversation. Dre was busy working on removing my tire. His hands moved rapidly as he rocked my tire from side to side while pulling it off the rim. Sitting the damaged tire up against the truck, he used the inside of his forearm to wipe sweat from his forehead.

"Helloooooooooo," Carmen's voice reverberated through the speaker, pulling me out of my trance.

"Huh? Did you say something?" My voice was shaky, like I'd been caught even though I knew she couldn't see me.

"Never mind that, what were you doing?"

"My bad, boo. I'm actually sitting in Dre's truck waiting for him to finish changing my tire."

I could hear the concern in her voice when she asked, "Damn. What happened?"

"Some asshole cut me off and I swerved to avoid hittin em. I hit the damn curve and must've ran up on somethin that popped my tire."

Her tone was calm and her cheery sing-songy voice had returned. "That sucks but I'm glad you're okay. So, what you and Dre about to get into when he's done?"

"We don't have plans silly. I didn't even call him to change my tire.

I was in the process of changing it when he showed up out of nowhere and took over."

"Now, if that ain't some Prince Charmin shit I don't know what is. Girl give that boy some as a thank you." Her voice was light and joking but I didn't miss the seriousness in her tone.

If only it were that simple.

Out of the corner of my eye, I saw Dre walking toward the truck, holding my busted tire in his hand. "Hey boo, it looks like he's done. I'll call you back."

"Alright be safe. Bye chica."

"Bye." I disconnected the call and rolled down the window as Dre neared the driver's side of his truck.

"Where you going with my tire?"

Dre smirked at me as he continued walking toward the back of his truck. Craning my neck, I turned toward the rearview window and looked out just as Dre was bending down to sit my tire on the ground. A few moments later he stood to his full height then used both his hands to grab the collar of his tee-shirt and drag it up his face. My eyes traveled south to his exposed flesh, admiring his sculpted abs. Silently I counted each one. Six beautifully chiseled rectus abdominis muscles glistened with tiny specks of sweat. His muscles flexed every time he inhaled and seemed to directly correlate with my accelerated breathing. Licking my lips, I quickly shifted my eyes back up to his face. Dre had shifted his hands from the inside of his collar to the front of his shirt and swiped it down his face, settling his eyes on mine.

Shit, he caught me.

Beautiful white teeth peeked from underneath his lips as he flashed me an amorous smile followed by a wink. A girlish giggle slipped from my mouth before I had time to catch it. Thankfully, Dre's attention had shifted back to his original task. Bending down, he picked my tire off the ground and tossed it on the bed of his truck. Clasping his hands in front of his face Dre wiped the dirt from them then trekked the short distance back to the driver's side of the truck.

"You're all set, Short Stuff. You ready to go?" he asked while placing his hand on the door handle and looking me in the eyes.

"Yes, but you never answered me. What are you doing with my tire?"

Shaking his head, Dre smiled down at me as he opened my door and stretched out a hand to me. "I'm gonna get it fixed if it's possible. If not, I'll replace it and return it to you once I'm done. Is that alright with you, Miss Independent?"

I grabbed my phone from my lap before accepting Dre's proffered hand and allowing him to help me out of the truck. "You don't have to do that. I can take care of it. I appreciate all that you've done already," I supplied, while tucking my phone inside the pocket of my shorts.

Dre frowned as he ran a greasy hand down his face. "Stop it. I told your hardheaded ass to call me if you needed anything, yet your ass was out here in the blazin sun about to change your own tire. I told you I got it, so let me handle it."

Again, there was finality in his words. I held my hands up in defeat. "Okay, just let me know the cost and I'll pay you back."

As soon as the words left my mouth, I wanted to take them back. I watched as Dre stepped back and pinched the bridge of his nose. He shook his head in disbelief. It was clear he was offended, but that wasn't my intention. I wasn't trying to be difficult but previous encounters taught me that men always had ulterior motives. So, as a rule I never accepted gifts unless the terms of said gifts were outlined from the gate. However, Dre and I weren't involved, we were friends and friends didn't do tick for tack favors. I knew that, and I needed him to know I knew his offer was genuine. Fiddling with my hands, I considered my words. I wanted, no scratch that, I needed him to know how much I appreciated him and what he did for me today.

Nervous, I licked my lips before speaking again. "Dre that didn't come out how I meant it."

"Well, what did you mean Rocky?" His voice was slightly elevated, and his tone was clipped.

I felt myself getting agitated with my inability to articulate my feelings. I took a deep breath and attempted to keep the frustration out of my voice. "I'm just sayin, Dre, foreign parts, even tires are expensive and—"

A frown donned his handsome face, halting my words. "I'm well aware of the going rate for a BMW X5 tire Rocky. And if I couldn't afford it, I wouldn't have offered to replace it."

I took a step forward, closing the gap Dre created moments ago when he stepped away from me. Waiting for my rebuttal, Dre cocked his head to one side and glared down at me. I opened my mouth to speak but quickly snapped it shut, fearful anything I said at this point would make things worse. Neither of us spoke as we stood staring at one another. Unable to interpret his silence I remained quiet as I implored him with my eyes.

Dre appeared unaffected. Annoyance was etched all over his face as he pinned me with his unwavering emeralds. I squirmed underneath his intense glare, purposely diverting my eyes I explored his face. My gaze started at his clinched jaw, then laggardly slid down to his full lips. Lips that were too enticing to still be fixed in a languid frown. Sweeping my eyes upward, I observed the slight crinkle of his nose and the furrow of his full brows.

Damn, all of this over a freakin tire.

Finally settling my eyes on his again, I attempted once more to formulate the words needed to kill the tension between us. An apology sat on the tip of my tongue, but pride kept it trapped there. I was being stubborn, and I knew it. Guilt tugged at my subconscious as I fought like hell to keep my eyes focused on Dre's. The ire I'd seen moments ago was no longer present, what I saw left me miffed.

"I'm sorry. Please stop lookin at me like that," I blurted out, suddenly hit with the realization that Dre wasn't just pissed, he was hurt.

Finally straightening his neck Dre relaxed his shoulders while releasing a cool stream of air from his parted lips as a soft grin slowly eased across his face. I hated how I felt knowing he was upset with me. I wasn't sure why it bothered me so much, or at least I wasn't ready to explore the why. But seeing Dre's teeth peek through his lips as his grin morphed into a full smile made me giddy, causing an unexpected chuckle to escape from between my lips. My eyes ballooned as a hand shot up to my mouth. I attempted to hide the gargantuan smile plastered on my face.

Dre gently removed my hand from my mouth and enclosed it in his. "No harm no foul, but if it will make you feel better you can pay me back by cookin a nigga a good home cooked meal. Then we'll call it even. Coo?"

Again, I chuckled as I placed my other hand on my forehead, attempting to block out the sun that was now shining directly in my face. "Deal. But who said I know how to cook? And when would you like this meal, tonight or on another night?"

Deliberately shifting his body to the side Dre intentionally blocked the sun. "Better?"

I removed my hand from my forehead and shook my head.

"Quit playin. You already know who told me. Ryker swears if he wasn't an athlete, he would be big as hell from eatin your cookin growin up. And yes, dinner tonight sounds great if you're up for it. I don't want to impose on your time tho. So, if tonight doesn't work, we can pick a different day."

"Well I'm sure changin my tire in this hot ass sun wasn't part of your plans today, so I think I can manage to whip you up a nice thank you meal."

"The heat doesn't really bother me, but your little ass look like you're about to melt," he joked, as he used the thumb of his free hand to wipe sweat from my cheek. Dre removed his hand from my face and instantly I missed his touch. Diverting my eyes, I tried to ignore the fluttering in my stomach.

Dre's deep bravado resonated over my head, prompting me to look up at him as he spoke again. "Bet. I need to go home and get cleaned up first. What time is dinner?"

I smiled at the excitement in his tone while glancing at my watch. "Well, it's three-thirty now. So, is six cool with you?"

"Six is perfect. Do you need me to bring anything?"

"Just your appetite. Do you have a preference on what you want to eat?"

Dramatically Dre placed his index finger up to his lips and shifted his eyes toward the sky, humming he pretended to be in deep thought. I snatched my hand from his and playfully shoved him in his muscular arm then took a step forward. Dre laughed while quickly grabbing me by the back of my arm and halting my steps. He dropped his hand to my waist and pulled me backward into his chest while wrapping his other arm around my midsection, locking his arms at the wrists he let them rest against my thighs. I melted into his embrace as I felt the warmth of his breath on my earlobe.

"I'm not picky. I'll eat whatever you prepare, Short Stuff."

I tilted my head back so I could see his face. "My kind of guest. I stopped cookin for Egypt's picky ass a long time ago. She has way too many restrictions for my kitchen," I joked.

"Well let's get you home so you can get to work on that delicious meal you're about to cook for me."

Tickled and relieved to hear the amusement return to his voice, I giggled while rotating my head forward as Dre gently nudged me. Falling into a comfortable silence, Dre and I walked to my truck while I enjoyed the comfort of being wrapped in his arms. That comfort was short-lived as we arrived at my SUV. Reluctantly I peeled myself out of his grasp and Dre took a step back, allowing me enough space to open my door.

I turned to face him and looked up into his eyes, noticing they had resumed their intrinsic hazel hue. "Seriously Dre, thank you. I really appreciate your help."

"No thanks necessary Short Stuff. I would've done the same for a stranger, so for you it was nothing," he stated nonchalantly.

Stepping forward, I perched on the tips of my toes intending to press my lips to Dre's cheek. However, he shifted abruptly, and my mouth landed directly on his. Eyes open, lips still pressed against his, I craned my neck up in search of his eyes. I felt Dre's lips curl into a smirk as his amused eyes met mine.

He took his time removing his mouth from mine, stepping back he continued to peer down at me. "Six o'clock right?"

What. The. Hell. Was. That?

Speechless, I held his gaze while nodding my head. Dre's smirk remained plastered on his face as he instructed me to get into my truck. Slowly, I eased into the driver's seat and allowed him to close the door behind me. I started the engine and paid him one last glance before pulling away from the curb and cautiously easing into the flow of traffic.

Shifting my eyes forward, I pulled my bottom lip in between my teeth and savored the memory of his lips pressed against mine. Lips that had intentionally made contact with my lips. Warm, buttery soft, succulent, full lips that I wanted to feel again and on different parts of my body.

Damn you, Andre Cameron.

I pulled into my apartment complex a little after four, and my mind was still racing. I exited my truck while trying to make sense of what happened as I trekked the brief walk to my door. A few moments later I stepped inside my apartment to find Creed eagerly awaiting me. I lowered my backpack to the floor and tossed my keys into the dish next to the door then slowly dropped to my knees and greeted my beefy canine. Excited, Creed jumped in my lap, throwing me off balance he almost knocked me on my ass. Quickly regaining my composure, I laughed as I briskly ran my hands over his massive head.

"I missed you too, yes I did," I roused, giving Creed one final pat before standing to my feet. "You ready to go outside?" Creed wagged his tail excitedly while playfully pouncing around me.

That was my cue. Stepping away from the door I walked into the living room and headed straight to the patio. I opened the door and chuckled as Creed bolted past me, damn near knocking over one of my patio chairs in his haste to get to the open field. He wasn't outside long. After a few high energy laps around *his* area he relieved himself then lazily ambled back over to me.

"Un hun. You wore yourself out that quick, didn't you?"

Perched on his hind legs, tongue dangling from his mouth, Creed cocked his head to the side and stared up at me.

"Yeah, yo ass tired. Come on." I waved a hand at him while shuffling off to the side.

Amused at how quickly he tired himself out, I watched as Creed trotted past me and plopped down on the living room floor. *He gonna be there for a minute.* Shaking my head, I turned back toward the door and slid it shut while looking across the courtyard. I was surprised as hell to see my neighbor engaged in a steamy kiss with a man who was not Rashad, her live-in-boyfriend. I looked down at my watch and noted she had approximately forty-five minutes until Rashad would be home.

An insidious smirk spilled onto my face as I shifted my gaze back in her direction just as she and her side piece disconnected. Her head whipped from side to side, eyes scanning the yard, surveying her surroundings before finally noticing me. Her lips curled up into a mischievous smile while hints of a blush heated her tan cheeks. Acknowledging me with a wink, she returned her attention to her lover. Completely enthralled in something I knew wasn't my business I remained posted up in the door. My eyes bounced between her and her lover as she watched him trek through the parking lot and head for his car. After seeing him get inside his car, she did one final sweep of the area before turning on her heels and sauntering into her apartment.

I continued staring out the door as I recalled the day Paige and Rashad moved into the apartment complex. I was sitting out on my patio studying when I heard yelling. Annoyed by the distraction I sat my textbook down and looked in the direction of where the commotion was coming from. Immediately, my eyes landed on the newly occupied apartment where I saw a woman standing on the patio half naked. She was wearing only her panties and a bra, screaming out into the parking lot at a frustrated-looking man. My annoyance quickly shifted to curiosity as I watched the angry man sprint toward the half-naked women. Her voice had elevated and on top of tossing some pretty vulgar insult, she'd started shouting obscenities at him. He damn near tackled her little ass back into the apartment once he reached her. Later that night she came over with a bottle of wine and apologized for making a scene.

That was a little over a year ago, and we've been sharing wine ever since. I wouldn't say Paige and I were friends, but we were definitely cool. On nights that I couldn't sleep and found myself sitting on my patio enjoying the calm of the night, I'd likely find Paige on her patio doing the same. It was during those moments we gravitated to one another, talking over wine or silently sipping while appreciating each other's company. I could always count on her for a good story and equally good bottle of wine. Paige was cool people, but she definitely rocked to the beat of her own drum. Rashad seemed pretty cool too, from what I could tell based on the few interactions I had with him since they moved in. According to Paige he worked a lot. She complained of being lonely, so she entertained others in his absence. I didn't judge, nor did I make it my business to involve myself in their affairs. So, whenever I caught her with her flavor of the month I would observe in silence and wait until our next late-night meeting for her to provide me with all the salacious details. I couldn't wait to hear about this one because homeboy was fine as hell.

I was eating into my running time being nosy. I peeled my meddlesome ass away from the door and walked into the kitchen. I headed straight for the freezer, removing a pack of frozen chicken breast I sat it on the counter then checked the refrigerator and the cabinets for all the other ingredients necessary for tonight's meal. Satisfied that I had everything I needed, I returned to the counter and placed the frozen poultry inside the sink then filled it with hot water. After shutting off the faucet I turned away from the sink and leaned against the counter. My thoughts were everywhere but before they could get away from me, my phone chirped. Rubbing my damp hands down the back of my shorts, I withdrew my phone from my pocket and glanced at the screen.

Instantly, I became aroused. My heart rate increased, body temperature spiked, my hands felt dank, and the hairs on the back of my neck tingled. *What. The. Hell?* Without reading Dre's text, I laid my phone on the counter and left out the kitchen, heading straight for my bedroom. I needed to run. I had to clear my head before he got here or else, I would be a complete mess. As soon as I crossed the threshold of my bedroom I started stripping out of my clothes, leaving them sprawled across the floor wherever they landed. Quickly I opened my drawers and retrieved my running gear. I was dressed in record time.

The only thing left was my footwear. I sprinted into my closet and stepped into my running shoes, wiggling my feet from side to side until they were all the way on. Bending at the waist I tied my laces then walked out the closet, snatching my headphones from my nightstand as I passed and exited my bedroom.

I walked back into the kitchen and stood over the counter gawking at my cellphone. Deciding I was wasting time and being ridiculous I grabbed my phone and opened Apple Music then scrolled through my playlists. I located the list labeled *motivation for yo ass*, plugged my headphones into the receiver and hit play. Drake's "HYFR" blared through the speakers as I traipsed out of the kitchen and into the hall. Reflexively my head bobbed to the beat as I snatched my keys from the bowl by the door and rushed out of my apartment. Outside the door I secured the lock then rested my forehead against the cold metal on the doorframe while inhaling the fresh humid air through my nose. I allowed it to fill my lungs before slowly blowing it back out through my mouth. Feeling comfortable with my breathing in the searing heat, I removed my head from the doorframe and hit the home button on my phone. Before I could change my mind, I opened my message app and quickly scrolled to Dre's text. As a warmup, I started a light jog out of my apartment complex and almost tripped over my feet when I read his message.

Dre: I hope dinner tastes as good as your lips <tongue emoji>.

CHAPTER FOUR

Stretched out across my couch, I sipped my brew while half listening to the TV. I wasn't really paying attention to the sport show that was blasting from the large screen but hated the sound of silence. Placing my beer on the table I picked up my cellphone and checked the time. I had a little over an hour before I needed to be at Rocky's. I'd already showered so there wasn't much left for me to do. However, I needed to make a quick stop before I headed her way. Which meant I needed to be dressed and out the door in the next twenty minutes.

I laid my phone back on the table and picked up my brew as I peeled my big ass off the couch. I gulped down the rest of the grainy hops and smirked to myself as I envisioned the shocked expression on Rocky's face when I removed my mouth from hers. I didn't plan on kissing her, but when I saw her mouth coming toward my face I couldn't resist. Turning my cheek at that precise moment and feeling her sumptuous lips against mine was the highlight of my day. Hell, it took every ounce of self-control I had not to dig my hands in her unruly ponytail and shove my tongue down her throat. I had to be careful with her. Rocky had an allure that could make the strongest of men weak, something that became clear the more time I spent getting to know her.

Fuck it, it was worth it though.

I walked into my bedroom and pitched my empty bottle into the trash can then trekked into my closet. Leisurely, I removed my basketball shorts as I considered what to wear. I shifted my eyes straight ahead then upward as I looked between the hanging garments and the pile of clothes neatly folded on my overhead shelf. Unsure if I wanted to wear shorts or pants, I remained still in place as I continued shifting my eyes between the shelf and the hangers. I decided on shorts. Reaching above my head, I pulled my army fatigue shorts down from the shelf and tossed them over my shoulder then turned in the opposite direction where my shoes were lined up against the wall and surveyed my shoe collection. I moved over to the meticulously stacked shoe boxes and gingerly pulled the box containing my fight club Air Jordans from the pile before exiting the closet.

With my shorts and shoes in hand, I headed straight for my dresser where I retrieved a plain black tee. Less than fifteen minutes later, I was completely dressed and ready to go. Excitement had my ass damn near skipping as I headed toward my dresser to examine my appearance. My eyes swept down my lengthy frame, starting at my head and stopping just below my knees. Satisfied with my attire I slid my brush off the dresser and ran it over my hair, smoothing down my natural waves. I remained in front of the mirror staring at my reflection. I observed the freshly grown hair since getting my hair cut on Friday when my stomach growled, reminding me I hadn't ate since breakfast.

God please let this woman know how to cook.

I placed the brush back on the dresser and frowned as I ran my hand over my empty stomach. I hadn't planned on skipping lunch, but food was the last thing on my mind after I spotted Rocky stranded on campus earlier today. Once I saw her off, I came home and planned to grab a quick bite to eat, but the heat had kicked my ass. My body craved relief, relief that only a heated shower could provide. After my shower, I reclined across the couch and passed out.

Wandering into the living room, I grabbed the remote and my cellphone off the coffee table. I tucked my cellphone in the pocket of my shorts while hovering my thumb over the power button on the remote. I was prepared to shut off the TV but paused when I heard an ESPN sports anchor mention my name. Eyes glued to the TV, I increased the volume and listened for any negative or controversial commentary.

From the moment I showed interest in sports, my pops told me I needed to be just as conscious of my conduct off the field as I was on the field. He told me fans and especially critics would watch what I did when out of uniform sometime more than what I did when suited up. Pops said it was my responsibility not to give them anything to concentrate on other than how I played the game. With my pop's words always in the back of my mind, I worked hard to maintain a low profile, but I was smart enough to know the media could create a story even if there wasn't one.

When I didn't hear anything out of the norm, I clicked off the TV and dropped the remote on the couch. Shaking my head, I wondered if I would ever get used to the spotlight that came with being an athlete. According to my coach, this was only the beginning and truthfully that shit intimidated me.

Quickly pushing those thoughts out of my mind, I snatched my phone out of my pocket and glanced at the time. The screen was lit up with multiple text notifications, but one name was missing. A little disappointed but not at all surprised, I opened my message app and swiftly scanned through the threads. None of the messages required my immediate attention so I slid my phone back in my pocket and walked out of the living room and straight for the door.

Inside my truck I started the engine and immediately rolled down all the windows. It was still hot as hell outside, but I didn't really mind the heat. Summer was actually my favorite time of year. I loved the way the sun enveloped me in its warmth and caressed my skin with its fiery rays. I especially appreciated the tan it always left behind when it was done dancing upon my pale vellum.

Growing up, I was the kid who hit the streets as soon as his chores were complete and didn't return home until the sun had set. By the end of summer, I was always three shades darker from spending so much time outside. However, I considered it a small price to pay to enjoy the summer heat and time spent playing with my friends. My pops never understood how I could tolerate the heat. I, on the other hand, never understood why people made such a big deal over it. It's wasn't like we lived in Florida or Nevada, we lived in Ohio. On our hottest days we rarely reached a hundred degrees. Pops swore the only reason I loved the summertime was because I was born in May. I doubted there was any validity to his theory, but I didn't have one of my own, so I rolled with it.

The sound of laughter pulled me from my musing. Reflexively my head swung in that direction. Two small children were ducked behind an old beat up car. Their small hands covered their mouths, attempting to mask their mirth as they hid from a woman, I assumed was their mother. Tickled by their innocence and obvious amusement, a fatuous grinned spilled onto my lips. I continued watching the pair for a few moments before tugging my cell phone out my pocket and glimpsing at the screen. Seeing a text notification from Rocky instantly shifted my grin into a broad smile.

I shook my head and dropped my phone in my lap while reflecting on the effect Rocky had over me. I'd been crushing on this chick since eighth grade. Of course, as I got older and started dating girls my own age those feelings waned, and I chalked them up to just that, a child-hood crush. However, the time we've spent getting to know one another outside of our individual relationships with the twins had those old feelings crashing to the forefront. Undoubtedly, I thought Rocky was beautiful, so naturally I was physically attracted to her. But it was more than that, the more I got to know her the more I found myself wanting her. I wanted to love her. I wanted to love away the pain that JB's reckless example of a husband marred on her soul. I yearned to shield her from anything that would cause her harm while showing her I could be the man she could give her heart to. I wanted her to know that I would treasure it and her, never abusing her trust or her love. But she wasn't ready, so I would keep that shit to myself until she was. I just wasn't sure how long I could hide my feelings.

Remembering I had a text from Rocky snapped me out of my

reverie. Fully expecting her to cuss me out about our kiss, I picked my phone up from my lap and diffidently opened her text.

Rocky: Trust, dinner will be good but nothing tastes better than "my" lips <winking face emoji>.

Whoa, I definitely wasn't expecting that.

Stuck staring at the screen, I read her message over and over again, each time my eyes lingered over the word "my," clearly insinuating that the lips she was referring to weren't the ones on her pretty little face. Closing my eyes, I laid my head back against the headrest and tried to formulate a response that wouldn't scare her little ass. Unable to think of anything rated PG, my eyes fluttered open. I replied with a simple emoji.

Me: <tongue emoji>

I let my phone fall back in my lap before shifting my truck in gear and pulling out of my apartment complex. Forty-five minutes later, I was parked outside of Rocky's apartment building with no real recollection of the drive over. The entire ride I couldn't focus, my mind couldn't move past her text. *Fuck!* I ran a hand over my face while blowing out an exasperated breath as I acknowledged the fact that she had me feeling like the pimpled face fourteen-year-old boy who used to secretly draw her name inside all his notebooks.

My head shook softly on my shoulders as I quickly dismissed those unsolicited yet very familiar feelings. Focused on the present and the friendship Rocky and I had committed to building, I composed myself before rolling up my windows and turning off the engine of my truck. Reaching across the middle console into the passenger seat I retrieved the wine I picked up from Cooper's Hawk then grabbed my phone from my lap and plucked my long frame from my whip. Outside I took comfort in the warm air as I tucked my phone and keys in the pocket of my shorts before leisurely starting the short trek toward Rocky's door, using that time to try and shake off the emotions, I felt merely moments ago.

This shit is crazy, no other woman has had this kind of effect on me. What is it about her?

I knocked on the door and immediately took a step back when I heard Creed barking from the other side. *Shit, I forgot all about her big ass four-legged roommate.* I heard Rocky yell at Creed, and instantly he stopped barking. I chuckled to myself as I thought about her little ass having such a ferocious animal for a pet. Seconds later, Rocky flung the door open, and all traces of humor left my face as I stared down at her in a loosely fitted UC T-shirt and nothing else. An innocent smile was splayed across her face as she moved to the side and waved me into her apartment. Closing the gap between us, I stepped forward and stood directly in front of her. Rocky pushed the door close while sucking in a big gulp of air and dropping her head. My eyes dusted over the top of her head as I slowly raised a hand to her face and softly rubbed the back of my fingertips along her silky cheek. I felt her cheeks rise as she gradually raised her head and smiled up at me. I wanted to taste her lips again but knew better than to press my luck.

I removed my hand from her face while locking my eyes on hers. "I know you said I didn't need to bring anything, but I stopped and got you a bottle of wine. Barbera right?"

Indolently, Rocky's eyes lowered to my hand then returned to my face. "You remembered."

Holding her gaze I shook my head. "I pay attention to everything."

Approbation danced in her slanted eyes as her teeth clamped down on her bottom lip. She tried hiding her smile by turning her head away from me, but it was hard to miss the ascent of her cheeks and the deep dimples piercing her flesh.

Slowly swiveling her head back in my direction, she spoke in a low and absconded tone. "Thank you, that was sweet. Dinner is almost ready, so I hope you're hungry."

"I'm starving actually."

Bemused by our close proximity, I decided to create some space between us, languorously walking past her I stepped further into her apartment. Immediately I stopped in my tracks when my eyes landed on Creed. We were in the middle of a stare off when I felt Rocky's small hand on my middle of my back. Refusing to take my eyes off killer, I remained frozen in place. I heard Rocky chuckle behind me before commanding Creed to go lay down.

"Dre, you really are gonna have to get use to him if you're gonna be chillin over here. I don't make it a habit to put him up for company since this is his home too, but if it will make you feel better, I'll lock him up this one time."

Turning to face her I couldn't help the frown that settled on my face. "Don't say it like I'm some kind of bitch. That's not a normal dog, Raquel." I felt my face relax as she stared up at me with a teasing smile. "It's cool. You're right, I do need to get use to him because if you can cook imma be over here once a week for dinner."

"Oh yeah?" Cutting her eyes at me she waved her hand dismissively in my direction. "Nigga I can burn, you're about to see," she joshed, as she sashayed past me.

I bent down and removed my shoes before following behind her. Inside the kitchen I sat the bottle of wine on the counter before pulling a bar stool back and plopping down on it while I watched Rocky fiddle around in the kitchen.

"It does smell good Short Stuff."

"Thanks. You want a beer, or do you want me to open the wine?"

I hiked a brow. "What kind of beer?"

With her hands on her hips she turned and faced me. "The kind you drink," she answered sassily.

I smirked as I watched her laugh at her own joke while sauntering over to the refrigerator. The gentleman in me told me to look away but the savage quickly overruled that thought. I took full advantage of her having her back to me, taking my time I swept my eyes down her shapely body. I watched her ponytail bounce up top of her head while the material of the thin tee-shirt swayed along with the bounce of her cheeks. I licked my lips as my eyes rested on her toned thighs, watching the muscles in her hamstrings tighten each time she stepped forward on the balls of her small manicured feet. I continued watching her as she opened the refrigerator and casually bent over to look inside.

Completely enraptured in her beauty I barely heard a word she spoke as she ran down a list of beers. Instead, I found myself gawking in awe as her tee-shirt gradually hiked up her back, exposing her voluptuous ass. Ass that was now spilling out of her snuggly fitted boy shorts, that had been hiding underneath her large shirt. My eyes remained glued on her backside as I hopped off my bar stool and marched tenuously into the kitchen. I continued admiring the curves of her athletic frame as I stood behind her, careful not to place my growing erection on her ass. Gently I placed my hands around her petite waist, reveling the closeness of the moment. Slowly she stood up and stilled in place.

I lowered my mouth to her ear. "Please go put on some real bottoms," I growled.

Listlessly I removed my hands from her waist and leaned back against the wall. No words were spoken between us as Rocky padded out of the kitchen and down the hall. Closing my eyes, I let my head rest against the wall. Slowly I felt the tension leave my body as I relaxed my shoulders and ran my fingers along the bridge of my nose. Suddenly my eyes flashed open at the sound of Creed's collar jiggling. Eyes trained on the floor I found Creed resting at my feet. Calmly I dropped down on my haunches and ran an uneasy hand over his massive size head.

"Now ain't this cute."

I was so consumed with watching Creed's reaction to my touch that I didn't hear Rocky come back into the kitchen. Slowly I stood to my feet as she walked timidly toward me. I could see the apprehension on her face as she stood in front of me chewing on her bottom lip. Unsure how to comfort her I did the only thing I could think of, I pulled her into my chest and gently ran a hand down her back.

"What's wrong Short Stuff, did I do something to upset you?"

She wrapped her small arms around my waist and shook her head against my chest.

"Then why you look so sad?"

"Because we can't do this," she mumbled against my shirt.

"Do what?"

Unhurriedly she removed her arms from around my waist and peeled herself out of my embrace. Her head remained down as she answered me. "This." She used her index finger to point between us. "We can't do this, be like this."

"Be like what, friends?" I tried to keep the annoyance out of my voice.

Her head snapped up and for the first time since she entered the kitchen a slight smile adorned her face as humor danced in her eyes. "Really Dre? So, I'm trippin? There is absolutely nothing going on between us?" She blinked away the traces of mirth previously present in her soft ambers. "I mean, do you kiss all your friends Andre?"

I didn't like her tone but at least I had a better understanding of her somber mood. "You're right, there is something between us and no, I don't kiss all my friends. Is that what has you upset; you think I just go around kissing anybody?"

She tried turning away from me, but I grabbed her arm, preventing her from moving. "Thank you," she whispered.

I hiked a brow. "For what?"

"For not making me feel crazy, like I was making this up." She pointed between us again.

"Nah, you're not crazy. There is definitely some undeniable shit going on between us."

She chuckled but I didn't find shit funny. "It's too bad we can't explore it."

I let her arm go and looked down into her doleful eyes. "Why not?"

"Dre," she whined.

"I'm serious, why can't we see where this goes?"

"Because you're my brothers' best friend and I don't want to mess that up."

"What do the twins have to do with us Rocky?"

"Everything," she yelled.

She walked away and this time I didn't stop her. I watched as she walked over to the stove and retrieved the food from the oven. Placing a large baking dish on the counter she turned and faced me. "Dre I'm not like your typical woman. I don't do relationships. I date for fun and when the fun is over, I'm done. I don't want to complicate your life or hurt you."

I was speechless, I knew Rocky wasn't ready for love but I wasn't expecting her to admit she had feelings for me then shoot down the idea of exploring those feelings all before giving me a chance to process it. My confusion must have registered on my face.

Rocky walked over to me and grabbed my hand. "Please don't be mad. I really enjoy your company and I want us to continue to be friends. Please tell me that's possible?"

Shaking off the disappointment of her admission I decided to focus on the positive, Rocky felt something for the kid. "We can be friends but only under one condition."

"What?"

"I still get to flirt with you. Deal?"

She pulled her hand out of mine and smiled. "I wouldn't want it any other way."

I used the back of my hand to playfully wipe invisible sweat from my brow. "Now that we got that out the way can we eat? A nigga starvin." There was no hiding the gaiety in my tone as I teased her.

"Yes, let me fix your plate." Rocky walked back to the counter then turned toward me. "Seriously Dre, are we good?"

I shook my head and pushed off the wall then walked back to my stool. I sat silently mulling over our conversation while watching Rocky fix our plates. Coming in the door I fully expected Rocky to cuss me out about our kiss. Instead, I found out the woman I used to crush on as a teenager and was developing feelings for as an adult also had feelings for me. A soft smile eased upon my face as the realization of having my feelings reciprocated sunk in. However, I had to admit I was disappointed when she shot down the idea of exploring a relationship between us, but I was happy as hell just knowing she thought about it.

Conversely, Rocky mentioned something I never considered, her brothers. Not once since I acknowledged my feelings for Rocky did I consider how my relationship with the twins would be affected once she and I hooked up. Royce and Ryker were my day one niggas and we'd never had any real static between us. I just hoped it remained that way. I needed them to be receptive to me dating their sister. Because although Rocky said she wasn't willing to take it there, it was definitely headed there. It was just a matter of time. The shit that was happening between us was undeniable and no matter how much she tried to fight it, the shit was inevitable. I knew in my heart Rocky's little ass was going to be mine. The sound of Rocky clearing her throat snatched me out of my musing.

"Sorry to interrupt your daydreaming but I thought you came to eat."

I shook my head at her snarky comment, allowing an amusing smirk to settle on my face as I watched her switch out of the kitchen. Hopping off my seat, I pushed the bar stool back in place and joined Rocky at the table. I sat in the empty seat where she had placed my dinnerware and looked down at the artfully decorated plate loaded with a heaping portion of food. The delicious aroma streaming from my dish elicited an involuntary groan from my stomach. Caught off guard I placed a hand on my stomach as my eyes shifted up from my plate to across the table, settling on Rocky.

"Huh, let me bless this food so you can eat," she offered, sliding her hand across the table toward mine. I encased her hand in mine. I relished the feel of her delicate skin as I closed my eyes while she said grace.

"Amen," we uttered in unison.

Slowly fluttering my lids open I looked down at my plate and ran my tongue across my lips. "Damn Short Stuff this looks amazing. What is it?"

She flashed a coy smile as her eyes darted to her plate sitting in front of her. "Chicken parmesan, I hope you like it."

"I'm going to love it because you made it for me."

Rocky's eyes shot up from her plate and found me staring back at her. "Okay, I know I said I wanted you to continue to flirt with me, but you don't have to do it all the time," she joked, as she playfully rolled her eyes at me.

"I wasn't flirting I was being honest. I know we made a deal so you would stop fighting me about your tire, but I really appreciate you taking time out of your day to cook for me. So, like I said, I'm going to love it."

She flashed me a soft smile and picked up her fork then began eating. I followed suit, grabbing my own fork I dug into my plate. A soft moan escaped from my lips as I savored the deliciousness of my first bite. Embarrassed, my eyes ballooned out of their sockets as I shifted them up from my plate. I wasn't surprised to discover Rocky smirking at me. That was my undoing. I dropped my fork in my plate and pushed away from the table, hunching over I laughed uncontrollably. My laughing spell intensified when I heard Rocky's gut-wrenching laughter above my own. We carried on for a minute, until the sound of Creed's collar jiggling in the distance caused us both to look in his direction. Slowly regaining my composure, I pulled my chair back up to the table and watched Rocky dab her napkin at the corners of her eyes before returning my eyes to my plate.

"So, I take it you like my cooking?" she asked before sipping from her glass.

I smirked while nodding my head as I finished chewing the forkful of food I had shoved into my mouth. "Oh, you can burn baby girl. I haven't had a meal this good since I left home. Looks like your stuck wit my ass."

"I'm glad you like it. Besides the twins and my daddy of course, you're the first man I've ever cooked for."

I sat my fork on the table and picked up my glass, taking a hearty sip I looked across at Rocky. "Word, why?"

She sat her fork next to her plate and returned my gaze. "Because cooking for a man is something you do when in a relationship."

My mouth formed an O as I absorbed her words. "So, does that mean you won't be cooking for me anymore?" I asked sadly, placing my glass back on the table.

Picking up on my tone Rocky's lips curled up into a slight grin. "Nah, I'll cook you a nice home cooked meal once a week like you suggested but only because you're cute though." She winked at me as she picked up her fork and resumed eating.

A comfortable silence settled between us as I picked up my fork and continued eating. A few moments ticked by before either of us spoke. Holding my fork next to my plate I settled my orbs on my gracious hostess.

"So, what are your plans for the holiday? You going home?"

Rocky shook her head while simultaneously placing a hand in front of her mouth. "Yeah, my daddy threatened to come down here if I didn't." She rolled her eyes and dropped her hand from her mouth as she finished chewing her food. "Besides, the holidays are kind of a big deal in my family. Miss Brenda and daddy are cooking out. Are you coming? I know the twins won't be there but you're more than welcome to come join the shenanigans. Speaking of the holidays, are you going to Atlanta at the end of August for Labor Day too?"

I shoved the last forkful of food in my mouth and closed my eyes, enjoying the flavorful taste as it traveled down my throat. Slowly I fluttered my lids open and swallowed the remainder of my food before I answered her. "All I needed was an invite. I'm there. Yeah, I'll be in the A that weekend. Royce already called and made sure I was coming. J and I will probably roll out that Thursday night. I'm just glad they finally settled on a weekend because the football season starts Labor Day weekend."

"And we can't have our star wide receiver gallivanting in strip clubs in the A when he's supposed to be on the field, now can we?"

"Who said anything about strip clubs?" I asked, sitting my fork on my plate and resting my elbows on the table.

Rocky waved a hand at me dismissively as she stood from her seat. I watched as she gathered her dinnerware then walked toward me and picked up my plate. "Boy bye. We are definitely hittin up a strip club or two."

I wasn't really surprised since the strip clubs in Atlanta were more like regular clubs. You were likely to see just as many women there as men. But I was shocked to know Rocky was one of those women.

I got to see this shit.

"We'll see. Anyway, is it cool if I bring J on the 4th? He's coming back next week and will be coming home with me." I attempted to change the subject, feeling slightly roused at the idea of Rocky inside a tittie bar.

"That's cool, E is coming home with me and you know Carm is already there. E is gonna be happy as hell when I tell her you're bringing Jamison." She smiled at me over her shoulder then sauntered out the room.

I stood from my seat, grabbed both our wine glasses off the table, and followed behind her into the kitchen. "Why is Egypt gonna be happy?"

Rocky kissed her teeth as she took the glasses from my hand. She turned on the water in the sink and began rinsing the goblets. "Don't act like you didn't know E has a crush on Jamison," she stated apathetically.

"Word? Does J know she's crushing on him?" I stepped behind Rocky and gently moved her to the side. Taking the glasses out of her hand I turned to face her. "Am I washing these or rinsing them for the dishwasher?"

Rocky leaned on the counter and crossed her arms in front of her chest. "Dre you don't have to do that."

I looked down at her before returning my attention back to the sink. "Now this we're not going to argue about." I reached for the dish-washing detergent when I felt her small hand on top of mine. I paused and turned my head in her direction, placing a soft smile on my face I kept my tone light. "We have reached our max on arguments for the day Raquel. You cooked for me, the least I can do is clean up."

Slowly she removed her hand from mine. "Can we do it together?"

I released an exasperated breath and shook my head. Hands down Rocky was thee most stubborn and independent woman I'd ever met, she was exhausting.

"Thank you. I'm far from the neatest person you know but I am particular about my kitchen and bathroom. Now the rest of my house, that's a different story," she joked.

"I get it, I have to get used to your extra independent ways. Tell me what you want me to do."

She smiled at me while playfully bumping me with her hips. "First, you can let Creed out and I will finish getting the stuff off the table. When you come back, you can rinse, and I'll load the dishwasher."

"Wait what?" I looked at her like she was speaking French. "You want me walk the beast?"

Rocky laughed as she shoved me out of her way. "Not walk him. Let him out the patio and wait for him to finish then let him back in. Y'all gotta get used to each other."

I hated to admit it, but she was right. I planned on spending a lot of time with her which meant I would be at her place often, so yes, I needed to get use to Creed. *Shit!* Rocky giggled behind me as I turned to leave the kitchen. Stopping in my tracks I spun around and smacked her on the ass before casually resuming my walk out the room. The expression on Rocky's face was priceless. Her mouth looked like it was ready to hit the floor as she stood speechless with a hint of a blush dusting over her ebony hued cheeks. I smirked to myself, tickled by how easily she was frazzled by me.

My humor was short lived as I stood at the apex of the living room staring at Creed who was sprawled out by the patio door. I approached him judiciously. Lowering to my knees I hovered my hand above his head, watching him closely as he raised his massive dome to meet my hand.

"I'on want no static. You dig?" I spoke out loud, while rubbing his head gingerly.

As if he understood what I just said his large tongue fell out of his mouth and swiped me across the knee. Relieved that we had an amicable understanding I stood to my full height and stepped over Creed's large body, opening the patio door to let him out. Creed jumped up on his beefy legs and ambled out the door. To kill time, I pulled my phone out of my pocket and checked for any missed calls or messages. I noted a missed call and text message from Payton. Deciding to respond to her later I dropped my phone back into my pocket just as Creed strolled up to the door. Still a little uneasy around the massive canine I kept my eyes trained on him as he trotted back into the apartment. Closing the door behind him I waited until he rested his large frame on the floor before returning to the kitchen.

"Ready?"

Rocky sat down her newly filled glass of wine. "I am. Do you want another glass of wine or a beer?"

I snickered as I recalled the beer debacle earlier this evening. "Wine is cool."

Rocky retrieved a new glass from the cabinet and poured me a hearty dose of her favorite wine. I stood silently admiring the view of her from the back as I felt my manhood waking up again. Grateful for the black capris leggings that was now covering her ass I quickly diverted my eyes and waited for her to finish. Turning toward me Rocky handed me the fresh glass of wine then stepped to the side of me. An appreciative mien donned my face as I accepted the glass from her hand and took a hefty sip of the pungent cocktail. I savored the oaky full-bodied spirit before sitting my goblet on the counter and turning on the water, starting the task of rinsing our dinnerware. Fifteen minutes later Rocky and I were finished cleaning the kitchen.

I used my shirt to dry the small amount of water from my hands before grabbing my glass off the counter and looking down at Rocky. "So, what you got going on for the rest of the night Short Stuff?"

Swallowing the remaining contents of her glass I watched as her lips pursed up from the bitterness of the wine, causing her mouth to make a loud popping sound when she opened it to speak. "I planned on studying but now I don't feel like it. I don't have class tomorrow, so I'll study then. Why, you ready to leave me?"

"Nah, not at all. Just didn't want to overstay my welcome."

Her dimples retreated into her cheeks as she smiled at me. She sat her empty glass on the counter and walked out of the kitchen, taking the few steps over into her living room. "Good because I'm not ready for you to leave."

"Really? I thought your lil spoiled ass would've had enough of me by now."

"Spoiled? Who me?" Turning in my direction Rocky held her small hand up against her chest, feigning shock.

A clamorous chuckle spilled out of her mouth as I strolled out of the kitchen and made my way into the living room. I placed my glass on the coffee table and sat next to her on the couch. "Yes you."

Rocky crossed her arms in front of her chest while poking out her bottom lip. "And how do you figure I'm spoiled?"

I angled my lengthy frame on the couch, ensuring I was able to look her in her potty face. "For starters you drive a newer year BMW X5 with license plates that say daddy's girl and—"

"It's a 2012 Dre" Rocky retorted, cutting me off.

"It's a BMW Raquel and one that is less than five years old."

Rocky rolled her eyes up in her head. "That's just one thing, I hardly see how that qualifies."

"Oh, I wasn't finished princess. Do I have your permission to continue?" With my head cocked to one side and a brow slightly hiked I waited for her to acknowledge my question.

Smirking she waved a hand at me, imploring me to continue.

"Like I was saying, your spoiled ass drives a 2012 BMW X5 that you don't pay the note on. Wait—" Placing a finger up to my chin I tapped it a few times for emphasis. "As I recall from one of our many conversations, you don't pay any bills with the exception of groceries, cell phone and car insurance. You did tell me that right?"

She stared at me through her lashes while pursing her lips and ignoring my rhetorical question.

A chortle flew from my mouth. "I'll say this then I'm done, because I do believe I have proven my point. I have seen your lil ass in more designer brands than the Kardashians. And at least one pair of red bottoms that I know of, but I'm sure you have a closet full. Not to mention the designer bags you—"

Rocky held up her tiny hand, then placed it on my chest. "Okay okay, you can stop. Point made. Sheesh, I never should've asked."

I hiked a brow while allowing a grin to spread across my face. "So, we agree you're a brat?"

Removing her hand from my chest she held it out in front of her face. She used her thumb and index finger to align them parallel to one another, leaving just a tiny space in between them. She squinted her already slanted lids and peeked through the tiny opening between her fingers. "I may be about this much of a brat and—" barely widening her fingers she continued to peak through the little slit, "this spoiled."

I softly smacked her hand as I turned my body forward and rested my back against the couch. "Yeah, okay."

81

Rocky burst out laughing. "Fuck you Dre."

"Don't be like that Short Stuff," I goaded.

"Whatever. You wanna play cards?"

I looked at Rocky out of the corner of my eye. "I'on think you want none of this."

"Boy please. Tunk?" she asked, with a raised brow.

"Hell yeah, what you know about some tunk?"

"I know I'm about to beat that ass. So, don't be mad when I do."

"Go get the cards then witcha shit talkin ass."

Without hesitating Rocky hopped off the couch and strolled out of the living room, leaving me alone with Creed while she retrieved the cards. I looked down at the fury canine and grinned when he looked at me and lifted his head like he knew what was going on. Moments later Rocky returned with a deck of cards, two shot glasses, and an unopened bottle of Rémy.

I looked at the bottle of liquor before sliding my eyes up to hers. "What's with the Rémy?"

"Loser answers the winner's question and takes a shot," she answered nonchalantly.

"Oh, you trynna get fucked up on a school night I see."

"I told you I don't lose, and I don't have class tomorrow, so. . ."

My chortle was barely audible, but my smile was clearly evident. "Okay, shuffle and deal em. But don't say I didn't warn you."

Sitting the shot glasses and Rémy on the table Rocky took her seat next to me. She removed the cards from the box and offered them to me. "You shuffle and deal and I'll find us some music. Deal?"

I took the cards out of her hand and began shuffling them while she fiddled with her cell phone. "Niggas in Paris" by Jay Z and Kanye West boomed through a speaker I hadn't noticed sitting on her side table. Rocky tossed her cell phone beside her on the couch while I bobbed my head to the beat and dealt the cards. With the cards on the table I looked up as Rocky helped herself to my glass of wine. A smile danced on my lips as she offered me my cocktail. Leisurely I accepted the glass from her hand, turning it to the side she drank from I chugged back the last of the balmy liquid. Instantly, Rocky jumped off the couch, grabbing the empty glass from my hand she walked out the room. Seconds later she returned with two beers. She took her seat while placing a cold Heineken in front of me on the table. Folding one leg underneath her she took a quick sip of her Redd's Apple Ale before sitting it on the table.

"I needed a chaser for these shots, and I wasn't about to repeat the episode from earlier, so I made an executive decision. You look like a Heineken man anyway." She winked at me as she picked up her cards.

"Thanks, Short Stuff but before we start, I got a question."

"You do remember me telling you the loser answers the winner's question, right?" she asked with sass.

"I know but I don't wanna waste my questions once I start spankin that ass."

A smirk adorned her beautiful face as she eyed me suspiciously. "Alright, I'll give you this one freebie."

"Where did the name Rocky come from?"

Picking up her fruity beer she took a quick sip then returned it to the table. "It's nothing spectacular really. My father wanted a boy and when he found out I was a girl he and my mother went back and forth about what to name me before finally settling on Raquel. According to my mother daddy only agreed because he thought Rocky was a cool nickname for Raquel. She said he wanted to name me a boy's name, something like Erin or Devon but she wasn't havin it. So, he got his boy name for his daughter by way of my nickname."

"Interesting. Alright, I'm ready."

"Let's go."

Rocky won the first round. Leaning forward I grabbed the bottle of Rémy and removed the protective sealing. In my peripheral I saw Rocky staring at me while I poured my shot. "Shoot, what's your question?"

"How come you don't have a girlfriend?"

I tossed my shot back and slammed my glass on the table as the hot liquid burned its way down my esophagus. Eyes trained on the sexy woman sitting next to me I picked up my beer and gulped down a few swigs. "Because you turned me down." I couldn't resist teasing her. I winked at her as she rolled her eyes at me. "No seriously, I can't afford the distraction. School and football are my top priorities right now."

Rocky bit down on her bottom lip while I shuffled and dealt our next hand. I won the second round. Picking up the liquor bottle I poured Rocky's shot and slid the glass toward her. "Inquiring minds want to know, aside from your ears and your two nose piercings do you have any other piercings?"

Rocky picked up her glass and threw back her shot. She smirked at me while taking a quick swig of her beer. "I have four other piercings besides my ears and the two in my nose."

My eyes shot up in disbelief and curiosity as she shuffled and dealt the cards. I won the third round. As bad as I dying to know what other parts of her body she had pierced I choose not to ask. I decided it would be more fun to discover them on my own. Rocky took her second shot like a G while I mulled over my next question.

"If I weren't the twins' friend would you," I placed my hands in the air and made air quotes, "date me?"

Rocky poured herself another shot and took it to the head, before staring me dead in the eyes with the most serious expression plastered on her face. "If you weren't the twins' friend, I would date you, fuck you, and eventually leave you."

Completely caught off guard I drew in a deep breath of air and immediately started choking on my spit. A concerned expression washed over Rocky's face as she leaned into me and patted my back until my coughing fit settled. Sliding back to her area on the couch Rocky picked up the cards and began shuffling. I bore a hole in the side of her face while she dealt our next hand.

"Stop staring at me Dre. I told you, I wasn't your average girl," she stated casually.

Picking up the Rémy bottle I poured myself a shot and tossed it back then picked up my cards. Rocky fucked up my head with her last answer, so I wasn't surprised when I lost. My concentration was fucked. Pouring myself another shot I chugged it back while I waited for Rocky's next question.

"Have you ever tried to reach out to your birth mom?"

What the fuck? Was she using these questions and answers to throw me off my game? Because the shit was working.

My expression was stoic while I tried to level out my voice. "First of all, you're a cheater but two can play that game. No, I've never looked for her. She didn't want me as a kid, so I'd be delusional to think she wants anything to do with me as an adult," I answered honestly.

I grabbed my beer from the table and gulped down the remainder of the bitter liquid before hopping off the couch and gaiting into the kitchen. I quickly retrieved two more beers, then returned to Rocky on the couch. I sat both drinks on the table and picked up the cards, shuffling and dealing the next round. Peeking at me through her long lashes Rocky slid her cards off the table and smirked at me.

"You called me a cheater, why?"

"Because your Q&A is throwin me off my game and I think that's your strategy."

"Nope, just answerin honestly and askin questions I really wanna know the answers to."

I shook my head acknowledging her last statement as I laid my cards face up on the table. "Ten Short Stuff." I winked at her as I picked up my beer and sipped from it.

"Or maybe my Q&A put a fire under that ass. Damn Dre."

"Yeah, whatever." I sat my beer on the table, poured her shot, and handed her the shot glass. "Drink."

Rocky sat the glass on the table, picked up her beer, and took a big gulp. Placing her beer back on the table she tossed back her shot. "I'm ready, what's your question Andre?" she asked mischievously.

"Favorite sexual position Raquel?"

"Any that involves me being on top," she fired off without hesitating.

Her little ass is something else.

Rocky picked up the deck of cards and began shuffling. "I know you didn't think that little punk ass question was gonna stump me." She cut her eyes at me before shifting them back to the deck of cards in her hand.

85

"Whatever smart ass. Just deal the cards. I'm going to the bathroom. You better not cheat either," I joked.

I stood from my seat and almost fell back onto the couch. Instantly, my eyes shot over to Rocky who was grinning up at me. Regaining my balance, I walked out the room to relieve myself. When I returned Rocky was standing at the patio door sipping from her beer. Sluggishly I plopped down on the sofa and waited for her to return. I watched as Rocky let Creed back into the apartment then padded back over to the couch where she took her seat. Placing her beer on the table she tucked both her legs underneath her and sat facing me.

"Last hand, you ready?"

I picked up my cards and nodded my head. I won the last round so I grabbed the liquor off the table and poured a shot for the both of us. I slid Rocky her glass while I picked mine up from the table. Holding the shot glass in my hand I waited until she picked up hers.

"Good games Short Stuff. Toast?"

"Sure."

"To good food, better company, and a blossoming friendship." I tapped my glass against hers then chugged down my drink. "Let the record reflect, I spanked that ass tonight."

Rocky laughed then tossed her drink back. "Last question, make it a good one."

I ran my hand over my goatee while looking directly in her soft brown eyes. "Are you a squirter or a shaker?"

"Oh wow. Go hard or go home huh?" She uncrossed her legs, leaned forward and grabbed her beer. I watched as she took a big swig before sitting it back on the table. Rocky licked her lips seductively as she returned her eyes to mine. "I'm a shaker but I must confess I've never had a vaginal orgasm so. . ."

Just like that, she left those words hanging in the air while I tried processing that shit through my slightly inebriated haze.

"Wait what? What do you mean you've never had a vaginal orgasm? How is that shit even possible?" I asked, honestly confused.

Rocky giggled. "It's not uncommon Dre. I've had orgasms from manual stimulation and oral sex, just never from penetration," she supplied, like I was the crazy one for asking.

I was truly flabbergasted, I sat quietly with my mouth hanging open. Rocky giggles turned into full on laughter as she leaned into me, raising her small hand to my mouth she gently nudged it shut.

"Stop being dramatic Dre, that's my department," she teased.

I remained stuck in place as I watched her pick up her cell phone and cut off the music. She tossed her phone back on the sofa then gathered our shot glasses, placing them upside down on the tops of the empty beer bottles before picking them and the Rémy bottle up from the table. I continued watching her in silence as she traipsed out of the room and into the kitchen. Rocky sat all the containers on the island then moved further into the kitchen. I was unable to see her but heard her open the refrigerator.

Moments later she walked back into the living room with two unopened bottles of water in her hands. She sat both bottles on the side table and cut off the speaker while looking down at me. I was still perched up on the couch and completely speechless. Moving directly in front of me Rocky stretched out her hand for mine. I placed my large hand inside of hers and allowed her to help pull me up from the couch. Not really sure what was going on I looked down into her slanted orbs, patiently waiting for her to speak and give me further instructions.

"You can't drive home after all the shots we had. Come on, let's go lay down."

That snapped me out of my haze real quick. "Ummm, I'm good," I protested.

Without saying another word, she tugged at my hand, pulling me a few feet away from where I'd been standing. In what I could only describe as a fog I watched as she grabbed the water bottles off the table and turned off the lights. Like a little puppy dog, I followed behind her, allowing her to guide us out of the living room. Halfway down the hall Rocky stopped at the bathroom where she retrieved a bottle of aspirin. She handed me the bottle then grabbed my other hand and continued the walk toward her bedroom. The closer we got to her room the heavier my legs felt. Sliding my hand from hers I stopped walking.

Rocky turned to look at me. "What are you doing Dre?"

"Not going in there, that's for damn sure," I stated adamantly.

Rocky continued walking the short distance to her room. She reached the threshold of her bedroom and flicked on the light before turning back toward me when she realized I wasn't behind her. "Dre stop being silly. You are too damn big to sleep on my couch and I sure as hell ain't sleeping on the couch. I know we got some shit between us but surely you can share a bed with me even if we're not smashin."

I conceded, shaking my head I reluctantly followed her into the room. She was right, I was being silly, but I also had been drinking. "I will do my very best not to press up on you, but I want it to be known, I'm not comfortable wit this shit. I'm a damn man Rocky, a slightly intoxicated one at the moment," I pointed out.

"It has been duly noted. Now get your gigantic ass in bed. Wait, do you have on basketball shorts or do you need a pair?"

The look I gave her must have shown my confusion because she spoke again before I could respond.

"You ain't gettin in my bed in your street clothes. I have a pair of basketball shorts I took from one of the twins, you can borrow em."

Rocky walked over to where I was standing and gave me one of the bottled waters. "Drink this and take some aspirin."

I did as she said while watching her shift through one of her drawers. She pulled out a pair of basketball shorts then she closed the drawer and walked back toward me. I remained paralyzed in place as she removed the aspirin and water bottle from my hands and tossed me the shorts. I was left standing there looking stupid as Rocky walked over to her bed and plopped down. I continued watching her as she sat one of the water bottles on her nightstand before opening the other one and popping the top of the aspirin. Rocky took two pills and chased them down with her water. My eyes remained on her as she placed both items on her nightstand and picked up the remote, clicking on the TV.

"Dre," she whined, not bothering to look at me.

"I'm sorry Short Stuff."

I quickly shimmied out of my fatigues before stepping into the basketball shorts Rocky had given me then pulled my tee-shirt over my head. I folded my discarded clothes and dropped them by the dresser. Turning toward the wall, I found the light switch and flicked it off. Unhurriedly, I strolled over to the bed and paused. Rocky turned toward me and pulled back the thick comforter draped over her king size mattress. She peered up at me, her reticent eyes pleading with me. Tired, I eased my fatigued frame onto the plush bed and allowed my body to melt into the comfort and softness of the mattress. I closed my eyes as Rocky's scent enveloped me. The pillows and blankets were saturated with her scent. The delicate crisp aroma of cocoa butter mixed with coconut oil permeated my nostrils.

Umm...

Suddenly my eyes sprang open, I turned in the direction of where Rocky was sitting just as she stood to her feet and started removing her pants. She must have felt my eyes on her, looking back over her shoulder she smiled at me. I felt like I was watching a movie in slow motion while peeking at her through half mass lids as she pulled the comforter back on her side of the bed and climbed inside. Shifting underneath the thick bedspread Rocky fought to find a comfortable space. Meanwhile, I was rested on my back with both of my hands tucked underneath my head, laying stiff as a board.

Turning on her side Rocky positioned a pillow underneath her head and looked at me. "You good Dre?"

Slowly rolling my neck in her direction I nodded my head. "I'm good as long as you stay on your side of the bed."

With her eyes half closed she grinned. "I'll try but can't make no promises. I'm kinda a wild sleeper and I'm not used to sharin my bed."

"Raquel," I growled.

"Hmmm."

"Alright, bring yo ass over here if you want to and see if I don't have yo ass walkin funny in the mornin," I warned.

Rocky giggled. "Go to sleep Dre."

Closing my eyes, I switched to my side, yielding my back to

Rocky. I shuffled a few pillows around while I struggled to get comfortable. Eyes wide open I stared out into the dimly lit room when the sounds of Rocky's heavy breathing blended with the voices from the TV hit my ears. She was out.

Fuck! It's about to be a long ass night.

CHAPTER FIVE

Stuffing the last item inside my mother's Louie Vuitton Keepall Bandouliere duffle bag I surveyed my office for my cell phone. I walked around the small room looking for my ringing phone while giggling to myself as I thought about how my mom would react when she saw me walk into the house with her tote. The sad part was she had so many bags she hadn't notice it was missing, I've had this bag for the past six months. Hopefully, I'd make it back home with it. Spotting my phone sitting on top of a few textbooks on my desk I swiftly picked it up and answered the call.

"Hey boo, what's up?"

Carmen's animated voice came blaring from the other end of the phone. "What time y'all hittin the city?"

"Hi Rocky, how are you? I'm good Carm. That's good to hear. What time are you and E coming into town?" I teased, trying my best to imitate her voice.

"My bad boo, I'm just excited. I miss the hell out of my girls."

"We miss you too. I actually just finished packing. E should be here within the next thirty minutes or so. Then we'll jump right on the highway."

"Uggh, y'all gonna hit rush hour in Cincy and Columbus."

I positioned my cell phone between my shoulder and ear as I grabbed my bag off the futon and walked out of my office. "Yeah I know but I don't want to wait too late to leave. You know me, if we wait, we won't leave until the morning."

Carmen chuckled. "This is true. You are the oldest twenty-seven-year-old I know." She smacked her lips before she continued. "I swear you're an old ass lady in a young person's body," she finished with another chuckle.

I dropped my bag next to the one already by the door then stopped in the kitchen and poured myself a glass of wine. I grabbed my glass off the counter and headed to my bedroom to make sure I wasn't forgetting any essential items to survive the next couple of days. "Whateva, heffa, I'm not old I'm just—" I couldn't think of an adjective to describe my versed ways. Carmen was right, I definitely acted like a middle-aged woman at times. "Not old—mature," I finished my thought.

"Mature, elderly, old-fashioned, geriatric, they all mean the same thing, old. Just admit it, you act old." Carmen burst out laughing at her own joke.

"Yeah okay, well this pussy ain't old and that's all that matters," I spat.

"Eww, you so damn nasty. That mouth ain't old either I see. Old gutter mouth heffa," she teased.

"My old ass is about to hang up on you if you keep talkin shit," I threatened playfully.

"I'm done. Let's talk about that young kitty tho. We still haven't talked about your hot ass lettin Dre spend the night with you."

Inside my bedroom I did a quick inspection of my dresser before walking into my closet. "You're the one who was indisposed while you callin somebody hot. Glass houses bish, glass houses."

"Yeah yeah, we're not talkin about me right now. We're talkin about you. Now spill it bitch! I want every little freaky detail and start with how big his dick is. Please and thank you."

Taking a sip of my wine I almost spit out the balmy liquid as I listened to Carmen laughing on the other end of the phone. "I already told yo nasty ass we didn't have sex."

"And, that doesn't mean other shit didn't pop off."

I wish.

"No freak nasty, nothing happened. We drank too much playin cards, so I refused to let him drive home. I damn near had to fight his big ass to get him to spend the night. But that's all he did, spend the night," I admitted somberly.

"So, you mean to tell me you had fine ass Andre Cameron drunk and, in your bed and no freaky shit jumped off? Please tell me you at least rubbed up against his wood?" I could hear the suspicion in her tone.

I took another nip of my wine as I examined the objects in my closet for any items I may have overlooked while packing. Satisfied I had packed everything I needed I exited the closet just as Creed starting barking.

"What da fuck got Cujo going crazy?"

"Hell if I know. Let me go see."

I walked out of my bedroom and ran smack dab into Egypt. I almost knocked her over and nearly spilled my wine. "Hey boo. I didn't hear you come in."

"I don't know how; Creed was ready to eat my ass," she joked.

"Who is that?" Carmen yelled in my ear.

I placed the phone on speaker as Egypt and I walked into the living room.

"Hi Carm, it's me E."

"Hey chica. I miss you."

Egypt smiled at the sound of our best friend's voice. "I miss you too, can't wait to see you later."

"You're just in time, Rocky was tellin me all about her co-ed sleep-over," Carmen sassed.

Egypt turned to face me with her brow raised in question. I shook my head at her while rolling my eyes up in my head. "Stop it. I already told yo crazy ass nothin happened. I don't speak any other languages or else I would say it again in another one."

Egypt laughed when Carmen smacked her lips. "Welp, I know he woke up with mornin wood. Tell me you at least got a glimpse of what he's workin wit."

A huge smirk eased across my face as I recalled the size of Dre's bulge that next morning. I quickly tried to turn away from Egypt whose eyes were glued to my face, but she was having none of it.

"Oh, hell nah. Carm she's over here grinning like a kid in a candy store. Out with it, hooker."

"I was smilin thinkin about how pissed Dre was the next mornin when he found out there was a futon in the second bedroom. Y'all should've seen his face."

Egypt squinted her eyes at me. "Nah boo, that ain't gonna fly. That may be true but that wasn't what your smile was about."

Careful not to drop my cellphone I placed my hand on my hip and smacked my lips. "So, what kind of smile was it?"

"That was a replaying a good ass time in my head kind of smile," Egypt sang.

I chuckled while removing my hand from my hip. "Like I said nothin happened, our night was innocent. But Carm you're right I did get to see, or should I say feel his mornin wood." I couldn't help the chuckle that fell out of my mouth. "Homeboy is definitely packin," I admitted.

An unexpected hush fell upon the room after my disclosure. I was sure the girls would've had something to say after that admission. A few seconds passed before anyone spoke.

"I fuckin knew it," Carm yelped. "Wait what do you mean felt?"

I knew that was coming, I purposely dropped that little nugget to see which one of them would call me on it first. I wasn't at all surprised it was Carmen's raunchy ass.

"Well, we're waitin bitch," Carmen stated impatiently.

"Okay, okay but it's nothin like what you're thinkin freak nasty." I flashed a smile at Egypt before continuing. "Dre and I fell asleep on opposite sides of the bed but that wasn't how we woke up. At some point during the night I slid over to where he was sleepin and laid as close to him as I could, I did my best not to wake him but—"

"Shid, you better than me. All that ass you workin wit, I would've pushed all that shit up on his dick and dared him not to touch me," Carmen interrupted.

"Can I finish?"

"My bad, please continue," Carmen said sarcastically.

Laughing I shook my head at a smiling Egypt. "Dre must have felt my movements because without so much as crackin an eyelid he pulled me into his chest and wrapped his arms around me. I buried myself underneath him and fell back to sleep. Well the next mornin I woke up because I couldn't get comfortable. No matter how I positioned myself I kept feelin somethin pokin me. I shifted to my side, it poked me in the back. I shifted up, it poked me in the ass. I shifted on my stomach, it poked me on my other side. Finally, I turned to face him and that's when it dawned on me, it was his dick. Now my ass was super curious at that point, but I couldn't just go liftin the covers and risk him catchin me starin at his junk."

"So, what you do?" Egypt asked.

"Shit nothin at first. I stared at him for what felt like forever y'all."

I stopped speaking when Egypt burst out in a rich contralto laugh causing Carmen and I to join her. Tears were falling from my eyes as I tried to regain my composure. Swiping the dampness from the corners of my eyes I looked at Egypt.

"What the hell, what was that E? You almost made me pee on myself."

"I'm sorry Rocky, I could just picture that shit. I know Carm and I don't always agree but I'm with her on this one, I mighta jumped on his shit."

I waved at hand at her dismissively while trying to contain the lascivious smile on my face. "You heffas asked for this story so y'all gonna let me finish it."

"Our bad," they spoke in unison.

I cleared my throat dramatically before I spoke again. "I watched Dre until I was certain he was still asleep. My goofy ass laid there peekin at him through my lashes while I listened for changes in his breathin. That shit felt like forever but once I was sure he was still sleep I discreetly and slowly lifted the comforter to get a quick peek at what he was workin wit. Man listen, I dropped that cover so fuckin fast and turned my ass back on my side so quick I'm surprised he didn't wake up. I made sure I left a small gap between us because truth be told if I would've pressed up against it again, I might've climbed on it."

"Well all I know is, if you find yourself in bed with him again you better jump on his shit or we gonna have a problem," Carmen sassed.

"Just because you got a friendly coochie don't mean imma let you peer pressure me," I teased.

Egypt shoved my shoulder gingerly while laughing. I winked at her before retuning my attention back to the phone in my hand, waiting for Carmen to respond.

"Fuck y'all. E you slip on just as many dicks as I do, our reasons are just different. Yo ass be lookin for love while I'm chasin orgasms. And Rocky, you just a stingy bitch with the best coochie control I've ever seen," Carmen spat. She barely got the words out of her mouth before she started giggling. "Anyway, back to Dre's dick. So about how big is it?"

I grinned to myself at Carmen's quick CoochieFax while Egypt held her middle finger up to the phone. Snickering I swatted her hand away then placed it up near my mouth as I prepared to answer Carmen.

"I can't say for sure, but I don't think I've ever seen a dick that big. He had on basketball shorts so it's hard to say but I know it was thick like a damn water bottle." Mechanically my eyes slid shut as I licked my lips, envisioning the outline of Dre's dick.

"Dayum! Fine, smart, and athletic. Girl you better snatch his young ass up before some bird gets a hold of him and destroy him," Egypt chimed in.

Snapping out of my head my tight lids fluttered opened and landed on Egypt. "I'm not a bird but I would destroy him E. We're better off being friends. Dre is too good of a dude to get mixed up with someone as fucked up as me."

Egypt gently ran a hand up and down my arm. "Rocky you are way too hard on yourself. I think a dude like Dre is exactly what you need to dispel your backwards ass thinking."

"You could be right, but we'll never know."

"And why the fuck not?" Carmen practically shouted.

"Because he's the twins' best friend and I don't want to come between them," I answered honestly.

"Girl bye. They would get over that shit once they saw y'all all happy and in love. Besides, the twins have smashed some of your so-called friends, so they have no room to talk," Carmen contended.

"Yeah and look how well that worked out. I fought one of them hoes, and the others stopped talkin to me once the twins were done with their asses."

"That's because they weren't real friends," Egypt countered.

"True but I'm not riskin that for Dre and the twins."

"So, you just gonna decide for the both of y'all? That's fucked up Rocky," Carmen asserted.

"It is what it is. Let me off this phone so E and I can hit the high-way. We'll see you shortly. Love you."

"Love you Carm," Egypt called out.

"Bye, drive safe. Love y'all too."

I ended the call and looked at Egypt who was staring at me like my dog just died.

"I'm good boo. You ready to go?"

Egypt stared at me a few seconds longer before shaking her head. I was messed up. I knew it and my friends knew it, but I didn't need their pity. My shit was just that, mine. Besides, I'd come to terms with it a long time ago. Forcing a smile on my face I dropped my eyes to the drink in my hand and gulped down the remainder of my wine while leaving Egypt in the living room and walking into the kitchen. Ready to get on the road I quickly rinsed all traces of the red residue from my oversized goblet then sat it inside the sink and called for Creed. He was on my heels before I could exit the kitchen.

At the front door I bent down and rubbed the top of Creed's head while he excitedly licked my arm. His merriment was contagious and just that quickly I felt my lugubrious mood shift. A faint smile dusted across my lips as I reached onto the bottom shelf of my console table and grabbed Creed's collar, attaching it to his leash I stood to my feet and looked at Egypt who was leaned against the door completely absorbed in her phone.

"I'm ready boo," I called out loud to get her attention.

Egypt's head swung in my direction as she pushed off the door. A soft pair of inquisitive ambers peered at me. She didn't speak. Instead, her questioning orbs bounced around my face, attempting to gauge my mood. No longer bothered by the tail end of our conversation I flashed her a confident smile. She held my gaze for a beat before sliding her head forward and bending down to grab my bags. She tossed my mother's Keepall Bandouliere over her shoulder and balanced Creed's bag in her other hand all while continuing to fiddle with her phone. Shocked, I watched as she kept her head buried in her mobile device while flinging the door open and walking out. Shaking my head, I grabbed my purse and keys off the console table next to the door and followed behind her, securing the deadbolt on the door behind us. With Creed's leash tightly secured in my hand I strolled into the courtyard, stopping momentarily to allow him to relieve himself.

After Creed finished his business, I continued the short walk to the parking lot where I found Egypt leaned against the back of my truck still engrossed in her phone. Hitting the key fob, I unlocked the doors and stood directly in front of her. Egypt looked up from her phone and shifted to the side, allowing me enough room to open the trunk. I bent inside and retrieved Creed's blanket from the floor of the trunk then stepped over to the back passenger door. After getting Creed settled inside, I returned to the trunk to assist Egypt with my bags. For the first time since I spotted her at my door, she pulled her face out of her phone and stuffed it in the pocket of her blue jean romper then removed my tote from her shoulder, tossing it on the floor of the trunk along with Creed's bag.

"I was coming back here to help you," I told her.

"I got it. Go start the car and blast the air. It's hot as hell out here. I'm parked right next to you. I only have one bag, so I'll be quick."

"You sure?"

Egypt waved her small hand at me as she walked over to the back door of her car. Not wanting to spend another minute in the heat I didn't bother arguing with her. Instead I walked to the driver's side of my truck, opened the door, and hopped inside. Starting the engine, I immediately turned on the air and adjusted the frequency to the highest level. Hot air blasted through the vents and smacked me in the face. I quickly rolled down all the windows, grateful for the subtle breeze blowing through my truck.

Glancing up at the rearview mirror I checked for Egypt. Her small frame was tucked inside her car, I assumed fidgeting with her luggage. Tickled by the image of my best friend's ass hiked in the air a soft chuckle fell from my mouth as I gradually shifted my eyes to my purse. I slid my bag in my lap and dug around the cluttered space searching for my cellphone. After rummaging through several stacks of papers I located my phone wedged between my wallet and a bottle of lotion. With my phone clutched in my hand I pulled it out my bag and returned my purse to the center console before checking my messages.

"Why you cheesin so hard?"

Startled I dropped my phone in my lap and placed a hand over my racing heart. Slowly I turned and face Egypt. "What the hell E? I didn't hear you get in the truck."

Egypt smirked at me as she reached into her pocket and retrieved her cell phone. "I see," she stated with humor in her tone. "Your ass was too busy in your phone. Who got my girl blushing like a hooker in church?"

Rolling my eyes, I faced forward while trying to wipe the smile from my face. "I was just checking a text from Dre."

"Hmph."

Ignoring her, I grabbed my phone out my lap and responded to Dre's text.

Me: We're just now about to hit the road. I'll text you when we touch down.

I plugged my phone into the port of my car charger and started searching my music app when my phone chirped in my hand. Quickly exiting out of Apple Music I went to his text.

Dre: Safe travels Short Stuff and don't forget.

My grin started off subtle, ploddingly blossoming into a full fledge smile as I sent Dre a quick response. After making sure my text was sent, I switched back to my music app and shuffled through a variety of albums before selecting Beyoncé's latest project, Beyoncé. Although it wasn't my first choice, I knew it was something Egypt and I could vibe to during our drive. Track list set to shuffle, "Partition" streamed through the speakers. Sitting my phone inside the cupholder I placed my truck in reverse and backed out of the parking space. As we pulled out of my apartment complex cool air flowed through the vents competing with the heated wind flowing in from outside. Swiftly rolling up the windows I adjusted the frequency of the air then glanced at Egypt who sat silently fiddling with her phone. Curiosity piqued I turned my attention back to the road and decided to inquire about what or who had her attention.

"Excuse me Miss but why are you so quiet and what are you doing in your phone?"

Egypt looked up from her bright screen and flashed me a coy smile. "My bad. I been texting with Raheem all day. We're trying to coordinate our schedules."

"Oh, now I see why you've been so preoccupied. Y'all hookin up this weekend?"

"That's the plan," she admitted zealously.

Catching the giddiness in her voice a small grin eased onto my face. I liked Raheem for Egypt and dude had been putting in major work to capture her attention. It seemed like the only thing that kept the two of them from spending more time together was the fact that he lived in Cleveland and E was in Cincy.

Egypt's sultry voice pulled me out of my head. "He's coming up to spend some time with me. I'll still be available to kick it with my girls but I'm definitely trynna make time for him. I'll probably stay with him too."

"That's what's up. I ain't mad at you. Get some for me too," I joked.

Egypt playfully tapped me on the arm. "I plan on it. It's been a minute."

"Well if he's still here on Sunday bring him to the cookout."

"Cool, I'll see how long he plans on staying. He won't be here until later tonight. I told him he could pick me up from your parent's once we were done hanging out."

Egypt and I settled into a comfortable silence, my focus was on the road and she went back to her phone. To kill the dead air between us I turned up the volume on the radio, relaxing in my seat while the sounds of Beyoncé serenaded us as I maneuvered through the congested traffic on 71-North. Less than two hours later Egypt and I exited the freeway in Columbus, pulling into a gas station off 104.

After letting Creed out the back so he could stretch and relieve himself. I loaded him back into the truck and headed inside to empty my bladder and grab something to drink. Five minutes later I was back inside my truck waiting for Egypt to return from her own potty break. With a few minutes to spare I grabbed my phone from the cupholder and opened my message app, scrolling to our message thread I sent Dre a short text.

Me: Hey, we're here. Stopped to use the restroom and about to head to my parent's.

The thirst was real. I stared at the screen until I saw the tiny word delivered underneath my text before switching over to my music app, selecting shuffle I placed my phone back in the cupholder and zoned out. I hadn't realized Egypt was back until the sounds of her hearty laughter filled the truck. My lids flickered open. I peeked at her from the corner of my eye as I continued bopping my head while rapping along to Chris Brown's "Look At Me Now". A crafty smile tugged at the corners of Egypt's lips as she held her phone up and aimed it at me. Swiveling my head in her direction I moved my hands animatedly in rhythm with the beat of the music while I continued rapping and simultaneously nodding my head as my friend recorded me.

After about forty seconds or so Egypt ended her recording and placed her phone in her lap. "I swear you can be such a thug," she teased.

I flipped her the bird. "Whateva lets ride out, I'm so over bein in this car and my ass hurt."

"Im ready," Egypt declared through a little giggle while pulling her door shut.

I pulled out of the gas station, hopping back on 104 Egypt and I did our best rap impersonations as the tracks switched between some of my favorite hip hop artists. Before I knew it, I was maneuvering onto 70-East, cautiously navigating through rush hour traffic as swiftly as I could. Thirty-five minutes later we pulled up to my parent's house.

Sitting in my parent's driveway I looked out the window staring at the place I once called home. Although this wasn't the house, I remembered from my earlier years it was definitely the one that held the most memories. The extravagant five-bedroom house sat atop a freshly manicured lawn surrounded by exotic shrubbery. Pristine floor to ceiling windows aligned the front and side of the estate, drawing in natural sunlight. An assortment of colorful plants and flowers decorated the custom paved walkway leading up to the wood encased doorway. There wasn't a flower out of place, or a blade of grass not cut to precision. From the outside looking in it all looked perfect, from their home to their cars and especially their marriage. But it was all an illusion. An illusion my mother spent the last twenty-five years of her life protecting.

A hard gush of air pushed through my lips as I continued sweeping my eyes around the beautiful edifice. When I was younger, I often wondered why my daddy had such a large house built for just three people. But the older I got I realized our house was never intended for just the three of us. I think my daddy believed eventually my mother would come around and his sons would be welcomed in his home. Unfortunately, that never happened. Instead, my mother found other uses for those extra bedrooms, filling them mostly with expensive unused items.

The smooth stroke of her soft hand moving gently up and down my arm snatched me from my thoughts. Slowly I turned and looked at my best friend, my melancholy eyes landing on her empathic ones. "Are you okay?"

I allowed my head to rock softly on my shoulders while placing my hand on top of hers and smiling. "I'm good." Silently Egypt held my gaze, imploring me with her eyes. "I promise," I declared.

She looked at me a few seconds longer before removing her hand from my arm and turning forward in her seat. Egypt and Carmen knew me better than anyone, so I wasn't surprised Egypt picked up on the change in my mood. Coming home for me has always been bittersweet. I loved my family and we were very close but there was a division of households and that separation always left me feeling fucked up.

My lids slammed shut as I took my time counting to fifteen, pulling in long draws of air through my mouth I slowly released them through my nose. Anxiety tapered, I fluttered my eyes open and allowed a convivial grin to settle on my face.

"C'mon boo. My ass can't take another minute in here." I tossed my head toward the window before flinging the door open and hopping out.

Egypt followed suit, hurriedly peeling her small frame from the truck she trailed behind me. Luggage spilling out of our hands Egypt and I stood inside my parent's foyer, absorbing the comfort of the cool air while dumping our bags at our feet. Instantly, my earlier feelings of angst dissipated as I took in my familiar surroundings. Very little had changed since my last visit. Sweeping my eyes around the open area I smirked to myself, noticing my mother had switched out her "winter" canvases for her "spring" pieces.

Only Vivika had seasonal décor. Such a damn diva.

The sounds of pots and pans clanking in the distance snatched me out of my head, drawing my attention to the most delicious aroma. Excited I kicked off my shoes and reminded Egypt to do the same. I waited for her to remove her shoes then latched my arm around hers, matching my pace with Egypt's we playful skipped down the hall and headed toward the kitchen. Barely out the foyer our childlike gait came to a halt when Gigi rounded the corner and immediately started barking. Eyes locked on Creed her tiny body shuddered as her yapping increased. My eyes shifted toward the floor where Creed sat perched on his hind legs, completely unbothered.

Amused by the feisty Yorkshire Terrier trying to establish dominance, I unhooked my arm from Egypt's and scooped the small dog off the floor. I attempted to calm her by rubbing her small belly as we resumed the short walk into the kitchen. As I suspected, I found my mother standing at the stove looking inside a large pot while humming to herself. Placing Gigi back on the floor, I instructed her to be nice before strolling over to my mother. Quietly I stood behind her and waited. Totally oblivious to my presence my mother continued humming while adding ingredients to the pot on the stove. Tickled at her lighthearted temperament, I leaned in and planted a soft kiss on her cheek. Damn near jumping out of her skin, she turned around with a manicured hand covering her heart. A warm smile graced her face as she dropped her hand from her chest and pulled me into a tight embrace.

Slowly releasing me she flashed her characteristic beauty pageant smile as she scanned my body, starting at the crown of my head and leisurely drifting her eyes down to my feet. "Dammit little girl! You almost gave your mother a heart attack." I could hear the mirth in her tone as her eyes returned to my face.

Standing eye to eye with the woman who gave me life, I smiled while admiring her beautiful features. Although my mother was fifty-two, she didn't look a day over forty. We were the same short height and carried the same petite frame, except somewhere in the gene pool I inherited a fat ass while my mother's backside was as flat as a board. My years of running track also gave me thicker toned thighs while Vivika's legs were thin but shapely. My mother and I also shared the same thick curly hair, slanted brown eyes, and high cheek bones. But that's where our similarities ended. The remainder of my physical features came from one Johnathan 'JB' Banks. I inherited my father's small nose, dark chocolate complexion, full lips, and deep dimples. Vivika had a narrow pointy nose, thin lips, and a skin tone so light she could damn near past for white. My mother was a beautiful woman and she knew it. She was also a diva in our own right and today was no different.

After a few minutes of my mother and I taking each other in and absorbing the other's energy, she turned her attention to Egypt. She wrapped my best friend in her little arms, holding Egypt close to her chest my mother playfully fussed at her for taking so long to come home with me. Eyes fixed on the pair, I chuckled at their spirited exchange while observing my mother's less than casual attire.

Dressed in a pair of khaki knee-length shorts and a cream silk quarter sleeve button up blouse, she paired it with a sexy pair of Jimmy Choo Portia wedge sandals. A simple pair of small pearl earrings donned her small lobes and matched the single row of pearls around her slim neck. Her naturally long hair was pulled into a neat bun on top of her head with a few loose tresses dangling neatly next to her ears. Per usual, her face was beat to the gawds. Yeah, my mother was a true diva. As my mother released Egypt from her embrace, I couldn't help noticing how healthy she looked.

"Mommy you look amazing. You got a hot date?" I teased.

My mother waved a hand at me as she went back to the stove. "If you count Gigi."

"Seriously, are you feeling okay?"

Putting down the spoon she used to stir the contents inside one of the pots, she turned and looked at me. "I feel great. The new meds my doctor has me on seem to be working for now. Thanks for asking sweetheart."

"Just checking, I only have one mother so I wanna make sure she's around for as long as possible," I stated, keeping my tone playful even though I was dead serious.

My mother smiled at me before coming over to take my hands into hers. "Your mother isn't going anywhere anytime soon. Now go put your things away so I can put some food in those bellies."

I looked toward the stove. "This is for us?"

Releasing my hands my mother returned to the stove and glanced over her shoulder with a smirk on her face. "Of course, dear. Who else would I be cooking for?"

I caught the sarcasm in her tone but chose to ignore it. Instead, I turned toward Egypt and motioned for her to follow me out the kitchen. We'd made it to the threshold of the kitchen when I slowed my steps as a digital voice from the alarm notified us that the garage door was open.

His deep baritone resonated through the walls. "Where's my baby girl?"

"Daddddddy," I screeched.

My father came into the kitchen with two bouquets of roses in his large hands. I took off in a full sprint toward him almost knocking the beautiful arrangements on the floor. My father quickly adjusted the flowers in his hand while laughing heartily. Scooping me off my feet my father pulled me into his strong arms, hugging me tight against his chest. I giggled like a schoolgirl in my daddy's arm as he twirled me around while planting kisses all over my face.

Slowly lowering me back down to the floor my father held me at the wrist as he looked me over. "You look good princess. How is school going this semester?"

I rolled my eyes up in my head. "School is school. Nothing I can't handle."

A boisterous chortle spilled out of my father's mouth. "That's my girl, future Dr. Raquel Banks," he stated proudly.

Placing the roses on the island, my father walked over to my mother and kissed her cheek. He pretended not to notice when she rolled her eyes before stepping away from him and retrieving a glass of wine. A glass I hadn't noticed until now.

"Mommy are you allowed to drink on your meds?"

My mother took a sip of her spirit while waving a hand at me dismissively. "And who is the mother here?"

I didn't want to argue in front of Egypt, so I decided to drop it, resolved to address it later. I looked at my father who was staring a hole in the side of my mother's face. "Daddy are these flowers for me?"

My father turned his attention to me, walking over to the island he picked up the bouquet of white roses and handed them to me. "Yes princess, here you go."

"Thank you handsome."

A purple hue tinted my father's tawny cheeks as he placed a soft kiss on my forehead. "You're welcome princess."

A childlike giggle crept up from my throat and spilled out of my mouth as my father turned back toward the island and grabbed the other bouquet of red roses. Head held high, shoulder squared my father walked over to my mother and stared down in her indomitable face. I watched them closely as my mother straightened her spine, placed her glass on the counter, and tugged at the ends of her shirt. She nervously fiddled with the hem of her blouse while tooting her nose in the air and fixing a spurious grin on her flawless face. My father stood towering over her, gazing into her hardened pupils.

I continued watching them, curious to see how things were going to play out. It felt like time stood still before either of them made a move. Slowly, my mother's face relaxed and her eyes softened while my father's ambers danced with mischief. He ran the back of his hand along her cheekbone before handing her the colorful arrangement. I be damned, he was flirting with her. Closing the small space between them my father leaned into my mother's petite frame and whispered something in her ear. My mother's pale cheeks turned crimson as she ran her small hands up and down my father's chest.

These two.

Surprised would've been an understatement, it had been a long time since I saw my parents display any kind of affection toward one another. It was weird but refreshing. Shaking my head, I put a pin in it, deciding to ask my mother about it later. A slight rumble in my stomach reminded me I was hungry, looking at Egypt I motioned for her to follow me. She paid my parents one final look before strolling toward me with a silly smirk on her face.

"So… You just gonna act like you ain't peep JB flirtin wit Mrs. Vi?" she asked as we grabbed our bags out the foyer and carried them upstairs to my room.

Plopping down on my bed I sat my purse in front of me and dug inside to retrieve my phone. "Yeah, I saw that bullshit." I knew my answer was dismissive, but I really didn't want to think about it.

"I'm sorry I wasn't—"

"You have nothing to be sorry about. I just ain't trynna think about my parent's dysfunctional ass marriage," I admitted, opening my phone and smiling at the sight of Dre's name in my alerts.

"You sure you're good?"

I looked up from my phone. "I promise." I held Egypt's gaze until I saw a smile tug at her lips then I returned my attention to Dre's text, scrolling down to his name I read his message.

Dre: Glad you made it home safely. I know u & ur girls are about to hit da streets. Let me know where y'all land.

Me: Deal <winking face emoji>

"So, what you and Carm trynna get into?" I asked, face still buried in my phone.

"She's on her way over. I told her Mrs. Vi cooked and her greedy ass was on it. She said she was stopping at the liquor store then she would be here."

I chuckled while opening my social media account, clicking on Facebook I scrolled through my newsfeed when I came across his name. His massive frame damn near filled the tiny box containing his profile picture. Subconsciously I licked my lips as I clicked on his name. As soon as his page loaded, I clicked on his profile picture, enlarging it to its original size. The picture was from the back. A, a University of Cincinnati jersey clung to his muscular torso. His arms were curled up on each side of his head. The bulging muscles in his biceps curled the sleeves up on his jersey, pushing them up toward his shoulders. The cursive initials on the underside of his biceps were barely visible but there was no mistaking the large A and C inked on his skin.

Goddamn, this boy is fine.

Exiting out of the picture I scrolled down his page, stopping when one of the pictures we took the night we first hung out appeared on his timeline. There I was snuggled underneath his tall frame, head tilted upward toward his face with my hand halfway in front of my mouth as I pretended to blow a kiss at him. Dre stood next to me, hand around my waist, smiling down at me. The caption read, #twinning. It had more than two hundred likes.

Damn how many people follow this dude?

Shocked, I stared at the image of us appearing more like a couple rather than two people hanging out for the first time.

"Rocky," Egypt yelled.

I popped my head up from my phone as Egypt walked over to the bed and snatched it out of my hand. "What are you looking at?"

"Damn Rocky," Egypt shrieked. "When did y'all take this pic? Y'all look hot together."

I gently plucked my phone out of Egypt's hand and clicked out of Facebook. "C'mon, Carm should be about to pull up."

Egypt smirked at me as I stood from the bed with my phone in my hand and walked out my bedroom door. "The night we first hung out," I said, answering her previous question.

Egypt and I made our way down the stairs just as the doorbell rang. Instantly, Gigi and Creed started barking as they charged for the door. At the bottom of the steps I glanced over my shoulder at both yapping dogs, instructing them to stay I waited until they stilled then flung the door open. A light giggle spilled out my mouth as I watched Carmen Milly Rock all while holding a brown paper bag in one hand.

"Girl, if you don't bring yo silly ass in here."

Carmen dropped her arms to her side, causally strolling into the house like she wasn't just cutting up on the porch less than ten seconds ago. "Don't act like y'all ain't trynna turn up wit me."

I chuckled while closing the door behind her and taking the bag from her hand. "Quit playin. You know we stay ready, but can we eat first?"

Carmen pulled me into a quick hug, kissing my cheek before letting me go. "I guess." She rolled her eyes while sashaying past me and wrapping Egypt in a tight hug. "Alright, now let's eat so we can drink and catch up."

After planting a brisk peck on Egypt's cheek Carmen eased away from her and discarded her shoes by the side of the door then headed down the hall. Egypt shot me a look before taking off behind Carmen, leaving me trailing leisurely behind them. In a single file line, we trekked into the kitchen just as my mother was walking out. My mother's eyes bounced around the three of us before focusing on the woman she considered her second daughter, her eyes lit up as a wide smile blossomed on her face.

"Mommy," Carmen shrieked while damn near sprinting into my mother's outstretched arms.

I smiled at the duo while easing past them, ambling over to the island I sat the bag down and chuckled as the two exchanged pleasantries. My mother really enjoyed when I was home and she especially loved how my friends doted on her when home with me. Lucky for Vivika, Carmen didn't disappoint. Gushing over my mother, Carmen complimented her on her appearance as well as her fashionable ensemble. And true to my mother's diva nature she feigned humbleness while her eyes beamed with pride.

"Alright, I'll leave you ladies to your fun. On the stove is oxtail stew." One arm still draped around Carmen's waist she looked at Egypt. "And in the oven is your meal dear: baked salmon and asparagus."

A Kool-Aid size grin formed on Egypt's face as her head swung over to the stove before returning her gaze to my mother. "Thank you, Mrs. Vi. You didn't have to do that."

My mother waved a hand at Egypt as she turned to walk out the kitchen, slowing her steps she picked up Gigi and glanced over her slender shoulder. "Oh, the bar is fully stocked. Feel free to help yourselves to whatever you want. However, I expect if any of you consume too much you will sleep here tonight." Not waiting for a response, she gracefully slid her head forward and sauntered out the kitchen.

Simultaneously, Egypt and I both turned and looked at Carmen.

"What?"

"You know she was talkin to your alcoholic ass," I teased.

Carmen smacked her lips. "Whatever heffa."

We all burst into laughter as we walked over to the cabinets and grabbed dinnerware. Settling into a comfortable silence we sat around the island and enjoyed the food my mother prepared for us. After we finished eating the girls and I retreated to the basement to partake in libations and good old fashion gossip. Three and a half hours later we were caught up on the current happenings in each other lives and I was tipsy. We managed to kill a little more than half a bottle of Remy and a full bottle of red wine. Stretched out across one of the sofas I fiddled with the remote while Egypt and Carmen laid across another, engrossed in their cellphones.

Egypt stood from her seat and looked between Carmen and I. "Welp, it's been fun ladies, but Raheem should be pulling up in ten minutes." Egypt ran her tongue over the front of her top row of teeth. "I need to brush my teeth and grab my bags. I'll call y'all tomorrow."

Carmen scrapped herself off the couch and walked over to Egypt. "Hol'up, I'm out too. Eric is pulling into the housing development now." Carmen turned and faced me. "Rocky I parked on the street. I'll have Eric bring me back to pick up my car tomorrow."

I looked at both my best friends and smiled. "Cool, but I'm too drunk to walk y'all to the door. Make sure y'all lock it behind y'all and call me tomorrow."

Egypt and Carmen chuckled as they ascended the stairs, leaving my inebriated ass on the couch. Once again, I found myself home alone on a Friday evening. Dropping the remote on the couch beside me I picked up my phone and considered calling Emery when my phone chirped, alerting me I had a text. Curious to see who texted me, I wasted no time unlocking my phone and opening my message app. A soft grin tugged at the corners of my lips as I read Dre's text.

Dre: I see how it is. U didn't want me poppin up on u huh? I'm hurt <sad face emoji>

Me: Huh????

Dre: U didn't text me. I told u to let me know where u and ur girls were going.

Me: My bad, I didn't text b/c we didn't go out. The girls just left, they ditched me for their boos <sad face emoji>. I'm home alone as usual. Where are you & Jamison?

Not really expecting him to respond, I sat my phone down and peeled myself off the couch. I walked over to the patio doors and let Creed out. Eyes cast out into the expansive yard I waited for Creed to finish relieving himself when the sound of my phone chirping caught my attention.

Although I was surprised by the alert, I knew it wasn't nobody but Dre. Instantly a mischievous smiled stretched across my face as I envisioned all the attention his fine ass was most likely attracting wherever he was posted up. Before I could get lost in my thoughts Creed trotted up to the door and stared up at me. I eased the door open, wide enough for him to enter and watched as he ambled back into the house and flopped down on the floor. Closing the door behind him I walked back to the couch and grabbed my phone, sinking down into the cushions I read Dre's message.

Dre: That's funny b/c J ditched me too. My pops and stepmom just went to bed so I'm just sitting here flippin thru channels trynna find something worth watching on TV. Whatcha doing?

Me: The same thing as u except my TV perusal isn't going so well. Why, u trynna keep me company?

I knew it was a stretch asking him to come see me this late, but the alcohol had lowered my inhibitions and in my current state of mind I didn't have a filter. Not to mention that spending time with him was quickly becoming one of my favorite pastimes. *Oh well. Ask not, want not.* With my phone in one hand I picked up the remote with the other and flipped through the channels, stopping on Keeping Up with the Kardashians. Tucking my legs underneath me I looked down at my phone when it alerted me, I had a new text message.

Dre: Send me ur address. U need me to bring anything?

Oh shit! I didn't really expect him to say yes.

Me: Nope. But I must warn u, I've been drinking so I can't be held responsible 4 my actions. LOL

I quickly texted Dre's my parent's address as I stood from the couch and tossed my phone on the ottoman before heading for the stairs. I moved as fast as my short legs would carry me, taking the stairs two at a time I dashed up the second flight of steps and made a beeline for my bedroom. Once inside I went straight to the ensuite bathroom. I flicked on the light and checked my appearance in the mirror. Starting at my head I swept my eyes down my body, paying attention to the smallest details.

The two French braids I'd placed in my hair earlier in the day sat neatly atop my head and hung down over my breast. My edges were aptly aligned to my braids, giving the illusion of finely laid baby hairs. Donned in a peach rayon crepe strapless maxi dress with a flounce top I noticed a few wrinkles. Running my hands down the front of my dress I smooth down the creased fabric before returning my attention back to my face.

I was happy to see the minimum makeup I applied earlier was still visible. The eyeliner and blush hadn't moved but my lips could definitely use some gloss. I stared at my reflection and debated on pushing my septum piercing inside my nose but quickly decided against it. Satisfied that I still looked presentable I grabbed my toothbrush off the sink and went about the task of freshening my breath. After brushing my teeth and gargling with mouthwash I grabbed my Chanel careese rouge coco gloss from my makeup bag perched on the counter and applied an amble amount to my lips. Chucking the lip gloss back inside my bag I paid myself a final glance then toed out the bathroom and headed back to the basement to wait on Dre.

Back on the couch I stretched my legs out on the ottoman in front of me. I attempted to taper my excitement, which was probably why I was hyper focused on the latest rerun of Keeping Up with the Kardashians. Typically, I wouldn't be caught dead watching this shit, but I needed the distraction. I'd just finished the last thirty minutes of the episode when my phone chirped. Kicking my legs out from in front of me I leaned forward and grabbed my phone off the ottoman. I wasn't at all surprised to see Dre's name flashing across the home screen. Mechanically my cheeks rose on my face as the corners of my mouth formed into a wide ass smile as I opened my phone and read his message.

Dre: I'm outside. I didn't want to knock or ring the doorbell and wake ur ppl up.

Me: Here I come

A hard gush of wind passed through my lips as I stood from the couch. I tried like hell to ignore the butterflies that were fluttering around my stomach but the truth of the matter, I was giddy as hell. Taking my time climbing the steps I silently counted backwards from fifty while breathing in my mouth and blowing air out my nose. By time I'd reached the door I'd managed a slight level of calm. However, my resolve was short lived once I flung the door open. Standing on the other side with his hands tucked inside his pockets Dre looked like something out of a sports magazine. I fought to contain the smile while forcing myself to stare up at him.

Smiling down at me I watched as Dre's eyes raked over my body. "Hey Short Stuff."

I pried my eyes away from his mouth while quickly sweeping my curious ambers down his massive frame. Dre was dressed comfortably in a pair of heather grey sweat shorts, a plain white tee-shirt, and a crisp pair of all white Nike Air Force 1's. His hair was longer than I was used to seeing him wear it. His usually low waves were starting to form a natural curl, peeking out from underneath the grey University of Cincinnati fitted cap covering his overgrown hair. His usual neatly trimmed facial hair was also grown out. Untamed hair was splayed across his defined jawline and scattered along his chin, creating a subtle five o'clock shadow. *Goddamn!* Once again, I found myself forcing myself to look him in the eyes.

A sheepish grin covered my face. "Hey Dre. Come in." I grabbed him by the hand and softly pulled him inside the house. I closed the door and secured the lock before turning to face him. "Leave your shoes here," I instructed in a hushed tone.

Dre removed his shoes and followed closely behind me as I walked out the foyer and down the hall, in the direction of the basement. Peeking over my shoulder I watched Dre take in his surroundings. His head moved from side to side while his eyes scanned every room we walked past. A small grin spilled onto my lips as I returned my attention forward.

"Damn Rocky. I figured JB made good on those NBA checks, but I had no idea y'all were livin it up like The Fresh Prince over here," Dre joked, as we walked down the stairs to the basement.

I smiled to myself at his comment but didn't reply. Most people who knew my father knew he retired from the NBA after a career shattering injury in his late twenties. And since he'd dropped out of the spotlight most assumed, he went broke, squandering away his NBA fortune. So no, I wasn't surprised by Dre's response to my parent's house, it wasn't atypical. Carmen and Egypt had the same reaction the first time they visited my family's home.

Dre and I approached the couch, rousing a sleeping Creed who lifted his head from the carpet and stared up at us. Not paying him any attention I plopped down on the sofa while watching Dre from my peripheral. He paused before slowly taking a seat on the large sectional.

These two.

Picking up the remote I stretched my hand out toward Dre. "Maybe you'll have better luck than I did. Want something to drink?"

Dre took the remote from my hand and studied me before answering. "Sure. You gonna make me drink alone?"

Slowly I stood up from the couch and walked over to the custom built-in bar. "We have a little of everything. What would you like to drink?"

Turning his attention my way Dre lowered his eyes as he scanned my body. "That all depends on if you're drinkin with me," he answered in a low tone.

I felt heat pulsating through my entire body. I moved behind the bar and shuffled bottles around to avoid his penetrating stare. "Under normal circumstances I would call it quits but since you are a guest and you don't want to drink alone; I'll indulge you this onetime."

A chortle slipped from his mouth as he continued staring at me from the sofa. "In that case I'll take something dark with Coke please."

"Two Rémys and Coke coming right up." I promptly made our drinks and returned to Dre on the couch. Sitting both cocktails on the ottoman in front of us I turned toward Dre. "So, were you able to find something to watch?" I asked, tucking my legs underneath me.

Dre picked up his drink and looked at me. "I think so, do you like scary movies?" His brow hiked up on his forehead as he stared at me, waiting for my response.

I sucked my bottom lip in between my teeth before quickly releasing it while studying his handsome face. The extra hair gave him a sexy rugged look that I really liked. It looked good on him. "Ummm, not usually but since I have such a big handsome movie partner, I think I'll be fine," I answered, coquettishly.

Placing his drink up to his lips, Dre peered at me over the top of his glass as he sipped his cocktail. "Oh, so you think I'm handsome?"

I nudged him in the shoulder then picked up my drink and took a hearty sip. "Quit playin, you know you're fine as hell," I answered honestly.

A subtle blush formed on his sun kissed cheeks as he closed out the guide and selected the channel with a movie titled *Let Me In*. "Hmm... that doesn't mean I knew you thought so."

"Well now you know." I kept my tone light and face neutral while hunching my shoulders.

Dre smirked over his glass. "Thanks, Short Stuff. I happen to think you are, how did you put it—" Dre's tone dropped an octave as he attempted to mimic my voice, "fine as hell also. Actually, I think you are fuckin gorgeous and sexy as sin."

Fuck, I'm way too intoxicated for this shit.

I tried hard as hell to mask the humongous smile that threaten to ease onto my face. Unable to stop it, I shifted in my seat, turning my body forward on the couch I stared at the TV. "So, what's this movie about?"

I heard Dre snicker on the side of me. "It's a vampire movie but if we're really gonna watch this you gotta kill these lights. Scary movies need to be watched in the dark."

I turned and looked at Dre only to find he was staring at me. His hooded lids damn near hid the tiny specks of emerald surrounding the natural hazel of his eyes as they danced around my face before finally settling on my mouth. I licked my lips and diverted my eyes as I tried ignoring the sudden heat coursing through my body. *What the hell? I can't believe this little boy has me shook like this.* Suddenly feeling

116

nervous I gulped down the reminder of my drink and sat the empty glass on the ottoman before carefully standing to my feet. I walked past Dre, purposely brushing against him as I added a switch to my hips while sauntering over to the bar. A mousy giggled tumbled out my mouth as I felt my ass jiggle underneath the light material of my dress.

I could feel Dre's heated gaze, glancing over my shoulder a mischievous grin tugged at the corners of my mouth when I found him gawking at my ass. Unbothered, a salacious leer eased across his face as his eyes lingered on my backside. *Men.* Swinging my head forward I picked up the remote to the lights and surround sound then padded back over to the couch and lowered myself onto the fluffy cushions, leaving a sizable gap between us. Intentionally keeping my eyes trained forward I stole quick glimpses of Dre from the corners of my eyes. He was completely oblivious to my creepish ogling. Glass pressed against his lips he drained the remainder of his cocktail then placed his empty tumbler next to mine and gently pulled me to his side, closing the gap I'd purposely created.

"I don't bite Rocky, well not unless you want me to."

A chill surged down my spine as I mulled over his licentious words while slowly turning to face him. I didn't respond, instead I watched him closely as he stood up from the couch and grabbed my hands. I didn't resist when he pulled me to my feet and stared down at me, pinning me with an intense gaze. Head completely still and mouth clamped shut, I followed him with my eyes as he propitiously raised a hand to my face and ran his thumb softly across my lips. He delicately pulled my bottom lip down as he removed his thumb and dropped his hand at his side. My breath hitched in the back of my throat when I watched in what felt like slow motion as Dre brought his mouth down to mine, lingering over my slightly parted lips his eyes searched my questioning orbs.

The fluttering in my stomach and quickening of my pulse made it difficult to maintain his gaze. Lowering my eyes to his mouth I watched as he curled his full lips into a delicious smile before gently pressing them against mine. Sluggishly my lids drifted shut as Dre wrapped his arms around my waist, pulling me up against his body he increased the pressure of his kiss. An involuntary whimper spilled from my lips as I draped my arms around his neck, relishing the feel of his mouth on mine as he littered my lips with a swarm of torrid kisses. Caught up in the moment I felt deprived when Dre's arms slid from around my waist and gripped my hips. With his large hands settled on each side of me he gradually removed his mouth from mine and stepped back, creating a tiny gap between us.

Listlessly, Dre swiped his tongue over his lips as he looked down into my confused ambers. "I'm sorry Short Stuff, I know you friend zoned me, but I couldn't help my—"

Before Dre could finish his sentence, I lunged forward, closing the space between us I pressed against his solid frame. My hands lifted to each side of his head, pulling his face down to mine I attacked his mouth. I felt his hesitation as I planted an onslaught of heated kisses on his pillowly soft lips. However, with each peck Dre's body relaxed. Languidly submitting to me he became an active participant, willingly meeting my pecks with puckered lips.

Ignoring the small voice in the back of my head telling me to stop I relaxed my head against one of Dre's large hands as he grabbed the back of my head while his other hand fell from my waist and caressed my ass. Too far gone, I parted my lips and ran my tongue across his top lip, then his bottom. Gently sucking his bottom lip into my mouth I softly nibbled it. A deep groan escaped from his mouth when I released his lip and hurriedly inserted my tongue. Fully engaged, Dre allowed my exploration as his tongue danced with mine.

Wrapped in a cloak of pure euphoria I snaked my hands up his neck to his head and snatched his hat off, tossing it to the floor I ran my fingers through his soft wavy mane while enjoying everything he was giving. Dre was a skillful kisser. Blindly navigating through the depths of my mouth he swiped, twirled, masterfully pulsated, and unexpectedly suckled, all while keeping his tongue in rhythm with mine. He heard my non-verbal and incoherent cries, using them as a guide to please me. Feeling lightheaded I released a throaty moan into his mouth before slowly detaching my lips from his. Unhurriedly, Dre removed his hands from my head and ass, bringing them up to my hips he held me at the waist.

I wasn't really sure what to say after such an unexpected and heated encounter. So, I did what I did best, I opted to ignore the shit. "I've never seen you with this much hair before."

"It'll be gone tomorrow. I skipped my weekly appointment with my barber in Cincy since I was coming home. I have an appointment in the morning with my regular barber."

I ran a hand over his outgrown beard then quickly dropped it to my side. "Umm, so about that movie."

Dre leaned down and pressed his forehead against mine. "Whatever you want Short Stuff."

"I want," I whispered.

Dre pecked my swollen lips before lifting his head and intertwining his fingers with mine, pulling me back toward the couch. Detaching his hand from mine I stood silently watching him. Dre sat down on the edge of the sectional and looked up at me.

"I wanna hold you, that coo with you?"

I shook my head and waited for him to get comfortable. Dre repositioned himself on the large sofa, pulling his long legs up onto the couch he stretched his ample frame back into the cushions. Propped on his side Dre reached for my hand. I lowered myself onto the couch and laid on my side with my back to his chest.

"Lights Rocky."

I slid to the edge of the couch, reaching onto the ottoman I grabbed the remote and hit the button to shut off the lights, then tossed it back on the ottoman and glided back into Dre's firm body. Relaxing against him I let go of a breath I hadn't realize I was holding as Dre wrapped his strong arms around my torso. I tried to get comfortable. I shifted back, pushing my ass into his midsection. I continued to wiggle my body in an effort to find a comfortable space when Dre firmly gripped my hips.

"Rocky," he gritted out.

I instantly stopped squirming and glanced over my shoulder to see his face. "What's wrong?"

Loosening his grip on my hips Dre locked his eyes on mine. "You can't keep grindin all that ass up on my—" His voice trailed off as he lowered his eyes. The only light illuminating in the huge room was from the TV, so I was unable to see directly where his eyes landed.

An O formed on my mouth when I realized he was referencing his dick. Turning my head forward I grinned to myself. "My bad, I was just trynna get comfortable."

Dre shuffled his body behind me as I settled back against him, leaving a tiny gap between us. His grip tightened around my waist again, pulling my body flush against him. "Just don't start that wigglin shit again," he spoke over my head.

I grabbed a throw pillow from the floor and propped it in front of my face while settling into the coziness of Dre's arms. Focused on the TV I tried filling in the gaps from the first ten minutes of the movie that we missed. Five minutes of my undivided attention and I was able to determine some weird little boy had befriended a creepy little girl who I assumed was the vampire. I tried concentrating but my mind kept wondering, consumed with thoughts of the man lying behind me. Closing my eyes, I allowed Dre's intoxicating scent to consume me. *Damn he smells good as hell. I bet he taste even better. Umm. Yeah, he looks like his cum is sweet.* Subconsciously I started rocking my hips as lecherous thoughts played out in my head.

"Rocky, you're doing it again," he growled.

My eyes fluttered open as I stilled my hips. "Sorry."

Dre buried his face in the crook of my neck. "That was your last warning Short Stuff. You can wake him up if you want to, but I won't be responsible for what happens once he rises," he breathed into the back of my neck.

The feel of his silky lips pressed against my flesh combined with his lascivious words opened my well, moisture instantly gathered in the bottom my panties. As bad as I wanted to call his bluff I knew better. Dre was a grown ass man and if I kept taunting him, he would give me what I was asking for right here on my parent's couch. Besides he had a point, I was the one who drew the line. And I was the one who said we couldn't take our relationship there but the more time we spent together the blurrier that line was becoming. The feel of Dre's balmy breath on my skin snatched me from my reverie. Dre placed a soft kiss on the back of my neck then raised his head and placed it gently on top of my mine. His large hand moved up and down my hip. Suddenly my lids felt heavy and before I knew it sleep settled in my core.

A loud thunderous voice woke me from my slumber. My eyes flashed open, trying to focus in the direction of where I heard his voice streaming. "Raquel Marie Banks."

I jumped up from underneath Dre's arms and stood from the couch. Dark eyes stared into me as he moved closer to the sofa. My father squinted his dark mahoganies while peering at Dre sleeping where I left him. "I know you don't think you're grown enough to be laid up in my damn house with some nigga," he roared.

In my peripheral I saw Dre stir, slowing he lifted himself into a sitting position and looked in my father's direction. "Hello Mr. Banks." His usually raspy tenor sounded deeper when mixed with the groggy bravado in his cords.

Damn his sleepy voice is just as sexy as his every day one.

My father took another step closer to the couch, eyes widening as recognition set in. "Dre?"

I heard Dre chuckle on the side of me. "Yes sir, it's me Andre."

My father looked between Dre and I, the scowl slowing leaving his face as confusion took its place. My father stood staring at us a few seconds longer before he started toward the stairs. Stopping at the base of the steps he glanced over his shoulder, his eyes danced between the two of us. "Set the alarm behind your company."

That was it, my father had spoken. It was time for Dre to leave. I watched as my father started up the stairs mumbling underneath his breath. "Daddy what are you doing here anyway?"

My father paused, looked back at me then turned back around and continued to ascend the stairs. "I live here," he huffed.

Shit. I offended him.

Blowing out an exasperated breath I turned and looked at Dre. "I'm sorry." I bent down and grabbed my cellphone off the ottoman to check the time. "Oh wow, its two-thirty. I didn't mean to keep you out this late."

Dre stood up from the sofa and walked over to me. Sliding his hand in mine he gently tugged, prompting me to follow him toward the stairs. "It's cool Short Stuff. I enjoyed myself. Let me get out of here though before JB comes back down here with his gun," he joked.

I chuckled softly as I allowed Dre to lead us out of the basement. I couldn't believe my father. Who was he to come in my mother's house flexing his muscles? I mean seriously, who did he think he was fooling? I talked to my mother damn near every day and most of those conversations occurred at night. Whenever I would ask my mother where my father was her response was always the same, *somewhere being JB*. So why was he even here? Shaking my head to myself I tried ignoring the irritation that was bubbling in my core.

Dre and I reached the door, sliding his hand out of mine he looked down at me. "Let it go Short Stuff, he's your father. If I came home and saw my baby laid up on some dude I would've flexed too." His statement was matter of fact but felt like he'd been reading my mind.

A small grin eased onto my face and just like that Dre had calmed the anger that was boiling inside of me. "Thanks again for coming to hang out with me. Sorry I fell asleep on you. I owe you another movie night, when we get back home."

"No problem Short Stuff. Sleep or not I enjoyed myself especially the part where you attacked me," he finished, while winking at me.

I playfully shoved him in the shoulder as he walked out the door. "Bye Andre, text me when you get home."

Dre didn't reply. Instead he planted a soft kiss on the base of my forehead and stepped onto the porch. Leaned against the door jamb I waited until I could no longer see his tall muscular frame before closing the door and heading to the basement to straighten up. Stepping off the last stair in the basement I trekked over to the ottoman and picked up the remote for the lights. I clicked on the lights and glanced over at Creed who was nipping at something in between his paws. I stepped closer in his direction and smiled. Bending down I snatched Dre's hat from his mouth and placed it on my head then grabbed the empty glasses from the ottoman and walked over to the bar, sitting them in the sink with the ones I placed there earlier. Once I moved from behind the bar, I did a quick survey of the large room before clicking off the TV and the lights.

With Creed on my heels I traveled up the two flights of stairs to my bedroom. Once I made it inside, I shut the door behind myself and quickly disrobed before climbing into my childhood bed and sinking into the comfortable mattress. Propped up on a plethora of pillows I opened my cellphone and set my alarm. Tomorrow was going to be a long and busy day. I needed sleep, or I wasn't going to be any good. Dropping my phone in my lap I grabbed the remote from the night-stand and clicked on the TV. I started surfing channels for something to fall asleep to when my phone buzzed in my lap. Positive it was Dre I didn't waste any time picking it up and opening my message app. As expected, there was a text from Dre.

Dre: Hey Short Stuff, I'm home. Thx again for 2night, I REALLY enjoyed myself <winking face emoji>

Me: I'm glad u made it home safely. I'm also glad u had a REALLY good time. I did 2. Sweet dreams handsome got an early day 2mrw with my mother. Btw, I have your hat. I'll bring it to the cookout on Sunday.

Dre: Oh, they're gonna be amazing. I have a feeling a certain chocolate goddess is gonna visit me in my dreams. And good look-ing, 4got all about it. Goodnight beautiful.

Tired I plugged my phone into the charger and sat it on the night-stand then buried myself underneath the covers. The events from earlier tonight played over in my head as sleep settled in my core. The last thing I remembered before dozing off was my unexpected rendezvous with Mr. Cameron.

The sound of my alarm blaring from my nightstand snatched me out of a peaceful sleep. Annoyed I peeled the covers from my head and groggily reached for the noisy device. Hurriedly I silenced the alarm and dropped my phone on the bed while lying back against the pillows and staring up at the ceiling. I found myself thinking about the same thing I thought about before falling asleep last night, Andre Cameron.

Smiling I thought about his mouth. A mouth I was finally able to explore and taste. A mouth I so badly wanted to be more acquainted with.

"Fuck, why did he have to be my brothers' best friend?" I asked myself out loud.

An exaggerated breath flew out my mouth as I kicked my feet and threw my arms in the air, causing the covers to fall from my upper body and lay haphazardly off the bed. The feel of my cellphone buzzing interrupted my mini temper tantrum. I ran my hands across the sheet while sitting up and searching the bed for my buzzing phone. Annoyance etched across my face as I stared at the name displayed on the home screen. *It is way too early for this shit.* Deciding to let the call go to voicemail I scrambled out of bed and headed to the bathroom to relieve my weighted bladder. I knew I couldn't avoid the twins forever, but caffeine was definitely necessary before I talked to them.

CHAPTER SIX

*S*itting my phone down I looked across the table at my mother as she sipped from her dirty martini. I stuffed a piece of salmon in my mouth while I continued studying her immaculately made up face. My mother appeared carefree and relaxed, a complete contrast to the angry woman I heard screaming at my father earlier this morning.

After finishing my morning routine, I sauntered downstairs to make a cup of coffee when the sound of my mother's voice stopped me in my tracks. Her usually soft rosy voice was loud and shaky. I could tell she was trying to keep from crying. Something that didn't sit right with me, but I knew better than to interrupt them. She and my father were in their bedroom with the door closed but their elevated tones could be heard throughout the entire first level. I heard my mother tell my father she hadn't seen him in two weeks and questioned why he was home. When my father tried to reply my mother cut him off with a series of curses. I hated hearing my parents argue. I decided to forgo my morning coffee and headed back to my bedroom where I spent thirty minutes on the phone being questioned and chastised by my younger brothers. When I finally ventured back downstairs my father was gone.

"So, your father told me he found you laid up with some young man last night. Do tell dear," my mother spoke, bringing me back to the present.

I giggled at my mother's use of slang. "Laid up mommy, seriously?" I quipped.

My mother swatted my hand. "Don't play with me young lady. Who is he?" she asked, placing her elbows on the table she intertwined her manicured fingers together and rested her chin on top of them.

My mother and I had spent the morning at Lulu's Spa and Grand Salon enjoying a mother daughter spa day. Between sipping on endless mimosas, facials, full body massages, mani and pedis we'd caught one another up on the few new events in our lives. Now we were seated outside on the patio, feasting on a late lunch at Cooper's Hawk Winery in Easton Town Center.

Leisurely I pushed my plate aside as I mimicked my mother's gestures. "His name is Andre and there really isn't anything to tell."

"Uh huh, well at least tell me the basics dear. Where did y'all meet, how long have you been dating, what does he look like, what does he do for a living—"

Holding up my hand I stopped my mother's rant. "Bring it back in Vi. One question at a time," I teased.

I signaled for our waitress and ordered my mother another dirty martini and a Washington apple for myself. During one of our many talks at the spa my mother assured me that the symptoms associated with her medical condition of multiple sclerosis was effectively being managed due to a combination of new medications prescribed by her specialist. She'd also politely reminded me she was my mother and drinking had no ill effects on her health or medication regime. All of which helped quash my previous concerns.

I grabbed my glass from the table and polished off the remnants of my current cocktail as I looked at my mother. "I've known Andre for a while. He went to high school with Carmen but he's younger than us, so we didn't really hang out then." I gave her the bare minimum while choosing my words carefully.

Although I wasn't lying, I knew I wasn't telling her the whole truth. I hated that there were parts of my life I couldn't share with my mother. However, I learned very early on never to mention my brothers to her. Vivika Marie Banks spent the twins' entire life ignoring their presence, like that somehow made them non-existent. Although I never judged the way my mother decided to handle my father's infidelity or his illegitimate children, I would never pretend to understand it. Swallowing the bitter taste that omission left in my mouth I watched my mother process my words as she continued peering into me with her slanted eyes.

I sat my empty glass on the table and continued. "He also attends UC, so we have been hanging out over the summer. It's nothing serious. In fact, we're not dating. Just two old acquaintances becoming good friends. So, what he looks like doesn't matter. Satisfied?"

Our waitress returned with our freshly prepared drinks. Happy for the interruption I glanced at her as she placed our cocktails in front of us and cleared the table, removing our lunch plates and empty glasses.

My mother picked up her glass and smiled at me as she sipped her from her beverage. "Okay dear, whatever you say. However, I do hope you have a much better poker face with your father because you haven't stopped blushing since I mentioned that young man."

The sound of my phone chirping recused me from my mother's probing. I quickly picked up my phone grateful for yet another distraction. I heard my mother excuse herself from the table as I opened my phone and went to my message app.

Dre: I waited a minute b4 reaching out, I hope u and mom dukes are having a good day 2gether. So, did the twins call or text you yet?

I rubbed the back of my neck as I thought about the awkward ass conversation, I had with my brother earlier today. I wondered what they said to Dre.

Me: 1st thing this morning. I spent 30mins on the phone w/them fools. U?

I was so engrossed in my phone I didn't realize my mother had returned to the table until I heard her ask the waitress for our bill. Looking up from my phone I found my mother's eyes glued to my face.

"Nothing to tell my ass," she whispered under her breath.

Ignoring her I grinned as I went back to my conversation with Dre.

Dre: Me 2. Call me later when ur free so we can kick it about em. Coo?

Me: Cool

I laid my phone face down on the table and purposely avoided my mother's gaze while looking out into the distance. A teenage couple standing on the corner across the street caught my attention. I smiled to myself as I watched the young boy grab the shopping bags from the girl's hand before they stepped into the road, making their way across the street. The girl seemed to be pleased with her young suitor. She lovingly grabbed his free arm, hooked her arm around his, and rested her head on his shoulder as they continued their stroll. I found their naïveté cute. There was something sweet about their innocence. I continued watching them as they walked arm in arm down the street. I thought back on my teenage years and tried to recall if there was ever a time I believed in the fairytale of love. I don't think there was, but it always made my heart smile seeing others revel in the illusion.

"Finish your drink dear so I can turn you over to your father." My mother's clipped tone snatched my attention away from the young lovers. Turning to face my mother I stared at her as she looked at her watch. "We don't want to keep him waiting," she stated, through a tight smile.

I hated the dynamics of my parent's relationship. For the life of me I didn't understand why they were still married. It was clear that after twenty-five years of marriage they weren't in love anymore, but they seemed committed to keeping up the facade.

Shaking my head, I picked up my drink and feigned a smile. "Yes ma'am."

After our bill was paid my mother and I walked in silence to her vehicle. Forty-five minutes later we pulled up to our house where my father was waiting for me in the driveway. My mother looked out her rearview mirror and rolled her eyes. I chuckled at the indignation splayed on her face as I propped my elbow on the armrest and kissed her on the cheek. My mother's face quickly shifted into a partial grin before turning to face me, saying our goodbyes I hopped out of her car and trekked the short distance to my father's SUV.

Climbing inside the large SUV, I sat my bag on the floor of the truck and leaned across the console, giving my father a quick peck on the cheek. "Hi daddy. Where we going first?"

My father smiled at me before turning his attention to the rearview mirror as he proceeded to back out the driveway. "I figured we go to Sam's Club first and whatever we don't find in there we can pick up from Walmart."

"Cool," I replied nonchalantly as I dug in my purse for my cell phone.

Honestly, I was still annoyed at my father for the shit he pulled in the basement last night. If I thought I could've gotten away with it, I would've skipped this grocery spree altogether and just met Miss Brenda at her house. However, I knew my father wasn't the one to play with. On top of the fact I knew it would hurt his feelings. Although he would never admit it.

Fiddling with my phone in my hand I stared out the window while my father hummed along to an old song by Will Downing Jr. The deep bravado of my father's voice brought a smile to my face, prompting me to turn away from the window and look at him. He was relaxed. Posture slack but not exactly erect. His left hand gripped the steering wheel while his right draped off the armrest. A jubilant beam donned his chocolate face as he continued humming while bobbing his head. I wanted to stay mad and be my usual bratty self but it was hard staying mad at him when he was in such a sprightly mood.

My father must have felt me staring at him. Turning toward me, he began to sing out loud, encouraging me to join him before turning his attention back to the road. Unable to resist his cajoling I sang along, laughing at my off-tempo rendition of one of his favorite songs. Song after song my father and I did our best impersonations of some of his favorite old school classics, chuckling every time one of us fumbled over the lyrics. Our overly exaggerated father daughter mini concert was just what we needed to kill the perceptible tension between us.

We'd just finished destroying an old Whitney Houston track when my father pulled into a parking space at Sam's Club, placing the truck in park he looked over at me. "Am I gonna need to buy you some shoes in here so you can shop?" he asked, as he stared at my feet draped in a pair of wedge sandals.

I chuckled as I dropped my phone inside my bag. "No silly, I have shoes in my purse."

My father raised a brow while staring at my Louis Vuitton Neverfull GM. "You have shoes in there?" He lifted his arm off the armrest and pointed down at my purse.

I nodded my head while snatchin my bag off the floor, digging inside I retrieved a pair of Toms. "See." I waved the shoes in his direction. "There are benefits to carrying bags this big."

"Well I'm glad to see my money isn't going to waste," he teased.

I quickly removed my sandals and eased into the flats. Chucking my discarded shoes into the backseat I climbed out the truck and waited for my father. A few moments later he rounded the truck, taking his time as he strolled toward me sporting a pair of aviator Ray-Bans and his classic GQ smile. My father was that man. At fifty-five he still had the swagger of a thirty-year-old. And he knew it too. It didn't help that women never seemed to let him forget it. His presence commanded attention, attention that he readily soaked up. But to his credit he never indulged in anything further than a little harmless flirting. Johnathan Banks was a real lady's man. No matter where he went my father was constantly being hit on by women of all ages and race, and today was no different.

Standing off to the side of the entryway I rolled my eyes up in my head as I watched my father and the woman checking membership IDs engage in what appeared to be a very friendly conversation. Clearly, she missed the platinum wedding band on his ring finger because baby girl was all tits and smiles as she pushed her perky double D's into my father's face. Annoyed and just a tiny bit amused I pulled my phone out of my bag and snapped a quick picture. After sending the photo to Carmen and Egypt with the caption, *somebody come get this thirst box* I dropped my phone back in my purse and waited for my father to finish entertaining the flirtatious greeter. I was relieved when I saw him stuffing his membership card back into his wallet. Shaking my head, I couldn't help but smile as I watched him flash his signature JB grin topped off with a wink before he walked away. The poor girl stood silently watching my father's every step. She was damn near drooling as he strolled over to where I was standing.

"You ready princess?"

I shook my head as I linked my arm inside his while smirking at his young admirer. "Let's do this."

After spending over an hour parading through the aisles of Sam's Club my father and I were finally back in his SUV and headed to Miss Brenda's. Fatigued, I closed my eyes and leaned my head against the headrest as my father started humming, picking up where we left off before our shopping spree. It didn't take long for sleep to find me. Unfortunately, my nap was short lived, the ringing of my phone snatched me from my slumber. Sluggishly my lids fluttered open and my attention went to my purse. I rifled through my bag and grabbed my phone, smiling at the name displayed on the home screen. I snuck a peek at my father before deciding to let the call go to voicemail. I waited until the phone stop ringing to unlock my device and go into my message app. I clicked on our old message thread and shot Dre a text.

Me: I haven't 4gotten about u I promise. I'm with my father right now. I'll be in your neighborhood soon. We're headed to Miss Brenda's now.

Message sent, I exited out of our thread and noticed an unopened text from Carmen. I clicked on her name and read her message. She let me know she picked up her car and asked me to call her when I was free. Again, I peeked at my father who seemed to be in his own world. Not really sure how our conversation would go I opted to send her message instead, promising to call her later when I didn't have extra ears around. Just as I was about to close out of the app my phone pinged with a new text from Dre.

Dre: Coo. I ain't want shit 4 real. Walk down here if u can. Would love to see your pretty face.

I felt my cheeks heat while in my peripheral I saw my father staring at me as we waited at a red light. Slowly I turned to face him. "Daddy, why are you looking at me like that?"

"I'm trying figure out who got you blushing. It better not be Dre's ass. I already told the twins to check his big ass."

Frowning I stared at my father in complete shock. I knew he told the twins about last night, but I didn't know exactly how that conversation went, until now. "How come you follow the rule when it comes to Royce and Ryker but not me? That's not fair daddy," I whined.

My father turned his attention back on the road as the light changed. "Because you're my princess. I only got one daughter damnit."

"But daddy it's your rule," I argued.

"I know whose damn rule it is. I don't need you to remind me." The muscles in his jaw flexed as he fought to remain calm. "Just not him Raquel," he huffed.

"Daddy you're not serious, are you? Dre and I are just friends but why do you say not him? You don't even know Dre."

My father paid me a quick glimpse before turning his attention back on the road. "I don't know Dre? Andre Cameron? Now you're the one who can't be serious. Dre and the twins have been inseparable since before they had pubic hair. I'm very familiar with Dre, Raquel."

I felt myself getting more and more agitated with the conversation, so I decided to dead it. "Welp, since Dre and I are just friends there is nothing for you to worry about."

My father didn't respond but the way he pushed a hard gush of air from his mouth I knew he wanted to say more. Rolling my eyes, I turned and looked out the passenger window as we pulled up to Miss Brenda's house. Grateful that our uncomfortable ride was coming to an end I shifted my head forward and glared at my father from the corner of my eye.

Coasting up the driveway my father hit a button below the sunroof, raising the garage. "Just make sure it stays that way," he ordered, as he pulled into the garage.

I couldn't believe this shit. My father never interfered in my dating life so I couldn't understand his interest now. When the twins and I were old enough to date my father told us our dating/love life was our personal business. He said he wouldn't interfere in our affairs unless we asked. In exchange, he asked the same of us. I guess in his crazy ass mind he felt he had no right to give love advise or make demands since he was sleeping with both our mothers.

Frustrated I closed my eyes and quickly counted backwards from fifty before flicking my lids open and picking up my phone to text Dre.

Me: Will definitely be down there shortly. U won't believe the convo I just had w/my father <angry face emoji>

I chucked my phone in my bag and hopped out the truck as soon as my father placed it in park. "You bet not slam my damn door." His deep voice echoed off the walls of the garage.

My eyes lowered to a squint as I looked across at him, careful not to roll them I left the door open as I made my way over to the stairs leading into the house.

"Fuckin smart ass," I heard him fuss behind me.

Served his ass right. He'd really gotten under my skin with that entire conversation. I knew I was being dramatic, but I didn't care. He was being hypocritical. So as far as I was concerned, we were even. My father continued fussing as I pushed the door open and walked in the house. I left that door open too as I headed for the kitchen. Still seething, our conversation played on repeat in my head as I plopped down in a chair at the kitchen table. I tried making sense of my father's unreasonable request when my phone chirped, drawing me out of my head. I welcomed the distraction. I sat my purse on top of the table and retrieved my phone, going straight to my text app.

Dre: Damn, that bad huh? I can't wait to hear all about it. I'll be here whenever ur ready.

Exhausted just thinking about repeating my conversation with my father I placed my phone on the table and pushed my purse back then lowered my head to the hard, wooden surface. I had just closed my eyes when I felt the soft touch of someone's hand on my back. My eyes fluttered opened. Slowly I raised my head from the table and turned around. Miss Brenda stood over me looking down at me with concern in her big brown eyes.

133

"You okay baby?"

I shook my head while looking into the eyes of the woman who helped raise me. Miss Brenda and my mother were complete opposites. Miss Brenda was a beautiful woman in her own right, but she and my mother didn't share a single physical feature. No one could accuse my father of having a 'type' that was for damn sure. Miss Brenda was a thick woman with a full waist, wide hips, a huge backside, and enormous breast. However, she carried her weight well. Her statuesque frame allowed those extra pounds to spread evenly throughout her body. Miss Brenda was tall, standing at five-foot eight in flats. She had big soulful light brown eyes, a wide nose, and full puffy lips. Her skin was the color of caramel with hints of a red undertone. A sprinkle of freckles donned her beautiful face complimented by two moles on her left temple. She wore her relaxed hair in a medium length bob complimented by razor sharp bangs. Unlike my mother who dyed her hair regularly to hide her greys Miss Brenda embraced hers. Her blackish brown hair was highlighted with hues of gray throughout. To a stranger it would appear that she had it professionally done but it was all natural just like the woman underneath the hair. Miss Brenda truly subscribed to the old adage that less was more. She rarely wore makeup outside of a little bush, eyeliner and colored lip gloss and even that was rare. Miss Brenda's beauty shined from the inside out. Yes, Miss Brenda was physically attractive but what made her exceptionally beautiful was her kind spirit.

Growing up there was never a time that Miss Brenda treated me differently than she treated the twins. In her eyes and her heart, I was her daughter. She genuinely loved me and in return she gained my trust and love. Emotions I often found myself struggling with because of my love for my mother. Loving both of them made me feel conflicted. I struggled with the idea of being disloyal to one by loving the other. For the most part I'd learned how to compartmentalize my conflicting emotions but there were times when the guilt wouldn't allow me. It was during those times I despised my father for putting our family in this situation.

Pushing those thoughts out of my head I forced a smile onto my face. "I'm okay," I lied.

I stood from my seat and eagerly walked into Miss Brenda's open arms. She wrapped me into a tight embrace while gently running her hands up and down my back. I melted into the comfort of her arms while closing my eyes and exhaling slowly. With each stroke of her soft hands I felt the tension gradually leaving my body. My shoulders relaxed while my breathing evened out and the pressure weighing down on the back of my neck eased up. I'd just gotten comfortable in my relaxed state when my father's heavy footsteps resounded from the hall.

And just that quickly, I was annoyed again. Tiny pockets of pressure formed behind my eye sockets, causing a bit of discomfort as I flicked my lids open. Listlessly peeling myself from Miss Brenda's arms I shifted my head toward the kitchen entrance just as my father walked in with both his hands full of groceries. Without hesitating Ms Brenda quickly walked toward my father and grabbed several bags from his overstuffed hands. Irritated, I rolled my eyes in my head while grabbing my bag and cellphone off the table and stalking past them.

"What did you do to my baby?" I heard Miss Brenda ask behind me, as I traipsed out of the kitchen.

I couldn't get out there fast enough, ascending the stairs I wondered what version of the story my father was down there telling her. I was sure it wasn't the one where he basically prohibited me from dating Dre. I reached the second level and shook my head as I walked down the hall toward my bedroom. Passing Royce's bedroom on the right side of the hall I peeked inside and smiled at the tidiness of his space. His bed was neatly made and there wasn't a single item out of place. Quickly moving past the Jack and Jill bathroom the next door over was Ryker's room. A complete contrast to his older brother's. Pushing the ajared door open I peeped inside. Clothes were scattered everywhere; across the bed, over the chair, and of course on the floor. His bed was disheveled and a few of his dresser drawers were slightly opened. I pulled my head out the messy room and chuckled as I tugged the door close behind me.

No wonder Miss Brenda left the door pulled up.

I continued walking to the end of the hall where my room was located and stepped inside, pulling the door shut I dropped my bag at my feet and rested my tired frame against the door while surveying my room. Everything was just how I left it. Although not as neat as Royce's room it was nowhere near as messy as Ryker's.

Mentally and physically drained I peeled my fatigued body from the door and padded over to my bed, plopping down on the firm mattress. I tossed my phone on the bed beside then took a beat to collect myself before kicking off my shoes and massaging my throbbing feet. Satisfied that I relieved some of the aching I stood from the bed and walked into my bathroom.

Standing in front of the sink I turned on the hot water and waited for it to heat up while staring at my reflection in the mirror. I looked tired and the frustration with my father was present on my face. Exasperated, I released a hard gush of air through my nostrils as my eyes drifted to the faucet. Languidly lowering my torso, I inserted my hands underneath the running stream then cupped them together to scoop water into my palms. After a few quick splashes to my face I dabbed it dry with a hand towel laid across the sink then sluggishly walked back inside my room and headed straight for my dresser. I grabbed a container of shea butter and unscrewed the top then scooped a dollop into my palm before returning the container to the dresser. Hurriedly I gently applied the creamy substance to my face before looking up and paying myself a quick glance in the mirror. Satisfied that I no longer looked as tired as I felt, I stepped over to the bed and retrieved my phone. I clicked on the home button and cleared my alerts as I walked out my room and headed back down the hall, toward the stairs.

The soft sounds of R&B streaming through the built-in surround sound greeted me as I stepped into the hall. Rounding the corner, I trekked into the kitchen where I found Miss Brenda and my father engaged in a playful two step. His vast arms hugged her possessively from behind as he guided them around the island, swaying to "Between the Sheets" by the Isley Brothers. Miss Brenda giggled like a schoolgirl as my father sang along to the track in her ear. I hated the fact that my father was involved in a relationship with another woman but seeing the two of them together and happy made it hard to feel anything other than love. Leaned against the wall I wondered what happened between my parents that lead my father here. My thoughts barely had time to manifest when my father's eyes landed on mine. Lifting his head from Miss Brenda's ear he kissed her on the cheek and swatted her on the ass before casually sauntering over to where I stood.

My father looked down at me before grabbing me by the arms and pulling me into his chest. "You know I don't like it when my princess is mad at me. Although I stand by what I said earlier I know you're grown and will try to mind my business."

I lifted my head from my father's chest and cut my eyes at him. I felt the rumble of his chest when he snickered. "I said I will try," he stated with humor in his tone.

Knowing my father, I knew this was as close to an apology as I was going to get. "Thank you, daddy."

My father kissed me softly on the forehead before releasing me from his embrace. "Alright, I'll get out y'all's hair so y'all can get things together for tomorrow."

I watched as my father walked over to Miss Brenda who stood by the island where she'd observed our entire exchange. Placing his hands on each side of her face he lowered his head and kissed her passionately. Grossed out, I turned away until I heard my father's deep boisterous laughter behind me.

"I'm done. Y'all have fun."

My father winked at me as he strolled by. Shoulders erect and head held high he trekked out the kitchen. My attention shifted to my surrogate mother, shaking my head I walked toward her. There was no doubt in my mind she was responsible for my father waving the white flag.

I stood in front of her with my head cocked to one side and my lids lowered to a squint. "I know you had something to do with that."

A coy smile danced on her semi-glossy lips as she pretended not to know what I was talking about. "What?" she asked with a hint of a smile in her tone while walking to the refrigerator.

I giggled while watching her dig items out of the fridge. "Yeah okay."

She sat the ingredients she took out the refrigerator on the island and turned to me with her hands on her broad hips. "You know I can't have anybody messing with my baby," she asserted, with sass and a smirk on her pretty face.

A few determined strides had me standing face to face with her. I threw my arms around Miss Brenda's waist and pulled her into a quick hug before walking into the pantry and gathering the remaining items we needed to prepare for tomorrow. Hands and arms full of everything necessary to get started I unloaded everything on top of the counter. Miss Brenda and I wasted no time getting to work. I prepped the macaroni and cheese, loaded the green beans into the crockpot, and made the pasta salad. Almost finished prepping for tomorrow's festivities I picked my cellphone up from the counter and texted Dre while Miss Brenda finished patting the burgers.

Me: U still good w/me stopping by?

I sat my phone down and made my way over to the fridge, pulling out a Red Bull I cracked it open and guzzled down half the small bottle before returning to the island. Sitting the can on the counter I picked up my phone and checked my text. Dre's name was displayed in bold at the top of my message thread.

Dre: Of course. U on the way?

Me: Give me like 10mins and I'll be down there. Cool?

Immediately, I received a new a new text notification. I didn't bother checking it. Instead, I stuffed my phone in my pocket and walked over to the sink where Miss Brenda was rinsing chicken wings. I playfully bumped her with my hip to get her attention.

"Is there anything else you need me to help you with?" I asked when she looked at me.

"No baby, I got it from here. I'm about done. I appreciate all your help." She playfully bumped me back. "You going down to Dre's?" She kept her voice low while sweeping her eyes around the room.

I shook my head as I leaned into her tall frame, standing on my tippy toes I kissed her cheek. "Well in that case, I'm out." I flashed her a silly grin while throwing up the peace sign.

I heard Miss Brenda chuckle as I walked over to the island and picked up my half-consumed energy drink. Chugging down the remainder of the carbonated drink I headed toward the entryway when something occurred to me. I slowed my steps and glanced over my shoulder to where Miss Brenda was standing.

"Hey," I called out.

Miss Brenda turned and looked at me. "Yes baby?"

"If daddy ask, you don't know where I went."

Miss Brenda brought a hand up to her mouth. With her index finger and thumb pinched together she dragged them from the left side of her mouth to the right then winked at me. That was all I needed to see. I shifted my head forward and accelerated my steps out the kitchen, pitching the empty can in the trash as I passed by. Grateful to have Miss Brenda as a buffer I made a mad dash up the stairs and darted into my room. I snatched my bag off the floor and dug inside, removing my lip gloss I lowered my purse to floor and ran back down the stairs. I flew out the garage door and climbed inside my father's truck. Reaching into the backseat I grabbed my sandals and quickly put them on. I then pulled the visor down and flipped the mirror up. I did a quick sweep of my face before focusing on my lips and applying a fresh coat of lip gloss. *Slow your ass down, he ain't going nowhere.* Leisurely, I exited the truck while digging my cellphone out of my pocket and going directly to my text app. Without hesitating I clicked on Dre's name.

Dre: I'll be waiting <winking face emoji>

I stood at the end of our driveway and took a second to calm myself before crossing the street and casually strolling the short distance to Dre's. Just four houses down from Miss Brenda's it took me less than a minute to reach his front door. I felt a twinge of nervous energy as I stood on the porch. Closed fist just inches away from the door I prepared to knock when it was pugnaciously flung open. Without warning, I was snatched into a pair of strong arms while being lifted off my feet. Burying his face in my neck Dre ran his nose softly across my flesh then inhaled deeply

"Dre that tickles," I squealed.

Slowly dragging his face out of the crook of my neck Dre peered into my eyes while lowering me back on me feet and pulling me into his house. "Im sorry, you just smell so damn good," he growled, while greedily raking his eyes down my body.

Unable to stop the blush from creeping onto my face I dropped my head and looked down at the phone in my hand. "Thanks."

Dre placed his hand underneath my chin, lifting my head he forced me to look him in his exotic colored eyes. "You never have to hide this from me." Dre ran the back of his hand down my cheek then repeated that motion with the tip of his thumb across my lips. "I love making and seeing you smile, and I especially love these," he finished, while poking me in one of my dimples.

I closed my eyes while shaking my head. Flashing my lids open I smiled freely at the sincerity in Dre's eyes. "Thank you. You are the best thing on my worst day," I admitted softly.

A perceptive grin settled on Dre's face as he laced his fingers in mine. "C'mon Short Stuff." Dre pushed the door shut and gently tugged on my hand, urging me to walk.

Staying close to Dre's side I followed him down a long hallway until we reached a large sitting room. My eyes swept around the spacious area, taking in the beautiful décor and luxurious furniture as Dre lead me to an oversized couch. Damn near standing on top of me Dre unhooked our hands and instructed me to sit. Completely engrossed in my surroundings I took in everything my eyes could see, hoping to catch a glimpse of Dre's life in order to understand him better. I almost forgot he was there until those raspy cords rumbled above my head. Tearing my eyes away from a family portrait hanging on the wall I lowered myself onto the sofa and melted into the plush cushions.

"I'll be right back Short Stuff. Make yourself comfortable. The remote to the TV is on the table in front of you."

I nodded my understanding as I watched him disappear out the room. Immediately I made myself comfortable, tucking my left leg underneath my butt I grabbed the remote off the table and switched on the TV. Not really interested in watching anything in particular I leaned into the back of the couch and flicked through the channels while waiting for Dre to return. Unable to find anything remotely interesting I looked down at my phone when a shadow in my peripheral caught my attention. Slowly I turned my head to find a tiny figure creeping up on me.

"Rocky," she squealed, as she ran over to where I was sitting and threw her small frame into my body.

Laughing I fell further into the couch as I opened my arms to catch her. I kissed her almond colored cheek as I lifted her onto my lap. "Well, hello lil Miss Madison. Where did you come from?"

Giggling soft brown eyes peered into mine. "My room," she answered, as she placed her tiny hands in my curly mane.

"Maddy get out of her hair and get your big butt off of Rocky's lap," Dre ordered.

Startled, Madison and I jumped at the sound of Dre's voice. Madison's little face scrunched up in pout as she removed her hands from my hair and slid out of my lap. Damn near sitting on top of me, Madison planted her small body right next to mine and grabbed my phone out of my hand.

"Do you have games on your phone," she asked, while pressing the home key in an attempt to open my phone.

"Yes, let me see." I pressed the home button, unlocking my phone while she held it tightly in her little hands.

I helped Madison navigate through my gaming apps, pausing momentarily when I noticed Dre sitting two glasses on the coffee table. Peeking at me through lowered lids a sly grin eased across his face as he took a seat next to Madison. My eyes bounced between the siblings before I turned my full attention back to Madison who was still engrossed in my phone. After a few minutes of swiping through various games Madison found one she liked and instantly zoned out.

Satisfied that Madison no longer needed my help I looked at the glasses on the table then turned my head toward Dre. "And what do we have here Mr. Cameron?"

Dre looked at me and winked then turned his attention to his little sister. "Madison finish that game then I want you to give Rocky her phone back and go back up to your room."

"But Cam Cam I want to stay down here with you and Rocky," she whined.

"I know munchkin but Rocky is my company, not yours. We have some grownup stuff to talk about," he offered kindly.

"Okay, but next time she comes over I get to play with her." I chuckled at the sass in her voice. "Here you go Rocky, that game was boring anyway." She handed me my phone then hopped up from the couch.

I sat the phone on the table and shook my head as I watched her skip out the room. Her long full pigtails bounced on top of her small head with each bop of her feet.

Once Madison was gone, I turned to face Dre who was staring at me with humor in his eyes. "She is the cutest, how old is she now?"

"That's because she looks like her big brother," he responded with a wink. "She's six."

"Oh wow. I think the last time I saw her was about two years ago."

"Well it looks like time hasn't diminished her affinity for you."

"I have that effect on people."

"Yeah I know," Dre murmured, as he reached for one of the glasses on the table and handed it to me."

Accepting the proffered drink, I raised a brow. "Again, what is in this glass. Did you slip me a micky?"

Dre picked up the other glass from the table and offered it to me. "You want this one instead?"

I lightly swatted his hand while taking a sip of my drink. "Ummm. Barbera?"

Shaking his head at me Dre sipped from his glass then sat it back on the table. "Yes. And for the record I would never spike your drink. Although if it gave me an opportunity to taste your lips again, I might consider it."

His words did something to me, or maybe it was the man behind the words. Either way, it had my hot ass sliding over, closing the gap Madison's absence created between us. I took another quick nip of my wine before sitting my glass back on the table and leaning into Dre's hard frame. Confusion danced in his glowing hazels as he peered at me. Making my intentions clear, a salacious grin spilled onto my lips as I softly placed my mouth on Dre's. In complete contrast to last night, there was no hesitation. Dre was fully engaged and a willing participant.

Grabbing a fist full of my hair Dre deepened our kiss while threading his fingers into my loose curls and tenderly massaging my scalp. Tiny sparks of pleasure started at the base of my neck and coursed down my spine. His minty breath laced with a hint of Barbera filled my nostrils as a soft moan escaped from my lips. Completely enthralled in our oral foreplay I climbed into his lap. I straddled his colossal thighs while wrapping my arms around his neck. Inching his hands from my hair Dre slid one hand down the back of my neck. He pulled me deeper into his mouth as his other hand palmed my ass.

I felt so needy, but I couldn't get enough of him. My nails clawed at his shoulders while my hips took on a life of their own, grinding rhythmically against Dre's growing erection as his tongue intertwined with mine. Passionate, intense, and damn right messy, we freely explored each other's mouths, kissing until we couldn't breathe. Panting, I cracked my lids open while listlessly removing my tongue from his mouth. I watched him in awe as I traced his full lips with my tongue and gently sucked his bottom lip into my mouth, lightly running my tongue across it before releasing it.

Dre placed his hands on each side of my face as his eyes slowly fluttered open. "Fuck," he growled into my mouth, while slowly lowering his head back and resting it on the back of the couch.

Bringing my hands up to his I removed his large hands from my face and gently held him at the wrist. I kissed the back of his right hand then his left. Dre raised his head and gazed at me through hooded eyes. Suddenly aware I was still straddling him I climbed out of his lap, careful of his engorged manhood I sat silently next to him on the couch.

"Fuck Rocky. I wasn't going to say shit about last night because you were tipsy, but you can't friendzone me then—" his voice trailed off as he ran a hand down the front of his face while slowly turning to face me. "Don't get me wrong, I enjoy kissing you but—"

"You're right and I'm sorry," I offered sincerely, cutting him off. I reached over and clutched his hand in mine, running my thumb back and forth over it, I stared into his eyes. "Dre, I like you. A lot actually. And if our circumstances were different, I would jump at the opportunity to be in a situationship with you but—" I stopped speaking. Timidly I removed my hand from his, closed my eyes, and pinched the bridge of my nose.

Dre grabbed my hand, removing it from my face he held it firmly in his hand. I opened my eyes but was unable to look at him. Instead I focused on the TV as I tried to control my emotions.

Dre tugged on my hand. "Look at me Rocky."

I shook my head no.

"Raquel," he barked, as he roughly pulled me into his lap.

Using his hand to lift my face to his I looked into his eyes. "For the record, I like you a lot too and I'm trying real hard to respect your words. But I need your actions to match those words or else I will make you eat them," he asserted firmly, while running the back of his hand along my cheekbone. "You understand?"

I shook my head while holding his penetrating gaze.

"Use your words Rocky. Because if you kiss me again, I won't stop you and you will have to deal with what follows after wakin a sleepin giant." His eyes lowered to his pelvic area.

A soft smirk formed on my face. "I hear you loud and clear Andre."

"Good, now get yo ass off of me before I start some shit you ain't ready to finish." He was smiling but I heard the seriousness in his tone.

As bad as I wanted him, I knew he was right. I was definitely playing with fire and if I kept on my ass was going to get burnt. For the second time in less than a minute, I climbed out of his lap and sat next to him on the couch.

I leaned forward and plucked my glass off the table, taking a hearty sip while turning my body to face Dre. "Since we can't kiss anymore, we might as well talk," I gibed, as I strummed my fingers on my glass. "Tell me about your convo with the twins."

Mimicking my movements Dre picked up his drink, took a nip of his spirit, then turned his body toward me. "It was an expected and somewhat surprising conversation that occurred way too early in the damn morning," he stated flatly.

"Really Dre, that's all you have to say? Aren't you the one who texted askin to talk?" I implored, with a raised brow, hoping that would prompt him to continue.

Smirking Dre took another gulp from his drink. "Ryker woke me up screamin through the phone askin me what the fuck was goin on with us. He said JB called him and Royce last night after findin you asleep in my arms. After tellin his ass to calm the fuck down I told him there was nothin goin on. I let him know I was doin what they asked and nothin more."

"And?"

"And what?" he asked as he stood from his seat. "Be right back, you need anything?"

"Only for you to finish tellin me what the fuck you and my brothers talked about."

"Yeah okay. I got you smart ass," he called out, as he walked across the room.

I watched as Dre causally strolled out of the room. He returned just as quick as he left, in his right hand was an opened bottle of Copper's Hawk Barbera. Walking over to where I was sitting Dre grabbed my hand holding my wine glass and topped off my drink. He then poured more wine into his glass before sitting the bottle on the table.

"After I got Ryker calmed down, I talked to Royce. He was nowhere near as turnt up as his twin. Royce asked what was going on between us. He asked if I was fallin for you then warned me to be careful. He said some shit about you not being like the average woman and that he didn't want me to get hurt. He said you had a habit of chewin dudes up and spittin their asses out when you were done. Oh, and he said no matter what we were both grown but he didn't want whatever was happenin between us to affect our friendship." Dre took his seat beside me. "Is that enough info for your nosy ass?" he teased.

I winced hearing Dre recite my brother's perception of me. "Thank you. Now was that so hard Cam Cam?" I asked, calling him by the nickname Madison used earlier.

Dre softly pinched my side. "Your turn, what did the twins say to you?"

Flinching I swatted at his hand before taking a quick sip of my newly poured drink. "Basically, the same things they said to you. Ryker was extra. He was in protective brother mode askin me a thousand questions per minute. After answerin everything he asked I had to pull rank and shut his ass down. I ended my call with Royce who took the same approach with me as he did with you. He asked once if you and I were an item then warned me not to hurt you after I told him we were just friends."

Dre chuckled as he ran a hand down his neatly trimmed goatee. For the first time since I arrived, I noticed Dre's freshly groomed face and crisp haircut. "You got a haircut," I exclaimed excitedly.

That made him laugh. Dre's deep baritone filled the large room as tears formed in the corners of his eyes. Wiping the tiny drops from his face he looked at me. "Damn Rocky, you only been here for over an hour now. You just now noticin a nigga?"

I ran my tongue across my bottom lip while smirking at the sarcasm in his tone. "What can I say, you're sexy either way."

Dre cut his eyes at me as he sipped from his glass. "Yeah okay. So, tell me what JB said that had you pissed off earlier."

I rolled my eyes up in my head. "You got something stronger than this?" I tilted my glass toward him.

"Damn, that bad? Let me check my pop's stash."

Dre sat his glass on the table and prepared to stand. I quickly placed my hand on his muscular thigh. "I'm playin with you, this is good. I don't wanna go back wasted. That will just be another thing for my father to talk shit about."

Dre picked up his glass and sat back on the couch, stretching his long legs out in front of him. "I'm listening."

"Long story short, he told me not to date you. He basically said anyone but you," I said heatedly, as I felt myself getting agitated again.

"Don't sweat it Short Stuff"

I took a swig of my wine and peered at him over the top of my glass. I licked the corner of my mouth, swiping the dribble of wine that fell there after my sip. "That doesn't bother you?"

"Nah, not at all. JB may think he knows me, but he has no idea the man that I've matured into. JB knows the silly, nerdy, Bishop Hartley football star who thought he was a lady's man. Since the twins went away to school the only time, he sees me is when, three months out of the year when we're on summer break? He has no idea of the grown man Andre Cameron is. So, no. His warning for you stay away from me doesn't bother me in the least."

"Wow."

Dre chuckled while digging his phone out of his pocket. Looking at the screen he slid forward on the couch and sat his glass down. "You about ready for me to walk you back to Miss Brenda's? I forgot all about J's ass. I gotta go pick him up from some shorty's house."

"Let me find out Jamison out here messin with broads with no whips," I teased, while shaking my head.

Dre chuckled. "Nah, she has a car, but I guess something happened. J said he would tell me when I picked him up."

I finished the contents in my glass then sat the empty goblet next to his. "You don't have to walk me, it's only four houses down."

Dre stood to his feet and reached down for my hand. "I'm fully aware of where my best friends' live. Get your feisty ass up so we can go."

I didn't protest, taking his proffered hand I allowed him to pull me to my feet. "Such a fuckin gentleman," I sassed, bending over I grabbed my phone off the coffee table and damn near jumped out of my skin when Dre's hand made contact with my ass.

To take the sting out of the mild blow Dre rubbed the area where he just swatted and looked down at me. "And you're such a fuckin lady," he countered, with mischief in his eyes.

Laughing, I trailed Dre out the room as he guided us back down the hall and out the front door. He pulled the door closed behind us and locked his finger in mine. Something I'd noticed was becoming our new norm. I smiled to myself while relishing the feel of his hand in mine. I would never admit it to him, but I loved how affectionate he was toward me. We walked hand in hand, allowing a comfortable silence to settle between us as we traveled the short distance down to Miss Brenda's.

Although I had just spent the last two hours with him, I wasn't really ready to leave his company. Clearly, he must have felt the same way because he stood silently holding firmly onto my hand. Turning to face him I slowly retracted my hand from his.

"Thanks for walking me back," I spieled softly, while titling my head to look up and into his eyes.

Low hazels gazed down at me. "It was nothin Short Stuff. Thanks for comin and kickin it wit a nigga. As always, I enjoyed spendin time with you. You and the girls goin out tonight?"

I hadn't thought about my girls or anyone else for that matter since I stepped foot in his house. Shaking my head, I chuckled at that revelation. "Honestly, I have no idea what we're gettin into tonight. I'll call them when I get inside. I'll see you tomorrow, tho right?"

Dre smiled down at me. "Of course. What time does it start and what do I need to bring?"

"We typically get started about three and go until, so you can come whenever you like. You don't need to bring anything. There will be plenty of food and drinks."

"Coo, I'll make sure to wear my bulletproof vest tho. You know, just in case JB is feelin froggy."

I playfully pushed him in his diesel chest. "Yeah okay. JB better be on his best behavior tomorrow or imma put my mama on his ass." I was smiling but I was dead ass serious.

Grabbing me by the arms Dre pulled me into his chest. He looked down at me and grinned. "I can handle JB. Don't let him bother you.

We are gonna have a good time tomorrow without any problems," he asserted coolly, while running his hands up and down my arms.

A soft smile spread across my face as I absorbed his words. "Okay." Although I wasn't sure how my father would react to seeing him tomorrow, his confidence was soothing.

Lowering his head Dre softy placed his forehead on mine. A chill ran down my spine as the minty scent of his breath filled my nostrils. In that moment I found myself longing to feel his lips against mine again. I fought the irresistible urge to kiss him as his words played in my head. Instead, I sucked my bottom lip in between my teeth while enjoying just being in his space. I hated that he had such an effect on me when I knew I couldn't have him.

"I gotta get out of here Short Stuff." His deep tenor snatched me out of my head.

Languidly I shifted my eyes up, stopping at his succulent lips. Slowly, his lips eased into a delicious smile as he used his hand to raise my dipped chin. "Whenever you're ready to change the terms of our relationship just say the word." His tone was deathly serious, words dripping with lechery.

Gazing intensely in my eyes Dre lowered his head again, pressing his silky lips on the corner of my mouth. Briefly closing my eyes, I reveled in the intimacy of that simple act. My lids cracked open when he removed his lips from my face and slowly backed away from me. He walked backwards down the driveway while keeping his eyes focused on me. I placed a soft smile on my face as I stood silently watching him until he was no longer within my eyesight. Exasperated by so many unexplainable emotions I turned toward the garage and tried ignoring the tingling sensation coursing through my entire body.

What. In. Thee. Entire. Fuck?

CHAPTER SEVEN

*D*ropping my phone in my lap I picked my brew off the table and chugged back the last of the grainy hops. I slammed the empty bottle on the table harder than I intended as I snatched up the PlayStation controller.

"You ready to get cha ass beat?"

"Man whatever, ain't nobody trynna hear that shit. Just pick your team so I can beat that ass right quick," he stated confidently.

I angled my body toward Jamison who was sitting adjacent to me in our large recliner. "Put something on it then nigga."

Jamison waved his hand at me. "You don't want them problems nigga."

I laughed while shuffling through the teams displayed on our flat screen TV. After selecting the Cleveland Cavaliers, I sat the controller on the table, tossed my phone from my lap, and stood to my feet. Reflexively my arms shot up in the air as I leaned backward to loosen the tightened muscles in my lower back. I did that a few times before dropping my hands to my hips and twisting slightly from side to side, stretching the other constricted limbs of my solid frame. Satisfied that I'd relieved some of the tightness in my body I let my hands fall to my side as I bent over and grabbed my empty beer bottle from the table.

"You want another brew?"

Jamison picked up his bottle from the side table and studied the contents inside. "Yeah, I let this one get warm. Can you toss it for me?"

I swiped the half empty bottle from his outstretched hand as I walked past. "Only if you ain't gonna babysit it this time."

"Babysit these nuts."

A light chortle slid from my mouth as walked into the kitchen and discarded my empty bottle in the trash. Standing in front of the sink I poured Jamison's wasted brew down the drain then pitched that bottle in the garbage as well. I then moved over to the refrigerator inside our small kitchen and quickly retrieved two Coronas and strolled back into the living room, handing Jamison one of the cold brews as I took my seat on our oversized couch.

Chugging back a hearty amount of the cold lager I sat my beer on the coffee table and picked up the controller. "You ready for this ass whippn?"

"Just hit play nigga."

I didn't hesitate as I hit play on the controller to start the game. I was prepared to serve my friend a royal ass whipping. Jamison was a gamer more so than I was, but I enjoyed kicking back with him; playing video games, throwing back a few brews, and talking cash money shit while doing it. During the school year, especially football season we rarely had time for social activities. So, when our schedules synced this was typically how we passed the time. Halfway through the game Jamison was up by ten points. And as usual, he was hyped and talking shit. His player had just scored on one of my men, prompting him to jump his big ass up from his seat while stretching his long arms in the air and imitate shooting a basket.

"Man sit cha black ass down. The game ain't ova yet nigga," I stated, while shaking my head at his animated antics.

"Might as well be. Your punk ass Cavs ain't shit against my Bulls."

I felt my phone vibrate next to me on the couch. Grateful for the distraction I paused the game while laying the controller in my lap and picking up my phone. Pressing the home screen, the phone opened and displayed a text notification from Rocky. Immediately going into my text app, I clicked on her name.

Rocky: Hey handsome, don't worry about the bread I picked some up. See u when u get here <winking face emoji>

Me: Cool, you need me to bring anything else?

Rocky: Just you

I couldn't help the prodigious smile that eased onto my face as I re-read her last message. It was crazy that something so simple from her could bring out the bitch in me. Laying my phone on the table I picked up my beer and took a swig, trying desperately to remove the images of her that were bouncing around in my head. I'd chugged back a few sips of my beer before returning my drink to the table and grabbing the controller from my lap to resume the game.

Jamison paused the game and looked over at me. "Nah nigga, who da fuck got you cheesin at cha phone?"

I ignored his ass while unpausing the game. My eyes stayed fastened the buttons on the controller as a means to avoid Jamison's unwavering stare. "Ain't nobody cheesin, I was just textin Rocky." I tried hard as hell to hide the smile in my tone.

Again, Jamison paused the game and sat his controller on the accent table next to his beer. "So, we lie to each other now? That's what we doin?" he questioned, calling me on my bullshit.

I turned to face him, finally allowing my eyes to meet his. I sat silently trying to figure out how to articulate into words the shit that was going on between me and Rocky as Jamison studied me through squinted lids.

"What da fuck is going on between the two you anyway?" he asked, before I could address his initial inquiry.

I ran a hand down my face as I sat the controller on the table and picked up my beer. "Long story short, nothin. Her choice not mine." That was the shortest way to give him an honest answer.

Grabbing his brew from the side table Jamison placed it to his lips then quickly removed it. "So, you mean to tell me, shorty cooks for you every week and y'all just friends? Not even fuck buddies?"

I chugged back a mouth full of my brewski, swallowing the frosty ale I shook my head. "Not a damn thing. We are strictly friends."

"Hmm, well I don't see that arrangement lastin too much longer," he stated, as he took a nip of his own beer.

My eyebrows shot up on my head as I drank the last of my beer and sat the empty bottle on the table. "Why you say that?"

"I was for sure y'all were already smashin and just trynna keep it on the low. Hell, anybody with eyes can see y'all got hella chemistry." Jamison returned his bottle to the accent table and grabbed his controller, unpausing the game he paid me a quick glance before he started pressing buttons on the handheld device. "Shid I thought she was gonna swing on ole girl at her family's cookout when she plopped down in your lap durin our spades game," he finished, while laughing.

I picked up my controller and laughed as I thought about the expression on Rocky's face when Carmen's thirsty ass cousin made my lap her chair. Jamison wasn't lying. I thought Rocky was going to leap out of her chair and snatch shorty out of my lap or worse, knock her ass to the ground. However, I made no efforts to remove Charmaine from my lap. I meant it when I told Rocky her actions needed to match her words. If she only wanted to be friends, then she didn't get girlfriend privileges. I typically didn't engage in childish antics, using one female to make another one jealous but the look Rocky was giving us made it hard to resist. The ball was in her court and I wanted her to take that shit to the hoop. Lucky for baby girl not so much for me, Carmen peeped the death stare Rocky was shooting our way and quickly reacted. Carmen hopped out of her seat and snatched her cousin out of my lap, dragging the poor girl by her arm across the yard. I had no idea what Carmen said to her but when they returned to the table baby girl sat silently next to Carmen. She didn't look my way the rest of the night.

Jamison's deep baritone roared on the side of me, bringing me back to the present. Why I was off in lala land he secured the win. I shook my head while placing the controller on the table.

"Rematch?" I asked as I stood up from the couch.

"Sure, I got another ass whippn in me. I thought you were goin over to Balboa's tho."

I chuckled hearing Jamison refer to Rocky by the nickname he coined for her since her family's barbeque. "I am but—" raising my left wrist in front of my face I glanced at my watch for the time. "I got time. She's not expectin me for another hour or so," I stated, while walking past him.

"Where you goin?"

"To take a leak and when I come back imma need for you to stop bringin up old shit."

"Old? Nigga that shit was just last month," he shouted to my back, as I continued down the hall toward the bathroom.

After handling my business, I trekked back into the living room where I found Jamison hunched over on his phone, whispering to the person on the other end.

Looking up at me as I walked past Jamison abruptly ended his call. I smirked as I continued toward the couch. "Don't stop on my account," I mocked, looking down at the phone in his hand.

Jamison flicked me the bird then tucked his phone in his pocket. "Fuck you."

I laughed while dropping back down to the couch and snatching the controller off the table. "No thanks. You can save that for the shorty you were whisperin to."

"Nigga wasn't nobody whisperin. You just worry about this second ass whoppin I'm about to serve you. I should've bet cha high yellow ass."

"Why, so your black ass could cry like a bitch when I took your money?"

"Aye. Bitch these nigga," he roared, while animatedly grabbing his nuts.

"Just press play foo," I muffled through my laughter.

Jamison started the game and immediately started talking shit as he scored the first points in our rematch. Slowly I turned and looked at him, laughing I extended my middle finger then turned back toward the TV but not before Jamison returned my gesture. Determined not to lose again I decided to employ the same strategy Jamison utilized during our last game, distraction.

Eyes fixed on the TV my fingers danced around the multiple buttons on the PlayStation controller. I passed the ball from one of my players to the next, scoring my first set of points and picking up a foul in the process. "And one nigga."

"What the fuck ever nigga. Just shoot," he grumbled.

While studying the shot meter on the game I glanced over at Jamison and smirked. "What's up with you and Egypt?"

My player made the free throw while Jamison's player secured the rebound. "Whaa, whaa... what da fuck you mean," he stuttered over his words, as my player stole the ball and scored.

"Why you stutterin? Nigga just answer the question."

Jamison's fingers moved quickly over the buttons on his controller while he tried to regain the lead. "Ain't shit goin on wit me and E. Why da fuck you askin nigga?" I could tell he was completely baffled by my question.

A soft smile settled on my face at the uneasiness in his tone while I watched my player dribble down the court after rebounding a missed shot by one of Jamison's players. My smile broadened as the computer-generated version of Lebron James made a successful alley-oop.

"Now what were you sayin about whoppin my ass?" I boasted, rubbing in my small lead as I paused the game.

Jamison waved a hand at me dismissively. "Whateva nigga, this game ain't nowhere near over. Now why da fuck you askin about Egypt?"

"I'm askin because you had that same stupid look on your face..." I turned and glanced at him, "as you do right now, when she walked into the cookout with old dude," I finished, while turning back toward the TV.

"Nigga what? Ain't nobody checkin for E. Don't get me wrong, baby girl is fine as hell, but she can't handle my ass. And I definitely wasn't worried about that Nick Cannon wannabe she was with."

Laughing hysterically, I dropped the controller on the floor as I bent over holding my stomach. I could hear Jamison's boisterous laughter on the side of me. And I be damned, if I didn't laugh even harder. My head whipped over toward Jamison while shaking on my shoulders as I tried to settle from my laughing fit. But the look on his face only triggered more laughter. Jamison smacked his knee with his large hand while using his other hand to dab away a tear from the corner of his eye. Turning away from him I did my best to regain my composure while swiping my hand across the carpet, blindly searching for the controller.

"You a foo for that shit," I stated, through mild laughter as I scooped up the controller.

"Say I'm lyin," Jamison challenged. "His skinny ass came in there looking like Devon."

"Who?"

"Devon, Nick Cannon's character in Drumline. I was surprised he didn't have a drum strapped to his chest. And who da fuck still rockin a tight fade? Nigga either go bald or let some hair grow on top of yo fuckin head."

A guttural howl flew from my mouth as I shook my head, agreeing with Jamison's assessment. I didn't pay dude much attention, but I had to admit, Jamison was spot on with his comparison. I also had to admit that although Jamison was being his usual silly self there was definitely hostility in his tone. He was salty about seeing Egypt with another man. Two months ago, I didn't even know Egypt had a thing for J but once I saw the two of them together, I wasn't sure how I missed it. There was definitely a mutual attraction. Jamison was right though; Egypt was too sweet for his wild ass. So, I understood why he kept his distance.

"Aye, you ready nigga?" Jamison called out from the side of me, snapping me out of my head.

"Let's go so I can finish beatin yo ass."

Jamison started the game again. "Yeah yeah, just play so I can catch up with this shorty and you can get over to Balboa's before she put hands on your soft ass."

"Soft?" I looked to my left then to my right as if I was looking for someone else in the room. "Who you talkin bout?"

Jamison snickered while his player posted up. "You nigga."

"Nah, you can't be. I ain't Devon. I'll beat yo black ass," I declared jocosely.

"You can't see me nigga. Never forget that."

Slightly turning my head, I looked over at Jamison with a hardened scowl set on my face. Not one to back down from a challenge Jamison returned my icy glare. Cold emeralds glared into dark mochas. Slowly the corners of his eyes loosened as a smirk formed on his ebony colored face. Unable to continue with the façade I released a deep chortle as Jamison flicked me off. Returning our attention back to the game we resumed playing NBA 2K15. Forty-five minutes later I had succeeded in earing my revenge. I beat Jamison by twenty points.

"Tie breaker tomorrow?" I asked, sitting my controller on the table and picking up my phone.

"Fa sho," he responded, while rising from his seat.

I glanced down at my phone before pressing the home button and going directly to my text app. I clicked on Rocky's name and sent her a text.

Me: Hey Short Stuff I'm headed your way in the next 15mins. U sure you don't need me to bring anything?

From my peripheral I noticed Jamison moving toward me. He sat his controller on the table and looked down at me. "I'm out."

With my hands positioned on each side of me I pushed up off the couch and stood to my feet. Forming a fist with my free hand I lightly tapped Jamison's balled fist, giving him dap. "Which flava of the week are you blessin with your company today?"

Picking up on my sarcasm Jamison saluted me with his middle finger. "Green is not your color bro," he replied, while walking toward the door. At the door he glanced over his shoulder with a smirk plastered on his face. "I'm meetin up with some shorty I met at the gas station the otha night."

"By the size of the smile on your face I take it she's a baddie?"

Fully turning his body away from the door Jamison threw his hands in the air dramatically. "Bro, baby girl is cold and her body—" paus-ing, Jamison ran a hand down his face, "baby girl is shaped like a damn coke bottle. My dick is gettin hard just thinkin about that shit."

"Da fuck nigga? Ain't nobody trynna see that shit," I stated through light laughter, as I bent over and clicked off the TV.

"And ain't nobody trynna show you. I'm just sayin. Shit, I might strap up in the car."

I stood upright and damn near dropped my phone while bringing my hand up to my mouth, releasing a gut-wrenching laugh. "I swear you a whole fuckin foo," I managed through fits of laughter.

Jamison lips kissed his teeth while he waved a hand at me. "Nigga don't act like you ain't neva done it or thought about doin it. I bet you think about that shit every time yo ass on your way to see Balboa."

"Fuck you."

Jamison laughed as he turned back toward the door. "Nah nigga. You ain't my flava. Now what you need to do is creep yo ass up out that friend zone and tap Balboa's ass," he finished, as he strolled out the door.

"Gettin inside her pants wouldn't be hard but I'm aimin for her heart and that shit is damn near impossible," I declared, out loud to the empty room.

I exited the living room and headed down the hall toward my bedroom when my phone vibrated in my hand. Glancing at the home screen I quickly opened my phone and went to my text messages. I clicked on the first name on my message thread.

Rocky: I'm good. Just bring your appetite <winking face emoji>. See u soon.

A soft smile sprawled across my face as I walked into my bedroom. Sitting my phone on the dresser I headed straight to my closet. I quickly removed the basketball shorts and white tee I was wearing and tossed them on the floor. My eyes roved the closed area. Swiftly surveying the plethora of hanging clothes I grabbed a pair of khaki joggers, a sleeveless hoodie and a pair of tan low top Vans then ambled out of the closet. I trekked over to my bed and tossed the items on top of my mattress. For some odd reason "FWYB" by Trey Songz popped in my head. I found myself humming the racy lyrics as I put on my clothes. Once I was dressed, I strolled over to my dresser and picked up the bottle of Armani Code. I sprayed a few squirts of the cologne on my wrist and neck then returned the bottle to the dresser and fetched a pair of ankle socks out of one of my drawers. Shoving the socks in the pocket of my hoodie I grabbed my phone and trekked out of my room. Halfway down the hall I unlocked my phone and opened Apple Music. I searched my library for the song playing on repeat in my head as I envisioned a certain chocolate goddess who managed to invade my every waking thought.

"Come Fuck with ya boy/I'm trynna fuck with you baby/I'm trynna hook up with you baby/I'm trynna make sure you saying/Sooner than later, that I'm the only nigga fucking you later/See I've been watching you baby/Seen you in all of these spots you be slaying/Fucking with all of these thots, I be playing/In case you forgot/I was saying," I belted out the chorus along with Trigga, as I walked into the kitchen and headed straight for the refrigerator.

I stood in front of the fridge with the door propped open, bouncing my eyes between the two different bottles of wine I'd purchased earlier. I tried to decide which one to take. Unsure, I grabbed the one recommended by the hostess and strolled out of the kitchen. Spotting my keys splayed across the table, I picked them up when I passed and stuffed them along with my cellphone into the pouch of my hoodie as I continued toward the door. From my pocket, Trey continued to plead for some shorty to give him a chance. Suddenly, it dawned on me why I couldn't shake this song. In my feelings, I thought about the woman I wished would rock with me while bobbing my head to the muffled tune as I alternated between humming and singing out loud. Fully engrossed in the track, I waited until the song ended before sliding a hand into my oversized pocket and silencing the music as I ambled out of my apartment.

As usual thoughts of Rocky danced around my head as I trekked through the parking lot toward my truck. It was still hard to believe that she had become a major part of my life in such a short amount of time. However, now that she was, I had no plans on changing it. True to her word Rocky had been cooking for me every week since I fixed her flat tire. And baby girl could burn. But what I enjoyed most, was simply being in her presence. Rocky had a hard exterior but underneath it all she was truly a sweetheart. She tried like hell to keep me outside of the invisible wall she built but the more time we spent together I felt those bricks tumbling down, regardless of whether she wanted them to or not.

Completely consumed with my thoughts I arrived at Rocky's sooner than I expected. Traffic must not have been that bad or I was too occupied to notice. Either way I didn't mind. Placing my truck in park I cut the engine and reached across the center console, plucking the bottle of wine out of the passenger seat. I took my time easing out of the truck when it occurred to me that I always zoned out thinking about Rocky on the drive over to her house. If I wasn't thinking about something she said, or did I was thinking about what she was going to say or do. Rocky was nothing short of amazing and she always seemed to do some shit that blew my damn mind.

"What da fuck? Raquel," I barked, as I strolled up the walkway.

Startled, she turned and looked at me. "I'm waitin for Creed," she stated innocently, while pointing in the direction of the massive canine.

"Go inside and close the goddamn door," I growled, while waving a hand at her. "I'll let Creed in."

Her facial expression was a mix between perplexed and pissed as she mumbled something underneath her breath while rolling her eyes and stepping back inside her apartment. I shook my head then cut through the field, heading toward Creed. Sensing my movements, he lifted his head from the grass and cocked it to the side as he stared up at me.

Bending at the waist I rubbed the top of his head. "Go finish your business so I can handle your mama," I instructed, as I stood upright.

Creed didn't hesitate to follow my command. He turned on his hind legs and sniffed patches of grass as he roamed the modest courtyard. Placing the wine in the crook of my arm I stuffed my hands inside the pocket of my hoodie and waited for Creed to finish. A few moments later he trekked over to where I was standing. His cropped tail wagged as he looked up at me like I was the one taking too long. Dude had a big personality. Snickering I removed my hands from my pocket while turning toward Rocky's apartment and walking the short distance through the courtyard to her patio door. Creed and I entered the apartment and went our separate ways. He headed out the living room while I moved over to the coffee table and placed the bottle of wine on top of it. I scanned the room for Rocky while bending over and removing my shoes. Pulling my socks out of my pouch I secured them on my bare feet then stood back up.

"So, you wanna tell me why you ordered me back into my apartment like your name is Jonathan Banks?" she asked arrantly.

I released a deep breath before slowly running a hand down my face. "I think the better question is, why da fuck were you outside with no fuckin clothes on?"

A scowl rested on her pretty face as she marched up to me. She tugged at the material of her shirt then her shorts. "And what da fuck do you call these Dre?"

Staring down at her I allowed my eyes to slowly rake over her body. The corners of her mouth languorously eased into a smile as my eyes returned to her face.

"The shit ain't funny Raquel."

Humor danced in her eyes as she removed the smile from her face. "No, it's not but I didn't hear you complainin while you were undressin me with your eyes."

"I didn't have to work very hard," I fired back.

Placing her small hands on her hips she cocked her head to the side and glared up at me. "And what the fuck is that supposed to mean?" she asked, enunciating every word clearly.

I took a step closer to her. "It means, all of your ass is hangin out of these itty bitty ass shorts. And I now know where five out of six of your piercings are." My eyes descended to her breast before traveling back up to her face.

Smirking she stepped around me, grabbed the wine off the table, and proceeded to walk out of the room; leaving me standing in the middle of her living room. "What da fuck ever Dre. I'm about to put

the bread in the oven. Dinner will be served in ten minutes," she called
out over her shoulder, as she sauntered into the kitchen.

"You're welcome," I hissed.

"Thank you, Andre," she responded, sarcastically from the kitchen.

I swear she drives me crazy.

Walking over to the sofa I plopped down and closed my eyes,
resting my head against the back of the couch. Once again, the lyrics to
"FWYB" played on repeat in my head while visions of Rocky flooded
my mind. I could still see her standing in front of me oozing with attitude. A hardened grimace was set on her otherwise flawless face. Her
hair was fixed into a neat bun positioned at the back of her head,
donned by a few loose tresses curled on each side of her ears. A simple
gold stud decorated her small nose accented by her septum piercing.
She wore a loosely fitted midriff t-shirt that hung off one shoulder and
stopped just below her breast. Her small mounds sat up high as her
erect nipples poked through the thin material of her shirt, revealing a
barbell piercing in each nipple. Subconsciously, I licked my lips as the
visual played out in my head. Lazily, my eyes traveled down her body,
peeping the rose gold belly button ring resting against her flat stomach.
Lowering my eyes past her abdomen she wore the shortest pair of
shorts I'd ever seen. The insides of her pockets hung below the bottom
of the cutoff denim shorts. Completely enthralled I let my eyes settle
there before wandering back up to her face.

"That's my song."

Flashing my eyes open I stared up into the most beautiful face I'd
ever seen. "Was I singin out loud?"

"Nah, just hummin but it sounded just as good," she answered
libidinously.

With a licentious smile crest upon my face I stood up from the
couch. "That shit turns your lil ass on don't it?" I asked, smacking her
on the ass.

She couldn't hide the blush on her cheeks as she shook her head
before turning away from me. "C'mon, dinner is on the table. I called
you twice, but I guess you were in here in your own world."

If only she knew.

"Alright. Let me use the bathroom and I'll be right there."

After I finished in the bathroom, I met Rocky at the kitchen table. As usual she had fixed my plate and prepared the table with all the necessary condiments. I quickly took my seat as I looked across the table and slightly nodded my head, indicating I was ready for her to bless the table. After reciting a brief but eloquent prayer Rocky opened her eyes and peered at me skittishly. Picking up my fork I smirked to myself at the sudden change in her disposition. I had rattled her, and that shit was amusing to me. Rocky was feisty as hell and could give as good as she could get but there was also a softer tamer side to her. A side that she only revealed when she was feeling frisky or I bossed up on her ass. As I watched her fiddled with her eating utensils, I wondered which one was responsible for the timid woman sitting across from me.

"It has been a super long day. I cooked and cleaned my junky ass apartment. I was feelin like. . . I don't know, blah. So, after I showered, I just threw on some shit I knew I would be comfortable in." She paused, briefly looking up from her plate. "I wasn't trynna advertise my shit for the world, I was just watchin Creed," she supplied, breaking through my thoughts as she lowered her head.

Sitting the forkful of lasagna back on my plate I stared at the top of her head. "Look at me gorgeous."

Slowly she raised her head, allowing her eyes to rest on mine. I hated the somber expression crest on her perfect face. Even more, I hated that I was responsible for putting it there. Pushing away from the table I rose out of my seat and took the three steps to stand in front of her chair. I kept my eyes fastened to hers as I dropped down to my knees and pulled her chair away from the table. Confused, she pulled her bottom lip in between her teeth while fidgeting with her hands.

I grabbed her hands, stilling her movements I brought them up to my face and placed a soft kiss on the inside of each of her palms. "Get up," I instructed, as I stood to my feet and stepped back to give her space to do as I asked.

Without hesitating Rocky removed her petite frame from her chair. Her eyes were everywhere but on me as she slumped her head toward her chest. I placed a hand underneath her chin and tilted her head upward. "I need you to look at me when I say this. You understand?"

She shook her head while matching my intense gaze.

"What's understood don't need to be explained. I know you weren't advertising. I was just surprised to see you outside like that so my reaction was probably harsher than it should have been. But I need you to be mindful that you are a beautiful single woman who lives alone. You don't know who is watching you."

Slowly, a wide grin stretched across her mocha face. "Look at you usin that private school edumacation to get your point across. Not a single slang word used," she joked.

"Oh, I got some slang for yo lil ass." Grabbing the pockets of her little ass shorts I stared down into her face. "Seriously, your shorts are so small the fuckin pockets hang past the shorts." I didn't give her a chance to respond as I reached around and grabbed a handful of her cheeks. "So, you mean to tell me you didn't feel half your ass hangin out the back of these damn shorts?" I asked, as I released her juicy buns.

Rocky twisted her face up, causing a crease to form in the middle of her forehead while her lips pouted out on her face as she flicked me off. "Fuck off." Humor danced in her mahoganies as she turned and tried to take her seat.

"Hol'up, I ain't finished," I stated, while grabbing her tiny wrist.

She tugged her arm out of my hand and placed both her hands on her hips while rolling her eyes up in her head. "Hurry up, our food is gettin cold."

I took a small step backward, purposely creating a tiny gap between us. With my eyes fixed on hers I cautiously raised my hands and palmed her apple sized breasts while slowly running my thumbs across her now hardened nipples. Instinctively Rocky's lids slithered shut but before I could truly enjoy the feel of her in my hands, she fluttered her eyes opened and stepped out of my embrace.

I allowed my hands to fall back at my side while peering into her slanted orbs. "Why da fuck don't you have a bra on in this itty bitty ass shirt?"

A salacious smirked tugged at the corners of her lips as she waved a hand at me dismissively. "Okay, I'm done with you. Your point has been made. This is inside gear only," she retorted, while taking her seat.

I remained standing while looking down at Rocky in her chair. "What about when Creed has to go out?"

"I'll throw on a robe. Now go sit cha giant ass down so we can eat."

Satisfied that I made my point I returned to my seat and immediately picked up my fork. Shoving a hearty portion of lasagna into my mouth I closed my eyes and relished the flavorful dish. Careful not to moan, I parted my cracked lids and was surprised to see Rocky staring at me.

"How may I help you beautiful?"

"Why do you always close your eyes when you first bite into your food?"

A knowing smile swept across my face. "It's a habit that started when I was young. My pops said I was a picky eater growin up. He was constantly trynna find foods that I would eat. One day he made a pasta dish and as soon as I placed it in my mouth, I loved it. Pops said I closed my eyes while I chewed my first bite. Guess I've been unconsciously doing it ever since whenever I eat something that taste good to me."

Rocky finished chewing the bite of food she had placed in her mouth. "Well then I guess I should be flattered because I don't think there has ever been a time, I haven't seen you do it."

"You most definitely should," I stated, as I winked at her. "Although I have outgrown my picky phase I don't eat just anybody's food," I admitted.

"Hmm," she breathed out, as she plucked her wine glass off the table.

Drinking from my own glass I watched her sip the clear substance before placing the goblet back on the table. "Do you like it?"

"I do, thank you. But you don't have to bring wine every time you come over."

Running the back of my hand across my forehead I blew out a dramatic breath. "Whew, I wasn't sure if you actually drank white wine. I've seen it in your stash but can't recall ever seein you drink it. And I bring wine as a way to express my gratitude." I held her gaze while sitting my glass on the table.

"I'm glad you enjoy this." She extended her arm and waved it toward the spread on the table. "But a simple thank you would suffice."

I shook my head while releasing a soft chortle. "Just enjoy the wine smart ass."

Right on cue, Rocky picked up her glass and took an affable nip of her spirit. Twirling the glass in her hand she fixed her eyes on mine. "I packed you and Jamison a big ass Tupperware container full of leftovers."

An unexplainable surge of jealousy coursed through my veins. "Come again."

A soft giggle flew from her mouth as she sat her glass down and used her napkin to dap at the corners of her mouth. "I made a big pan and I know I'm not gonna be able to eat it by myself. So, I packed the majority of it for you and J. I know you heard me the first time tho."

"Yeah I heard you. I just wanted to make sure I heard you right," I answered in between bites of my food.

"Don't act like that. Do I need to text J and let him know I'm sendin food home with you?" Her smirk was cute and annoying at the same time.

Although I didn't find shit funny, I let a small grin settle on my face. "And how am I actin Short Stuff? I asked, using every ounce of control I could muster to keep my tone leveled.

"Like you're feelin some kind of way about me sendin food for J."

With her elbows propped on the table she leaned forward and pinned me with her eyes as she picked up her glass again, finishing the last of her wine. Mulling over her accusation I shoved another forkful of lasagna into my mouth. I chewed my food in silence while staring across the table at her amused face. Rocky returned her empty glass to the table, picking up her fork she dug into her plate. A comfortable silence settled between us as we ate while our eyes engaged in a sound-less war the entire time.

"So, you just gonna ignore me?" she questioned, stuffing the last piece of bread into her mouth.

I wasn't sure how to answer her without sounding like a bitch, but I knew I couldn't ignore her. "Nah, I ain't feelin no kind of way," I answered, lying through my teeth.

She sat her fork on top of her plate and waved a hand at me. "Boy bye. Lyin is not your forte."

"I'll share *my* food wit J, but that nigga will know it's mine not *ours*. Now answer me this, why you got J's number?"

Plucking her plate off the table she stood and walked toward me, picking up my empty dish she sauntered into the kitchen. "I've had Jamison's number longer than I've had yours. I told you, E has a thing for him," she called out behind me.

"That better be all it is," I shot back, as I gathered our glasses and used napkins off the table and walked into the kitchen. I dropped the napkins in the trash then sat the glasses on the counter.

Rocky glanced at me as she grabbed the glasses, rinsing them under the running water she peeked at me before returning her atten-tion back to her task. "You can't be jealous over someone who isn't yours Dre."

I moved to stand next to her and placed my hands on each side of her waist, pinning her petite frame between the sink and my body. I lowered my mouth to her ear and pressed my body firmly against hers. "You are already mine Short Stuff. You just don't know it yet." I couldn't help the gruffness in my timbre.

Rocky squirmed against me. Removing my hands, I took a step back to give her space to move. Slowly she turned and faced me, angling her head upward she peered into my eyes. A coquettish mien danced in her slanted ambers. "Is that right?"

"Yep. And the sooner you realize it the sooner we can move past this bullshit phase you got us in," I declared assuredly, as I gathered the remaining items off the table.

There was an air of confidence in my steps as I strolled back into the kitchen and placed the condiments back in their rightful places. Rocky hadn't denied my claim that she was mine and that had me feeling pretty damn good as I rested against the wall and waited for her to finish rinsing and loading the dishwasher. Less than five minutes later Rocky closed the dishwasher and propped her small body up against it. She crossed her arms in front of her and rested them on her chest. Shifting my weight, I placed my right foot up against the wall while quietly watching her. Rocky's eyes darted around the small kitchen as she nibbled on her bottom lip.

"What's wrong, Short Stuff?"

Uncrossing her arms, she turned her head toward me. "Nothin. I'm just tired. I really need to wash my hair, but I don't feel like it. Was just thinkin, if I don't do it tonight, I don't know when I'll have time to do it later this week."

I pushed off the wall and stepped in front of her. "You want me to do it?"

Her head shot up, astonishment evident in her wide eyes. "Stop playin."

"Do you see me smilin, who's playin?" I asked, as I raised my hand and placed it on her bun. Carefully I removed her hair tie.

Rocky's already wide eyes stretched to the size of saucers as her boundless tresses cascaded past her shoulders. "Dre!" she shrieked, while attempting to grab her hair tie out of my hand.

I couldn't help the errant smile that eased across my face as I extended my arm above my head. "Stop being dramatic and go get your hair products," I stated, while looking down at her.

I snapped her hair tie around my wrist and yanked my arm out the air. Grabbing Rocky by the hips I snatched her off the counter and twisted her little body toward the entrance of the kitchen.

Rocky glanced at me over her shoulder while taking baby steps away from me. "You're serious?"

"Dead ass."

With my eyes glued to her ass I watched as Rocky put a pep in her step and swayed out the kitchen. Shaking my head to myself I walked into the living room in search of Creed. I spotted the beefy canine lying on his dog bed next to the fireplace. It was crazy how quickly Creed and I became acclimated with one another. Thankfully, neither of us saw the other as a threat, making it easier for us to be comfortable around each other. Calling his name, I walked over to the patio door and cracked it open. He raised his body off the bed and extended his forearms out in front of him. Butt in the air he stretched his muscular frame then moseyed over to the door and cocked his head to the side, looking up at me.

"I gotcha boy," I stated, as I widened the door and watched him trot outside. I stayed in the doorway waiting for Creed to finish when I caught a glimpse of her shadow. Mechanically my head swung in her direction just as Rocky started the short trek toward me.

"I'm ready," she muttered softly.

I acknowledged her statement with a subtle nod. "Here I come, soon as your dog finishes."

I shifted my head back toward the door, looking outside for Creed. Seconds later he came barreling through the door. Closing the door behind him I noticed her silhouette on the wall. Slowly I turned around to find Rocky quietly staring at me. A closed mouth smile settled on my face as I approached her.

"What's up Short Stuff?"

"Just trynna figure you out is all." There was an inquisitive beam in her eyes as she let her head fall to one side.

"There is nothin to figure out. What you see is what you get," I explained, as I gently grabbed her by the arm.

I ran my thumb up and down the inside of her small wrist while leading her into the kitchen. Walking over to the sink I surveyed the items she had laid out on the counter. "You ready?"

Staring up at me she flashed a reticent smile. "You sure you wanna do this?"

I tugged at her wrist, positioning her directly in front of the sink. "Girl quit playin. I think I can manage somethin as simple as washin hair. It's not like you need a nigga to go half on a damn baby."

A soft giggle tumbled out of her mouth as she turned on the water and placed her hand underneath it, testing the temperature. I stood behind her watching as she toggled between the hot and cold until she got the temperature she desired.

She tilted her head back toward me. "Okay, I'm ready."

I tapped her on the hip. "Let's do this."

Propping herself up on her tippy toes she bent over the sink, dipping her head underneath the running water. It took her a minute to get comfortable. She shifted her weight, wiggling back and forth on her toes until she was close as she could get to the sink. Placing my hand on my chin I took a step back and admired the front row view her position gave of her voluptuous ass. Ass that was almost completely exposed as her cheeks spilled out the bottom of her tiny shorts. Gradually she stopped squirming and I took a step forward, resuming my place behind her. Careful not to place my mini boner on her ass I reached over and grabbed the shampoo off the counter. I opened the bottle and squirted a quarter size amount of the creamy substance into the palm of my hand before returning the bottle to the counter. I used my free hand to push the faucet into the second half of the sink then rubbed my hands together and placed them in her damp hair. Spreading the shampoo evenly throughout her bounteous mane I firmly massaged her scalp.

"Mmmm. Shit Dre, that feels amazin."

After several minutes of scrubbing I moved the faucet back to her head and let the water stream down her hair as the suds flowed down the drain. Scooping the large cup off the counter I filled it with water and poured it over her hair. I repeated that step several times before dropping the cup into the sink and planting my hands back in her hair to ensure I had rinsed out all the shampoo.

"I told you, I got this."

Swinging her hand back Rocky smacked me on the thigh, just missing my dick. "Oh hush. Can you wash it twice?"

Again, I moved the facet out of the way of her hair, grabbed the shampoo, and emptied another quarter size amount into the palm of my hand. "I'm all over it," I stated, as I scrubbed my hands together and submerged them back in her hair.

Satisfied that I had worked the shampoo meticulously through her hair, I concentrated on kneading the crown of her head as I hummed softly. Belting out a sensual moan Rocky swayed her hips rhythmically to the sound of my voice. Instantly, my fingers stilled as a small knot formed in my throat, halting the melody I was previously humming. Impetuously, I took a step back as my dick started losing its flaccidity.

Shit!

Releasing a hard gush of air, I stepped behind Rocky again and snatched the cup out of the sink. I hurriedly filled it with water then pushed the facet over Rocky's head and watched as the water cascaded down her curly mane. I repeatedly dumped cups of warm liquid over her hair until all traces of shampoo were gone.

I placed the cup in the sink and reached onto the counter to retrieve the medium sized hand towel Rocky had laid there and draped it over her wet hair. "Stand up Short Stuff."

Straightening her spine Rocky stood upright, turned off the water, and held the towel over her head. "Thank you."

"No problem," I muttered, lowering my eyes to her protruding nipples.

With her head titled back she closed her eyes and dabbed the towel vertically along her sodden locks. The extension of her arms caused her shirt to rise as the underside of her breast peeked out from underneath it. Slithers of her dark brown areolas taunted me as blood rushed to my dick. Running my hand down my erection I quickly adjusted myself as my eyes remained stapled to her chocolate mounds.

FUCK!

Lazily peeling my eyes away from her chest, I grabbed the conditioner from the counter and placed my hand over hers. I gently tugged the damp towel away from her head and tossed it over my shoulder. "Last step."

"Who taught you how to do this?" she asked, taking the bottle from my hand after I'd squirted a dollop into my palm and started applying the conditioner to her hair.

I finished smearing the creamy substance on her hair then stepped around and rinsed my hands in the sink. Flashing her a smile I pointed to my head. "I mean, I do have hair Short Stuff."

"Okay, I give you that, but your way too good at it for you to only have washed your hair."

"Are you askin if I've washed another woman's hair before?" I couldn't help my smirk as my brow hiked toward my hairline.

Rocky shook her head and placed her hands on her hips. "That's exactly what I'm askin."

"Why, does it matter?" I implored mockingly.

Stepping around me Rocky began gathering the items off the counter. She clutched the shampoo and conditioner in her small hands and attempted to walk past me with her head aimed at the floor.

I curbed her steps by grabbing her by her elbow. "Now look who is actin jealous. And after you talked all that shit about me earlier," I goaded.

Quickly spinning around to face me, Rocky glared into my eyes. "Ain't nobody jealous. I was simply askin a question."

"No. I was the one who formulated your whack ass insinuation into a question but to answer you, no I have never washed another woman's hair. You are the first, but I have washed Madison's hair a time or two."

Scrapping her bottom lip with her teeth Rocky tried to conceal the smile that was already present in her eyes. I shook my head while grinning down at her. "Go put that shit back and I'll comb the conditioner through all this damn her," I stated, while tugging at her hanging tresses.

Without saying another word Rocky switched out of the kitchen. Moments later she returned with a small circular object with teeth sprouting out of it.

"What the hell is that?" I asked, pointing at the odd-looking object.

She looked at the item in her hand and giggled. "It's called a be-bop brush. I use it to detangle my hair. Just use it like you would a regular brush."

I took the brush from her proffered hand and stared at it while lightly running my fingers across the bristles. "Interesting."

Rocky stepped over to the island and dragged a stool into the kitchen. "I know my hair is super curly and it gets really tangled in some areas. I need you to take your time and not force the brush through or you'll pull my hair out," she instructed calmly.

"Thanks for the pointers, now sit cha ass down."

Rocky hopped up on the barstool and sat silently as I worked the brush through her wavy locks. "I swear, I had no idea you had this much hair."

"A lot of people don't. It's hard to tell since I usually wear it balled up in that messy ass bun on top of my head. But when I straighten it, it stops just below my waist."

"Damn, why you hidin all this pretty hair? Your ass is like a black Rapunzel."

Rocky glanced over her shoulder at me. "Not hidin it, it just gets to be a lot sometimes. It's much easier to wear it curly or in that messy bun. Don't worry, I'm not gonna make you suffer through blow dryin it."

I tapped her on the shoulder as I finished running the brush through her lengthy mane. "I don't mind. If you want me to I will."

Rocky hopped down from the bar stool and placed it back at the island. "Nah, it's cool. I'm gonna throw two braids in it and be done with it."

"I like the braids," I admitted, as I watched her saunter back into the kitchen and position herself in front of the sink.

Shit! Imma have blues balls fuckin wit her ass.

Resuming my place behind her I turned on the faucet and adjusted the temperature. I tapped Rocky on her hip. "Let me know if that's coo."

Rocky placed her small hand underneath the running stream and shook her head. Propped on her tiny toes she dipped her head beneath the water flowing from the spigot. Using the faucet and the cup I left in the sink earlier, I repeatedly rinsed her hair until all traces of the conditioner were removed. I dumped the cup in the sink for the final time before turning off the water and snatching the towel off my shoulder, placing it across Rocky's head. Planting her heels flat on the floor Rocky squirmed in front of me. Suddenly aware that I was crowding her space and prohibiting her from standing up I took a small step back and folded my arms across my chest. Completely enthralled by the woman standing in front of me, my eyes swept down her body before landing back on her face. I watched as Rocky used one of her hands to hold the towel in place while straightening her spine and standing upright. Wiping down her saturated mane she held the damp towel firmly around the ends of her hair. In need of a distraction I peeled my eyes away from her and retrieved my phone from my pocket checking my notifications.

Rocky removed the towel from her head and bumped me with her hip. "Meet me in the livin room."

I looked up from my phone just in time to see her sashaying out of the kitchen. Shaking my head, I walked into the living room and sank into the couch. A deep sigh flew from my mouth as I went back to my phone and clicked on a text from Jamison. *What da fuck? J a foo for this shit. Shorty is cold tho.* Flipping my phone over I dropped it in my lap, looking up just as Rocky plopped down next to me on the couch.

"She's cute but for some reason I thought you had a propensity for chocolate," she scoffed.

I plucked my phone from my lap and handed it to her, showing her Jamison's message. "I do but J is into redbones."

Rocky looked everywhere but at me as she placed my phone face down into the palm of my hand. Staring at her I waited for her to give me her eyes. Instead, she leaned forward and grabbed the remote off the coffee table then tossed it into my lap. I stared a hole into the side of her face while watching her purposely avoid my gaze.

She's a mess.

Rocky picked up a bottle from the side of her and squeezed a clear sticky substance into her hand then rubbed them together before working it through her hair. Her eyes remained forward, fixed on the blacked-out TV. Wiping her hands on the towel sprawled across her shoulders she picked up a paddle brush and placed it to her head.

Enough was enough, laying my phone next to me on the couch I placed my hand on top of hers. I slid the brush out of her hand and dropped it in my lap. Slowly her eyes traveled up to mine. Unspoken questions danced within her doleful eyes as she peered at me. Scooping the brush and remote out of my lap, I leaned forward and tossed them onto the table before snatching Rocky by the wrist and pulling her into my lap. Her little legs dangled beside my calf while her shoulder rested against my chest. The fresh scent of her hair invaded my nostrils, sending a tingle down my spine. A soft smiled settled on my face in acknowledgment of my body's automatic response to her.

Softly running my thumb across her velvety thigh, I kept my eyes focused on her face. "I would never disrespect you by entertainin another woman while I'm with you. And if you ever want to know somethin all you have to do is ask. I'll always tell you the truth."

Rocky chewed on the inside of her jaw, seemingly pondering over my words. Unexpectedly, she wrapped her arms around me and buried her face into the crook of my neck. "What da fuck are you doin to me?" she mumbled against my neck.

I couldn't stop the chuckle that lurched from my belly and escaped out of my mouth. "Being me. But this shit—" I hunched my shoulder, forcing her to lift her head and look at me, "is what happens when two people have organic chemistry."

She held my gaze as she placed a hand in my hair, tenderly running her fingers along my waves. "I'm not ready Dre but clearly my emotions don't give a shit," she conceded.

"I know Short Stuff and that's why I don't push you. I'll still be here when you are."

"Promise?" She sounded like a little kid a she removed her hand from my hair and held up her pinky finger.

I snickered as I locked my pinky with hers. "I promise. But you're closer than you think," I whispered, as I pressed my lips against her neck.

Shifting her body, she placed her back to my chest and titled her head back, granting me access to her isthmus. "How you figure?" she asked, breathlessly as I trailed my tongue down her neckline, along her collar bone.

"Because when we first started this journey you said fuck no and now, you're askin me to give you time," I explained, while running my callous hands across her toned stomach.

Rocky didn't respond. Instead, I heard her breath catch in the back of her throat as I continued to rub my hands across her abdomen.

Fully expecting her to stop me I cagily I trailed my hands up her torso. When she didn't, I dipped my hands underneath her shirt and cupped her bare breasts, strumming my thumbs across her nipples. A loud moan flew from mouth as she pressed her head into my shoulder. The dampness from her hair soaked through my shirt, sending a mild chill through my entire body. I continued to caress her, enjoying the soft moans rolling from her pursed lips. Arching her back, she widened her legs and gyrated in my lap. Blood flowed to my nether region as I used my index fingers and thumbs to gently knead her engorged nipples while planting feather soft kisses on her neck. Curiosity got the best of me when she pivoted her upper body toward me. Raising her shirt, I lowered my mouth to her breast and traced a circle around her swollen mound, slowly swiping my tongue across her nipple ring while relishing the feel of the jewelry against my tongue.

"Ummm," she muttered, as her hand flew to my head.

Smashing my face into her tit she damn near cut off my air supply. Undeterred I clamped my mouth around her breast and brushed my tongue rapidly across her nipple before sucking it firmly into my mouth. Another round of unabashed moans flew from her mouth as her hips moved wildly against my dick. Groaning I removed her swollen flesh from my mouth and slowly journeyed over to her other breast, repeating the same oral manipulation I performed just seconds ago. With her head still rested on my shoulder her moans filled my ears, becoming the soundtrack that fueled me. Trilled by her reaction to me, I placed my hand between her legs and stroked her on top of her shorts while twirling my tongue across her nipple. Imagine my surprise when I felt the evidence of her arousal. Her wetness had seeped through the thick material of her denim shorts.

Da fuck. Where are her panties?

Still in disbelief that this was happening I allowed myself to enjoy her, why telling myself I would stop before we went too far. I knew I needed to dead this and soon, but my dick was overruling my head and Rocky wasn't helping. Placing her hand on top of mine she shifted my hand to her thigh and slid it underneath her shorts. *Stop. Stop. You gotta stop this shit. You know she ain't ready.* Reluctantly, I removed my hand from her shorts and laid it on top of her thigh then slowly withdrew her breast from my mouth. Pulling her shirt back down I gently lifted her off my lap and sat her next to me.

Slowly her eyes fluttered open and traveled up to mine. "Thank you."

"Ain't no thing but I need a minute," I stated, looking down at my massive erection.

Rocky followed my line of sight as her teeth clamped down on her bottom lip and her eyes stretched wide. "Goddamn Dre."

Shaking my head, I leaned back into the sofa with my eyes stapled to her face. "What?"

"Dude your shit is like the size of a fuckin Sprite can," she stated, while still staring at my junk.

An exasperated breath passed through my lips as I ran my fingers down the bridge of my nose. "A Sprite can? That's a first."

With her eyes still focused on my lap she licked her lips. "Ummm, I can rub one out for you if you want me to. I don't want you to get blue balls."

I released a soft chortle. "Nah, I'm good. But if you really wanna help me, go put on some clothes. Clothes that cover all that ass and your tits."

Without hesitating Rocky hopped off the couch and damn near sprinted down the hall.

"And stay your ass back there until I call for you," I barked.

"Okay," she yelled, from somewhere in the back of her apartment.

Ten minutes passed, and I was still sitting alone on the couch, dick just has hard as it was when she left the room. "Aye, Short Stuff."

"Yeah?" she called out from I assumed her bedroom.

"C'mere please."

Strolling back into the living room she sported a pair of baggy sweatpants and an oversized t-shirt. Her loose curls were now pulled back into two long French braids cascading down her back.

I lowered my eyes to my swollen cock before slowly shifting them upwards to meet hers. "Umm, is that offer still on the table?"

Without saying a word Rocky padded over to the couch and dropped down on her haunches in front of me. Bringing her arms up to my waist she gazed into my eyes as I raised my hips off the couch. She placed her small hands inside the waistband of my joggers and pulled down my pants and boxer briefs in one swift motion, freeing my painful erection. With hooded eyes fixed firmly on hers I watched her eyes bulge open as she gaped at my dick. Tickled by her reaction the corners of my mouth curled upward into a sly smile. A soft moan passed through her parted lips as she wrapped a tiny hand around the shaft of my dick. Unable to fully close her hand around me she adjusted her grip, fitting as much of me into her small hand as she could. Flinching I closed my eyes and sank deeper into the couch, anticipating my needed release. Slowly Rocky's hand glided down the lenght of my erection. My eyes fluttered opened when I felt something cold and wet.

Eyes glued to my face; Rocky stared at me through the cracks of her slanted lids. "Sorry. Give it a minute, it will warm up."

Asking no questions, I closed my eyes again and enjoyed the feel of her hand working up and down my swollen member. Gradually increasing the pressure, she held the head of my dick firmly then smoothly lowered her hand down my shaft. I released a deep guttural moan when I felt her other hand massaging my balls while she simultaneously worked her hand up and down my dick. Flashing my eyes open, I stared down at her. With her bottom lip secured in between her teeth she held my gaze as she continued working me over.

My breathing quickened as sweat formed on my brows, the heels of my feet felt like they were on fire, and a tingling sensation coursed through my testicles. Involuntarily my lids drifted shut as I relished the feel of my impending orgasm. "Fucck," I growled.

Mechanically my hips took on a life of their own, thrusting in accordance with the movements of Rocky's hand. I felt cheated when Rocky removed her hand from my balls until I felt her place it on the shaft of my dick, just above her other hand. She moved her hands in opposite directions, creating a friction that intensified the tingling sensation in my balls.

"I'm abo—fucck. I'm about to cum," I muttered through uneven pants, as I cracked open my tightened lids.

Releasing her lip from in between her teeth a lecherous smile splayed across her face. "Cum for me, daddy," she breathed out sensuously.

That was my undoing. My ass tightened, and my back jolted up off the couch as cum shot out of my dick and oozed down her hands. Licking her lips, she looked at the creamy white liquid as she continued to stroke me, milking me completely dry. Gingerly removing her hands from my dick, she leaned forward and grabbed the towel that fell from her shoulders when I yanked her onto my lap.

Rocky used the towel to clean my semen from her hands and the tip of my dick then sprang to her feet. "Don't move."

Before I could reply she dashed out of the room and headed down the hall. Less than a minute later she returned carrying a small wash-cloth with steam emitting from it. Satiated, I remained slouched on the couch, my pants and boxers still draped around my ankles. Unable to speak or move I followed Rocky with my eyes as she headed in my direction and dropped down to her knees in front of me. Placing her soft hand on my deflating manhood she used the warm cloth to wipe away my residual juices. After ensuring she'd cleaned me up, she tossed the soiled rag onto the table behind her and grabbed my clothes bunched at my feet.

Finding my voice as feeling returned to my relaxed limbs I leaned forward and placed my hands on top of hers. "I got it Short Stuff. Thank you," I stated, looking down at her. "For everything."

Rocky stood to her feet and slid the rag and brush off the table before turning around and gathering her hair products from the couch. "That's what friends are for," she supplied, while shifting back toward me.

"Oh yeah? Well consider us besties now," I joked, while shimming my underwear and pants over my hips and securing them on my waist.

A soft smile eased onto her face while her eyes danced in mine.

There was so much emotion hidden behind her piercing ambers. Her smile was a front, concealing the questions that I knew she'd never utter, at least not now. Slowly she peeled her eyes away mine and traipsed out the room. Amused by her determination to keep her wall up a dry chortle fell from my mouth as I leaned forward and snatched the remote off the table and clicked on the TV. Not really interested in anything in particular I aimlessly flicked through the channels while I waited for Rocky to return.

"I hope you're not ready to go," she spoke from the kitchen.

"Not unless you're puttin me out."

"I would never put my bestie out," she stated, through a smile as she walked back into the living room carrying two martini glasses filled with a crimson liquid.

Taking the glass from her outstretched hand I looked at her with a hiked brow. "And what is this?"

"A drink silly." She giggled while sitting down next to me. Tucking her leg underneath her butt she pivoted her body in my direction.

"I can see that smart ass. But what is it?" I raised the glass and studied the contents inside.

Kissing her teeth Rocky placed her hand underneath my glass and tilted it toward my mouth. "Just drink it."

I stared at her over the rim of my glass as I sipped my drink. "Umm... Now tell me what you got me drinkin?"

Mischief danced in her soft ambers. "Fist, tell me if you like it."

I took another nip of the fruity concoction then nodded my head. "Now spill it."

"It's a sangria made with Rémy VSOP. I made it before you got here. You know how we do," she replied, while grinning at me.

"I do," I admitted, leaning forward and sitting my glass on the table. "We eat then drink ourselves silly while talkin all damn night."

She steered her glass toward her lips, stopping midway. Holding her drink inches from her face she peered at me. "Wait. Are you sayin you don't like our routine?"

I held my hands up. "Whoa! Did you hear me say that?" I couldn't help the smirk that tugged at the corners of my lips.

Rocky rolled her eyes up in her head. "You know Dre, if I were you, I wouldn't piss off the person who cooks my food."

"Are you threatenin me Short Stuff?" I asked, reaching for my glass again.

"Not a threat playboy. Just a little sound piece of advice."

I took a sip of my drink and locked eyes with hers. Slanted gingers silently battled against low bronzes. But behind the playfulness of her heated gaze was a hint of uncertainty. Maintaining eye contact I softened my eyes and reached for her empty hand.

I choose my words carefully. "I like our routine. Hell, I find myself lookin forward to it every week. I especially love spendin time with you. I wouldn't care if we sat and stared at the walls in silence as long as it meant I got to be in your presence."

I watched as her face relaxed. She released a deep breath and slowly withdrew her hand from mine. Lowering her eyes to the glass in her hand she took a gulp from it. I gave her time to process my words as I turned my attention toward the TV while drinking from my own cocktail.

"I promise I'm not always this emotionally off balance," I heard her whisper on the side of me.

Swinging my head toward her, I studied her pretty face. Rocky was so fucking beautiful to me. Even now, sitting next to me in baggy clothes, a make-up free face, and two braids she looked absolutely ravishing.

"I know. I tend to have that effect on women," I teased, attempting to lighten the mood.

Rocky smacked her lips as a soft smile eased across her face. "Shut up crazy."

I decided to change the subject and venture to something less stressful but still a little uncomfortable. Balancing my cup on my knee I ran my free hand down the back of my neck. "So, about that hand job."

Rocky's smile spread wide. Liquid dripped down her chin when she removed her glass from her mouth. Her hand flew to her face, catching the excess fluid. "Damn Dre. Straight in no Vaseline huh?"

I chuckled at her choice of words. "You know I don't bullshit. But speakin of Vaseline, what did you use for lube?"

Finishing the last of her cocktail Rocky leaned forward and placed her glass on the table. "Coconut oil."

"So, what, you just keep that shit on deck in case your company needs a quick hand job?"

Rocky cut her eyes at me. "No smart ass. I kinda figured you needed it, so I stuffed it in my pocket before I came back out."

After chugging back the last of my own drink I sat my empty glass next to hers and adjusted my body, turning sideways on the sofa. I picked my right leg off the floor and swung it over her head, stretching it out behind her. Leaning back, I placed my right shoulder against the back of the couch.

"Do tell."

Rocky chuckled while taking in my relaxed posture. "When you hadn't called me back out after five minutes, I figured your shit didn't go down on its own. So, I put the oil in my pocket and waited for you to call for me. Figured if I was right there was no point in makin you wait any longer for your release."

"That's some G shit," I stated, extending a closed fist toward her.

Rocky bumped her tiny fist against mine. A silly grin donned her face as she stood from the couch and grabbed the empty glasses off the table. "Another round?"

"Sure."

Rocky sauntered out of the living room and disappeared in the kitchen. Moments later she returned with two freshly filled glasses of Sangria. Plopping down next to next to me she offered me one of the glasses. "You know this has to be your last one or imma make you spend the night."

A knowing smirk eased onto my face as I accepted my glass from her. "How you know that wasn't my plan?" I asked, seeking her eyes.

Laughing Rocky shook her head at me. "What am I gonna do wit yo ass?"

"Whatever you want," I answered, gulping down a hearty amount of my drink.

"Umm…I don't know, I've seen and felt what you're workin wit. I don't know if lil ole me can handle all that, Andre Cameron."

"I'm good at squeezin into tight spaces. You'll see, when you're ready." I softened the reality of my statement with a wink.

She spit out the sip of liquor she just took into her mouth while instinctively holding her glass out in front of her. Coughing she sat up and tried to catch her breath. I leaned forward, sat my glass on the table and took hers out of her hand, sitting it next to mine. I patted her on the back until she stopped coughing.

Still trying to catch her breath, she couldn't help the Kool-Aid size smile plastered on her face. "What da fuck Dre?"

Laughing I picked up my glass and took measured nips while watching Rocky over the top of the rim. I paid close attention to her natural reaction to my words, to me. With her eyes trained on the TV she plucked her drink off the table and sipped her cocktail conspicuously, taking long deep gulps with each swallow. Her breathing was erratic although she tried her best to control it. Her mocha skin was flushed, and her high cheekbones held a subtle crimson hue. From her peripheral Rocky noticed my unapologetic ogling.

Slowly she allowed her head to follow her eyes. Sucking her bottom lip in between her teeth she tried to hide her smile. "Stop it Dre," she whined.

"Make me."

And with that challenge hanging in the air I grabbed the remote off the table and clicked off the TV. Nudging Rocky I prompted her to stand. Rocky hoisted her middle finger in the air then took her time rising to her feet. Finally giving me access to my leg that was trapped behind her, I shuffled off the couch and threw back the last of drink in one quick swallow. Tapping the pockets of my hoodie and joggers I searched for my phone. Rocky pointed behind me. Turning around I bent over and swooped my phone off the couch, stuffing it inside the pocket of my sweatshirt while turning back toward Rocky.

I looked at Rocky's glass with a hiked brow. "Finish that shit so we can lay down. I need to stretch out."

Rocky rolled her eyes up in her head then chugged back the

remainder of her cocktail. No words were spoken between us as she took my glass out of my hand and walked toward the kitchen. Calling out for Creed I strolled over to the patio with him on my heels. As usual I waited by the door while Creed handled his business when the shadow of her passing caught my attention. Turning my head, I caught the back of her as she headed down the hall toward her room. Automatically, I ran my hand down my dick while shaking my head to myself.

This chick really got me on one.

I knew I wasn't going home tonight regardless of how many drinks I had once she mentioned it. That was her indirect way of asking me to stay. And like the previous times before, I conceded. The sound of Creed's collar called my attention back to the door. Ambling inside, he walked past me and plopped down on his bed. After closing the door and securing the lock I cut across the room and turned off the light then headed down the hall.

I swear to God if she test me in even the smallest way tonight, she gonna find out just how much of me I can make fit.

185

CHAPTER EIGHT

"*R*ockkkyyy . . ." He stretched out the last part of my name, drawing my attention back to the phone.

"Huh? What did you say?"

He snickered although I was sure he didn't find my lack of attention funny. "I was trying to tell you I need to get ready for practice but clearly somethin else has your attention," he complained, almost whining.

I rolled my eyes up in my head. "I'm sorry Emery. I was watching Creed trying to see what he was chewing on," I lied. Lifting his head from the carpet Creed looked over at me as if he knew I was lying on him.

"It's cool, I'm just glad to finally catch up with you. Until next time beautiful." And with that the phone went dead. Classic Emery, he never said bye. He always ended our calls with the same closure.

Holding the blacked-out device in my hand I stared out my patio door. I really wondered why dude still fucked with me. We had tried the situationship thing, but I had to call it quits when he started catching feelings, I was incapable of reciprocating. Generally speaking, when I was no longer involved I deaded all ties, but Emery was insistent on us remaining friends. So, after months of dodging his calls and texts I finally caved. I agreed to let him fly me out to see him for a weekend. That was the wrong move. We kicked it like old times and of course that lead to us fucking the entire weekend. Which in turn made him think we were back on. It took another two weeks to convince dude nothing had changed on my end.

That was a little over six months ago and yet he still sent random texts and called every now and again just to check in on me. I didn't mind the calls or texts, but I didn't want him confusing our friendship for anything more than just that, a friendship. I wasn't one of those girls who got her kicks by leading dudes on then crushing their feelings. No, I was simply a woman who was emotionally unavailable for anything beyond good conversation and great sex. Unfortunately for me Emery was both but none of that mattered after he broke the number one rule. He fell for me, and hard. I would be lying if I said a part of me didn't miss his company, but I refused to hold onto him knowing I couldn't give him what he wanted. What I knew he deserved. So, I gave him the next best thing, genuine friendship.

The sound of Creed's collar jiggling caught my attention, snatching me from my reverie. Turning away from the patio I looked down as he placed his enormous head in my lap. I dropped my phone on the couch beside me and placed my hand on top of his head, rubbing his freshly washed fur. Instantly thoughts of Dre rushed to the forefront of my brain. A light snicker escaped my lips as I recalled our conversation when I told him I was about to bathe Creed. Dude was funny as hell. I wasn't sure how he thought my dog stayed clean, but it was apparent he didn't think I was the one who bathed him.

Crazy ass.

It was crazy because in complete contrast to Emery the closeness that Dre and I shared didn't make me want to run. If anything, it made me curious. He made me curious. I would never admit it to anyone but on more than one occasion I found myself wondering what a relationship with Dre would be like. I can't even begin to explain it. He made me feels things no other man has and probably ever will. Somehow in the short amount of time that we'd spent building our own friendship he managed to spark emotions in me that even after a year of being involved with Emery I never felt. There was just something about him, about us. He was right, we had a natural organic chemistry that even I couldn't deny or explain. I was adamant about not crossing that line with him for the sake of his friendship with my brothers but the more time we spent together the harder that was becoming.

Caught up in my thoughts I had all but stopped rubbing Creed's head. Over me, he lifted his head from my lap and strutted over to his bed and plopped down. I chuckled at his dramatic response as I swooped my phone up from the couch and opened it. Going directly to my text app I scrolled down to his name, clicking on it I instantly started typing.

Me: Whatcha doing?

Dre: Besides thinking about you?

I swear this muthafucka has game for days. I bet he has no idea what it feels like to work for a piece of ass.

Me: Yeah, besides that.

Dre: Just leaving the gym. What you up 2?

My eyes drifted shut as I envisioned Dre's sun kissed skin glistening with sweat as his muscles bulged out his workout gear. Flashing my lids open I shook my head to myself as I clicked away at the small letters on the keyboard of my phone.

Me: I ain't doing shit. Just finished studying about 30mins ago. Let me see what post workout Dre looks like.

Suddenly I felt thirsty and not just figuratively. My throat was parched, my hands felt clammy and my heart beat wildly against my chest. I was clearly having a physiological reaction to my request for Dre to send me a picture. *God, what is this dude doing to me?* Laying my phone on the table in front of me I peeled myself from the couch and traipsed into the kitchen. I quickly grabbed a bottle of water from the refrigerator and popped the top. I gulped down a mouthful of the cool beverage as I strolled back into the living room. Surprised Dre hadn't responded, I tried to fight off my disappointment when I noticed a blinking light emitting from my phone. My ringer was off. A fact I'd clearly forgotten. Placing the top on my water I swapped it out for my phone then plopped down on the couch. Before I did anything else, I

189

flicked the small button on the side to turn the ringer back on. Slowly a wide grin spread across my face when I saw Dre's name displayed on the home screen. Excited, I placed my thumb on the home button and waited for my phone to open. A few seconds later I was staring at our message thread.

Goddamn.

Inside our thread was a full body picture of Dre. Hurriedly I clicked on the image to enlarge it. His picture covered the entire screen, giving me a better view of him. He looked better than I imagined. Standing in front of a row of full-length mirrors he held his phone out in front of his face. A white tee clung to his solid arms but was pushed behind his head, leaving his torso completely exposed. Sweat gathered around his neck, laid across his firm pecks, and trailed down his well-defined six pack. Using my index finger, I traced over the V cut of his abs while subconsciously licking my lips. I shook my head to myself as I removed my hand from the screen and continued examining the picture. On the lower part of his body he wore a pair of loose fitting basketball shorts over a pair of grey compression tights.

What, what da fuck?

A noticeable bulge started below his waist and ended mid-thigh. It was obvious he wasn't hard but there was no hiding his package in those white shorts. Placing my fingers on the screen again I used my index finger and thumb to enlarge the image, zeroing in on his junk. *Whoa! That shit should be illegal.* Zooming out I stared at his phone for the longest, trying to see around it. I couldn't see his face because his phone was blocking it, but I was able to see sweat there also, resting on his forehead. Slowly running my tongue across my lips, I continued studying his picture, committing to memory every inch of his beautifully sculpted body. After a few minutes of lust filled ogling I reluctantly exited out the picture and sent him a text.

Me: Now that was the sexiest thing I've seen all day. If all the men in the gym looked like you there wouldn't be any fat bitches <laughing face emoji>.

Dre: Stop playing.

Me: Dead ass. Almost had an orgasm just looking at that shit.

Dre: See now you playing for real. You ain't gotta have an orgasm from no pic when I'll happily give you one whenever you want.

That shit instantly made my panties wet.

Me: And a fucking hysterectomy. I bet there's a lot of chicks walking around here who can't have babies fucking wit you and that anaconda between yo legs.

Dre: It's not that big Raquel. You'll see.

Me: I've seen it with my own eyes remember? It's huge Andre.

I sat my phone in my lap and reached for my water. I needed to quench my thirst, literally. Dre's picture and his nasty ass texts had me ready to rub one out. It had been six months since I last had sex and the shit was getting harder by the day. The sound of my phone chirping startled me. Water drippled down my chin as I removed the bottle from my mouth. Using the back of my hand I quickly wiped my chin while chuckling to myself. Not bothering to screw the cap back on I sat the bottle of water and the top on the table then grabbed my phone from my lap and unlocked it, going straight to Dre's message.

Dre: Oh, I remember. I'll never 4get. You made me cum using only your hands, u handled that shit like a G. I can't wait to see what u do wit me when I'm inside u.

Another surge of moisture oozed into my panties.

Me: Now u the one playing, got me needing to change my damn panties fucking wit u.

Dre: Let me see <tongue emoji>

Dre and I rarely engaged in sexual conversations and I couldn't recall a single time we sexted so I wasn't sure what had gotten into him, but I'd be lying if I said I didn't mind. In fact, there was very little about Dre that I did mind. Whether he was playing it lo-key or being aggressive. I found it all sexy as hell. He was sexy as hell, so I had no problems giving him what he was requesting. I trusted Dre and I knew what I shared with him was between us. Holding my phone in my hand I debated on how to fulfill his request when it chirped. A soft smile spread across my face at the sight of his name on the home screen. I quickly unlocked my phone and snickered at his message.

Dre: <inquisitive face emoji>

Fuck it I'll let him decide how he wants it.

Me: U do know patience is a virtue, right?

Dre: I exercise a lot of patience when it comes to u Short Stuff. Now show me or imma think u bullshittin.

Me: I'm a lot of things but a liar I am not. I was just trynna decide how to give u your pic. U wanna see em on me or just a pic of my wet undies?

Dre: ON!!!!!!!!!!!!!!!!!!!!

With my phone in my hand I hopped off the couch, dashed out of the living room and down the hall. Stopping in my bathroom I retrieved a handheld mirror from underneath the sink and sprinted toward my room. Walking over to my bed I sat my phone on the night-stand and positioned myself on the oversized mattress. With my legs spread eagle I propped a few pillows behind my head and leaned back into them scooting my butt out, leaving my girl exposed. Dragging my phone off the nightstand I used my thumb to slide the home screen over, activating the phone's camera. In my other hand I angled the mirror at my vagina while resting my hand holding my phone on top of my stomach. *Almost got it.* I shifted the mirror down just an inch which allowed me to see in between my legs perfectly. Clicking the small circular button on the screen I captured a perfect image of my saturated thong. I ignored the butterflies fluttering in my belly as I tossed the mirror to the side and sat up on the bed, examining the picture. *Nice.* Unlocking my phone, I went into my message app and clicked on Dre's name. I hit the small camera located on the side of the text bar and loaded the picture, studying the photo one final time I added a written message before sending it.

Me: Call me a liar again <raindrop emoji> <raindrop emoji> <raindrop emoji>

A minute passed, no response. Five minutes passed, no response. Ten minutes passed, no response. Tired of waiting I scooted off the bed and walked out my room. Halfway down the hall my phone chirped, then it chirped again, and again. Flipping it over I looked at the home screen. Only one name was stretched across it. Dre. A wide smile settled on my face as I made my way back into the living room. Scooping my water bottle off the table I finished off the last of its contents before opening my message.

Dre: Now that is the sexiest thing I've EVER seen. I just want to put my mouth on it.

Dre: I'm on my way. U gonna let me taste it?

Dre: Fuck, just peeped your piercing.

Yeah, fuckin wit his ass imma end up rubbin one out.

Me: I'm glad u liked it. Was starting to think I sent the shit to the wrong number or u didn't like it & was just trynna figure out how to tell me.

Dre: My bad Short Stuff. I was chopping it up with my coach when u sent it. Didn't wanna open it and risk him seeing it. And for the record, I fuckin love it. Thx.

Me: Ur welcome <winking face emoji>

Dre: So, I take it I can't cum put my face in it?

Me: Dreeeeeeeeeeeeeeeeee

Dre: LMFAO. It's coo I didn't expect u 2 say yes. I do want to swing by in a lil bit tho if you don't have plans. I wanna see u b4 u leave, b4 we're around the twins. I promise to be on my best behavior.

Me: When do I ever have plans? Just text and let me know when ur on ur way so I can make sure I'm dressed.

Dre: Coo but clothing really is optional <winking face emoji>

If only it were that simple.

I sat my phone on the couch beside me and thought about Dre's request to see me when suddenly it clicked, he missed me. No wonder he was bold in his flirting and aggressive with his request. I smirked to myself while acknowledging I missed him too. It was going on two weeks since we'd seen each other and that was rare since we started our weekly tradition of eating and getting to know one another. But last week I had to cancel, I had caught some sort of bug. He tried to come over and even offered to cook for me, but I refused. I didn't want to run the risk of getting him sick. Today would've been the day I cooked for him but because we were preparing for Atlanta we opted to wait until we got back. Well, that was until he asked to see me. I didn't think I had it in me to cook but I was more than willing to entertain him. I was actually looking forward to it.

Needing to calm my raging hormones I decided to take a shower. Slowly plucking myself from the couch I stood on wobbly legs and trekked out of the living room. Walking into the bathroom I immediately peeled my clothes from my heated frame, leaving them in the middle of the floor where they landed. I stepped over to the shower and pulled back the shower curtain before twisting the nozzle to turn on the hot water. Not waiting for the water to heat up I stepped into the shower and waited for the temperature to adjust to my liking.

Lukewarm water cascaded down my body as images of Dre danced around in my head. Before I knew it, my hands took on a life of their own. I grabbed my small swollen mounds and kneaded my rock-hard nipples between my fingers. A low moan escaped from my lips as my thumbs and index fingers rolled over my pebbles. I felt hot in spite of the cool water running down my body as a tingling sensation surged through my core and moisture gathered between my legs. Lazily dragging my left hand down my torso, I glided it over my stomach and lowered it between my legs. My eyes felt heavy. Sluggishly my lids drifted shut as I parted my legs to allow myself access to my hidden treasure.

In my head I pictured Dre standing in the shower with me. He stared at me through hooded lids as he held his bottom lip in between his teeth. Lasciviously lowering his eyes, he took his time drinking me in before dragging his eyes back up to my face. Beautiful emeralds cascaded over his natural hue. Captivated, I watched as his soft hazels slowly transcended to an exotic blueish green while running my middle finger over my piercing and sucking my bottom lip into my mouth.

Ummm. . .

Lowering my eyes to his chiseled pectorals I released my lip and ran my tongue across it. Slowly I parted my labia and carefully inserted my middle finger. With my palm resting against my clit I applied pressure to my piercing while dipping my finger in and out of my slippery canal. Brazen moans spilled from my mouth as I shifted my eyes from his chest and slid them past his sculpted abs, concentrating on his large appendage. Spry manicured hairs started at the base of his two-toned rod. Light colored flesh a shade darker than his skin blended deliciously into a darker caramel hue as my eyes continued roaming down his shaft. I'd never seen mustard and mocha merged together so perfectly. The bulbous head of his dick was the shape of a mushroom, a beautiful syrupy colored mushroom.

My imagination lingered there as I slipped my index finger inside my vagina, sliding my fingers deeper into my slickened flesh I rested them against my bud. I wagged my fingers forward. Purposely stirring that sensitive spot while rubbing my thumb over my clit and caressing my piercing. The muscles in my stomach tightened and a loud moan lurched from the pit of my belly. *Ummm. . .* A chill shot up my spine as my eyes rolled back up to his face. Gazing at me Dre dipped his head forward, encouraging me to finish. And finish I did. My fingers moved quickly against my bud as my palm crashed against my piercing with every forward thrust. I parted my lips, but no sound came out. Slowly I withdrew my fingers, rubbing my clit gingerly while my body jerked uncontrollably. Unable to take anymore stimulation I removed my hand from between my thighs and clinched them shut. I rode out the wave of my orgasm then fluttered my eyes open as Dre's image faded away. Adjusting the temperature of the water I reached for my rag.

Goddamn that was intense.

Fifteen minutes later I emerged from the shower feeling satiated and clean. I grabbed my discarded clothes off the floor and sauntered down the hall toward my bedroom. In the distance I heard the distinct chirp of my phone. Instantly a wide smile blossomed on my face as I fought the urge to shift my direction and check my message. Crossing the threshold of my bedroom I headed straight for my closet where I dumped my clothes inside the hamper and swept my eyes around the spacious area. I studied the small section of hanging garments containing my summer dresses before deciding on an all-white flowy halter dress.

I plucked the gown off the hanger and draped it across my arm then ambled out of the closet, moving toward my bed. Laying the dress across my disheveled sheets I stepped over to my dresser and grabbed the tube of shea butter. I took my time completing my routine. I made sure every inch of my body was covered with the creamy lotion before replacing the cap and sitting it back on the dresser. I then scurried over to the bed and retrieved my dress, stepping into the flowy gown I carefully shimmied it up my body. The material felt so light and airy, perfect for the muggy August weather. *Dre would flip his shit if he knew I was completely bare underneath here.* Hunching my shoulders, I trekked over to my full-length mirror and studied my reflection. An impish smile spread across my face as I ran a hand up my ponytail and smoothed down a few loose tresses. Satisfied with my appearance I turned away from the mirror and left out of the room.

I walked into the living room to find Creed perched up on the couch. His large head sprang up from the cushions at the sound of my footsteps. "Really dude? Get yo spoiled ass off my furniture."

Tail wagging his tongue spilled out his mouth as he jumped off the sofa and trotted toward me. Tickled by his excitement I bent over and gave him a quick pat on the head then headed toward the couch where I scooped up my phone. As expected, there was a text notification from Dre. I unlocked my phone and went directly to my messages while stepping over to the patio to let Creed outside.

Dre: Hey Short Stuff. I just got home, bout to hop in the shower then head your way.

My eyes inched close and a surge of heat coursed throughout my entire body as I thought about Dre in the shower. Vivid images of his sculpted frame danced behind my closed lids. A licentious grin tugged at the corners of my mouth as I flashed my eyes open and scrolled up to the picture he sent earlier. Again, I clicked on the photo to enlarge it, sweeping my eyes from his head down to his feet while my tongue dusted lightly over my lips.

Damn, it should be a sin for one person to look this good.

I exited out of the picture but not before saving it to my photo gallery. I'd just clicked inside the message box when the sound of Creed's collar called my attention to the door. Propping it open I watched as he waddled past me and headed toward his bed. I pulled the door shut and secured the lock then moved over to the couch, propping myself up on the plush cushions I responded to Dre's text.

Me: Coo. I'll be waiting.

Dre: I was starting to think u 4got about me.

I couldn't even if I tried.

Me: Never.

I decided to kill the time with some mindless TV but couldn't find the remote. I swept a hand over the cushions of the couch while my eyes shifted around the room. Both attempts, I came up empty. Irritated I scooted to the edge of the couch to get up and survey the room when my phone chirped in my hand.

Dre: I got bad news Short Stuff. J just got called into work and now I'm stuck here waiting on the cable guy. They gave a crazy window so not sure when I'd be able to make it ur way <angry face emoji>.

Furrowing my brows, a grimace settled on my face. Damn, I was really looking forward to seeing him. I sucked my bottom lip into my mouth as my fingers hovered over the keys on my phone. I nibbled on my lip while contemplating on how to respond.

Fuck it.

Me: I can come to you.

Dre: Word? I would love that. U sure?

A goofy smile splayed across my face as I read his message. I wasn't surprised at his reaction to my offer especially since I'd never been to his place before. I guess what I found funny was his disbelief that I wanted to. Shaking my head, I responded.

Me: I wouldn't have offered if I wasn't <winking face emoji>

Dre: I swear ur such a smart ass. When u coming?

Me: Don't act like u don't like it.

Dre: U right, I fuckn love that shit.

A chill ran through my entire core as I read over his words repeatedly. It was something about seeing the word love in association with me coming from him, I couldn't explain it. Those five little words roused me, making it difficult to ignore the fluttering in the pit of my stomach.

Me: Send me ur address wit ur flirty ass.

Dre: I'ght but wasn't nobody flirting. I was being honest.

I tossed my phone next to me and hopped off the couch like lava was spreading through the cushions. Looking over my shoulder I paid my phone on last glance then sprinted toward the small dining area, going straight to my liquor stash. I shuffled through the assortment of bottles gathered atop of my mini bar before settling on tequila. Grabbing the bottle of Patron, I walked into the kitchen and placed it on the counter. After grabbing a shot glass from the cabinet, I yanked the top out of the Patron and poured the clear liquor into my glass, filling it to the brim. I tossed back the shot in one swift motion. An audible roar tumbled out my mouth as I slammed the glass down on the counter. I needed that, my damn nerves were shot.

My eyes darted toward the living room at the sound of my phone chirping. *Fuck that, one more.* I poured myself a second shot then tossed it back just as quickly, ignoring the burning sensation as it glided down my throat. After returning the top to the Patron I headed out the kitchen. Bypassing the living room, I sprinted down the hall, toward my bedroom where I sprayed on a few dollops of perfume and retrieved a pair of pearl T strap Chanel tong sandals then walked back down the hall as I tried to make sense of my sudden anxiety.

Strolling into the living room I walked over to the couch and grabbed my phone. I pressed my thumb on the home key, feeling a calmness that wasn't present just moments ago. I stared at the screen, reading Dre's message. He had sent his address followed by a happy face emoji. A relaxed smile gradually inched across my face as I copied and pasted his address into Google maps. Grateful I was able to quiet my mounting anxiety I relished the slight buzz sparked by Patron that was now settled in my system as I slipped on my sandals and headed for the door. Tapping the screen of my phone I waited until it displayed our message thread then responded to Dre's last text.

Me: Omw.

Not waiting for a response, I picked up my purse from the console table next to the door and exited my apartment. The August heat was unapologetic as the humidity smacked me in the face and cloaked itself around me. *Shit*. Hurriedly I dashed through the courtyard, cutting through the parking lot I maneuvered by a few cars as I headed to my truck. Hopping inside I started the engine and immediately blasted the air. Hot air blared through the vents, hitting me on the shoulders and face. Not wanting the wind to blow my bun out of place I opted to ride it out, biding the time until the temperature adjusted.

A little over twenty minutes and I was pulling into Dre's apartment complex. I eased into a parking spaces close to his building and grabbed my phone out of my lap. Exiting out of the navigation app I clicked on my text app and opened our message thread. There was a message from Dre sent approximately fifteen minutes ago, no words just another smiley face emoji.

This dude.

Ignoring the giddy feeling stirring inside my gut I sent Dre a text.

Me: Outside.

I chucked my phone inside my bag and turned off the engine then hopped out my truck. Once again, heat greeted me at the door like an old friend. I looked down at my dress and was grateful for the light material as I gathered the sides in my hands and hiked it up to avoid tripping. Over the heat I took long determined strides toward Dre's building. Lucky for me, the walk was short. I'd reached the last step leading to Dre's building when I finally felt comfortable releasing the hem of the flowy garment. With my eyes cast low I watched as it draped across my feet, almost sweeping the ground.

"How you doing beautiful?" a male voice asked.

My head shot up from the ground as my eyes landed on a short chocolate man with a protruding belly. I flashed the stranger a smile while pointing a finger at my chest. "Are you talking to me?"

A sly smile spread across his handsome face as he took a step toward me. "You're the only beauty I see standing out here."

I took a step back as I lowered my eyes to my hands, pretending to brush something off my dress.

"Then I suggest yo big ass look somewhere else then nigga," his raspy tenor barked.

Quickly shifting my eyes up, I looked over the stranger's head. His hazels stared at me while walking up on the chocolate brother. Clasping his hand around the man's shoulder Dre slowly peeled his eyes from mine. He leaned his tall frame into the man, speaking near his ear. I watched as the man's eyes traveled over to me, growing big as two inflated balloons.

Holding his chubby arms in the air he kept his eyes stapled to me but spoke to Dre. "No disrespect intended my dude."

Dre released his grasp on the man's shoulder and stood to his full height. His eyes were on me again, sweeping down my body. "It's all goody. C'mon Short Stuff." He stepped in my direction and extended his hand.

I looked between the two men before stepping forward and taking Dre's proffered hand. Gently tugging my wrist Dre pulled me into his solid frame while possessively tucking me underneath him. Lowering his head, he buried his face in the crook of my neck and sniffed. I couldn't help the schoolgirl giggle that passed through my lips as he ran his nose along my collarbone. I felt his tongue and then his lips. He lingered there; his soft lips planted tenderly against my flesh. Slowly Dre raised his head from my neck as he guided us past his *friend*, who I hadn't realize was still standing there until we started moving.

With his hand rested just above my ass Dre looked back over his shoulder. "Aye Dale."

There was a pause, but no words uttered from Dale. I assumed he indicated his attention with a head gesture or some form of eye contact because Dre looked over at me then tossed his head over his shoulder again, toward Dale. "Rocky Dale, Dale Rocky."

I heard Dale chuckle behind us as Dre escorted me into the building. He kept me close as he guided me down the short hallway to his door. Once inside, he closed the door behind us and swept me off my feet, hugging me close to his chest while nestling his face in the crook of my neck again.

"Dre," I whined.

"Fuck that whinin shit Short Stuff. I missed the fuck out you.".

Heat coursed through my body at his words, his honesty, and his ability to share his feelings so freely. Letting down my guard I allowed myself to enjoy the moment, to enjoy him.

I planted my hands on each side of his head and raised his face from my neck, forcing him to look at me. "I missed you too."

A wide smile spread across his face as he lowered me to the floor. Clasping his hand in mine Dre walked me over to his living room. He sat back on a large sofa and positioned me on top of his lap. I swept my eyes around the modest size room, taking in the mix match furniture and big ass flat screen TV. I was surprised at how clean it was.

Pivoting in his lap, I adjusted my upper body so I could look into his eyes. "Damn Dre if I knew I would get this kind of greetin I would've went every two weeks between seein you a long time ago," I teased.

He lowered his eyes to a squint causing a V to form between his brows. "That shit ain't funny Raquel."

I placed my hand on the side of his face, gently stroking his cheek. "I'm playin."

His face relaxed, the corners of his mouth ascended toward his eyes as he ran his hand along my hip. Pausing his movements his eyes lowered to my waist then quickly shot up to my eyes. "Rocky, how come I don't feel a panty line?"

Skirting my eyes away from his I looked toward the blacked-out TV. "Huh?"

He placed his large hand under my chin and swiveled my head back toward him. "You heard me."

I held his gaze before planting a quick kiss on his cheek and hopping out of his lap. A coquettish grin eased across my face as I reached for his hand. "Show me around," I demanded, trying to avoid his question.

Slowly standing to his feet Dre stood in front of me, peering down at me. Again, I peeled my eyes away from his. Pulling me by the waist Dre snatched me into his body, running both his hands down my backside.

"What da fuck, Raquel?" he growled.

Slowly I allowed my eyes to meet his. "It's too hot for all that," I stated nonchalantly, while reaching behind me and grabbing his arms, tugging them away from my ass. "Don't make a big deal out of it."

Dre shook his head at me while gently pulling one of his arms out of my hand. Running his hand down the front of his face he blew air out of his mouth. "I swear you drive me crazy Short Stuff."

I used my free hand and flicked it under his chin. "And you like it." There was so much sass hidden behind my smile.

"I fuckin love that shit," he spoke in a low growl.

I refused to break eye contact but couldn't ignore the jolt of electricity that shot through my body as his words echoed in my head. This was the second time today he said that shit and just like the time before, it evoked an emotion in me that I wasn't familiar with.

Running my tongue across my top lip I shook my head to myself while placing a faux smile on my face. "So, about that tour."

Slowly a smile eased onto his handsome face. Sliding my hand down to his he intertwined our fingers as he led me out the living room and down the hall. Dre walked me from room to room, showing me him and Jamison's living space. My tour ended at his bedroom. A nice size room furnished with a king size bed, matching nightstand and dresser. A flat screen TV sat atop an old TV stand positioned across from his bed. A few free weights were neatly lined up against the wall next to his closet. His walls were completely bare, with the exception of a few plaques he earned from high school. To my complete surprise Dre's room was extremely neat.

I lowered myself on the bed and looked over at him. "So how long did it take you to hide all your groupie's paraphernalia?"

Pushing off of the doorjamb, Dre walked toward the bed, and plopped down next to me. "I see somebody got jokes. Wasn't shit to clean up because very few make it back here." His tone was light, but his eyes blazed with intensity.

"Now don't I feel special," I teased, trying to escape the fervor in his gaze.

"You are," he stated, standing to his feet he reached down for my hand. "Now I need to get your special ass outta here since you decided to come over here with no panties on."

I grabbed ahold of his hand and allowed him to pull me up from the mattress. No words were spoken between us as we walked out his room and strolled down the hall. Dre led us back to the living room and instructed me to make myself comfortable. I sat back on the couch and watched as he causally strolled out the room. Less than a minute later he returned with two beers in his large hands.

"We don't have wine, but we have a few of these fruity ass beers left," he supplied, handing me a Mike's Hard strawberry lemonade.

I hiked a brow as I accepted the colorful brew. "Thanks."

A knowing smirk settled on his face. "They been here since school ended. J and I had a lil kickback before some of our people left for the summer."

I placed a hand in the air. "You don't owe me any explanations playboy."

Taking a seat next to me, Dre sipped from his beer. "I got yo playboy. Come over here with no panties on again and you gonna leave wit a wet ass."

FALL SEMESTER

Pre-Labor Day Weekend

CHAPTER NINE

I pulled off of I-75 and coasted into the gas station. I placed the truck in park and snatched my phone out of the cupholder just as it was powering off. Looking at the empty USB port I cursed underneath my breath.

How did I forget my damn car charger?

Sitting my phone on the center console I looked at Jamison in the passenger seat then swept my eyes up to the rearview mirror. "Aye, either of got a car charger?"

Jamison shook his head no.

I heard shuffling coming from the backseat. In my peripheral I saw the outline of his tribal tattoo on his pasty outstretched arm. "Here bro."

"Good looking." Taking the charger from his stocky hand I connected it to the USB port, slid my phone off the console, and plugged it into the charger.

I pressed the power button to turn my phone back on but was quickly alerted it didn't have enough juice to power up. Irritated but not really having another option I sat my phone back on the console and opened my door. My bladder was screaming for relief.

"I'm about to take a leak then grab a Red Bull from inside. Y'all want anything?" I asked Jamison and Brayden.

The light inside the truck illuminated, indicating a door was open. Looking over my shoulder I saw Brayden easing out the backseat. "I gotta piss my damn self. I'll grab somethin when I'm done."

"Aye bring me back a MtnDew," Jamison called out.

"I got cha," I stated, while hopping out of the truck.

Inside the gas station I walked toward the back of the store, heading in the direction of the sign for the restrooms. Out of the corner of my eye I spotted Brayden standing by one of the coolers hollering at a thick redbone. I gave him a quick head nod, smirking to myself as I continued to the bathroom. Brayden was a chick magnet. Always had been and I imagine he always would be. Being a blonde hair blue eyed attractive white boy with the swag and confidence of black man didn't hurt either. The four of us, me the twins and Brayden met in elementary school, but it wasn't until the introduction of organized sports in middle school that our bond was cemented. So, when he called up and asked if he could ride to the A with me, I quickly said yes.

It's funny because as the only white dude in our crew I think he pulled more sistahs than we did. Growing up Bray took a lot of flak from the kids at school and a few in our neighborhood, he was constantly being accused of acting or trying to be black. But what a lot of people didn't understand was, Bray wasn't acting. He was simply being the only him he knew how to be. Bray was a product of his environment. He became what he saw in his own home. Bray's mother died when he was one and he never knew his father. His mother's best friend adopted him when he was two. She was married when he was five and her husband instantly fell in love with him, adopting the precocious boy when he was seven years old. Bray had a good relationship with his biological mother's side of the family, but he identified more with the family who raised him, two black parents. So no, Bray wasn't acting. Bray was a black man in a white man's body. His words not mine. The twins and I never saw Bray as anything other than our boy, we didn't care what color he was. He was cool as hell. He liked the same things we did, listened to the same music as us with the exception of his affinity for country music, and he absolutely loved black people especially black women.

Brayden Smith was my nigga.

I shook all thoughts of Bray from my mind as I entered the men's restroom. Securing the lock on the door I proceeded to the urinal. After emptying what felt like seven hours of liquid from my bladder, I stepped over to the sink to wash my hands. Turning on the water I stared at my reflection in the cloudy mirror. I let a little hair grow on my face, giving me a semblance of a tapered beard. I pumped soap into the palm of my hands then rubbed them together before placing them under the running water. A soft smile settled on my face as I thought back to that time in Rocky's basement when I needed to shave. My smile broadened as I recalled how she liked the rugged look on me. Although this was a lot cleaner it was still different than the usual clean cut shave I normally wore. I just hoped she dug it. The sound of someone pulling on the door snagged my attention. I paid myself one last glance before using my elbow to shut off the water. The person on the other side of the door must have needed the restroom bad because now they were knocking on the door.

"Almost finished," I hollered out, slightly irritated.

Snatching a few paper towels from the dispenser I dried my hands and used the old towels to unlock and open the door. A goofy ass smile was plastered on his face.

"I should've known it was yo silly ass," I said through a smile.

"What the hell were you doin in there? You better not have been takin a shit," Brayden joked.

"Man go on wit that bullshit," I stated, walking past him.

I heard his high pitch laugh as the door closed behind him. Making my way over to the coolers I grabbed a Red Bull and a MtnDew. At the register I placed my items on top of the counter and waited to be cashed out. Patting my hands down my pockets I searched for my cell-phone. *Shit, I forgot it was dead.* After paying for our drinks I made my way outside, walking back to the truck.

I handed Jamison his drink as I climbed into the driver's seat. The sound of his phone ringing snatched his attention. Lowering his eyes to the phone in his lap he picked up the ringing device and placed it to his ear.

"Hey Balboa. What's up?"

That caught my attention. I turned my head to face him, practically staring down his damn throat. Once again, a twinge of jealous spiked through my veins. I knew it was silly, but I couldn't help how the shit felt. Ignoring the grimace on my face Jamison continued his conversation.

"Yeah he right here. His phone died. Okay cool, I'll tell him. See you soon."

Jamison disconnected the call and burst out laughing.

"What y'all in here laughin about?" Brayden asked, while hopping into the backseat.

"Y'all ain't laughin," Jamison said through a deep chortle. "I'm crackin up because yo boy here…" he pointed at me, "is shitty because his shorty just hit my line."

Brayden's boisterous laughter boomed from the backseat. "Aye, are you serious?"

"Man, fuck both y'all," I shouted over top of their laughter, while smirking to myself.

"Oh man, I gotta meet this chick. She gotta be bad as fuck if she got my boy up in his feelings," Brayden declared.

I cut my eyes and slowly swiveled my head toward Jamison, shooting him a warning glare.

Completely ignoring me a menacing grin spread across his face. "Oh, you know her alright."

"Word? Well who is she?" Brayden asked, completely oblivious to the what he was asking.

Before I could stop Jamison, her name rolled seamlessly off his tongue. "Rocky."

Sucking in a lung full of air I slowly blew it out my nose as my eyes slid up to the rearview mirror. I watched Brayden mull over Jamison's words.

"Rocky who?" Brayden implored. Leaning forward he positioned himself in between the passenger and driver's seat.

"Rocky is not my shorty, we are just friends," I stated through gritted teeth. I tried to soften the blow I knew Jamison just hit Brayden with.

"Wait, what da fuck? Y'all takin bout Rocky, Rocky? Raquel Banks? As in our boys' . . ." Brayden pointed to himself then me, "sister?"

Jamison nodded his head. "Yep, the one and only."

I placed my head on the steering wheel.

I swear I'm going to kill Jamison. His ass can't hold fuckin water. I should've left him back in Cincy.

"Oooooooh, the twins gonna kick yo ass," Brayden stated, as he fell back into his seat.

I raised my head off the steering wheel and launched it toward the backseat. "Ain't nobody kickin nobody's ass. And ain't shit goin on between me and Rocky."

"Bro you can lie to yoself but I know you and I'm tellin you now, I don't believe you. You just better hope you and Rocky have better luck convincin the twins ain't shit goin on between y'all," Brayden stated through a cunning smirk.

Slowly I turned my head toward Jamison. I mouthed, "Imma fuck you up."

Jamison threw his hands up in the air and burst out laughing. Brayden quickly joined in. Reaching for my phone I hit the power button and waited for it to power on.

"Yo." I looked over at Brayden's hand on my shoulder.

"What?" I snarled.

"Seriously, that's a good look for you. Hell, it's a good look for her hard ass too," Brayden stated.

I refused to acknowledge his comment. Instead, I placed the truck in gear. I was ready to get the remainder of our drive over and put some space between me and dumb and dumber. Brayden removed his hand from my shoulder and sat back in his seat.

"You gotta admit tho, that shit was funny as hell," Brayden said.

"It's funny as fuck," Jamison added.

I looked over at Jamison then into the rearview mirror. "I swear I'll put both of y'all out," I threatened, with a mischievous smile set on my face.

"Whateva nigga. By the way, Rocky said to tell you she and Carm landed. She said Royce is pickin em up, but Ryker is at the house waitin on us."

I glanced over at Jamison as I merged back onto the expressway. "You could've just said that and skipped all the other bullshit."

"Yeah but where is the fun in that?" Jamison taunted.

Thirty-five minutes later we had reached our destination and not a moment too soon. I was ready to kill Jamison and Brayden. They had jokes the entire ride. Pulling into the twins' driveway I cut the engine and turned to face Brayden.

"Aye, I know y'all had a good laugh at my expense, but I need y'all . . ." I swung my head toward Jamison, "to dead this Rocky shit. We're here to have fun. I don't want no smoke."

"Not my business to tell bro," Jamison declared.

I looked in the rearview mirror at Brayden, waiting for his response. "No worries bro. I don't know shit, I ain't sayin shit. And for the record, when this shit does come out, I ain't know shit."

"Understood."

I unplugged my phone from the portable charger and sent Ryker a text, letting him know we were outside. Tucking my phone inside my pocket I swung my door open and peeled my cramped frame from the oversized truck. Although I was grateful my father lent me his truck, the Chevy Tahoe was still no match for the six and half hour drive.

"Welcome to the muthafuckin A," Ryker shouted. His long arms stretched wide into the air as he made his way down the driveway.

He reached me first. Pulling his arms out the air he extended a hand my way. I clasped my hand in his as he pulled me into a man hug, patting me on the back before releasing me. "My nigga. How was the drive?"

"Nothin I couldn't handle. But a nigga is a little tight after being in that truck all those hours," I stated, looking at one half of my childhood best friends.

"Aye," Brayden shouted, walking toward the front of the truck where Ryker and I were standing. Ryker greeted him with the same friendly man shake. "What da fuck you been eatin bro? Yo ass done beefed da fuck up? You on roids ninja?" Brayden asked, with a wide ass grin plastered on his face.

"Get da fuck outta here wit that shit," Ryker shot back.

I took in Ryker's massive size. He was never a skinny dude, standing at six feet nine inches he maintained a sleek athletic build. But Bray was right, dude had definitely packed on a good twenty-five pounds of muscles. Never one to be outdone by his brother I was willing to bet Royce was packing the same extra muscles.

"For real bro. What's up?" I asked, piggybacking off Brayden's question.

"Ain't shit up. A nigga put on a lil muscle and y'all trippin like some bitches."

"A lil my ass," I quipped, raising a brow.

A deep chortle flew from his mouth as he ran a hand down his beard. "My coach actually suggested I bulk up, said it would be better for my game."

"Now I get it. Your coach was tired of your skinny ass gettin knocked on your ass in the post," Brayden razzed.

Ryker chuckled. "Fuck you doughboy."

"Doughboy my ass. Just cuz you finally got your weight up don't be playin me like I'm a fat kid. I'll still beat yo ass," Brayden threatened playfully.

Ryker and Brayden squared up, playfully throwing light blows at one another. The sound of a door closing snatched my attention. I turned toward the truck and watched as Jamison strolled over, I'm sure curious as to what all the commotion was about.

"What da fuck y'all out here cacklin about like some ratchet ass broads?" he asked, stopping next to me.

Ryker and Brayden froze. Unclenching their fist, their hands fell idly at their sides. Jamison looked between the three of us as three set of eyes stared back at him.

"Ninja do broads have guns like these?" Brayden asked Jamison, while simultaneously curling his arms in the air, displaying his hefty biceps. Slowly he drug his head over to Ryker. With a sly smile rested on his face he winked at him before snatching his arms out the air.

"Ninja? What da fuck is that?" Jamison asked.

The three of us broke out in laughter while Jamison stood looking confused.

"Since yo boy here . . ." Ryker dipped his head toward Brayden, "is of the Caucasian persuasion he knows he can't say nigga so he adapted to sayin ninja instead. It's kinda an inside joke from when we were kids."

Jamison's mouth formed a soft O as he shook his head, indicating his understanding. Clearly amused by Jamison's reaction Brayden couldn't contain the wide grin set on his olive- toned face. I released a low snicker as I tapped my roommate on the shoulder before walking toward the back of the truck. I raised the back door and dipped my head inside. My eyes swept over the assortment of luggage, looking for the two duffle bags I packed. I shuffled through way too many bags for a weekend trip when I finally spotted the largest of my two bags. I rested my hand on the handle of my bag and paused when I heard the sound of car doors closing behind me. I didn't need to turn around to know she was there. I could feel her. Snatching my tote out of the pile of luggage I dropped it at my feet and pushed the remaining bags further into the back of the truck. Slowly turning around I ducked my head down and rested my ass on the bed of the truck while crossing my legs at the ankle and resting the palms of my hands on each side of me.

I tuned out the obstreperous chatter of my friends and the humming of the motor from the hoverboard ridden by a neighborhood kid. I even managed to ignore the sound of my own heartbeat thumping loudly in my eardrums. I reserved every ounce of my attention for her. Raking my eyes down her body I stopped my perusal as soon as my orbs landed on her juicy peach. Rocky was dressed comfortably, sporting a pair of black Capri leggings and a sleeveless tank top that rested on her hips. Both of which left her ass on full display. She had a denim jacket tied around her waist but there was absolutely no hiding that ass. Feeling like a creep I gradually drug my eyes back to her face. A face I could barely see thanks to the oversized sunglasses and the baseball cap atop her head. The blinged out cap was pulled down low, meeting the top of her eyewear. Her usually wild mane was pulled back into a curly ponytail hanging out the back of her snapback. Thankfully, I didn't need to see her face to know she was beautiful. I had committed to memory every single feature on her flawless face.

Engrossed in their own private conversation Rocky and Carmen walked arm in arm up the driveway. Carmen noticed me first. Using her index finger, she tipped the top of her sunglasses down her narrow nose, sweeping her honey colored eye up and down my relaxed frame. I smirked while acknowledging her playful inspection with a simple head nod. Carmen tugged on her friend's arm and I watched as Rocky stopped talking. The corner of her full lips curled up and settled into a wide smile. I couldn't see her eyes, but I knew that smile was reserved for me. Uncrossing my legs, I pushed off the back of the truck and started the short walk toward her, stopping at the sound of Ryker's loud ass voice.

"It's about muthafuckin time," Ryker shouted. Leaving Brayden and Jamison he sprinted down the driveway and scooped Rocky into his arms, swinging her tiny body from side to side.

Still laughing when Ryker placed her back on her feet Rocky removed her shades. Folding what I was sure were a pair of designer sunglasses she tucked the temple inside her shirt and titled her head up. "Take that up with Ace," she instructed, dipping her head back in the direction of where she last saw Royce. "That nigga drive like he's drivin Miss Daisy."

"You right," Ryker agreed while glancing over his shoulder at Royce who was now walking up the driveway. "Damn, Raxs I missed you."

"I missed you too Deuce," Rocky declared, rubbing her hand down the side of his face.

"Man, fuck both y'all," Royce spat out through a chortle, stopping next to his twin.

Carmen placed her hands on her hips and tilted her head to the side. "So, you just gonna act like you don't see me standin right here?" Her eyes were locked on Ryker.

Snatching one of Carmen's hands from her hip the other flared in the air as Ryker pulled her toward him, wrapping her in his long arms. "Ain't nobody forget yo dramatic ass."

I had seen enough. It was impossible to be so close to her and not touch her. Walking up behind Rocky I gently tugged on her elbow. Slowly she turned around with a closed mouth smile fixed on her face. Elation danced in her slanted ambers but behind her mirth was a semblance of worry. Reading her hushed expression, I bent down and hurriedly pulled her tiny frame into my body before releasing her just as quickly as I had scooped her into my arms.

I turned my attention to the rest of the group and forced my eyes away from Rocky. "Damn bro, you gonna let Carmen go so the rest of us can say hi?" I teased.

With Carmen still engulfed in his huge frame Ryker looked at me over her shoulder. "You say hi witcha yo mouth not cha hands nigga."

Carmen giggled while playfully shoving Ryker in the chest as she stepped out of his embrace. Looking Rocky dead in the eyes Carmen opened her arms and summoned me with a wave of her small hands. Rocky held the same tight-lipped smile while rolling her eyes up in her head.

Shaking my head, I couldn't help the smirk that settled on my face as I stepped into Carmen's arms. "Hi Carm," I sang, using the nickname I'd heard Rocky call her.

"Ummm," Carmen purred while wiggling inside my arms. "Hi Dreee." She dragged out the last part of my name, pulling me closer into the little space I'd left between us.

"You know she gonna kick yo ass for this?" I whispered in her ear, as I placed my hands on her hips and slowly backed out of her embrace.

"Alright alright, enough of all this huggin shit. The three of y'all see enough of one another in the city. Shit, it's hot as fuck out here. And I'm startin to sweat like a whore in church on first Sunday," Royce joked. Leaving us where we stood, he started walking up the driveway toward Brayden and Jamison.

Following behind Royce I clasped Ryker on the shoulder. "C'mon bro."

As we strolled up the driveway, I couldn't help but wonder how this weekend was going to play out. Would Rocky and I make it without letting on that there was some serious shit brewing between us and more importantly, would my boys keep their mouths shut? I wasn't worried about Bray as much as I was J. Once dude got some liquor in him there was no telling what would come flying out his big ass mouth.

Catching up to Royce I stopped in front of Brayden and Jamison, with Ryker on my heels. Determined to have a good time I tried my best to check my paranoia. That is, until my eyes landed on Jamison and Bray. Both stood quietly amongst us, their eyes darting between me and over my shoulder at Rocky. It was hard to miss the suspect look on both their faces as they continued to bounce their eyes between us.

Yep, this is gonna to be an interestin ass weekend.

Friday night went off without a hitch. After unloading our luggage and throwing our shit into the twins' spare room we decided to stay in for the night. Rocky and Carmen stayed for about two hours before taking Ryker's car back to their hotel a few blocks away. After the girls left, we decided to kickback the way we always did when it was just the fellas. We ordered takeout, turned on some music, and played a few rounds of cards. Shit talking and drinks flowed until damn near three in the morning.

Now I was posted up outside of Rocky's hotel waiting for her and Carmen's slow asses to come down so I could run them past Lenox Mall before heading back to the twins'. Ryker needed his car for work, so I drove him to pick it up. I agreed to play taxi for Rocky and Carmen since Royce left for some shorty's house after our kickback and still hadn't returned.

Glancing at the dash I checked for the time. It was a little after one in the afternoon but still too early because it was clear I hadn't slept enough for all the liquor I consumed to flush out my system. I closed my eyes and placed my thumbs on my temples, resting my fingers on

217

my forehead. Moving my thumbs in a circular motion I firmly kneaded the sides of my head, hoping the pressure would help calm the midget in Timberlands stumping around in my head. My eyes flashed open as the sound of her rosy voice filled my eardrums. Slowly I swung my head in the direction of where I heard her voice. Rocky was standing outside the truck holding the passenger door open, peering at me.

"Are you okay Dre?" she asked, with a concerned expression on her otherwise perfect face.

I winced as I tried and failed to offer her a smile. "I'm good Short Stuff."

"Bullshit. Your ass look like you been ran over by a Mac truck," Carmen stated, climbing into the backseat and closing the door.

Although I was sure she used the normal amount of pressure to pull the door shut it sounded like she slammed that bitch close with the strength of the Hulk. Again, I found myself wincing as the throbbing in my temples increased.

"Shut up Carm," Rocky admonished.

"Uggh, don't be mad at me because your boo can't handle his liquor," Carmen teased.

I extended my arm into the backseat and flipped Carmen the bird. I heard her chuckle as I drug my arm forward and pulled down the visor, looking in the mirror I checked my reflection. She was right, I looked like shit. My eyes were unusually low with a hint of red in the sclera. I had small puffy bags underneath both eyes and somehow what little melanin I had was drained from my skin, giving me an ashen tone.

"You don't have to take us to the mall Dre. I really want you to go sleep this shit off so you can be ready to turn up again tonight," Rocky stated, closing her door as she positioned herself in the seat across from me.

I released a light snicker while flipping the visor back in place and pulling away from the curb, heading South on Peachtree. "I got you Short Stuff. I'll go back to the house to sleep. And you and Carmen can take the truck to the mall. Coo?"

Rocky placed her hand on top of my arm lying on the center

console, using her thumb she gently traced small circles on the back of my hand. "That's cool."

Less than fifteen minutes later we pulled up to the twins' and not a minute too soon. I could now add bubble guts to the list of my hangover symptoms. *This is what the fuck I get for drinkin vodka. Fuckin with Bray's ass. Uggh!*

Placing the truck in park I left the engine running and quickly hopped out. Rocky met me on the driver's side before I could head toward the front door. She stood in front of me. With her head tilted up she looked me directly in my swollen eyes. Gingerly lowering my head, I placed my aching dome on her forehead as Rocky raised her hand and placed it on my face. My heavy lids drifted shut as I absorbed the warmth emitting from Rocky's body. Her heated touch felt good on my clammy skin as she ran her hand slowly along my jawline.

Fluttering my eyes open I slowly lifted my head from hers. I grabbed the hand she used to stroke my face, placed it up to my mouth and planted a firm kiss in her palm before sliding it out mine. The corners of her mouth curled up as a bright smile spread across her face, displaying her deep dimples. Her widespread smile caused the slits of her slanted eyes to appear close as she silently examined me. Leaning forward I softly kissed her on the forehead before taking a step back where I forced myself out of her personal space.

"I'll be A1 before we hit the streets tonight, I promise."

Rocky acknowledged my comment with a quick nod of her head. "Here," she whispered, placing two small pills in the palm of my hand.

Looking at the tablets an appreciative grin settled on my face as I slid the medicine in my pocket. "Thanks, Short Stuff. See you in a lil bit," I stated, while rushing toward the door. My stomach wouldn't allow me to linger any longer.

I rushed in the house and sprinted past Royce, who to my surprise was standing by the front door. *When did he get here?* As I made my way down the hall I glanced over my shoulder. Yep, he was still standing where I left him except now, he was turned facing me. There was no doubt in my mind that he was watching me. But why? Standing with both his hands tucked inside the pocket of his shorts his usually big eyes were low and an impish grin was fixed on his face. *Shit! Did he see me with his sister? I sure as hell hoped not.* The gurgling of my stomach quickly shifted my attention. I swiveled my head forward and clutched my stomach then raced to the bathroom.

That was close.

I exited the bathroom feeling ten pounds lighter and slightly better since my body extracted some of the filth, I consumed the night before. My head was still pounding but I was convinced a nap and some meds would have me back to normal in due time. Sticking my hand inside my pocket I felt around for the pills I dumped there before my trip to the bathroom. I palmed the tablets and snatched my balled fist out my pocket. Placing one weighted foot in front of the other I traipsed languidly down the hall. The house was in full swing. The sound of my boy's voices pierced the air as I rounded the corner of the kitchen. The three of them were in the living room in front of the TV. Jamison and Brayden were sitting on the couch while Royce was stretched out on one of the accent chairs. I had no idea what they were talking about, but I was sure they were talking shit to one another. Brayden's high-pitched laugh vibrated off the walls, causing me to wince. Hurriedly I entered the kitchen, stalked over to the refrigerator and plucked out a water bottle.

"I see you still can't handle light liquor," Royce chaffed, as he strolled in the kitchen.

Chucking the pills in my mouth, I unscrewed the top off the bottle, and swallowed a big gulp of water. "What gave it away?" I asked sarcastically, while wiping away a dribble of water from my lip.

A light chuckle passed through his lips. With squinted eyes he stood staring at me.

I placed the cap back on the bottle of water and leaned against the counter, twirling the bottle in my hands. "What's up Ro?"

"Ain't shit. Just wonderin what's up with you and Raxs," he responded drily.

Taking in a mouth full of air I swallowed the lump that seemed to magically appear in my throat. "What you mean?"

Royce crossed over to where I stood and placed his large hand on my shoulder. "Nothin bro. Go lay your hungover ass down," he advised, giving me a firm squeeze before removing his hand from my shoulder.

"Yeah, Imma do that." My voice was lower than usual as I turned toward the fridge.

Yanking the door open I sat my water bottle on the top shelf. I stood in front of the open refrigerator for a few seconds while mulling over Royce's question. There was no doubt in my mind now, he definitely saw my interaction with Rocky. Closing the fridge, I spun around on my heels, prepared to leave the kitchen and all thoughts of what he did or did not see when the sight of him still standing at the edge of the kitchen stopped me in my tracks.

A glint of a smile shimmered in his large eyes but was absent from his face. Instead a captious expression was settled where one would have expected to see a smile. "Be careful bro. JB's lifestyle really did a number on her. She's not like any other woman you've dealt with," he warned.

His words hung in the air like a thick cloud of smoke. A million questions bounced around in my head as I stood with my mouth slightly parted. I stared at my best friend as I search my brain for the words to address his warning. I found none. Royce paid me one last glance before he walked out the kitchen, leaving me alone with my thoughts. I replayed his words over and over while trying to decipher the meaning behind his cryptic warning. It wasn't like he told me something I didn't already know but it was something about hearing those words from someone who knew Rocky better than I did that knocked the wind right out of me.

Suddenly my entire body felt weak. The strength in my legs seemed to diminish while a knot formed in the pit of stomach, causing an unexpected queasiness. Leaning my fragile frame against the refrigerator I clamped my eyes closed. I used my thumb and index finger to pinch the bridge of my nose as I took in a lung full of air. I needed to lay the fuck down. Between battling this hangover and the blow Royce just issued I was fighting a losing battle. Flashing my eyes open I pushed off the refrigerator door and walked out the kitchen. Jamison and Brayden's backs were to me, but I had a side view of Royce's face. He must have caught a glimpse of me in his peripheral because his head swiftly turned my way.

Watching my slow steps Royce's bushy brows shifted toward his hairline. I offered him a quick head nod, indicating I was good. In order to sell the lie, I put a little more pep in my step as I climbed the stairs to the second floor. Entering the guest room, I closed the door and looked around at Jamison and Brayden's shit scattered throughout the room. *How the hell did two people manage this much mess in less than twenty-four hours?* Lucky for me the bed was clear of any clutter, just messy sheets and a crumpled comforter. Not bothering to remove my clothes I kicked off my shoes then dove face first onto the unmade bed. I used the last of my energy to clear my mind. I pushed my evolving feelings for Rocky, the eerie conversation with Royce, and the uneasy feeling I felt as a result of that conversation out of my head. Slowly my body relaxed as I melted into the softness and comfort of the mattress. It didn't take long for sleep to find me.

The loud thumping of bass vibrated the floor below me, jarring me from my sleep. Groggily I pried my eyes open. Sunlight peeked through the blinds slightly illuminating the otherwise dark room. Slowly pushing up off the mattress I sat up and scooted to the edge of the bed where I planted my feet on the floor. I took a minute to gather myself before dragging my ass out the bed and standing to my feet. The muffled sounds of lively chatter and boisterous music from down-stairs resonated through the halls as I left the guest room and made my way over to Royce's room, where I stored my belongings.

Sticking my hand inside the pocket of my shorts I fetched out my cellphone, glancing at the home screen I checked the time. I had managed to sleep the entire afternoon. It was ten till six. I shook my head as I walked into the dark room and flipped on the light. I surveyed the spacious room, settling my eyes on my two totes neatly stashed in the corner by Royce's closet. Sitting my phone on top of Royce's dresser I gaited over to my bags. I dropped down on my haunches, unzipping the larger of the two totes I shuffled through the assortment of clothes when I heard a noise behind me. I swung my head toward the door, a soft smile eased onto my face. Rocky stood in the entryway, leaned against the door jamb with her arms folded loosely across her chest.

"I was just comin up to check on you," she stated, uncrossing her arms and walking toward me.

"Oh yeah? And why is that?"

She stopped in front of me and peered down at me through her long lashes. "Well for starters, the last time I saw you, you didn't look too good," she answered, while sweeping her eyes over my body.

I hiked a brow and smiled up at her. "I feel a lot better. The meds and nap helped. Thanks."

"Good. I was comin to wake you up."

I stood to my feet. "Why?" I asked, taking her by the wrist I pulled her into my chest and wrapped my arms around her small waist, letting my hands rest on her ass.

"Royce said you came up here around two and it's almost six. I figured you had enough time to sleep off your hangover," she responded against my chest.

I let my head rest gently on top of hers. "I miss this. It's hard being around you and not being able to touch you."

Rocky ran her small hands up and down my back. "I know," she whispered. "But I appreciate you—"

"What da fuck goin on in here?" Ryker roared from behind us.

Lifting my head, I slowly removed my arms from Rocky's waist. A startled expression rest on her face as she backed away from me.

"Somebody answer me," Ryker commanded, while walking over to where Rocky and I stood.

Rocky's eyes skirted up to mine. I turned toward Ryker and looked him square in his angry eyes. "Ain't shit goin on bro. I was just thankin Rocky for the meds she gave me earlier," I lied, while studying his face, hoping he believed the bullshit I just fed him.

"That ain't what that shit looked like," Ryker spat out.

"Stop it Deuce," Rocky ordered.

Looking down at his sister, Ryker's eyes softened. His tense posture relaxed, and a cunning smirk eased upon his face. "I'on want no static sis. But I know this nigga . . ." his eyes shifted to me, "bet not be trynna press up on you."

Rocky softly placed her hand on Ryker's flexed pectoral. "Ain't nobody pressin up on nobody. Now stop it," she demanded, shoving Ryker in the chest and walking past him out the door.

Following behind his sister Ryker headed toward the door. "Hey," I called out to him.

Ryker stopped walking and turned toward me. "What's up bro?" Ryker asked, with a weak smile fixed on his face.

"We good?" My brows furrowed as I waited for his response.

"We're good," he replied, turning back toward the door and walking out.

Fuck!

I felt stuck in place as I stood staring into the empty hallway. Twice in one day I had managed to get caught in some sort of encounter with Rocky by both her damn brothers. And both encounters left me feeling some type of way.

"Ain't that some shit," I spoke out loud to the empty while turning back toward my luggage.

"What's some shit?" Royce asked from somewhere behind me.

Spinning around I looked across the room at my friend. "Nothin, just talkin to myself."

Royce chuckled. "Ryker caught you and Raxs together didn't he?" he asked, walking closer to where I stood.

I shook my head. "It wasn't like that tho. We were huggin and dude almost lost his shit," I clarified.

"Bro it's me, your day one. You ain't gotta lie to me. I know you almost . . . nah fuck that. I do know you better than you know yourself. You and Raxs may not be a thing right now, but there is definitely some shit goin down between y'all. I won't ask so you won't have to lie. All Imma say is, be careful."

I didn't bother to refute anything he just said. Instead I stood quietly trying to process his words. Running a hand down my face I released a long heavy sigh. "Can I ask you a question bro?"

"Anything," he answered coolly.

"Why do you keep tellin me to be careful? That's the second time you said that shit to me today."

Royce walked over to his bed and sat down. Bending over he slid an ashtray from underneath his bed and pulled a Black & Mild from his ear then sparked a light from a lighter I never noticed in his large hand. Taking a quick toke of his cigar he looked up at me.

"Imma say this shit once and its not to be repeated. Okay?"

I shook my head while looking at him intently, curious as fuck about whatever it was, he was about to say.

Placing the filtered tip to his lips Royce inhaled his cigar. He smirked at the grimace on my face as he blew rings of circles into the air. "Crack the window you damn baby."

I saluted him with my middle finger before turning and walking the short distance to the window. I slid the window up and humidity instantly oozed through the screen. I moved away from the heat and pulled out the chair nestled under his desk. Sitting backward in the chair I draped my legs on each side of the front legs while resting my arms across the top rail.

"Spit that shit out," I ordered.

He stared at me as smoke streamed from his mouth. "I ain't bout to give yo ass no long as spiel just some quick game. Raxs is twenty-seven and has never and I mean never had a boyfriend. I know that ain't no new info to you but think about that shit bro. My sister is fine, smart, and has a body that puts most video vixens to shame but her ass is grown as fuck and has never had a man. That shit ain't right." He paused to take a toke of his Black & Mild.

"I say all that to say, she has definitely had some good contenders, but Raxs is brutal bro. She ain't nothin to fuck wit and I don't wanna see you get hurt. Don't think I ain't remember yo ass use to have a crush on her back in the day. I just want you to be careful. Big sis don't love nobody but fam. I don't think she knows how. Our dad fucked her up. She like straight don't believe in that shit. And Dre, you a good dude. Don't let my sister fuck you up," he finished. Surveying me, he waited for my reaction to his warning.

I had none. Nothing he said was new to me, but I knew I would definitely analyze that shit later. "I hear you bro but I'm good. I know how to handle Rocky."

Royce put out his cigar in the ashtray and slid it back underneath his bed. Sitting back upright he locked his eyes with mine and shook his head. "If you say so but don't say I ain't warn you. Because nigga we brothers for life. So, if you let my sister break yo heart you still gotta fucks with me. Understood?"

"Most definitely," I said, standing up from the chair.

I met Royce between where we both were sitting, we bumped fist and locked arms for a quick man hug. Pulling back, I looked at my best friend. "Real quick, what you mean she had some good contenders tho?"

A deep chortle flew from his mouth. "I ain't finna tell her business but I'll give you this one for free since I know you've heard her mention his name before. Does the name Emery sound familiar?"

I shook my head as a scowl settled on my face.

"Chill bro, ain't shit gonna on wit them but Emery ain't yo average dude and Raxs gave that nigga the business. I don't know why dude still fucks wit her especially since he can have any chick he wants."

"Your point," I growled.

"My point is, my sister ain't shit to be fucked wit if she dismissed Emery Brackus, and he still sniffin around her ass hopin she will take him off the bench and let him wife her," he finished, while strolling toward the door.

My eyes ballooned big as saucers. "Emery Brackus that plays for the Pittsburgh Steelers, Emery Brackus?" I asked, my voice sounding louder than I intended.

"The one and only," he stated, as he walked out of his bedroom.

And just like that he was gone. Once again, I was left alone with my thoughts following a crazy ass convo with one of my best friends. Royce was right, I had definitely heard Rocky mention Emery before, but I had no idea she was referring to the 2012 number one draft pick. The up and coming second string quarterback for the Pittsburgh Steelers.

I made a mental note to ask Rocky about it later as I walked over to my luggage for the third time and snatched it off the floor. Moving over to Royce's bed I sat my bag down and quickly fetched out a clean pair of boxers and a white tank top. With my undergarments in hand I walked out the room, stopping at the linen closet I grabbed a fresh rag and towel then proceeded down the hall toward the bathroom. I needed a shower and for more reasons than one. I needed to wash last night off me but more importantly, I needed to clear my damn head.

I used my time in the shower to process my conversation with Royce. His words played on repeat in my head. I tried like hell to find holes in his theory, telling myself he was biased and didn't know Rocky the same way I knew her. Hell, I even tried to convince myself that he was lying to make me uninterested. But every scenario I drummed up lead me back to the same conclusion, dude was right. I needed to be cautious with my heart and how I approached this thing I was determined to build with Rocky. There was only one problem, my heart had a mind of its own. After spending what felt like too much time going back and forth with myself, I decided to let the shit go.

Thirty minutes later I emerged from the bathroom feeling clean and refreshed. With a newfound determination I trekked back to Royce's room, discarded my worn clothes, and threw on a pair of basketball short. It was time for me to get back to enjoying my weekend with my friends. All the other shit could wait. Grabbing my cell off the dresser as I passed by, I dropped it into my pocket and walked out the room. The sound of "Cheers" by Rihanna resonated through the halls as I navigated through the long corridor, heading toward the stairs. *How appropriate.* Stepping off the last stair I heard my friend's voices. Voices that blended together while they competed against the deafening sound of the music. I walked in the direction of the boisterous chatter and found everyone gathered in the living room, leisurely spread across the different pieces of furniture and the floor.

"Aye, there he is," Brayden called out, as his baby blues landed on me.

The corners of my mouth instantly curled upwards. "No thanks to yo ass," I ribbed, while tossing my middle finger in the air.

"What was that for? I didn't make yo ass drink vodka. I merely

227

suggested you stop actin like a bitch and drink what we were drinkin," he countered, snickering as the words left his mouth.

His quick comeback garnered a laugh from everyone in the room, including me. Walking further into the crowded room I spotted an empty space on the floor next to Jamison. He sat leaned over on his side next to one of the accent chairs propped up on his elbow with his legs stretched out in front of him. I stepped over Brayden and crossed in front of the sofa where I eased my solid frame down onto the carpet, resting my back against the chair occupied by Rocky.

"What's the game plan for tonight? I know y'all decided on somethin why I was sleep," I asked, to no one in particular.

I felt her little hand rest on top of my head. "Well, we figured we'd pre-game here until about nine or so then head out and get somethin to eat. After that—" Rocky's voice trailed off.

I shifted my head underneath her hand, tilting my head back to look up at her.

"Then it's on to Vixens," Carmen finished Rocky's statement.

"Wait, what?" I asked, completely caught off guard by that answer.

Rocky and Carmen giggled in unison.

"You heard em," Ryker stated, staring at his sister's hand on top of my head.

I watched him watch us as I slid my head back down, shifting my eyes between Royce and Ryker who were sitting in my direct line of sight. "Y'all serious?"

Rocky ignored her brother's icy glare. She continued rubbing her hand back and forth through my hair, gently massaging my head in the process. "Dead ass," she answered above me."

"And y'all legit coo with this?" I asked, swiveling my head to look at Carmen then tilting it back to rest my eyes on Rocky.

"It was their idea," Jamison answered from the side of me.

I didn't bother to look at him. Instead I continued to stare at the woman whose fingers were digging into my scalp, giving me the best head massage. "Have y'all been to a strip club before?"

Carmen smacked her lips. "Only every time we come to Atlanta," she stated, sarcasm dripping from each word.

I opened my mouth to reply but quickly snapped it shut. I vaguely remembered Rocky mentioning the strip club during one of our dinners, but I didn't really take her serious. *This chick is full of surprises.* The sound of Rocky giggling snatched me from my thoughts. A one cheek smile settled on her face, giving me a glimpse of one of her dimples. Slowly I shifted my head forward again with a mischievous grin splayed on my face. Out of the corner of my eye I noticed Jamison watching me. His eyes bounced from me to Rocky.

This is going to be an interesting ass night.

Thirty minutes after I joined my friends Rocky and Carmen took Rkyer's car back to their hotel to change. They agreed to meet us back at the house in an hour. While the girls were gone Royce and I made a quick run to the liquor store, replenishing our stash for the pre-game festivities. By eight-thirty everyone was back at the house.

Leaning against the kitchen counter next to the refrigerator I sipped from a red Solo cup while bobbing my head to the music. Music that was streaming loudly through speakers strategically hidden throughout the living room so they could be heard from anywhere on the lower level. As if on cue Rocky and Carmen sauntered into the kitchen just as the music switched from a bass thumping high energy rap song to a mellow mid-tempo R&B track. Instantly their presence commanded the attention of the room full of men. Taking another gulp of my cocktail I watched Brayden sweep his eyes up and down Carmen's body. He licked his thin lips, settling his sapphires on her full breast. I smirked to myself at his reaction. Both women looked extremely sexy, but my focus was on the short chocolate woman wearing all black.

Discreetly drinking her in I slowly raked my eyes down her body. Rocky wore a pair of very short black denim shorts paired with a sheer lace bustier top underneath an all-black cape that draped past her knees on each side. The high heel black boots with red soles sat comfortably just above her knees on her toned thighs, adding an extra four inches to her short frame. Multiple gold bangles donned her left wrist while a combination of black and gold bracelets along with an all-black watch sat on her right. A simple gold chain with disc beads and a stick accent rested around her neck, hanging down into her exposed cleavage. I couldn't tell if she was wearing earrings because her long mane was silky straight, parted down the middle and draped over her ears, flowing down her back, past the strap of her bustier. Tonight, she wore more makeup than I was accustomed to seeing on her but not enough to make you question her beauty without it. Her slanted eyes were decorated in a combination of dark hues, a goldish shimmery blush accentuated her high cheekbones, and a deep crimson gloss donned her full lips. Yeah, I had it bad, I had studied every detail of her down to her accessories and makeup.

I used my foot propped up on the cabinet to push off the wooden surface and stand up straight. Taking the few steps over to the table where everyone was gathered, I found an open space between the twins and slid into the gap between them. Ryker stood to the right of me holding his phone in his hand, tapping away at the keyboard. On my left was Royce, he was the only one sitting. Nodding his head to the beat of the music he concentrated on the task in front of him. Twisting off the lid of the grinder he sprinkled pieces of green with purple specks evenly into a sweet-smelling wrapper. Carefully picking the wrapper off the table he strategically twirled the paper between his fingers, forming a smoothly rolled blunt. He held the blunt out in front of his face and admired his handwork before lowering his hand and sparking a flame, burning the tip of his spliff.

"Ace," Rocky shouted over top of the music.

Royce looked across the table at his sister but continued rotating the blunt around the open flame. Titling his head to the side he hiked a brow and placed the marijuana filled cigar up to his lips.

"Royce Malik Banks," Rocky called out, as she drew her hands up to her abundant hips. "Ain't nobody trynna smell like weed when I leave here. Take that shit outside."

Royce smirked as he fanned out the spliff and stood from the table. "My bad. I got you sis." Shooting his eyes over to Brayden he dipped his head and walked out the kitchen.

Brayden grabbed his cup from off the table and trailed out the room behind Royce.

"Stop playin Carm, you know you wanna hit this shit. Now bring yo ghetto fabulous ass out here," Royce called out from the hall.

Winking at Rocky, Carmen switched away from the table and sauntered out the room. Rocky shook her head and turned toward Jamison as he slid into Carmen's space. Bending down he leaned into her space, speaking into her ear. *This nigga.* I shifted my eyes away from the pair, raising my cup I looked inside and noticed it was empty. Looking down at the table, I surveyed the various liquor bottles spread across it. I bent over and reached out for the bottle of Rémy Martin 1738 when I felt someone staring at me.

I slid the bottle toward me and looked up to find Rocky watching me. Instantly a smile sprang to my face. Returning her gaze, I pulled the top off the bottle and lifted it in the air, extending the bottle in her direction. She looked inside the cup in her hand and shook her head no. I mouthed, "suit yourself." I watched her flash me a smile before dropping my eyes to my empty cup. I quickly refilled my drink before adding a splash of Coke to the amber colored cognac.

Turning to my right I looked at Ryker, he was still engaged in his phone. I cleared my throat to get his attention. "What time your shorty gettin here? I'm hungry as hell and I think we need to get ready to bang out."

He looked at me then his phone again, a wide smile stretched across his face. "She's on her way. And you sure you good with her drivin your pop's truck?" he asked for like the third time that night.

Honestly, I didn't see any other option. Homegirl didn't drink or smoke and since everyone here planned to engage in at least one of the two we needed a designated driver.

"You makin me nervous bro," I admitted honestly. "You keep askin me that shit like babygirl can't drive."

Ryker chuckled. "Nah, we good. Just wanna make sure you sure is all."

I nodded my head.

"Coo," he stated, sitting his empty beer bottle on the table and backing out the kitchen.

Dear God, please don't let me regret this.

I fluttered my eyes open as her scent infiltrated my nostrils. She smelled like a combination of a woodsy musk, vanilla, and flowers, with a hint of coconut oil. Slowly I rolled my head in the direction of where I smelled her. Rocky stood to the right of me, with her head titled up she smiled at me.

"You smell amazing, what are you wearing?"

"Thank you. It's called Flowerbomb."

Leaning over I placed my nose against her neck, inhaling deeply through my nostrils. "You smell good enough to eat," I growled.

Rocky giggled and squirmed underneath me as I playful ran my nose across her collarbone. "Dreeee," she squealed.

Lifting my head, I looked down at her. "That's your fault. Ain't nobody tell you to come over here smelling like that," I stated, while running my tongue across my already moist lips.

Rocky's eyes were glued to my mouth.

"Uggh, y'all do know I'm standin right here?" Jamison asked from across the table.

Neither one of us looked at him. Instead, I offered him my middle finger as I continued to stare down at Rocky.

"Oh okay, it's coo. But if y'all start kissin I'm tellin like a lil bitch," he teased.

That caught our attention. In unison we swung her heads toward him.

Jamison burst out laughing just as Ryker came waltzing back into the kitchen, standing next to him.

"What's so funny?" Ryker asked looking across the table at me and Rocky, then turning his head to look at Jamison.

This time it was Rocky who was quick on her toes as she offered Ryker a response to his question. "J was talkin shit about me and . . ." she swept her eyes down my body, "Dre being dressed alike," she finished, turning her attention to her brother.

Ryker darted his eyes between us, sliding his sable orbs down our bodies he took in our matching attire. Something I hadn't paid attention to until this very moment when she mentioned it. A goofy grin spread across his face, taking me by complete surprise.

Ryker waved a hand in our direction as he stepped away from the table and walked over to the fridge. "They ain't do that shit on purpose," he spoke to no one in particular.

Out of the corner of my eye I looked down at Rocky. She was staring up at me, with a sly grin fixed on her face. "This is the second time this shit has happened. The next time somebody has to change," she teased, elbowing me in the ribs.

Ryker strolled back up to the table as Brayden, Royce and Carmen walked back in the house along with Ryker's shorty. Ryker made quick introductions and poured his female friend a glass of juice. Tuning out the music and the loud conversation between my friends I reflected on Rocky's words. She was right, this was the second time we'd been together, and our outfits accidently coordinated. I was dressed casually in a pair of relaxed fit black jeans with holes in the knees paired with an all-black tee that hung longer in the back than the front. Finishing off my look was a pair of all-black Air Jordan 1 Retro High Anodized sneakers. Hanging on the back of one of the chairs was a light all-black cloak hooded jacket; I would throw on before we left the house.

"Aye," Ryker shouted, gaining my attention.

"Huh?"

Ryker snickered. "Damn bro, you were out of it. You bout ready?"

I ran my hand across the back of neck. "Yep but let me snap a few pics wit my twin first," I responded, sitting my drink on the table and looking over at Rocky.

"Man, hurry that shit up," he sneered, looking between me and Rocky.

Rocky stuck her tongue out at him. Ryker couldn't help but smile while waving a hand at her silliness. Turning toward Simone, at least I think that's what he said her name was, Ryker tuned Rocky and I out.

I grabbed Rocky at the hips, pulling her small frame into mine. "You already know the routine."

Rocky flashed me a wide smile, exposing her deep dimples. Reaching into my pocket I pulled out my phone and went straight to my camera. Rocky and I took multiple pictures in various poses. Toward the end of our mini photoshoot we had the attention of everyone in the room. Carmen started it off with a slow dramatic clap, soon the entire room joined in. Laughter and applause filled the room, almost muting the boisterous music.

I stuffed my phone back in my pocket and removed my jacket from the chair on the other side of Carmen. Picking my cup back up from the table I looked across at Ryker as I pulled my jacket on. "I'm ready whenever everyone else is."

"Coo. If you takin your drink with you put that shit in somethin other than those Solo cups. I suggest water bottles for those of you drinkin light and a pop can for the dark drinkers," Ryker instructed, before grabbing his girl's hand and walking out the room.

From chugging down the last of drinks, switching cups, to pouring unwanted liquor down the drain everyone got themselves ready to leave. Royce shut down the stereo system and cut out all the lights. One by one we headed out the door. Standing in the driveway we tossed around restaurant ideas before agreeing to find someplace downtown. Once that was settled, I plucked my keys from my jacket pocket and tossed them over the truck to Ryker. Ryker handed shorty the keys then walked over to the passenger side and climbed in. Following suite, everyone filed into the oversized SUV. After everyone was settled inside, we drove to downtown Atlanta to Gladys Knight's Chicken & Waffles. With a party of eight it took close to two hours for us to order, eat, and cash out.

Around eleven forty-five we filed out the restaurant and headed to the truck. Fifteen minutes later we pulled into the parking lot at Vixens. It took three laps around the lot before we found a spot. Royce was the first one out the truck, followed by his twin. One by one we hopped out until all the men stood outside waiting on the ladies. As expected, mirrors were snatched out, lights flicked on, and makeup was being reapplied. Taking advantage of the girl's mini primping session Royce and Brayden stepped to the back of the truck and sparked a blunt. Instantly the pungent stench of weed permeated the air.

Rocky was the first of the women out of the truck. Immediately her nose scrunched up at the skunky odor as she bounced her eyes around the parking lot. Tickled by her reaction I snickered as

Carmen and Ryker's shorty stepped out the truck. Gathered in a circle we waited for Royce and Brayden to finish blazing. A few moments later they emerged from the rear of the truck and joined our group.

"Y'all good now?" Rocky looked directly at Royce with a snarky grin on her face.

Royce chuckled at his older sister while wrapping an arm around her neck. Rocky playfully fought against his hold as he started walking them toward the club. Following suite, we all trailed behind the pair while laughing and talking shit about our expectations for the night. I lagged the pack, watching the women I looked for any signs of discomfort. I wasn't naïve. I knew women attended strip clubs. I'd just never been to one with a lady. Let alone, one I was trying to link with romantically. To my surprise, the only person who seemed bothered was me. Even Ryker's shorty seemed confident in her strides as she walked beside Carmen. So, I let the shit go.

As we approached the club, I looked at the line stretching along the building well into the parking lot. "Damn. Maybe we should've gotten here earlier."

"Don't sweat it. Your boy already worked it out," Ryker stated, while waving his hand for us to continue following him.

Ryker strutted toward the front of the line and instructed us to give him a second. With Royce on his heels they walked up to the bouncer and gave him dap. They then looked back and pointed at the six of us. The huge man in charge of watching the door stood up from his stool and looked at each us individually. His squinted eyes lingered on the women in the bunch longer than I liked. Especially since the woman he seemed enamored with was Rocky. Thankfully Ryker quickly shut that shit down. Tapping the ogre on one of his muscular arms he whispered in his ear. I didn't hear what was said but I could tell by the look on the man's face that he had been warned. Reluctantly he peeled his bug eyes off Rocky. He redirected his gaze toward Carmen, flashing her a gold tooth smile. Watching the entire exchange Ryker laughed while motioning for us to join him. One by one we approached the burly doorman. He patted down the men and cleared us through. The ladies were ushered over to a female guard who searched them then allowed them entrance.

Stepping inside a set of tinted glass double doors we bypassed a beautifully made up woman in charge of collecting cover. A fringed metallic curtain separated the small lobby from the main room. Ryker pulled back the curtain and stood off to the side as each of us passed through, stepping into a dimly lit room. Observing my surroundings, I scanned the crowded club. A large oval shaped stage illuminated with LED light strips sat in the middle of the room surrounded by at least a dozen chairs filled with energetic patrons. A few stood from their seats throwing money onto the stage as a thick red bone slid headfirst down one of the poles. Another pole on the opposite side of the stage was occupied by a petite dark skin woman with the biggest set of tits I'd seen on someone her size. Balancing her weight on her hands she flipped upside down and rested her ass against the pole. Slowly she spread her legs open seductively until they resembled the letter V, giving those up front an up-close view of her pantyless crotch.

Slowly shifting my eyes past the stage, I noticed a bar on the other side. It started at the front of the stage and stretched past it, wrapping around toward the back of the club. There were no chairs aligning the extended strip, just a plethora of energetic customers waiting to be served. A sheer purple curtain covering an all-black wall draped down on either side of multiple shelves containing neatly stacked bottles of liquor. A neon purple sign with the word Vixens flashing from it sat perched up on the top shelf. The barmaids wore short black skirts paired with purple cropped tops with Vixen written across them in black glitter. The décor was nice, the entire room was decorated in black and various shades of purple. Several purple disco balls hung from the ceiling in various locations. The DJ booth was strategically positioned between the stage and the bar.

Pulled from my musing, we were greeted by an innocent looking light skin woman wearing nothing but a thong and a pair of high heels. She seductively swept her eyes over every male in our group before escorting us to two private tables in the section labeled VIP. A bucket of ice sat on top of each table, one contained Rémy Martin 1738 and the other Patron. Mixers sat beside each bucket in tall clear containers.

Turning to look at the twins I felt my brows hiking toward my hairline. "Let me find out y'all got pull," I yelled over the music.

Pulling the Patron from one of the buckets Royce smiled at me. "Stop playin bro. You know we do," he boasted playfully.

Ryker patted his brother on the back and stepped next to me. "Gotta love his arrogantly humble ass," he said through a chuckle. "No but for real, we have a lot of connects since we host a lot of parties. We rarely pay to play anymore."

"That's dope as fuck," Brayden stated, from the other side of Ryker.

"Yep, so drink up. Let's have some fun," Ryker commanded, while looking at Brayden then shifting his eyes in my direction.

"Nuff said," I responded, clasping his shoulder and walking over to the booth with the Rémy on the table in front of it.

Plopping down on the cushy sofa I leaned forward and plucked the bottle from the bucket. I peeled off the protective seal and popped the cork out of the bottle before placing it back on the table. I slid a glass to the edge of the table when I felt someone bump my arm. Sweeping my eyes upward I found the innocent looking woman who directed us to our section staring down at me while gyrating her hips to the beat of the music. I removed my arm from the glass and fell back into the base of the couch, watching her sway her tiny hips. With a lascivious grin crest upon her otherwise sweet looking face she pinned me with her colored eyes as she continued to dance provocatively next to me.

The DJ slowly faded out the fast track and blended in a slow tone. She caressed her small breast as she padded in between my legs and lowered herself onto my lap. Grinding against my dick she dipped her head, lowering it to her feet. As the hook to "Motivation" by Kelly Rowland dropped, she slowly lifted her torso. Arching her back, she placed her head on my shoulder and continued to wind her hips against me. Out the corner of my eye I saw Rocky watching me, a sly grin donned her beautiful face. Shifting my attention back to the woman in my lap I reached into my pocket and pulled out a wad of ones. I placed a few inside her G-string while rubbing my hands along her hips. Strategically she rotated in my lap, now facing me she placed her small mounds in my face. For some reason that shit tickled me, a deep chortled escaped from my lips as I tossed a couple more dollars in the air. The song ended and so did my lap dance. Scooping the dollars off the floor she winked at me before strolling off.

Resuming my original task, I hurriedly poured myself a drink when Rocky dropped down next to me.

"You enjoy that?" she asked, licking her painted lips.

I chugged back the shot I poured and stared at her. "It was coo."

Rocky chuckled. "Well the next lap dance I send you will include me," she stated, popping up from the sofa just as quickly as she sat down.

I opened my mouth to respond but she was already walking away, heading back to the other sofa where Carmen and Ryker's shorty were sitting.

I poured myself another shot and quickly gulped it down then fixed myself a mixed cocktail. I was definitely in need of a buzz to take the edge off. Snatching the bottle out my hand Jamison sat down next to me. I acknowledged his presence with a simple head nod while sipping from my drink. About an hour into our arrival I had succeeded in obtaining a buzz. Between the shots, lap dances, and Rocky's words playing over in my head I happily welcomed my semi-inebriated state. Hell, one more drink and I would definitely be drunk. Looking around our section I noticed the girls were missing.

I turned toward Royce who was now sitting where Jamison had been. "Aye, where are the girls?"

Looking at me over the top of his glass he smiled and pointed to the stage. I followed the direction of hand, shifting my eyes through the crowd of people gathered around the stage. It took me a few minutes, but I spotted them, rather her. Standing in front of a short stalky man Rocky threw dollars onto the stage as a thick ass chocolate sistah twerked her ass practically in her face. Carmen and Ryker's shorty stood on either side of her. Carmen picked up a few of Rocky's dollars from the floor of the stage and slapped them on the girl's jiggling cheeks. Darting my eyes from one end of the stage to the other I looked for the rest of the gang. Ryker stood behind the chairs lining the stage talking to one of the dancers while periodically sweeping his head in the direction of the girls. I knew his ass wouldn't be too far behind them.

"And where is J and Bray," I asked, picking up a fresh water bottle from the table.

A tall ass caramel skin dancer sashayed over to Royce and me, dropping down to her haunches in between us she rested her small hands on Royce's thighs. With hooded eyes he stared down at her, completely ignoring my question. With my eyes glued on the half-naked cutie gyrating in between Royce's legs I elbowed him.

"Huh? Oh, they thirsty asses went to the back with two dancers." His eyes never left the dancer as he grabbed the woman's wrist and pulled her into his lap.

Placing the bottled water back on the table I stood up from the couch and shook my head as I walked toward the exit of VIP. I made my way down the short row of stairs and maneuvered through the crowd, bogarting my way to the stage. I stood a few people back from the girls, but kept my eyes glued to Rocky. I watched as she swayed her hips to the up tempo beat while laughing with Carmen and Simone. Yep, I had figured out that was her name a little after we arrived.

The dude that was standing behind Rocky slowly pressed up against her, attempting to catch her rhythm. Sliding out of his path Rocky continued to dance as one of the chicks exiting the stage joined her and danced in front of her. Rocky laughed and danced while placing ones inside the woman's loose G-string. Not taking the hint dude moved behind Rocky again and pressed his body against her. This time he grabbed her by the hips, locking her in place as she tried to dance out of his hold. I had seen enough, shuffling through the few people in front of me I walked up behind Mr. Grab Ass and clutched him by the shoulder. An agitated look was fixed on his face as he turned around to face me.

"My man she's with me," I stated, loud enough for him to hear me over the music.

He swept his beady eyes up and down my body and chuckled. I stepped closer into his personal space when out of nowhere Ryker jumped in between us. Leaning into dude he whispered something in his ear. Dude threw his hands in the air and slowly backed away from us.

Shaking his head Ryker darted his eyes between Rocky, Carmen and Simone. "Alright, its back to VIP for y'all."

Without question the girls shifted through the crowd and made their way back to our section.

I turned and looked at Ryker. "You know I could've handled that right?"

He snickered and clasped me on the shoulder. "Yeah I know but your way would've got us kicked out" he stated, while guiding me out of the crowd.

Back in the VIP I sat down on the couch next to Rocky. Looking at me out of the corner of her eye she slowly allowed her head to follow. Her slanted eyes were low and glassy, triggering a sly smirk to spread across my face.

"You drunk Short Stuff?"

"Yep and lucky for you that means I don't give a shit about my brothers right now. You ready for our lap dance?"

Before I could answer she hopped off the couch excitedly, almost stumbling over the table in front of us. I attempted to snatch her by the wrist, but my reflexes were off thanks to the liquor streaming through my system. Taking a few steps forward Rocky turned and looked at me over her shoulder. Her eyes were low, and a coquette grin donned her beautiful face. Due to my inebriated state I was still sprawled across the sofa, laid on my side with my elbow propped on the soft cushions and my head resting on top of it. Unable to stop whatever Rocky had planned for us I remained slumped over as I followed her with my eyes. Paying a quick glance in Simone's direction Rocky winked at her then sauntered off. My eyes remained fixed on her, watching the sway of her hips with each step she took until she disappeared down the stairs. The ruffling of the cushion snatched my attention, alerting me that I was no longer alone on the couch. Pushing up off my elbow I sat upright and snaked my head to the right. Brayden sat a few inches away from me with a Kool-Aid size grin plastered on his face.

"What?"

"I ain't said shit," he answered, as his smile spread wider.

"Then why da fuck you starin at me like that?" I asked, reaching for my water bottle.

Taking a nip of his brew Brayden held the bottle stilled at his lips. His grin faded as he slowly withdrew the bottle from his mouth. "I'm just trynna figure out how long you and Rocky plan to keep up this lil charade."

I gulped down a hearty amount of the cold water before giving Brayden eye contact. "I got this."

"Yeah okay, but I don't think Ryker is buyin it," he stated, tossing his head in the direction of the other sofa.

Following his gaze, I turned to my left to find Ryker staring at me through squinted lids, a deep grimace was set on his face. *Shit!* I couldn't look away, I refused to look away. Lucky for me I didn't have to. As if she could sense the silent tension boiling between us Simone placed her small hand on the side of Ryker's face, gently tugging it toward her. Slowly the muscles in his face relaxed as his eyes settled on her. Stilled in place I watched the couple's interaction. Simone stroked his jawline while mouthing the words to the sexy up-tempo song blaring throughout the club. Listlessly she inched her face toward him, hovering her mouth over his lips. The corners of Ryker's lips curled upward as he placed a hand around her neck, pulling her into him, smashing their lips together. As if they were the only two people in the club they engaged in a passionate kiss. Suddenly I felt like a creep, like I was lurking on a moment that should've been private. Peeling my eyes away from them I sat back on the couch and gulped down the remainder of my water, crushing the empty bottle between my palm.

Leaning forward I tossed the distorted bottle on the table then placed my elbows on my knees and closed my eyes. I relaxed my shoulders while allowing my head to dip toward the floor. Humming along to T-Pain's "5 O'clock" I tried my best to shake off my shitty disposition when I sensed her. Instantly all the tension I was previously feeling melted away. Fluttering my lids open I swung my head up, swiveling it in the direction of the steps. Rocky sashayed up the stairs with two attractive half naked women trailing behind her. Engrossed in the beat of the music Rocky swayed in place as the woman directly behind her moved to her right, leaned into her, and whispered something in her ear. Slowly a coquettish grin settled on her face as she drew her bottom lip into her mouth. Then, two sets of eyes peered at me.

Placing a smile on my face I lazily swept my orbs down the mocha complexion woman standing next to Rocky. She stood an inch and a half taller but shared the same small waist, toned thighs, and voluminous ass. Ass that I was sure was medically enhanced. I trailed my eyes back up her body, taking in her perky breast covered by rhinestone pasties before settling on her pretty face. Big brown eyes continued to watch me while a salacious grin donned her thin lips. A silky straight weave extended down her back, just past her ass. Once again, my eyes shifted to her juicy backside then quickly rose up to her face. She held my gaze while grinding on Rocky. Giggling Rocky skirted her eyes over to her personal dancer and nodded her head.

She smacked Rocky on the ass then padded toward me seductively, leaving Rocky alone with the other dancer who followed behind the two of them. With one eye trained on the woman gaiting my way I watched Rocky with the other. Perched on her tippy toes she leaned into the tall light skin woman with huge breast and a small ass, speaking in her ear they both slid their eyes in the direction of Ryker and Simone. The fair skin woman licked her full lips while placing her hands inside the waist of her thong as she sauntered toward the couple.

This is going to be interesting.

Her soft hand grazed the hairs on my chin, gently stroking my goatee. She waited until she had my full attention then stood to her feet. Pivoting in her heels she spun around and peeked at me over her shoulder. Slowly she wound her hips down to my lap, making it her resting place. I stuffed a hand inside the pocket of my jeans and snatched out a wad of bills, sprinkling ones down her torso. Moving against my crouch she extended her arm out in front of her face and wagged her middle and index fingers at Rocky. Her slanted eyes were unusually low, bouncing between me and the ebony woman gyrating in between my legs. Placing one foot in front of the other she took slow measured steps as she sauntered toward us. Once again, I found myself juggling where to settle my eyes. Mesmerized by Rocky I paid her one long glance before giving my attention to the woman in my lap.

Swaying with the beat of the music my eyes slid down to the mocha dancer's rotating hips. With her hands positioned on my knees she dipped her head toward the floor while arching her back and hurling her ass up near my face. She continued to move rhythmically, snaking her torso until she was standing upright. She shifted from in between my legs and took the few steps to reach Rocky, grabbing her by the wrist she pulled Rocky into her small frame. Twirling Rocky in her arms she spun her toward me and gingerly placed her in my lap. I wrapped my arms around her tiny waist, pulling her closer to me I nuzzled my face in the crook of her neck. Rocky snickered on top of me as the chocolate woman danced provocatively in front of us.

The music lowered, and the DJ's voice came booming through the speakers. "Y'all havin a good time tonight?"

The crowd roared. Hands shot up in the air and applause could be heard over the lowered music.

"Make sure to tip yo servers, bartenders, and especially the dancers."

A light I hadn't noticed previously began to shuffle to various parts of the club, stopping at our section in VIP.

"As usually I see it's goin down in VIP. I see you Onyx. Show them why they call you the queen of the stage baby," the DJ goaded.

Winding her hips, Onyx brought her hands up to her breast and cupped her perky mounds. She removed the pasties hiding her nipples and tossed them on the floor behind her. Stepping forward she placed her hands on Rocky's knees and gently spread them apart, subsequently causing my legs to stretch along with hers. Onyx leaned forward dipping into Rocky's body then stood to her feet in between our legs. In one swift motion she spun around and bent over, placing her hands inside her thong she slid them down her legs and stepped out the flimsy undergarment. Completely bare and exposed to us she jiggled each cheek in accordance to the beat of the music. Rocky giggled as she brought a hand up to Onyx's ass and slapped her cheeks.

"Alright, I need to see some money flyin," the DJ announced, before returning the music to its earsplitting volume.

Slowly the spotlight faded, granting us the illusion of privacy under the dim lights illuminating throughout VIP. Reaching into her clutch Rocky pulled out a stack of ones, pouring a few loose bills over Onyx's bouncing romp. Backing up Onyx glanced over her shoulder as she parked her ass on Rocky's lap. She leaned back and raised her arms, resting her smalls hands on my shoulders. Strategically she hiked her right leg then her left, extending them into the air while grinding her hips as she stretched her legs open, simulating the letter V. Rocky's left hand rested around Onyx's petite waist while her right reached off to the side in search of mine. Finding my closed fist draped lazily on the couch she pried it open and placed it on Onyx's leg. With her hand on top of mine Rocky drug it from Onyx's calf back toward her ass.

What the da is happenin right now? Am I the only person seein this shit?

Through squinted lids I scanned our section in search of the people we came with, hoping they were too enthralled in their own fun to notice the shenanigans going on between Rocky and I. Jamison and Brayden were nowhere to be found. Royce and Carmen stood in front of the railing separating VIP from the rest of the club. Their attention was directed toward the stage. Shifting my eyes to the left I noticed Ryker and Simone engaged in their own private lap dance. Slowly I turned my attention back to the women in my lap but not before I noticed Ryker's side-eye sneer. I blew out an exasperated breath.

Fuck it, if I was gonna go toe to toe wit one of my best friends I might as well make it worth my while.

Onyx carefully removed her legs from the air and flung her body forward, sliding her hand off my shoulder she placed them on the floor and her ass took the place of her previously outstretched limbs. Rocky tossed dollars in the air as Onyx's cheeks bounced wildly to the music.

Imitating Rocky's prior move I took her free hand and placed it on Onyx's ass. Another round of giggles spilled from her mouth as Rocky repeatedly swatted Onyx on her backside while I slapped money on the opposite cheek. Suddenly without warning Onyx kicked her leg out in front of her and slid down into a split, bouncing repeatedly.

Impressed, Rocky hopped off my lap and tossed a handful of dollars over Onyx, giving the illusion of money raining from the sky. "Aye, aye, aye," she chanted playfully.

Onyx dipped, twirled, and twerked her ass off until the DJ switched songs. The entire time Rocky sprinkled her with ones until her hands were empty. I wasn't sure who was enjoying themselves more, me or her. Honestly it didn't matter because there was something erotic as fuck about watching two beautiful women with one another even if it was PG-13. *And for everyone's sake it better stay that way.* Erotic or not, I wasn't willing to share Rocky with anyone, man or woman. The loud uproar from the club snatched me out of my head as the DJ played the latest release by Atlanta's own, Truth. He blended the up-tempo track into a mini mix of songs by some of Atlanta's popular artists. The dancers went crazy, performing their most exotic moves as T.I, Young Jeezy, Outkast, Ludacris and Young Dro boomed through the speakers.

I leaned forward in my seat and fixed my eyes on the woman who consumed my every waking thought. I watched Onyx slowly turn and face Rocky, placing a hand on her hip she pulled Rocky toward her. I continued to study the pair, observing their interaction with one another like they were old friends. Taking note of my perusal, a sly grin stretched across Onyx's face as she gazed at me over Rocky's shoulder. She placed her crimson stained lips next to Rocky's ear while I concentrated on her mouth, trying to decipher her words. Rocky's dimples dipped into her cheeks as she shook her head. Pivoting on her heels Rocky turned in my direction. Two sets of hooded eyes stared at me, concupiscence oozing from their cores. Hit with a sudden feeling of déjá vu I held their gaze, uncertain of what to do.

"Thirty minutes until last call. So, get yo wallets out and make it rain in this bitch," the DJ announced, animatedly as T-Pain's "I'm N Luv" started playing.

Rocky peeked over her shoulder and tilted her head toward the ceiling. Onyx placed her hands around Rocky's waist, speaking into her ear again. *What the fuck are these two up to?* Rocky slid her head forward, her slanted brown orbs landed on me again. Placing her small hand on my shoulder she timidly hoisted a leg up on the couch. Instinctively my eyes shot over to her leg then quickly returned to her face. Onyx smirked, I assumed at the confused expression fixed on my face. Placing her other foot on the sofa Rocky carefully stepped behind me and hoisted herself up on the back of the couch, her short legs dangled on the side of my arms.

Onyx rocked her hips from side to side while her eyes bounced between me and the woman sitting above my head. I felt her small hands on my shoulders, tugging me backward. Giving in to her unspoken request I allowed my back to rest against the cushions, anxiously waiting for what was about to happen next. I angled my head upward and stared into her beautiful face. With her eyes trained forward she smiled at Onyx while bringing a hand up to my face, gently stroking me along my jawline. Then out of nowhere she bent down and brushed her lips against mine. Before I could register what was happening, she removed her mouth from my lips and placed them next to my ear.

"Stop thinkin so hard, and just enjoy the show." Her voice was low, her words steady but there was no hiding the alacrity hidden behind her smirk.

I swept my eyes down her legs then shifted them to my left. Relief washed over me when my eyes landed on the back of Ryker's head. Blowing out a gush of air I relaxed my shoulders and slid my eyes forward. Rocky removed her hand from my face and sat upright. Onyx winked, I wasn't sure if it was at me or Rocky but before I had time to figure it out, she was on me. Her perky breast jiggled in my face as she twirled her hips against my cock. Ones rained down from over top of us. Cupping her swollen mounds Onyx stroked her nipples with her thumbs then brushed them across my face. An uninhibited groan escaped from my parted lips. Gripping a handful of Onyx's ass, I allowed my shoulders to sink back into the cushions of the couch. Onxy melted against me as she continued winding her hips.

Her minty breath filled my nostrils stealing my attention away from the woman on my lap. "Ride that shit sexy," she breathed out throatily, tossing more ones down Onyx's body.

Onyx's hips seem to take on a life of their own as she gyrated wildly on top of me. Suddenly remembering I still had a stack of ones in my pocket, I reached my hand inside and yanked out the wad of bills. Onyx slowly disconnected her torso from mine, placed her hands on my chest and advertently lowered her back to my knees.

Damn, this chick is flexible as hell.

"Alright it's that time, it's last call and this is the last song. I wanna see asses bouncin, titties jigglin, and money fallin from the mutha-fuckin sky. Ladies get em up so these niggas can go home and let they misses put em down. Let's geaux."

The bass reverberated through the walls making the floors shake as Waka Flocka Flame's "No Hands" streamed throughout the club. Lowering her arms to the floor Onyx planted her hands firmly on the soiled carpet and hoisted her legs in the air. Slowly she spread her legs open while rhythmically grinding her hips. Taking a few of the ones from my right hand I swiped them over her breast, drug them down her flat stomach and rested them between her open legs. Once again, Rocky's little hands were on my shoulder while her head rested next to my face. Onyx put on a hell of a show, twirling her hips, bouncing her ass, opening and closing her outstretched legs.

At one point she pulled one hand off the floor and swatted her crotch repeatedly while I continued to toss and place dollars all over her grinding frame. Placing her hand back on the floor Onyx scooted closer to my dick, raised each leg one at a time and placed them over my shoulder, pumping her bare vagina close to my face. Rocky removed a hand from my shoulder and rained money down Onyx's body while chanting and cheering her on excitedly. Carefully lowering her legs from my shoulders Onyx clutched her legs together and snaked them from side to side before flinging them open again forming another perfect V.

Rocky ran her soft hand down my arm and lifted it from my side, placing a few dollars in my palm she sat it directly on Onyx's exposed crotch. "Her shit pretty but mine is better." She ran her tongue across my lobe then threw the remaining dollars from her tiny hand into the air.

Her lecherous words, the naked woman on my lap, the alcohol coursing through my system, combined with her close proximity sent blood flowing straight to my dick. I mulled over her words and wondered if she was referring to Onyx's vagina or her piercing, either way I couldn't wait for the day she finally let me find out. Pulling her legs out of the air Onyx wrapped them around my waist and raised herself off her back. Her low eyes bounced between me and the woman draped over my shoulder. Slowly she untangled her frame from mine and stood to her feet just as the music cut and bright lights illuminated throughout the entire club.

"Y'all sexy as fuck. Thank you for choosin me to dance for y'all," she stated, eyes locked on Rocky.

Seeing Onyx clearly underneath the bright lights it was evident why Rocky had chosen her. Not only did they share similar body frames and cocoa colored skin, but they actually resembled one another. A sly grin eased on my face at that revelation as I shifted my head to the side, catching the wide grin crest on Rocky's face.

"Thank you. We had fun and you did the damn thing," Rocky responded, lifting her head and shuffling behind me.

Onyx dropped down on her haunches and went to work gathering all of her tips. She used her hands and feet to sweep the loose bills into a big pile. Stuffing the last of her money into a second trash bag given to her by a security guard I hadn't noticed until now, Onyx stood to her feet. Using my shoulders as an anchor Rocky moved from behind me, climbed down from the couch, and stood next to me. Unhurriedly I peeled myself off the sofa and inconspicuously adjusted my inflated manhood.

Picking up her two bags full of money Onyx stood to her feet and walked over to us. "If y'all ever wanna add more chocolate . . ." her small eyes swept down Rocky's body then skirted over to me. She stared me dead in the eyes as she produced a card from out of thin air and extended it toward Rocky, "in the bedroom please don't hesitate to call." She continued to stare at me for a few more moments then drew her full lips into her mouth, pivoted on her heels, and walked away.

I turned my head toward Rocky and hiked a brow. "Did she just—"

Smirking Rocky shook her head and tossed the card to the table in front of us.

Wow!!!

I looked down at the small black card decorated with shimmery gold letters and mimicked Rocky, a lecherous smirk donned my face as I shook my head. Rocky's hand brushed against mine, snatching my attention away from the table.

"Aye, y'all ready?" Royce asked, walking over to us.

Intertwining her fingers with mine Rocky locked eyes with Royce. "Yep, let's go."

Royce's eyes slid down to our conjoined hands then skirted back up to his sister's face. A knowing smirk etched across his face as he turned and walked toward the rest of the group, gathered by the steps of VIP. Rocky moved first, prompting me to walk next to her as she led us over to everyone else. As we neared the group Rocky discreetly disconnected her hand from mine.

"Man, tonight was epic," Carmen declared out loud to no one in particular.

Ryker brushed his hand down his face while turning to face a blushing Simone. "Fuck yeah, definitely wasn't expectin it to go down like it did," he agreed, while pulling Simone into his lanky frame.

We filed out of VIP and quickly made our way out the door. The women stayed back while the men walked to retrieve the truck. Jamison and Royce shared stories while Ryker and I listened, laughing at their animated hand gestures and boisterous banter. Noticing Brayden was missing I tapped Ryker on the arm.

"Where's Bray?"

Ryker chuckled. "Do you even have to ask? Dude went home with one of the dancers."

The entire group burst out laughing. Talking shit about Bray's playboy antics we continued our walk. Ten short steps later we were at the truck piling inside before driving back to the door and picking up the ladies. The drive back to the twins' was a quiet one as sleepiness settled upon us.

Simone pulled into the driveway and cut the engine. Silently we all climbed out and headed to the house. Inside everyone disbursed to various parts of the house. Rocky, Carmen, Jamison and I found our way into the living room, dumping our fatigue bodies on the furniture. Royce and Ryker headed straight to their rooms. Minutes later Ryker entered the living room, tossed Rocky his keys and left back out with Simone.

Slowly peeling her body from the couch Rocky tapped Carmen on her way up. "C'mon Carm."

Carmen lifted her face out of her phone as she stood from the couch and followed Rocky out the room.

"Goodnight fellas. See y'all tomorrow," Rocky called out from the hallway.

Jamison took their exit as his cue. Standing up he looked over at me. "I'm going to bed. You sleepin down here again?"

Too tired to reply I shook my head.

Jamison ambled out the room leaving me alone with my thoughts. I lifted my tired frame from the chair and kicked off my shoes then trekked over to the couch. Plopping down on the soft cushions I stuffed my hand in the pocket of my jeans and pulled out my phone. There was a text notification from Rocky. Instantly I unlocked my phone and waited for the phone to open. The small screen lit up and I quickly clicked on my text app.

Rocky: Carmen got action. U trynna come lay with me.

Bending over I stretched out my arm and slid my shoes in front of me. I quickly stuffed my feet back in my shoes and peeled my ass off the couch. I dashed down the hall toward the stairs, taking the steps two at a time I hit the second floor in no time. I sprinted down the dark hallway and strolled into Royce's room, snatching my duffle bag off the floor I exited just as quickly as I entered. I made my way back downstairs and proceeded out the door. As I walked down the driveway I responded to Rocky's text.

Me: OMW.

I was tired as hell but there was no way I was passing on an opportunity to lay with Rocky. Besides I'd take a soft bed over a couch any day. Scrolling through my message thread I clicked on Jamison's name and added Royce's to the address bar. I shot them a quick text, letting them know I was leaving and would be back in the morning. Comfortable that my buzz had wane I hopped inside the truck, started the engine and backed out the driveway. Instantly thoughts from earlier tonight came crashing to the forefront of my mind. I couldn't help the face splitting grin stretched across my face as I replayed the erotic events over and over in my head. Fifteen minutes later I was parked outside of Rocky's hotel. Pulling my phone out of the cupholder I sent her a text.

Me: I'm downstairs. What's your room number.

Before I could pull the keys out of the ignition she responded.

Rocky: 369. The latch is holding the door open, just come in.

CHAPTER TEN

J sat my glass of wine down on the patio table and shook my head to myself. *I can't believe I let Carmen talk me into this shit.* Our old asses had no business going to anybody's mid-semester icebreaker. But here I was sitting out on my patio stalling for time before the girls got here to pre-game. Once again, I fell victim to my best friend's persistent coaxing. And poor Egypt, she'd do anything we asked her to do as long as we were doing it together. I swear that girl would walk into a cage full of hungry pit bulls wearing a suit made of meat if Carm and I were right by her side. We'd do the same for her ass but trust and believe there would be a lot of cussing and fussing. A giggle slipped from between my pursed lips just picturing the shit.

The crazy part was I knew Egypt's little ass would've much rather spent her Friday evening in her apartment binge watching one of those ratchet ass reality shows she was addicted to. But I also knew she was salty as hell she missed the ATL trip and was excited to kick it with us this weekend. *I guess I have one more turnup in me before classes really get into the full swing of things.* Not to mention, there was really no comparison. Reality TV vs icebreaker.

I swear for the life of me I couldn't understand how grown ass women went on national TV and made a complete ass out of themselves for a man and a check. Let's not forget the check. Now days people did anything for a dollar, but my mama always told me, all money ain't good money. Besides, I ain't rode a dick yet that would allow me to push my morals, values, and pride to the side while chasing behind a cheating ass man on national TV all for 15 minutes of fame and a few coins. Unfortunately, I had definitely played myself a time or two for the wrong man, but I learned quick and moved the fuck on. Let Dre tell it, I was a brat and brats didn't do too well with sharing. My phone buzzed on the patio table temporarily quieting my music and pulling me from my musing.

Bestie1: We otw bitch. Be ready!!!!

Me: Yeah okay <rolling eye emoji> I know what you're on the way means <rolling eye emoji>.

Bestie1: Whatever, just be ready b/c we finna turn da fuck up.

I didn't waste my time responding to Carmen's message. Instead I picked my glass up from the table and walked inside my apartment with Creed trailing behind me. Securing the lock on the patio door I walked into the living room and sat my empty glass on the coffee table then headed straight for the bathroom. Dumping my robe on the floor as soon as I entered, I placed my phone on the bathroom counter and started bobbing my head as music boomed from the speaker. I stared at my reflection in the mirror before quickly pulling my hair out of the bun that was on top of my head and running my fingers through it. I checked for tangles or matted pieces as my fingers glided over my loose tresses. Grateful that I didn't have to add detangling to my process I reached underneath the sink and pulled out my tub of coconut oil. I wasted no time rubbing the light oil throughout my curly mane. Satisfied with my curls I placed the coconut oil back underneath the sink and pulled out a bottle of styling gel. I applied a small amount to my edges and smoothed them out. Tonight, I was rocking my natural curls in a wild curly afro.

Shit! I need to get a move on it.

I stared at myself in the mirror again but this time my focus was my face. Earlier after I let Carmen convince me to attend this damn party, I took a shower and attempted to beat my face. I wanted to get a jumpstart on my makeup in case I needed to apply it more than once. Looking at myself now I must admit, I was pretty impressed, considering I was a novice when it came to the makeup game. Hmph. I managed to successful create a sexy smoky eye without making myself look like a freaking clown.

Happy with what I saw I decided to add the finishing touches. I applied my favorite mascara, *better than sex* before adding my new Marc Jacobs eyeliner gifted to me by Carmen. When I was finished, I tossed both container on the counter and gave myself another onceover in the mirror. I contemplated what color lipstick I wanted to wear. Before I could settle on a color, I heard a knock on my door. Immediately Creed started barking and took off toward the door. I paused the music on my cellphone and exited the bathroom, following behind my over-protective pocket size bully I headed to my front door.

Without asking who was at the door I flung it open. "It's about damn time."

"Shit!!!"

Immediately I turned on my heels followed by Creed and proceeded to walk away from the door. I left my girls and unexpected guests outside. As I was walking down the hall toward my bedroom, I heard the door close and his deep raspy baritone.

"What da fuck Raquel?"

I walked into my bedroom and closed the door but not before Carmen came bursting in practically screaming her apologies.

"OH! MY! GOD! I'm so sorry Rocky. I had no idea you wouldn't be dressed. I texted and told you we were on the way."

I continued toward my bed picking up my True Religion distressed denim jean shorts that I placed there after my shower earlier. I shimmied my way into the tight-fitting shorts as Carmen continued rambling. I turned toward her when I realized she had stopped yelling.

"It's cool boo, no worries."

I turned back toward the bed, picking up my denim deep v-neck top I contemplated the best way to put it on. I decided to step into it rather then pull it over my head when I realized Carmen hadn't said a single word since I let her off the hook. Leisurely I turned toward Carmen to find her looking at me like I had three heads.

"What?" I couldn't help the smirk on my face.

Suddenly the look on Carmen's face transformed from shock to amusement. She slowly and deliberately looked at my head as she scanned down to my toes before returning her eyes to mine.

"Bitch, you think you slick. You wanted Dre to catch that ass half naked. No wonder you ain't pissed. Got me in here apologizin like you my damn mama and your hot ass planned that shit." Carmen smirked while shaking her head at me.

I looked at her like I was offended or at least that's what I was attempting before my eyes landed back on hers. Simultaneously, we burst out in a fit of laughter.

Coming down from my laughing fit I addressed my bestie. "Carm I had no idea Dre and Jamison were with you and E. I don't have a peep-hole, remember? Besides, why would I want Dre to see me naked?" I attempted to sound serious as hell asking that last question. I waited for Carmen to answer and when she didn't, I continued.

"I keep tellin yo lil nasty ass Dre and I are just friends."

"Y'all looked like more than friends at Vixens," she declared, with her hands planted on her hips.

I rolled my eyes at her, refusing to acknowledge her claim.

Undeterred by my lack of a response Carmen removed her hands from her hips and tossed them in the air. "But why, why can't y'all be more than friends?" she whined.

I sucked my teeth and attempted another angel at this redundant conversation. "C'mon Carm, Dre is barely twenty-two."

Carmen smacked her lips while rolling her eyes at me "So."

"So? Carmen I'm almost thirty—"

Carmen cut me off. "Bitch twenty-seven is not almost thirty. Besides Raquel, the last time I checked twenty-two was grown."

"Barely. I mean dude has only been allowed to legally drink for a year." I laughed at my own joke. "Wait, you used my government. You're serious huh?"

Carmen flicked me off.

Going back to my original argument I told Carmen for what felt like the hundredth time the main reason I couldn't go there with Dre. "Dre is the twins' boy, like their day one. Even you have to admit it could get messy. You know I don't do messy."

Carmen looked me in the eyes. "Your ass don't do relationships, but I digress. Seriously Rocky, what if it is great, like what if y'all got married great?"

I waved a hand in Carmen's direction. "Girl bye. That sounds like some shit Egypt would say. If my ass don't do relationships you know I definitely won't be doin marriage so you can miss me with that bullshit." Changing the subject all together I asked, "Where the hell is E anyway? I thought she would've been right behind you chastisin me for openin the door half naked and shit."

"You know good and well little Miss Hospitality wasn't gonna leave guest unattended."

I nodded my head in agreement and walked into my closet. I yelled out, "And it doesn't hurt that Jamison happens to be one of those guests." I exited the closet with a pair of peep toe booties and a bomber jacket in hand.

Carmen giggled as we exited my bedroom and joined Egypt, Jamison and Dre in the living room.

"Creed, down. Dre what did I tell yo ass about lettin him sit in your lap on the furniture when he's dirty?" I asked, lightly slapping him on the back of his head while dropping my shoes on the floor then draping my jacket on the back of his chair.

Creed hopped out of Dre's lap as he jumped up out of his seat. Smacking me on the ass Dre pulled me into his lap while descending back into his chair. "Don't get fucked up in front of yo girls. I should be on yo ass for answerin the door wit no damn clothes on. You lucky J didn't see you or we'd be beefin right now," he whispered in my ear.

I adjusted myself on his lap, moving my ass from his junk I sat on one of his massive thighs. I nudged him with my left elbow while taking his glass out of his hand with my right. Taking a swig of the dark cocktail I looked up to find the entire room staring at us. Ignoring them I turned to face Dre, placing my mouth next to his ear.

"Um, it looks like we have an audience."

Dre licked his lips and I could smell the cognac mixed with spearmint on his breath. I swiveled my head back toward our friends when I felt the vibration from Dre's chest as he addressed them.

"Y'all keep starin at us and we gonna give y'all a fuckin show."

Carmen's nasty ass moved her butt to the edge of the couch, placed her elbows on her knees, and looked between me and Dre. "Oh! Please do. I bet it will be better than the one that dancer gave y'all at Vixens."

"Carm," Egypt yelled in shock. Although I'm not sure why the shit that came out of my or Carmen's mouth still surprised her.

Jamison's goofy ass didn't make it any better. Egypt's eyes damn near bugged out of her head when he moved from his chair, walked over to us and placed a Magnum in the palm of Dre's hand.

Carmen shrieked, "Fuck yeah, that's what I'm talkin bout."

I heard Dre chuckle behind me as he tried to mask his amusement with a fake cough.

Egypt on the other hand was not amused. She looked at Jamison on his way back to his seat and rolled her eyes. "Did you just give him a condom?"

Jamison responded with a simple head nod and a face splitting smile on his chocolate face.

"Clearly, I missed somethin, or I haven't been drinking enough." Egypt's tone matched the shitty look splayed across her pretty face.

Ignoring all their ignorant asses, I tossed back the last of Dre's drink and removed myself from his lap.

Turning to face him I held the empty glass out in front of my face. "What were you drinkin?"

Dre ran his tongue across his already moist lips. Leisurely he swept his eyes down my body before returning them to my face. "Rémy and coke."

I turned toward Egypt and waved my hand, requesting her to join me. "C'mon Boo let's get you on their level."

Egypt grimaced while standing to her feet. "I don't think you have enough liquor in your stash to help me achieve such crass and tacky ass behavior." She finished her statement with a deep eye roll as she followed me into the kitchen.

"Well excuse the fuck out of us for havin a sense of humor," Carmen shouted behind us.

In the kitchen, Egypt and I burst out laughing. Egypt's laughter died out before mine did. Calming myself I looked at my best friend, trying to decipher her mood. "You good Boo? You know Carmen and Jamison don't mean no harm."

Egypt looked me in the eyes then diverted her somber gaze toward her hands that were resting on the counter. "Yeah, I'm good Rocky. I think I'm a little tight because I haven't talked to Raheem since Wednesday and Jamison treats me like I'm his kid sister."

Now I was the one diverting my eyes as I looked in the cabinet for my shot glasses. Egypt caught it and called me on my shit. "Wait. Rocky what the fuck was that?"

I pretended not to know what she was talking about while I continued to stare into the cabinet. "What? I don't know what you're talking about."

Egypt wasn't going for my lackluster performance. "C'mon Rocky. Why'd you look away when I said Jamison treats me like his kid sister? Did Dre tell you somethin and you're not telling me?"

I had never been good at keeping shit from my friends but seeing the mood Egypt was in I wasn't sure how well she was going to take what I was about to say.

Fuck it, my intentions were good.

Looking Egypt directly in her eyes I blurted out my confession. "I threatened Jamison when you admitted to me you had a crush on him, and he started showing interest."

Egypt hopped off the stool she was sitting on and shouted at me. "You did what?"

Carmen came running in the kitchen, her eyes bouncing between me and Egypt. "What is goin on in here? Egypt why are you yellin?"

Egypt turned toward Carmen with a scowl set on her face. "Did you know?"

Carmen looked at me then directed her attention back to Egypt.

"Know what chica?" Her tone was soft but there was no hiding the concern in her voice.

I spoke before Carmen had a chance to answer. "No, E she didn't know. I didn't tell her because I didn't want to hear her mouth. Look E, I'm sorry if I overstepped but you know I'm very protective of you two. I be damned if—"

"You know what, it doesn't matter. Jamison is a grown ass man and if he let whatever you said to him stop him from pursuing me that's his loss." Egypt cut me off as she took her seat back on her stool and for the first time this evening she was smiling.

That was the thing about Egypt, she was so easy going. She was the only person I knew who could go from steaming to cool in less than a minute. She was definitely the calm one of our trio.

True to Carmen's nature her instigating ass turned to me and asked, "I'm glad you're good E, but Rocky what did you say to the boy?"

Smacking my lips, I looked at Carmen, ready to dead this conversation and get back to having fun. "I simply let Jamison know if he liked his dick as much as we all know he does he wouldn't stick it in my friend if he was gonna keep stickin it in every other chick on campus."

Egypt gasped, and Carmen burst out laughing just as Dre and Jamison walked into the kitchen. Two sets of suspicious eyes surveyed our group. After a few quiet minutes of trying to figure out what we were fussing about Jamison took a seat on the stool between Carmen and Egypt while Dre walked up and stood behind me. Reaching over my head he grabbed the shot glasses I was searching for earlier during my uncomfortable conversation with Egypt.

Dre placed a shot glass in front of each of us then looked between Carmen and Egypt. "What's your pleasure ladies. Light or dark?"

Carmen chimed in first. "Tito's for me please."

Dre waited for Egypt to reply. On cue, Egypt skirted her eyes over to me then back to Dre. "I'm drinking what Rocky is drinking tonight."

A deep chortle flew from Dre's mouth as he walked past me, strolling into my dining area to retrieve the alcohol requested by Carmen and Egypt. With bottles in hand he returned to the kitchen and sat the liquor on the counter. Feeling like we needed some music I headed out of the kitchen in search of my phone while Carmen and Egypt engaged in a petty debate over one of Egypt's ratchet ass shows. Completely engrossed in his phone Jamison appeared oblivious to it all. I shook my head to myself as I trekked down the hall toward my bedroom when I remembered I left my phone on the bathroom counter. Spinning on my heels I made a quick detour for the bathroom, snatching my phone off the counter I gaited back down the hall and sauntered into the kitchen.

I unlocked my phone to find Apple Music already opened on the small screen, pressing play I sat the phone on the counter while bobbing my head as Drake boomed through the speaker. My eyes shifted to the handsome man playing bartender. I watched while he poured Tito's in Carmen's shot glass, Patron in Jamison's and Rémy in his, mine and Egypt's. He then walked over to the fridge and took out two Coronas, three Redd's Apple Ale, and a small bottle containing lemon juice. Dre distributed the beers, squirted some lemon juice in his beer and passed Jamison the tiny bottle.

Watching Dre play bartender in my crib had my mind racing. Before I could stop myself, I was thinking about us and how quickly our friendship had taken a turn toward a situationship. No matter how hard I tried to fight it we always seemed to land right back there. Teetering the line between platonic friends and a damn couple.

Fuck! It seemed like I was battling the inevitable.

I attempted to dismiss those thoughts. Instead I made myself focus on the reasons or should I say the primary reason Dre and I shouldn't hookup. My brothers. The biggest reason I kept telling myself and Carmen that I'd never let things go there with Dre was and has always been his friendship with my brothers. Dre and the twins have known each other practically their entire life and I couldn't handle it if I was responsible for altering their friendship in any way. Lord knows I'd lost an associate or two over my hot in the pants brothers. Hell, I fought my college roommate in undergrad over their dumb asses. So, no Dre and I hooking up wasn't an option no matter how smart, charming, funny, and fine he was. And Dre's ass was definitely fine as hell.

Dre cleared his throat, snatching me out of my reverie. "So, we drinkin or what?"

Shaking the thoughts of a situationship with Dre from my mind I stepped up to the counter and took a swig of my beer. "Let's geaux."

First round of shots down and Dre refilled our glasses. I looked over at Egypt. "You good boo? You don't have to match us."

Egypt stuck her tongue out at me. "I'm good, we're not driving so f'it."

I chuckled at Egypt's use of proper grammar. "That's right E. Fuck it."

Picking up my glass I tossed back my second shot then slammed the tumbler on the counter and looked at Dre then shifted my eyes toward Jamison. "So, how'd y'all end up with my girls?"

Jamison looked over at Egypt then quickly dipped his eyes down to his hands.

"What da fuck was that J?"

Egypt squirmed in her chair, fiddling with her shot glass she refused to look at me.

"Y'all can't be serious right now. Somebody answer me," I shouted, louder than I intended.

Dre walked up behind me and placed his hands around my waist, pulling me back into his chest. "Chill Short Stuff. Does it really matter anyway?" he asked, with his lips pressed against my ear.

I stared at Egypt through slit lids then dragged my eyes over to Jamison. For the sake of not ruining everyone's fun, I opted to drop it for the time being.

"So, last shot for which one of y'all?" I asked, while nodding my head at Jamison then tilting it back to look up at Dre.

Jamison scrunched up his face. "What cha talkin bout Balboa?"

A goofy grin stretched across my face as my eyes simultaneously rolled up in my head at Jamison's new nickname for me. "Don't play wit me. I know Dre told you the rules when you pre-game at my house. Whoever is drivin has a two drink max. I'm lettin y'all slide since y'all threw in beers with these shots."

I spun around in Dre's arms and slowly backed out of his embrace.

Looking up into his eyes I started patting him down. Slowly I lowered my head and started with his back pockets. I took my time as my little hands stroked his ass and linger longer than needed. When I didn't find what I was looking for I took a step back and peered up at him only to find him staring down at me with his bottom lip tucked in between his teeth. I tilted my head to the side and allowed my brow to stretch toward my forehead. Slowly he released his lip and a sly grin settled on his face as he placed both his hands in the air like he was under arrest.

I resumed my search, bending down imperceptibly I placed my hands on each side of his left knee. Ploddingly I raised my hands until I reached the middle of his thigh. I dropped my right hand and resumed moving up his thigh until I reach his pocket. Again, I came up empty. Relentless in my pursuit, I placed my hands on each side of his right knee when he reached down and grabbed my left wrist, holding my hand in place. He then reached into his pocket and pulled out his keys. Smirking I stood upright, licked my lips and winked at him. He gazed down at me through hooded lids as he dropped his keys in my outstretched hand.

"That shit was sexy as fuck. Which one of y'all gonna frisk me like that for my keys?" Jamison asked, looking between Egypt and Carmen.

Carmen gave Jamison the bird. "Negro please, don't look at me."

Jamison turned to Egypt, "E?"

Egypt giggled, hopped off her bar stool, and stood in between Jamison's legs. "You know that ain't me Jamie and the fact that you didn't have a preference of who frisked you is the reason yo ass ain't gettin frisked. Now give me yo damn keys."

Damn, that brought the ghetto out of her ass real quick.

Everyone burst out laughing as Jamison reached into his pocket and yanked out his keys. Looking like a toddler being scolded by their parent, Jamison dumped his keys into Egypt's hand. With a warm smile plastered on her face she turned away from Jamison and walked over to me, grabbing Dre's keys out of my hand she quietly trekked out of the kitchen. With my eyes fixed on my best friend's back I recalled the night the three of us made the pact to never drink and drive.

It was our senior year of undergrad and we had just got back from a big campus party. We had been drinking all night and we weren't concerned with how we would get home since we walked to the party. However, once we reached our dorms, we realized we were starving. Two girls that we hung out with occasionally suggested going up the street for food. Not giving it much thought, we decided we would ride with them. As Trish and Tanika gathered a few orders from some of the other girls on our floor I noticed that the driver, Tanika kept stumbling and stuttering over her words. I asked if she was drunk and she got offended. We got into a mini argument which lead to us staying back in the dorms. Needless to say, we didn't get takeout that evening but neither did Tanika, Trish or the others they took orders for. Barely off the strip Trish and Tanika were in a serious car accident. Thankfully no one was critically injured, but that incident had a major impact on us. From that night forward, we vowed to never drink and drive or ride with anyone who was intoxicated. Typically, we rotated an assigned designated driver out of the three of us but on nights like tonight if we all decided to drink, we found safe alternative ways to and from our destination.

I was pulled back to the present by the sound of Egypt dropping both set of keys in the ceramic dish sitting on top of my wooden console next to the front door. I looked up as Egypt walked back into the kitchen with her phone in her hand.

"Are you fellas riding in the Uber with us or do y'all want y'all own?" Egypt asked, as she made her way back over to her stool.

And just like that lil Miss Proper was back.

Dre responded first, "Nah, we all ridin together."

I turned toward Dre who was sipping his beer and to my surprise, staring at me. Subconsciously, I ran my tongue across my lips and turned back around. "What time did you request the Uber?"

Egypt looked up from her beer. "Thirty minutes. Enough time for us to take a few more shots and freshen up our faces." Egypt looked at Dre. "Next round, bartender."

Thirty minutes later we were lapped up in the back of our Uber.

*T*he Icebreaker was packed, and the girls and I had a good ass time. I was glad I let Carmen talk me into going. However, standing outside waiting on our Uber all I could think about was taking a nice hot shower and diving in my bed. I looked over my shoulder and saw Carmen flirting with some dude she danced with earlier in the night. When she made eye contact with me, I mouthed, "Where's E?" Carmen pointed to her right and my eyes followed the direction of her hand. I spotted Egypt ducked off to the side a little further down from where Carmen and I are standing. Egypt had one hand covering her ear while the other held her cellphone which was placed on her other ear. I walked toward her to ask if she was okay when I heard her cussing at the person on the other end. I stopped a few feet from where she was standing to give her some privacy but at a distance where I could see her and Carmen. Since both my girls were occupied, I pulled out my phone and texted Dre.

Me: Hey, we left. Don't forget I have y'all keys. Call or text if you're going to come pick them up tonight.

I looked at my phone a few times to see if Dre responded but after the third time with no reply, I chucked it in my clutch and waved Egypt over when I saw our Uber had arrived. Egypt disconnected her call as she approached me. Not bothering to ask what that was about we strolled to the waiting car in complete silence. After we were settled inside, I looked over at a brooding Egypt. Baby girl was in her own world, clearly consumed in her own thoughts.

"Hey E, what's wrong? Who were you arguing with?"

Egypt rolled her eyes but not at me, more so at the answer she was about provide. "Girl, Raheem's lying ass."

My mouth formed an O and in my peripheral with the help from the streetlights shining in the car I saw Carmen roll her eyes. Deciding I was too tired to discuss Raheem I changed the subject.

"Sooooo Carm, did you give ol' boy your number?"

"Girl bye. I was only being nice because he insisted, he walk me out and wait with me for our Uber. I'm like damn dude it was just a few dances. I can't do these young dudes. They get sprung too easy. I don't know how you do it Rocky."

I chuckled. "First of all, y'all were definitely boo'd up like y'all were a couple or some shit. Second, y'all danced to more than. . ." I made air quotes with my index and middle fingers, "a few songs. So, don't act like you don't know why he was stalkin yo ass. And lastly, what the hell you mean you don't know how I do it? Girl that shit works for me because young dudes don't need, nor do they want a girlfriend. And since I have no interest in bein anybody's girlfriend it's a win win for all parties involved."

Carmen and I burst out laughing. When we calmed down Egypt looked at us solemnly. "I wish I could be carefree like y'all. I still believe in happily ever after. I just haven't found it or him yet. I could've sworn Raheem was different, but that nigga switched up on me after the fourth of July."

I hugged my best friend. She was inebriated but I knew she meant that shit. I also knew Raheem was the reason why she was no longer enjoying her buzz. Maybe I should've threatened his ass too but like E, I thought he was different. I released Egypt from my embrace and looked in her doleful eyes.

"It's gonna be okay E. Your Prince Charming is out there. He's just being prepared for you and all your greatness."

Egypt teared up. "Thanks Rocky." She looked between Carmen and me. "I love you ladies so much. I don't know what I would do without y'all."

I saw a tear fall down Egypt's cheek and it took the calm of the Lord to keep me from dialing Raheem's number myself and cussing his ass out. I used my thumb to swipe the tear from Egypt's face.

"E don't start that shit. Don't be the crybaby drunk. Besides, your ass is the reason we left early. So, don't try and turn this into a Waiting to Exhale moment. Bring back my turnup queen," I teased.

That got a laugh out of her and helped calm my surging temper.

Carmen cleared her throat. "Since we're talkin about men, Rocky you and Dre got a little um . . ." she dramatically cleared her throat again, "rated R. Hell, y'all damn near got X rated on the dance floor.

You might want to take a pregnancy test tomorrow to make sure that boy ain't get cha ass pregnant through your clothes the way y'all were bumpin and grindin."

I pushed Carmen on the shoulder and rolled my eyes. "Yeah, whatever. We only danced together on two songs. Plus, Dre was trynna turn me out when "Put It Down" came on and you know "Refill" is my shit."

Carmen laughed a high pitch hoot, causing Egypt and I to wince. "He was trynna put it down alright and you definitely looked like you wanted a refill of what he was servin."

The three of us laughed simultaneously as our Uber pulled into my apartment complex. After paying our driver we exited the car still giggling from Carmen's silly ass comment. Slowly we settled from our laughing spell as we gave each other hugs and said our goodbyes. I told them to text me when they got home then walked in my apartment with my shoes in my hand and immediately dropped them at the door. I damn near tripped over Creed's hefty ass trying to close the door. Creed raised his head off the carpet and sluggishly moved out of my way. I managed to close the door behind myself then locked both locks. Feeling relieved to be home I bent down to greet my fury friend, rubbing the top of his head until he jumped up on my thighs. After giving him the attention, he was craving I stood upright and walked into the living room, tossing my clutch on the coffee table I removed my jacket and heaved it onto the chair. On shaky and tired limbs, I walked over to my patio and unlocked the door, pushing it open I watched as Creed trotted outside. After Creed handled his business, I called him back into the apartment, locked the door behind us, and headed down the hall to my bedroom.

Stripping out of my clothes I threw them on the floor in my closet and walked back into the living room. I picked up my clutch and dug out my phone then dropped my purse back on the table. *Damn, I'm tired.* I walked out the living room and headed straight for my bathroom. Flicking on the light I ambled over to the shower and turned on the water. I had a few minutes before the water heated up so I closed the shower curtain and glanced at the toilet, checking to make sure the seat was down. I plopped down on the cold porcelain top and unlocked my phone, clicking on my text app I scrolled down looking for any messages from Dre, still nothing.

A hard gush of air passed through my lips as I sat my phone on the counter and hopped off the toilet. Stepping over to the mirror I pulled my wild mane into a messy bun on top of my head and threw on a shower cap. Studying my reflection in the mirror I made sure all parts of my hair were covered before plucking my toothbrush and toothpaste from the sink. I took my time cleaning my teeth. The entire time my eyes bounced between the mirror and my phone resting on the counter beside me. I felt thirsty as hell. I was really pressed for Dre to text. I tried not to think about it as I reached underneath my sink and grabbed my makeup remover wipes but that was a fail. The entire time I was scrubbing my face my eyes repeatedly glanced at the screen of my phone. *Uggh!* I don't know how, seeing that I couldn't keep my eyes on my face long enough, but I managed to successfully wipe all traces of makeup from my face. And like the thirst bucket I'd been since grabbing my phone from my purse I snatched it off the counter and took one last peek for any missed calls or text notifications. Again, there wasn't a single one. Frustrated, I damn near threw my phone back on the counter before padding over to the shower. I wasn't sure why I was so pressed, but I could feel my mood turning sour. I tried to shake off my shitty disposition as I pulled the shower curtain back and checked the temperature. *Perfect.* I climbed in the shower and attempted for the umpteth time to think of anything other than Dre. Closing my eyes, I stood underneath the hot stream and let it run down my tired body.

This is just what I needed.

I let the hot water sooth me body and relax my racing mind. It felt like I stood there for an eternity before deciding I needed to wash before the water turned cold. Fluttering my eyes open I grabbed my favorite body wash and loofa and of course, thoughts of Mr. Cameron popped in my head. Lucky for me I was too tired and if I was being honest with myself, I was salty, so I wouldn't be rubbing one out to his image tonight. I squirted a healthy amount of clear liquid onto the puffy pad and placed the body wash back in the shower caddy. Stepping back out of the way of the flowing stream I scrubbed my body from head to toe. I'd just finished my second scrub down when I felt the temperature drop as water splashed on my toes. It was time to end my shower. I stepped back into the water and ensured my body was clear of all soap or residue before placing my loofa back in the shower caddy and turning off the shower.

Shit, I left my towel on the back of the bathroom door.

I hopped on to the rug in front of the tub to the rug in front of the sink and reached for my towel on the door. Then before I could stop myself, I looked down at my phone as I dried off. The screen was black and since I was almost positive there wasn't any texts or calls, I forced myself not to hit the screen to check for any notifications. After I cleared my body of all excess water, I returned my towel to the back of the door then clicked off the light. For a quick second I contemplated leaving my phone but before I could finish that thought I snatched it off the counter and traipsed down the hall into my bedroom. Against my better judgment I flipped the screen toward me while pressing a button to display any notifications. Again, nothing. I tossed my phone on the bed and walked over to my dresser. I placed a small amount of deodorant under both arms then grabbed my shea butter and padded over to my bed. I sat on the edge of my bed and applied the rich substance to every inch of my body. When I was done, I didn't bother returning the bottle to my dresser instead I laid back on the soft mattress and closed my eyes.

Ding dong.

Ding, ding, dong.

I jumped up and grabbed my satin robe off the stool in the corner of my room. I wrapped the robe around my body and tied it securely. Walking out my room I glanced at the clock on my nightstand. *Damn, I dozed off for thirty minutes. It felt like I just closed my eyes.* I walked to the front door and again without asking who was there, I slowly pulled it open. Dre stood on the other side with a scowl fixed on his face.

Dre held his phone up toward me. "What da fuck is this Raquel?"

She didn't answer me right away instead she stood there staring at me like I was crazy. I was sure my elevated tone and the grimace on my face threw her little ass for a loop, but I didn't care. I was pissed. Been pissed since I got her text. I responded to her little raggedy ass message but deleted that shit as soon as I finished typing it. Nah, we needed to talk face to face.

So here I was, at her apartment at 2:45 in the damn morning with my cellphone in her face. "Answer me Raquel. What's up with this text? And why the hell you leave without comin to tell me?"

Rocky took a few steps back and widened the door, allowing me to enter. I closed the door behind myself and waited for her to respond.

She turned toward me; attitude evident on her otherwise pretty face. Her arms were folded across her chest as she glared up at me. "What was wrong wit my text Dre?"

Now it was my turn to look at her like she was crazy. "Are your serious Raquel? Why would you think I wouldn't be back here to get my keys? How else was I gonna get in my crib? Or did you have plans to be somewhere else tonight? Is that why you bounced without tellin me bye?"

Rocky smirked at me. I watched as her expression changed and she looked at me in shock. Her eyes ballooned like they are going to pop out of her head. "Whoa Dre, whoa." She unfolded her arms and licked her lips. "Okay first, I asked if you were comin back here because I thought you might be goin home with one of your lil fans." Rocky rolled her eyes at me. "Second, who the hell would I be laid up with Andre? You know I'm not involved with anyone."

For the first time since she opened the door, I realized this was the second time today I'd seen her half naked. Her little ass was standing in front of me with her hair on top of her head and her face completely makeup free. She looked even more beautiful than she did earlier tonight. Naturally my body responded, and I discreetly adjusted myself.

Suddenly, my mood shifted. *Fuck, this chick has me trippin.* I looked down at Rocky to find her staring up at me with a look in her eyes I couldn't identify. Deciding to approach the conversation in a different way I took a deep breath before speaking again. "Look, my bad Rocky. I didn't mean to come at you like that, but I didn't like how you just bounced on me then assumed I'd be laid up."

That got a chuckle out of her although I wasn't sure what I said that was funny. "Isn't that what you did, assume I was laid up?"

She had a point, less than five minutes ago I accused her of that very thing. And if I was being honest with myself it was the main reason, I was tight. Yeah, I didn't like that she left without telling me bye but the real reason I was over here flexing at damn near three in the morning was because I thought she was trying to curve me for another dude. It shouldn't have mattered to me but at this point we were past that. The fact of the matter was it did. Even if I would never admit that shit to her. My ass was salty.

"Dre." Rocky called my name demanding my attention. "I did look for you. In fact, I walked around for about fifteen minutes lookin for you, so I could tell you bye. When I didn't find you, I went back to my girls and that's when E told me she saw you outside on the patio. I came out to say bye, but you were um, occupied." She diverted her eyes from mine when she finished her last statement.

Using my index and middle fingers I tilted her head back, forcing her to look at me. "What do you mean I was occupied?"

She ran her tongue across her lips again. Something I'd noticed she does subconsciously when nervous. "I came to say bye but when I saw you Lyric was sittin on your lap and y'all looked . . ." she used her index and middle fingers to make air quotes, "occupied."

Rocky turned away from me and tried to walk away. I grabbed her arm and spun her little ass back toward me. "Nah, that wasn't me."

I remembered talking to Lyric for a hot second while outside smoking a cigar, but I definitely didn't recall her sitting on my lap.

Rocky smacked her lips. "You don't have to lie to me Dre. Why would I make that shit up?" A glimpse of jealousy flashed behind her heated gaze. I don't think she intended for me to see it though. She quickly flashed me a fake smile.

Shit, I do remember Lyric's thirsty ass sitting on my lap. She sat down to light my cigar and tried to linger there until I pretended like I wanted to stand just to get her off me.

I rubbed a hand over my head. "I wasn't lyin, I didn't remember that shit until just now. However, what does Lyric bein on my lap have to do with me and you?"

"Nothin, but I ain't trynna look like another member of your fan club."

This girl is exhausting.

"You will never be . . ." imitating her move I made air quotes, "a member of my fan club as you call it. We're friends. You're not one of these thirsty ass chicks who only wanna fuck with me cuz I catch a damn ball." That shit came out more jarring than I intended but it was the truth.

Ready for this conversation to end I pulled Rocky into my chest, wrapped my arms around her, and rested my chin on top of her head. "Rocky aside from my family, there ain't no other female especially Lyric's thirsty ass that matter more to me than you do. Got it?"

Rocky pulled back but not completely out of my embrace and looked me in the eyes. "Dre don't say shit like that."

I kissed her forehead. "It's the truth."

We stood there for what felt like forever staring at one another. Slowly Rocky stepped out of my embrace. She licked her lips then slowly pulled it in between her teeth. My eyes raked over her body. She didn't move or speak as I drank her. It was no secret that I was attracted to Rocky but for the past couple of months I'd been playing by her rules, trying to be understanding of the limits she placed on our friendship. However, right now all I could think about was how sexy she looked standing in front of me and how whatever lotion or oil she was wearing complimented her natural scent. It was all so erotic and right now it was fucking with my self-control. I needed to get the fuck out of apartment and fast.

As if she could read my mind she asked, "You stayin or goin?"

I opened my mouth to tell her I was leaving but found myself standing there with it gaped open when she grabbed the tie on her robe. Her eyes were stapled to my face as her lids lowered to a slant. Her tiny hands moved at a snail's pace as she untied her robe. I couldn't take my eyes off her as the silky gown spilled open. A lascivious mien spilled onto her face as she shimmied out of the tiny garment and let it drop to the floor. Rocky stood in front of me completely bare.

Goddamn!

With her arms extended out at her side she rested her hands on her hips. A mixture of confidence and lust oozed from her pores as she welcomed my brazen perusal. I took my time drinking her in. My eyes slid past her face and slowly glided down her body. Her small mounds sat high on her chest. Walnut colored areolas blended deliciously into her hardened nipples. The unyielding curves of her waist molded flawlessly into her shapely hips, giving her the perfect hourglass shape. Rocky was toned. There wasn't an ounce of fat on her entire body. A washboard flat stomach drove my gaze to the manicured hairs covering her hidden treasure. The small landing strip was the only hair on her entire body. After spending an undetermined amount of time fixated on her womanhood, I trailed my eyes down to her solid thighs. I didn't linger there long, dropping my eyes I scanned her shapely calves and manicured feet then returned my gaze to her face. Smoldering mahoganies bore into me as the smile disappeared from her face. In its place was pure unadulterated lust.

Fuck!

"Lock the door Dre."

Speechless, I watched as she turned and sauntered down the hall in the direction of her bedroom. I didn't move until she was no longer in my line of sight. Turning around I locked the door and kicked off my shoes, then damn near skipped my happy ass back to her bedroom.

When I entered Rocky's room she was stretched across her bed, lying on her right side. Her right arm was slightly bent, and her head was propped on her little fist. Her smooth chocolate skin glowed underneath the dim lighting and was a direct contrast to her all white comforter. She looked erotically angelic. Unquestionably, Rocky was the most beautiful woman I'd ever laid eyes on. Unsure if this would be the last time, I'd ever have the pleasure of seeing her like this I stood in the doorway and admired her beauty. My eyes roved over her body. Committing to memory every curve, scar, blemish, and imperfection that made her imperfectly perfect.

Unhurriedly my eyes traveled back up her body, stopping at her face. Unable to move I continued to stare at her. I watched as she licked her lips and adjusted her body on the bed. She removed her head from her fist and fully stretched out her petite frame, lying flat on her back. The entire time her eyes remained focused on me.

Fuck, she is gorgeous.

"Dre," she purred.

I felt my dick twitch against my leg as I watched her slowly spread her legs open. She raised her arm from off the bed and placed her index and middle finger up to her parted lips. Slowly she inserted both fingers into her mouth, lubricating each digit like they were her favorite dessert. Her eyes lazily drifted shut as she removed her fingers from her wet mouth and trailed them down her body. Settling them in between her legs her eyes fluttered opened as she parted her lower lips. She pinned me with her gaze while inserting her pre-lubricated fingers into her sex. I bit my bottom lip while watching in complete awe as she dipped her fingers in and out of her sex. Her soft sensual moans filled the air as she warmed herself up for me.

Goddamn, this shit is hot.

I remained stuck in place, glued inside the doorframe watching her. I couldn't move or speak. All I could do was stare. I watched her remove her glistened fingers and sit up on the bed. An enthralling smile adorned her beautiful face as she stood from the plush mattress and padded toward me seductively. With her head tilted up she stood in front of me, silently gazing into my eyes. Her body communicated what her mouth kept hidden. I felt her breath on my chest and the heat emitting from her core. The smell of her natural musk permeated my nostrils as she brought the hand, she used to pleasure herself up toward my face.

Finally, gaining control of my body I softly grabbed her wrist halting her movements. I saw the question behind the seduction in her eyes. My movements were slow and deliberate as I lowered my mouth to her hand and pulled her index finger into mouth. Swirling her finger around my tongue I sucked until I could no longer taste her essence. Rocky closed her eyes and let her head fall back as a soft moan escaped from her parted lips. Slowly I removed her finger from my mouth. Rocky's eyes flashed open and returned to mine as I took her middle finger in my mouth and repeated the same oral play, I performed on her index finger. I wasted no time cleaning her finger before pulling it out my mouth and planting a soft kiss on the palm of her hand. Rocky whimpered while closing her eyes again and placing her tiny hands on each side of my face. Slowly I lowered my mouth to her waiting lips. I hovered just above her mouth and stared into her face, waiting.

I didn't have to wait for long, leisurely Rocky's eyes fluttered open and skated up to mine. I held her gaze, searching for any signs of uncertainty. I needed to know she was sure before we went any further. Because once we crossed this line there was no turning back. "Are we really doin this?" I breathed out, still hovering above her mouth.

Rocky shook her head while snaking her arms around my neck and lowering my mouth to her soft lips. Mechanically, I enfolded her in my arms while sliding one hand up her back and the other down to her ass. Still slightly in disbelief that we'd finally arrived at this moment I took my time, savoring every detail. From the feel of her lips against mine to her breath lightly dusting across my philtrum. I relished the warmth emitting from her tiny hands tugging at the back of my neck while basking in the beauty of her muffled whimpers filling my ears.

I teased her with measured and deliberate kisses. Purposely littering her mouth with chaste lingering pecks, I laggardly slid my tongue over her bottom lip and gently sucked it into my mouth. Another soft moan spilled out of her mouth and into mine as I slipped my tongue over her lips and thrusted it into her mouth. The faint taste of her womanhood clung to my tongue, mixing deliciously with the spearmint flavor coating her tongue. My dick twitched against the constricted material of my pants at the thought of Rocky tasting herself on my tongue. Palming her ass, I voraciously fed her the last of her essence. I groaned from the back of my throat as she greedily accepted. Her brazen appetency was intoxicating and so goddamn erotic. Rocky's small hands clawed at the back of my neck. She pulled me deeper into her naked frame as I fervently poured the past four months of emotions into her mouth.

Bending slightly at the knees I trailed my hand down her back and gripped her under her ass, lifting her small body off the floor. Instinctively, Rocky wrapped her toned thighs around my waist. She secured herself in place by locking her feet at the ankles behind my back. Her slickened sex coated my stomach and a chill surged down my spine. I relished the feel of her arousal as I cracked my lids. Continuing to ravish her mouth I carefully walked us over to the bed. Gently lowering her onto the mattress I slowly pulled away from her mouth and gazed down at her as she unhooked her legs from around my waist.

Hovered above her, I placed the bulk of my weight on my arms as I planted a soft peck on her lips before dragging my mouth down to her neck. I buried my face in the crook of her neck. Licking, nibbling, and finally biting down on her spot. Rocky's back arched up off the bed as unabashed moans tumbled out of her mouth. Her head sunk deeper into the mattress as her little hands found their way to my face. Kneading the tips of her fingers against my jaw she wiggled underneath me as I replaced my teeth with my tongue. Traces of my saliva coated her collar bone and her sternum, stopping at the apex of her breasts.

Lazily I drug my head away from her heated flesh and directed my attention to her engorged mounds. I admired the diamond barbells that decorated her protruding nipples before clasping a hand around her left breast. An appreciative moan spilled from my mouth as I lowered my head and circled her erect nipple with my tongue before slurping it into my mouth. I gently sucked her petite mound, increasing my suction as she arched her back feeding herself to me. I continued to feast on her breast as I placed my free hand between her thighs, making contact with her final hidden piercing.

Goddamn, she is so fuckin wet.

Another growl escaped from between my lips as I dug two fingers deep inside her sex. A sense of pride and excitement washed over me at her natural reaction to me. I moved my fingers in a circular motion applying moderate pressure each time I stroked her soft nub. Paying close attention to every moan and movement of her body I gently caressed her clit while rubbing against her piercing with my thumb. Rocky screamed incoherent curses as she moved against my hand and mouth. Moving my mouth to her right breast I flicked my tongue across her pierced nipple before clamping my mouth around it.

"Oh My God, Dre. I'm about—"

I removed my mouth from her breast and placed it next to her ear, I lightly traced her lope with my tongue before whispering in her ear. "You're about to what sexy?"

Rocky didn't respond, she couldn't. Enveloped in the throngs of pleasure she moaned and cursed before falling completely silent. I continued caressing her nub while gingerly massaging her clit as I stared into her face. Eyes clinched shut, mouth slightly parted, and head titled back deep into the mattress, she slowly came undone as I took in every movement. Rocky made the most beautiful ugly cum face I'd ever seen. Mesmerized, I couldn't take my eyes off her as she clutched her thighs around my hand and surrendered to her orgasm. Her body shuddered uncontrollably as her vagina gripped my fingers like a vise. I wasn't sure how it was possible, but she became more lubricated. Slowly I withdrew my fingers and hovered above her, allowing her to come down from her orgasm I waited for her to open her eyes. Gradually, her breathing evened out and her lids cracked open. Hooded brown eyes gazed up at me.

"What. The. Fuck. Dre?"

I smirked, planting a soft kiss on her swollen lips I pulled up and stared down at her. "That was just an appetizer sexy. But now I'm ready for dessert. And I like my dessert before my main course. You ready to feed me sexy?"

Her eyes ballooned, brows hiked, and lips parted then closed. Eyes fixed on me she watched me closely as I moved from above her and stood in front of the bed. Rocky readjusted her body on top of the mattress, flipping over on her stomach she perched her ass in the air and bent her arms in front of her. Head cocked to the side, she rested it on her hands as she smiled up at me. Returning her gaze, I took my time as I removed my clothes. I snatched off my blazer and dropped it at my feet then unfastening my belt. Slowly and deliberately I unbuttoned my shirt as Rocky followed my every move. Removing my shirt, I discarded it in the same pile as my blazer then quickly pulled my t-shirt over my head. I stood bare chest in my jeans and boxer briefs looking down at the most beautiful woman I'd encountered as she stared up at me with lust and wonderment in her eyes.

Rocky parted her lips and slowly ran her tongue over her top row of teeth. Bending down I placed a brisk kiss on her lips and quickly stood back up.

"And all this time I thought only women teased."

Unable to hide the coquettish grin on my face I hiked a brow while reaching inside my pocket and pulling out my wallet. Shuffling through one of the compartments I retrieved a gold foil packet then tossed the wallet on the floor. I purposely took my time unbuttoning my jeans before letting my pants fall down my legs.

"Patience is a virtue sexy."

I stepped out of my jeans and smirked to myself as Rocky's eyes traveled from my face to the only part of my body not fully exposed. Her eyes grew big as saucers and her breath caught in her throat as she gaped at my ridged member. I wasn't sure why she seemed surprise when she'd seen it before. Shrugging it off I placed my hands inside the waistband of my boxer briefs and pulled them down, finally freeing myself. I studied her face, noticing when she let out the breath she'd been holding as her bulging orbs returned to mine. All traces of humor were removed from her face. In its place was the undeniable look of desire.

With my eyes still focused on her face, I slowly approached the bed. Tossing the condom near her head, I placed a knee onto the mattress and hoisted myself onto the bed. Instantly Rocky slid on her side and attempted to turn onto her back. I placed a hand on her waist, halting her movements. Gently pushing her back onto her stomach I hovered over top of her outstretched body as I raked my eyes down her naked frame, admiring her petite athletic physique.

Fuck, she is absolutely stunnin.

Lowering my head, I ran my tongue over her right shoulder and up her neck. I repeated that task on the left side then ran my tongue down the back of her neck before settling on her spot and lingering there. Rocky moaned into the mattress as she crumbled a fistful of the bedspread in between her hands. After a combination of sucking, licking, and biting I slowly trailed my tongue down her spine, stopping once I reached her ass. Scooting down the bed I raised her right leg slightly off the mattress while lowering my head to her foot. I parted my lips and swiped my tongue across her big toe. Rocky squirmed underneath me but quickly stopped moving as a soft whimper escaped from her mouth.

I continued my oral assault, running my tongue across each of her toes until I reached her pinkie. I then placed a chaste kiss on her ankle before trailing my tongue over her calf and up her thigh, stopping at her sex. Slowly I placed her leg back on the bed and moved over to her left. I paid the same attention to her left foot and leg as I did her right before lying it back on the bed. Back at the apex of what made her a woman I swiped my tongue down the crack of her ass as I planted my face deep inside her opening. Indolently swiping my tongue over her slick lips, I relished the taste of her sweet essence. Reflexively, Rocky bounced her ass against my face as I devoured her like she was favorite meal. Listening to her moans and paying attention to her movements, I lapped my tongue over her clit before dipping it inside her warm juicy canal and sucking gingerly on her piercing.

She pressed her face into the comforter and bit down, muffling her cries. "Fuck Dre. I'm cu . . . I'm cu . . . fuuck," she breathed out, while lifting her head from the bed.

Determined to bring her the release she was craving, I inserted my middle finger and slowly ran my tongue over her lips then repeatedly swiped it over her clit. Rocky shuddered as she moved her sex against my tongue.

"Argh, Dreeee."

I rolled my tongue over her clit one final time before stilling my finger and carefully sliding it out of her, at the same time I pulled my face out her ass and sat back on my haunches, watching her submit to her orgasm. *Umm. That shit is sexy as fuck.* Rocky continued to quiver as I leaned forward and grabbed the condom off the bed. Ripping the packet open with my teeth, I tossed the wrapper on the floor and quickly applied the latex to my engorged member.

"Get up baby."

Sluggishly Rocky lifted herself from the mattress and settled in the doggy style position.

Sliding up to her rear, I aligned my dick with her opening. "You ready sexy?"

Glancing over her shoulder she peeked at me through the cracks of her slanted lids and nodded her consent. I planted my hands firmly on each side of her waist as I took my time easing inside of her. I gave her just a few inches of me while slowly rocking my hips. I stayed right there, maintaining the same slow rhythmic movement, giving her time to adjust to my girth. Her tight walls clung to my rod, softly pulsating against me. Eyes fixed on Rocky's tiny frame I looked for any signs of discomfort. When I didn't see any indicators that she was in pain I eased in a little further.

A sensuous purr spilled from her mouth as she rocked her hips against my dick. Subsequently, her lubricated sex pulled me deeper inside of her and my own groans filled the air. Increasing my speed, I tightened my grip on her waist and plummeted deep inside of her soaking canal. Her unabashed moans mixed with the sound of her dripping pussy sent a quiver up my spine. Placing a hand on the small of her back I pushed her down into the mattress, opening her up to me. Rocky slid her arms out in front of her, resting them on each side of her head she arched her back. Going balls deep I grounded my hips, withdrew my rod, then thrusted it back in.

"Fuccck," I hissed, as I continued stroking her.

Rocky found her rhythm, throwing her ass back on my rod she matched my strokes. Her uninhibited cries of pleasure filled the air as I stretched my arm forward and placed a hand in her hair. Grabbing a fistful of Rocky's bun, I tugged her head away from the bed. I slowed my strokes as I applied a little more force, yanking her body off the mattress I pulled her back against my chest. With my free hand, I placed it on her clit and swiped my finger gingerly over her slickened bud. Instantly, her walls tighten around me, stealing a moan I tried to keep composed.

"Umm, Dreee."

I ran my tongue over her ear. "Don't overthink it, listen to your body and cum for me sexy."

As if she was waiting for my permission Rocky moved in accordance with my strokes while calling out for her savior as her body shook uncontrollably. Sliding my hand from her hair to her face I turned her face toward me, capturing her mouth I stifled her cries. Her soft whimpers spilled into my mouth as she rolled her tongue ardently over mine. Close to my own release I removed the hand resting against Rocky's clit and wrapped my arm around her waist. I locked her in place, flush against my chest while gradually ending our kiss. Still in the midst of her orgasm, Rocky's face contorted, shuffling between various ugly faces as she rode out her climatic wave.

There was something very arousing about watching a woman experience the pinnacle of pleasure, especially when you were the one responsible for the beautifully ugly expressions that involuntarily stretched across their faces. Rocky's orgasmic mien was now my favorite.

I waited until Rocky's body stilled before slowly pulling out of her, flinching as I left her tight pulsating grip. "Lay on your back. I want to see your face when I cum."

Obeying my command Rocky turned around and lowered herself onto the mattress. I mounted her and looked down at my dick while smiling at the evidence of her explosive climax. Running my hand along the shaft of my erection, I leisurely entered her again. Slowly I glided further into her warm lubricated fold until my balls slapped against her ass. Mechanically her legs wrapped around my waist as she rounded her hips while digging her nails into my back.

"Urgh."

I dipped my head down to her breast and swiped my tongue across her nipple while pumping fervently into her. Rocky's small hands flew up to my head, pressing my face into her tit. I sucked her small mound into my mouth while simultaneously twirling my tongue over her nipple. Releasing my head, her hands were on my back again, clawing at my flesh as she pulled me deeper into her. Lifting my head, I stared down into her face then placed my mouth on hers. Reflexively, her lips parted as Rocky thrust her tongue into my mouth.

"Ummm . . . I can't hold off much longer sexy," I breathed into her mouth.

Gradually slithering her tongue out of my mouth Rocky bit down on my bottom lip as her eyes fluttered opened. After a few edacious nipples she released my lip and threw her head back into the mattress. "Umm, cum for me daddy."

I placed my hands on her thighs and removed her legs from around my waist, hoisting them straight up in the air I rested her ankles on my shoulders. I pulled completely out of her then forcefully rammed back inside of her sex, grinding my hips in a circular motion as I filled her. I repeated that move three more times before my stomach lurched, and heat coursed down my spine. I felt that unmistakable tingle in my balls as I continued to stroke her slow and hard. With my eyes fixed on her pretty face I let go of my orgasm, blasting off inside the latex shielding us.

She flung her legs off my shoulders and wrapped them around my waist as she pulled me down to her, kissing me passionately while grinding against my dick. Completely empty, I pecked her lips before raising my head and gazing down at her. A wide ass smile spread across her face as she cracked her lids open.

"Oh. My. God. Dre. That was—" She looked away then quickly brought her eyes back to mine. "I don't want you get the big head or anything, but I've never experienced anything like that before, like ever," she admitted.

Reluctantly I peeled myself from her tight embrace and hopped off the bed. "Thank you, Short Stuff. I aim to please. And for the record, me either." I headed toward the door. "Where are your rags?" I asked, while strolling out the room.

"First closet on the left," she called out behind me.

Less than five minutes later I returned with a warm rag. Sitting down on the bed I tapped Rocky on her leg, instructing her to open. She stared up at me sleepily as she spread her legs.

Gently I sat the warm cloth on her vagina. "You think you can sleep with it there?"

A warm smile eased onto her face as she scooted across the mattress and climbed underneath the covers while rolling onto her side. "I'll make it work. Thank you. Now come hold me while I sleep."

Reaching over to the nightstand I turned off the light and peeled back the covers before hoisting my legs onto the bed and sliding over to her. I wrapped my arm around Rocky's small waist and pulled her into my chest. Adjusting a few pillows underneath my head, I closed my eyes and surrendered to sleep.

I rolled over and swiped my hand across the bed in search of her. Coming up empty, I cracked open an eye lid. The sun peeked through the curtains, casting a dull light into the room. I threw my arm over my head to block out the sun while flashing my other lid open. Peeling the covers from my body, I slid to the edge of the bed and sat up, planting my feet on the floor. Instantly I was hit with the delicious aroma of bacon and some sort of bread. I stood to my feet and surveyed the pile of clothes next to the bed for my boxers. Bending at the waist I plucked my briefs from the top of the pile and gaited out the room, heading straight for the bathroom to relieve my heavy bladder.

I emptied my bladder and ambled over to the sink. Cutting on the water I stared at my reflection in the mirror, smirking as images from last night flooded my mind. It didn't help that I could still taste her. Her scent was not only on my tongue but in my mustache and goatee. Sliding my eyes down to the counter I noticed a fresh rag laid across the sink. I grabbed the rag off the counter and dragged my eyes back up the mirror. I had half a mind to skip cleaning my face just to have her scent with me a little while longer. I quickly shook that crazy ass thought from my head as I placed the rag under the water and washed my face. My next task was my teeth which also meant the last traces of her would be gone. *Damn nigga, you got it bad.* Reaching into the cabinet I pulled out my toothbrush and brushed my teeth. Once I finished my morning routine, I shut off the water and put my toothbrush back where I got it then exited the bathroom, damn near tripping over Creed on my way out the door. Barely paying me attention, Creed lifted his head from the carpet and sluggishly moved out of my path. Strolling into the kitchen I found Rocky bent over looking inside the refrigerator.

I stood on the balls of my feet and trekked quietly over to her, bending over I threw my arms around her waist and lifted her off the floor. Rocky shrieked while giggling in my arms. I took a nice whiff of her natural scent before planting a kiss on the side of her face and placing her back on her feet.

"Good morning Short Stuff."

Rocky turned and faced me. Standing on her tippy toes she placed her mouth on mine, quickly peeking my lips then pulling back. "Ummm. Good morning Dre."

"It smells amazing in here. You making breakfast for me?"

Rocky turned back toward the fridge and finished digging inside. "Uh hun. After last night I figured you'd worked up an appetite. But you do know it's after twelve, so technically it's not breakfast," she spoke with her head still inside the refrigerator.

I swatted her on the ass before walking over to a barstool and taking a seat. "Such a smart ass," I joked, while popping a grape in my mouth from a bowl of fruit on the counter.

Rocky shut the refrigerator with her hip and stepped over to the counter carrying a carton of eggs, cheese, and milk. Sitting the items on the counter she batted her lashes at me. "Carmen is on her way over for a hot sec so you might . . ." her eyes swept down my body and settled on the bulge in my boxer briefs, ". . . want to put some shorts on."

I waited for her eyes to return to my face before speaking. "Say no more."

Hopping up I turned to leave the kitchen. I stopped in mid stride at the sound of Rocky's high pitch scream. I turned back around to find Rocky staring at me with a hand covering her mouth.

"What's wrong Short Stuff?"

She didn't speak, instead she walked over to me and timidly placed her hands on my back, causing me to flinch. Her misted eyes traveled up to mine. "Your back. Your shoulders. I'm. . .Oh my god Dre. I'm so sorry," she whispered.

Grabbing her tiny hands, I brought them up to my mouth and kissed them. Slowly I released her hands, watching as they fell by her waist. "Don't trip, it was well worth every scratch sexy."

A sly grin stretched across her face as I turned and walked down the hall. Less than a minute later I returned with my phone in hand, wearing a pair of basketball shorts and a sleeveless t-shirt. Rocky looked up as I took my seat and picked through the bowl of fruit.

"You sure you good?"

I finished chewing the fresh strawberry I'd just popped in my mouth and looked across the counter at her. "Girl stop it. I'm a grown ass man, these lil punk ass scratches ain't shit. I'm light skin so they look worse than they really are."

Rocky nodded her head then went back to whisking the eggs in the frying pan.

"By the way, thanks for not throwing away my toothbrush this time," I teased, in attempt to assuage her guilt.

Plucking a grape out of the bowl Rocky tossed it at me. "It was one time Dre. You ever gonna let me live that shit down?" she asked through a giggle.

"Nope," I stated jokingly, picking the grape up from my lap and chucking it into my mouth.

Shaking her head at me Rocky removed the pan from the burner and scooped out a hearty portion of cheese eggs 0nto a plate. Rocky sat the skillet on a potholder then quickly added four strips of bacon, two buttered biscuits, and two sausage links. Scooting the plate in front of me she moved over to the fridge and pulled out a bottle of strawberry jelly and a container of orange juice. Rocky sat the jelly and a set of eating utensils next to my plate and nodded her head, indicating it was okay for me to eat. She didn't have to tell me twice. Saying a quick prayer, I immediately dug into my plate. I stuffed a forkful of eggs into my mouth and looked up at the sound of Rocky snickering.

"Did I do it again?"

She shook her head and placed a tall glass of OJ in front of my plate. "I actually find myself looking forward to it every time you eat my food."

I placed a hand in front of my mouth and slid my eyes up to hers. "Your food ain't the only thing you've fed me that made me moan because of how good it tasted."

Dropping the spatula, she was using to scoop eggs onto her plate she stared at me. "Oh yeah, and what part of my body would you be referring to, seeing as you licked me from head to toe last night?" she asked, while running her tongue across her top row of teeth.

"All of you tasted delicious but my favorite was your juicy pussy." That admission had my dick rising.

Rocky picked up the spatula and resumed making her plate. "Well, I can't wait to return the favor."

That shit had me out my seat and on her ass. Startled Rocky dropped the serving utensil again and placed her hand on my chest. Slowly she skirted her eyes up to mine. I lowered my head to hers, prepared to attack her mouth when the doorbell rang. *Damn it.* Placing a quick peck on her lips I stepped back out of her space and returned to my seat.

"Ummm, it smells amazing in here. Did you save me some food?" Carmen asked, as she entered the apartment.

"Wasn't really expecting you Carm but you know what's mine is yours."

"I'm just fuckin wit you my fat ass already—"

I think the first expression was shock as Carmen's light-colored eyes crashed with mine. Then a knowing smirk settled on her face as she slid her eyes down my body, observing my relaxed attire. Slowly she turned toward her friend and examined her closely. Rocky waved a hand at her before strolling over to the island where she finished fixing her plate. Carmen remained stuck at the entrance of the kitchen; eyes still glued on Rocky. I watched her watch her best friend. Suddenly it clicked. Carmen had been studying Rocky's walk. It was off, her steps were careful, and she moved slower than usual. Something I hadn't paid much attention to until this very moment. Now I felt bad, just moments ago I was ready to jump on her ass when clearly, she was in pain or at the very least uncomfortable. I knew it was temporary until her body became acclimated with my size but that didn't make me feel any better.

A loud thud snatched me out of my head. My eyes swept around the room, landing on Carmen who was standing at the edge of the counter staring between me and Rocky.

"It's about muthafuckin time," she yelled.

Rocky finished chewing a piece of bacon and rolled her eyes at Carmen. "Stop being dramatic."

"Dramatic. Bitch you can barely walk, and you want me to stop being dramatic. Nah fuck that, I need all the nasty—"

Carmen's words were halted at the sound of Rocky's fork hitting her plate. Walking over to Carmen Rocky snatched her by the arm and dragged her out of the kitchen.

"Oh my God. Bitch did you turn into Wolverine while y'all were—" Carmen stopped mid-sentence and made a loud popping sound with her mouth. "Bitch is that a muthafuckin hickey?" That was the last thing I heard as they headed down the hall.

Going back to my plate of food I snickered to myself at how quickly Carmen deduced that Rocky and I had been intimate. I found her reaction comical, although Rocky didn't seem to think so. Five minutes later both women returned to the kitchen. Rocky's eyes bounced around the room as she walked up to the counter and picked up her plate. Opening the microwave, she sat it inside, punched at the number pad, and closed the door. Turning away from the microwave she leaned against the counter with her arms folded across her chest.

My silent ogling was interrupted when Carmen tapped me on the arm. Slowly I turned my attention away from Rocky and looked over at her best friend. A sly grin rested on her face as she discreetly extended her balled fist toward me underneath the counter. Shifting my eyes forward then back down at her fist, I quickly bumped it with mine.

"You have no idea how long I've been waitin for this shit. Now that the easy part is out the way I need you to prepare for the hardest shit to penetrate," she whispered.

I didn't speak for fear my voice would alert Rocky to our covert conversation. Instead I hiked a brow, letting her know I wanted her to continue.

"Her heart. Nobody and I do mean nobody has ever gotten in. But for some odd reason I think you're different."

I nodded my understanding just as Rocky turned around to grab her plate out of the microwave. Rocky's eyes landed on us then quickly went to her plate.

"Welp I got what I came for. Imma let y'all get back to y'all's day. Call me later Rocky."

"Maybe," she answered, eyes still in her plate.

"Bitch whateva, don't make me have to come back ova here."

Rocky giggled as she sat her fork in her plate then walked with Carmen out of the kitchen. I was glad to see Carmen's outburst hadn't messed up her mood. A few moments later I saw her tiny hand reaching for my plate. Sitting my phone on the counter I grabbed her hand and pulled her toward me.

Shifting on the stool I turned my body to face her, placing her in between my legs I smirked to myself as I noticed the dark purplish mark in the crook of her neck. "We good?"

Rocky shook her head against my chest.

"Did I hurt you last night?"

Rocky spun around and placed her hands on each side of my face as she stared at me. "No. You were attentive and passionate. You took your time allowing me to adjust to you. This…" her eyes swept down to her crotch, "is the price one pays for sleeping with a well-endowed man. I'll be fine. My girl just has to get used to having a damn water bottle inside of her for over forty minutes."zx

"So, this will happen again? This wasn't just some drunk one-night stand shit?" Not that her answer really mattered because after last night there was no way I was going to let her put me back in the friend zone.

A wide grin settled on her face. "I'm not sure if no one has ever told you or you just want me to stroke your ego but I gots no shame about mine. Ain't no way in hell after experiencin the shit you did to me last night could I eva just hit it and quit it. I'm already trynna think of ways to ease my swellin so I can return all the favors you bestowed on me last night."

I couldn't help the Kool-Aid size smile that spread across my face. "Nah, I wasn't lookin to have my ego stroked. I was just hopin this wasn't a one-time thing," I supplied, even though I knew damn well I wasn't going to let it be even if she tried. "I can't lie tho, knowin I'm the only person to ever give you a vaginal orgasm did make a nigga feel some kind of way."

"Yeah, that part. How'd you know I was on the brink of an orgasm?" she asked, turning back around and resting against my chest.

"I paid attention to your body," I answered honestly.

She tilted her back and looked up at me. "And what, it just told you I needed a release?" Her tone was mocking, and doubt danced around her slanted orbs.

"That's exactly what it told me."

Rocky shifted her head back forward. "Boy stop."

A chortle flew from my mouth. "I'm serious Short Stuff. My pops was very real and honest with me about all things, including sex. He taught me that sex is not a solo sport. He told me as the man it was my job to pay attention to my partner and make sure she enjoyed herself as much as I did. He said to always make sure she got hers before I got mine."

I paused giving her time to absorb my words. When she didn't speak, I continued. "Last night when my fingers were inside you, you told me when you felt like your orgasm was near. But your pussy told me before your mouth did."

"How?" she breathed out barely above a whisper.

"Your breathing hitched in your throat and the walls of your pussy pulsated around my dick like a heartbeat. Plus, the way you were throwing it back on my dick I knew you were chasing somethin."

"I can't wait to chase that shit again."

Unfuckingbelievable.

CHAPTER ELEVEN

"*O*h my god. My feet are throbbing," I announced to no one in particular, while plopping down on the sofa in Carmen and Egypt's living room.

Carmen's head shot over to me. "Are you serious? Who the hell wears heels to a football game?"

Egypt chuckled as she sat down beside me on the couch. "Somebody who is smashing the school's star wide receiver," Egypt answered, although the question was directed at me.

I laughed as I bumped Egypt with my shoulder and flipped Carmen the bird. Leaning forward I tossed open the pizza box and carved out a slice. I held the steaming square up to my mouth and blew, attempting to cool it off before stuffing it in my mouth. Following suit, Egypt reached over and grabbed a few slices and tossed them on a paper plate. I finished chewing the piece I shoved in my mouth a few moments ago before reaching in the box for more. I loaded a plate and sat back on the sofa, going back at the greasy treat.

"Ummm."

Carmen paused her movements and peered at me. "What da fuck was that?"

Opening my half-closed lids, I slid my eyes in her direction and burst out in a fit of laughter. "Oh my god. I can't believe I just did that," I admitted, as I calmed myself.

Carmen finished loading her plate and sat back in her seat. "So, you gonna share with us what the hell that was about and why you found it so funny?"

"The first time Dre ever ate somethin I cooked for him he closed his eyes and moaned. It's a subconscious thing he does that stems from when he was a kid. I guess I picked it up. I swear I've never done that before," I stated, slightly embarrassed.

Carmen hiked a neatly arched brow while biting into a slice of pizza. "I guess when a man gives you your first vaginal orgasm you start picking up his little quirks," she teased, in between bites.

I rolled my eyes up in my head while tending to my own plate of food. "Yo ass ain't ever gonna let that go, are you? I wish I never told you."

"Like you can keep anything from me," Carmen goaded.

"Speaking of, I feel left out. I know I'm late to the party, but I need to be brought up to speed. It feels like forever since we've hung out like this," Egypt stated solemnly, while looking between me and Carmen.

Neither of us spoke, allowing Egypt to vent.

"I swear I love being nurse, but I think I'm over these twelve-hour shifts." Egypt repositioned herself on the couch, tucking a leg underneath her bottom she turned and faced me. "I ain't the nasty friend so I don't need a play by play but give me some details."

I leaned forward and sat my empty plate on the table. Shifting back on the sofa I kicked my legs up and propped them on the table as I directed my attention toward Egypt. "I'll tell you whatever you want to know but you can't tell. . ." I swung my head toward Carmen, "that bitch."

Egypt and I burst out laughing. Carmen stood from her seat and sat her plate on top of the pizza box then knocked my foot off the edge of the table. Sashaying back to her chair, she sat down, crossed her legs, and stared at us.

"Y'all done?"

Egypt placed a hand over her chest, calming herself. "I'm sorry Carm, but that was funny, and you know it."

Carmen smacked her lips, narrowing her eyes she stared at me then flicked me off.

Sobering from my own bout of laughter I winked at Carmen. Slowly I slid my head back toward Egypt, giving her my attention. "What cha wanna know boo?"

"You know the basics, how'd it happen? Was it good? And how long has it been happening?"

I closed my eyes as I thought about the night Dre showed up at my door flexing. In retrospect I think that was my undoing. It was like all the months of pent up sexual frustration came to a head. I was done fighting what I wanted and willingly gave myself to him. And it didn't hurt that I was still slightly intoxicated but liquor or not, it was time.

Fluttering my eyes open I held Egypt's gaze. "Dre and I have been gettin it in since the icebreaker." I paused, giving Egypt time to absorb my words.

She didn't speak, just simply nodded her head as a wide grin eased across her face.

"He came back to my apartment after the party, mad because I left without sayin bye. He was feelin some kind of way because he thought I played him to be with someone else. I dunno, the entire time he stood in my face demandin answers to his ridiculous assumption all I could think about was seein him naked. So, I dropped my robe and left his ass standin by the door. Needless to say, he followed me to my room, and it went down from there," I finished animatedly, feeling my cheeks heat up at the memory of that night.

"Dayum," Egypt breathed out barely above a whisper.

"Girl she ain't even got to the good part yet," Carmen chimed in.

A light giggle slipped from my parted lips as Egypt looked at me, waiting for me to finish.

"To answer your last question, the shit was better than good, it was amazin. Like lil freak nasty stated earlier..." I dipped my head toward Carmen, "I had my first climax during intercourse but that was after already havin two. The first from his fingers and the second from his mouth."

"Shut the front door," Egypt shouted, making me flinch.

My eyes were low, but my smile was wide. I shook my head in the affirmative.

"Nah bitch, that ain't even the best part," Carmen declared.

I looked at Carmen out of the corner of my eye. "So, tell me what the best part was Miss Know It All?"

Sitting up in her seat Carmen bounced her golden orbs between me and Egypt. "After you left, I went over Rocky's to borrow her YSL clutch and imagine my surprise to find Dre sittin at her counter while her ass was at the stove playin Susie homemaker. I stood back watchin both of them and noticed our homegirl could barely walk."

She paused for dramatic effect while staring at me. I smirked but didn't utter a word.

"So, I stated the obvious and Rocky's ass snatched me out the kitchen wit the quickness but not before I saw her handiwork on Dre's back and shoulders," Carmen finished, while resting back in her chair with a satisfied smirk splayed across her face.

"Say swear?" Egypt exclaimed.

"Bitch I could walk," I stated, trying to downplay her claim.

"Barely," Carmen barked.

Egypt slapped her small hand on my thigh while trying to hold in her laugh.

"No bullshit but I understand why. Dre is hung like a damn elephant," Carmen announced, while holding her two index fingers parallel from one another, about ten inches apart.

"Carm," Egypt gasped.

"What? Dude's dick almost spilled out the bottom of his basketball shorts. He may be off limits but that don't make me blind," Carmen blurted out through a chuckle.

I couldn't help the gut-wrenching laugh that started in my belly and tumbled out of my mouth. I could feel Egypt's eyes on me but was too caught up in my fit of laughter to acknowledge her. Bending over I wrapped one arm around my waist and reached onto the coffee table with the other. I snatched a napkin off the table and slid back in my seat while attempting to calm myself. I used the napkin to dab at the corners of my eyes, catching the tears gathered there before they streamed down my face. Slowly I craned my head toward Carmen.

"You a foo for that shit," I stated, still giggling.

"But I ain't no liar," Carmen declared, with a knowing smirk on her face.

I shook my head in acknowledgement of her statement while plucking my cell phone out of my pocket. Unlocking the device, I clicked on my photo gallery and immediately scrolled through the rolls of pictures, tapping on the picture Dre sent when he was at the gym, I handed Egypt my phone.

"Dayum," she hollered, as she dropped my phone in her lap.

Another uncontrollable giggle escaped from my mouth as I picked up my phone. Minimizing the image, I exited out of the photo gallery and sat it next to me on the couch.

"I told you," Carmen stated, eyes bouncing between me and Egypt.

"That shit has to be—" Egypt's eyes ascended toward her brows. "I mean, does it hurt?"

"Nah, Dre is a very attentive lover. Dude knows his shit ain't regular size, so he takes his time easin me into it. The soreness comes after, well it used to. Now I'm used to it."

"And how long did that take? Because the way you were walkin after that first encounter, I wasn't sure you'd go back," Carmen teased.

"Ain't no way in hell I wasn't goin back. I didn't care how long the recovery time was. The shit was too good to be a one-time thing," I admitted, feeling my cheeks heat up.

"So, do you still get sore afterwards?" Egypt implored softly.

"Nah, after about the third time my girl adjusted." A full-blown smile now decorated my fully made up face.

"I know that's right." Carmen leaned forward in her chair and extended her au lait colored arm toward me.

I leaned over the arm of the couch and touched my palm to hers. Settling back in my original position I slid my head over toward Egypt.

"Now that we got that out of the way." I swept my eyes down her body then returned them to her face. "So, you J and fuckin or y'all just sextin?"

Egypt thrust her hands up in the air while shaking her head vehemently. "We aren't doing either. Who told you that, Dre?"

I smirked at her proper response. Unlike Carm and I Egypt rarely spoke slang. We switched back and forth from our private school educations to street vernacular so much our parents probably wondered why they bothered paying for it.

"Nah Dre ain't said shit. Y'all did, that night at my house before the icebreaker."

Egypt's eyes grew big at that revelation. "J and I talk and text from time to time but nothing more than that. Definitely no sexting. Maybe some harmless flirting every now and again. Jamison thinks I'm a good girl and I know where he stands regarding relationships. Besides, I really think you scared dude with your threat."

"You are a good girl." I held Egypt's gaze. "And there is nothing wrong with that. The fact that J recognizes it means he will never try to play you and if he does—"

"You're coming for his dick. He knows," Egypt stated, cutting me off.

"Damn skippy."

"And I'll be right behind her ass to finish him off," Carmen piggybacked.

The three of us broke out in laughter. Although we knew none of us could beat a man that didn't mean we wouldn't try. We were that protective of one another. Egypt sobered first, her soft brown eyes bounced from Carmen to me.

"So, you and Dre aren't hanging out tonight?" she asked silkily.

I snickered, looking at her out the corner of my eye. "Nope, y'all stuck with me for the rest of the day."

"E may be stuck witcha ass but dependin on how shit shake I may be leavin both you heffas," Carmen chimed in.

Egypt waved her hand in Carmen's direction while rolling her eyes up in her head. "I know I said I missed y'all, but you don't have to stay if you want to hang out with Dre."

"Dre and I don't have plans boo. He has some frat thing he's gettin into tonight. Besides, we been together almost every day this week."

Egypt squealed while scooting toward the edge of the couch, excitement emitting from her core. Without giving her eye contact I rested my hand on her thigh and shook my head to myself, tickled by her dramatic reaction.

Carmen sucked her teeth. "Calm the hell down, you act like the girl just announced her engagement or some shit," she stated, through a light giggle.

That made me chuckle. "She's right E, it's not that serious. Ain't shit changed between Dre and I except now we're havin sex."

Egypt swatted my hand off her thigh and hopped off the couch. "You two bitches. . ." she pointed a finger at me then slid her head over to Carmen, jabbing that same finger in her direction before returning her gaze to me, "kill me with that shit. I don't know who da fuck made y'all the authority on men but you bitches need to get a fuckin clue. I know y'all think I'm naïve when it comes to men and that's cool but I ain't neva been stupid."

Egpyt's Cincinnati roots had come out swinging. She ditched her usual proper grammar and jumped in our lane, throwing slang and curses as if it was her typical way of speaking. I wasn't sure why our small digs pissed her off, but she wasn't having it, not today. So, I sat quietly waiting for her to get her shit off.

Bouncing her eyes between me and Carmen she waited to see if we were going to refute her last statement. When neither of us spoke, she continued. "I know there are some niggas you can fuck and walk away from wit no strings, but I also know there are some niggas that you fuck who take a piece of yo soul wit em every time you lay down wit they asses. And trust, Dre is the latter. You gone fuck around and fall in love wit that man, then you gone be forced to boss up cuz Dre ain't Eric, Tyson or even Emery. Dre is a grown ass man and I don't see him goin for yo bullshit. Yo gone have to decide if you ready for a grown-up relationship or watch that man walk outcha life. And when he does best believe he takin yo heart wit him. Then yo ass gone be the one standin somewhere lookin pitiful cause you got rocked by love."

She glared down at me, again waiting for a response. I had none. I was completely speechless. Paying me one last glance Egypt turned on her heels and stomped away from me.

"Silly ass bitches," she mumbled, as she stalked out the living room.

What the fuck just happened?

I heard ruffling on the side of me but kept my face forward, frozen in place mulling over Egypt's words. Carmen's spat out a string of curses as she rose up out of her seat. Everything else was a blur. I vaguely recall seeing her frame past by me. Blowing out an exasperated breath I allowed my shoulders to sink back into the couch. I rested my head against the cushion and quickly snapped my eyes shut. Concentrating on my breathing I counted backwards from fifty.

"Here bitch."

I fluttered my lids open and stared into a glass containing a clear liquid. Without asking any questions I accepted the drink from Carmen's outstretched hand. I didn't bother asking what was inside as I placed the small goblet to my lips and chucked it back. Relishing the burning sensation as it traveled down my throat, I thought about Egypt's read.

After a few quiet minutes I sat my glass on the table and looked over at Carmen. "Bitch you should've brought the bottle in here."

"Here."

I looked up to find Egypt standing in front of the coffee table with the bottle of Patron in her hand. "I'm not going to apologize because I meant everything I said. However, it came out harsher than it should've. I know you all. . ." she looked over at Carmen before settling her eyes on me again, "don't mean no harm but sometimes it feels like you guys are double teaming me."

I accepted the bottle from her proffered hand as she rounded the table and plopped down next to me. Refilling my glass, I passed the bottle over to Carmen. She quickly refilled her tumbler then held the small goblet out in front of her face. Egypt and I got the message and quickly mimicked her gesture.

"This one is to Egypt. I'on want no fake friends and that mini read proved I'on have none. You said how you felt and we ain't got no choice but to respect it. We love you and mean no disrespect when we clown you. It's always out of love." Carmen raised her glass from in front of her face and extended it in the air. "Cheers bitches."

Glasses clinked, and laughter filled the air as we tossed back the shots of tequila.

I sat at my desk inside my modest-sized office staring at the stack of papers in my hands. Shuffling them around for what felt like the hundredth time I tried to come up with a system. School had resumed in mid-August and I had returned to my role as a paraprofessional to the school's guidance counselor at the beginning of October. I needed to meet individually with the graduating seniors, so I purposely stayed late tonight in order to develop a plan on how to get that done. However, I was having a difficult time concentrating. My stomach was empty, and my libido was at an all-time high. I laid the papers on my desk and picked up my phone, unlocking it I tapped on my messaging app. Dre's name was at the top of the list. Clicking on his name I sent him a message.

Me: Whatcha doing????

Before I could sit the phone down it pinged in my hand.

Dre: Thinking about you. What u into?

Me: Why is that always your answer?

I sat my phone down and stared at the stack of papers again. I shifted through a few when my phone chirped. Gazing at the screen I picked it up and read his message.

Dre: B/c I'm always thinking about u.

I couldn't contain the wide smile splayed across my face as my fingers pecked away at the tiny keyboard.

Me: U do know you don't have to run game anymore seeing as we're already sleeping together <winking face emoji>

Dre: It's never game wit you, always the truth. And for the

record getting you in bed was a bonus not the end game. I got my sights set on somethin more valuable.

Whoa! Egypt's words echoed in my head as I read his message for the third time. Unsure of how to respond I sent him an emoji, the one with hearts for eyes.

Dre: LOL. U never answered my original question.

My mind drew a blank. Scrolling up our thread I read through our messages in search of the question he was referring to, locating it I sent my response.

Me: My bad, I'm at work. Trying to finish up some things before I come back on Wednesday, but my hunger is making it hard for me to concentrate.

Dre: Say no more. What do u want to eat? I'll bring u dinner.

I quickly typed back, telling him he didn't need to do that but erased it before I could hit send. I knew he would've had some sort of smart ass reply and truthfully, I missed him. We hadn't seen each other since Friday but it felt more like weeks. So instead of being difficult I simply responded with my restaurant of choice.

Me: Umm, Penn Station.

Dre: Coo, send me your order and I'll be there in 30. Give or take depending on traffic.

I sent Dre my order and sat my phone down on my desk. Hopping out of my seat I gaited over to the closet inside my office and flung the door open. I stared at my reflection in the full-length mirror, scanning my body I made sure I still looked presentable. My hair was pulled back into a neat bun resting at the back of my head, accentuated with a small neat part down the middle. I wore a long sleeve denim shirt tucked inside a high waisted black leather pencil skirt that stopped just below my knees. On my feet were a pair of black Tom Ford high heels. My makeup was light, a natural hue covered my lids while a soft plum blush decorated my cheeks. I was happy to see my Mac Ruby Woo lipstick was still intact. Placing a hand up to my non-prescription Chanel frames, I adjusted them on my nose before closing the door and returning to my seat. The notification light flickered from my phone, picking it up I unlocked it and noticed a message from Dre.

How the hell did I miss this?

Dre: Finish whatever you're working on b/c I'm taking you home after dinner.

I didn't bother responding, instead I did as he instructed. I scooted the stack of papers I had been studying to the side and pulled my laptop forward. Opening the lid, I waited for it to wake then clicked on the Excel spreadsheet I compiled earlier.

Forty minutes later there was a light rasp at the door. Not bothering to look up from the screen I instructed whoever was there to come in.

"Hey Short Stuff." His raspy baritone carried into the small office.

My fingers stilled on the keyboard as I swiveled my head in the direction of his voice. He stood in the frame of my door, head damn near touching the top. Two grease stained bags were in his large hands and a sexy grin crest his sun-kissed face. I took my time drinking him in as my eyes scanned his body. Today he sported a preppy look. He wore a white vest decorated with the letters of his fraternity in red outlined in white over top of a stone washed denim shirt. My eyes lingered at his chest where he left the first two buttons undone. Reluctantly I slid my gaze down his frame, continuing my perusal. A pair of fitted khaki pants that stopped just above his ankles covered his toned legs. Finishing off his look was a pair of caramel colored loafers.

Gawd, it should be a crime for one person to look this damn good.

Pushing my chair away from my desk I stood to me feet and took the few steps to meet him at the door. I perched up on the tips of my toes and wrapped my arms around his neck as I pulled his face toward mine, crashing my lips against his. Initially the kiss was gently but when I heard the groan tumble out of his mouth into mine, I lost all control. I attacked his mouth with fervor, running my tongue over his bottom lip I dipped it inside his parted lips. Dre matched my passion, wrapping his arms around my waist I felt the heat from the bags on my ass as he allowed me to explore his mouth. Removing my hands from his neck I moved them to his face, grabbing him on each side I pulled him closer into me.

"Ummm," I moaned into his mouth.

The sound of chatter behind him reminded me that we were

standing inside my office door. Slowly I withdrew from his mouth, placing a hand on his muscular chest I stared up into his eyes. Dre held my gaze. Again, a sexy grin donned his handsome face.

"Hi," I breathed out huskily.

"Somebody missed me."

"I did." It was a simple truth. One I had no problem admitting as I removed my hand from his chest and backed out of his personal space.

Dre's smile widened as he took a step toward me. Glancing back at the door he pushed his leg back and kicked it close with his foot. I couldn't help the smile that stretched across my face as I drank him in again. *Damn I missed his ass.* Remembering my manners, I grabbed one of the bags out of his hand then turned around and strolled over to my desk. I sat the greasy bag down and spun around. To my surprise Dre was right there, in my face. Reaching around me he emptied his hand of the other bag then placed his large hands around my waist.

"I missed you too," he stated, while burying his face in my neck.

I light giggle slipped through my lips. "How'd you know where to find me? I expected you to text when you were outside. I would've came and got you," I said, barely above a whisper.

"I didn't want to disrupt you, so I came in hoping I'd see someone who could direct me to you. I got lucky. A student getting water walked me down here," he breathed out against my neck.

I hunched my shoulder, prompting him to lift his face from the crook of my neck. Dre peered down at me and waited for me to speak.

"What student?" A freshly arched brow hiked up on my forehead.

"She said her name was Nevaeh. She talked my ears off the entire walk to your office."

"I bet she did. She was probably sizin you up, trynna figure out if she should shoot her shot." There was more attitude in my tone than I intended.

Dre kept his eyes on me as a resounding chortle flew from his mouth. "I'on know bout all dat but it's dead for that shit. I'on do jail-bait. Besides, I kinda gotta a thing for cougars," he teased, while removing his hands from my waist.

I playfully shoved him in the shoulder before moving over to my chair and taking a seat. "I got yo cougar youngin."

Dre winked at me as he took a seat on the other side of my desk. Sliding both bags toward him he opened them both and peeked inside. He slid the one containing my order back across the desk.

"C'mon let's eat so I can get you home. I need to show you how much I missed you."

"Say no more."

After saying a quick blessing, Dre and I dug into our food, stealing glances at one another while silently enjoying our meal. Fifteen minutes later I watched as Dre stuffed the last bite of his sandwich into his mouth. My eyes were glued to his lips while my mind raced with lecherous thoughts.

Dre's lips curled upwards. "So, you just gonna watch me eat instead of finishin your food?"

I shifted my eyes up to his. "I'm full."

Dre chuckled. "You barely touched your food."

I looked down at my half-eaten sandwich and the picked over fries before shifting my eyes back to his. "I thought I was hungry for food, but my appetite seems to be craving somethin else." I kept my eyes glued to his as I stood from my seat.

Low emeralds brushed down my body before returning to my face. "And what exactly are you hungry for Short Stuff?"

I walked over to the door and turned the latch, securing the lock. Spinning around on my heels I turned my attention back to the handsome man in my office. "I can show you better than I can tell you," I proclaimed, while stepping over to him.

Placing my hands on either side of his chair I pulled it away from the desk and spun it toward me. With my hands still on the arms of his chair I stepped in between his legs and bent at the waist. I looked into his hooded eyes then planted my lips against his. Opening his mouth Dre slipped his tongue over his lips and dipped it in my mouth. I willingly accepted the expected intrusion, lashing my tongue against his. Dre's hands moved to my waist. In one quick motion he snatched me into his lap.

"Ummm."

Slowly I disconnected my lips from his and gazed into his confused eyes. A sly smirk slid across my face as I climbed off his meaty thighs. Dropping down to my knees I slid my hands up his thighs, over his erection, and up to the waist of his pants. I wasted no time unfastening his belt and unbuttoning his pants.

Easing back on my haunches I continued to stare up at him while running my tongue across my top row of teeth. "Take em off," I instructed, dropping my eyes to his lower half.

Without saying a word Dre stood from his seat and removed his pants.

"The draws too," I commanded, staring at his massive erection.

Once again, he complied. Placing his hands in the waist of his boxer briefs he slid them down his baronial thighs. I felt the saliva gathering in the corners of my mouth as I studied the part of his body that made him a man. It was perfect. From the mushroom shaped head, to the pulsing veins, and the two-toned hue of his girthy shaft. It truly was a beautiful piece of anatomy, a piece I had been dying to taste since the day I rubbed one out for him.

I lifted my ass off the heels of my feet and removed my glasses, placing them on the desk. Shifting my head back toward Dre I gently wrapped as much of my hand that I could fit around him. Caught off guard by my initial contact Dre flinched. Eye fixed on his I lowered my head and swiped my tongue across the tip of his dick, trilled by the presence of his pre-cum. Savoring its sweetness, I twirled the tiny bit of fluid around my mouth, running my tongue across both cheeks and over the roof my mouth.

Instantly moisture dripped from my pussy and gathered in the crotch of my panties. Tightening my grip around the shaft of his erection, I wrapped my mouth around his head, slowly sucking him in an inch at a time. I took my time easing him into my mouth, sliding down his shaft until my lips brushed against my hand. Relaxing my grip, I glided my hand further down his cock, resting it against his pelvis. I followed the direction of my hand as I slid my mouth further down his swollen rod while relaxing the muscles in my throat. I moaned against his dick as I slowly trailed my way back up toward the tip. Spit collected in my mouth as I found a steady rhythm. With my tongue rested against my bottom lip, I moved vigorously up and down his lengthy rod.

Dre's hands flew to my head, holding me in place as the crown of my head made contact with my hand. "Fuck," he growled.

I twirled my tongue around his dick until he eased up and allowed me access to move again. Drifting backward I removed my hand from his pelvis, looping it around him I stroked and sucked. I repeated that motion over and over as Dre uttered incoherent words above my head. Adding my other hand to his rod I moved them in opposite directions, creating friction as my mouth whisked up and down his dick.

"Goddamn," he breathed out through gritted teeth.

Completely turned on I removed my hands from his dick and placed them on his thighs, sliding him further and further down my throat until I felt him at the back of my tonsils. Holding him there I released a moan from the back of my throat then slowly pulled back.

Dre's knees buckled. "Where. . . ummm, fuuck. Where am I releasing this? Because you got. . . Fuuck. About thirty more seconds before I blow."

For the first time since I put my mouth on him, I fully removed him. I shifted my eyes up to his and held his gaze. "I wanna taste you, daddy."

I swiped my tongue across the head of his dick, twirling it over the mushroom shaped cap over and over before wrapping my lips around him again. Slowly I eased down his shaft then back up, sliding my tongue firmly against his large vein with each stroke. Dre's hands were on my head again but this time they rested there, allowing me the freedom to move up and down his engorged manhood. Increasing the suction of my jaws I slid down his shaft and paused. I felt the twitch in his cock and then warm semen shot down my throat. Slowly I resumed my movements, rolling up and down his dick until he had completely emptied himself. Sluggishly I removed him from my mouth as I stared up at him and parted my lips, revealing his juices sitting on my tongue. Slowly my lips curled into a devilish grin as I swallowed his seeds. I winked at him while giggling at the expression on his face.

Dre fell back into his chair with his eyes still locked on mine. "Fuckin freak."

A satisfied smirk donned my face as I wiped the corners of my mouth. "You ain't bout to have me turned out by my damn self," I stated, as I stood to my feet and walked over to my side of the desk.

I heard Dre snicker as I went to work clearing my desk. Ten minutes later I was set. I had cleaned up my food, packed my laptop and put away the two piles of paper I had sorted earlier. I looked over at Dre to find him quietly staring at me. He was fully dressed and looked completely sated.

"You ready handsome?"

Hopping up from his seat he pushed the chair up to the desk and walked around to me. "Oh yeah. I can't wait to get you in bed, so I can return the favor," he growled while enfolding me in his arms.

silenced the volume on the TV, picking up my phone I smiled at the name displayed on the caller ID.

"Hey pops, what it do?"

"Ain't shit youngin, just checkin in on my first born," his mellow tone answered from the other end of the line.

I smiled at the sound of my father's voice. "I'm good, just got back from meeting with my coach."

"Oh yeah, how'd it go?"

"It was cool," I answered flatly.

"Just cool?" he asked, picking up on my tone.

I chuckled at my father's ability to read me. "He talked with me about some things that I can improve on to make me more marketable. Then we talked about the deadline for the draft."

"And? Has something changed that you ain't trynna tell your old man?"

I ran a hand down the back of my neck as I pondered my father's question. "Nah it's just—"

"Just what? he asked, cutting me off. "I don't understand where this uncertainty is coming from. You've worked your entire life for this moment. What's changed?

I blew out an exasperated breath while trying to find the right words to articulate my feelings. "No, nothing has changed."

"So, help me understand. Since you were a boy you've dreamed of playing professional ball. You've dedicated your time to perfecting your gift and you've made sacrifices for it. So, what's the problem son?"

I started to answer him when my phone beeped, alerting me there was another call. I looked at the caller ID and frowned. The name THIRSTY flashed across the screen. I swear I hated ever hooking up with her ass. It seemed the more I ignored her the more she pursued me. *She is fuckin relentless.* Everyone else had gotten the memo even Payton had fell back. But not her ass. Lyric hit my line at least twice a week. Every message was the same, an open invitation to come blow her back out. Just like the hundred times before I ignored her ass.

Pressing decline, I placed the phone back up to my ear. "You still there?" my father asked.

"Sorry pops, I'm here."

"So, you gonna tell me what has you second guessing your dream?"

"I'm not second guessing it I'm just considering everything that will come along with it," I admitted somberly.

"Like?"

"The loss of my privacy for one. You know I'm not comfortable being in the spotlight. Once I go pro everything I do on and off the field will be critiqued by the world. My life won't be my own anymore. I'm not sure I'm ready for that. If I can be who the world or should I say the media wants me to be. And don't let me mess up or fall out of the perception they have of me. Then what?"

My father chuckled. "I hate to be the one to tell you this, but your life has never been your own son. Who you are and what you do has and will always impact those who love and support you. It's the same for me, Shalonda, your grands, your baby sister, hell even your mother," he stated passionately.

I winced at the mention of my birth mother as I blew out a heavy sigh.

"You can't live your life in fear of fuckin up or being scared of what those who don't matter think when you do. Because guess what?"

"What?"

"You're gonna fuck up, you're human. But how you handle those fuck ups and not repeatin your mistakes is how you grow. I raised an amazin man. A strong man with good morals and values. A man with a strong sense of self. As long as you don't lose sight of him, I have no doubt in my mind that you will be okay. Don't let fear keep you from your dream son." He paused for a moment I assumed giving me time to process his words. "Now you said lack of privacy was one reason, are there other reasons you're rethinkin entering in the draft?"

I smiled for the first time since we started this part of the conversation while contemplating his question. "No, that was it. Thanks pops."

"Thank me by fulfillin your dreams. If you told me, you no longer wanted to play pro ball because you lost your passion for it, I'd understand but I can't get behind you givin up out of fear. I know I ain't raise no punk."

That made me laugh, a deep hearty chortle. "No, not at all," I agreed, as I sobered from my laughing fit.

"That's what I thought. So, I don't wanna hear no more of this scared of the public eye shit. I'll leave you with this and we can dead this convo."

"Shoot."

"You are my son and there is nothing you can do that will ever make me stop loving you. I want you to live your best life and not out of fear but with passion. Don't let the world's expectations of you stop you from living the life you want to live. We only get one life son and I want you to ride it until the wheels fall off. Time is something we can't get back. Just make sure you use yours wisely. Your family loves you and we are so proud of you."

"Damn pops that was dope. Thank you, for everything. I love you."

My father chuckled. "I love you too. I just hope you don't get drafted to the Browns or the sorry ass Avengers," he teased.

"I just hope I get drafted."

"Oh, yo ass is gettin drafted and you're gonna kick ass in the NFL."

"From your lips to God's ears," I spoke quietly.

"For where two or three have gathered together in My name—"

"There am I in the midst of them," I finished.

"And don't you ever forget it," he instructed with authority.

"I won't."

"Alright son, I didn't call to talk your ears off. I just wanted to check on you. You comin home for Thanksgiving? I got some stuff we need to chop it up about and it needs to be done face to face."

I picked up on the seriousness in his tone but decided to ignore it. If he said we needed to talk in person I'd wait until then. "Yeah I'll be there. We have a game that Saturday in North Carolina, so it'll be a short visit. I'll probably hop on the road after classes on Wednesday and leave back out early on Friday."

"Cool. I'll see you then. I love you son."

"I love you too pops. Bye."

I disconnected the call, dropping my phone on the couch next to me I smiled. My father always had a way of making me feel better. After my meeting earlier today, I had my doubts on whether I was actually going to enter the draft but now I knew exactly what I was going to do. For the first time since my coach talked to me about going pro, I was confident in my decision. And I had my pops to thank for that.

Kicking my legs up on my coffee table I reflected on my conversation with my father as his words echoing in my head. I welcomed the new sense of calm that washed over me as I silently recited Matthew 18:20. I didn't necessarily consider myself to be a religious man, instead I thought of myself as spiritual. Growing up it was just me and my pops until I was fourteen. Shalonda had been around for some years but they didn't marry until then. Therefore, she didn't really have a motherly role in my life until after her and my pops said I do. So, my father relied on his parents for support. My grands introduced me to religion and my father imparted spirituality in me. Pops taught me the importance of having faith and developing my own personal relationship with God.

A low chortle passed through my lips, recalling my father's favorite quote regarding church. He would say, "Son going to church don't make you a Christian any more than standing in a garage makes you a car." He taught me that it was what was in my heart that mattered while encouraging me to know God for myself.

The sound of my phone chirping pulled me from my musing. I swiped a hand over the cushions of the couch, trying to feel for my phone. Brushing against the small devise I picked it up and looked at the screen. *Seriously.* Annoyed, I went into my messaging app and clicked on the moniker I used in place of her name. As expected, she let me know she was available if I was looking to get into something tonight. Shaking my head, I exited out of Lyric's message without replying. Instead, I tapped the tiny square with the pen icon at the top of the screen. When the blank message thread popped up, I started typing in the address bar until my coach's name populated. Going into the body of the text I keyed in two words, I'M READY.

After hitting send I allowed my shoulders to relax as I sank further into the plush cushions on the back of the couch while reveling in the sense of peace I felt with my decision. I snapped my eyes shut but quickly fluttered them open when my phone pinged, alerting there was a notification from one of my social media accounts. I looked at the screen of my phone and saw a notification from Facebook. *I thought I turned these alerts off.* Clicking on the blue icon I waited for my newsfeed to load, interested to see what foolishness I was sure awaited me.

What. The. Fuck?

Confused I stared at a picture of me that I didn't post, a picture I didn't recall taking. I studied the image trying to figure out when she could have taken it. Enlarging the photograph, I examined the background, searching for clues. For anything that would jumpstart my memory. I was able to determine that it was taken at my crib. And by the looks of my outfit it was some time during the warmer months. Although it was a picture of me from the side there was no mistaking it was me. I stood by the window in my living room with a brew in one hand while the other rested against the window seal above my head. Only one side of my face was exposed. The sun combined with the flash of her camera created a slight shadow over the picture. Frustrated, I blew out a hard breath while exiting out of the photo. For the first time since discovering the invasive image I looked at the caption. In bold letters it read, *HE GIVES ME BUTTERFLIES.*

Shaking my head, I slid my eyes down the picture, taking note of the many likes. Pissed and somewhat curious I tapped on the comment button. I skimmed through the plethora of comments all with the same basic theme, congratulating Lyric and complimenting me. I had seen enough. It was time to shut this shit down. I stopped scrolling, ready to exit out of the comment section when my eyes landed on a comment unlike the others. She_Slay wrote, *can somebody say THIRST TRAP!!!*

Exactly.

I was happy to see someone recognized this shit for what it was. I studied the small circle containing She_Slay's profile picture. It wasn't of her face. The photo was of a woman with long hair layered in bountiful curls cascading down her back. Curiosity got the best of me, I clicked on miniature picture and waited for her page to load. I was surprised to see She_Slay and I were already Facebook friends. Not recognizing her from the many pictures displayed across her page I clicked on the photo tab near the top of her page. A huge smile seeped across my face as a dozen images of Carmen's face popped up on her different photo albums. *I should've known.* Exiting out of her photo section I went back to her profile picture. Narrowing my eyes, I examined the image of the woman with a head full of curls. Carmen wore her hair in a short platinum mohawk, so I doubted it was her. My eyes skimmed down to the date, the picture was posted last month. Suddenly it clicked, the photo was Rocky.

Fuck!!! If Carmen saw this bullshit, then that meant Rocky had to too.

Dropping my phone in my lap I closed my eyes and ran my fingers down the bridge of my nose, trying to calm my raging temper. Foolishly I thought if I ignored Lyric, she would get the message and move the fuck on. Clearly, I was wrong. Slowly I cracked open my lids and plucked my phone from my thighs. I didn't have the energy for an actual conversation, so I choose to send her a text. Going into my messaging app I clicked on our message thread and started typing. My message was short and simple but definitely clear, TAKE IT DOWN NOW!!!

I didn't bother looking at the caller ID when my phone rang seconds after I hit send. Instead I tossed it on the table, slid my legs onto the floor and stood up from the couch. I didn't have time for this shit. I hated when people mistook my kindness for weakness. Reaching down onto the coffee table I clicked off the TV, snatched up my phone and gaited out the room. My phone rang again as the front door closed behind me. I glanced at the screen then quickly sent her ass to voicemail.

I was halfway to Rocky's when I decided to stop ducking her calls. "Yes Lyric."

"I'm sorry Dre. I took it down, but I really don't understand why you're so pissed," she whined on the other end of the line.

I didn't speak at first, debating on if I had any words to offer her. "I'm pissed because you're playin games," I breathed out slowly.

"How?" she shrieked.

"C'mon Lyric don't try and play me. So, you gone act like it's a coincidence dat you put that shit up after yo girl ran back and told you she saw me wit Rocky at the ESPN photoshoot earlier this week?"

"Yeah, Brooke told me she saw y'all but that didn't have anything to do with me posting that picture." Her tone was controlled, voice strong. If I didn't know her, I would've believed her.

"Cut the shit Lyric. I don't know what cha issue wit Raquel is but if you try that dumb shit again it's gone be me and you that have issues. Understand?"

"Dre. . . I'm so. . . I wasn't trynna—"

"I ain't askin for all dat. I just need to know that we have an under-standin," I barked out, cutting her off.

"Yeah we do," she answered barely above a whisper.

"Preciate it." I disconnected the call before she could spew more lies.

I stuffed my phone inside the pocket of my hoodie as I shut off the engine of my truck and released a long sigh. Needing to get this shit over with I flung the door open and slowly peeled my ample frame from the truck. I took my time walking through the parking lot while I tried to mentally prepare myself for whatever reaction Rocky had to Lyric's little stunt. With my eyes trained to the ground I cut through the courtyard, pausing at the sound of my name.

I looked up to find Carmen walking toward me. "What's up Mellow Yellow? Rocky ain't tell me you was comin over."

Snickering I draped an arm around her shoulder while matching her pace. "She can't tell you what she ain't know."

Carmen cocked her head to the side, angling it to look up at me. "My nigga," she stated, as a wide grin stretched across her face.

Enfolded underneath my arm Carmen guided us the short distance to Rocky's apartment. Without knocking Carmen flung the door open and immediately strolled inside, leaving me standing in the doorway. Rocky smiled as her best friend approached while I played the back-ground. Posted up against the doorjamb I waited for her eyes to find me. I waited while watching her and Carmen exchange hushed words. I continued to wait as I crossed my arms in front of me and rested them on my chest. I stood inside the door silently watching the woman who was quickly taking root in my heart, looking for a sign that she was okay, okay with me being at her home uninvited. As if she could feel my eyes on her Rocky looked at me over Carmen's shoulder. Leisurely she slid her eyes up to mine. Instantly I felt the tension leave my shoul-ders as her smile widened. In what felt like slow motion I kept my eyes fixed on her as she stepped around her friend and walked up to me and threw her arms around my neck. I quickly unfolded my arms and placed my hands on her waist, holding her flush against my chest.

"Well isn't this a pleasant surprise," she gushed out giddily, gliding her hands up to my face.

I stared down at her, trying to decipher the sincerity in her words. "Sorry to just pop up on you, Short Stuff."

Rocky planted a soft kiss on my lips then quickly pulled away. "No worries handsome. Did you come over, so you could have me feelin butterflies too?" Her tone was light but there was no hiding the sarcasm hidden behind her words.

I brushed a hand down my face. "That's actually why I'm here," I admitted, while holding her gaze.

Rocky backed out of my arms. "I'm fuckin witcha. Ain't nobody thinkin bout Lyric's thirsty ass. But I appreciate you takin the time to make sure I was good."

Rocky turned to walk away but I grabbed her by the wrist, halting her movements. My eyes bounced between her mouth and her soft brown orbs. "Just so you know I deaded that shit."

Sucking her lip in between her teeth, Rocky tried to hide her smile. The sound of Carmen smacking her lips stole her attention from me, glancing over her shoulder she shook her head.

"Man fuck that sac chasin bitch," Carmen spat.

"Carm," Rocky shrieked through a chuckle.

I tugged on Rocky's arm, prompting her to slide her head back toward me. "We good Short Stuff?"

She shook her head in the affirmative. "Carm and I were about to go get some food, you trynna roll or do you want me to bring you somethin back here? I mean, that is if you were plannin on hangin out."

I hiked a brow. "I'm rollin, where we eatin?" I asked, still holding onto her tiny wrist.

"Alabama but ain't nobody trynna be y'all's third wheel. I'll drive my whip and you two can ride together," Carmen chimed in.

"Sounds like a plan," I responded to Carmen, while still staring down at Rocky.

"Dre. You have to let go of my wrist." She looked down at my hand, still hooked around the small of her arm. "I need to grab a jacket and get my phone."

Reluctantly I loosened my grip, allowing her to slide her arm out of my hand. Spinning on the balls of her feet, Rocky padded into the living room. She retrieved her phone from the coffee table and a light-weight jacket from the arm of a chair then ambled back toward me with a wide smile crest on her pretty face.

"I'm ready."

The three of us exited her apartment, Carmen headed to her car while Rocky and I made our way to mine. Buckled in, I started the engine and slid my eyes over to Rocky, watching her closely.

"You gonna do that all night?" she asked, eyes fixed on mine.

I didn't answer her, instead I shifted my head forward as I placed the truck in gear and backed out of my parking space. I trailed behind Carmen doing my best to keep up with her speed demon ass. Weaving in and out of traffic we navigated through the slightly congested streets, heading into Over-the-Rhine. Fifteen minutes later we had reached our destination. We stood outside the modest sized restaurant wedged between a nerdy looking brother and a petite white woman dressed in gothic garb from head to toe.

It was late October but the steady decline in temperature made it feel more like the dead of winter. Pulling my hood up over my head I tried to block out the wind that was slapping the back of my neck. *Shit, if I was cold Rocky has to be freezing.* Focused on the tiny woman standing in front of me I watched as she wrapped her arms around herself and vigorously ran her hands up and down her arms. Unzipping my hoodie, I pulled her back into my chest, wrapping my arms around her waist I covered as much of her tiny frame as I could.

Rocky tilted her head back against my chest. "Thank you."

I gazed into her eyes for a short moment then planted my lips against her forehead, lingering there before lifting my head. I fixed my mouth to reply when the line finally shifted. Rocky stepped forward and I quickly matched her pace, stepping in accordance with her strides in order to keep her shielded underneath me. Less than five minutes later we made it inside and placed our orders then stepped off to the side to wait for our food.

"Damn this place is always packed." Carmen looked around at the dozen or so of patrons standing inside the small eatery. "I swear it don't matter what time of day you come here this joint stay jumpin like the damn club."

I heard the light sound of Rocky's giggle as I walked back up to the counter to pick up our orders. Food in hand I met the girls at the door. Cool autumn air greeted us as we filed out the packed restaurant. Again, Rocky's arms flew up and around her upper body. *I don't know why her ass put on that little ass jacket.* Shaking my head, I handed Carmen both bags of food then removed my jacket, gingerly draping it across Rocky's shoulders. A soft smile decorated her slanted orbs as she stuffed her arms in the sleeves and zipped the oversized hoodie.

Once again, I found myself playing the background while Carmen and Rocky engaged in girly chitchat as we walked Carmen to her car. After making sure Carmen was tucked away safely inside her car Rocky and I started the short walk to my truck, parked on the next block.

"So, what did you have planned before I interrupted your evening?" I asked, lacing my fingers with hers.

"Nothin for real. This was kinda spontaneous. Carm saw Lyric's post and called me all pissed. She was halfway to my apartment by time she finished the story. We decided on food after I got her ass to calm down," she explained, with her eyes fixed forward, refusing to look at me.

I hated the solemn tone I heard in her voice. I knew she said we were good, but something didn't feel right. Like now that we were alone her true feelings about Lyric's post were quietly seeping out, even if she wasn't verbalizing them. I tugged at her hand and waited until she looked at me before I spoke.

"Hey, talk to me." I ran my thumb over the top of her hand, waiting for her to speak.

She giggled but not in a way that meant she thought what I said was funny. "I thought that was what we were doin Dre."

I stopped walking which in turn halted her steps as well. I shifted my body so that I was standing directly in front of her. Looking down I stared into woeful eyes as I took my time studying her. "No, I mean talk to me not around me. We've come too far for you to put your wall back up. Cuss me out if that's how you feel but don't keep that shit bottled up."

Another giggled spilled out her mouth but this time it was a genuine gut-wrenching laugh. Calming herself she looked at me, a smile now present in her eyes. "No walls just processing. But I mighta picked up my phone once or twice to cuss yo ass out," she admitted.

"There she is," I teased, stepping back on the side of her and resuming our walk.

Rocky snatched her hand out of mine and nudged me in the side with her elbow. I snickered, pulling her tiny frame into mine while tossing my arm over her shoulder. We settled into a calm silence as we rounded the corner where my truck was parked.

What da fuck?

She didn't see us, not at first. Her head was down, stuffing something inside the bag draped across her body. I narrowed my eyes and zoomed in on my windshield where what looked like a small piece of paper was lodged in between one of the wipers.

Slowly she raised her head and that's when our eyes connected. Mine held a look of confusion while I saw something different in hers, a look I couldn't identify. Placing a faux smile on her face she walked toward us with measured confident strides.

Fuck!!!

Sliding my eyes toward the woman underneath my arm I studied her out the corner of my eye. Her expression was murderous, eyes fixed straight ahead, locked on Lyric. Five more steps, that was the number of strides it was until we reached her.

One.

Two.

Three.

Four.

Five.

Lyric stood directly in front of me, her eyes larger than usual bounced between me and Rocky. Again, I found myself looking out the corner of my eye at Rocky. For the first time since we noticed her

Rocky gave me her eyes. Eyes filled with questions mixed with something unidentifiable. Swiping a hand down my face I turned my attention back toward Lyric.

"Lyric."

"Oh, hey Dre. I . . . um, I just left a note on your truck."

I looked past her toward my parked SUV. "I see," I stated, as I drew my eyes back to her.

"I . . . um. . . I didn't know you weren't alone," Lyric responded, with her eyes now fixed on Rocky.

"I guess that's somethin else you didn't think through," I stated, while smirking, although I didn't find shit funny about her being here in this very moment.

"Dreeee," she whined, skirting her eyes back over to me.

"Oh Dre, don't act surprised. Lyric is used to doin shit without thinkin," Rocky spoke up, surprising both of us.

"Excuse me?" Lyric asked.

"What? You hard of hearin too?" Rocky questioned, while stepping out from underneath my arm.

I stepped forward, positioning myself in between the two of them but was quickly pushed aside as Rocky stepped closer to Lyric.

"Did I stutter?"

Lyric's eyes bugged out of her head then slid over to me. "Dre."

Before I could respond Rocky spoke. "Why are you callin him when I'm the one who said it?"

"Whatever Raquel, I don't have time for this." Lyric swiped her hair over her shoulder.

"Neither do I. You ready?" Rocky asked, looking up at me.

I shook my head, not bothering to look at Lyric more concerned with Rocky. Moving past Lyric, Rocky strolled casually toward my truck, with me in tow behind her.

"Well fuck you too, black bitch," Lyric mumbled underneath her breath.

Before I had time to react Rocky had spun around on her heels and was in Lyric's face. "What da fuck did you say?"

Lyric took a step back. A mischievous smirk donned her immaculately made up face. "Did I stutter?" she asked, repeating Rocky's previous statement.

Her hands were posted up on her hips with her head cocked to one side. She gave off the illusion of confidence, but I could tell she was anything but. She was intimidated by Rocky but tried to disguise it. Who she was putting on for I wasn't sure. I knew Lyric wasn't from the streets but yet and still she stood her ground, body language oozing of attitude as she waited for Rocky to respond.

I took a step forward but quickly stopped in my tracks when Rocky shot me a look that said, *nigga I will kill you where you stand if you take one more step.* So instead I waited with my eyes stapled to her, silently praying she didn't swing on Lyric.

"See what I thought I heard was your ignorant ass call me out of my name and make reference to my skin tone in a derogatory manner. Now I know earlier I said you were accustomed to saying stupid shit, but I thought you had enough sense not to say them in the presence of someone who you know can beat your ass."

I couldn't help the smirk that eased upon my face as I stood by watching their exchange. Rocky delivered that warning purposely without the use of slang. She knew Lyric prided herself on her suburban upbringing and boasted on her Princeton City School education in order to make others feel inferior. Yep, right now Rocky was challenging her and doing so in a way that she knew Lyric would understand.

"Listen, everybody gets one. That was yours." There was a finality in her words as she turned away from Lyric and prepared to walk off.

"One what?"

Fuck. What the hell is wrong with this chick?

Rocky spun back around and faced Lyric. "One warning. Now the next time you call me out my name be prepared to pick your fuckin teeth up off the ground." Rocky stared Lyric dead in her eyes, waiting for a response. When she offered none, Rocky spoke again. "Matter of fact, if you see a bitch smack a bitch."

Again, Lyric was dead silent. Instead her eyes slid over to me, but I

had nothing for her ass. My only concern was Rocky and how I was going to keep her from going upside Lyric's head.

"That's what I thought. And I'on know why you keep lookin over at Dre, he can't help you. Because if I decide to beat cha ass it's gonna take Jesus himself to pull me off you." She was pissed. That quick she slipped back into slang. With her head cocked to the side she waited for Lyric to make a move.

Lyric dropped her hands from her waist and relaxed her posture while softening her voice. "Look Raquel, I don't have no beef with you and I'm definitely not trying to fight you."

"You might wanna think about that the next time you decide to call me outta my name. Because the next time there won't be a conversation." Rocky held Lyric's gaze while taking a step closer to her.

Lyric took a step back.

"And FYI, that's me." Rocky glanced back at me over her shoulder then slid her head forward, looking at Lyric again. "So, you remember that the next time you think about postin one of your little thirst traps."

Lyric's eyes stretched wide. She opened her mouth to respond but quickly snapped it shut. Nodding her head, she paid me one last glance then silently walked past Rocky. Unsure of what to do I found myself waiting yet again.

"What in the hell possessed you to fuck that chick?" Rocky asked, as she strolled over to where I stood.

Caught completely off guard I chocked on the spit I was swallowing while preparing to answer her. I thumped my fist against my chest and waited until I caught my breath to respond. "What. . . Why would—"

"Oh, stop it Dre. We're grown. I'm just wonderin what you saw in her besides her pretty face. The bitch is dumb as a box of rocks. Not to mention, she thinks she better than everybody."

"Honestly?"

"No for play. Yeah honestly, dude."

"I was drunk," I admitted, slightly embarrassed by the topic of conversation.

Rocky stared at me for a beat, her eyes bouncing around mine.

"Every nigga's excuse for smashin a chick he knew he had no business stickin his dick in."

She turned away from me and started walking in the direction of my truck. I quickly followed suit. Grabbing her elbow with my free hand I jerked her toward me, forcing her to stop walking. In no hurry I waited until she looked at me. Slowly she turned and faced me, sliding her eyes up to mine.

"We only hooked up twice. First time she gave me a terrible ass BJ. I was sober for that shit. The second time we smashed and like I said, I was drunk." Suddenly it hit me, that's when she took that picture. The night we had the kickback at my apartment before summer break.

Rocky drew her bottom lip in her mouth while maintaining my gaze.

"You mad?"

"Depends."

"On what?" I asked, anxious as fuck to get this conversation over with.

"You still fuckin her?"

"Hell no!" I shouted, louder than I intended.

"Then nope, I'm not mad. We good," she stated, as a sly grin stretched across her face.

Naturally a wide smile donned my face in response to her. Rocky snickered while shifting her body forward.

"Now can we get out of this cold? I did give my jacket to a certain lil person and now I'm freezin my balls off," I teased, while weaving my fingers inside hers as I started the walk toward my truck.

"I'll warm em up for you."

"Well in that case let's hurry up and get you back home."

Rocky chuckled as I opened the passenger door for her. Handing her the bag of food I rounded the front of my truck, stopping momentarily to grab Lyric's note from the windshield. Not bothering to read it, I ripped it into a bunch of tiny pieces and stuffed them in the pocket of my jeans. Standing at the driver's side door I couldn't help the Kool-Aid size smile plastered on my face as I stared at the woman in the passenger seat. I replayed her words in my head, feeling a sense of pride hearing her stake her claim to me. Swinging my door open I climbed in, paying her another quick glance before turning my attention forward. After starting the engine, I buckled my seatbelt then navigated out of the tight parking space.

"So, are we gonna talk about you claimin me to Lyric?" I asked, hiking a brow up toward my hairline.

"Nope."

CHAPTER TWELVE

"*Y*ou're serious?" he asked, his usually low eyes stretched wide as he watched me pull a gold foil packet out of my pocket and drop it on the table.

"Dead ass. Besides, I did win the bet." I swept my eyes low, staring at his semi erect penis. "And by the looks of it, your wit it," I finished, slowly bringing my gaze back to his face.

Dre smirked while reflexively running a hand down his rod. "I ain't opposed to it if that's what you're implyin. And for the record, I never renege on a bet."

"That's what I thought," I declared confidently, while taking a step toward him.

Dre opened his mouth to speak but before he could formulate a response, I attacked his mouth, crashing my lips against his. He willingly accepted my unsolicited peck. Parting his lips, he released a low groan from deep within his throat. Trilled by his reaction to me the corners of my mouth curled up into a smirk as I slid my tongue slowly across his velvety soft lips. I took my time tasting him before gliding my tongue into his warm mouth.

Grabbing a palm full of my ass Dre pulled me into his chest, deepening our kiss. His minty breath filled my nostrils while his tongue rolled silkily over mine. I had initiated contact, but Dre had quickly taken over, devouring my mouth while his hands freely explored my body. With one hand cupping my ass he placed the other in my hair, gingerly massaging my scalp. Instantly a chill shot down my spine causing the tiny hairs on my arms to stand up. I relished the feel of his body against mine as I raked my hands greedily over his back. Brushing over his deltoids, I clawed at his rhomboids, then trailed the tips of my fingers down his spine. I let my hands rest at the small of his back as I released the moan, I'd been concealing from the moment my lips made contact with his.

Slowly I detached my face from his. "Shit," I panted, trying to catch my breath.

His chest heaved up and down, inhaling a lung full of air he peeked at me through half open lids. "Damn girl, you literally just took my breath away."

I smirked but didn't speak. Instead, I dropped my head and slid my hands on either side of his waist. I stared at his now fully erected dick while swallowing the excess salvia that had gathered in mouth.

Ummm.

I discreetly dabbed at the corners of my mouth before lazily raising my head. Sweeping my eyes up to his I got lost there, watching the specks of emerald glisten above the flame from the candle perched on the table. Neither of us spoke as we stood underneath the quiet of the night drinking each other in. I wasn't sure how long we'd been standing there when I felt Dre's hand underneath my chin. Shifting my eyes to his hand I watched as he slowly traced his thumb over my lips. First my top then the bottom, gently dragging my lip down as he slid his hand from my face and rested it on my wrist.

"So, we really doing this?"

I drew my bottom lip into my mouth and closed my eyes as I ran my tongue across the brim. The sound of Dre clearing his throat snatched me out my head. Flicking my lids open I stared up into his amused face. Slowly a grin swept across my face as heat spread through my cheeks. Dre tugged at my wrist while hiking a brow, waiting for my answer. I nodded my head, feeling my arousal dripping down my thighs.

Peeking over his shoulder Dre looked in the direction of the wicker loveseat located in the corner of my patio, on the other side of the small table next to us. Taking the few steps over to the sofa Dre pulled me along with him. Carefully he lowered himself onto the coach while still holding firm to my wrist. Then his hands were on my hips again, positioning me in between his outstretched legs. I stared down at him and watched as he lowered his head and dipped a hand underneath my skirt. Using the tips of his fingers he trailed my calf then slowly slid his chaste tips up the inside of my thigh. His head shot up while his squinted lids ballooned to the size of quarters as he discovered the moisture oozing down my legs.

"Where da fuck are your panties?" he growled, while traveling further up my leg.

I parted my lips prepared to reply when I felt his fingers brush against my labia. Tilting my head backwards I closed my eyes when Dre entered me with his index and middle fingers while swiping against my clit with his thumb. Tiny burst of tingles started at my neck, slid around my shoulders, coursed over my arms, shimmed down my spine, and skirted over my thighs down my calves to my toes. I was hypersensitive, and my senses were on overload. Dre's long fingers twirled skillfully in and out of me, sending sporadic chills up my spine.

"Aaah." I flung my head upward while fluttering my lids open. Feeling my knees starting to buckle I leaned forward and rested my hands on Dre's broad shoulders.

Beautiful hazel eyes slid over to mine. "I'm gonna let you fuck the shit out of me out here. After which I'm gonna take you in the house, make love to you, then watch you fall asleep in my arms."

I swallowed back the lump that had formed in the back of my throat the moment he opened his mouth to speak. Nodding my head, I turned my face slightly, attempting to hide my blush. Dre released a deep chortle then placed his free hand underneath my chin, slowly dragging my face back toward his. His hand was soft, his touch was tender, but his eyes. His eyes held a hint of lust and an emotion I was starting to become accustomed to seeing whenever he looked at me. There was so much emotion, so much so I almost thought I imagined seeing lust. Batting my lids rapidly I tried to blink away the fresh wave of emotions that washed over me as my eyes danced in his. But the longer I stared in his eyes the more lost I got. Lost in my feelings, lost in what he was clearly communicating without the use of words. Suddenly I felt weak. The unusually warm winter night started to feel more like the dead of summer. Sweat started forming above my upper lip. *Shit.* Turning away from him I ran a hand across my lip.

Again, Dre tugged at my chin. Reluctantly I slid my face back to his. "Stop fighting what's inevitable Short Stuff. Don't let how I feel intimidate you. It doesn't matter who gets there first, the destination is the same." He held my gaze, giving me time to process his words.

A warm smile adorned my face as I nodded my understanding.

"Just know that when you get there, I'll be there waiting for you," he finished, peering at me with the same emotions from before. Then slowly it faded from his eyes. In its place was somethin I was much more comfortable with. Something I knew how to handle. Pure unadulterated lust.

Dre wiggled his fingers, reminding me he was still inside of me, deep inside of me. Instinctively, a high pitch moan flew from my mouth as I returned my hand to his shoulders. Using the length of his middle finger to his advantage he pressed against my nub in a come here motion. Again, an unabashed moan escaped from my parted lips as my body responded to him, releasing a new gush of moisture. Moisture that Dre seemed enthralled with as he stared at his fingers fresh out of my sex. A sly smirk donned his face as he held his slick fingers up to his lips. Locking his eyes on mine he placed both digits in his mouth and cleaned them of all traces of me.

Holy fuck that was sexy.

I stood upright, prepared to take over when the breeze from the wind caught my attention. Sliding my gaze down to my leg I watched as Dre hiked my skirt up over my hips. He placed his large hand on my calf and gently lifted it off the ground. Resting the ball of my foot on the cushion next to him he brushed the inside of my thigh with his nose. The warmth of his breath against my skin sent a quiver up my spine as my hands flew to his head. Digging in his scalp I relished the feel of his smooth silky tongue coursing up my leg. He angled his head as his hands grasped at my ass and his tongue lashed against my sex. *Oh. My. God.* I was already on the brink of a mind-blowing climax thanks to the earlier ministrations of his gifted fingers, now this. I didn't know how much more I could take but Dre had every intention on finding out. His tongue moved repeatedly in a circular motion, licking every inch of my lubricated sex. Aware that we were outside I tried to conceal my moans but was failing miserably. At one point, I heard Dre chuckle as he lapped up my juices while craftly snacking his tongue inside of me before slowly withdrawing it and sliding it across my clit. That was it, that was undoing. Holding firmly onto his head I gave into my orgasm. My eyes clamped shut and my head rolled back as my muffled screams pierced the quiet skies.

I felt the softness of his lips on the inside of my thigh, sensed his movements around me as I released my grip from his head. I heard the sound of the wrapper tearing; I even felt the still of his hand on my calf as he gingerly placed my leg back on the ground. But it wasn't until I felt his hands on my waist that I opened my eyes. Staring down at him I covered his mouth with mine. Rolling my tongue over his I straddled his lap, carefully lowering myself onto his sheathed erection.

"Ssssh," I mumbled against his lips.

"Umm. . . don't hurt yourself sexy."

I locked my eyes on his while sedulously gliding down his rod. Finding a comfortable space, I held him there as I slowly wind my hips, allowing myself to get acclimated with his size. Placing the bulk of my weight on my thighs I wrapped my arms around his neck then glided up his shaft and back down. Dre's hands quickly moved from my waist down to my ass. He gave my cheeks a firm squeeze then dropped his head to the back of the couch while rolling his eyes in the back of his head. Completely aroused I felt my sex lubricate between us as I moved rhythmically up and down his pipe.

Dre's lids creaked open as he lifted his head from the back of the couch. "Goddamn sexy."

I had no words I was too busy trying to ride out the emotional wave that had suddenly taken ahold of me. Shifting my eyes to his mouth I quickly slid my tongue over his parted lips, rolling it smoothly around his. Dre released a moan in mouth as I continued to ride him like my life depended on it. Easily keeping up with the fervor of my kiss Dre's hand returned to my waist. He attempted to control my speed, but I wasn't having it. Ignoring his tightening grip, I bounced up and down rapidly, thrusting forward each time I came down. I felt tiny beads of sweat gathering at the crease of my forehead as my palms misted, making it difficult to hold onto to his shoulders.

Removing my hands from his body I swiped them down my skirt then judiciously unmounted him. "Don't move," I commanded.

I turned around and placed my legs on either side of his then slowly lowered myself onto his throbbing rod. I leaned forward and placed my hands on the table in front of us for leverage. Gliding down his dick I watched as he disappeared inside of me. Pivoting his hips Dre matched my strokes as I slid up and down, taking all of him in each time I came down. *Fuck, I'm cumin.* Before I had time to process it my body jerked uncontrollable as my pussy pulsated around his stiff rod.

"Get that shit," he coaxed, while wrapping an arm around my waist.

I lifted my hands off the table and pressed my back into his chest, rocking my hips slowly I rode out my orgasm. Dre's lips were in the crock of neck then his teeth clenched down, sending a jolt of electricity through my already sensitive body.

"Fuucck," I screamed, not caring about my neighbors, or being discovered.

"Can I cum now?" he asked, barely above a whisper.

Completely spent, I shook my head as I continued to rock and swirl my hips on top of him.

"Lean forward," he breathed into my neck, as he released his hand from around my waist.

I did as he instructed, leaning forward I placed my hands on the coffee table again. Moving behind me Dre scurried to his feet all while still inside of me. Those hands were back at my waist, gripping firmly as he piled aggressively into me from the back. Leaning into me he rested his chest against my back, placed his mouth on my neck, and released himself into the condom. His strokes slowed as he rode out his climax. Panting, he rose sluggishly while pulling me up with him.

"Remind me that yo ass is a freak the next time I decide to bet against you." I could hear the humor in his voice as he leisurely pulled out of me.

"Why? You love this shit," I countered, while glancing back at him over my shoulder.

"Damn right but it ain't the only thing I love." He made that declaration with confidence while removing the used latex and pulling up his pants.

I didn't hide my smile, instead I held his gaze. I needed and wanted him to see my emotions even if I couldn't verbalize them. Never one to push me, tonight was no different. Dre pulled my skirt back down my legs and grabbed my hand with his free hand. I placed the cap back on the candle then allowed Dre to escort us back into the house where we quickly made our way back to my bedroom.

If I thought, he blew my damn mind out on the patio I had no words to describe what he'd just done to me in my room. Stretched out across my bed, covered up with just a sheet I stared at him confused by the sudden shift in our evening.

"Wait, you're serious? You're mad?" I asked, feeling slightly annoyed.

"I'm not doin this shit wit you Raquel."

"Doin what? I'm being serious as fuck. Please tell me why you're mad." I heard myself begging as I sat upright on the bed, holding the sheet close to my body.

"I don't know. Maybe it's because the woman I've been gettin to know for the past five and half months and who I thought I had a fuckin bond with wants to go home and leave what we've built here. Or maybe it's becuz you're askin me to hide—" his voice trailed off as his eyes remained glued to my face.

"I'm not trynna hide shit," I yelled, feeling myself getting more and more pissed by the minute. "I'm just askin for more time, that's all."

"Time for what Raquel? What's gonna change between now and God knows when?" he barked, scooting over to my side of the bed and staring directly in the eyes.

"I don't know. I just nee—"

"Exactly. You don't fuckin know. But you want me to be okay with this undetermined amount of time."

My eyes burned but I refused to let the tears fall. I refused to let him see my emotions, not now and definitely not like this. Blinking excessively, I turned toward the wall, watching him from the corner of my eye. "Dre please, I don't want to argue."

"Too fuckin late." He stood from the bed and walked over to our pile of clothes by the dresser.

I snapped my head in his direction, not caring about my impending tears. "Why are you gettin dressed?" My voice was so low, I barely recognized it as my own.

Shifting between our discarded garments Dre found his clothes and quickly began tugging them on. Fully dressed he turned and looked at me. "I need to go. I can't do this shit wit you right now. Not after—" he paused, staring down at me he shook his head. "I'll call you later."

I hopped out the bed and sprinted toward him. "Dre wait. I don't want you to go. Not like this," I pleaded, as I grabbed him by the wrist.

Dre didn't look at me, instead he stared at my hand on his wrist. "Let me go Raquel."

"No."

His eyes quickly shifted up to mine then slowly raked down my body. A sly smirk seeped across his face as he took in my nudity. A fact I was oblivious to until that very moment. Subconsciously I wrapped my arms around myself as my eyes darted toward the floor.

"Lock the deadbolt behind me."

My eyes shot up from the floor as my hand flew back up to his wrist. Dre stared down at me while my eyes darted capriciously in his. His smirk had disappeared, in its place was a deep grimace. Our moment was gone, ruined by my ability to live in my truth. *Shit, this is not how I envisioned our night ending.* A knot formed in the pit of my stomach as I fought back tears. Like the coward he was basically accusing me of being I let my eyes drop, staring at the wall behind him.

"Let me go Raquel," he gritted out, while snaking his wrist out of my grasp.

Before I had time to reply he was out my bedroom door and down the hall. I stood stuck in place, trying to gather my emotions as the front door slammed close. *Why am I so upset?* This wasn't the first time Dre and I had argued but for some reason this felt different. This hurt.

FUCK!!!

Taking slow measured steps, I padded out my room toward my front door. I quickly secured the deadbolt then traipsed back to my room where I stood inside the doorjamb. Pressing my back against the wall, I let the tears I tried to hold back fall freely down my face. *How da fuck did we get here?* I wasn't sure how long I stood there when I finally willed myself to move. I wiped a hand down my face to clear my cheeks of the unwanted moisture only to have fresh tears stream over my hand. Giving up, I removed my hand from my face, allowing my body to eradicate the pain as I slowly gaited over to my bed.

It had been an hour since Dre left my apartment, and he still hadn't called or texted. Throwing my pride to the side I sent him a text only to be ignored.

This is exactly why I don't do relationships. So why the fuck did I care so much?

"So, tell me again how you got Dre to agree to keepin y'all shit a secret?" Carmen asked, while giggling into the phone.

I smacked my lips, still feeling raw from our fight damn near two weeks ago. "I already told you."

"Yeah well tell me again becuz I swear you must have kryptonite in yo pussy."

I rolled my eyes up in my head and smiled at Carmen's last statement. "He agreed to wait since he won't be home the entire weekend.

He said it wasn't fair to leave me alone to explain or defend our. . . um—"

"Relationship bitch. It's called a relationship Raquel," Carmen stated, cutting me off.

"Whatever." I chuckled to disguise my discomfort.

"You can laugh all you want but I know you and I know this is different. Can you honestly tell me what you and Dre have is the same as all the others?"

"It's definitely different," I whispered.

"Huh? What was that? I couldn't hear you."

"You know what? You really ain't funny."

"Yes I am. But seriously Rocky, Dre is a good dude and he is good for you. Don't let your parent's shit fuck up what could potentially be the best thing to happen to you. You deserve to be happy," Carmen implored passionately.

"I hear you, I really do. But I'm dealin with twenty-seven years of fuckedupness."

"Have you ever thought about talkin to somebody?"

I sucked my teeth. "Like a shrink? Nah, I'm good."

"Now ain't that some shit. Yo ass in school to be a damn shirk but you opposed to seein one. Help me understand that shit."

"People go to counselin for mental health issues not becuz their daddy has two damn families." I found myself giggling again although I didn't find shit funny about my parent's situation.

"Okay, well what about talkin to your mom? Hell, or even Miss Brenda? I mean maybe they can give you some insight on their situation that would make it easier for you to open up to love."

"I'm good. That sounds like some Iyanla Vanzant shit. I'll pass," I stated, trying to imagine talking to my mother or Miss Brenda about their blind dedication to my father.

"Bitch you can use the help to fix your life." Carmen chuckled at her own joke.

"Fuck you. My life ain't broke boo boo."

"Suit yourself but one way or another you gonna have to deal wit your shit or risk losin Dre. Let that shit sink in."

"Thanks for the counselin session but I need to get off this phone, so I can finish packin. I'll see you when I get there," I finished, while shuffling through the pile of clothes on my bed.

"Bye boo. Safe travels."

I disconnected the call and dropped my phone on the bed. Staring at the array of garments I reflected on Carmen's words. Although I hated to admit it, my best friend was right. The situation between Dre and I was unlike anything I'd ever experienced. If someone was to ask me how, why, or when things shifted in our relationship, I don't know that I would have an answer. All I knew was that he was different and that this thing between us was unlike anything I'd ever experienced.

Throwing a few items inside my tote I continued to reflect on my situation with Dre. Never in a million years would I have imagined we'd be here. Yes, I was attracted to him and yes, I enjoyed the sex but this, this was some next level shit. Dre invoked feelings in me I'd never experienced before. And for the first time in my adult life I wanted to explore those feelings. I wanted to give myself to him, but I was scared. Scared of getting hurt but more importantly I was scared of hurting him.

Suddenly aware of the time I pulled myself out of my haze. Studying the items in front of me I quickly selected a few, tossing them in my bag I pulled it close and zipped it. The next fifteen minutes consisted of me flying through my apartment gathering everything I needed for the next four days. Luggage strapped across my chest, phone tucked away in my pocket and Creed secured on his collar I walked out the door and headed for my truck.

Shit it's cold.

Pulling my hat over my ears I unlocked the doors and hurried Creed inside. Once he was settled, I opened my door and climbed into the driver's seat. Warm air from the vents circulated throughout the truck, instantly warming me. On days like this I was truly grateful for my aftermarket remote car starter courtesy of the twins. Pulling my gloves off I tossed them in the passenger seat then hit the button for the steering wheel heater. I placed my truck in reverse prepared to pull off when my phone chirped. I kept my foot secured on the brake while pulling my phone out of my pocket. Looking at the home screen a smile stretched across my face. With my thumb pressed on the home button I waited for the screen to open then went into my text app and immediately clicked on Dre's name.

Dre: Hey beautiful, u on the road yet?

Me: Was in the process of pulling out when u texted. What time u getting on the road?

I stared at the three small dots on the screen, anxiously waiting for his reply.

Dre: Imma leave here in about an hour. Can't seem to get out of bed. U have any idea why that is?

I chuckled as my fingers typed on the small keyboard.

Me: Because somebody wouldn't let me leave last night so I had no choice but to put it on em <smiley face emoji>

Dre: I told yo freaky ass to stay because I didn't want u driving home late. I didn't expect u to wear my ass out.

Me: You wanted it so stop complaining.

Dre: I'll never complain about spending time with or in u.

Me: And u call me a freak.

A few minutes passed before he sent a response, prompting me to place my truck back in park.

Dre: Sorry Short Stuff I had to use the bathroom, but I never said I wasn't <winking face emoji>

Me: And I can't be?

Dre: Only wit me.

Me: Okay daddy but u gotta promise me the same.

Dre: Promise. Alright, I ain't gonna keep you. Just wanted to check on u. Text me when u get home and be careful.

Me: K

Sitting my phone in the empty cupholder I placed my truck back in gear and pulled out of my parking space while smiling from ear to ear as I replayed our conversation over in my head. It was crazy how easily Dre could affect my mood. Like those two days following our fight when he refused to accept my calls or return my texts. Those few days were hell for me. Not knowing where we stood fucked me up more than I cared to admit.

Coasting onto the highway I shook my head, thankful we made it past that point. In retrospect it was Dre's reaction to me asking that we keep things between us during the holiday that made me realize how much he meant to me. I stopped denying my feeling that night I watched him storm out of my apartment.

Dude had my head gone.

Turning the dial on the radio I blasted the music from my hip hop playlist as I navigated down the highway. Traffic was light, making me glad I waited for rush hour to pass before getting on the road. Zoning out I welcomed the random thoughts of Dre that seemed to invade my head during my drive. Before I knew it, I was pulling into my parent's driveway. Retrieving the garage opener from the center console I pushed the open button and tossed it back as I watched while the door slowly rose. While I waited, I grabbed my phone out the cupholder and sent Dre a text, letting him know I made it home safely. Once the door was open, I coasted inside, cut off the truck, and quickly hopped out.

I entered my parent's home fully expecting to hear old school tunes blaring through the custom built in surround sound while my mother dashed through the house packing last minutes items for her trip. Instead I found the house dark and eerily quiet. Leaving my boots inside the mud room I closed the door behind myself and dropped my bags on the floor while swiveling my head around. The curtains were still drawn close and Gigi was inside her crate.

That's weird mommy hardly ever crates Gigi.

I freed Gigi from the confinements of her cage and walked down the hall, sweeping my eyes over each room I passed looking for my mother. I made it to the kitchen without so much of a trace of her. Letting the dogs out the back door I headed back down the hall toward her room. The door was slightly ajar, no lights or movement reflected into the hallway. Cautiously I opened the door and stepped inside. Laid underneath an expensive comforter on her oversized bed I found my mother sleeping peacefully. I stood inside the doorway watching her.

Even in her sleep she was flawless. With my eyes fixed on her peaceful face I padded toward the bed.

"Shit," I cursed under my breath after stubbing my toe on a small Louie bag at the foot of the bed.

"Watch your mouth young lady."

A hushed giggled slipped through my lips as I perched myself on the edge of the bed. "Sorry, I thought you were sleep."

"I was until some vulgar mouth young lady came into my room cursing," she teased, as she propped herself upright on the bed while pulling her face mask up and resting it against her forehead.

"Mommy why are you bed? Do you feel okay?"

My mother frowned at me. "I feel fine just a little more tired than usual."

I hiked a brow. "Why? Are your meds not working?"

"They're working just fine. I just didn't plan very well. I had my injection yesterday and I've been extremely tired ever since. Didn't think it through."

"Are you okay to travel? If not, I can stay home and cook us Thanksgiving dinner."

"I'm fine little girl. I pushed my flight back until seven. I'll be ready way before then." Her lips curled into a one cheek smile as she tossed the covers off her body and swung her legs off the bed.

"Are you sure?" I asked, watching her closely.

"I'm positive. Besides I know you don't get to see your brothers that often, and I would hate to be the reason you missed spending time with them," she asserted, while glancing at me over her shoulder as she lifted herself off the bed.

To say I was shocked would've been a major understatement. My mother rarely if ever talked about my brothers, and I couldn't recall a single time she mentioned them to me. Picking up on my silence my mother snickered as she gaited into the bathroom.

After my mother finished her bathroom routine she sauntered back into the room with a face full of immaculate makeup, a satin robe wrapped around her tiny frame, hair absent of the curlers that were present when she entered, and a beauty pageant smile plastered on her face.

"Have you eaten?" she asked, walking past me toward her bedroom door.

I quickly hopped off the bed, trailing behind her. "I had some fruit earlier, before I got on the road."

My mother halted her steps. Startled I almost ran smack dab into the back of her. Spinning on her heels she turned and faced me. "That is not acceptable," she proclaimed, while making a tsk sound with her mouth. "Let's get some food in you then you can help me pack." With that she turned back around and traipsed down the hall, toward the kitchen.

She's such a damn diva.

I followed my mother into the kitchen without question or complaint. She immediately strolled over to the refrigerator and began pulling out items for what she considered an acceptable meal. I stood in the entryway of the kitchen observing her. My mother was a strong woman, but multiple sclerosis had a way of weakening even the strongest of people. Although my mother had gotten her condition under control, I could still remember a time when it had taken over her ability to function. Sweeping my eyes down her small frame I watched her closely, looking for signs of discomfort.

Casually strolling over to the stove my mother looked over her shoulder at me. "Stop staring at me and let the dogs in. Their barking is starting to annoy me."

Again, I didn't say anything I simply did as she instructed. After letting Creed and Gigi into the house I walked over to the island and took a seat. Resuming my perusal of my mother I studied her movements as she went about the task of fixing us brunch.

"Little girl, if you don't stop minding my business and get some of your own, I'm going to know something." She belted out that command without looking at me.

I snickered while pulling my phone out of pocket. Unlocking the device, I quickly cleared my alerts then began browsing my social media accounts. Fifteen minutes later my mother joined me at the island, holding two plates containing what I was sure were veggie omelets accented with three slices of turkey bacon. Sitting both plates on the counter my mother took a seat next to me. After saying grace, we settled into a comfortable silence while digging into our individual plates.

Once we had eaten and I cleared away our dishes my mother and I spent the rest of the afternoon prepping for her trip. By the time five o'clock rolled around I was dog tired, my early morning activities had definitely caught up to me. However, I refused to let that prevent me from enjoying my time with my mother. So here I was, propped up on the edge of her bed watching as she stuffed the last piece of clothing inside her designer bag before zipping it. Moving the oversized luggage from the bed to the floor my mother rattled off a list of instructions for Gigi and the house. I pretended to pay attention as I stood from the bed and snatched her bag off the floor.

Offering me a cinematic smile accompanied by a wink my mother turned on her heels and sauntered out the room. I trailed behind her as I followed her down the hall, through the mud room, and into the garage where I quickly loaded her luggage into the back of my truck.

"You ready beautiful?" I asked, climbing into the driver's side of the vehicle.

"I am," she responded, while gingerly lifting herself inside the truck.

While waiting for my mother to get settled I started the engine then searched my music app for an appropriate album to listen to while she was in the car. Selecting Jill Scott's radio station, I shifted into reverse and carefully eased out of the garage.

"Thanks again dear."

I smacked my lips as I peered at my mother from the corner of my eye. "You don't have to thank me. What I look like letting you take a cab when I'm home?"

My mother didn't answer me instead she leaned over and placed her soft lips on my cheek then returned to her side of the truck. Once again, we found ourselves settled in a comfortable silence as I navigated out of the neighborhood. Forty-five minutes later I said goodbye to my mother then watched as she proceeded to the curbside check-in. I waited as long as airport security would allow before shifting my truck in gear and pulling off.

It was still fairly early when I returned to my parent's, but my body didn't give a damn about the time. Leaving my coat and shoes in the mud room I marched down the hall toward the steps where I took the stairs two at a time, speedily trekking up to the second floor. Dashing down the hall I opened the door to my room and practically threw myself across the bed. I hadn't intended to fall asleep but that's exactly what I did, waking up three hours later to the sound of my phone buzzing from my pocket. Rolling on my side I reached onto the nightstand and flicked on the light then plucked my phone from my pocket, grinning at the name displayed across the screen.

Dre: Hey Short Stuff. Sorry I didn't text earlier, being running around like crazy since I touched down. I hope your night is going well. Just wanted to let u know u were on my mind <winking face emoji>

Unable to ignore the fluttering in my stomach I wasted no time responding.

Me: No worries I'm just glad u made it home safely. Enjoy your family we'll talk later <kissy face emoji>

Dre replied with the same emoji I'd just sent him; a kissy face followed by the smiling with heart eyes emoji. My modest grin instantly spread into a face splitting smile as I sat up and swung my legs off the bed.

I dropped my phone on top of the comforter as I shook my head to myself at the giddiness, I felt over two little emojis. *Damn, I really need to get my shit together.* Running a hand down my face I slowly peeled myself off the mattress, walking just as slowly toward the door. Even with three hours of unexpected sleep I was still exhausted but the way the dogs were bouncing around my feet I knew I needed to let them out.

Taking my time, I trekked into the hallway and was immediately greeted by darkness and the quietness of the night. The only sounds I heard came from Gigi and Creed trotting excitedly behind me.

Talk about déjà vu.

Strolling down the long corridor I quickly made my way down the stairs and into the kitchen. I flicked on the light and watched as Creed and Gigi rushed over to the patio door, wagging their tails they bounced their heads between me and the door. There was no urgency in my steps as I walked over and let them out. Taking advantage of not having them on my heels I refilled Gigi's bowls with food and water then grabbed Creed's eating dishes and food from his bag, quickly adding food and water and placing them next to Gigi's. I stood in front of the door impatiently waiting for them to finish. Less than a minute later both dogs ambled up the steps of the deck, lazily trotting through the cracked door.

Securing the lock on the back door I walked over to the stove and flicked on the light over top of it. I paid the dogs one last glance before strolling out the kitchen, flipping off the light as I passed. I made it upstairs as quick as my short legs would carry me. Repeating my earlier movements, I lunged forward onto the bed but instantly popped up, remembering I was still fully clothed. I stripped down to just my socks and panties before pulling back the covers and diving underneath them, relishing the feel of the soft warm material against my skin. Using the last of my energy I plugged my phone into the charger and cut off the light. I didn't bother turning on the TV because sleep was my only mission.

---

*S*tanding in front of the full-length mirror inside my bedroom I swept my eyes down my body, checking my appearance for what felt like the hundredth time since I got dressed. Although I knew I could be particular I was especially self-conscious today. As usual Thanksgiving dinner was at Miss Brenda's and the majority of her family was in attendance, including her youngest sister Stephanie. Stephanie hated my father and barely tolerated me. She made no qualms about her feelings toward either of us. In order to keep the peace, I tried to make myself invisible when in her company and that typically started with my appearance. Taking in the long cream sweater dress with a modest side split accented with a pair of cognac knee high heeled Christian Louboutin's I decided I wasn't calling too much attention to myself.

"You look amazing as usual. Now can you hurry up, so we can eat. Everyone is waitin on yo slow ass."

I jumped at the sound of his voice before slowly turning around. "I'm ready," I stated, turning back toward the mirror while running a hand down the front of my dress, smoothing out the bunched-up material.

"Well come on then," Royce instructed, stepping into my room and walking over to me.

I looked at him over my shoulder. "Are you sure I look okay?"

He wrapped his arms around my waist and pulled me back into his chest. "When are you gonna stop lettin Stephanie get to you?" He looked at me through the mirror while resting his chin on the top of my head.

I spun around, dragging my eyes up to his. "Ain't nobody pressed about yo bitter ass aunt." I attempted to sound confident as I pushed him in his chest and strolled past him.

"Uh hun. Just know I'll cuss her out if you want me to, all you have to do is say the word," he responded playfully, catching up to me at the door.

I couldn't help the wide smile that eased onto my face as I looked over at him. "I'm a big girl. I'm good."

"Big where?" He hiked a brow, waiting for my response.

"Don't forget who used to beat yo ass."

"Thanks for the reminder. I owe you one," Royce joked, while pinching me in the side.

I took off down the hall in a full sprint, giggling while Royce chased behind me. Miraculously I made it down the stairs without falling on my ass. Arriving just behind me Royce scooped me up in his arms, cradling me like a baby up against his chest. He walked with me in his arms, carrying me into the formal dining room where everyone was gathered just like he said.

"The princess is here. Now let's eat," he announced, as he placed me on my feet.

"Well it's about damn time," Stephanie mumbled loud enough for me to hear.

Suddenly the entire room went quiet as all eyes were on me. In that moment I wanted to disappear. Looking down at me Royce shook his head then walked over and stood behind his aunt. Placing his hands on either side of her chair he bent down and placed his mouth next to her ear. He whispered something I couldn't hear but knew was about me by the look on Stephanie's face as she peered at me through squinted lids.

Being the peacemaker of the family Miss Brenda also addressed Stephanie. "Ain't gone be none of that today. If you can't control your mouth in my house you know where the door is," she admonished, while staring at her sister.

Stephanie threw her hands up in submission while not so subtly rolling her eyes just as my father causally strolled into the room carrying the turkey. Sensing the tension, he turned and looked at Miss Brenda then quickly swung his eyes toward Stephanie. Neither woman said anything as my father bounced his blazing orbs between the two. I remained in the same place Royce had left me. I watched the entire ordeal somewhat shocked that my mere presence had caused tension.

My father sat the turkey on the table while paying Stephanie one last glance. Slowly he turned toward me. "You look beautiful princess. C'mon take a seat so we can eat."

"Thanks daddy," I responded quietly, while walking up to the table and taking an empty seat in between the twins.

With his eyes focused on me my father gaited over to Miss Brenda and stood next to her at the head of the table. Reflexively her hand moved to the small of his back. In an attempt to sooth the silent rage she knew was underneath his calm veneer she ran her hand up and down his spine. Unhurriedly he turned his attention away from me, sliding his face over to Miss Brenda he placed a kiss on her cheek. With a soft smile set on her lips she took her seat adjacent to my father who remained standing. Asking everyone to bow their heads my father blessed the table then took his seat.

Despite the earlier incident dinner was filled with good food, rambunctious conversations, and an overall peaceful atmosphere. Afterwards everyone dispersed to various parts of the house while me and one of Miss Brenda's nieces helped her clean up. We packed food inside Tupperware dishes, wiped down the counters and table while working diligently in a peaceful silence until there wasn't a single item out of place. Closing the door to the dishwasher I stepped over to the island and poured myself a hefty glass of wine.

Miss Brenda came over and stood next to me. "You are glowing sweetheart and I'm not just talking about a I've had some good sex type of glow either," she stated, playfully bumping me with her shoulder.

Damn near chocking on my wine, I raised a hand to my mouth, catching the excess liquid that almost dribbled down my chin. "Miss Brenda," I squealed, while wiping my mouth, thankful the wine hadn't made its way to my dress.

"What?" she asked, placing her hands on her hips.

I didn't answer her, instead I took another sip of my drink while holding her gaze over the top of my glass.

"Tell me I'm wrong. Tell me there isn't something different about you. Like you don't have an extra pep in your step and a beautiful aurora surrounding you."

Dropping my eyes toward the glass in my hand I shook my head. "I don't know what you're talking about," I lied, hoping she didn't pick up on the change in my tone.

Miss Brenda opened her mouth to speak when the doorbell chimed, leaving her words caught in the back of her throat.

Ryker hopped up from the couch in the family room. "I got it," he announced to no one in particular.

Still in disbelief of Miss Brenda's previous comments I bounced my eyes around the room while I tried to avoid her inquisitive gaze. Undeterred by my attempt to avoid her Miss Brenda perched her elbows on top of the island, rested her chin on her balled fist, and stared a hole in the side of my face. I smirked while keeping my eyes trained forward, catching a glimpse of Ryker as he casually strolled through the kitchen with not so much of a glance our way as he trekked toward the front door.

The electronic voice from the alarm announced that the front door was open just as his deep raspy baritone resonated through the halls. Instantly a chill surged down my spine causing me to straighten my already erect frame.

"Un hun. There's my answer," Miss Brenda whispered in my ear.

I hiked a brow, pretending not to know what she was talking about. "Excuse me?"

"You heard me just fine little girl. That handsome young man making his way down here is the reason my baby is glowing," she asserted, while sweeping her eyes down my face. "Don't worry, it doesn't leave here," she finished, using her index finger she pointed between the two of us.

Smiling I placed a kiss on her cheek in acknowledgement of her promise. Miss Brenda winked as she backed out of my space, standing an arm's length away her eyes bounced between me and the entryway of the kitchen. I placed my glass in front of my mouth and tried to hide my smile as Dre and Ryker entered the kitchen. Shuffling from behind the island Miss Brenda walked over to Dre and wrapped him in her arms as she whispered in his ear. Dre flung his head in my direction as his eyes descended to mine. A knowing smile adorned his beautiful hazels as Miss Brenda continued to speak in his ear. Slowly Miss Brenda released him from her embrace just as my father walked into the room.

"What up young blood? I see you came through for our annual spade's tournament. You ready to get that ass spanked?" my father teased, walking up and extending a closed fist toward Dre.

"I'on know bout all dat, JB. You know the kid slick wit it on the spades table," Dre boasted, as he bumped my father's fist with his own.

"Well we finna see. See you in the basement. Royce down there settin up now," my father stated, while walking out the kitchen and heading toward the basement door.

"Hi Rocky, you ain't speakin today?" Dre asked, as his smile stretched up to his eyes.

I swallowed the last of my wine and placed my empty glass on the counter. "Hey Dre. I always speak but I was waitin my turn." I couldn't help the sass in my voice as I drug a hand up to my hip.

"Fuc— I mean, forget all that. You ready to go bust some ass?" Ryker asked, stepping to the side of Dre and clapping his hand on Dre's shoulder.

"You already know," Dre responded, eyes still focused on me.

"What you want to drink? Hard liquor and beer are in the basement, but we got wine and juice up here," Ryker yelled over top of the music that started blaring from the basement.

"Let me get a glass of ice and a coke," Dre responded, watching me with his eyes as I walked over to the sink.

I rinsed my glass out and sat it inside the sink. Turning on my heels I headed out of the kitchen when I heard my name being yelled, causing me to pause my steps.

"Aye yo sis, you ain't playin tonight?" Ryker inquired.

"Of course, I am. I just need to get my phone out my room," I replied, glancing over my shoulder at him.

"Bet. See you downstairs."

Adding an extra sway to my hips I took my time walking down the hall toward the stairs. Even though I couldn't see him I knew he was watching me. Once I was out of his sight, I dashed up the steps and down the hall to my room. I flicked on the light, snatched my phone off the bed, and quickly headed out the door. Walking back down the hall I checked my notifications. I was surprised to see a text notification from Dre less than a minute ago. Clicking the phone onto the home screen I went into my text app and pressed his name.

Dre: U wearing the fuck out of that dress. But why da hell don't u have any panties on <angry face emoji>?

Me: What is your obsession with panties? And who said I didn't have any on?

I made it back down to the main level of the house when my phone buzzed in my hand. Walking toward the basement I instantly clicked on his message.

Dre: I could give a shit about panties but what I do care about is yo ass always walking around without em.

Me: Again, who said I wasn't wearing any?

I stepped off the last stair in the basement with my face fully engrossed in my phone, waiting for his response. After a minute of no reply I clicked out of the app and strolled over to the bar. Stephanie's daughter, Mia was behind the large wooden structure fixing a drink. Looking up a wide smile stretched across her face as she sat the bottle of Rèmy on top of the counter.

Since when did I earn such a greeting from her stuck-up ass.

All thoughts of Mia were quickly snatched from my head as his raspy tenor vibrated in my ear. "Yo ass, that's who," he whispered, accepting a drink from Mia's proffered hand.

I rolled my eyes as I spun around to face him. "Thongs are panties too Dre," I stated loud enough for only him to hear.

Sitting his glass on the bar he nodded his head at Mia who I assumed was still back there cheesing like a damn Cheshire cat. Without saying a word, he returned his attention to me. Staring down at me he placed both his hands on the small of my back, leisurely moving them lower until he felt the material of my thong. Satisfied, he quickly removed his hands from the apex of my ass and picked up his drink while smiling down at me.

"C'mon, come watch me whip your pops and uncle's asses." He grabbed my wrist as he prepared to walk toward the card table.

Slightly irritated, more at her then him I snatched my wrist out of his grip. "You sure you don't want Mia to watch you instead?"

Dre spun around, confused hazel peering down at me. His brows were scrunched together damn near meeting in the middle as a subtle scowl seeped onto his handsome face. "Don't start that shit Raquel before you make me do some shit that will have both our asses fightin up in this bitch."

Feeling defiant and unable to shake off the shitty feeling that settled over me when I realized Mia was all goo goo eyed over him, I placed my hands on my hips and cocked my head to the side. "Like what Andre?"

Using his free hand Dre knocked one of my hands from my hip and wrapped his arm around my waist while pulling me into him, closing the already small gap between us. "Like announcin to this whole muthafuckin room that we're more than just friends. Or how bout I'm fallin in love wit your stubborn ass. You take yo pick," he growled in my ear, while silently challenging me with his eyes.

That knocked all the fight out of my ass, taking my breath along with it. Slowly I fluttered my lids, processing his words while I tried to play it cool as I attempted to control my breathing. I had no idea what I expected him to say but that was definitely not it. I parted my lips prepared to finally speak when Royce tapped Dre on the shoulder. Reflexively Dre tightened his grip around my waist as he looked at Royce over his shoulder.

"Aye, y'all been over here doin this lover shit too long. Y'all startin to draw attention. So, unless y'all ready to let this. . ." Royce looked at Dre then slid his eyes over to me, "be known. I need y'all to break this shit up."

Slowly Dre loosened his grip, allowing me to slide out of his hold. With his eyes still locked on mine he quietly challenged me. His low hazels bounced around mine, flashing specks of emerald as he waited to see if I was going to keep with the bullshit. When I didn't speak, he took that as my answer. He turned away from me and followed behind Royce over to the card table. I heard her smack her lips, prompting me to turn towards the bar. I almost forgot about her hot ass. With her hands propped on her narrow hips she perspicuously raked her eyes down my body.

"Can I help you?" I asked, not bothering to hide the attitude in my tone.

Slowly a mischievous smirk spread across her face as her eyes returned to my face. "No but I think I'll go and see how I can help Dre though," Mia goaded, holding my glare longer than I liked.

"Beat it bitch. Dre is good."

I heard Mia smack her lips as a wide smile etched across my face.

Ignoring her, I spun around and stood face to face with my best friend. "Oh my God. I'm so glad you're here. When did you get here?" I asked, throwing my arms around Carmen's neck.

"Just now. Actually, I been here for about ten minutes. Got caught up by one of the twins' cute ass cousins," she stated, while easing out of my embrace.

"Bitch I got some shit to tell you."

Carmen's eyes ballooned wide. "Word?" Lowering her stretched orbs, she looked in Dre's direction then returned her eyes to me. "Well can it wait til tomorrow? Cuz I got a can of hoe repellant in my purse I think we need to use tonight," she replied, looking back toward the card table where Mia was posted up next to Dre.

I laughed while hooking an arm inside of hers. "It can but it's juicy. Now let's get somethin to drink before you pull out yo can of spray."

Carmen and I stepped behind the bar where I quickly fixed us drinks. Linking our arms together again we strolled over to the first card table where Royce and Dre faced off with my father and the twin's uncle. Ryker and Brayden were at the other table playing against Miss Brenda and Stephanie. Each table played until one team reached a total score of two hundred and fifty. The winning teams from each table would face off with the other making them the champs until the next round of players battled it out to determine the winning team from that group. Then the two champion teams played each other for bragging rights. This typically went on for hours. Teams were often shifted; games were sometimes forfeited but one thing remained the same; constant fun loaded with a gang of shit talking.

Carmen removed her arm from mine then causally strolled around the table, stopping next to Mia. Mia looked up and rolled her eyes. I snickered as I stood behind Royce, peeking at his hand before walking up behind Dre and glancing at his spread. Both had good hands and if they played them right, they had a chance of running a Boston.

"You gonna just lurk behind me or pull up a seat?" he asked, staring up at me over his shoulder.

I sucked my bottom lip in between my teeth as I sat my glass on the table next to his. "Imma sit."

Dre sat his cards face down on the table then pushed away from it, standing he took the few steps over to the wall where a few fold-out chairs were stacked together. Grabbing one he returned to where I was standing and sat it out for me.

"Thank you."

"You're welcome. Now sit cha ass down so you can watch us beat these old dudes." He winked at me before returning his attention back to the table.

"Don't be lying to my princess," my father shouted above the music, as he slammed down his card.

Looking at me out of the corner of his eye Dre slid his card across the table, cutting my father's suit. "I never lie to Raquel."

Feeling all eyes at the table on me I picked up my drink and gulped back a hefty sip. Royce released a chortle as he raked up their winning book. Dre and my father talked shit their entire game while Mia and I sat on opposing sides watching one another as we pretended to pay attention to the game. Ultimately, Royce and Dre won. Ryker's table was still playing so there was a break before the next round started. Turning toward me Dre looked at the empty glass in my hand.

"You want another one Short Stuff?"

Before I could respond I saw Mia stand from her seat and tap Dre on the shoulder. Annoyance eased across his handsome face but was quickly replaced with a fake smile as he slid his head in her direction.

"I'll make you another one," she stated, taking his glass from his hand as she prepared to walk away.

Dre hopped to his feet and grabbed her wrist, gently taking his glass back. "I'm good Mia. Imma go and fix me and Rocky a drink. Thanks, tho." Not giving her a chance to respond he turned his attention back to me.

Dre grabbed me by the hand and helped raise me out of my chair. "C'mon Short Stuff."

Looking across at Mia I couldn't help the smug grin that settled on my face as I watched the dumbfounded look on hers. I rested my hand in Dre's, allowing him to guide us over to the bar. Unhurriedly I eased out of his grip and stepped behind the bar.

"Let me take care of you Mr. Cameron. Rémy and coke, right?" I asked, taking his glass out of his hand and sitting it on the counter next to mine.

Dre hiked a brow while leaning into the counter. "If you really wanna take care of me you'll come home with me tonight." His tone was low so that only I could hear him.

I topped off his glass with coke then slid it toward him. "It's too risky."

Dre picked up his drink and took a nip. He shook his head in under-standing but there was no hiding the disappointment in his eyes.

I picked up my own drink and sipped the pungent cocktail while staring at him over the top of my glass. "But you're more than welcome to come home with me."

"Say no more. We're out after this last round of cards."

CHAPTER THIRTEEN

I held my phone in my one hand and a single loose-leaf piece of paper in the other, staring at the number scribbled on it. It was only a number with no name assigned to it because I couldn't bring myself to write her name. Like writing her name would somehow make this nightmare a reality. A reality I wasn't ready to face.

"What the fuck bro?" Jamison asked, walking toward me on the couch.

I looked up from that weighted piece of paper, dropping it next to me. "What?"

"What the hell has your attention? I been callin your name for the past two minutes."

"My bad bro." That was all I could offer because I wasn't ready to share with him the reason I had zoned out.

Jamison took a seat on the couch, picking up the paper I'd let fall next to me.

"Whose number?" he asked, looking at the small sheet of paper.

"Nobody worth mentionin'," I declared, gingerly taking it out of his hand and tucking it inside my pocket.

"I can't tell by the way yo ass was spaced out. It must be one hella important number."

"Nah, not really but I promise to share when I'm ready," I stated blandly, looking over at him.

Jamison tossed his long arms up in the air. "Aye, I know when somethin ain't my business. But I'm here whenever you're ready to talk," he responded, pounding a fist on my knee.

"Thanks bro. I appreciate it."

"It ain't shit. You trynna get on these sticks?"

I glanced at my phone; suddenly aware it was still in my hand. Looking at the time I shook my head. "Sorry bro, I can't. Rocky is treatin yo boy to Pappadeaux," I explained, as a smile settled on my face for the first time since I pulled that piece of paper from my wallet.

Jamison's hand flew up to his mouth. "Oh word, what cha celebratin?"

I snickered at his animated response. "Nothin really. Just kickin it since we're both done for the semester."

"That's what's up. Make sure you bring yo boy some leftovers."

"Nigga please."

Jamison snickered. "It's coo, Balboa will hook me up."

I narrowed my eyes and stared at him as he continued to laugh at his own joke.

Sobering he reached onto the coffee table and grabbed the remote, clicking on the TV. "I quit. But for real, I hope she can help with whatever has you fucked up."

Initially I didn't respond. That quickly my mind had drifted back to that sheet of paper. *This is some bullshit.* Shaking my head to myself I attempted to shift all thoughts of Alexandria to the back of my mind while pushing up off the couch.

I extended a closed first toward Jamison, giving him dap. "I'll holla."

"Later," he called out behind me, as I made my way to the door.

Just like the millions of times before, I arrived at Rocky's without any real recollection of my drive over. However, instead of my thoughts being occupied by Rocky all I could think about was her. Pulling the creased piece of paper from my pocket I stared at the number again, contemplating if or when I'd work up courage to dial it.

My head shook softly on my shoulders as I folded the small sheet of paper and pulled out my wallet, stuffing it behind one of my credit cards. Tucking my wallet back inside my pocket I found myself trying my damnedest to push all thoughts of her and that dreadful conversation with my pops out of my head.

I shuffled out of my truck and attempted to focus my thoughts on the woman who had quickly made my heart her home. With my head aimed toward the ground I forced a smile on my face as I trekked the short distance to Rocky's front door. Pulling my hand from my pocket I held it up to the door when it flung open. Rocky stood on the other side with a bright smile on her beautiful face.

"Hi handsome. You didn't have to get out in the cold. I would've met you in the car," she stated, moving out of the doorway.

I walked inside and instantly scooped her up in my arms. Burying my face in the crook of her neck I relished the feel of her in my arms. Rocky ran her small hands gingerly up and down my back, providing a comfort I didn't know I needed until that very moment.

"What's wrong baby?" she asked, slowly withdrawing from my embrace.

Staring down at her I let go of my façade, allowing my face to reveal my true emotions. "I just got a lot of shit on my mind."

Rocky grabbed my hand, pulling me further into her apartment as she walked with me behind her into the living room. "You wanna talk about it?" she implored, letting go of my hand while watching me as I removed my coat and tossed it on the adjacent chair. I then kicked off my boots and sat on the couch.

Perched on my lap she angled her body toward me, looking me dead in the eyes while waiting for me to respond. Too emotionally spent I simply shook my head. Rocky sat quietly peering into my eyes, giving me the time I needed to articulate my thoughts.

Snapping my eyes closed I leaned back and rested my head on the back of the couch. Slowly and with much hesitation I cracked my lids open. "I'm ready but can I get a shot first?"

Rocky hopped up from my lap without saying a word, paying me one quick glance she strolled out of the living room. Less than a minute later she returned with two shot glasses filled with an amber colored liquid. She handed me one of the glasses before taking her seat on my lap. I held the glass up to my lips prepared to down the drink when I felt her hand on my wrist.

"To open and honest dialogue and peace of mind when you're done," she asserted, clinking her goblet with mine.

"Cheers Short Stuff."

I tossed back what I promptly identified as Rémy, in one quick swallow then held the empty glass in my hand as I stared off into the distance. The feel of Rocky's hand on mine drew my attention back to her. Gently she removed the glass from my hand, sitting it next to hers on the table in front of us.

Leaning back into me she ran a hand along my jawline. "Okay baby spill it."

I held her gaze as I contemplated if I was really ready to disclose my truth. Running my fingers along the bridge of my nose I released an exasperated breath. Rocky's eyes never left mine as she sat patiently waiting for me to speak. Thirty minutes later I had bared my soul, finally verbalizing what I'd been keeping close to my chest for the past two weeks. As hard as it was to put into words there was something freeing about telling her. Initially she said nothing, I assumed processing the load I'd just dumped in her lap. Suddenly I felt bad. Maybe it was too much for her to deal with.

Feeling uncomfortable by the silence I opened my mouth to speak but my words were quickly silenced by Rocky's mouth on mine. The kiss started off soft almost timid, as if she was expecting me to stop her. Placing my hands on her tiny waist I deepened our kiss, placing chaste firm pecks on her soft lips as I shifted her toward me. With her mouth still pressed on mine she lifted off my lap only to turn fully toward me as she straddled my legs. Her hands cupped each side of my face as she slid her tongue in my mouth. Inhaling I breathed her in, delighting in the minty taste of her tongue as it skillfully rolled over mine. A deep groan emerged from the pit of my stomach, slithered up my throat, and passed through my mouth into hers. Rocky's lips curled into a smile. Slowly she slid her tongue over my top lip then my bottom, sucking it into her mouth while softly nibbling on it. Again, I released a moan completely unbothered by the level of vulnerability I was displaying. I needed this, I needed her.

Unhurriedly she released my lip but not before placing her warm mouth on mine again. Fluttering my eyes open I watched as she climbed out of my lap. Extending a hand toward me she looked down at me, her own set of emotions present in her slanted eyes. Without question I took her hand and allowed her to help me rise from sofa. With our hands clutched tightly together Rocky led me out of the room and down the hall.

"Where we going Short Stuff? I thought you wanted Pappadeaux," I inquired, my voice so low I barely recognized it.

"Another time handsome. Tonight, I need to take care of you. Your energy is off, and I need to fix that. Right now, that's my priority then I'll feed you. Afterwards if you want to resume our convo we can. But not until you're ready. I know that was hard to share," she stated, her tone matching mine.

Plating my feet, I halted her steps. I threw my arms over her shoulders, pulling her small frame into my chest. "Thank you."

Spinning around in my arms she looked up at me. "You never have to thank me for taking care of you. It's what I'm here for. Besides, I'll always have your back." With that she turned back around and grabbed my hand again. "C'mon baby."

Lacing my fingers with hers I willingly followed behind her as she resumed walking down the hall. Rocky stopped in the bathroom where she retrieved a bottle of oil then continued guiding us toward her room. Once inside she instructed me to strip down to my boxers and lay on my stomach across the bed. Consumed with my thoughts I didn't ask any questions as I did as she instructed. I quickly discarded my clothes, leaving them splayed on the floor next to her nightstand then dived onto the plush mattress. Shuffling through the assortment of pillows I grabbed two and placed them underneath my head. The softness of her mattress mixed with her scent emanating from the pillows provided a calm my body needed. Closing my eyes, I attempted to shut off my mind while waiting for Rocky to finish whatever it was, she was doing.

I felt the mattress shift underneath her weight as she climbed onto the bed. Her warm hands rested on the blades of my shoulders as she mounted me, placing the majority of her weight on my butt as she sat down. Her thighs were bare letting me know she had removed the high waisted black jeans she wore when I first arrived. Curious, I cracked my lids open and peeked at her over my shoulder. Straddling my waist, she sat comfortably on my ass wearing a pair of short ass cotton shorts and a cropped long sleeve Pink sweatshirt. Her big bountiful curls no longer hung at her shoulders. She had pulled her hair up into a high bun on top of her head. Noticing me staring, she leaned forward and placed her lips on mine, kissing me softly. Just as I was ready to roll over and take this somewhere else Rocky pulled her mouth away from mine.

She winked at me as she sat upright, and her small hands returned to my deltoids. Unhurriedly I swiveled my head back toward the head of bed. For the first time since opening my eyes I realized the room was damn near dark. Perched up on my elbows I swept my eyes around the room, noticing soft lights illuminating throughout the expansive room from various candles strategically placed on different pieces of furniture. I turned toward Rocky ready to question her when the soft sound of jazz filled the air. Taking the hint, I clamped my mouth shut while shifting my head forward again. Burying my hands underneath the pillows I rested my chin on top of them.

I felt Rocky moving above me as her hands slid off my shoulders. Moments later they returned to my body, this time on my lower back, just above my ass. Her hands were warm, and her touch was firm. Taking her time, she massaged my obliques, applying varying degrees of pressure as she worked out knots, I wasn't aware were there until she loosened them up. Closing my eyes, I relished the feel of her oily hands as she worked her way up my spine. Kneading and rubbing she managed to successfully relax my entire body, sending me into a light sleep. I wasn't sure how long I'd dozed off, but I woke up to the feel of Rocky's breast pressed against my back as her small hands massaged my trapezius. She used the tips of her thumbs pressing firmly as she kneaded that knotted area. Reflexively, a soft moan slipped from my parted lips as I lazily opened my heavy lids. *Damn, I really needed this.* Gliding up my neck she gently stroked my splenius capitis. Finding a rhythm, she alternated between firm and soft strokes, sending a chill throughout my entire body.

I felt the warmth of her breath on my ear as she removed her hands from my neck, placing them on the mattress. "You good baby?"

Careful not to knock her off of me I rolled onto my back. "Yes, but now I need you to take care of something else," I growled, as my eyes traveled down my body, in the direction my growing erection.

Rocky's mouth formed an O as she glanced over her shoulder then returned her slightly bulged eyes to mine. "I think I can handle that. You sure you're up for it tho?"

Again, I swept my eyes toward my swollen rod. "Um, I'd say so," I stated, while propping up on my elbows.

Rocky leaned into me, crashing her lips against mine. Skillfully she slid her tongue over my lips and dipped it inside my mouth.

"Mmmm," I moaned, as her tongue slowly intertwined with mine.

Shuffling underneath her I sat up and wrapped my arms around her waist. Quickly adjusting to my movements, she looped her legs around me then slowly wound her hips, gyrating against my dick. Her arms rested on my shoulders and her fingers were in my hair, tenderly stroking my scalp while she made love to me with her mouth. There was something different about the way she was handling me. Her touch was soft and delicate, her kiss passionate and deliberate. Even the way she grinded her hips was methodical and controlled. I wasn't even inside of her yet and I was already losing my mind.

What the fuck is this chick doing to me?

Gradually withdrawing her tongue from my mouth, she placed a soft peck on my lips before softly pushing me back onto the mattress as she unhooked her legs from around my waist. With my eyes locked on hers I placed my hands underneath my head and waited. What I was waiting on I wasn't sure, but it was clear that this was Rocky's show, I was simply a willing participant. Her thick mocha thighs rested on each side of my chest while her perfectly manicured feet laid splayed across the bed next to my ears. Staring down at me through the tiny slit of her slanted eyes she took her time drinking me in, lazily sweeping her eyes down my upper body. Her perusal started at my head, slid down my face, grazed over my neck, swept from one shoulder to the other, eased down my chest, and landed on my abs. Slowly she returned her eyes to mine as a mischievous grin adorned her beautiful face.

Goddamn that was sexy as fuck.

Completely enthralled with the woman propped on my crotch I watched as the tip of her tongue slithered out of her mouth and rolled seductively over her top lip. Her eyes were no longer focused on my face. Instead they bounced between my triceps, studying the ink etched there. Placing her hands on my chest she lowered her body to mine then used the tip of her index finger to trace the scripted A on my left tricep. She then shifted her head to the right and repeated that motion on my right arm, trailing the outline of the italic C. Closing my eyes I reveled the feel of her delicate touch. Just as I was getting used to the feel of her skin on mine, she removed her hand from my arm and rose up from my chest. I flashed my eyes open, staring up at her.

Rocky held my gaze, quietly studying me. "Do you trust me Dre?"

Unsure why she was asking I hiked a brow. "Of course, I do. Why?"

Her tiny hands returned to my chest. This time she used it as a means to balance herself as she climbed out of my lap. "Because I want to try something, but it won't work unless you trust me," she answered quietly, hopping off the bed.

Rolling over onto my side I watched as she sashayed into her closet. "I'm down for whateva yo lil freaky ass wanna do as long as it doesn't involve anything goin in my ass," I called out to her.

I heard her snicker from inside the closet. Moments later she walked out with a wide smile on her face and a silk scarf in her hand. Curious, I kept my eyes focused on the thin material in her small hand as she strode confidently over to the bed. Placing a knee onto the mattress she carefully mounted the bed.

"You ready daddy?" She didn't wait for me to answer as she pushed me over onto my back.

I shook my head against the pillow, sweeping my eyes up from her hand to her face.

Rocky straddled me, resting her ass on my dick. With her eyes fixed on mine she leaned forward and grabbed my right arm, placing it above my head. Trailing her tongue down my neck she reached for my left arm, sliding it up and placing it next to my right.

"Tonight, is all about you. I want you to relax and let me please you. All I want you to do is tell me what you need," she breathed next to my ear, while strategically binding my wrist together with the scarf.

Lifting up from my chest she studied her handiwork before returning her eyes to mine. "Cool?"

Swiping my tongue across my lips I nodded my understanding.

"Use your words Dre."

"Agreed sexy."

Rocky smiled at me as she began to wind her hips in my lap. "Oh, one more thing."

I scrunched my brows together but didn't utter a word.

"If you remove your hands from that scarf I will stop. If you try to take over, I will stop. This is not about me tonight. Understand?"

I started to nod my head when I remembered her instructions from less than a minute ago. "I gotcha Short Stuff."

Her soft ambers danced in mine as she slowly removed her sweatshirt, tossing it on the floor beside the bed. Sweeping my eyes down her face to her breast I stared at her perky mounds as she swiped a hand across the mattress. A few seconds later she drug her hand up to her face and clicked a button on a remote I hadn't noticed until the music changed. Trey Songz "Slow Motion" streamed through the speakers as she leaned forward, dropping the remote somewhere on the bed. With her hands planted next to my head she dipped her face into the crook of my neck, swirling her tongue over my sensitive spot. Instantly a shiver of pleasure shot down my spine causing my ass to lift off the mattress. I felt Rocky's lips curl into a smile as she trailed soft wet kisses down my chest.

"Fuck Raquel," I grumbled, as her mouth traveled further down my body.

Propped on her knees in between my legs she placed her hands inside the waist of my boxers, gently tugging them down over my massive erection. Tossing them on the floor with the other discarded clothes she stared up at me. I held her gaze as a low groan involuntarily flew from my mouth when one of her tiny hands gripped me. Slowly she slid her eyes down to my rod while lowering her head. She swiped her tongue across the tip of my dick, gradually lapping up the pre-cum oozing from my slit.

Clamping my eyes shut I squirmed as she inserted the head of my dick into her mouth, rolling her tongue laggardly around me before smoothly sliding down my shaft. Her movements were controlled and carefully executed as she took her time drawing me fully into her mouth. Wiggling my arms underneath the scarf I cracked my lids as I brought my hands down to her head, resting them on top of her fluffy ponytail.

Rocky's eyes fluttered open and quickly found mine. She continued to peer up at me as she leisurely slobbed up and down my engorged pole. Using her hand to control her pace, she took slow measured gulps, sucking me in slowly while simultaneously running her tongue along my shaft. She was driving me crazy, and the fact that I had limited use of my hands added to my heighten sensitivity. I was a fucking mess, cursing and moaning while she concentrated on working me over. I had my dick sucked countless times before but never like this. Rocky wasn't just giving me a blowjob; she was making love to my dick with her mouth.

Fuck this, I needed to level the playing field before I blew my fucking load too soon. Lifting my hands from her wild mane I stretched them out above my head while looking down at her. "C'mere sexy."

She slid her eyes back up to mine as she slowly withdrew my dick from her mouth. *Fuck. Even that shit drove me wild.* With her hand still on my rod she used her excess salvia as a lubricant, indolently gliding her hand up and down my erection.

"Where would you like me?" she breathed out huskily.

"On my fuckin face. Now," I growled, squirming underneath the ministrations of her tiny hand.

"Nice try Mr. Cameron but I told you already tonight is about you, not me," she stated, dipping her head back down to my dick and sucking me into her mouth.

I released a deep groan as her tongue swirled around my rod. "You also said to tell you what I needed—" I paused at the feel of her other hand massaging my balls. Blowing out an audible breath I closed my lids then quickly fluttered them back open. "I need to taste you," I explained through gritted teeth.

Ignoring me she continued stroking my dick while gliding me further down her throat. Moaning as I hit the back of her throat, she slowly slid up my pipe then steadily slid back down. She was teasing me and doing a hell of a job too.

"Rocky," I barked.

Flashing her eyes up at me she curled her lips into a smile around my dick. Although I was on the verge of losing my shit, I kept my face neutral as I watched her take her time dragging her mouth up my rod. Unhurriedly she removed her hand from my balls while listlessly sliding me out of her mouth. Grateful for the temporary relief of unbridled pleasure I watched Rocky move from in between my legs and stand on the bed, carefully removing her shorts to expose her bare crotch.

I swear her ass never wears panties.

She took her time dropping down to her knees before crawling up to my face. "Where do you want me?" she asked teasingly.

Moving my constricted wrist, I placed my hands on her thigh. "Quit playin and bring yo ass here."

Tossing my arms above my head she mounted my face, slowly lowering her sex down to my mouth. Breathing her in I wasted no time running my tongue over her slick labia. An unabashed moan sceped from her mouth as she lowered her body to mine, lavishing my stomach with kisses until her mouth found my dick again. Wrapping both her hands around my rod she gradually sucked me in as she swirled her tongue down my shaft while twisting her hands around me. Moaning I slid my tongue inside of her, greedily lapping up her wetness. Rocky squirmed above me, moving her hips against my tongue while bobbing her head up and down my dick. I was slowly losing my mind as she continued devouring me at the same pace she had been doing before I interrupted her to have her sit on my face. I needed to make her cum before I did. Gliding my tongue out of her slickened flesh I slithered it over her clit, wildly flicking it back and forth until she stilled her movements. Holding me tight in her tiny hands she rode my face, moaning loudly as I sucked and licked her sensitive spot. She was close I could tell. Determined to bring her to a climax I slowed my tongue, dragging it repeatedly over her clit while softly sucking her into my mouth.

"Got. Damn. Dre," she exhaled, breathlessly.

"Cum for me sexy," I demanded, smothered underneath her.

She returned her mouth to my dick while slightly increasing her speed, grinding her hands in different directions while her warm mouth slid down my rod. Fuck, it was now or never because I was about to blow. Softly sucking her clit into my mouth, I swirled my tongue around her. Again, her movements halted as her body shook uncontrollably above me. Lightly lashing against her clit, I relished the feel of her juices dripping in mouth and down my face. Moaning incoherent curses her body slowed as she shuddered one final time before placing her mouth back on me. Slow and steady she inched down my pole while rolling her tongue around my shaft. Letting me rest at the back of her throat she released a husky moan. That was my undoing, I couldn't hold it any longer. A guttural moan eased from my mouth as my seeds spilled down her throat. She swallowed every ounce of my semen then slowly slurped her way up my rod while gradually easing me out of her mouth.

"Mmm," she moaned, as she carefully climbed off my face.

"You can say that shit again."

Rocky smiled down at me as she reached over to her nightstand. Opening the drawer, she pulled out a Magnum. "Round two or do you need a minute?"

Shifting my eyes down to my rock-hard dick I smirked. "Nah, I'm good but I do have a request."

Kneeled next to me she placed her lips on mine, kissing me tenderly. "What daddy?"

I looked at her hand with the gold foil packet in it. "No condom. I want to feel you without any barriers between us," I spoke, looking her directly in her slanted eyes.

"Dre, I've nev—"

"I know baby and I promise I won't be mad if you say no."

Rocky's eyes dance in mine, I assumed pondering my plea.

Not wanting her to feel pressured I clarified the reason for my request. "It's just everything about this night has felt different and I want to experience something with you that you've never shared with anyone else. But if you're uncomfortable don't do it," I finished, bringing my clasped hands up to her face.

She tilted her head into my hand and briefly closed her eyes. Fluttering her lids open she looked at me with questions dancing in her beautiful orbs. Without saying a word, she slid down the bed and tossed her leg over my stomach, straddling me. Her eyes slid from my face to my arms as she raised them back above my head.

Dropping the wrapper near my head she laced her fingers in mine while looking me dead in the eyes. "Has there been anyone else since we became intimate?"

"No," I answered honestly.

Placing her mouth on mine she traced my lips with her tongue before dipping it inside my mouth. I willingly accepted her as she slowly rolled her tongue over mine. Rhythmically grinding her hips against me she kissed me until I couldn't breathe. Panting, she eased away from my face while placing her hands on my chest.

"I'm trusting you with my body Dre you better not make me regret it," she whispered through uneven breaths, with her eyes fixed on mine while carefully inserting me inside of her.

"Fuuuuck." The words flew from my mouth as she gingerly slid down my dick. "I won't. I would never disrespect your body or betray your trust," I groaned through half slit lids, as pleasure seared through my entire core.

Forgetting that my wrists were bound I launched my arms forward only to toss them back above my head. Smiling, Rocky sucked her bottom lip in between her teeth as she rolled her hips, sinking further down my rod. Her pussy was dripping wet, allowing her tight walls to easily adjust to my girth. I watched her nibble at her lip while taking measured glides down my dick, inching me in slowly until she rested comfortably in my lap. With her knees planted firmly on the mattress she threw her hands on the bed, arched her back, and rocked steadily against me. My head shot up from the pillows as waves of pleasure washed over me. *Fuuuuck!* Throwing my head back onto the cushions I watched her lip ease from between her teeth as a soft whimper escaped from her mouth while her eyes rolled to the back of her head. She felt amazing, she always felt amazing. But sex without the barrier of latex between us intensified the sensation.

Lifting her hands off the mattress she placed them around my neck and pulled me toward her. I sat up in a seated position, drug my restricted arms over her head and down her body, resting them on her ass. Carefully moving one knee at a time she stretched her legs out and wrapped them around me, locking them at the ankles she smoothly wound her hips. Palming her ass, I pulled her deeper into me as I dipped my face into the crook of her neck. Frustrated that I didn't have the use of my hands I took it out on her neck, sinking my teeth into her flesh. She squirmed on top of me as I continued my oral assault. I greedily licked and nibbled while using my hands to try and control her movements. True to her word she stilled in my lap causing me to lift my head and lock my eyes with hers.

"Use your words Dre. What do you need me to do? You want me to move faster?" She resumed a rhythmic grind, moving her hips swiftly while staring me in the eyes. "Or do you like it slow?" She stilled her hips then quickly changed the direction of her movements, winding slowly against me.

"I need my hands sexy. Please," I begged.

"Tell me why. Why do you need your hands baby? I'm not pleasing you?"

I attempted to answer her, but my words got stuck in the back of my throat as she purposely constricted her walls around me, pulling me deeper into her wet canal. An involuntary moan seeped through my parted lips as she continued to stroke me. She was fucking with me and doing a damn good job too.

"What did you say daddy? I didn't hear you." She was fucking with me and she knew. A cunning smirk spilled onto her face as she stared down at me.

Resting my hands on her ass I tilted my hips, matching her strokes the best I could under my confined state.

"Ummmm. See, you don't need your hands," she muttered softly as I continued to thrash my hips against hers.

"Baby please. I want to touch you, I need to touch you," I pleaded, not caring that I sounded like a complete bitch.

"Lay down."

Without asking any questions, I unloosed my arms from around her body and allowed my back to fall onto the mattress. Rocky leaned forward and placed her mouth next to my ear. "I'll give you your hands if your promise to let me take you to the finish line. Deal?"

She slid her face up to mine, looking me directly in the eyes. "I'll do whatever you want, just give me my hands."

Stretching her arms up to mine she took her time untying me then slowly dragged her hands down my chest, sitting up in my lap. "Better?"

I moaned my approval as she shifted to the balls of her feet, gradually sliding up and down my dick. She kept with the same slow and concentrated pace, sending tingles down my spine as I brought my hands up to her breast. Cupping her mounds in my hands I flicked my thumbs over her erect nipples.

"Argh."

"I promised to let you make me cum but only after you," I stated, dragging my face up to her breast and drawing her left nipple into my mouth.

Whimpering she pushed my head away from her body and carefully climbed out of my lap. I watched as she shifted down the bed and in between my legs. My eyes bulged out of my head and my mouth flew open as she took me in her mouth. Her tongue slithered smoothly over my head and down my shaft. Again, her movements were deliberate and un-rushed as she took her time licking her juices off me.

"Fuck." I slammed my fist into the mattress as stars flashed behind my pupils, making it difficult to see.

I clamped my eyes shut and placed my hands in her hair as she continued to slide her mouth up and down my rod. Twirling her tongue around me she firmly sucked in her jaws as she glided up toward my head. Shifting her hands up from the bed she wrapped them around my dick. Instantly my eyes flashed open. If I didn't stop her, I was going to cum, and I didn't want to finish like this. I wanted to experience the intimate act of releasing myself inside of her.

I removed my hands from her head and slid them down to her shoulders. "Get on top of me."

She flicked her tongue across the tip of my dick then judiciously removed me from her mouth. Mounting me from the back she carefully lowered herself onto my engorged rod. My hands flew to her hips as a deep guttural moan slid from my mouth. Bending at the waist she slid her hands down my legs and rested them on my ankles. Beyoncé's "Drunk in Love" reverberated throughout the room as her ass bounced to the beat. Swaying her hips, she glided up then dropped back down, slow and hard.

Goddamn, she feels amazin.

Twirling indolently, she kept with the semi-fast tempo of the music as she moved methodically up and down my rod. I sank my head deep into the mattress, tossing the pillows aside as my body surrendered to the inexplicit pleasure she was doling out. I was on the brink of an explosive orgasm when I felt her walls tighten involuntarily around me, letting me know her own release was near.

Although she had been adamant that this wasn't about her, I was determined to make her cum. Something I made my personal charge the moment she told me she never had an orgasm from penetration. Lucky for me that mission came easier than I expected and had become the norm as I quickly familiarized myself with her body. And tonight, would be no different. I be damned if I blasted off before she did.

Gripping hold of the sheets I fought off my release. I thrusted my hips and quickly matched her pace, relieved when her rhythm faltered. Her nails dug into my ankles as she rocked her hips sluggishly. Her walls clinched around my dick and a loud gasp spilled from her mouth as her body trembled above me. I slowed my hips as I continued to stroke her, allowing her to ride out her orgasm. Gradually her tremors subsided. After a few choppy moans she resumed her usual pace, jiggling her cheeks on beat as Jay Z joined his wife rapping about their love. Snapping my lids closed I snatched a pillow from the side of me and covered my face. I bit into the fluffy material while moaning uncontrollably as I shot my load into her. Slowly she shifted above me, sitting upright she swirled her hips steadily until I was completely empty.

Tossing the pillow away from my face I leisurely lifted at the waist, wrapping my arms around her. "I fuckin love you," I growled, holding her flush against my chest.

Rocky chuckled as she ran a hand down my arm. "Um, that's post orgasmic jibber babe."

I buried my face deep into the crook of her neck, not caring about the small beads of sweat gathered there. "Nah, that's real talk. I love yo spoiled ass," I breathed against her dank flesh.

Sliding her face over her shoulder she placed a soft kiss on my forehead. "Dre," she whined my name, as she removed her lips from her face.

"Don't sweat it Short Stuff. It is what it is. I'm not ashamed to admit it. Your head hasn't caught up to your heart yet and I'm okay with that. For now." I shifted my face from her neck and looked into her eyes. "It's all about the destination remember?" I stated hoarsely, as I fell back onto the bed.

Rocky looked back at me, her eyes saying what her mouth couldn't articulate. I didn't need to hear her say she loved me to know that she did. My pops always told me to not to give a lot of weight to what people said, rather pay attention to what they did. And Rocky had been showing me every day. I was okay giving her time to process her feelings as long as she remained open to what was developing between us.

Flashing me a soft smile she turned back around and carefully climbed off my dick. I was spent, stretched out across the bed I followed Rocky with my eyes as she sluggishly slid out of the bed and padded across the room, disappearing out the door. A few moments later she returned with a warm rag and a bottle of water. She sat next to me and handed me the bottle then proceeded to gingerly clean my deflating rod.

"Thank you."

"You're welcome handsome. Are you hungry?"

"I'm famished," I answered before taking a sip of the cool liquid.

Rocky giggled. "Famished? Really Dre?"

A light chortle slipped from my lips as I screwed the cap back on the water bottle. "My bad. You know that good ole private school edumacation slips out every now and again." I slid my tired gaze over to her. "A nigga could eat but I don't think I have the strength to get out of this bed right now."

"No worries, I got you. I'll be back in a minute. I got some leftovers I can heat up. Cool?"

"Hell yeah."

Standing up from the bed Rocky grabbed the remote to the TV from off the nightstand and extended to me. In complete awe of the woman standing in front of me I accepted the small device while watching her scurrying around the room. Rocky clicked off the radio, blew out all the candles, then rummaged through our discarded clothes. Grabbing my tee shirt from the pile she quickly draped it over her tiny frame and padded out the room.

Fuckin amazin, that's what she is. Simply fuckin amazin.

Clicking on the TV I thought about everything that led up to this moment. If Rocky's mission tonight was to turn me out, she had definitely succeeded. From the moment she wrapped that scarf around my wrist she had blown my fucking mind. Sex with Rocky had always been incredible but what we just shared was different, it was special and unlike anything I'd ever experienced. Every action was planned, and every move was calculated. She anticipated my needs and made it her mission to execute them with precision. Tonight, was not about her but solely about me. Rocky and I had made love before but on those rare occasions it was me anticipating her needs and delivering. Yeah, she may not have said I love you too but the way she took care of me tonight spoke volumes.

I flicked through the channels trying to find something worthy of my attention when I stumbled upon a sports segment on ESPN. The announcer was discussing the upcoming 2015-2016 NFL draft. Shuffling a few pillows behind me I propped my back up against them and tuned into the TV, curious to hear who they were predicting to go first in the first round.

"Damn you're sexy as hell."

Turning away from the TV I slid my head toward the door where Rocky stood with a plate in one hand and a glass in the other. A soft smile decorated her beautiful face as she swept her eyes down my body.

"Thank you sexy. What you got?" I asked, looking at the plate in her hand.

"Seriously Dre?"

"What? I can't ask what you trynna feed a nigga?"

Rocky smacked her lips. "I'm not talking about that silly." Her eyes lowered, zeroing in on my junk. "So, you not gonna put on some clothes?" she questioned, as she casually strolled toward the bed.

Smirking I rolled onto my side and sifted through the pile of clothes next to the bed. Grabbing my boxer briefs I held them loosely in my hand while sliding my eyes up to hers. "What? My nudity bothers you now?" I implored, while frowning, pretending to be offended.

Rocky sat the glass and plate she was carrying on the nightstand then plopped down on the bed next to me, snatching my underwear out of my hand. "Bothered?" She hiked one of her perfectly arched brows. "Never. Distracted is more like it. So, unless you trynna get it back up I suggest you put these on," she stated in a low sexy tone, as she tossed my boxers at me.

I watched the under garment roll off my leg and fall onto the mattress. Snickering I reached over and grabbed her, pulling her on top of me. "Don't challenge me lil one or imma have yo ass walkin funny for the remainder of the week."

"See you ain't playin fair."

"I never claimed to be a fair player, but I can tell you this, I do play to win," I growled, rolling her onto her back and staring down into her face.

A soft moan crept up from the back of her throat as my hands glided up her thighs toward her sex. Tracing my index finger over her lips I smiled when her eyes closed, and head sank further into the mattress. Unable to resist, I slid a finger inside of her while keeping my eyes fixed on her face. *Fuck. She is soaking wet. She was always so fuckin wet.* My lips shifted into a lascivious smile as I continued to stroke her, twirling my thumb over her clit while dipping my finger in and out of her.

"Dreeeee," she whimpered, while fluttering her lids open.

"What beautiful?"

"Your food. Ummm—" she rolled her hips in accordance with my movements.

"What about my food sexy?"

"It's. Fucccck. It's gonna get cold," she responded breathlessly while maintaining my gaze.

"Fuck it. I'm hungry for somethin else now," I groaned while slowly removing my finger from her pussy and bringing my hand up to my face. Parting my lips, I placed the finger I extracted from her into my mouth, licking every trace of her essence from it before dropping my hand at my side.

Lifting her torso off the bed she looped her arms around my neck and crashed her lips against mine, pulling me into her as she fell back onto the mattress. I traced her puffy lips with my tongue then slid it into her mouth. Rocky moaned while slithering her tongue over mine and winding her hips against me, slowly bring life to my flaccid penis.

I placed my hands on her hips and stilled her movements while laggardly slipping my tongue out of her mouth. I slid my hands down her thighs when my stomach rumbled, reminding me I was starving. Rocky chuckled as she pushed up off the mattress.

"Your stomach has spoken. Now move so I can feed you."

I fell back onto my knees snickering as I watched her shuffle from underneath me. Scooting off the bed she dug through our disheveled clothes and picked up her shorts, sliding them up her legs she sat on the edge of the bed. Since she had decided to add more clothes I reached for my boxers and slid them on.

"You ready daddy?"

I moved to the head of the bed and adjusted a few pillows behind my back, resting against them. Stretching my legs wide out in front of me I shook my head while patting the empty space in between them. Rocky grabbed the plate from the nightstand then carefully mounted the bed. Handing me the dish she sat in between my outstretched legs, pressing her back lightly against my chest.

"Let me know if it's cold and I'll reheat it," she stated, tilting her head up to look at me.

Smiling I planted a soft kiss on her forehead. "It's fine Short Stuff. I appreciate you making me a plate." I stuffed a forkful of food into my mouth. "Ummm."

I felt the vibration of her tiny frame against my chest. Ignoring her laughter, I held my fork up to her lips. She opened her mouth, willingly accepting the bite of food. We spent the next fifteen minutes in a comfortable silence as I ate and fed her from my plate.

"Thanks again Short Stuff. That was good as hell and much needed," I stated, sitting the empty plate on the nightstand and grabbing the glass she placed there earlier.

Rocky picked up the remote and turned up the volume. "No thanks necessary. I told you I was gonna take care of you then feed you," she responded absently, while dragging her legs toward her and folding them in front of her.

Wrapping my arms around her I shifted my eyes up to the TV, curious to know what had captured her attention. Various clips from this year's football season flashed across the screen. Each one highlighting my stats as the sports anchor announced his excitement about my declaration for the upcoming draft and his prediction of when I'd be picked.

"Oh My God Dre!" she squealed, turning toward me and throwing her arms around my neck. "You really did it baby. I'm so happy for you."

A chortle seeped from my mouth as I folded her underneath me. "Chill lil one, it's not like I've actually been drafted. All I did was enter my name."

Pushing off me Rocky shoved me in the shoulder. "Quit being modest. This is huge Dre."

I hunched my shoulders feeling tension building there as thoughts of her flooded my brain. Hearing my name mentioned as a top prospect for the upcoming draft felt surreal but it also made me think of my pending graduation thus bringing my thoughts back to her. Sensing my change in mood Rocky muted the volume on the TV and dropped the remote on the bed. Concern danced in her eyes as she silently swept them down my face. I attempted to avoid her inquisitive gaze, taking a nip of my drink as my suppressed emotions came crashing to the forefront.

Rocky placed her hand on mine, lowering the glass from my lips. "Talk to me Dre," she implored, while taking the glass from me and sitting it on the nightstand. Slowly she shifted her eyes to mine as she sat back on her knees in front of me.

"I don't know what you want me to say."

"Okay, I'll start. Do you want to meet her? I mean are you willing to start the conversation and see what she has to say?"

I chewed on my bottom lip, mulling over her question. I had spent the last two weeks trying to block out everything that my pops had told me, that I never really considered what a conversation with her would look like let alone had I given any thought to actually meeting her. I mean, what does one say to the woman who gave birth to them then gave them away and never looked back. At least that's what I'd believed up until two weeks ago.

However, the reality of the situation was yes, she had given me to my father to raise but she was never far away. According to my pops my birth mother hadn't missed a single milestone of my life. Kinder-garten graduation, she was there. Eight grade graduation, she was there. My first varsity game, she was there. My high school graduation, she was there. Alexandria Evans didn't miss a single event. Instead she watched me grow up from a distance, present for all my important life events. Posted up in the crowd, blended in with the faces of people I didn't know just for a glimpse of me during those special moments. In fact, she was so vested in my life she had sent monthly child support checks and had set up a million-dollar trust to be awarded to me the day I graduated from college. Her only request was for the opportunity to meet me. The trust was mine regardless, but my pops asked that I consider it.

"ANDRE."

The deep inflection in her otherwise soft voice snatched me out of my reverie. "I'm sorry Short Stuff. What was your question?"

Tilting her head to the side Rocky's eyes bounced around my face, studying me. "I asked if you considered talking to her to hear her side of the story and if you wanted to meet her," she repeated softly.

"Honestly, no. I've been too busy trynna block the shit out that I haven't considered either."

"I get it, trust me I do. You're talkin to someone who's family unit is dysfunctional like a muthafucka. But you can't continue to act like she doesn't exist. The ball is in your court babe. What you gonna do wit it?"

I released a breath I didn't realize I'd been holding. "I know but seriously? What. The. Fuck. It's so much to process. I've spent my entire life thinkin my birth mother didn't give two shits about me only to find out that couldn't have been further from the truth. And I wanna be mad at my pops but he was only doin what she asked."

"Sounds to me like you have your answer," she stated softly, but in a very matter of fact tone.

I hiked a brow while reaching for her, pulling her up off her knees. Rocky settled between my legs, snuggling her back against my chest. "How you figure?" I asked, resting my chin on top of her head.

"Your father gave you all the information he had but the answers you need lie with the woman who birthed you. Even if you don't want a relationship with her, you're gonna have to talk to her for closure. However, I really want you to be open because based on what you've told me it sounds like she had her reasons for keepin her distance."

I released an exasperated breath. "I'll consider it but only if you do somethin for me."

Shifting her head upwards she looked me in the eyes. "Anything you want."

I couldn't help the smile that spread across my face as I stared down at her. "Make love to me again. Make this shit go away, even if it's just for the night," I pleaded, barely recognizing my own voice.

Slowly she rotated her tiny frame, turning her entire body toward me. Drawing my legs together she climbed on top of me and hooked her arms around my neck. Her mouth quickly found mine. She littered my lips with soft firm pecks before slipping her tongue into my mouth. I willingly accepted her, following her paces as our tongues danced together. A soft moan spilled into my mouth as her hands ascended my neck and landed in my hair. Her nimble fingers threaded over my coils, gingerly massaging my scalp. Placing my hands on her ass I drew her deeper into me and was rewarded by a slow wound of her hips. And just that quick blood flowed to my nether region, waking up my dick.

Removing a hand from her cheeks I placed it in her hair, gently pulling her face away from mine I buried my face in her neck. I ran my tongue along her collar bone and sank my teeth into her flesh. I softly nibbled on her spot, applying varying degrees of pressure as she continued to rock on top of me.

"Argh. Goddamn."

Slowing her hips her hands flew in between us. She clumsily tugged down my boxers, leaving them resting on my thighs. Moving her shorts to the side Rocky placed her mouth on mine as she lifted her ass and carefully lowered herself onto my swollen rod.

"Fuuuck, sexy."

Rocky balanced herself on the balls of her feet, wrapped her arms around my neck, and bounced her ass skillfully up and down my dick. Lazily I clamped my eyes shut and let her ride the stress out of me.

CHAPTER FOURTEEN

J sat up in my bed and I wiped the sleep from my eyes before sliding my phone off my nightstand. Checking the time, I sat up and opened my text app. I scrolled through my messages and clicked on her name.

Me: What time you getting on the road?

Peeling the covers from my body I sat my phone on the bed and swung my leg to the floor. I placed my hands on either side of me, prepared to stand when my phone chirped. I quickly picked it up and read her text.

Rocky: I'm here. Bout to have brunch with my mother. Whatchadoing?

Me: Just woke up.

Rocky: Well damn. What u get into last night that made u sleep past noon?

Me: Foolin wit yo damn brothers. We went to Scully's. Didn't get in til after 3.

Rocky: Sounds fun. What you got planned today?

Me: Not a damn thang. Am I gonna get to see you today?

Sitting my phone on the bed I dragged my tired limbs from the mattress and ambled out the room, toward the bathroom. After emptying my bladder, I stood in front of the sink studying my reflection in the mirror. As expected, my night of partying was evident on my face. I went about my business, quickly washing my face and brushing my teeth before exiting the bathroom. Feeling refreshed I prepared for whatever the day had in store, I just hoped that included some quality time with a certain chocolate woman who consumed my every waking thoughts. Walking into my room I scooped my phone off the bed and checked my notifications. A goofy grin stretched across my face at the sight of her name. Hurriedly I opened the home screen and clicked on our message thread.

Rocky: If that's an invitation, yes.

I wasted no time responding.

Me: Hell yeah it is. I miss yo sexy ass <winking face emoji>

Rocky: I miss u 2 <kissy face emoji>. I'll text u later after I'm done shopping. Cool?

Me: Say no more. See u later sexy.

Stuffing my phone in the pocket of my basketball shorts I walked over to my dresser and grabbed a tee shirt, dragging it over my head I pulled it down my body and exited the room. It was crazy how quickly I'd become accustomed to seeing her. It had been damn near a week since we last saw each other yet it felt like an eternity. Shaking my head to myself I strolled down the hall toward the stairs. Taking the steps two at a time I made it to the main level and headed to the kitchen. Maddy was sitting at the kitchen table watching one of her shows on her iPad while Shalonda stood at the stove, preparing her something to eat.

"You make enough for me?" I asked, kissing Shalonda on the cheek.

"If you want ravioli I did," she teased, knowing I hated ravioli.

"Nah, I'll pass." I walked over to the pantry and grabbed a box of Cap'n Crunch.

Grabbing a bowl out of the cabinet I stepped over to the refrigerator and pulled out the milk. I sat all the item on the table next to where Maddy was sitting. I greeted her with a kiss on the head then took my seat.

"What you watchin small fry?" I asked her while pouring cereal in my bowl.

"Proud Family." Her little face never came up from the iPad.

"Proud Family? What you know about the Proud Family?"

"Please don't get that girl started," Shalonda stated, from behind me. "Your dad got her hooked. Now all she does is watch old episodes on that thing all damn day."

Madison smacked her lips while glancing over her shoulder to look at her mom. "You owe the curse jar mommy," she sassed, then quickly turned her attention back to her show.

Chuckling I added milk to my bowl only to realize I'd forgotten to grab a spoon. Shalonda walked over to the table, snatched the mini device from Madison's hand, and sat her food in front of her.

"Mommy," Madison whined.

"You'll get it back after you eat your food."

"But why can't I watch it while I eat," Madison complained.

Shalonda sat the device on the island and rested a hand on her hip. "Because you haven't mastered the art of doing two things at once. And if you say one more word about that damn iPad you won't get it for the rest of the day. Now be quiet and eat your food."

Madison picked up her fork while sliding her eyes over to me. "Sorry small fry. Mommy has spoken," I stated, standing from the table to retrieve a spoon.

With my spoon in hand I strolled back up to the table and plopped down in my seat. "Pops at the office?"

"Yeah but he's only working half days all this week. Said he wanted to spend as much time with you as he could since you gotta cut out early on us."

"That's what's up. I hate that I'm going to miss Christmas with the fam but I'm geeked about going to Hawaii," I responded, as I scooped a spoon full of cereal into my mouth.

Shalonda came around the island and took a seat across from me at the table. Her soft brown eyes swept down my face as she watched me scarf down my food. Looking up from my bowl I smiled while chewing the sugary meal.

"What's on your mind?"

"Nothing, just trying to get a feel for your energy. We really haven't had a chance to talk since your father dropped that bomb on you at Thanksgiving."

Sitting my spoon in my bowl I gave her my attention. "I'm better but still shocked."

"That's understandable. Have you given any thought to at least speaking to her?" she asked, while studying me.

"Yes and no. Initially I tried not to think about it, but I've worked through that part. I guess it's just a matter of when versus if. Don't know if I'm ready but truthfully, I'll probably never be ready. I told myself I'd decide on when after the New Year."

She clasped her hands together in front of her as a soft smile settled on her face. "I'm glad to hear that. I know you probably have a lot of questions that your father and I can't answer so for your peace of mind I think it's a good idea that y'all talk."

"Yeah," I stated absently, while picking up my spoon and shoving the last of my food into my mouth.

"Well I'm not going to beat you over the head about it. I've said my peace, but I want you to know I'm here if or when you need to talk."

"Thank you."

Shalonda stood from her seat and took the few steps over to me. Placing her lips on my forehead, she kissed me softly then patted me on the shoulder. "I love you so much Cam. I've never desired to replace your mother but to show you a mother's love in her absence. Please keep an open mind and know that regardless of what happens your father and I will always be here."

Tilting my head back I looked up into her eyes. "That means more to me than you know. I love and appreciate all you've done for me."

Madison chewed the last bite of her food, her little head shifted to the side, looking at me and her mother. "What cha talkin bout," she asked innocently.

"Grown folk business. Now go wash your hands and you can have your iPad back," Shalonda stated, while reaching across the table and picking up Madison's empty dish.

"Okay mommy but can I have some juice when I come back?"

"Yes baby, now go."

That was all she needed to hear, pushing away from the table Madison stuck her tongue out at me before skipping off down the hall toward the bathroom. Snickering I gathered my empty bowl and the rest of the items I brought to the table then stood to my feet. After placing everything back where it belonged, I rinsed my bowl and placed it in the dishwasher. I stood upright and looked over my shoulder at Shalonda who I hadn't realized was there until I heard her sit Madison's bowl in the sink. Turning toward her, I wrapped her in my arms, holding her tight against my chest. Her tiny hands made circles on my back as we stood silently embracing one another.

"Okay I'm ready for my juice now," Madison announced, as she walked back into the kitchen.

Slowly I let Shalonda go so she could tend to my sister. Placing a hand on my chest she smiled up at me before turning her attention to Madison.

"Mommy is Cam Cam okay," I heard Madison ask, as I strolled out the kitchen.

Back upstairs in my room I laid across my bed with my wallet in one hand and that damn piece of paper in the other. Hyper focused on Alexandria's number I contemplated calling her when my phone chirped from my pocket. I welcomed the distraction, pulling my phone out my pocket I saw a notification from Rocky. Stuffing Alexandria's number back inside my wallet I tossed it on the nightstand and opened my phone, going into my text app I read Rocky's message.

Rocky: Headed to Polaris now. Tentatively I can be to u around 7. Does that work for u?

Me: Yup. I'll be anxiously waiting <winking face emoji>

Rocky: Cool, see u then <kissy face emoji>

Now I just need to find something to occupy my time until then.

Dropping my phone on the mattress I sat up and quickly hopped off the bed. I walked into my closet and surveyed the clothes I'd packed for my trip. Deciding on comfort over style I selected an all black Nike sweat suit then gaited out of the closet. I tossed the outfit on the bed then grabbed my undergarments from my dresser and exited the room. I used my time in the shower to reflect on my conversation with Shalonda. It was clear there was more to the story than what my pops knew or was willing to share. If I really wanted to know why Alexandria left me with my father only to watch my life from a distance, I had to talk to her. It was then that my decision was made, standing underneath the steaming brook of water I decided to reach out to my birth mother.

Forty-five minutes later I emerged from the bathroom with a clear head. I reveled in the calm settled in my spirit as I trekked down the hall. Halfway to my room I felt a set of tiny hands loop around my legs, halting my steps.

I slid my eyes down to her as I bent over and scooped her up in my arms. "What's up small fry?"

"I'm bored," she whined, while digging her tiny fingers into my cheeks. "Wanna play Xbox?" Her eyes lit up, matching her animated tone.

"Sure. Let me get dressed first. Deal?" I inquired, setting her back on her feet.

"Deal. But hurry up," she demanded, while turning on her heels and skipping toward the stairs.

Releasing a soft chortle, I continued the short walk to my bedroom. Once inside I walked into the closet, dumped my worn clothes on the floor and quickly exited. Heeding Madison's warning I got dressed in lightning speed, grabbed my phone off the bed, and strolled out my room. I made it to the main level of the house to find Madison in the family room sitting with her legs folded underneath her in front of the TV with a controller resting in her lap and the iPad in her tiny hands.

This little girl is something else.

Thanks to Madison, my afternoon went by fairly quickly. After spending damn near two and a half hours on the Xbox my father came home and asked for some of my time. He sent Madison off to play while he and I ventured off to the closed in screened porch to kick it over brews and cigars. My father and I sat on the porch politicking for hours. We covered all bases, from the situation with my birth mother to my feelings about the upcoming draft. Initially I wasn't looking forward to my trip back home since the Thanksgiving fiasco but now that I was here, I was happy I came. These last few days being home, surrounded by my family was exactly what I needed.

Sitting my stogie inside the ashtray I grabbed my phone off the coffee table. A wide smile stretched across my face as I peeped my notification.

"I've been lettin the shit slide but now that I put my cards on the table it's your turn. Who got my boy open?"

Opening the home screen, I went into my messaging app and clicked on her name.

Rocky: I'm leaving Polaris now. I'm starving? Have you ate?
Me: Nah but let me see if Shalonda is cooking.

I looked up from my phone and slid my eyes over to my pops. "Huh?"

"Nice try nigga. You heard me," he stated, reaching over and sliding my phone out of my hand.

I didn't bother trying to stop him. Instead, I dug my stogie out the ashtray and took a toke. My father took his time going through my phone, I assumed reading my message thread with Rocky. A few moments later he sat my phone on the table and turned to look at me.

"JB's girl?"

I shifted my eyes to my phone before letting them settle on him. "Yeah."

My father released a soft chuckle. "They don't know yet, do they?"

I shook my head slightly embarrassed by that admission.

"Don't sweat it. Things have a way of working themselves out in the time they're supposed to," he supplied, while clasping a hand on my shoulder.

I took another pull of my cigar then dabbed the ashes in the ashtray. "Do you know if Shalonda is cooking," I asked, attempting to change the subject.

My fathered patted me on the shoulder as a hearty chortle flew from his lips. "I doubt it. She left about an hour ago. Took Maddy to get her hair braided so they'll be out for a while."

"Thanks."

I snatched my phone off the table and sent Rocky a text.

Me: No dinner here Short Stuff. Wanna pick something up & I'll give u your money back.

Rocky: No worries. How does pizza sound?

Me: Delicious <tongue emoji>

Rocky: Say no more. See u in about 30.

I dropped my phone in my lap as a silly grin eased across my face. Subconsciously, Rocky had started taking on small pieces of my personality, from my mannerism to my coin phrases. I was sure I'd picked up on a few of hers as well.

"So, my boy is in love with JB's daughter," my father stated, eliciting my attention. A quiet chuckle spilled from his mouth. "Now ain't that some shit," he spoke out loud, more to himself than to me.

"Imma marry that woman," I asserted, putting out my cigar and locking my eyes on his.

"Love is a beautiful thing son especially with the right person. Rocky is a good woman and it don't hurt that she's fine as hell. I'm happy for you Cam," he proclaimed, as he stood up from the couch.

"Thanks pops."

My father tilted his head then quietly walked into the house. I stayed seated, using the quiet time to reflect on my conversations with my father and Shalonda. *Damn, I'm so glad I talked to them.* There was nothing like the love and support of those who genuinely loved you. Twenty minutes later I grabbed my phone from my lap and peeled myself off the couch. I strolled into the house just as the doorbell sounded.

Walking out of the kitchen I continued down the hall toward the door. Flinging it open I gingerly plucked the two large boxes from her hands and pulled her into me with my free hand.

"Umm, hi Short Stuff," I breathed out, once I removed my lips from her cheek.

Rocky chuckled. "Hi handsome. You know you smell me more

than Creed does?" she teased, as she stepped inside and pushed the door closed with her hip.

"I can't help it. You always smell delicious," I growled, while watching her come out of her coat and placing it across my outstretched arm.

Rocky moved to the side of me and followed me down the hall into the kitchen. I sat the two pizza boxes on the table before pulling out a chair and waiting for her to be seated before turning on my heels and trekking the short distance to the coat closet. Pulling a hanger from the rack I draped the heavy coat around it and quickly surveyed the garment before hanging it up and closing the door.

"North Face and Pink huh?" I hiked a brow as I took the adjacent seat at the table.

"What? You don't like?" she asked, holding my gaze.

Slowly I swept my eyes down her body, observing her casual attire. She was dressed in a heather grey University of Cincinnati Pink sweat suit accompanied by a pair of bailey bow grey Uggs. It was rare that she rocked sports attire, but she looked good in everything she put on.

"You cute babe but I think I'll like it better when it's spread across my bedroom floor," I whispered.

Rocky quickly swiveled her head around the room before returning her eyes to mine. "Stop it. You crazy as hell if you think imma spread these cheeks. . ." she swatted a hand across her ass, "in your parent's house."

I hopped up from my seat, pulling her little ass up in front of me. "You ain't gotta spread shit. Imma handle that," I declared, while wrapping her in my arms and burying my face in her neck.

A hushed moan seeped from between her lips as she snuggled deeper into me.

"Whoa. What the hell I done walked in on?"

Rocky tried to free herself from my arms, but I held her tighter, sliding my hands up from her ass as I pulled my face out of her neck. "Relax," I spoke into her ear.

Swinging her head to the side Rocky looked up at my father. "Hi Mr. Cameron."

"Hello gorgeous."

Rocky snickered while still trying to wiggle out of my arms.

"You gonna let her go so I can get some love?" my father asked, placing a hand on my shoulder.

Reluctantly I allowed Rocky to squirm out of my embrace. She stepped to the side of me and walked into my father's waiting arms. "You have to excuse this one..." she joked, as she looked over her shoulder at me, "he's a lil possessive."

That made me laugh, a hearty rumble from the pit of my stomach kind of laugh. "Now ain't that some sh—" I shook my head; grateful I caught my slip before the words fell from my mouth.

"I wasn't sure if y'all ate so I got two pizzas," Rocky stated, backing out of my father's arms and taking her seat at the table.

"Shay and Maddy aren't here but I could definitely eat. If it's okay," my father stated, looking over at me.

Rocky waved a hand in my direction. "Please eat." She looked at my father while flipping open the first box of pizza.

"Tommy's? Damn I haven't had their pizza since they closed their location on Hamilton. Where'd you get this?" my father questioned, while walking back to the table with three plates after washing his hands.

"On 161. I think they have another location in Upper Arlington," she responded, while padding over to the sink.

After washing her hands, she returned to the table and dug in right behind my father. With her plate loaded with food she sat down and waited for me. Drying my hands on a paper towel I ambled up to the table and stacked my plate.

"It was good seeing you gorgeous. Thanks again for dinner," my father announced, as he strolled out the kitchen.

"My pleasure," she called out behind him, while sliding her hand over to mine.

Rocky blessed the food then released my hand. Per our usual routine we settled into a comfortable silence as we dug into our food. Twenty minutes later Rocky helped me clear the table. Rinsing our used plates, I loaded them in the dishwasher while Rocky placed the pizza in the oven.

"You want anything to drink?" I asked, walking up behind her.

"You got some wine?"

"Of course, I do. I stay prepared for my spoiled princess," I goaded, swatting her on the ass as I walked past her toward the refrigerator.

"Ain't that sweet." There was sass and humor in her voice as she lifted a hand to her hip.

"They were out of Barbera but I copped a bottle of Gewurztraminer. Coo?" I inquired, glancing at her over my shoulder before returning my attention back to the fridge.

"Sounds delish."

"Say no more. I'll grab us some glasses and meet you in the livin room."

I didn't bother turning back to look at her. Instead I rummaged through the refrigerator for the wine I placed in there two days ago. Locating the bottle behind the jug of milk I snatched it from the fridge and quickly prepared us two full glasses.

"Here you go sexy," I stated as I rounded the coffee table and sat next to her on the couch.

"Thank you."

Rocky took a sip from her drink then slid her slanted orbs over to me, quietly examining me.

"What's up Short Stuff?"

"Nothing, just digging your vibe. It's nice to see you back to your usual self."

"It's nice to be back to myself," I admitted, before taking a nip of my wine.

"So, I take it this time home has helped clear your head?" she asked, sipping from her glass.

I shook my head as my eyes drifted down to my own glass in my hand.

"You ready for y'all's bowl game?"

"I am but I'm still a lil salty about missing Christmas with the fam."

"Yeah, I can understand that, but Hawaii is a nice consolation prize," she responded, sitting her half empty glass on the table.

"It would be even better if you were going with me," I muttered, moving closer to her as I sat my glass next to hers on the table.

"I would've loved to join you but the shit I would get from my mother doesn't compare. She takes holidays serious, especially the ones she has deemed as hers."

I pulled her up from the sofa and into my lap. "I know. I remember you telling me. We'll be back before the New Year, so don't make no plans. I want to bring it in with you."

Before she had a chance to reply I placed my lips on hers. Slowly I slid my tongue across her parted lips, relishing her natural taste mixed with the light flavor of the spirit she recently sipped. Reflexively a moan seeped from her mouth as I dipped my tongue inside. Rocky welcomed my invasion, silkily intertwining her tongue with mine. With our bodies pressed together we took our time exploring each other's mouths until neither of us could breathe. Backing away from me Rocky placed her hands on either side of my face and stared down at me.

"I'm still not screwin you in yo parent's house," she panted.

"Its coo because the shit I want to do to you can't be done discreetly."

"Ummm," she breathed huskily, before placing a soft peck on my lips. "Sounds like my type of a good time. How bout this? Tomorrow night I'll get us a room at the Hilton in Easton. Send you off to your bowl game depleted and satisfied. How that sound?"

Furrowing my brows, I couldn't help the grin that slid across my lips. "Say no more."

After calming our hormones Rocky and I spent the next three and a half hours playing catch up on our day to day lives. There wasn't too much that either of us missed since we talked or texted everyday but there was something refreshing about having a face to face conversation versus talking over the phone or through text.

I heard the garage door rising and took that as my cue. "Alright beautiful. It's time for me to let you get home," I stated, raising up from the couch and reaching back for her hand.

Placing her hand in mine Rocky allowed me to pull her up. "I already can't wait to see you tomorrow."

Brushing my lips across her hand I ushered her out of the living room and into the hall. Shalonda came in through the garage door carrying Madison in one arm and holding a bag in the other. I quickly moved around Rocky and plucked Madison from her arms.

"I'll be right back Short Stuff. Your coat is in the closet to your left."

I heard the two women greet one another as I proceeded down the hall, heading toward the stairs. I made it back downstairs to find Rocky propped up on a chair at the island and Shalonda digging in the oven, removing one of the pizza boxes.

"Oh my god. You are a godsend for this," Shalonda stated, sitting the box on the counter next to the microwave.

Rocky chuckled. "I take it sitting and waiting on Maddy didn't include food?" Rocky implored.

"Hell no and I wasn't about to leave my baby to go get none either. I packed snacks for her but didn't think about myself."

"Oh, the joys of motherhood."

"Joys my ass. Don't nobody tell you all the non-joy shit that comes along wit the title," Shalonda responded, sarcastically.

The two women shared a laugh over that comment as Shalonda placed her plate full of food into the microwave.

"Alright Short Stuff, c'mon."

"See you next time. And if I don't see you again before Christmas, enjoy your holiday," Rocky declared, as she hopped off the stool and pushed it up to the counter.

"You too baby. And thanks again," Shalonda offered, stuffing a slice of pizza in her mouth.

Lacing my fingers with Rocky's I walked out the kitchen and lead her to the front door. Tossing my hoodie over my head I placed a hand on the doorknob. Rocky's small hand landed on top of mine, halting my movements. I swung my head in her direction, locking eyes with her.

"Dre its cold outside, you don't have to walk me to my car."

I didn't bother responding as I opened the door and lead her outside. "Where's your car?" I asked, turning to look at her.

"I drove my mom's whip, so the twins wouldn't know I was down here," she answered, barely above a whisper.

My mouth formed an O before I shifted my head forward. Silently trekking down the driveway toward her mother's car, I tried to process how that shit made me feel. I'd be lying if I said I wasn't bothered. Rocky picked up on my change in mood. Yanking her wrist, she garnered my attention. Slowly I allowed my eyes to find hers.

"Don't do that Dre. Don't overthink this. I've already decided to have a talk with my brothers after the New Year."

Before I could stop it, a wide ass smile splayed across my face as I scooped her up in my arms. "I think this is the best gift I could've gotten this Christmas. What a nigga do to deserve it?"

Rocky placed a hand on my cheek. "You are an amazing man, and no one has the right to keep you a secret."

"I fuckin love you. You know that, right?"

Rocky shook her head then placed her lips on mine. Neither of us moved at first. We simply just stood in that moment; lips pressed together absorbing each other's energy. Resting my hands on her hips I closed the small gap between us, fully prepared to deepen our kiss when the sound of a horn stole our attention. Instinctively I tightened my grip on her waist as I looked out into street. Rocky raised a hand to her forehead, shielding her eyes from the bright lights of the car. Recognition set in at the same damn time. Lowering her hand from her head she quickly scurried from underneath me.

Oh shit!

"Aye, yo. What the fuck?" he growled, moving around the front of the car and sprinting the short distance to where we stood.

"Calm down Deuce," Rocky demanded, placing a hand on his chest.

Just as he was about to speak the passenger door flung open and

Royce quickly jumped out. He was at his brother's side before Ryker had time to formulate his next sentence. Swatting Rocky's hand off his heaving chest Ryker turned angry eyes on me.

"I ask you to look out for my sister and this the shit you do?" he hissed, staring daggers at me.

"Calm the fuck down bro. You can't be out here wildin in front of his parent's crib at damn near midnight," Royce tried to reason.

"What the fuck bro? You don't have a problem wit this shit?" Royce shouted, at his twin as his eyes bounced between me and Rocky.

"It's not my business. They grown," Royce answered calmly.

"Nah fuck that shit. This our sister and muthafuckin best friend. Somebody need to explain this shit to me and NOW."

"I ain't explainin shit until I get good and goddamn ready to explain it. It's my shit to explain not Dre's. Now carry yo big ass home and I'll call you when I get home," Rocky shouted.

Royce placed a hand on his twin's shoulder, firmly pulling him back in the direction of their parked car. "C'mon bro. Let them handle their shit and Rax will call us when she gets home. Ain't that right Rax?" Royce coached, silently pleading with his sister.

Rocky shook her head but kept her blazing ambers fixed on Ryker who was still glaring at me. Reluctantly he allowed Royce to walk him back to their car. With one leg propped inside the door and a hand resting on the roof he called out to me. "Aye Dre."

"Yeah," I gritted out.

"This shit ain't ova. My house when she leaves," he demanded, before sliding inside the car and peeling off.

Rocky stood on the tips of her toes and placed her lips on mine. Slowly she peeled her mouth away and slid her eyes up to mine. "I'm sorry. I'll handle Ryker," she promised, as she gaited around to the driver's side of her car and quickly climbed inside.

I watched as she drove off, stuck in that same spot for what felt like forever while I replayed the last seven minutes over in my head.

Ain't this some shit. FUCK!!!

2016

CHAPTER FIFTEEN

Sitting up I watched as the sheet slid down my body and bunched at my waist, leaving my torso exposed. Squinting my eyes, I attempted to adjust to the dark room while using the slither of light shining in through the cracks in the blinds to check the time. The clock read two-thirty which meant I'd only been sleep, well attempting to sleep for about an hour.

This is some bullshit.

Frustrated I peeled the covers off my legs and carefully slid off the mattress. I padded quietly around the foot of the bed in search of our discarded clothes. Dropping down on my haunches I rummaged through the pile.

"Whatcha doing sexy?" The bravado in his raspy tenor sent a shiver down my spine.

I looked up from the disheveled garments, eyes shifting toward where I heard his voice. "Finding something to put on so I can use the bathroom. Go back to sleep," I stated softly, while pulling his tee shirt over my head and sliding it down my body.

"Grab a pair of basketball shorts from the bottom drawer before you go out there."

I smirked as I rose from the floor. "Now why do I need shorts when your shirt hangs past my knees?"

"Because you might run into J. Now hurry up. I sleep better when you're underneath me snoring," he responded, while sluggishly shutting his lids and rolling onto his back.

"I do not snore."

"Yes, you do princess. Now go," he growled, staring at me through the cracked slits of his eyes.

A soft chuckled spilled from my mouth as I closed the drawer and quickly shimmed into a pair of his shorts. "I'll be right back," I announced, as I walked out the door and pulled it close behind me.

Inside the hall I rested my head against the doorframe, reflecting on the events from earlier tonight. Dre and I finally made it to Pappadeaux. After dinner we came back to his apartment where we made love until we passed out. Almost immediately Dre fell into a peacefully post orgasmic coma while I laid beside him tossing and turning because I couldn't turn my brain off.

It had been a little over two weeks since the blowup outside of Dre's and I'd yet to resolve things with my brother. True to my word I called Ryker when I got back to my parent's but that conversation only lasted five minutes. The remainder of my time at home I avoided his calls, ignored his texts, and only visited Miss Brenda when I knew he wasn't there. I knew I couldn't dodge him forever, but I needed to let my anger subside before we talked. We were both too emotionally strung. But I'd be lying if I said I wasn't bothered. My brothers and I were extremely close, and I wasn't used to this level of tension.

Lifting my head off the door I ambled down the hall while trying to push all thoughts of my situation with Ryker out of my head. Halfway down the hall Jamison's door swung open and the last person I'd expected to see gaited out. Holding her phone in one hand she used her other hand, the one her coat was draped over to gently pull Jamison's door shut. I folded my arms across my chest and cleared my throat. Surprised, she damn near jumped out of her skin before slowly turning in my direction. Her eyes bulged out of her head as her outstretched orbs landed on me.

Smirking I casually strolled up to her. "Now ain't this a pleasant surprise," I stated sarcastically.

"Rocky." Her chords trembled making her soft voice sound shaky.

"Lyric." I ran my eyes down her body while planting my hands on my hips.

"Umm, I don't want no problems. I was. . . I was just leaving."

"Yeah, I can see that, but the question is, what were you doing here in the first place?"

Lyric fumbled with her coat as her eyes bounced around the dimly lit hallway. "I don't really see how it's any of your business. Just be happy that it's not Dre's room I'm creeping out of," she proclaimed, as her eyes finally settling on mine.

I chuckled not because I thought what she said was funny but because I thought she was pathetic. "Bitch please, like that's an option."

A sly smile etched across her made-up face. "Option?" she snick-ered. "I guess you missed the memo sweetie. Been there, done that, and—"

I stepped closer into her personal space. "Nah sweetie," I placed emphasize on sweetie. "Oh, I know all about the two encounters you had wit my boo. And that's exactly why I know it will never be an option again," I declared, cutting her off.

Lyric looked mortified. "I don't have to stand here and listen to this shit," she huffed, taking a step away from me.

"Suit yourself, I'm just calling it like I see it boo."

"You don't know shit about—"

"What the hell is taking you so long?" His deep gruff tone stifled Lyric's words.

Lyric jumped at the sound of his voice while a smile splayed across my face.

"Lyric? What da fuck are you doin here?" he asked, walking to where we stood.

"I wa... I wa... I was just leaving," she stuttered.

Dre looked at the coat in her hand then slid his eyes over to me before returning them to her. "Yeah I can see that, but it still doesn't tell me what da hell you were doin here in the first place."

"I'll tell you what she was doin here. She decided to move on to J since she couldn't have you. I mean, an NFL prospect is an NFL prospect to a groupie. She doesn't care who it is as long as she has one," I stated, dragging my eyes down her face in disgust.

"I'm not going to keep letting you insult me," Lyric proclaimed.

"It's not an insult when it's the truth."

"What da hell is goin on out here?" Jamison asked, stepping out of his room in nothing but a pair of boxers.

"That's what we're trynna figure out," I announced, unable to mask the giggle in my voice.

Jamison looked down at Lyric. "I thought I told yo ass to bounce."

Sliding her eyes between me and Dre she quickly turned toward Jamison. "I was trying to, but I got stopped by. . ." she glanced at me over her shoulder then returned her attention to Jamison, "Raquel."

"Bro go put on some damn clothes," Dre ordered, sweeping his burning hazels down Jamison's half naked frame.

Following Dre's perusal Jamison smirked. "My bad bro."

Jamison stepped back inside of his room, returning a few seconds later in a pair of jeans hanging low on his narrow waist.

"Thanks. Now would one of y'all please explain why da fuck she. . ." Dre directed his angry gaze at Lyric then relaxed the scowl on his face as his eyes returned to Jamison, "is here in our apartment."

Jamison released an exasperated breath while running a hand down his face. "I went out tonight and got a lil too drunk. I was on my way out the club and in the process of ordering an Uber when I bumped into…" Jamison dipped his head toward Lyric, "she offered to drive me home and I accepted. When we got here, she asked to come in and use the bathroom. She went to the bathroom and I dragged my drunk ass—"

"Jamison please," Lyric begged, cutting him off.

Jamison shot her a menacing look. "Nah fuck that shit, you foul shorty."

"I'm leaving. I will not continue to stand here and be insulted."

Turning away from Jamison she looked at me and Dre, pleading with us with her eyes to step out of her way. Neither of us moved. Instead we looked at one another then returned our attention to Jamison, forcing her to remain in the hall. With her head hung low Lyric swiveled back around, facing Jamison.

"Go on bro."

Looking down at Lyric Jamison shook his head then slid his eyes up, bouncing them between me and Dre. "I went to my room and got undressed, dove my ass in the bed and started dozing off. A few minutes later I felt someone on my bed. I opened my eyes to find her. . ." again, his gaze was on Lyric, "sittin next to me in nothin but her panties and bra—"

"Jamison please stop," she whimpered.

Ignoring her plea Jamison cut his eyes at her. "Like I was sayin. I was drunk but not that fuckin drunk, so I sprung my ass off the bed and asked what the hell she was doin. That's when her thirsty ass told me I could hit it and when I politely declined, she offered to suck me off instead. Pissed, I cursed her ass out and told her to see her way out. After she got dressed, I climbed back in bed and fell asleep. I assumed she was long gone until I heard y'all out here," he finished, while sweeping his eyes across to Dre.

"Wow. That's some straight hoe shit. I can't wait to tell Carm," I stated before breaking out in a full-on laugh.

Embarrassment flashed across her face then quickly morphed into anger. "You better be glad I even offered to suck your little raggedy ass dick," she spat, as her ireful orbs settled on Jamison's face.

"Little where?" he asked, grabbing his crotch.

Dre and I snickered earning us a hard grimace from the saddity queen. Unfazed I rolled my eyes as she swung her head back toward Jamison and peered up at him.

"You're such an ass. I can't believe I was going to have sex with you."

"Bitch please." Jamison removed his hand from his dick and waved it at her dismissively. "I ain't want that shit. Dre said yo box was trash and yo head game was weaker than this bougie ass act you puttin on. So, miss me wit the bullshit."

Lyric spun around; her eyes big as a half dollar coin as she swept them up to Dre's face. "I can't believe you told him that."

"And I can't believe you just tried to fuck my nigga. So, consider us even sweetheart. Now get cha thirsty ass outta my crib," Dre commanded, while stepping out of her way.

Gasping she placed a hand over her chest as her brows dramatically shot up to her perfectly cut bangs. "Andre."

"Oh, girl please. Stop being so damn dramatic." I tossed her a quick look then ambled down the hall. I had my laughs, now I was over the entire situation.

Standing in front of the refrigerator I swung the door open and grabbed a bottle of water then instantly tossed it back inside. I needed something way stronger than water to help cure my insomnia. I stepped over to the cabinets when I caught a glimpse of Lyric walking past. With her coat tossed over her shoulders, chest puffed out, and nose tooted in the air she sashayed toward the door like her hoe card wasn't exposed less than a minute ago. I snickered then returned my attention to my original task. Opening one of the cabinet doors I took a step back, perched up on the balls of my feet, and scanned the shelves for a shot glass.

"What cha doin Short Stuff?" I heard him ask at the same time the door slammed shut.

"Looking for a shot glass", I responded, as I continued peering inside the cabinet.

Dre walked up behind me, placed his hands on my waist, and lowered his mouth to my ear. "And why do you need a shot glass?"

I released a deep sigh. "Can't sleep. Hoping a shot will help."

Dre spun me around. "Call your brother," he stated, staring down at me.

"I want to, but I don't want to argue no more."

"I understand but you ain't gonna resolve it if y'all don't talk. It's been two weeks. He's had time to cool off. He might surprise you."

"Speakin of surprise, how da hell y'all resolve y'all's shit so quick?"

"Men are different baby. We say what we need to say then move da fuck on. Besides that's my nigga and that wasn't our first disagreement. I knew we'd be good. I kept trynna tell a certain lil person that very thing but—" he intentionally cut himself off, as he continued holding my gaze.

"Whateva. And how exactly did that convo go?" I asked, cocking my head to one side.

"It was quick and to the point. He was pissed, he said he couldn't believe I was fuckin his sister. I told him what we did or didn't do was between us then politely informed him that I wasn't just fuckin you but that I loved you. That changed his tune real quick. That nigga went from being mad to warnin me, tellin me to be careful. After which, we exchanged some otha shit that will remain between us. But long story short, we good. Now I need for y'all to be good."

I giggled. "That may be easier said than done. You know we're both stubborn as hell."

"True but y'all love the shit out of each otha. Please talk to him," he implored.

I closed my eyes then quickly fluttered them open again. "I'll call him tomorrow but right now I need a shot."

"Make me one too," Jamison stated, walking into the kitchen and standing next to us.

"Yo ass ain't had enough?" Dre asked, looking over at him.

Jamison stuck up his middle finger. "My ass is sober now. Thot box killed my buzz. So, what we drinkin?"

Dre and I burst out laughing as Dre stepped in front of me and pulled down three shot glasses. Sitting them on the counter he looked at me. "What you want sexy?"

I hiked a brow. "You drinkin too?"

"I ain't gonna let you drink alone."

"And what da fuck am I?" Jamison chimed in.

"A non-factor," Dre stated, gazing at me like we were the only two people in the room.

Jamison's hearty chortle filled the air. "Fuck you. What we drinkin Balboa?"

I shook my head as a subtle grin eased across my face. "Um, Pat Ron should do the trick," I answered, while inching next to Dre.

"Patron it is," Dre agreed, while bending over and grabbing the liquor from underneath the sink.

Dre filled our glasses and slid them toward us. Picking up his tumbler he held it out in front of his face while waiting for me and Jamison to join him. Hoisting our glasses in the air Dre looked down at me.

"What we toastin to Short Stuff?"

"Good riddance to any and all thirst buckets who will try and use y'all for y'all's money and celebrity."

"Hell yeah," Jamison bellowed, clinking his glass with ours.

We gulped back our shots then slammed our empty glasses on the counter. Stacking the empty tumblers inside of each other Dre sat them in the sink then shifted his eyes over to me.

"C'mon Short Stuff let's get you in bed."

"Goodnight J," I sang, while turning and looking up at Dre.

"Goodnight Balboa. Night bro."

Cupping my hand in his Dre saluted Jamison with a head nod then escorted me out of the kitchen. Blanketed in silence we strolled the short distance to his room. As soon as we crossed the thresholds Dre kicked the door shut and immediately hoisted my shirt over my head then dropped down to his knees and tugged my shorts off.

"And what are you doing sir?" I asked, staring down at him.

Dre ran a hand up my calf as his eyes glided up to mine. "I'm about to put yo ass to sleep for good," he stated, as his lips made contact with my inner thigh.

"Umm," I purred, placing my hands on his shoulders as I clamped my eyes shut. "I see you trynna have me walkin funny in the mornin."

His muffled chortle tickled my skin as he slithered his tongue toward my sex. And just like that my body was ready to receive him. Evidence of my arousal trickled down my thighs as he continued to tease me, silkily rolling his tongue across my meaty flesh. I was always amazed at how quickly Dre was able to get me worked up with little to no effort on his part. It wasn't like this was a problem in my past situationships but with him it was different. It was instinctive and organic; it was unlike anything I'd ever experienced before. My heart told me it was because of the emotional connection we shared but my brain didn't know how to process that. Dre's hands moved to my ass while his tongue traced my lips, snatching me out of my head as a soft moan spilled from my mouth.

Fluttering my lids open I dug my nails into his deltoids. "Wait, we used the last condom," I uttered in panic, while trying to ignore the pleasure coursing through my limbs.

"No worries sexy. We don't need protection for this round," he mumbled, before gently lapping his tongue against my clit.

"Argh. Fuuuck, Dre."

With one firm swipe he removed his face from between my legs and lifted me into the air as he stood to his feet. Looping my legs around his waist I held onto his shoulders as he walked us over to his bed. Carefully lowering us onto the mattress he gingerly unhooked my leg from his waist.

"Relax and try and enjoy this as much as I'm about to," he instructed, easing slowly down the bed while littering my body with kisses.

Involuntarily my lids drifted shut as Dre settled between my legs. His hands traveled up my calves to my thighs, pushing my legs further apart. Resting his hands on either side of me he buried his face between my thighs, licking a trail up to my soaking pussy. He wasted no time diving in as he skillfully twirled his tongue over my lips and down my clit, giving special attention to my piercing. Squirming I sank my head deep into the mattress while my hands flew to the top of head. Sliding his tongue inside of my canal he alternated between soft and firm thrashes as he dipped in and out of me. Slow then fast, firm then soft. That was the rhythm he used to drive me crazy as he devoured me like I was his last meal. Just when I thought I had reached the pinnacle of pleasure he slithered his tongue over my perineum down to the crack of my ass. Instantly tiny burst of tingles glided over my toes, shot up my calves, slinked up my thighs and erupted in my belly as an unabashed moan parted from my lips.

"Oh. My. God. Dre."

I was granted temporary relief from the onslaught of pleasure as he leisurely pulled his face from between my thighs. "How many orgasms you need to fall asleep because I can stay down here all night," he growled, as he inserted two fingers inside of me.

My eyes sprung open, but I was unable to speak. Smirking he continued to stroke me while watching me closely, using my facial expressions and the reflexive movements of my body as his guide.

"Goddamn. You're sexy as fuck."

Again, I had no words. I was sheathed in euphoric bliss under the meticulous ministrations of his fingers. We stayed in the moment for what felt like an eternity. His hooded orbs fixed on my face, my half open lids fighting to hold his gaze all while he taunted and pleased me with his long digits. A soft whimper spilled from my lips as my walls began to tighten, gripping his fingers as he continued to stroke me while rubbing against my sensitive spot.

"Cum for me baby," he prompted, while gliding his thumb over my clit.

"Fuck. Fuck. Fuuuck!" I bellowed out, while grinding my hips against his hand.

"Un huh, give me all that shit."

Lazily my eyes slid shut as Dre worked his fingers inside of me, allowing me to ride out my climax.

"Open your eyes sexy."

Sluggishly I forced my lids open and slid them down to his face. When my body stopped shaking, he slowly withdrew his fingers, softly dragging them over my jewelry before bringing his hand up to his lips.

With his eyes fixed on mine he inserted his coated fingers into his mouth and licked them clean. "I would've stayed down there but I wanted to see you cum," he stated casually, while gradually moving up my body and lying next to me.

Rolling onto my side I placed my head on his chest and cocked my thigh over his. "Thank you."

"No thanks necessary, truth be told I think I could cum just from eatin yo pussy," he stated, rubbing a hand down my side.

"You so nasty.".

"Only wit you. You think you can sleep now, or do you need me to handle that again?"

"I'm good handsome."

He placed a soft kiss on my forehead then grabbed a handful of covers and pulled them over our bodies. "Goodnight Short Stuff."

"Goodnight baby," I responded through a yawn.

*P*icking up my phone I twirled it around in my hand while contemplating if I had the energy to entertain this conversation. It had been two days since I promised Dre, I'd call but hadn't made it a priority, using school as an excuse to put off calling him. Now here I was sitting on my couch trying to think of yet another reason why this call could wait another day.

Fuck it, time to put yo big girl panties on Raquel.

I opened my call log and clicked on his name before I could change my mind. Running a hand through my wild mane I counted the number of times the phone rang, wondering how long I'd wait before disconnecting the call.

One.

Two.

There.

Four.

"It's about time you called me back," he snapped, from the other end of the line.

"Don't start Deuce. That's not how I'm trynna start this conversation," I countered, as my eyes rolled up in my head.

"Miss me wit that shit Rax. You been avoidin me for more than two weeks, we're past the bullshit pleasantries."

"I been avoidin you becuz I ain't trynna argue. I'm willin to answer whatever questions you have, within reason. But after this I'on wanna hear no mo shit about it. Cool?"

"It's gone haft to be. You said it like I really have a say in the matter." His tone had decreased but there was no hiding the hostility behind it.

"I'm glad we have an understandin. Now ask me whatever you want to know."

Ryker snickered. "You're such a fuckin brat."

I chuckled before smacking my lips. "So, I've been told, but I think the word you're lookin for in this situation is bitch." I chuckled to myself. "But you know better."

"You right, I do. But seriously Rax, what da fuck? My boy tho? You can have any dude you want, why him?"

I sat up on the couch and grabbed my drink off the coffee table. I took a quick nip of the mixed cocktail as I absorbed his words, flinching at the sincerity behind his question. I wasn't really sure how to answer the why, hell I still wasn't sure how the hell Dre and I happened. Let him tell it, it was destined. Shaking my head, I pushed out a hard sigh.

"It wasn't intentional Deuce. Y'all sent him to check on me and we developed a friendship that accidentally blossomed into something else, something more," I supplied honestly.

"So, this shit is my fault? Is that what you—"

"Whoa, calm the hell down. Did you hear me say that?" I defended, cutting him off before he could finish his dumb ass accusation.

"No but you don't accidentally fall on dick. How long has this been goin on?" he asked, slightly calmer.

I didn't response right away, contemplating on how to answer what felt like a complicated question. Dre and I had only been intimate for a few months but if I was honest with myself, things had changed between us long before I shared my body with him.

"Rax."

"My bad Deuce, I was thinkin. Truthfully, it's been in the works since we became reacquainted," I supplied, knowing I was being vague.

"What da fuck does that mean Raquel?"

I took a sip of my drink then blew out another exasperated breath. "It means Dre and I had some shit brewin between us since the day he knocked on my front door. Initially I was hell bent on not goin there with him but as time went on, we got closer and it became harder and harder to ignore."

"Man Rax, I hear you sayin a bunch of shit but none of it is makin sense. So, make me understand this shit."

"The long and short of it is, there's been an undeniable chemistry between us from the beginnin, but we didn't start a physical relation-ship until mid September. Does that answer your question?"

"Okay, now I get it." His words dripped of sarcasm, as his deep chortle filled my ears.

"Wow Ryk, so you think this shit between me, and Dre is just sex? So, what, I'm screwin yo boy then gonna toss his ass back when I'm done huh?"

"Ain't that what you always do?"

"Fuck you," I shouted, before gulping down another taste of my much needed spritzer.

"Nah, explain to me how fuckin my boy is any different than the past bullshit you've engaged in?" he challenged, his tone matching mine.

"So, let me get this shit straight, you ain't mad that we fuckin? You mad cause you think imma play yo boy?"

"Pretty much. I think I could've took da shit better if it was Bray."

"Bray, Really?" A chuckle snuck out of my mouth. "Okay explain, cuz last time I checked they were both yo boys. So, what da fuck is the difference?"

"Bray can handle yo ass. He ain't lookin for shit but a good time. Don't get me wrong, I ain't trynna picture any of my niggas smashin my sister but at least wit Bray y'all would've been on the same page. Besides, you like white boys, right?" He snickered at his own joke.

"I'm glad you think this shit is funny. And for the record, I've only dated one and Emery doesn't really count."

"If you say so."

I smacked my lips. "So, what's the issue wit me and Dre?"

"It's simple. Dre ain't built for a woman like you."

I was fuming now. Our conversation had taken a turn I wasn't expecting. I knew Ryker was pissed when he found out Dre and I were involved, I even expected it. But what I didn't expect was his concern to be for Dre. He made it sound like I was some kind of cold-hearted bitch.

"And what kind of woman is that Ryker Malcolm Banks?"

"The kind that chew niggas up and spit their asses out."

"And what da fuck is wrong wit that? Nigga do it all the time. Besides, I ain't that bad."

Ryker's boisterous laugh reverberated from the other end of the line, causing me to remove the phone from my ear. Creed's head shot up from the floor and swung my way, staring at the phone in my hand.

I don't know what the hell is so funny.

"Seriously Deuce?" I called out, placing the phone up to my ear again.

Ignoring me Ryker continued laughing. His zealous cackle sounded like it emerged from the pit of his stomach and lurched out of his big ass mouth. It irked my soul, pissing me off even more. Standing up from the sofa I chucked back the remainder of my drink and galloped into the kitchen to refresh my cocktail.

"I'm not trynna insult you Rax, I'm just statin facts," he offered, sobering from his laughing spell.

I poured myself a shot and killed that shit before refilling my glass with dark liquid and a splash of cranberry juice. Snatching my glass off the counter I walked back into the living room and plopped down in my original spot. I sat my goblet on the table and pulled my legs up from the floor, folding them underneath me.

"Well it sure as fuck feels like it."

"Look Rax, I love you and you know that. All I'm sayin is, our father fucked us up in his own special little way. The way he decided to live his life has impacted how we approach our own love lives. You, you don't let niggas get too close and when they do, you cut em off. I get it, trust me I do. I know it's your defense mechanism becuz you're afraid of gettin hurt."

"I thought I was the one studyin to be a doctor," I joked, feeling his words tugging at my core.

"Yeah well, you ain't the only smart one in the fam. But seriously Rax, Dre is a nigga but he ain't like these otha niggas you've dealt wit. Dude comes from good stock and has a good heart."

"You say that shit like I don't already know this," I defended, leaning forward and plucking my glass from the table.

"Look Dre and I settled our shit and I promised to stay out of y'all's business but I wanted to talk to you first and see where your head was at. I love both of y'all. Dre is more to me and Royce than a friend, dude is like our brother. It's crazy cuz under normal circumstances I'd be worried about a nigga hurtin my sister but in this case its vice versa. I don't wanna lose my friend Raquel."

I winced hearing the sincerity in his unspoken plea. "Deuce I would never intentionally hurt Dre. Contrary to what you may believe I really care for dude."

Ryker snickered. "See that's what I'm talkin about. Dre is in love wit yo hard ass and you only like the nigg—"

"Don't do that. Don't minimize my feelings because they're not on a level you think they should be. I have a learning curve. Shit."

Ryker blew out a loud gush of air.

I gulped back a hefty swallow of my drink, relishing the slight burn as it traveled down my throat. "I've never experienced romantic love before, so I don't know what that shit is supposed to feel like. Hell, I don't even know what it looks like thanks to our father. But what I can tell you is this, what I feel for Dre is unlike anything I've ever experienced before. And yes, the shit scares me, but you know what scares me more?" I asked, feeling a burning sensation in my eyes.

"What?"

"I'm scared of fuckin this up and losin the one person who's come to mean more to me than I expected."

"Aaah Rax, that shit sounds a lot like love to me."

Dabbing at the corner of my eyes I took a nip of my cocktail. "I see you got jokes."

"Nah I'm serious as fuck."

"Since when did you become the authority on love lil brother?"

Ryker's light chortle sent a smile to my face. "I'm far from an authority on love. Like I said, dad fucked all of us up, but I know how to recognize love when I see it, just like I know bullshit when I see it."

"Okay, I can give you that."

Again, he snickered. "I want you to promise me somethin."

"What's that?" I inquired, returning my glass to the table.

"Just keep an open mind. If you feel in yo heart you love my nigga don't run from it, don't run from him. Just embrace that shit and hold on to it til yo heart tells you different, if it tells you different. Deal?" he asked, his tone deadly serious.

"I'll promise you my first born if it means you'll shut the hell up."

"Ha ha, I'm serious Rax. Can you do that for me? But more importantly, for you?"

"I promise."

"Thank you. Alright, I'm done beatin up yo ears. I'm just glad we talked. I thought a nigga was gonna have to jump on a plane, so we could hash this shit out. You had one mo week and I was bookin a flight."

"Now who's being dramatic?"

"I'm dead ass, you can ask Royce."

"I'm glad we talked too and I'm sorry Deuce. I should've made this call a lot sooner. Thanks for givin me my space tho. Unlike yo pushy ass father."

I heard Ryker suck in a lung full of air then slowly blow it out. "Man Rax, I'm sorry bout that. I was just pissed after seein you and Dre together and Royce was being so fuckin nonchalant, I—"

"It's all good. We just worked our shit out so I ain't sweatin it. I knew your punk ass was gonna run and tell daddy anyway," I teased, not caring about the rest of his sentence.

"Aye."

I couldn't stop the chuckle from easing up my belly and passing through my parted lips. Soon after, Ryker joined in. It was comical considering that out of the three of us Ryker held the most contempt for our father. But at the end of the day he was still a daddy's boy. And proof of that was him running back and telling on me.

"I love you Deuce," I stated, as I sobered.

"I love you more Rax. Talk to you later lil sis."

"Later big lil bro."

I disconnected the call, dropping my phone on the couch next to me. Sliding my glass off the table I gulped down the last of my drink then sat the empty chalice back down. Although I wasn't looking forward to talking to my brother, I was happy we'd finally worked our shit out. It was a conversation that was long overdue, and he definitely left me with some things to think about.

Unfolding my legs from underneath me I stood up from the coach and hurled my arms into the air, stretching my relaxed limbs. Reflexively a soft moan eased out of my mouth as I slowly drug my arms back down my body. Reaching onto the coffee table I picked up my empty glass and trekked lazily into the kitchen. After rinsing my goblet and sitting it in the sink I leaned up against the counter and reflected on my conversation with Ryker.

Was he right? Did I love Dre? I mean, I would know right?

The sound of someone knocking on the door pulled me out of my reverie. Rising from his spot in the living room Creed charged toward the door, barking non-stop.

"Hello beautiful."

A bright smile stretched across her face as she swept

her eyes down my body. "Hey handsome," she responded, reaching for my hand and pulling me into her apartment.

Kicking the door closed with my foot I scooped her up in my arms, earning me an exuberant shriek as she backed away from me.

"Dreec, you're cold," she whined.

"My bad Short Stuff," I offered, while unzipping my coat and shimming out of it before stepping out of my Tims.

She quickly relieved me of the heavy fleece as she draped it across her arm and reached for my hand. Lacing my fingers with hers I allowed her to lead me into the living room. Rocky tossed my coat on one of her accent chairs then turned and looked up at me.

"What are you doing here? You're supposed to be getting ready for the kickback."

"Yeah well, I was out your way picking up a few last minutes items and figured I'd stop by. I wanted to tell you about my conversation with Alexandria," I explained, lowering myself onto the couch and snatching her onto my lap.

Rocky's eyes stretched wide as she made herself comfortable on top of me. "Oh wow. You really did it. I'm proud of you baby."

I chuckled at the excitement in her tone and surprise etched on her face. "It was time."

"Well you tell me all about your convo with your mother and I'll tell you about mine with Ryker."

"Now that explains the alcohol on your breath."

Rocky's hand shot up to her mouth as she slid her face away from me. "Yeah, I needed a few in order to keep from losin my shit."

I placed my hand on her arm and drug it down from her face. "I didn't say yo shit stank. I just said I smelled alcohol. Stop being so damn dramatic," I teased, while nudging her face back toward me.

Rocky smacked her lips before placing them on mine. Wrapping my arms around her tiny waist I sucked her bottom lip into my mouth. A soft whimper spilled from her parted lips while her hands flew up to my chest. She gently pushed me back, forcing me to let go of her lip.

"No sir, not right now. You trynna start some shit and we don't have time for all that."

My lips curled into a smirk as I watched her climb out my lap. "Damn, its like that?"

"Hell, yeah it's like that. You know damn well we don't have an off switch once we get goin," she asserted, scooting further away from me.

"Scoot yo ass ova one mo gin and imma jump on you."

"Stop lookin at me like that then."

I hiked a brow. "And how am I lookin atchu?"

"Like you wanna take my clothes off."

My smirk stretched into a lascivious sneer as I purposely raked my eyes over her body. "I always wanna take yo clothes off but you right, we got shit to do. So, let me tell you about my call wit Alex so I can get up outta here."

Rocky stopped squirming as her freshly arched brows peaked on her forehead, getting lost underneath her wild mane. "Alex?"

"Yeah, that's what she prefers to be called."

Rocky's mouth formed an O as she pulled one of her legs off the floor and tucked it underneath her. Fixing her eyes on my face she waited for me to continue. I shifted my body toward her, resting my shoulder on the back of the couch I stretched my legs out in front of me.

Thirty minutes later I had shared with Rocky everything Alexandria and I talked about, including our tentative plans to meet sometime next month. It was crazy how life worked out. Less than two months ago I had no idea she existed outside of the fact that she gave birth to me. Now I was planning on meeting my birth mother and was open to the possibility of building a relationship with her. It would take some time which she said she was willing to give but I was proud of myself nonetheless for taking the first step.

"Baabby."

The excitement in her tone snapped me out of my head as I slid my eyes over to her. "I'm sorry Short Stuff, I got lost in my thoughts."

"No apologies needed but I wanna know how you feel now since you know her side of the story?"

"Honestly, I feel like a weight has been lifted off my shoulders. I mean, I still have some questions and some shit I need to process but

I'm glad I know her truth. Now it's up to me to decide if I'm willing to accept it. Does that make sense?"

"It makes perfect sense. I still can't believe it though. I mean, who forces someone to give up their baby because the father is black?"

"Force is a strong word. She did have a choice and she chose her inheritance."

"Don't do that Dre. You just said less than ten minutes ago you were gonna keep an open mind. She was young at the time and still dependent on her family for her basic needs. Try and see it from her point of view. I'm just glad she chose to keep you." She whispered that last part, relaxing her voice I assumed to soften the blow of the reality of the situation.

"I know but it's gonna take time. I'm trynna stay out of my head. Hence, why I agreed to meet her."

"I just have one question and then we can drop it," she stated, sliding across the sofa and sitting directly next to me.

"Shoot."

"Did she say, or did you ask why she wants to meet you now, after all this time?"

I nodded my head. "Her father is or was in control of the money. He was also the racist who gave her the ultimatum. He died six months ago." My voice trailed off as I felt myself getting emotional.

"And because of that she's earned her freedom. Freedom to pursue a relationship with the son she left behind?"

"And her inheritance without the threat of it being taken away."

"Wow. And her mother? So, she doesn't share the same prejudice views of her deceased husband?"

"According to Alex she doesn't. Apparently, she also feared losin her luxurious lifestyle, so she kept quiet and did as he said."

Rocky shook her head in disbelief while running a hand down my thigh. "Wow. Money truly is the root of all evil."

"You can say that shit again."

"So, my boo is a millionaire before ever steppin foot on a professional football field."

I snickered at the silly grin plastered on her face. "Hell nah. I'on want that money," I protested, unable to stop the scowl from dragging the corners of my mouth toward the floor.

"Why?"

"I ain't earn that shit. Nah, it's goin in a trust for my first born. The only millions I'll be spendin are the ones I earn."

"But it's your birthright babe."

I waved a hand at her ready to end this part of the conversation. "Alight, I've laid my cards on the table. It's your turn, tell me how yo convo wit Ryker went."

Rocky blew out an exasperated breath. "It was interestin to say the least. Long story short we're good. We cussed and fussed then came to an amicable agreement."

"Which is?" I asked, pulling her up from the couch and into my lap.

"He will stay outta our shit and I will not hurt you," she answered, while sliding a hand along my jawline.

I couldn't help the chuckle that spilled out of my mouth. "I'on know what you did to those otha lames you dealt wit before me but I ain't them and I damn sure ain't worried about yo lil ass."

Rocky threw her arms around my neck and rested her head on my shoulder. "As long as you know I would never hurt you."

"I know beautiful."

"As long as you know," she stated again, while lifting her head from my shoulder and standing.

"You wanna know what else I know?"

"What's that?" she asked, looking down at me and reaching for my hand.

"I don't know what I'd do without you. You've become my peace and the best thing on my worst days," I admitted, placing my hand in hers and allowing her to help pull me up from the sofa.

A broad smile stretched across her beautiful face. "Thanks baby. I feel the same way about you. Now quit wit this mushy shit. Come, let me show you what I got ready for tonight," she supplied, gently tugging on my hand.

I willingly followed behind her while raking my eyes down her body. My gaze roved past her tiny waist and focused on her fat ass. I licked my lips as my eyes bounced from one cheek to the other, enthralled with the slight jiggle underneath her fitted sweatpants.

I swear her body is the coldest. Goddamn.

"The meatballs are all set and ready to go with you when you leave. I cooked the mac and cheese earlier today and you can take that as well. You'll just need to put it in the oven thirty maybe forty minutes before you expect y'all's first guest." She looked at me over her shoulder.

"Dre," she whined.

I slid my eyes up from her ass. "My bad sexy, I can't help it. I heard everything you said tho."

She rolled her eyes while shifting her head forward. "The chicken is in that pan." She pointed to a large aluminum pan covered in foil sitting next to the stove. "It's already seasoned all I have to do is drop it in the deep fryer, but I didn't wanna cook it until I got there. It won't take long but reheated fried food is gross. Did you or J get a deep fryer?"

"Yep, J borrowed a turkey fryer from one of his—"

"I got it. That's perfect, I can fry more at one time with something that size."

"Coo coo. Thanks again for all of this Short Stuff. J owes you."

She turned and faced me, waving her hand at me dismissively. "Consider it his birthday gift."

"I'll make sure he knows."

Rocky chuckled. "I'm sure you will. I ain't gonna lie tho, I was surprised as hell when you said this was how he wanted to celebrate his birthday. I thought he'd want to be in the club in somebody's VIP poppin bottles and gettin wasted."

"After that shit wit Lyric and our talk wit our coach he decided it was time to chill. He needs to start workin on keepin a low profile," I replied, sliding my hands around her waist and pulling her up against me.

"That makes sense. Well I'm glad to see he's heedin the advice," she declared, running her hands up my arms.

"It doesn't matter where we are, we gonna turn up regardless. His brother and two of his cousins are comin in town so I'm sure it's gonna be lit."

"Aaah shit!"

A soft chuckled passed through my lips. "We should be good as long we can keep his ass off social media."

"Yeah, good luck wit that shit. You might need to collect cellphones at the door."

"Right. By the way, thanks for bein coo wit me invitin Payton."

Rocky shrugged her shoulder as she continued stroking my arms. "She seems cool. No thanks necessary."

"How'd I get so lucky?" I moved my hands down to her ass and squeezed her cheeks.

"And here I was thinkin I was the lucky one," she responded, while stepping up on her tippy toes and sliding her tongue across my collarbone. "So, how much time do we have before you need to leave?"

"Enough for me tear that ass up," I proclaimed, before attacking her mouth.

*S*itting the cooler on the floor next to the refrigerator I stepped over to Rocky. "You good Short Stuff? You need me to do anything?"

"I'm good. This is the last batch of wings then I'll be able to join in the festivities," she answered, just as she lowered the basket filled with uncooked chicken into the boiling grease.

"Aye Balboa. Let me introduce you to my big brother," Jamison interrupted, stepping up to where Rocky and I stood.

Rocky placed the lid on the turkey fryer then turned and faced Jamison and his brother. "Hi handsome, I'm Raquel but everyone calls me Rocky and this. . ." she slid her eyes over to Jamison, "foo calls me Balboa," she supplied, as she extended a hand toward Jamison's brother.

His regard went to her hand. Gently swatting it down he pulled her into his muscular frame. "I'm Hendrix beautiful."

Jamison cleared his throat while tapping his brother on the shoulder. "Back yo big ass up before I have to slam this one," he stated, pointing a finger in my direction.

Hendrix loosened his grip on Rocky as his head swiveled toward me. "My bad bro. No disrespect intended."

Rocky stepped out of Hendrix's hold and looked between the two of us. "It was nice to meet you Hendrix," she uttered softly, while turning back toward the counter and checking the food.

"Same here sweetheart," Hendrix returned while sweeping his eyes down to her ass then skating them back over to me and winking.

Lord please don't make me have to bust his ass.

"Good look," Hendrix mouthed, before walking off with Jamison.

Stepping up behind her I lowered my mouth to her ear while placing my hands on either side of her and resting them on the counter. "I gotta fight every night to prove my love," I recited against her small lobe.

Rocky spun around and looked up at me with a wide grin splayed across her face. "What yo young ass know bout The Five Heartbeats?" She barely finished, as a fit of giggles spilled from her mouth.

"You know I'm an old soul."

"Well can you carry yo old young ass over to where y'all got the drinks and fix me something?" she inquired, gently pushing me away from her.

"Anything in particular?"

"Surprise me," she answered, while turning back toward the counter.

"Say no more."

I heard her chuckle as I walked off. Five minutes later I returned to the kitchen area, but Rocky was nowhere to be found. Sitting her drink on the counter I held mine up to my lips and scoured the room. I spotted her across the room by one of the couches standing in between Egypt and Carmen. As if she could feel my eyes on her she looked up from her girls. A set of beautiful mahoganies landed on me. Reaching behind me I grabbed her cup off the counter and held it out in front of me. She acknowledged my gesture with a nod as she tapped Carmen on the arm then worked her way through the crowd of people, sashaying up to me.

"Thanks, handsome," she sang, taking the cup out of my hand.

"You're welcome sexy. When did E and Carm get here?" I adjusted my stance as she rested her tiny frame up against my body.

"Carm called right after you walked off to let me know they were outside. So, after I took the chicken out, I walked out to meet em. Oh. . ." she looked at me over her shoulder, "I made you and J a plate. They're in the oven covered in foil."

"My brows damn near met in the middle as I scrunched up my face. "What I tell you bout that shit?"

She playfully elbowed me in the stomach. "Stop it. It's his birthday so I wanted to make sure he got somethin to eat before it was gone."

"A'ight, I'll let this one slide since it's my man's bday but don't make that shit a habit," I teased, smacking her on the ass.

"Would y'all cut that lovey dovey shit out," Carmen shouted over the music, as she made her way over to us.

Giggling, Rocky moved herself from underneath me, taking the few steps to stand next to her best friend. I took a sip of my drink and approached the duo, greeting Carmen with a head nod.

"Hey Dre," Carmen called out.

"Sup."

Carmen swept her eyes around the large clubhouse. "Damn, its packed in here. I thought Rocky said J wanted to do somethin lowkey."

"This is his version of lo-key," I supplied, surveying the crowded room.

Carmen shook her head, but I could tell something else had caught her eye. Snickering I followed her line of sight. With lust filled eyes she stood silently peering at Hendrix who stood just a few feet away from where we were standing.

"Who is that?" she asked, swinging her head back over to us.

"Who?" Rocky questioned, oblivious to Carmen's previous blackout.

417

"Him," Carmen asserted, dipping her head in Hendrix's direction.

Just as I was about to answer, the man himself strolled over to us. There was no discretion in the way he raked his eyes over Carmen's body before lazily settling them on her face.

"Please don't tell me this one is one of yours too," Hendrix stated, while smiling down at Carmen then sliding his eyes over to me.

"One of?" Rocky implored, raising her free hand to her hip.

Hendrix's smile broadened. "I'm fuckin wit Cam. I know he don't get down like that beautiful. But seriously please tell me this cutie. . ." he skirted he eyes back over to Carmen, "ain't spoken for."

Finding her voice Carmen stretched out a hand to him. "She has a mouth and a name. And if you care to know anything about her, you'd do good to ask her yourself."

Hendrix used the same maneuver he used earlier with Rocky. He gently swatted Carmen's hand and pulled her into a hug. "I'm sorry sweetheart. I'm Jamie's older brother, Hendrix. And you are?" he inquired, unwrapping his arms from around her little body.

Carmen's lashes batted at the pace of windshield wipers on intermittent speed. She couldn't keep the sly smirk from etching across her face as she stared up at him. "I'm thirsty. Let's go get me a drink then maybe I'll tell you my name," she responded sassily, while hooking her arm onto his and pulling Hendrix away.

Rocky and I burst out laughing as the two walked away.

"Hendrix has definitely met his match wit that one," I asserted, while hooking a finger in Rocky's belt loop and pulling her back toward me.

"Fo sho."

I swept my eyes around the room, looking between the various games we had set up. On one table there was an oversize Jenga puzzle, a spades game was running on another table just a few feet over, and on the opposite side of the room there were two games of dominos being played.

Bringing my attention back to the beautiful woman standing in front of me I looked down at her. "You trynna get yo ass beat in one of these games?"

She giggled as she tilted her head to look up at me. "You just don't learn, do you? C'mon, let's get in on Jenga before the table fills up, but let me find E first. Cool?"

"Bet. I'll meet you over there," I agreed, letting go of her pants.

I watched Rocky walk away before strolling out of the kitchen. Shuffling through the crowd of partygoers I walked over to the game table and took a seat on an empty bar stool. I took a nip of my drink and zoned out. Absorbed in the music I bobbed my head to the up-tempo track when I felt someone tap me on the shoulder. I shifted my head in that direction, fully expecting to see Rocky. Instead my eyes landed on another set of familiar eyes.

"P Body," I exclaimed, standing from my seat.

"Hey Dre," she giggled, as I pulled her into my arms.

"Long time no see. I'm glad you came," I admitted, releasing her from my tight embrace.

"Yeah, it's been a minute. I ain't gonna lie, I was surprised as hell when I got your text."

"My bad Payton, life has been kinda hectic these past few months."

Payton chuckled. "You mean yo girl been keepin that ass under lock and key," she teased, raking her eyes down my body.

I snickered. "Well, that too."

"That's what's up. As long as she's treatin you right."

"She's definitely been good to yo boy."

"Then I'm happy for you," she stated, before taking a sip from the cup in her hand.

"Thanks, we need to catch up."

"Definitely. By the way, congratulations on enterin the draft. You gone kill em in the NFL," she declared excitedly.

I couldn't help the massive smile that spilled onto my face. "Thanks P Body, I appreciate it."

"Oh, hey Raquel," she greeted, looking past me.

I swung my head to my right, smiling down at Rocky as she approached my side.

"Hey to you too Payton and call me Rocky," she asserted, as she stepped around me and pulled Payton into a quick hug.

Surprise was an understatement for the look displayed on Payton's face. Giggling Rocky ignored her puzzled expression as she introduced her to Carmen and reminded Egypt of their previous encounter. I stood off to the side watching the entire exchange as I finished off my drink. The women chit chatted for a few minutes before Payton was approached by one of my team-mates, requesting a dance. Payton excused herself from the group and walked off with the school's second-string quarterback. That was my cue, stepping up to the trio I asked Rocky if she needed a refill. She looked inside her cup and shook her head then handed it to me.

"Hurry back so I can beat that ass," she teased, as I walked away.

Flipping her the bird I continued making my way over to the makeshift bar. After refilling our drinks, I weaved through the crowd, hurriedly making my way back over to the game table. I handed Rocky her cup then swept my eyes over to the game.

"What happened?" I asked, looking at the couple standing in front of the oversized Jenga game.

"You snooze you lose. We got next. By the looks of it, it won't be long. Her drunk ass. . ." Rocky slid her eyes over to the woman pulling a piece from the bottom rack, "bout to make it crash."

"Coo. Y'all playin too?" I asked Egypt and Carmen.

"Hell yeah," they chimed in at the same time.

"Bet. I'on wanna hear no cryin when I spank y'all asses tho."

"Boy please. I don't lose. Rocky you betta tell yo boy," Carmen stated through a chuckle.

"Yeah, well we finna see," I announced, as I watched the pieces come tumbling down.

Strolling up to the table Egypt giggled as the chick who lost fired off a string of curses while walking off with her friend. I followed behind Carmen and Rocky as they stepped on the side of Egypt. We played a total of three games before the table got crowded and other partygoers vied for a spot.

"I told y'all I don't lose," Carmen stated, as we shuffled through the waiting gamers.

"Hol'up. How you figure you won?" Rocky implored, staring at her best friend.

"Because I ain't knock that shit down in any of the games," she answered, before chugging back her drink.

I laughed while listening to the two of them go back and forth. I guided us through the packed room. I lead the girls over to the bar then told them I'd be back. I left the group and searched through the crowd for the birthday boy. A few moments later I spotted him ducked off in the corner with a light skin shorty on his lap. *I should've known.* Doing my best to navigate the crowd I quickly headed in his direction.

"C'mon. Time for your birthday shot," I shouted over the music, when I approached him.

Jamison whispered something to the woman in his lap then peeled his large frame from the chair, following behind me.

Back at the bar I noticed Hendrix had joined the women. With his arm draped around Carmen he whispered in her ear while Rocky and Egypt played the background.

"Now that I have the birthday boy y'all ready for these shots?"

"Let's do this shit," Jamison answered for everyone.

"Bet. Everybody good wit Patron?" I asked, bouncing my eyes around the group.

"Yep," everyone roared in unison.

I filled up six disposable shot glasses then passed them out with the help of Rocky and Egypt. Everyone held their glasses in the air and Egypt did the honors. She saluted Jamison with sentimental words of encouragement sprinkled with humor.

"Cheers," we shouted, before clinking glasses and tossing back the potent tequila shots.

"Fuck," Carmen howled, slamming her glass on the counter.

"Nah cutie, let's do one mo round," Hendrix coaxed, while picking her empty shooter back up.

Smirking I turned my attention to Rocky. I grabbed her by the waist and maneuvered her away from our friends, guiding her through the crowd onto the place designated as the dance floor. I spun her around in my arms and pulled her snug against my chest. Per usual my hands found their way to her juicy ass. Music blared through the clubhouse's speaker system controlled by one of Jamison's cousin, Trent. He'd programmed his phone to the Bluetooth and had been playing DJ all night. Currently he was on a slow jam kick, giving me an excuse to get raunchy with Rocky on the dance floor.

Keeping her close Rocky and I danced our asses off. Trey Songz "Neighbors Know My Name" was winding down when the music came to a complete stop. The crowd erupted in a loud roar; dudes were pissed their slow grind was interrupted while the women were just mad because they didn't know what was going on. Swinging my head around the room I tried to figure out what happened when Trent's voice came booming over the uproar of the crowd.

"I'm sorry for the interruption folks but we're all here to celebrate my cousin's birthday. He has requested a song, but I need y'all assistance first. Can I get a few dudes to push these couches and tables back along the wall please?"

Placing my mouth down to her ear I told Rocky I'd be back. I walked her off to the side then quickly helped the guys move the furniture around then waited for the next set of instructions.

"Thanks everybody. Aye yo J, Cam, Hendrix. Get cha asses to the middle of the floor. Everybody else back the hell up," Trent announced.

My confusion quickly turned to amusement as Jamison emerged in the middle of the crowd holding a red and white stripped cane. I had no idea where it came from because he damn sure didn't come in with it. Shaking my head, I moved to the center of the floor, standing by his side. Once Hendrix joined us Trent made one final announcement.

"I'ght, let's do this one time for the one time."

"Wipe Me Down" by Boosie Badazz resonated throughout the packed room. The crowd went wild, cheering as Jamison began twirling his cane before stepping off with his right foot, leading the pack. Following suit Hendrix and I trailed behind him. It didn't take long for the rest of our bruhs to join us. We gracefully strolled around the congested room. Legs swinging, shoulders bouncing, hips dipping, we worked our way around the room hitting every move with precision while randomly tossing up our fraternity's hand sign. We'd made our way around to where Rocky stood with her girls when we dropped down to one knee and started the infamous shoulder shrug. I could barely hear the music over the screams of the crowd as I wound back up from my feet. Smirking, I winked at Rocky as I continued past her, strolling until the song ended.

Slightly winded I dapped up Jamison and Hendrix then made my way through the crowd now gathered back on the dance floor. I found Rocky standing in the same spot I'd left her talking to Payton. Standing off to the side I ear hustled on their conversation.

"I'm surprised you didn't get out there," Payton stated.

Rocky shook her head. "I rarely stroll anymore. I used to, a lot in undergrad. Now, I let the young girls have it."

"Girl bye, you still young."

"Tell my body that shit the next day. How'd you know I was Greek?"

"I saw your keychain the night we left the club. It was an ivy leaf, right?"

Rocky nodded. "Good eye."

Payton chuckled. "I ain't gonna beat yo ears up. I just came over to say bye. I see yo boy is back so imma say bye to him then let y'all get on wit y'all's night. It was good seein you."

"You too. Be safe."

Payton stepped over to me. "Thanks again for the invite. Don't be a stranger."

"I won't," I declared, pulling her in for a hug. "Text me when you get home, so I'll know you made it," I finished, while unwrapping my arms from her body.

"Will do. You be safe."

I watched Payton shuffle through the crowd then moved next to Rocky. I stared down at the cup in her hand. "What you drinkin now?"

"Some shit Carm made," she answered, taking a sip from her cup.

I shook my head as a soft chortle eased from my lips. "I guess that means I'm the designated driver."

"Nah Egypt is, I don't think she drank anything other than that bday shot with us and J."

"Coo. You good or you ready to go?" I implored, moving closer into her personal space.

Rocky perched up on the tips of her toes and placed her soft lips on mine. She lingered there. I was ready to deepen our kiss when she slowly backed away from me. "I'm good. Go have fun wit cha boy. You don't have to stay under me all night."

Before she could get too far away, I snatched her by the waist, pulling her into me. "I like being under you, especially when you're naked."

Her slanted eyes were lower than usual letting me know she was feeling her liquor. She looked down into her cup then took a quick sip of her cocktail.

Looping an arm around my neck she smiled at me. "You betta stop before I find somewhere to put cha ass under me in here."

"Let me see what the hell you drinkin," I teased, gingerly taking her cup out of her hand and sipping her drink.

"Grown woman shit," she sassed, as she plucked the red Solo cup out of my hand.

"Yeah okay. That shit is fruity as hell."

"It's a slow creeper. Now go. Imma go find E," she demanded, trying to push me away from her.

"I'ght. Let me know before you leave."

"I gotcha baby," she replied, while turning on her heels and starting to walk off.

"Aye," I called out to her.

Rocky turned back toward me. She didn't say a word as she waited for me to speak.

I looked down at my wrist, checking the time. "We got about another hour in this bitch then I'm shuttin it down. Imma stay and make sure this place gets cleaned up then come get underneath you. Coo?"

Her slanted orbs swept down my body then slowly returned to my face. "Fuck yeah."

CHAPTER SIXTEEN

*M*y nerves were shot as I coasted into the hospital entrance. Following the signs for the emergency room I located the lot designated for emergency parking and pulled into the first empty spot I saw. My hands gripped the steering wheel as I tried like hell to settle my nerves. Slowly I removed my hands from the wheel and clasped them together in front of me. Instantly my eyes clamped shut and my mouth started moving but no words were audibly spoken. No, this prayer was spoken from my heart and uttered silently from my lips.

"Amen," I declared, out loud as I closed out my silent request to God and returned my shaking hands to the wheel.

Blowing out an exasperated breath I stared at the large red sign with bright white letters illuminating through the word EMERGENCY. Completely entranced by it I traced each letter with my eyes, quietly wishing it spelled out something else. Anything else, but most importantly I needed it not to be my mother's final resting place. It had been close to two hours since I got the call from my father and I'd been a fuckin wreck ever since.

God please let my mother be okay.

Loosening my grip on the steering wheel I tore my eyes away from that God awful sign just as my phone started ringing. Not bothering to check the caller ID I picked it up and pushed talk.

"Hello."

"Raquel, princess are you okay? Where are you? How come you ain't been answerin my calls?" he fired off question after question before I had time to answer.

"I'm sitting in the parking lot of the hospital," I answered, barely above a whisper.

My father blew out an audible breath. "I'm glad you made it safely."

"Thanks daddy. What room are y'all in?" I asked, turning off my truck and snatching the keys out of the ignition.

"Your mother is still in the emergency department. They haven't admitted her. Right now, they are just keeping her for observation. When you go inside go to the front desk and give them her name. Someone will direct you back to her room."

"Wait, you're not here?"

"No. I had to come back to the office to reschedule a meeting and close up. I'm on my wa—"

I disconnected the call before he could finish his sentence. I was pissed. Right now, nothing was more important than my mother. Not even work. Chucking my keys inside my bag I snatched it off the passenger seat and hopped out the truck. I hauled ass across the parking lot. I entered the hospital through a set of sliding glass doors, then sprinted down the short corridor to the emergency department. Walking past the security guard perched at a desk next to the entrance I gaited across the crowded room. My legs felt weighted as I approached a twenty something Caucasian women sitting behind another desk positioned diagonal from the one I passed when I came in. I dropped my bag on top of the counter and lost all control of my emotions as warm tears streamed down my cheeks.

"Oh, honey don't cry. Tell me how I can help."

"I'm looking. . . I'm looking for—"

I felt a hand on the small of my back. "Hi ma'am. Can you tell us what room Vivika Banks is in?"

426

Instantly I felt a sense of calm that hadn't been present since I received my father's call. I wiped a hand down my face and slid my chin toward my shoulder. My gaze shifted up at the last person I expected to see. He smiled then diverting his eyes to the sympathetic woman working behind the desk. Her blazing blue pupils brushed down his face as a wide smile stretched the corners of her mouth.

"Of course, sir. Tell me the patient's name again," she inquired, batting her false lashes.

Dre repeated my mother's name then stepped to the side of me. He placed a hand around my waist and pulled me into him. "It gonna be okay Short Stuff," he whispered in my ear, while caressing my arm with his other hand.

"I hope so," I mumbled, with my head forward and eyes locked on Miss Congeniality as she searched for my mother's information.

A few moments later she looked up from the computer screen, directing her attention to the handsome man standing beside me. "Mrs. Banks is in an observation room. You'll enter through these double doors." She pointed to a set of doors to the left of us. "Continue down the hall past the nurse's station then turn right. Once you've turned right look for room forty-five. It will be about four doors down on the left," she instructed, as she handed us two visitor's tags.

"Thank you. . ." Dre slid his eyes down to the name tag pinned to her scrubs, "Kourtney."

"My pleasure," she sang in a sugary tone, as her electrifying cobalt's bounced around his face.

You got to be kiddin me. Is this bitch really flirtin with him in my damn face?

Picking up on my observation Dre snickered while simultaneously giving my wrist a gentle squeeze before returning his attention to the overly friendly nurse. A soft smile donned his face but didn't travel up to his eyes. He acknowledged her words with a head nod then tugged firmly at my waist. Comforted by his presence I allowed him to guide me away from the counter. Concern danced in his eyes, but a smile remained glued to face. Slowly he slid his hand from my wrist and draped his arm over my shoulder. I stood quietly enfolded underneath his gargantuan arm tucked closely at his side while waiting for the automatic doors to open.

"What are you doing here?" I asked, feeling my emotions threatening to spill from my eyes again.

"Does it really matter right now?" He implored, leading me through the double doors.

Deciding he had a point; I didn't press the issue. Instead I silently trekked beside him, absorbing his energy as he led me down the aisle. There was a peace in his presence that settled my frazzled nerves. I had no idea how he knew where to find me, let alone how he knew I was home, but I was glad he was here.

"Over here Short Stuff," he instructed, guiding me by the shoulders down another hallway.

"What number did she say again?"

"Forty-five, it's coming up on the left," he answered, while pointing to the small blue square plaque sitting above the door.

As we approached the door, I felt the corners of my eyes mist. I quickly shifted my head toward the ceiling to prevent the impending tears from falling down my face. Dre tightened his grip on my shoulder then used his other hand to dip my chin out the air.

"Don't do that. Not now and not with me."

I let the tears flow freely down my cheek as I swiped my head to the side, looking up at him. "Thank you. Thank you for being here."

"C'mon beautiful. Let's go check on your mother." His voice possessed a confidence I needed as he ushered me into her room.

I swept my eyes around the modest size room, scaling them over the walls and medical equipment before fixing them on the bed. My mother's tiny body laid across the twin sized mattress underneath a dingy white blanket draped haphazardly across her right leg and hung halfway off the bed. An IV pierced her right arm. Fluid dripped from a transparent bag suspended from an irrigation tower. She was asleep, completely oblivious to my presence. Not wanting to wake her I took a few careful steps toward the bed then paused when I noticed her moving. She ruffled underneath the sheet as her immaculate brows crinkled in the middle of her forehead. With her eyes still closed she tugged at the cover, pulling it over her chest.

A fresh stream of tears rolled down my cheeks as I stood watching her. I quickly drew my hands up to my face, trying and failing to wipe away my tears.

Pull it together Raquel.

His touch was soft but firm as he pulled my hands away from my face. Spinning me around he wrapped his arms around my waist and pulled me flush against his chest. His large hands stroked my back as I sobbed inaudibly against his chest.

"Stop crying little girl. I'm fine."

I spun around to find my mother sitting up on the bed with a soft smile on her beautifully made up face. I swiped away my excess tears and padded over to the bed, dropping my purse on the floor beside it I stared down at her. My mother returned my gaze and stretched out her hand.

"Sit down sweetheart," she instructed, cupping my hand in hers.

I lowered myself onto the bed, careful not to touch her as I attempted to make myself comfortable on the small mattress. With my hand still in hers she ran her thumb over the back of it. Neither of us spoke as two sets of identical slanted eyes studied each other. Slowly I scanned my mother's face then relaxed my shoulders as my eyes glided down her body. Aside from the IV sticking out of her arm my mother looked like her usual self. That simple detail allowed me to relax, just enough to enjoy the moment without the threat of tears running down my face again.

My mother's movements were slow, sliding her hand out of mine she brought it up to my face. Lovingly she ran the pads of her fingers along my cheekbone where she lingered as she stared into my eyes. Inching my lids closed I titled my head while simultaneously hunching my shoulder. I held her hand there, relishing the warmth of her touch while silently sending up another quick prayer.

"I'm okay sweetheart. I promise."

I dabbed at the corners of my eyes as I slowly flashed them open. I didn't respond to her comment. Instead I raised my head from her hand

and nodded. In turn she shot me her classic beauty pageant smile then directed her attention behind me.

"And who is this handsome young man?" she asked, sweeping her eyes behind me.

Smiling for the first time since I arrived, I turned my head away from my mother and slid my eyes over to Dre. He stood in the same spot I'd left him with his hands tucked inside his pockets. His low penetrating gaze bounced between me and my mother. Even under the shitty circumstances, my body responded to him. A chill surged down my spine and found its way to my lady parts. Embarrassed, I ignored the fresh moisture gathered in my panties while brushing off my licentiousness thoughts before waving him over. As if he could read my mind Dre's lips curled into a lascivious smirk as he withdrew his hands from his pockets and gaited casually over to the bed. Pulling my bottom lip in between my teeth I slowly swiveled my head forward, looking at my mother again.

"Please excuse my daughter. It appears she has forgotten her manners. I'm Raquel's mother, Vivika. And you are?" she implored, raking her eyes up his expansive frame.

Dre snickered. "Hello Mrs. Banks, I'm Andre."

"Andre?" Her eyes returned to mine as she dramatically hiked a brow.

"Yes mother, this is Dre," I responded, answering her unspoken question while rolling my eyes up in my head.

Playfully she swatted me on the thigh. "Well it is nice to finally meet you Andre. I'm sorry it's not under better circumstances but I'm glad you're here with my precious daughter."

"Thank you and please call me Dre," he stated, moving around me and placing a soft kiss on my mother's cheek.

"Oh my. Cute and chivalrous. You better keep this one."

Mischief danced in his colorful eyes as he glanced at me over his shoulder while backing away from my mother. "She doesn't really have a choice ma'am. Because I'm not going anywhere."

"I know that's right." She winked at Dre before releasing a soft chuckle. "I like him already," she asserted, returning her eyes to mine.

"Mother."

"Don't mother me. He's the first I've met so I know he's special and by the looks of him I can see why," she stated, in what she thought was a whisper.

I tapped her IV. "What the heck are they giving you?"

I heard Dre snicker behind me, triggering me to spin my head in his direction. "Don't laugh at her. Clearly, she's under the influence," I teased, swinging my head forward again.

"Hush little girl. I'm very lucid. This. . ." she pointed to the needle protruding out of her arm, "is just liquid. I was dehydrated when I came in."

That small admission sobered me, reminding me where we were. "What happened mommy? You scared the shi—" I stopped talking when I realized my emotions almost made me forget my home training.

"I can step out and give you two some privacy," Dre spoke up from behind me.

"That won't be necessary handsome. But please take a seat and make yourself comfortable," my mother coddled, staring at him.

I didn't turn around but heard Dre's boots moving against the linoleum floors. A few moments later I heard the ruffling of his jeans as he took a seat. Smiling my mother drug her eyes back over to me.

"I told you I am fine," she insisted, patting me on the back of my hand.

"People who are fine don't end up in the ER being kept for observation mommy. Stop playing and tell me what happened."

Inhaling a calming breath my mother released it as she adjusted her position in the bed. "What did your father say? So, I don't repeat what you already know."

The mere mention of my father's name sent a rage through my body. I hadn't thought about his ass since I hung up on him earlier. *Shit!!!* Mad or not that wasn't acceptable, and I knew it. I twisted my torso to bend down and scoop my bag off the floor. Digging inside I searched for my cell phone so I could send him a text. I released an exasperated breath as I pulled my phone out of my purse and dropped it back on the floor. I opened the small device and immediately opened my messaging app, scrolling down to my father's name I clicked on it.

Me: Hey daddy. Sorry for the late text, just got good reception. My phone disconnected us earlier. See you when you get here <kissy face emoji>

Closing out of the app I rolled my eyes up in my head, hoping he didn't see through my lie. Sometimes my father drove me crazy. He could be so selfish. I doubt that I'd ever wrap my mind around how my mother, hell even Miss Brenda could be so dedicated to him.

"Hey little girl," my mother called out, snapping her fingers inches away from my face.

"Huh?" I responded, breaking out of my haze.

"Where'd you go? You alright?"

"Sorry, what did you ask me?"

With her eyes locked on mine my mother studied me through squinted lids. "I asked what your father told you already."

"Oh, he didn't tell me anything. He just said you were in the hospital and told me to come home if I could." I purposely bounced my eyes around the room to avoid her gaze.

"Uh hun."

"Quit stalling and spill it. Why are you here?" I questioned, bringing my eyes back to her face.

My mother chuckled. "Long story short I woke up fee—"

"No ma'am, that is unacceptable. I need every single detail from the time you woke up to when you were brought here," I stated, interrupting her.

"Well excuse me, and here I was thinking I was your mother."

"Mommy," I whined.

I heard Dre snicker as my mother rested a hand on my knee. "You're such a damn brat but I digress."

I placed my hand on top of hers while giving her my undivided attention. "Okay, I'm listening."

The smirk on my mother's face reeked of sarcasm. "Like I was saying, I had been feeling a little off all week but today I woke up feeling like—"

"Wait, you haven't been feeling well all week and didn't tell me? I've talked to you every day this week and not once did you mention feeling. . ." I made air quotes with my fingers, "off," I interjected, while cutting my eyes at her.

My mother waved a hand at me dismissively. "Do you want to know what happened or not?"

"Yes, please finish," I breathed out, not bothering to hide my annoyance.

"Like. I. Was. Saying. When I woke up feeling like myself, I took advantage of it. I let Gigi out, showered, then checked with your father to see if he wanted breakfast." My mother paused as her mahoganies bounced in mine.

"Daddy stayed the night," I mouthed quietly, while leaning into her.

She shook her head. "He's been staying at the house all week since I wasn't feeling like myself," she responded, matching my tone.

I nodded my understanding as I moved out of her face.

My mother studied me for a moment before speaking again. "After getting dressed I went to the kitchen to start breakfast when my eyes started bothering me. Initially I blew it off until I was halfway through breakfast, and everything went black."

Gasping I squeezed her hand while covering my mouth with the other. "Mommy."

"I'm fine now and it only lasted for about thirty seconds. But when my vision returned, I took a seat at the island and called for your father."

"Did somebody say my name?" he asked, galloping into the room like it was a damn runway.

Shifting my head toward the door I placed a fake smile on my face. My father's eyes bounced between me and my mother before landing on Dre. *Oh shit. Please don't make a scene.* As if he could read my mind my father walked over to Dre with an unreadable expression cast on his handsome face. Slowly it morphed into what appeared to be a genuine smile.

433

"What it do youngin? Thanks for making sure my princess was good," he greeted, giving Dre dap.

"No thanks necessary. I'll always make sure Rocky is taken care of," Dre responded, looking past my father and staring at me.

What the hell was that about?

"Much respect," my father stated, as he turned away from Dre and walked leisurely over to the bed.

Placing a soft kiss on my mother's forehead my father shot his eyes over to me. "Hey princess. You doing better now that you've seen your mother?"

"Yes and no. Mommy was just in the middle of telling me what happened to get her here," I explained, holding his gaze.

"Well don't let me stop y'all's flow," he replied, sitting a bag of food I hadn't noticed until now, down on the table next to my mother's bed.

"Thanks, JB," my mother cooed, as she watched him move around the bed to kiss me then amble back across the room and take a seat in an empty chair next to Dre.

My father smiled at my mother then turned his attention to Dre. The two of them immediately engaged in sports talk, prompting me to turn my attention back to my mother.

"Go on mommy."

"When your father came to check on me, I told him what happened. He immediately suggested we come to the ER, but you know I hate unnecessary trips to the hospital. So I asked if he would give me a minute, to see if it was just a fluke."

"But you're here so. . ."

My mother shook her head at me, probably tired of me interrupting her. "He didn't want to argue so he agreed but when he went to help me off the bar stool I almost fell on my ass. My left leg had gone completely numb. At which point he didn't give me an option. He carried me to the bedroom and called my neurologist and told him we were headed to the emergency room. At that point I was worried, so I conceded. And here we are," she finished, running her hand softly up and down my thigh.

I turned and looked at my father. "And you let her get that off?"

My father's hands flew into the air. "Hey, her body her call but when she couldn't walk, I vetoed that shit."

"I'm right here you know, and I do have a say so in what happens to my body," my mother asserted.

"I swear the two of you frustrate me," I chuckled, while sweeping my eyes back over to my mother.

"And how the hell do you think you make us feel?" My father questioned.

My mother winked at my father as a sweet sugary laugh spilled from her painted lips. "Exactly. Frustration is an understatement when dealing with your spoiled butt," she chimed in, as her mini laughing spurt ceased.

"Y'all better stop. I am an angel." I batted my long lashes for emphasis.

This time it was Dre's chortle that stole my attention. Spinning my head in his direction I squinted my lids at him.

"And what the hell do you find so funny Mr. Cameron?"

Dre pointed at the small TV hoisted on the wall. "Oh me, I was just laughing at. . . um, something on the TV."

The entire room erupted in laughter.

"Well I'm glad to see everyone in good spirits," announced a petite Caucasian woman wearing scrubs, as she entered the room.

Instantly a hush fell over the room as the nurse stepped up to my mother's bed. Looking at the IV bag she raised my mother's arm from the stiff mattress and inspected her IV. "Are you feeling better Mrs. Banks?"

"I am. Thanks for asking Sarah. Do you know how much longer I have to be hooked up to this?" My mother's eyes slid down to her arm in Sarah's hand.

"I'm actually here to take it out," she stated, while placing my mother's arm back on the mattress. "The doctor will be in shortly with your discharge paperwork, instructions for your aftercare, and a detailed summary of today's visit for your neurologist."

"Thank you, Sarah."

"It's my pleasure. Hold on what do we have here?" she asked, eyeing the bag of food on the bedside table.

"It's just soup and a salad," my mother responded.

"Okay, just make sure you're eating from the approved list," she cautioned, as she carefully extracted the needle from my mother's arm.

"Understood." My mother rubbed her wrist where the IV was just moments ago.

"Alright Mrs. Banks you're all set. Just sit tight and the doctor will be in shortly."

My mother nodded her head as Sarah ambled out of the room. Once the door closed, I set my eyes on the woman who gave me life. Bringing a hand up to her face I ran it softly over her high cheekbones. My mother tilted her head and melted under my touch.

"I'm so glad you're okay. I don't know what I'd do if something happened to you."

"Well, thank God you don't have to worry about that any time soon." Her tone was soothing, relaxing my renewed anxiety.

"Now ain't that sweet," my father teased.

"Don't be jealous because my baby and I were having a moment," my mother countered, looking at my father.

My father waved a hand in the air as a light snicker fell from his lips. "So, she's still my princess."

"Wow. Now I see why you're so dang on spoiled," Dre chimed in.

Dropping my hand from my mother's face I shifted my head, so I could see Dre clearly. "Ain't nobody ask you."

Dre stared at me. Lust mixed with humor danced in his hazels.

"Aye Vi," my father called out, causing me to shift my attention to him.

My mother smacked her lips, pretending to be annoyed. "Yes JB."

"Did the doctor say how long it would be before you got the results from your MRI?" he asked, instantly changing the mood in the room.

"MRI?" I questioned, peering at my father before returning my eyes to my mother.

My mother flashed my father the look of death. "It's just a

formality to try and determine what caused my symptoms from earlier," she answered, sweeping her eyes back over to me.

Blowing out a gush of air I opened my mouth to respond when my mother's room door flung open. A tall, slender, attractive, black woman walked in wearing a long white medical coat. A stoic expression donned her immaculately made up face as she scanned the room over the top of her fancy frames. Her fingers drummed against the clipboard cuffed against her chest. Slowly her gaze settled on my mother and her expression softened.

"Mrs. Banks and family," she greeted, as she neared the bed and looked down at my mother.

"Dr. White. I heard you have my discharge paperwork," my mother stated, looking at the stack of papers in the doctor's hand.

"That I do but before I release you, I want to go over a few things with you." She swept her eyes over to me then looked over at my father and Dre. "If you all don't mind, I would like the room for a minute?"

Anger blazed in my eyes as I bore a hole in the side of the doctor's face. My mother's hand found its way to my thigh again. "That's fine but I'd like my husband to stay," she supplied, looking at Dr. White before sweeping her pleading orbs back to mine.

Smiling she silently pleaded with me as her light ambers danced in mine. Not wanting to upset her I fixed my face, allowing a soft smile to settle at the corners of my lips while cursing Dr. White out in my head.

"Thank you, sweetheart. Give us just a minute," she whispered, while patting me on the knee.

I held my mother's gaze for a beat before slowly rising from the bed. Stealing another glance at Dr. White from the corner of my eye I walked over to Dre and stretched out my hand. He smiled up at me and placed his hand in mine then peeled his large frame out of the chair.

Once on his feet he slid his hand out of mine and snatched me by the hips, pulling me back into his chest as he locked his arms around my waist. "C'mon Short Stuff, let's get something to drink."

Knowing I had little say in the matter I let Dre guide me out of the room while relishing the comfort his tight embrace provided. Just outside the door Dre pressed his lips against my ear. "Are you okay?"

I nodded my head against his chest. "Thank you."

Dre didn't respond, instead he ushered me down the hall. He kept me close. Tucked underneath him Dre led me out of the emergency department. I was so consumed with my thoughts I hadn't noticed we stopped walking until Dre removed his hands from waist.

"They don't serve alcohol, so I hope coffee will do."

"It's gonna have to," I stated, smirking up at him before walking up to the counter.

"Can a brotha get a cup of tea?" he called out behind me, as he took a seat at one of the empty tables in the small restaurant.

Smiling to myself I nodded my head while waiting for the barista to finish with the customer ahead of me. When she was done, I ordered Dre's tea and an iced mocha latte for myself. With both drinks in hand I joined Dre at the table.

"Thanks, Short Stuff," he stated, taking both cups out of my hands and sitting them on the table.

"You're welcome handsome. You didn't specify what kind of tea you wanted so I got you apple cinnamon. I hope that's cool," I implored, taking the seat next to him.

Dre nodded his head as I plucked my cup off the table and sipped the sugary drink through the straw while peering at him over the top of my mug.

"What's that look for?"

I couldn't help the enormous smile that snuck onto my face as I held my cup away from my face. "I'm just trynna figure out how you knew where to find me."

"What, you don't want me here?" he asked, blowing into his drink.

"Just the opposite actually. I'm relieved that you are but that still doesn't answer my question Mr. Cameron."

Dre chuckled before taking a quick sip of his tea. "Your pops called me."

I almost chocked on my drink. "Come again?"

Dre's grin spread wide across his handsome face. "He was

worried when you weren't answering his calls, he thought that we might be together. I told him the last time we spoke you were on your way to class. He told me what was going on with your mother and asked me to check on you. So, when you didn't answer my calls either I hopped on the road and headed straight here."

Unfuckingbelievable. What did I do to deserve this man?

"Wow."

Dre sat his cup on the table and slid a hand on top of mine. "Don't over think it Short Stuff."

I shook my head still trying to process his words. "It's not like that. I just can't, I just—"

"I think the words you're looking for are, thank you," he teased, cutting me off.

I snatched my hand back and playfully tapped him on one of his meaty thighs. "Whatever cocky ass. But seriously Dre, thank you. You have no idea what this means to me," I asserted, feeling myself getting emotional.

Wrapping his hand around my wrist Dre snatched me out of my seat and pulled me into his lap. "I was fuckin wit you. I know you appreciate me bein here," he claimed, dabbing his thumb at the corner of my eyes.

Sliding my cup onto the tabletop I gently placed my hands on either side of Dre's face. I stared into his beautiful eyes and let the tears flow freely down my cheeks, unashamed at the emotions behind them. I had no idea what romantic love felt like, but I knew what I felt for Dre surpassed anything I'd ever experienced.

Running one hand over my thigh he soothingly rubbed the other up and down my back. "I know Short Stuff."

Unhurriedly I removed my hands from his face, swiping them down my own in an attempt to clear away my tears. "I'm sorry. I don't mean to keep crying in front of you."

"Stop it. You never have to apologize for sharing your feelings with me," he admonished, kissing each of my eyelids one at a time.

"I know but I don't wanna be that girl."

"And what kinda girl is that?" he asked, trailing his fingers up my neck and digging them into my wild mane.

Reflexively my lids slid close as he worked his fingers through my hair, expertly kneading my scalp. "The kind that gets all emotional and clingy every time she's around her boo," I clarified, as I slowly fluttered my eyes open.

Dre smirked as he nudged my head forward. He met me halfway and placed his soft lips on mine. Instantly a chill surged down my spine causing a silky purr to escape from my mouth. Teasingly he ran his tongue across my top lip. I parted my lips ready to receive him when the sound of someone clearing their throat snatched my attention. Pulling my face away from Dre's I shifted my head in the direction I heard the sound to find my father standing next to my mother with a hard scowl crest on his face.

"If the two of you are done playin kissy face we're all set to go," my father stated, staring a hole into Dre.

Hopping out of Dre's lap I grabbed my cup off the table and ambled over to my mother. "What did the doctor say? Is everything okay?" I questioned, ignoring the wide ass smile splayed across her face.

"Everything is fine. Dr. White just wanted to stress to me the importance of listening to my body and she cautioned me on waiting to see if things would get worse before seeking medical attent—"

"Just so damn hardheaded," my father scolded, interrupting my mother as he tore his eyes away from Dre and peered down at her.

"Oh hush, wasn't nobody talking to you anyway," she countered, returning his stare.

"Umm, excuse me. Can you finish what you were saying please?"

"I'm sorry sweetheart. Dr. White just really wanted me to understand that waiting could do more harm than good. She reassured me that what I experienced wasn't uncommon for someone living with multiple sclerosis but could be indicators that the condition was progressing."

"Mommy," I gasped, feeling my eyes misting all over again.

My mother removed her arm from around my father's waist and

pulled me into her tiny frame. "No worries baby. I'm fine. Dr. White doesn't believe that to be the case, but we won't know for sure until we get the result back from my MRI."

Taking a step back I peered into her eyes. "Are you sure or are you watering it down, so I don't worry?"

"When have I ever lied to you?" she implored, holding my gaze.

"Never."

"And I never will. Can we go now? I want to wash this place off of me."

And with that she dropped her arms from my body, looked up at my father, and strutted gracefully away from us. Smirking I sipped my cold beverage and watched my father take off behind her.

"C'mon handsome," I stated, looking over at Dre.

Wearing a grin matching the one stretched across my face Dre slid his cup off the table, stood from his seat, and casually strolled over to me. He wrapped his arms around my waist and pulled me flush against his muscular body.

Dre lowered his lips to mine and hovered above my mouth as the corners of his lips widened. "Now where were we before yo pops interrupted us?"

CHAPTER SEVENTEEN

icking the door closed with my foot I stumbled into the kitchen and clumsily dropped the bags in my hand onto the counter. I then shimmed out of my coat and tossed it on a nearby chair before stepping back up to the counter and digging inside the first bag. I quickly emptied the contents onto the clean surface.

"Oh shit, is it that time already?" Jamison asked, as he walked into the kitchen and stretched out a closed fist toward me, giving me dap.

I looked down at the groceries splayed across the counter then shifted my eyes back to my roommate. "You good. I just picked up a few items I needed to cook for Rocky."

I shifted the bulk of my weight to my left foot and folded my arms across my chest, prepared for the bullshit. Instead Jamison stood staring at me with the most intense look in his eyes. Uncomfortable by the silence and his penetrating gaze I focused on a spot on the wall while waiting for him to say what was on his mind.

"Damn bro, so this shit between y'all is serious eh?"

I slid my eyes back to his face as a grin played at the corners of my mouth. "Depends on which one of us you ask."

Jamison cracked a wide ass smile, showing his gums along with his teeth. "Don't tell me there's trouble in paradise already. Y'all just started smashin."

I kissed my damn teeth like a fuckin bitch as I turned away from him. "Nah nigga, we good."

"Then what bro? Cause I ain't neva seen you cook for a chick before."

Sitting the pack of noodles, I was toying with back on the counter I turned and faced my friend. "To answer your original question shit is definitely serious between us but—"

"Nah, don't do that bro. I've seen y'all together and I know that she makes you happy. Focus on that and not her deficiencies. Balboa is a real one, even if it's takin her a lil longer to get to where you are."

My brows hiked in the air as a wide ass smile crept onto my face. "Wow! This comin from someone who hasn't had a real girlfriend since middle school."

Jamison released a gut-wrenching chortle as he hurled his long arms into the air. "Aye, we talkin bout you not me. I ain't trynna see no parts of a relationship until I retire from the league."

The mention of our pending acceptance into the NFL sobered me. "We gotta get there first bro."

"Oh, we're definitely going bro and we gonna kill that shit," he declared, with confidence while pulling his arms out the air.

"From your lips to God's ears." I tilted my chin toward the ceiling then slowly drug it out of the air, settling my eyes on Jamison again. "Retirement bro? You a fuckin foo for that shit. Ain't nobody gonna wait on yo ass that long," I supplied, allowing a smile to return to my face.

"You see all this," he stated, flanking his hands down his body. "Nigga please. Oh, she'll wait and do that shit wit a smile."

"Whatever nigga. You need to take your own advice."

Stepping around me Jamison gaited over to the refrigerator. He mumbled something underneath his breath as he flung the door open and ducked his head inside. "Like I said, that shit was for you. The kid is good," he asserted, while closing the refrigerator and standing with a beer in his hand.

I turned back toward the counter and started unloading the other bag of groceries. "Whatever you say but you might miss out on a quality relationship stickin to that whack ass timeline."

"Like who? Nigga you said that shit like you got somebody in mind."

"Like Egypt." I glanced at him over my shoulder before turning back to the task in front of me.

"Dude we been over this already. E can't handle my ass."

I finished unloading the second bag of groceries. Once that was done, I collected both empty sacks, smashed them into tiny balls and tossed them in the trash. I purposely took my time before turning around to face him. I knew Jamison was waiting on my comeback. He tried hard to act like he wasn't pressed about E, but I knew different.

Leaning against the counter I crossed my feet at the ankle and smiled across at my roommate. "I beg to differ my friend. I think it is you who is afraid of Egypt."

"Nigga please. Why would I be afraid of a five foot five one-hundred-and-thirty-pound female?"

A sly smirk inched across my face. "Damn bro, but you ain't pressed?" I hiked a brow, expressing my disbelief.

Jamison took a sip of his brew while waving a hand at me. "Egypt is too sweet to get caught up in my shenanigans and I need at least another two years before I could even entertain her ass."

"Now we gettin somewhere. You just went from like thirty-four to twenty-five. But I got a question."

"What nigga?" he asked, lifting his beer to his lips again.

My mischievous grin stretched wider knowing I'd flipped the tables on his ass. "What's the difference between now and the next two years?"

Jamison snickered letting me know something ignorant was about to spill out of his mouth. "I said two bein nice." He paused, taking another nip of his brew while I stared at him with my brows creased, ready for the bullshit. "Imma need at least two full years to sample all the celebrity pussy that's gonna be thrown yo boy's way once I hit the big boy league."

"Sounds to me like you gonna need some Valtrex and one hella lawyer to handle all yo child support claims," I roared, through a fit of laughter.

Jamison clutched his beer against his chest as a boisterous chortle spilled from his mouth. "Fuck you." He hoisted his free hand in the air and saluted me with his middle finger. "You know the kid stay strapped up. Won't be no herpes or illegitimate kids for yo boy."

"Yeah okay, but back to Egypt."

Jamison's smile melted from his face as his eyes lowered to tiny slits. "What about her mane?"

"I think you might be underestimatin her bro. She got fight in her and I know for certain that she's more than equipped to deal witcha ass."

The left side of his mouth curled upward like he smelled something stank. "How you figure bro?"

"Because she's the only woman I've seen bring out Jamie."

"Nigga you trippin. Just cuz yo ass is out here seein hearts and flowers don't mean the rest of us are. And what da fuck you mean she brings out Jamie nigga?" Easing the muscles in his face he lifted his brew to his lips and took a swig while still glaring at me through the tiny slits of his cracked lids.

Smirking I unloosed my legs and turned toward the counter, sorting through the ingredients scattered on the cluttered surface. "I'm just sayin there are two elements to one Jamison G. Carter. There's Jamison/J, the college all-star quarterback and campus whore. Then there's Jamie, the honor student and true gentleman at heart. Egypt appeals to Jamie and has an uncanny way of bringing him out. And bless her sweet lil heart becuz she accepts and understands J and is willin to deal with him as long she knows Jamie comes along with him," I surmised, while shuffling through the groceries and grouping them together in the order in which I'd need them.

Jamison guzzled back the last of his drink, stepped over to the trash and chucked the empty bottle inside of it. "Yeah you on that bullshit."

Snickering I reached into the cabinet, grabbed a large mixing bowl, and placed it on the counter. "Mark my words, you sleep on that one and you're gonna be the one to lose out."

"Okay Dr. Phil. Why you cookin anyway? Valentine's Day ain't til next weekend."

"Nigga I know when Valentine's is." I dumped the pound of chopped lobster inside the bowl. "Rocky has never celebrated Valentine's Day so she made plans wit her girls. They have some kinda girl's days endin in a slumber party at the Hilton. So, I'm gettin my time in today." I felt like a straight bitch saying that shit out loud. Tossing the empty packet on the counter I turned toward Jamison and propped up against it.

Jamison came charging toward me, flailing his hands, slapping them against my chest and lowered hands. "My nigga. I told you Balboa was a keeper. Let me find a chick who don't believe in these bullshit holidays. Now that's the one imma marry," he teased, while backing off of me.

I shook my head still embarrassed by that admission as I turned back toward the counter. Jamison snickered on the side of me and that shit grated at my nerves.

"A'ight, Imma leave you to it then chef Boyardee. Imma change clothes then I'll be outta yo hair. Tell Balboa I said whadup." He tapped his knuckles against the counter then turned on his heels and strolled out the kitchen, leaving me alone with my thoughts.

A light chortle slipped from between my lips as I slid the can of crab meat in front of me. Turning on the faucet I placed the can underneath the stream of running water while reflecting on my conversation with Jamison. Rocky and I were in a good place. The more time we spent together I could see her invisible walls crumbling down. *So why all of a sudden am I annoyed?* Shutting off the water I removed the can from the sink and sat it in front of the can opener. An exasperated breath flew from my mouth as I tried to shake off my unexplained shitty disposition. Bits and pieces of my conversation with Jamison replayed over and over in my head until it clicked. The source of my frustration and happiness were tied to the same person, Miss Raquel Banks. Once again, I found myself playing by her rules without any real consideration for my feelings and that shit had me tight. *Fuck! I knew this shit was gone be challengin but damn a nigga can't catch a fuckin break.* Again, a gush of air spilled out my mouth as I decided to focus on the one thing that stood out from my convo with Jamison, *she makes you happy, focus on that and not her deficiencies.* It had been a few months since I openly admitted I was in love with her stubborn ass and she'd yet to say it back. However, there was no doubt in my mind or heart that Rocky was in love with me too.

Then why the fuck are you standing here tripping?

I used my thumb to swipe the tip of my nose then rested both my hands on top of the counter and closed my eyes. I sucked in a mouth full of air then slowly blew it out through my nose. I repeated that calming maneuver two more times while concentrating on the woman who stole my heart.

"Aye, what da fuck you doin? I thought you blessed the food before you ate. I ain't know you prayed before cookin it too," Jamison joked, triggering me to flash open my closed lids.

"Shut yo silly ass up." I cut my eyes at him as the corners of my lips twitched into an errant grin. "I thought yo ass was leavin."

Jamison's boisterous laugh filled our modest sized kitchen. "I'm leavin nigga. Trust me, I ain't trynna be here for y'all's after dinner activities. I know how y'all get down and ain't trynna hear that shit tonight."

I glanced at him over my shoulder as an impish grin splayed across my face. "Plug your ears next time," I countered, placing the can of fresh meat underneath the can opener.

"Nigga that shit don't work. You muthafuckas sound like a porn movie in high definition playin on the big screen in a damn movie theatre. I'm willin to bet the whole damn complex can hear y'all." He picked up the package of shrimp, carefully wrapped in thick white paper and examined it. "Now it makes sense," he stated, lifting the package to his head and tapping it against his temples then tossing the prawns back on the counter.

"What makes sense?" I asked, removing the can from the can opener and dumping the meat into the bowl with the lobster.

"You cookin." I could feel his eyes on me but refused to meet his gaze. "I mean, if I had someone puttin it on me the way Balboa does yo ass I'd be in here cookin too."

I reached into the drawer and pulled out a knife, sitting it on the counter I looked over at Jamison. "Bro somethin is seriously wrong witcha ass. And for the record, I'm the one puttin it on her," I boasted, feeding into his bullshit.

"Yeah okay. Either way, I ain't trynna stick around to hear it. I'll see you tomorrow."

"Tomorrow? You won't be back tonight?" I questioned, as my brows stretched up toward my hairline.

"Hell nah. If I'm lucky I'll miss round one but if I bring my ass back here, I'm sure I'll get an earful of rounds two and three. Nah, I'll pass. I'll stay at shorty's and make my own soundtrack." A devious smile sparked in his dark eyes before he turned and headed toward the door. "Later." He chucked an arm in the air and saluted me with two fingers stretched wide in the shape of a V.

"Peace," I called out behind him, as I leaned over the stove and set the oven to three hundred and fifty degrees.

Chuckling to myself at our exchange I pulled my phone from my pocket and checked the time. I had a little over an hour and some change before Rocky would be knocking at my door. Not wanting to waste any more time I sat my phone on the counter and surveyed the remaining ingredients while silently checking items off my imaginary to-do-list. I still had a lot left to do with little time to do it. In addition to finishing dinner I still needed to shower and change clothes.

I clapped my hands together in front of my face. "Game time Cam. Time to finish this shit," I announced out loud to the empty room.

Dragging my hands out the air I placed them on the counter and slid my phone toward me. I opened Apple music and selected my 'turnt' playlist. Fetty Wap's "Trap Queen" blasted through the mini speaker of the small devise, giving me the energy boost I needed to wrap up dinner. I moved my phone back out the way and scooted a handful of vegetables toward me. Picking up the knife I sat aside earlier I zoned out. My head bobbed to the beat of the music and I recited the racy lyrics while cutting up vegetables and mixing together the dry ingredients and meats. When the track switched to another up-tempo song I continued rocking out, rapping along with the track as I prepared the sauce and boiled noodles. Twenty minutes later I was done and ready to load the baking dish I laid on the counter a few minutes earlier. After dusting the dish with an ample amount of cooking spray I sprinkled a light layer of white sauce on the bottom then neatly laid down my lasagna noodles until the entire pan was covered. I carefully scooped out the seafood mixture, sprinkling it over the noodles until they were completely covered. I added a generous portion of white sauce then drizzled it with cheese. *Damn this shit look good as hell. I hope she likes it.* Licking the tips of my fingers I cleared the dribble of sauce that had landed there. *Oh, hell yeah. This might have her professing her love for a nigga tonight.* I chuckled to myself after I finished layering the dish then loaded it into the oven.

Mindful of the time I worked on cleaning up my mess. I cleared away the dishes I used, chucked the discarded wrappers in the trash, and filed away the unused ingredients in the fridge and cabinets. Taking a step away from the counter I surveyed the kitchen to ensure I hadn't left anything out of place. Satisfied with my cleanup job I grabbed my phone from the counter and exited out of Apple music. I clicked on the clock icon from the home screen and set the timer for one hour and twenty-five minutes then gaited out the kitchen.

Forty-five minutes later I walked out of my room feeling clean and fully dressed, wearing a pair of heather grey Nike sweatpants and a crisp white tee. A pair of all white ankle socks and black Nike slides donned my feet. I had spent way too much time inside my closet, debating on what to wear. I didn't want to scare Rocky off with my attire, giving her the impression that I was forcing some kind of pre-Valentine's day celebration— so I opted for comfort over style. It wasn't my first choice, but it felt like the right choice.

Stepping inside the kitchen I ambled over to the oven and peeked inside. The dish looked and smelled delicious. Satisfied with the progression I closed the oven and checked my phone for the remaining time. With plenty of time still left I stuffed my phone in my pocket then grabbed a beer from the refrigerator. Settled against the wall I lifted my brew to my lips and took a hearty swig. I savored the crisp coolness of the grainy hops when my phone buzzed, momentarily stealing my attention. Fetching my phone from my pocket I smiled at her name stretched across the screen. I shifted my beer to the crook of my arm before pressing my thumb on the home button. The phone opened to the home screen where I instantly clicked on my message app and selected her name.

Rocky: I'm about 2 head your way. U need me to bring anything?

Me: Just all the sexiness that is Miss Raquel Marie Banks <winking face emoji>

I clutched my phone in one hand then maneuvered my beer to the other. I chugged back another swallow, waiting for her response. I didn't have to wait long. My phone pinged in my hand as I slid the bottle away from my lips. Smiling I walked over to the counter and placed my brew on top of it. Looking at my phone, still open on our message thread, I read her reply.

Rocky: Say no more. See you soon <kissy face emoji>

My smile widened across my face, partially because of her constant use of a phrase I introduced to her but mainly because I was excited to see her. Responding with the heart eye emoji I closed out the app and dropped my phone back inside my pocket. And just like that all the negative feelings I'd entertained earlier, and truthfully was still harboring, disappeared in that instant. Although I'd become accustomed to it, it still took me by surprise how easily Rocky could affect my mood. Smirking I slid my beer off the counter and walked out of the kitchen, giddy as fuck.

You really need to get yo shit together bro.

I stood at the apex of the living room and took a nip of my drink as I swept my eyes over the furniture in search of the remote. To my surprise it was lying next to the PlayStation on the console table underneath the TV. *Now that's a first.* Between me and Jamison we had the damnedest time keeping up with it which typically meant spending ten to fifteen minutes tearing the living room apart every time we wanted to watch TV. Trilled that wasn't the case today, I trekked across the room and grabbed the remote off the TV stand. With my beer in one hand and the remote in the other I stepped around the coffee table and plopped down on the couch, grateful to finally be off my feet.

I powered on the TV and wasn't surprised to see the station set on ESPN. But instead of the usual sports broadcast typically aired on this station an old game between the Tennessee Titians and Akron Avengers streamed what was supposed to be an easy victory for the Avengers. But true to their nature the Avengers found a way to blow their lead, resulting in yet another lost for the rookie NFL team. At the close of this season they held the second worst record, trailing behind the Browns.

Chugging back the last of my brew I dropped the remote in my lap and tuned into the game, watching closely the missed passes, the clumsy footwork of the starting wide receiver, and the obvious disconnect between the players and coaches.

Watch yo ass get drafted by these clowns.

The Avengers weren't as bad as their stats made them out to be. They were however, a relatively new team with a new coaching staff and an inexperienced front office. Add in the fact that they haven't had a consistent group of players due to mid-season trades and injuries, and the end result was being marked with the label as the second worst team in the NFL. However, they had potential. Potential that could make them a strong contender next season if the players and coaching staff could get on one accord. Something I would work my ass off to achieve if I was in fact selected to be a part of their franchise.

I tore my eyes away from the TV just as one of the Titian's linebackers broke free and sacked Akron's quarterback, forcing him to throw a wild pass that was intercepted. A rookie tight end fumbled with the ball in the air before securing it in his arms and running for over thirty-five yards into the end-zone. Shaking my head, I glanced at the empty bottle in my hand then placed it on the coffee table. I had enough of the fuckery, having experienced it the first time the game aired in real time. I shifted my weight to one side and plucked my phone out of my pocket to check the timer. There was still a little over thirty minutes left before dinner would be done.

Clearing the lock screen, I decided to check my social media accounts. I skimmed through Facebook, cleared my notifications on Twitter, and watched a few stories on Snapchat. I saved my favorite indulgence for last, smiling I opened Instagram and clicked on the search icon. I typed in the first initial of her name and stared at the screen as IG auto populated her name underneath the search bar.

You definitely got it bad dude.

I clicked on her name and couldn't stop the wide smile from stretching across my face as images of her loaded onto the screen. I clicked on a picture of Creed as I read the caption below and almost dropped my phone. I read it two more times before releasing a suppressed chortle as my phone toppled out of my hands onto the floor. Taking my time to calm myself I bent over and scooped my phone up from the carpet. *This chick.* I smiled at the image of Creed with his paw inside her hand. His large head filled the small square and was tilted to one side. His deep brown eyes stared at her behind the camera, making the perfect shot. Scanning down the picture I read over the caption again. *My #MCM. Not 4 real but here's a pic of my stud 4 all you nosy b!tches. #sorrynotsorry #runtellthat.* Again, a snicker slipped from my mouth, fully aware of the reason she fired that shot.

Last month Rocky had to make her account private. After word of our courtship hit campus and my formal announcement to enter the draft, she gained an extra thousand followers, most of whom were only on her page as a means to get to me. In addition to the unwanted followers she received daily inquiries about us as well as unsolicited and often times inappropriate love advice. Shaking my head, I exited out of the app and laid my phone on the table. This new-found noto-riety would take some getting used to on both our parts. I just hoped it didn't scare her off. Four light raps sounded against the door pulling me from my musing.

I shuffled to my feet and ambled out the living. Headed straight for the door, I swung it open and stood stuck with my eyes bugled wide and mouth gaped open. Rocky stood on the other side wearing an all-black full-length mink and a pair of patent leather red strappy high heels. Her usually wild mane was pressed bone straight, cascading neatly down her back with a few strands splayed over her right shoulder. Dark eyeshadow adored her slanted lids. Bronze blush highlighted her high cheekbones and a deep crimson gloss coated her full lips. A small rose gold hoop hung from her septum while a tiny diamond stud rested on her left nostril. An overnight bag hung over her right shoulder and a small black cutch was snuggled underneath her right arm.

Goddamn! This chick is the epitome of sexy.

"Hello handsome. You gonna keep starin or can I come in and show you what's underneath?" She dropped her purse down to her hand and ran the clutch along the hem of her coat.

I clamped my mouth shut as my eyes slowly raked from the top of her head down to the soles of her feet before landing back on her face. Smirking she kept her eyes locked on mine as I stepped to the side, allowing just enough space for her to enter my apartment. I removed the overnight bag from her arm and dropped it by my feet before pushing the door closed. Sweeping my eyes to her rear I watched her glide past me. Instantly I was hit with her intoxicating scent. A blend of sugary vanilla, coco butter, and her natural aroma filled my nostrils, sending blood directly to my lower region.

"Hello Sexy," I damn near growled, as I discreetly adjusted myself.

She sashayed deeper into the apartment and placed her clutch on the counter before turning to face me. A salacious grin tugged at the corners of her painted lips while her slanted orbs raked down my body. "I hope dinner ain't done yet."

My brows met in the middle of my forehead. "Why? You not hungry?"

She brought her hands up to her small waist. "I'm starvin but I wanted to give you your dessert first." Sliding her hands up the fluffy mink she placed them on each side of her collar and slowly pulled the fur open, leaving it pooled around her mahogany shoulders as her hands found their way back to her waist.

Running my tongue across my bottom lip I took my time drinking her in. I started my perusal at the tip of her heels and ascended to the crown of her head. I couldn't decide where to settle my eyes as I continued to bounce them around her perfectly toned body. Her petite frame glistened underneath a red lace one-piece teddy. Instinctively I ran a hand down my rod as my eyes settled on her small mounds spilling out the sides of the tiny fabric. Her beaded pebbles were rock hard, drawing my attention to the gold barbells of her nipple rings poking through the small holes of the lacy material. Following my line of sight Rocky shifted her eyes to her cleavage then drug them back up to my face.

"Close your mouth Dre," she breathed out in a low husky tone, while taking slow measured steps toward me.

Dragging my eyes up from her breast I pulled my lips together. Lips I had no idea had fallen slack for the second time since she arrived at my apartment. "So, what I do to deserve this?" I asked, reaching for her hips and closing the small space between us.

Rocky ran a hand up my arm, gliding it over my shoulder she grasped the back of my neck. "There are too many to name, but I'll start with this. I'm sorry if it seemed like I disregarded your feelings or wants regarding Valentine's Day." Her tiny fingers traced soft circles along my collar bone. "I've never been in a relationship before, so I've never cared about celebrating. I do, however appreciate your willingness to compromise and because of that I thought I'd show you just how much it is appreciated."

I closed my eyes, melting underneath her touch as I absorbed her words. "Wait, did you just say relationship?" My lids fluttered open.

Rocky's fingers stilled on my neck as her eyes locked on mine. "This has surpassed a situationship Mr. Cameron so yes, you and I are definitely involved in a. . ." she slid her hand from around my neck and placed it in the air along with her other hand, making air quotes with her fingers, "relationship. Is that a problem?"

I lowered my mouth to hers. "Hell nah. It's not a problem at all." I held her gaze for a moment before speaking again. "So, I'm your first and last boyfriend," I stated, my tone matter of fact as I hovered above her lips.

Hooking her arm around my neck she perched up on the tips of her toes and pressed her lips on mine. A suppressed groan spilled out of my mouth as I wrapped my hands around her waist again, pulling her flush against me.

"Umm, wait. I haven't even told you the best part," she mumbled, stepping out of my embrace and fully out of my reach.

I lowered my eyes from her face, sweeping them down her body. "What da fuck is better than this?" I questioned, returning my gaze to her face.

Rocky took a few more steps away from me while trailing her hands up the outside lining of her coat. Her eyes danced in mine and a sexy grin donned her beautiful face. "How bout dinner reservations next Sunday at Pappadeaux?" she asked, letting her mink drop from her body.

For the third time in less than ten minutes my mouth gaped open. Quickly snapping it shut I hiked a brow. "Oh word? On Valentine's Day?"

"Yes baby," she answered, stepping over the mink and padding up to me.

No other words were needed. Cuffing my palms under her ass I lifted her tiny frame off the ground, relishing the feel of her juicy thighs as she wrapped her legs around my waist. A soft purr escaped from her mouth as she placed her lips on the nape of my neck. I walked with her cradled in my arms into the kitchen, sitting her on top of the counter I reluctantly stepped out of her tight embrace.

"Let me change the temp on the oven then I'll handle you."

Rocky crossed her left leg over the right and rested her hands on top of her knee. "Kay. By the way, it smells delicious in here."

I pulled the oven door down and peeked inside. The sauce coated over the noodles while the cheese bubbled down the sides. Satisfied that it was practically done I set the oven to warm, then closed the door, and stepped in front of Rocky. "Not as good as you. And I'm willin to bet you taste even better," I surmised, while raking my hands up her thighs and nudging them apart.

"I guess you're just gonna have to find out for yourself."

"Say no more," I growled, lifting her off the counter and carrying her over to the kitchen table.

Rocky giggled as I lowered her onto the wooden surface. "Seriously Dre? The table?"

"What?" I implored, meeting her gaze. "You said you were my dessert and food is supposed to be consumed at the table," I reasoned, leaning into her and placing my mouth at the nape of her neck.

Her breath hitched in the back of her throat as I traced my tongue over her skin. "So, I'm just supposed to bust it open right here, on your kitchen table?" I could hear the humor in her voice.

I sprinkled feather soft kisses across her clavicle before peeling my face away from her neck. "That's exactly what's about to happen," I assured her, sliding my eyes down her face and over her breast before bringing them back up to her slanted mahoganies.

Rocky didn't respond, instead her eyes drifted shut as her head rolled back. Enthralled by her beauty I peered down at her as I rested one hand on the table and placed the other on her leg. Parting her lips, she sucked in a lungful of air as I slowly eased my hand up her thigh. Purposely, I stopped at the peak of her sex. I kept my eyes focused on her face while my digits hovered over her clit, absorbing the warmth emitting from her core.

She is so goddamn sexy.

I ran the tip of my thumb over her clit, not at all surprised by her arousal seeping through the flimsy material. "Lay back."

Fluttering her lids open she eased back onto the table and stretched her legs wide, letting her heels drape listlessly off the sides. I swiped my tongue across my lips and stared at her pussy. *Fucking beautiful.* A groan escaped from my mouth as I stepped back and pulled the chair away from the table. Bouncing my eyes between the chair and the woman stretched out on my kitchen table I debated on what position to take before deciding to sit. Plopping down on the soft leather cushion I placed my hands on either side of her thighs and carefully pulled her down toward me. I wasted no time diving in, trailing soft wet kisses up her legs until my nose grazed her moist opening. A sensuous purr oozed out of her mouth as her hands shifted to my head. Digging into

457

my scalp she wiggled impatiently against my mouth. I couldn't help the smirk that tugged at the corners of my lips as I swiped my tongue over the thin material of her teddy.

"Dreeee," she cried out, now clawing at my neck.

I shifted my hand from her leg to her crotch and slid the small strip covering her pussy out my way. A muffled growl seeped out of my mouth as I swiped my tongue down her slick opening. Cuffing my hands around her waist I buried my face deep in her sex, meticulously swirling my tongue over her lips. My tongue dipped inside of her and my mouth clamped closed, slurping up her moisture. Rocky's hand flew to my head again. She trapped me against her pussy as she grinded against my face. I alternated between long soft licks and short hard flicks before gingerly easing out of her tight grip. Her hands dropped onto the table as she cursed my name and called on God in one long breath. Turned on by her natural response to me I slithered my tongue over her clit while humming from the back of my throat. I was rewarded by a fresh wave of wetness as her ass bucked off the table. Lapping up her juices I stuck two fingers inside of her tight canal, wiggling them against her nub while slithering my tongue over her lips and up her clit.

"Oh my god. Dreeee. I'm. . . Fuuuuck. . . I'm. . . I'm abou—"

Before she could finish her sentence, her walls tightened, and her body quaked. Her tiny hands found their way to my head again, wildly rummaging through my hair as she gave in to her orgasm. I carefully withdrew my fingers while softly licking her clit, relishing her undoing. When her body stilled, I peeled my face from between her thighs and sat back in my chair. I grated my teeth over my bottom lip while roving my eyes over her body. I watched the heavy rise and fall of her chest as she struggled to regulate her breathing. Slowly she sat up, crossed her legs, and placed one hand on her knee while the other rested on her chest.

"That. Was. Fuckin. Phenomenal," she breathed out through uneven breaths.

Swiping a hand down my mouth I smirked at her as the timer from my phone rang out. "Perfect timing. You ready to eat?" I asked, standing from my seat and walking into the living room to retrieve my phone.

I returned to the kitchen to find Rocky still sitting on the table with a confused look on her face. "What's wrong Short Stuff?"

"We're not done," she answered, while hopping down from the table and padding up to me.

"No but we are going to pause so I can feed you. C'mon my lil nasty girl," I supplied, grabbing her hand and moving her toward the counter.

Rocky opened her mouth in protest but quickly snapped it shut when her stomach growled. Her eyes grew big as saucers as her hands flew to her belly. "Eww, my bad. That was kinda gross."

"Please. Did you forget that you snore?" I questioned, letting go of her hand and stepping over to the oven. "And I've never told you before, but you fart in your sleep. So ain't no point in being embarrassed by your body's natural reaction to being hungry."

"You are lyin," she shouted, stepping in my face and crossing her arms over her breast.

Looking down at her I couldn't stop the grin from spreading across my face. "Wish I was Short Stuff but what's been done can't be undone. Ain't no biggie. I still love you," I stated, in a teasing tone but was dead ass serious.

"You're for real?" she implored, staring a hole in the side of my face as I shut off the oven and pulled the lasagna out.

"Go sit down. Imma clean off the table then set it, so we can eat."

I peeked at her over my shoulder waiting for her to move. But true to her stubborn nature she remained stuck in the same place, glowering at me through her long lashes. Sitting the dish on top of the counter I turned toward her and gently knocked her hands down from her chest. I placed my hands on her hips and pulled her into me, resting my head on top of hers.

"Miss Banks, I know you're not about to fuck up our evening over some petty ass bodily function. I only mentioned it as a joke. If I don't care you shouldn't either. And if I recall, you're the same person who had my pick up a box of tampons for them last month. You weren't embarrassed then."

"That's different." She attempted to shuffle out of my arms but I tightened my grip, keeping her little ass in place.

"Shiiid. I was mad uncomfortable checkin out witcha feminine products, but I did that shit. And the damn self-checkout lines were closed so I had to use a regular register. The damn clerk couldn't stop cheesin at my big ass. Now please stop or you're goin on dick punishment."

That made her laugh. She shoved me as she stepped out of my arms and saluted me with a manicured middle finger as she strolled out the kitchen. I snickered then waited until she was seated at the table before turning back toward the counter and stepping over to the sink. Dropping down on my haunches I shuffled through the various cleaning products and retrieved a bottle of Clorox all-purpose with bleach, sitting it next to my feet I grabbed a sponge and shut the cabinet. Snatching the cleaning spray off the floor I stood to my feet and walked into the living room. I paid Rocky a quick glance then started the task of clearing the table of her climax. Out of the corner of my eye I saw Rocky fidgeting with her hands while bouncing her eyes between me and the table.

"What wrong Short Stuff?"

"Nothin. It's just, I kinda feel bad knowin what went down on this—" Her voice trailed off as she skirted her eyes over the table before shifting them back down to her hands.

A light chortle spilled out of my mouth. "Don't becuz I sure as hell don't. Besides, ain't no tellin what kinda shit J get into when I ain't here." I sat the bottle of cleaner and the sponge on the table then stepped over to her. "Look." I pointed behind me to the clean surface. "No one but me and you will know what went down here. And thanks to you I'll never look at that table the same."

Rocky's eyes slid up to mine as a sly inched across her face. "And you say I'm nasty."

"You are," I stated, moving back over to the table and gathering the cleaning supplies in my hands.

"Yeah okay, I wasn't the one eatin my box like it was the last supper," she teased, standing from her seat and walking behind.

I pivoted on my heels, halting her steps. "You right and after dinner Imma eat that shit again," I growled, sweeping my eyes down to hers. "Where you going?"

"To change. You don't expect me to eat in this." She looked down, scanning her body.

"Yes, the fuck I do." I took a step toward her, closing the small gap between us. "You said this. . ." I glided my hooded orbs down her body before bringing them back up to her face, "is my gift and I ain't done unwrappin it. So, the shit stays on until I can properly take it off."

Rocky tossed her arms in the air. "Say no more." She didn't move, instead she stood gazing up at me with lechery dancing in her soft ambers.

I shook my head while using my free hand to turn her back toward the dining area. "Go sit cha ass down."

"You know I like when you boss up on me like that," she purred, as she walked back into the small kitchenette, gracefully parking her ass in the chair she was posted up in less than a minute ago.

I turned back toward the kitchen. "I know you do."

Dinner was amazing. My seafood lasagna was delicious, and Rocky couldn't stop raving about it. I was happy we were able to get pass that awkward moment and back to enjoying each other's company. But what I wasn't expecting was the bullshit that just left her mouth as I loaded the last dish into the dishwasher. I didn't respond, instead I stayed facing forward while trying to control my breathing.

"Dre, did you hear me?"

Again, I didn't say shit. I closed the door on the dishwasher, cut off the light in the kitchen and walked into the living room without so much as giving her the privilege of seeing my face.

"Andre," she shouted my name like that was supposed to get me to answer her stupid ass question. "I know you heard me."

I swear she just don't know when to leave well enough alone.

"Yeah I heard you." That was all I could muster without losing my shit.

461

I heard her heels clanking against the linoleum floors but refused to turn around. I placed my thumb and index finger on the bridge of my nose while letting my eyes slide close. Dragging in a lungful of air I ran my fingers down my nose then slowly fluttered my lids open. The room was completely silent, piquing my curiosity. I turned around to find Rocky sitting with her legs crossed staring at me. Her elbows were planted on her knees, her head cocked to one side and an unreadable expression rested on her face. I noticed she had ditched her heels by the side of one of the coffee tables. She didn't speak, instead she studied me for longer than I felt comfortable giving the current circumstance, but I refused to give her my words.

Realizing I wasn't going to say shit she smacked her lips as her eyes rolled down to her hands. "So, you have nothin to say?"

"I'on think you wanna hear what I have to say."

Her balled fist went to the cushions of the couch, using it for leverage she shot up from her seat. "C'mon Dre say somethin."

No words left my mouth. I stood waging war with her through angry eyes. Defeated, she sat back in her original spot, sheepishly peering up at me.

"Please just talk to me."

Fuck it, she asked for it.

"Are you fuckin serious? Are you really sittin here askin, no fuck that—" I threw my hands up in the air, "becuz I don't remember a question comin outta yo mouth."

She didn't respond, instead she sat staring up at me as five different emotions splayed across her face. First there was shock, then came confusion, followed by anger. The fourth was the one I hated the most, pride. And lastly, came understanding but that shit was too late. I was fuming. Turning away from her I walked over to the patio and stared out the door. I wasn't sure how long I stood there when I heard the ruffling of the cushions from the couch. Glancing over my shoulder I watched as Rocky padded toward me, her eyes aimed at the floor. I refused to acknowledge her, to give in yet again to another one of her fucking requests. Stubbornly I slid my face back toward the door until I felt her tiny hands on the small of my back. I spun around and glared down at her. Appearing startled by my sudden movement she took a step back and held a hand up to her chest. I waited for her to speak as I continued to peer at her, wondering what bullshit was going to come out of her mouth this time. Finally giving me her eyes, she placed a hand on the side of my face and cocked her head to the side. We remained quiet in that space for what felt an eternity.

Then suddenly without warning Rocky's mouth was on mine. Her warm minty breath peppered with traces of tonight's dinner invaded my nostril as she sprinkled my lips with rushed kisses. Running her tongue across my bottom lip, she sucked it into her mouth and nibbled. I groaned into her mouth while welcoming her tongue in mine. She threw her arms around my neck and climbed up my body, wrapping her legs around my waist. Having no choice, I placed my hands underneath her ass and secured her in place against me. Rocky continued to attack my mouth with fervor. I gave in to what had always been natural between us. I allowed myself to enjoy her, to be present in the moment with her. Rocky must have sensed my change in disposition. Slowly she withdrew from my mouth and stared at me, imploring me with her eyes. I wasn't ready to speak. I had no words to offer her, only my body. Holding my gaze, she dropped a hand from around my neck and placed it at my waist. In one quick motion she yanked down my pants and boxer briefs, freeing my swollen manhood. Returning her arm around my neck she placed a soft peck on my parted lips then dipped her tongue into my mouth again.

This I could handle; this was the easy part. Had always been that way between us.

Removing one of my hands from her ass I slid it toward her crotch and pulled her teddy to the side while disconnecting my mouth from hers. I waited until her eyes landed on mine. I needed her permission, permission to enter her unsheathed. She sucked her bottom lip in between her teeth and nodded her head as her eyes clamped shut. That was all I needed. Lowering her ass down to meet my cock I hovered over her slick opening.

"Are you sure Raquel?"

Her eyes fluttered open. "Fuck me Dre," she groaned, before placing her warm mouth back on mine.

I felt conflicted as I eased into her lubricated folds. On one hand I wanted her, needed her, but I couldn't tune out the small voice in the back of my head screaming that I was a bitch. Oblivious to the thoughts running through my head Rocky worked her tongue around mine. Slowly she rolled it around my mouth as she coiled her hips and tightened her pussy on my dick. Gripping a handful of her ass I gave in to the surges of pleasure coursing through my body, tossing out all thoughts except one, *tear her ass up*. I bent slightly at the knees and plunged deeper into her until she stopped moving above me. Pulling her mouth away from mine her head fell back, and a soft whimper spilled from her parted lips. A confident grin etched across my face as I continued to dive inside of her, spilling my frustration and love into her.

"Goddamn Dre."

I clamped my teeth down on her neck then traced where I'd bitten her to take away the sting. I was rewarded by the sudden movement of her hips. Lifting my face from her flesh I stepped out of my pants and boxers then carefully walked with her out the living room as she bounced her ass on my dick. I managed to guide us to my bedroom without breaking contact. Tossing her little ass up on my dresser I stretched her legs wide, placing them in the folds of my arms. Rocky's back and head crashed against the mirror, prompting me to pause.

"Don't fuckin stop."

I took my time stroking her, inching out to point of disconnecting our bodies then ramming back in. Rocky lost her mind. Her eyes rolled in the back of her head as her legs trembled in the crook of my arms and sweat gathered above her lip. She begged for me not to stop while repeatedly calling on her savior. I gave her what she asked for as I continued to tease her. I pulled out, then grinded back in, filling her up whole. Her walls started to quiver, and her hands gripped for me as she pushed herself up from the back of the dresser. But I wasn't ready for her to cum yet.

Staring into her face I pulled my dick out of her and dropped her legs from my arms. I placed my hands around her waist and helped her off the dresser. She stared up at me confused as I stripped her of the flimsy lingerie, tossing it on the floor by our feet. Ranking my eyes down her body I rested my hands on her shoulders and nudged her to the floor. All traces of confusion fell from her face as she propped up on her knees and wrapped her small hands around my rod, tracing the head of my erection with her tongue. She kept her eyes trained on me as she slowly sucked me into her mouth.

Refusing to release the groan at the back of my throat I bit down on my lip. A muffled moan tickled my dick as Rocky slurped greedily down the length of me. Grinding her hands in opposite directions she created a beautiful friction as she continued to work her warm mouth up and down my hardened pole. Saliva spilled from her mouth onto her hands and down the sides her lips. Undeterred she maintained a steady pace, sending mini tremor down my spine while keeping her eyes locked on mine. I was close but couldn't determine where I wanted to release. As if she could read my mind Rocky slowly withdrew my dick from her mouth while her hands continued to caress my rod. Tightening her grip, she rolled up and down my shaft, pressing her thumbs into my main vein as she ascended to the tip. That was it, I shot my load without warning or care for where it landed. Milky white semen landed on her cheek, splashed on her shoulders and breast, dribbling down to her navel. Flipping my head back my lids drifted shut as I released a delayed moan while Rocky milked me dry.

My head sprung forward, and lids cracked open at the feel of her mouth on me again. This time her eyes were closed as she gently inched her mouth down my semi-flaccid dick. She took her time coasting up and down my rod, guarding her teeth while her mouth and tongue did all the work. I was hard again in no time. Placing a hand on her shoulder I gingerly pushed her away from me. Rocky sprang to her feet and climbed my torso before I knew what was happening. One hand rested around my neck while the other maneuvered between us. Grabbing hold of my dick she carefully guided me inside of her. Reflexively a deep gut-wrenching growl slipped out of my mouth as she sank down on me. The sounds of her arousal permeated throughout the quiet room as she swirled her hips on my rod.

"Shit," I hissed, while walking with her in my arms over to the bed.

"I let you fuck me. I even let you shoot jizz on my body. Now I want you to make love to me."

I didn't respond right away. Instead, I gently laid her on her back and gingerly removed myself from her tight hold. Looking down at her, I fixed my eyes on her face. "Tell me you love me Raquel."

Without warning she lurched forward, wrapped her arms around my neck and pulled me onto her as she fell back onto the mattress. "I love you Andre."

I was glad the room was dark, so she couldn't see the Kool-Aid size smile plastered on my face. Planting a chaste kiss on her shoulder I removed her arms from my neck. "Turn yo ass over so I can eat the booty like groceries. I owe you a few orgasms."

CHAPTER EIGHTEEN

"*B*itch you said what?" Carmen asked, as her perfectly microbladed brows ascended toward her platinum precision cut.

"Carmen," Egypt shrieked.

Carmen dismissed Egypt's admonishment with a flick of the wrist as her head rolled over to me. Sweeping her golden orbs down my face she waited for my response.

Chuckling I sat my glass on the table and pulled my legs off the floor, folding them underneath me. "Really Carm, what was wrong with what I said?"

Carmen shuffled to the edge of her seat and pointed her acrylic coffin shaped nail toward me. "Let me see, where do I start?" She placed that same nail on the tip of her chin as an errant grin slid across her lips. "You asked, no wait—" she placed both her hands in the air with her palms slightly tilted toward the ceiling, "you told, because I don't recall your version of events being formulated in a form of a question—"

I smacked my lips. "And yo point?" I implored, cutting her off.

"Bitch my point is, how you thought the nigga you're currently fuckin was gonna be cool wit you goin to dinner wit a nigga you used to fuck? I mean, how Sway?" Her hands dropped down to her lap, but her eyes remained glued to my face.

Damn she did have a point. A point I wasn't open to hearing when I first told Dre Emery wanted to meet for dinner this month. I was too focused on my response that I didn't listen to the reasons why he didn't want me to go. Hell, I even tried to bring up being cool with Payton attending Jamison's birthday kickback to justify my argument. But after hearing Carmen state the obvious, I had to admit, even if it was just to myself, she was right.

Man, this relationship shit is a lot of work.

"Oh, so now you ain't got shit to say?"

"Carm, stop it. I think she gets it now," Egypt responded, coming to my rescue.

I bounced my eyes between my two best friends as a dry chuckle eased from the back of my throat and spilled out of my mouth. As amusing as I found Carmen's brash delivery there wasn't a damn thing funny about the facts of her argument. Facts my stubbornness hadn't let me conceptualize until this very moment. It had been almost three weeks since I damn near ruined a very thoughtful and well planned out evening and it took just about all of that time for me and Dre to get back to normal. Even after professing my love and putting it on his ass that night it was a slow crawl out of the doghouse. In hindsight I could see why because it wasn't until now that I understood how fucked up the situation was. And I was sure my efforts to bring us back to a place of normalcy reflected that.

Damn Raquel, you need to do better.

Plucking my drink off the table I took a quick nip of the fruity cocktail before settling my sights on Carmen. "Message received."

"Good. Cause that was some foul shit and if the shoe was on the other foot you would've dismissed his ass." She nodded her head for extra emphasis before taking a swig of her drink.

"Bitch I said I got it."

"I'm just makin sure." She chuckled as she sat her glass on the table. "Take it from somebody who is out here dealin wit fuckboy after fuckboy, you got a good one wit Dre."

"Uh hun," Egypt chimed in.

"Not you too E. I thought you were on my side."

"I am I'm just agreeing with Carm about Dre being a good dude." Egypt's eyes dropped to the cup in her hand.

"I know he is, and I would never do anything to intentionally hurt him," I reasoned, before taking another gulp of my drink.

"Well imma need you to start thinkin about the unintentional, cuz hurt is hurt. And some shit you can't come back from. Lucky for yo spoiled ass this wasn't one of them."

"See this exactly why I don't do relationships."

"Didn't, you didn't do relationships as in past tense. Cuz yo ass is in a full blown one now," Carmen corrected.

"So, what all of a sudden I'm supposed to be psychic? How da fuck you predict unintentional hurt?" I tried to keep my tone even, but I was getting more and more annoyed by the second.

Carmen's lips kissed her teeth. "I swear, you're too smart to be this dumb. It's not that hard. Simply put, you put yourself in his shoes. If it's some shit that you know would piss you off or hurt your feelings, then don't do it. It's that simple."

"CARMEN."

Carmen swung her head in Egypt's direction. "Don't Carmen me. I ain't her mama and I ain't gonna sugarcoat shit." She shifted her head back toward me, locking her eyes on mine. "Right is right and wrong is wrong and Princess Raquel was wrong as two left feet."

"I get that but damn, do you have to be so—"

"Real," Carmen responded, finishing Egypt's sentence knowing damn well real wasn't what Egypt was going to say. "Cuz I'm a real bitch."

"You got the bitch part right," I teased, squinting my eyes at her before sliding them over to Egypt. "Don't mind her, she been talkin crazy to me since middle school."

"Damn skippy and imma be talkin to yo ass crazy when we old and grey and can't find our dentures and rockin Depends."

The three of us burst out laughing, killing the animosity that had built during what was supposed to be a light-hearted conversation.

Relived by the shift in the atmosphere I sank back in my seat and shook my head to myself. I loved my girls and even though we could push each other's buttons we always found our way back to this. My eyes shifted between the two of them.

"Why are you looking at us like that?"

"And how am I lookin?" I responded, making eye contact with Egypt.

"Like you trynna figure out where to bury our bodies," Carmen supplied, before Egypt had a chance.

I slid my eyes over to Carmen before dragging them down to my cup and taking a swallow. "Whatever crazy." I dismissed her with a wave of my hand as I held my cup away from my face.

Giggling Carmen stood from her seat and stared down at me. I cocked my head to the side and lowered my already slanted eyes, returning her gaze I waited for her response. A goofy grin tugged at the corners of her lips as her little arm flew in the air and her hand stretched out in front of her face. She flipped me the bird then turned toward Egypt and saluted her with the same gesture. That triggered a fresh round of giggles as Carmen stepped over Egypt's legs propped on the table.

"And where the hell you goin?"

Carmen glanced at me over her shoulder. "To the bathroom. Is that okay with you?"

I didn't respond, instead I kept my eyes fixed on her face as one side of my mouth twitched into a half smile. That melted the stoic expression off her beautifully made up face as a slick grin spread across her painted lips. We continued our playful stare off until Egypt cleared her throat, prompting both of us to shift our attention to her.

"Would you take your ass to the bathroom. We got other shit to talk about before you carry your hot ass out of here for one of your boos," Egypt declared, looking past Carmen and winking at me.

Smacking her lips Carmen added an extra sway to her hips as she sashayed out the room. Snickering at her dramatic exit I finished the rest of my drink as my thoughts turned to Dre. May was damn near two months away, marking a year since he came into my life and took over my world. Dre was nothing like anything I could've imagined and somehow, he managed to be everything I needed him to be when I needed him to be it. And to top it all off, he loved me. He loved me in spite of my spoiledness, beyond my relationship curve, and past my doubts. He made me feel special and appreciated. I really needed to do better.

"Okay I'm back. So, let's address the last elephant in the room." The sound of her voice snatched me out of my head. I looked up to find Carmen standing in front of the coffee table holding the pitcher of sangria.

"Yes please. So, spill it. Which one of you is holdin out?" I asked, happy to have the spotlight off me.

"Sorry boo boo, we're still on you," Egypt stated, humor dancing in her big eyes.

"Wait, what?" I placed my free hand over my chest, feigning surprise.

Egypt nodded her head as Carmen's eyes landed on me.

"Damn okay, but imma need a refill before y'all start diggin in my ass again."

Carmen sat her freshly filled cup on the table then stepped over to me and topped off my glass. "You good or do you need more?" she inquired, sliding her head over to Egypt.

Egypt lifted her glass in the air. "Yes please."

Carmen moved over to her original spot and refilled Egypt glass, then sat the pitcher on the table. "Inquirin minds wanna know how long you gonna play Russian roulette wit the box or is yo ass trynna get knocked up?" She swung her head over to me while sliding her glass off the table and sitting on the couch.

My hand flew up to my mouth, wiping away the dribble of liquid that spurted down my chin before Carmen finished her crazy ass statement. "Bitch what? You know damn well I'on want no muthafuckin kids."

I swear I tell these broads entirely too much.

"I can't tell." She brought her glass up to her lips but kept her eyes on me, waiting for my response.

Shaking my head, I sipped my drink. "Whatever." I rolled my eyes as I rested my glass on my knee. "For your information I had a doctor's appointment last week."

"And?" Egypt asked, scooting to the edge of her seat.

"And my coochie is fine, thanks for askin."

"Bitch quit playin. You know what we wanna know." Carmen pulled her legs off the floor and folded them underneath her.

"There won't be any kids for me. Dr. Peters insisted I take a pregnancy test before she would prescribe me the pill." I balanced my cup in one hand while reaching over the side of the chair and snatching my purse off the floor. Resting it in my lap I shuffled through the contents inside and pulled out the pack of pills, tossing them on the table I bounced my eyes between my friends.

Carmen's golden orbs brushed over the blue billfold as a sly grin distended across her lips. Satisfied that I had quashed the pregnancy bullshit I took a swig of my drink as a smug grin tugged at the corners of my mouth.

"That's good. Did you start them already?" The enthusiasm in Egypt voice made me giggle.

"Yes boo. Now, are we done wit me?"

Egypt chuckled before nodding her head and taking a nip of her cocktail. I blew out a dramatic breath while playfully swiping a hand across my forehead. That earned me an eye roll from Carmen, triggering a goofy grin to stretch across my lips. The three of us settled into a comfortable silence, the first since they arrived at my place.

I loved hanging out with my girls. Just the three of us being our authentic selves, talking shit while kicking back and catching up without judgement. Our girl's day shenanigans were cancelled due to Egypt being called into work. So, this was the first time the three of us were able to coordinate our schedules and really talk. I wasn't surprised that my shit was at the top of their list of things to discuss, I just couldn't wait until I wasn't the only one talking about their boo.

Dragging my bag out of my lap I slid my feet to the floor and stretched my legs out in front of me. "So, you mean to tell me neither of you. . ." I swept my eyes between the two of them, "don't got nothin new to share?"

Egypt hunched her shoulders while Carmen stared at me over the top of her glass.

"Seriously?"

"Sorry boo. I told you, it's one fuckboy after the next." Carmen sat her drink on the table and picked up her phone just as it chimed. "See, nothing but fuckboys," she stated, stretching her phone toward me and showing me the name of one of the dudes she entertained from time to time.

I giggled. "E?" I dipped my head toward her before looking into my cup.

"Nope, nothing. Not since I cut Raheem's lying ass off." Egypt sat her glass on the table and picked up the pitcher.

"Damn. Well, update us on one of those ratchet reality shows you always watchin." I leaned over the table and held my glass out for her to fill.

Egypt poured herself another drink then refreshed my glass. Her eyes grew wide and a big ass smile seeped across her face. "Now that I can do. Which one? Basketball Wives, Love and Hip Hop, The Real Housewives of—"

"Why the hell you get her ass started?" Carmen flashed me an evil look before picking up her glass and extending it toward Egypt. "Fill my shit up too. Imma need it to sit through yo ratchet recap."

Smacking her lips Egypt topped off Carmen's drink before returning the pitcher to the table and plopping down in her seat. She angled her body toward me and Carmen then started talking a mile a minute. Her usually husky tenor was high pitched and animated as she ran down the details of the latest episode of Basketball Wives. Chuckling at the look of disgust on Carmen's face I sat back in my chair and sipped from my glass, relishing the sweetness of my cocktail as it traveled down my throat. This was truly one of my favorite ways to bring in the weekend.

he sound of a door closing somewhere in my apartment jarred me from my sleep. Cracking my lids, I perched up on my elbow and surveyed the dark room. I damn near fell off the couch when my eyes landed on his arduous frame. A slither of light from the single lamppost in the courtyard spilled into the room, casting just enough light inside my apartment for me to see him clearly. His back was to me, but I could tell by the shift in his stance that he'd heard the ruffling of the cushions underneath my sluggish movements.

He didn't turn around right away. Instead, his head remained rested against his arm propped up on the ledge of the door. *That's weird.* Sliding my legs off the couch I pushed up off my arm and sat upright, resting my back against the cushions of the couch. Again, his body responded to my movements, but his head stayed facing the patio. *Why is he here?* I opened my mouth to speak but quickly clamped it shut when his head swiveled in my direction and his eyes landed on mine.

"Hey Short Stuff." His thick chords cracked, letting me know he'd been sleep before coming here.

"Hey to you." Still groggy I could hear the sleep in my own voice.

The room fell silent as Dre continued to peer at me over his shoulder. Imperceptibly he lowered his gaze and raked his eyes down my body. Suddenly self-conscious about my appearance I brushed my hands over my hair, fluffing down any loose strands before swiping my fingers at the corners of my eye.

A soft smirk formed on his handsome face. "You look beautiful as always."

"Thank you," I mumbled, dropping my eyes to my hands in my lap.

I couldn't see him, but I heard Creed's collar jiggling in the distance followed by the cool breeze from the night's air as the door was opened then pushed shut. Out of my peripheral I saw Creed amble past Dre's feet. Feet that remained stuck in place, prompting me to lift my head and look over at him. Something was off. He wasn't close enough for me to feel his energy but by the way he bounced his eyes around the room, refusing to settle them on me told me all I needed to know. This wasn't like the times in the past. He wasn't here because he needed me, he was here because something was wrong. And it had to be something serious for him to drive over here at— I looked down at my wrist only to realize I wasn't wearing a watch.

Dragging my eyes up from my arm I swept them around the room, in search of a clock. Unable to read the time off the cable box I turned my attention to the couch, gliding my eyes over the cushions while simultaneously running my hands everywhere my eyes landed. The ruffling of his sweater snatched my attention. Yanking my head up from the sofa I swung my neck toward him to find Dre pointing somewhere behind me. Instinctively I rolled my head in the direction of his outstretched arm, peeping my phone resting on top of the island where I left it after letting Carmen and Egypt out earlier.

"It's two-thirty," he stated, answering my unspoken question.

"Thanks." My voice was so low I barely recognized it.

I felt his eyes on me, prompting me to turn around and face him again. "What are you doing here Dre?"

He stuffed his hands inside the pocket of his joggers as his eyes lowered to the floor. "I wanted to see you."

I stood from my seat and glanced at him over my shoulder. "I can tell." Not bothering to hide the sarcasm in my voice I swiveled my head forward, stepped around the table and padded out the room, leaving him standing by the patio door.

As I strolled the short distance to the bathroom, I wondered why he was here and more importantly if it was something, I did wrong that brought him to my apartment in the middle of the night. Inside the bathroom I closed the door and rested my head against it. Sliding my eyes closed I sucked in two big ass breaths of air then slowly blew them out my nose. Gradually I felt the tension ease from my shoulders as a calm washed over my body. Fluttering my lids open I quickly went about my business, relieving my bladder then washing my face and brushing my teeth. I paid myself one last glance in the mirror before exiting the bathroom and ambling down the hall. I walked into the living room and stopped, shocked to see Dre still standing in the same spot I'd left him, the same spot he'd been in since I discovered him in my apartment. As if he could feel my presence, he swept his head over to me and locked his eyes on mine.

Yep, something is definitely wrong.

I forced a smile on my face as I took slow measured steps toward him, stopping just a few inches away from his body. "Baby what's wrong?" My tone was light as my eyes searched his for answers.

Doleful hazels flashed emerald green before sliding down my face and landing somewhere on the carpet. He didn't speak, instead his attention remained on the floor as the muscles in his jaws flexed every two to three seconds. Yes, I had counted. I counted every second there was dead air between us in hopes that he would answer me. An answer I somehow knew wasn't coming anytime soon.

Flustered, I slid my eyes close and counted backwards from fifty. I slowly breathed in a mouthful of air and exhaled it through my nostrils as my lids flashed open. Dre's head was still aimed at the floor, his eyes swept rapidly across the carpet while his hands fidgeted in his pockets. *This is stupid and I'm tired. Lord give me the strength to deal with this man.* Bouncing my eyes around his brooding frame, I took a step forward then stopped dead in my tracks. He didn't want me any closer, something made clear when he abruptly swung his head up from the ground and peered at me with a hard scowl crest on his tired face. I hadn't noticed it before, but it was crystal clear now. There was an invisible wall between us, one he'd put up to keep me out.

Stunned, I damn near tripped over my feet as I shuffled backward to move out of his personal space. Dre's eyes stretched wide as he reached out a hand to help me. Unconsciously I shook my head as my eyes shifted to his outstretched hand. I quickly regained my footing while sliding my confused orbs back up to his.

"Please just tell me what's wrong," I implored, while trying to remain calm, a battle I was slowly losing as he remained silent.

Again, Dre's eyes crept away from mine. His jaws tightened as he held onto his words.

"Fine. I'm going to bed. You can let yourself out the same way you came in." Tired of masking my frustration I rolled my eyes up in my head, spun around on my heels, and proceeded to walk away. A task that proved futile as Dre reached out and gripped my wrist.

I didn't bother turning around. I simply acknowledged his unspoken request not to leave by planting my feet and relaxing my shoulders. Dre released an audible sigh above my head as silence settled between us. I wasn't sure how long we stood there before he finally slid his hand from my wrist. A few seconds later I felt his hands on either side of my waist. He pulled me against him, laced his fingers together, and rested them on my pelvis then placed his chin on top of my head. Using every ounce of self-control I could muster I tried like hell not to melt against his taut frame, wiggling underneath him I attempted to create some space between us.

His brawny arms flexed around me as he tightened his grip. "Stop moving and let me hold you."

His words were laced with a desperation I'd never heard before, sending a pang directly to my heart. I stilled my movements as an exasperated sign spilled out of my mouth. "Talk to me. Please."

"I want to, that's why I'm here. It's just—" He ran his thumb over the back of my hand while blowing air out his nose. "It's just, I'on know how to say what I'm about to say without soundin like a bitch."

I shifted my stance, so I could turn and face him, but Dre stopped my movements by placing his hands on my shoulders and holding me in place. "Don't. It's easier to talk to you this way."

Damn this is serious.

"Wait. Are you here to breakup with me?" I couldn't hide the panic in my voice as I tried calming my erratic heartbeat.

Dre slid his hands back down to my waist. "What? Breakup with you? Hell no."

I pushed my head back, resting it against his chest. "Then what is it Dre? I can't help you if you don't tell me what's wrong."

Another hard sigh passed through his lips. "I just need you to listen. To hear me out without sayin anythin. And when I'm done if you want to cuss me out, I'll eat that shit."

"Okay, whatever you need."

Brushing his hands over mine he laced his fingers between my tingling digits. "I came over here tonight because I wanted to see if you were home." The bass in his voice decreased with each word until he fell completely silent.

Confused I snatched my hands away from his and turned around, staring up into his eyes I tried to make sense of what he was saying. "Where else would I be? I told you the girls were coming over."

Dre's eyes drifted to the carpet. "With Emery."

"Come again?" I stepped forward, closing the small gap created a few seconds ago when I pulled away from him.

Slowly he brought his doleful eyes up to mine. "I know it's fucked up and I'm sorry but it's my truth. I—" His eyes fell to the floor again before he turned around and faced the patio.

I was fuming, was beyond pissed but something told me to hear him out before flying off at the mouth. Taking a step forward I placed a hand on the small of his back. "Can you please explain. I mean, have I done something that would make you not trust me?" I kept my tone even. That was all I could do to keep from going off.

Dre looked at me over his shoulder and shook his head. "Did you know I used to be in counseling?" A gruff chortle spilled from his parted lips. "That was a stupid question, of course you ain't know," he reasoned, smirking at the surprised expression splayed across my face.

Unsure of what to say I kept my eyes locked on his while raking a hand up and down his spine. Dre held my gaze, bouncing his eyes around mine as the sardonic grin faded from his face.

Clamping his lids shut he scrunched up his face like he was in pain then slid his head back toward the door. "I'm sorry for rambling, I just thought you should know." His voice was so low he barely sounded like himself.

"I'm glad you told me. I'm just trying to understand what that has to do with you being here because you thought I was out with Emery."

The light shining in from outside allowed me to see his hazels flash open. "I said that to say, you're not the only one fucked up by shit that happened to you growing up." He paused and I saw him looking at me through the glass.

I nodded my head, encouraging him to continue.

"My pops put me in counseling the summer before I started six grade. I was a bad ass kid. I stayed getting kicked out of school and getting into fights in the neighborhood. So, my grandmother convinced my pops that maybe counseling would help. Exhausted from constantly beating my ass he finally relented." Dre peeked at me over his shoulder again.

I perched up on the tips of my toes, placed my hand on the side of his face and softly pecked his pouty lips. I lingered there, feeling his need for me before slowly backing away. "Keep going, please."

Shifting his body away from the patio he turned around and faced me. "I was so pissed at my pops for making me go to counseling that initially my behaviors got worse. But after a few months I finally opened up and—" He swept his eyes down my face as a heavy sigh poured out his mouth. "Dr. Reese determined that my acting out was my adolescent way of dealing with not having my mother in my life."

My heart ached for him. I threw my arms around his waist and ran my hands over his back while resting my head against his chest. "I'm so sorry you had to go through that."

The rumbling of his thick chords vibrated against my ear as a chuckle spilled from my lips. "Thank you but I'm good now, for the most part. I worked out my shit but—" his voice trailed off.

"But what?" I lifted my head and slid my eyes up to his.

"One of the biggest things Dr. Reese and I worked on was my feelings of abandonment and my lack of trust in people to stick around because of my mother leaving. Like I said, I'm good but sometimes that shit has a way of creeping into my subconscious and fuckin with me. To answer your question, no you haven't done anything to make me not trust you. I just, I—"

"Say no more." I slid my hands from around his waist, placing them on either side of his face I locked my eyes on his. "Listen to me and really hear what I'm about to say."

Dre nodded his head in my hands.

"From the bottom of my heart I apologize. It was selfish and inconsiderate to agree to have dinner with Emery. I didn't take into account your feelings and for that I apologize. It will never happen again. I'm sorry that my actions drug up old and painful feelings for you. I never want to be the source of your pain nor do I want you to doubt me or us. Dre, I love you and I take that shit serious. I'm new at this relationship thing but that's not an excuse. I promise I will do better. Can you forgive me? Can we get past this?"

For the first time since he arrived a wide ass smile spread across his handsome face. "Already done. So, you ain't finna cuss me out for comin over here to check on you like some fuckin stalker?"

Dropping my hands to my side I mimicked his facial expression, allowing a soft grin to settle on my face. "Not gonna lie, I was but after hearin you out, how can I? This is my fault. So, I gotta eat that shit. But like I said, Imma do better so if you pull this shit again, I'm takin my key back."

"Deal. Now seal it wit a kiss." He leaned into me with his lips puckered and eyes closed.

Standing on my tippy toes I threw my hands around his neck and placed my lips on his. Dre wrapped his arms around my waist, dropped his hands to my ass and squeezed. My giggles quickly turned into moans as I willingly accepted his tongue into my mouth. There wasn't a damn thing funny about the sensuous way he devoured me or the way he meticulously glided his tongue over mine while sliding his hands underneath my shirt and caressing my bare cheeks.

"Where are your panties Miss Banks?" he growled against my lips, while palming my ass and scooping me off my feet.

Slithering my tongue across his lips I fixed my eyes on his. "Why do you ask questions you already know the answer to?"

He sank his teeth into the crook of my neck while simultaneously smacking me on the ass. A loud shriek eased out of my mouth as a puddle formed in between my legs. He traced his tongue along my collarbone before slowly lifting his head and gazing into my eyes.

"Well answer me this smart ass, we makin love or are we fuckin?"

I shifted my head over to the coffee table, staring at the pack of birth control pills still resting on top of it. "I wanna make love. Slow, passionate love with no barriers between us."

I felt his dick twitch against my ass. "So, we really doin this? No more condoms?" he asked, prompting me to turn around and look at him.

"Only if you're comfortable with it. I'm back on the pill so—"

Dre's mouth was on mine before I could finish my sentence. Sliding his tongue across my lips he gingerly entered my mouth while carefully maneuvering us around the furniture and stopping in front of the table. His muffled groan filled the quiet room as he disconnected from my mouth.

"That's what you were lookin at? Are those it?" He looked down at the blue billfold containing the pills then slid his surprised gaze back to mine.

I clamped my teeth down on my bottom lip while shaking my head.

"And you're sure? I know you've—"

"I'm sure. I love you and if I trust you with my heart I know I can trust you with my body."

"Say no more."

Dre slid his hands up from my ass to my waist, slowly inching up my torso, lifting my shirt along the way until he reached my armpits. Removing one hand from his neck I allowed him to slide my arm out my shirt before returning it to his neck and watching him repeat the same gesture on the other side. Tossing my shirt on the floor he placed his hands back on my cheeks while his beautiful hazels danced in mine.

"I fuckin love you."

"Show me," I coaxed, while wiggling against him, soaking his shirt with my juices as he carried me out the room.

CHAPTER NINETEEN

I was on my third trip around the crowded parking lot when a man with his arm draped over his shorty walked down the aisle I was coasting through. Taking my foot off the gas I stepped on the brake and clicked on my blinker. Something about their interaction held my attention. I don't know if it was the way she stared up at him lovingly or the way he held her protectively underneath him, shielding her from ongoing traffic by walking on the outside lane. Either way, I kept my eyes glued to the couple as they neared their vehicle. Dropping his arm from her shoulder he walked to the passenger side of the car and opened the door. He held it open until she was comfortably seated inside. A proud beam donned his chocolate face as he pushed the door shut and casually strolled toward the front of the car. His eyes landed on mine, saluting me with a quick nod of his head he proceeded to the driver's side of his whip and hopped in. A few seconds later they were gone.

Placing my truck in gear I eased forward then slammed on the brakes, barely missing the Honda Accord attempting to turn into the parking space I'd been patiently waiting for. *You can't be fuckin serious!* Irritated I gripped the steering wheel with both hands while shooting daggers at the inconsiderate driver in the other vehicle. She kept her head facing forward, refusing to look at me. Neither of us moved. Her small car hung halfway out of the parking space while my truck rested just inches from her driver's side door. Blowing out an exasperated breath I rolled down my window and propped my elbow on the ledge. My head hung out the window as I lightly tapped on the horn. That got her attention. Swinging her head in my direction she rolled her eyes before cracking her window.

"What?" she barked, attitude present on her overly tan face.

Another sigh spilled from my mouth as I attempted to calm my flaring temper. *Let me try this from another angle.* Pulling my head back inside my truck I opened the door and hopped out. There wasn't enough space between our vehicles for me to approach her window, so I got as close as I could, resting my gangly frame against the hood, near the driver's side tire.

"I'm not sure if you didn't see my blinker but I was waiting on this spot." I kept my tone even in an effort to keep the situation from escalating.

A sardonic grin tugged at the corners of her thin lips. "Yeah, I saw it."

Although I didn't find a damn thing funny, I couldn't help the dry chortle that tumbled out of my mouth. "Now that we've established that can you please back up, so I can pull in?"

Sweeping her eyes down my face she looked me up and down. "Boy bye. If you don't take your extra tall Chris Brown wannabe lookin ass back to yo truck and move the hell outta my way."

"Really? This what we doin?"

"I ain't movin so I guess we are," she replied sarcastically.

My bottom lip poked out on my face as I shook my head while I suppressed the urge to call her a bitch. "Okay, but unlike your Oompa Loompa Honey Boo Boo lookin ass I ain't come here to eat so I can sit here all day." I slid my eyes over her robust frame, squished behind her steering wheel. "You know yo big ass hungry." I felt bad as soon as that shit left my mouth.

Her grey orbs stretch wide as the smirk dropped from her face. "Fuck you. Fuckin nigger," she shouted, as her orange face turned a

484

shade darker. Flicking me off she revved her engine and backed out of the parking space, almost hitting my truck.

Pissed, I took the few steps to my door and yanked it open. I jumped inside and quickly maneuvered into the empty spot. *I can't believe her fat ass called me a nigger.* The sound of my phone buzzing snatched my attention, temporarily silencing the rage bubbling in my gut. Shifting my weight to one side I placed my hand in my pocket and pulled out my phone. Instantly a smile spread across my face at the sight of her name flashing in my notifications. I wasted no time opening the small device and clicking on the messaging app, selecting her name I read her text. The three little words displayed on the screen quickly dissipated every negative feeling I was previously harboring.

I replied with a simple emoji, the one winking with puckered lips and a heart then stuffed my phone back inside my pocket. Those words were just what I needed to face the person waiting for me inside the packed restaurant. Shifting the gear to park, I rolled up my window and cut the engine, relishing the indescribable calm that washed over me. A calm that could only be attributed to having my feelings validated.

A week ago, when I set up this meeting, I shared with Rocky the biggest hurdle I'd worked through with Dr. Reese were my feelings of inadequacies as a result of not having my mother in my life. Her response was exactly what I needed even though I hadn't realized it until that moment. And today, it was like she could sense my apprehension and the silent whispers from my past fueling my insecurities. The words spoken that night was sent through a text today, giving me what I needed to squash the seeds of doubt that were trying to take root in my head. In all caps, those three words had glared at me, quietly reminding me of the man I had worked hard to become.

Snatching my keys out of the ignition I silently chanted her words; *you are enough* as I opened my door and hopped out. I repeated that mantra over and over as I strolled casually across the parking lot. I reached the steps of the busy restaurant when my phone chimed. Pausing my steps, I reached into my pocket and pulled out the buzzing phone. My breath hitched in the back of my throat while my heart felt like it stopped beating. I couldn't control the rapid fluttering of my lids as I stared at her name flashing across the screen. Blowing out a deep breath I swiped right and placed my phone up to my ear.

"Hello." Her greeting was short, but I could hear the uncertainty in her voice.

"Yes." It wasn't my intention to be curt, but I really didn't know what else to say.

"Umm, I'm here. Are you still coming?"

An audible gush of air passed through my nostrils. "I'm here, about to walk in now."

"Oh okay. If you let the greeter know you're here for Evans they will direct you back to my table," she responded, sounding relieved knowing I was actually here.

"Bet. I'll see you in a minute."

"I'll be waiting. Bye Andre."

I disconnected the call then stuffed my phone inside my pocket and opened the door, standing off to the side I waited for a young woman carrying a sleeping toddler to past through. I watched as soft brown eyes slid up my lengthy frame, settling on my face. A demure smile tugged at the corners of her full lips as color flooded her cheeks. Whispering her thanks, she slowly dropped her head toward the ground while angling her body away from mine. Careful not to brush up against me as she made her way through the door then judiciously down the stairs. Chuckling at her reaction to me I strolled inside the restaurant, weaving through the crowd of people gathered in the waiting area.

Relieved to see the hostess stand less congested I walked up and stood behind a Wesley Snipes lookalike holding a fair skinned, curly haired little boy who looked too big to be hoisted up on his hip. Looking at me over his father's shoulder he waved his tiny fingers in my direction before sticking his tongue out at me. Giggling he continued to stare at me as I bounced my eyes between him and the flamboyant hostess helping them. A few moments later they were escorted away from the booth but not before I returned his playful gesture.

Little bad ass.

"Welcome to Ruby's Rib Shack how may I help you?" A wide ass smile donned his extravagantly made up face as his man-made emeralds swept down my face, lingering on my mouth longer than I was comfortable with before sliding back up to my eyes.

"What's up my man. My guest is here already, the name is under Evans," I responded, keeping my expression neutral.

Again, those phony ass eyes drifted away from mine, bouncing over my frame. "Of course. Let me check on that for you."

My patience was waning, but I kept my tone leveled. "Thank you."

"It's my pleasure." Traces of baritone slipped through his clearly practiced high-pitched tenor as he shifted his eyes from my chest to a set of sticky notes aligned neatly on top of the podium next to a seating chart.

Picking up one of the small pieces of paper he dramatically flicked his wrist before holding it up to his face. One of his perfectly arched brows hiked toward his neatly pressed hair as he waved another staff member over to the booth. He handed his co-worker the sticky note and instructed me to follow her to my table.

Saluting him with a quick nod of my head I followed behind the short woman with long blonde pigtails draping over her shoulders. We'd made it a few feet away from the podium when a piercing shrill stopped us in our tracks. Simultaneously we turned in the direction of the exuberant hostess to find him flaring one of his arms out in front of him.

"I'm sorry Jessica but this woman. . ." he dipped his hand toward the lady standing in front of him at the booth, "is also seated in the same section as this handsome gentleman." His eyes shifted to me. "Can you take her with you please? Her table is in section two forty-two next to the window."

Mumbling something underneath her breath Jessica nodded her head in the affirmative then spun around on her heels. Amused, I snickered while keeping my eyes fastened on the woman standing at the counter. She was leaned over the booth whispering something to the hostess while her eyes timidly bounced from him to me.

"Don't be silly, it's no problem at all," he insisted, clearly missing what I suspected was the woman's request to wait for another worker to escort her to her table. Stepping around the podium he took the woman by the arm and walked her the short distance to where we were standing. "Now you are all set. Everyone enjoy their dinner," he supplied, dropping his hand from her body and switching back over to the booth.

A sly grin stretched across my face as I watched the woman dip her head toward the floor while fidgeting with the sleeves of her jacket. Jessica peered at us over her shoulder before turning back around and resuming her strides. Hurriedly the woman took off behind her, staying as close to Jessica's heels as she could get without bumping into her. Tickled by the woman's obvious discomfort I watched her closely as we neared what I assumed was her table. What I didn't expect was who was sitting waiting on her.

A few seconds later we stopped in front of a table where the Wesley Snipes lookalike and curly hair little boy sat. Jessica stretched out her right arm while positioning the other one behind her back. "Here you go ma'am. I hope you enjoy your dinner."

Looking up for the first time since we started the short trip through the restaurant, she looked at me out of the corner of her eye then quickly shifted her gaze to Jessica. "Thank you."

Jessica nodded her head at the woman before glancing up at me. Pivoting away from the table she motioned for me to follow her as she continued walking. My feet didn't move. Instead, I stood stuck in place in front of the table staring back and forth between the seated couple. Sensing something wasn't right Wesley Snipes stood from his seat and stepped to the left of me, leaning inches away from my face he asked if there was something, he could do for me.

I took a step back and dusted my eyes over his partner before bringing them back to his face. "No but I may be able to do something for you."

"Is this some kinda fuckin joke?" The lines on his forehead deepened as he stood scowling at me.

Disgusted by the entire situation I shook my head. "I wish it was my G."

"Well spit the shit out or move da fuck on."

I ignored the bravado in his tone, understanding how weird this shit must have seemed. "I'm not sure what kind of relationship you have wit baby girl but seein that you two have a child together. . ." sliding my eyes over to the rambunctious curly head kid I lowered my voice, "I think you should know; your lady is a fuckin bigot."

"Excuse me?" His dark eyes grew wide. "What da fuck you say?" His tone was slightly elevated, and his posture screamed confrontation, something I wasn't trying to get into but wasn't going to back down from either.

I didn't budge, maintaining my stance I couldn't help the smug grin that stretched across my face as I watched his fat ass girlfriend hop up out of her seat and stand next to him. "Listen I ain't trynna start no shit but I thought you should know." I slid my eyes over to his lady. "You might wanna ask yo girl why she called me a fuckin nigger earlier." I made sure to place emphasis on the er.

I wasn't sure what bothered me more, being called a nigger or finding out that she was the mother of a little black boy. The percentage of African American blood streaming through his system didn't matter because the world would only see the color of his skin and judge him accordingly. Add that to the fact that his mother had her own prejudices despite having a black lover and son. I never understood that shit, it reeked of old slave mentality. How back during those time blacks were held captive against their will and treated less than but that didn't stop massa from sneaking down to the slave quarters and laying with our women or slave owner's wives allowing our mothers to breastfeed their babies. Nothing about that shit made sense to me but it was something I'd learned a long time ago; I had no control over.

Shaking my head, I ignored the sound of her gasping behind me as I turned on my heels and walked up to Jessica who'd stopped a few feet away when she realized I wasn't behind her. I tapped her on the shoulder and asked her to show me to my table, leaving Wesley Snipes and Mama June arguing at theirs.

Jessica looked up at me with a perplexed expression crest on her ivory face. Ignoring her confusion, I winked and took a step forward, hoping it would prompt her to follow suite. Taking the hint, she shifted the bulk of her weight onto the balls of her feet and spun around, trekking forward like her feet were on fire. There was at least one table between us before I realized I needed to put some pep in my step or risk losing her. Using my height to my advantage I took long strides to catch up to her. I trailed her heels as she navigated around the confined space while being careful not to bump into the seated patrons.

"Where the hell are we going? I could've sworn old dude said we were in the same section as Mama June," I mumbled under my breath.

As soon as the words left my mouth, I saw her. Instantly my heart started racing and the palms of my hands began to itch while a slither of preparation gathered above my lip. Scrubbing a hand down my face I stared at the woman who gave me life. A woman who looked so familiar it was hard to believe she was a stranger. But how? I couldn't shake the eerie feeling that I'd seen her before, but I'd be damned if I knew from where. Then it hit me with the force of a ton of fuckin bricks. Rapidly blinking, I tried to process the onslaught of emotions that washed over me as I recalled the day, I found her pictures stashed in an old beat up box underneath my father's bed.

It was the day of my tenth birthday and my father had left to pick up my cake for my party. I remember standing in front of the window watching his car back out of the driveway before taking off down the hall. I had one mission, find my gifts before he returned. I ran around the house like a bat out of hell, searching all the obvious hiding spots only to come up empty.

Slightly defeated but still determined I headed to his room, hoping to find my gifts stashed somewhere in there. I started in the closet. I rummaged through his neatly hung clothes before stretching my little neck up toward his shelves, checking for any new boxes that could be gifts. Again, I didn't find a single present. Disappointment clung to my tiny frame as I ambled out of the closet with deflated shoulders and my head aimed toward the floor. With a pool of tears gathered in the corners of my eyes I plopped down on the floor next to his bed. I sat there pouting longer than someone who just turned ten should've when I decided to check one last place, underneath the bed.

Rolling onto my belly I swiped my hands across my eyes and scoured the tight dim space but didn't see anything that resembled toys. A fresh wave of tears streamed down my face when I noticed a raggedy shoe box back in the corner near the legs of his nightstand. Crawling toward the bedside table I reached under the bed and pulled the box toward me. I fell back on my knees and peeled the lid open. I wasn't sure what I was looking at but for some strange reason I remember not being able to look away.

A half dozen of opened envelopes addressed to my father were neatly stacked on top of some pictures. Tossing the letters to the side I found over two dozen pictures scattered inside the box. I hurriedly shuffled through each one, captivated by the beautiful woman in the photographs. Some of the pictures were of her and my father when he was much younger, but most of them were just her.

I couldn't explain the unnerving connection I felt toward the stranger as I peered through each photograph, stopping long enough to slide my tiny fingers over her tanned face before dragging them down her long auburn tresses. Shaking off what my ten-year-old brain couldn't process I continued digging through the stacks of photos. I had finally reached the end of the pile when I came across a picture of her pregnant sitting on my father's lap. His large hands rested on top of her round belly as they both looked up at the camera smiling. I studied that image for what felt like an eternity when I heard the garage door opening. Quickly stuffing everything back inside the box I shoved it back underneath the bed where I found it and sprinted out of his room. To this day my pops has no idea about my little discovery.

"Sir, I believe this is your table." The sound of Jessica's voice jarred me from my past, forcing me to look away from Alex and bring my eyes to meet hers.

I cleared my throat to ensure my emotions didn't come out when I spoke. "Thank you, Jessica."

The same confused look from just a few moments ago crossed her otherwise innocent looking face. "My pleasure. I hope you enjoy your evening." Fixing a faux smile on her fuchsia covered lips she slid her eyes down my face before glancing at my mother and swiftly shuffling away from the table.

Walking on heavy legs I stepped up to the table, standing in front of the chair directly across from her. Identical hazels slid up my lengthy frame as a soft timid smile swept across her thin rosy lips. Not wanting to be rude I matched her expression, tugging the corners of my mouth upward.

"Hello Andre." I heard the excitement in her voice as a full blown smile stretched across her pretty face.

"Hello Alex," I greeted, dropping my eyes to the table.

"Are you going to take a seat, or did you come to tell me to kiss your ass then leave?" She giggled after that question, but I could tell she was serious.

I chuckled, hoping to alleviate her concern. "I'm sorry, I'm just—"

"It's okay, I'm nervous too. But I am glad that you're here. I don't care if you stand the entire time as long as you stay."

"The hard part was getting here. Now that I am, I wouldn't deny you the opportunity to meet me," I answered honestly, shifting my eyes up to her face as I pulled out my chair and sat down.

"Thank you," she whispered.

"Don't thank me yet. I still might tell you to kick rocks then carry my big ass up out of here," I teased, knowing damn well I'd never disrespect her or anyone I considered my elder.

That made her laugh, a genuine chortle from the pit of her stomach kind of laugh. "That's fair. But I know you'd never disrespect me, stranger or not."

"How can you be so sure?"

"Because I know your father and I know he nor your grandparents raised you that way. You may be grown but I'm willing to bet Mable would have your ass if she found out you treated any adult with even the slightest form of disrespect." A glint of emerald flashed in her bright hazels.

"You know my grandparents?" I'm not sure why but hearing her mention my grandmother by name surprised me.

She shook her head. "Titus and Mable are probably two of my favorite people."

"Yeah, they are pretty awesome and you're right, they'd beat my big ass for being disrespectful."

A silly grin splayed across her slender face. "No worries but I wouldn't be mad if you did. Hell, that would only prove that there are pieces of me in you even though I was absent from your life."

Lifting the glass of water sitting in front of my place setting to my lips I hiked a brow. "Word?"

"Oh, yes. Once upon a time I had a rebellious streak." She leaned forward and plucked a martini glass off the table. A glass I hadn't noticed until she dragged it up to her lips.

I didn't respond, choosing instead to sip from my glass to avoid speaking. I tried like hell to keep my expression neutral while wondering where the fuck was her rebellious streak when she allowed her father to force her to give up her first-born child.

Gulping back a hearty sip of her spirit she sat back in her chair. "I sure as hell hope you don't play poker son."

"Excuse me?" I returned my glass to the table, running a hand over the tablecloth I waited for her to reply.

She giggled, a sound I found comforting in spite of the awkwardness between us. Opening her mouth to respond she quickly snapped it shut as a waitress approached our table. Too wired to eat I instructed Alex to order while I glanced over the drink menu. In a husky tone I discovered was her natural speaking voice, she rattled off her entrée order. A few moments later silence hung in the air, prompting me to shift my eyes away from the menu in my hand. Two sets of eyes peered at me. One set stared across at me with a look I couldn't identify while the other tried to mask her attraction to me, bouncing her bright ambers between the small notepad in her hand and my face. One side of my mouth twisted up into a half smile as I turned toward the timid waitress. I suppressed a chuckle as the color drained from her face while she jotted down my order. Releasing a breath, I'd be willing to bet she didn't realize she was holding she stuffed her pen behind her ear and asked if we needed anything else then slowly backed away from the table.

"You have quite the effect on women I see," Alex surmised, drawing my attention back to her.

"I don't know what you're talking about," I supplied, as a sheepish grin settled on my face.

"Handsome and humble, just like your father."

"Pride goes before destruction, and a haughty spirit before a fall."

"Aah, Proverbs 16:18. Now that's Titus and Mable."

I shook my head while resting my hands on top of the table. "I'm definitely a good mix of the three of them."

"I see. They did an amazing job raising you."

"Thanks. I'll be sure to let them know you approve."

She giggled. "There it goes again."

"There what goes?" I asked, leaning forward and fiddling with the straw inside my water.

"Your shitty ass poker face. You try but fail miserably at hiding your annoyance."

"I'm sorry. I'm not trying to be rude."

She sat her empty martini glass on the table. "Please." She waved a hand at me. "You don't owe me any apologies. I understand how difficult this is and I am fully prepared for your questions and any reactions you may have to my answers or me."

I sat back in my seat, absorbing her words while she watched me through squinted lids. I appreciated her candor, it made me comfortable, allowing me to relax my tense frame. For the first time since I sat down, I took in her features, noticing how many of them resembled mine. Growing up I was always told how much I looked like my father but now that I was face to face with the woman who gave birth to me I wasn't so sure anymore.

Our silent stare down was temporarily interrupted when our waitress approached the table and placed my drink in front of me. I thanked her while keeping my eyes fastened to Alex's face, memorizing every crease and crevice in case this was my last time seeing her. Out of my peripheral I saw our waitress nod her head before informing us that our meals would be out soon. Then she was gone, leaving me and my mother alone feeling each other out.

"So how do you want to do this?" she asked, breaking the silence clinging to the air between us.

"Honestly, I don't know. I have so many questions. I mean, there's just so much I don't know."

"I understand. How about I start with the basics about me. Get that out the way and you can jump in whenever you like. How does that sound?"

I peeled my drink off the table and took a swig, holding the glass away from my face I nodded my head.

"Well let's see, I was born and raised in Bloomfield Hills Michigan. I am the oldest of two born from the union between my father and mother. My father had one child prior to his marriage to my mother but I've never met my sister." Her eyes dusted the table after that statement. "That's another topic for another day if you ever care to know." Her gaze lifted from the table and was back on me.

"That sounds interesting and familiar at the same time," I responded, thinking about Rocky and her crazy ass family dynamics.

She snickered but I could see there was pain behind the smile she fixed on her face. "Yeah, that's definitely a story for a different day. Anyway, I moved away from home when I was eighteen to attend college. I was sheltered and wanted to establish some independence from my family, so I chose to attend school out of state. I applied to several ivy league colleges because that's what I was supposed to do but my heart was never there." She stopped speaking when Tiffany, I finally noticed the name tag pinned to her shirt, sat our dishes on the table.

"Thank you," we spoke in unison.

Tiffany's timid gaze bounced between me and Alex. "My pleasure, can I get you anything else?" she asked, settling her big brown eyes on me.

Sitting my drink on the table I shook my head no. I could see Alex grinning from the corner of my eye as Tiffany flashed me a coquettish grin before spinning on her heels and sashaying away from the table.

"You must have a girlfriend."

"Huh?" I slid my head toward her with a brow hiked in the air.

"You heard me. It's just an observation. Miss Thing is throwing you all kinds of signals and you ain't having none of it. So, one could only assume you have someone special in your life."

I couldn't stop the wide ass smile from spreading across my face as my thoughts turned to Rocky. "I do."

"Well good for you. She must be one hella catch because Tiffany is beautiful."

I chuckled. "Baby girl is cute but she ain't shit on my baby. Excuse my language."

Alex tossed her hands in the air. "No apology needed. Trust me, I understand. Well, if all goes well, I hope to meet her someday." Her voice lowered as she finished off her statement.

"So far so good but I can't make any promises yet."

"That's fair." She swept her eyes over the spread of food. "You want to bless the table?"

"Sure." I slid my hands across the tablecloth, enclosing her hands in mine I closed my eyes and said grace.

"Amen." She slowly withdrew her hands from mine. "That's all you wanted?" she implored, eyeing my appetizer.

"I'm not really hungry," I lied, refusing to tell her my nerves were too fried to eat.

"Suit yourself because I'm about to pig out."

A hearty chortle spilled from my lips. "Please do. But can you eat and talk?"

"Of course, as long as you aren't judging me on my table manners."

"I'm not judging you at all." I picked up my fork and held it up to my lips.

Winking at me she tossed a forkful of ribs into her mouth. "Where was I? Oh yeah, I was accepted into all the schools I applied to but decided to forgo the whole ivy league experience which lead me to OSU. That's where I met your father."

"Word? I think I remember hearing that before." I sat my fork next to my nachos and picked up my glass.

"Is that all you've heard about me?" She stuffed another piece of meat into her mouth while peering at me from her side of the table.

"Honestly—" I stared at her over the top of my glass while mulling over my words. "I stopped asking about you around eleven, maybe twelve. I think that's when I realized you weren't coming back. Ironically, that's about the same time I started wildin."

She placed her fork on her plate and propped both elbows on the table. "Hmm. I remember that phase."

"Why you say it like that?"

The green specks in her eyes overshadowed her natural hazels. "I was just remembering my conversation with Tony about it." A nervous snicker fell from her parted lips. "We didn't talk for six months after that."

I gulped down a hefty sip of my cocktail. "That sounds more like an argument than a conversation. Wait, you and my pops talked regularly?"

"Talk not talked sweetheart. Tony and I are really good friends. But you're right, it was a disagreement." She raised her glass off the table and sipped her water.

"Was the disagreement about me?" I asked, feeling a crinkle form in the middle of my forehead as my face scrunched up in surprise.

Her eyes lowered to the glass in her hand. "It was. He shared with me the change in your behavior and how he thought it might have been related to my absence. I suggested meeting you. . ." she shifted her colored orbs to my face, "ss a means to help but Tony didn't want to hear it. In hindsight I can see how selfish my request was but back then I pissed. For the first time since you were born, I felt like Tony was purposely keeping you from me."

A thousand questions bounced around in my head as a mix of emotions flashed across my face. I was having a hard time processing her desire to meet me back then and my father denying me the opportunity. I couldn't help but wonder what, if anything would've changed if I'd met her during that transitional period of my life.

Placing her water on the table she swept her eyes down my face before laggardly dragging her soft eyes back up to mine. "I have no idea what's running through your mind right now but if any of those thoughts are anger toward your father please discard them."

"You're right, you have no idea what I'm thinking. Nor do you have the right to tell me what to think." A reflexive scowl crept onto my face and I allowed it to settle there as I peered at her.

"This is true but any ill will you have should be directed toward me and only me."

"No ill will but plenty of anger and I have enough of the shit to go around," I gritted out through clenched teeth, not giving a damn about my manners.

"Shit! I didn't mean to up—" She clamped her mouth shut, shifting her attention to Tiffany, who'd just approached our table.

"Pardon my interruption. I was just checking to see if y'all need anything." She smiled at Alex before switching her gaze to me. "Sir, is there something wrong with your food?" Her eyes descended to my plate then shifted back to my face. "Would you like something different?"

I looked down at the plate of untouched nachos and shook my head. "Everything is fine. I just don't have much of an appetite." I lifted my angry sneer from my dish and looked at the woman sitting across from me.

"Thank you, Tiffany can you bring my so— can you bring him another long island and I'll take another dirty martini please."

"Topped off with Patron," I added, turning away from Alex and looking up at our waitress.

"Absolutely. I'll get those right out for y'all." A bashful smile flashed across her face before she turned and walked away.

"Andre can we talk about what I said that upset you?"

I swung my head in her direction, relaxing the grimace still present on my face. "Let's see, maybe the part about the woman who gave me up as a baby thinking it was okay to waltz back into my life at twelve or the fact that my pops knew I was having a hard time because she was gone and telling her no. Tell me which part would have you tight."

She didn't speak at first, instead she bounced her eyes around my face. "I'm sorry, that was a dumb question."

I guzzled down the remainder of my drink, placing the empty glass on the table I stared at her with a sardonic grin splayed across my face. Tiffany returned with fresh drinks, placed them on the table in front of us and quickly disappeared.

"Can I explain?"

"Please do," I responded, shuffling a few tortilla chips around my plate.

"Like I said, I realize now that my request was selfish. Although my intentions were good, I didn't consider how my sudden appearance in your life would affect you. Tony did, hence his reason for saying no. You're young and you don't have children but when you become a father you will understand. As a parent it's your job to protect your child at all cost. At the time I took that personally, like Tony viewed me as a threat to your well-being." She paused, picking up her glass she held it out in front of her face and gazed at me.

"I get that, I really do. It's just a lot to process. I'm sorry for—"

She held her free hand out toward me. "Stop. You're allowed to feel how you feel. I made my choices and I have to live with the consequences of those choices."

"I appreciate that." I released an audible sigh before running a hand down my face. "Ugh, Dr. Reese would be disappointed in me for losing my cool so quickly."

"I beg to differ. I think she'd be proud of you for even meeting with me. I'm sure she doesn't expect you to be perfect. This is a huge first step. If I haven't said it already, thank you Andre." She placed her drink to up to her mouth and sipped.

A soft smile seeped across my lips. "You can call me Dre; all my people do."

Placing a hand in front of her mouth she fell back in her seat as a boisterous laugh spilled from her lips. Tears formed in the corners of her eyes as she continued to chuckle.

"What's so funny?" I picked up my glass and took a nip of the potent cocktail.

She swallowed the liquid she just consumed before leaning forward and sitting her glass on the table. "I'm sorry. It's just that you remind me of him. Don't get me wrong, you look like me, a lot like me. But your mannerisms and facial expressions are all Tony."

I welcomed the chortle that spilled from my mouth, happy for the shift between us. "Yeah, that part. I can't believe how much we look alike," I admitted, sipping my long island before placing it back on the table.

"That's fair. Does it bother you?" She dug back into her plate while still watching me, waiting on my answer.

"What? That I look like you?" I chucked a tortilla filled with pulled pork and queso into my mouth.

Chewing her steamed broccoli, she shook her head.

"Nah, surprised is more like it."

She snickered. "I'm sure. I've watched you grow up and now that I'm sitting across from you, it's a lot to take in. So, I can only imagine how it is for you."

"Soooo, can we talk about that? The giving me away and watching me from a distance part?"

Chuckling she washed down her food with a swig of water then grabbed her martini off the table. "Of course. I'll give you the abbreviated version, but I'll make sure to hit the important parts. Cool?"

I leaned back in my seat, stretched my legs out underneath the table and rested my arms on the sides of the chair. I deliberately took my time responding to her, guiltily enjoying the excited nervous grin etched across her olive toned face. "That's cool."

She took a swig of her cocktail while rolling her eyes up in her head. "You're definitely Tony's child."

One side of my mouth curled up into a half smile, one I was sure reminded her of my father by the way she beamed at me over the top of her martini glass. "What can I say, I get it honest."

Balancing her drink in one hand she swept a strand of hair out of her face with the other "That you do. But on a serious note, I met your father my junior year of undergrad. We started dating exclusively the following year and fell in love shortly after. Tony was unlike any man

I'd ever dated. Before I knew it, we were inseparable until. . ." her eyes shifted to her glass then slowly glided back up to my face, "you were born."

"It's okay, take your time. I'm sure this is hard to talk about," I stated sincerely, while leaning forward and plucking my drink off the table.

"Thank you but it's my truth and I owe you an explanation."

I nodded my head before falling back in my chair, slowly sipping from my glass I waited for her to collect herself.

"Let me back up just a little. Is that okay?"

"Of course."

"When I started my college experience, I was a spoiled naïve teenager who had been sheltered from the outside world. However, living away from home and the bubble my father's wealth provided taught me a lot about me. I came to school to get an education but also to grow as a person, and an individual separate from who I was told to be. By the time I met your father I had no qualms about who my father was and what he would think of me dating outside of my race. None of that mattered to me. What mattered was how Tony made me feel. I never hid him from my family, nor did I give a shit when my father threatened to disown me if I continued my relationship. But all that changed around the time I found out I was pregnant." She stared off into the distance, shaking her head as a sinister chortle tumbled out her mouth. "Life has a funny way of forcing you to step back in line."

"Hmm."

She shifted her eyes back to my face. "What are you thinking? You don't have to guard your words."

"I'm just listening," I stated, not really sure how I felt about the tidbit of information she just shared.

"I was in my final year of grad school when we found out we were expecting. Outside of the bullshit with my father I was happy as hell. I was in love. I was already in my field, going to graduate school was just icing on the cake to ensure higher pay. I had established myself outside of my family and I felt pretty damn good about it. Then my world spun out of control." Fighting back tears she rapidly blinked her eyes before dipping her head toward her lap. "A week after my gradua-tion my baby brother was killed in a car accident by a drunk driver."

I sat up in my chair, feeling my heart ache as I watched her try to shake off the pain from the loss of her brother. "Alex I'm so sorry for your loss. You don't have talk about it if you don't want to."

Listlessly she raised her head and settled her misty gaze on me. "It's part of my truth. I'm okay."

"Are you sure?"

A soft smile donned her somber face. "I'm sure. Thank you."

Relaxing my posture, I rested against the back of my seat and sipped my cocktail. "For what?"

"Being empathetic even though I don't deserve it, not from you."

Matching her smile, I nodded my head. "No thanks necessary. I'm just being the man my pops and grands raised me to be."

She closed her eyes and released a lungful of air then fluttered her lids open again. "Let me wrap this up so I can get you back to your lady."

"No worries, she ain't going nowhere." I winked at her over the top of my glass.

"You are a mess. Anyway, when my father found out I was preg-nant he threatened me again. I refused to have an abortion, so he made good on his promise. We didn't talk for four months and honestly if Michael hadn't passed, I don't think we ever would've spoke again." Pausing, she sat her drink on the table and bounced her eyes around my face. "After Michael passed, I was lost. I went into a deep depression and the strain between me and my father didn't help. A month after we buried my brother, I gave into my mother's persistent request to meet with my father. I'll spare you the details, but I will say this, nothing changed on his part. He still wanted nothing to do with Tony or a half breed grandchild. His words not mine. I was too far along to terminate the pregnancy, so he begged me to give you up for adoption." Her words trailed off as she breathed out the last part of that sentence.

"Wow." I guzzled down the remainder of my spirit then rested the empty glass on my knee.

"Are you okay?"

I shook my head but kept my lips clamped shut.

"Initially I said no. I told him to kiss my ass and ran back home to Tony. But as the months went on my hormones were out of control combine that with my depression and my father's persistence, it was all too much. There were days when I couldn't get out of bed to take care of myself that I couldn't imagine being responsible for another person. And Tony, God bless his heart. He was amazing. He did his damnedest to comfort and support me, but grief had a stronger hold on me. Ultimately, I ended up pushing him away while sinking deeper into depression. At month eight I was still in my funk and honestly, I didn't think I'd ever come out of it." Taking a break, she released a heavy sigh.

Sweeping my eyes down her face I noted the change in her demeanor. There was a sadness in her eyes as they bounced anxiously around the table, refusing to settle on one particular thing. One of her tiny hands glided back and forth over the linen tablecloth while the opposite leg bopped rapidly underneath the table.

I slid my tongue over my lips and cleared my throat, prompting her to lift her lids and look me in the eyes. "Are you okay? We can take a break if you need to."

She slid her hand off the table and held it out in front of her face, positioning her thumb and index finger parallel to each other she created a small gap. "Just a tiny one." Shifting her hand back on top of the table she dragged her martini glass toward her while pushing a lenient smile onto her rosy lips.

"That's fine. Is there anything you want to know about me that you don't already?" I placed my glass on the table and picked up my fork, digging into my appetizer. "

"Do you still talk to Dr. Reese?"

That question caught me off guard, causing me to still my fork in mid-air. "Um, from time to time. Why?"

"Just thinking you might need someone to help you unpack all the junk I've unloaded on you tonight."

Weighted pressure lifted from my chest and pushed out through my lungs, making it easy for me to breathe again. "I ain't gone lie, you have definitely unloaded some heavy stuff on me, but it was to be expected. It's not Dr. Reese heavy but I will definitely be beating up my girl's ears when I get back to her place."

She raised her drink off the table and chugged back a mouthful of the clear liquid. "I'm glad you have someone you can talk to. How long have y'all been together?"

Chewing the bite of nachos, I'd just stuffed in my mouth I contemplated my answer. "It's complicated but the short version, we're creeping up on a year at the end of April."

She smirked at me as she sat her nearly empty glass back on the table. "Another story for another day?" Her thin neatly manicured brows hiked up on her forehead.

"Definitely."

Chuckling she turned her attention to her plate, picking up her fork she wasted no time attacking what I was sure was lukewarm ribs. "I'm ready to continue if you are."

I nodded my head in agreement as I looked down at my wrist, checking the time.

"I'm sorry, I know you need to go." I looked up to find her shifting her eyes up from my arm.

"Don't be. I'm good. Please continue."

"I was so lost that the only thing that made sense was to give you to Tony. But not before I made my father set up an inheritance for you. It was the only thing I could think to do to ensure you were financially provided for. Hell, I tried to sign over my rights after you were born but Tony wasn't having it. He always had faith that I'd come out from under my storm and when I did, he wanted me to know the door to you was always open." Those hazels that never looked like anyone on my father's side of the gene pool, grazed the table then slowly made their way back up to my face. "Unfortunately for me, he closed off his heart the day I climbed my broke down ass in my car and hit route 23."

"So why didn't you come back for me then?" I did my damnedest to keep the emotion out of my voice.

"Honestly, the longer I stayed away the harder it was to come back. After I tackled postpartum, I was able to address my grief which allowed me to deal with my guilt. But that took almost two years."

Clamping my eyes shut I ignored the tingling behind my closed lids. "Why are you here now then?"

"Because despite what you believe based on what I've shown you, I love you. I always have, and I always will. There hasn't been a day that's gone by that I didn't wish I did things differently. But I can't take it back. All I can do is own my mistakes and take whatever you are willing to give me."

I fluttered my lids open and stared at her, surprised to see streams of tears freely flowing down her face. "Twenty-two years is a long time Alex."

She shook her head in agreement.

"But I'm willing to take this a day at a time if you are."

Using the napkin from her lap to pat her tear stained face I watched as a gargantuan smile seeped across her painted lips.

CHAPTER TWENTY

*L*eaning against the counter I shifted the bulk of my weight to the right side of my body while kicking my left foot back and resting it against the wall. A coquettish grin dusted across my parted lips as I stared into the living room, settling my eyes on the beautiful man perched on my couch. I raked my eyes down his body while greedily drinking him in. My sights zeroed in on his crotch before slowly shifting back up to his face. Stretched out across the sofa he held a burning stogie in one hand and his cellphone pressed against his ear in the other. A boyish grin was splayed across his handsome face while he chatted animatedly with the caller on the other end of the line. Fully engrossed in his conversation he was oblivious to my salacious perusal, earning me a few extra seconds of uninterrupted ogling.

You are such a creep Raquel. Get yo shit together.

I chuckled to myself as I turned toward the counter and snatched up the drinks my thirsty ass made before I got stuck staring at him. Balancing a cup in each of my hands I took slow measured steps as I walked into the living room. I placed both drinks on the coffee table then sat down next to him. Again, my eyes scaled the length of him. Only this time my gaping wasn't undetected.

Smirking at me over his shoulder Dre pulled the phone away from his ear and held a hand in front of the receiver. "You betta stop lookin at me like that." His tongue slithered out of his mouth and ran silkily over his full lips as he shifted the phone back up to his ear and slowly angled his head forward.

I playful rolled my eyes while reaching onto the table to grab the coiled hose, placing the tip up to my lips I settled back against the cushions. "It ain't my fault you came over here wearin thot attire."

"Yeah that's her." He pushed up on his elbow and sat upright. Dumping the ashes of his cigar in the ashtray he slid his hazels over to my face. "I will. Take care Alex, I'll talk to you later." He disconnected the call and dropped his phone somewhere on the couch.

A cloud of smoke filled the air. Reflexively I stretched an arm in front of my face and swiped at the smog while meeting his gaze. "I'm so proud of you," I breathed out, as a fresh wave of smoke expelled from my mouth and nose.

"Thank you. Alex said to tell you hi."

Nodding my head, I took another toke before leaning forward and placing the hose on the table. Before I could sit back Dre snatched me off the couch and into his lap. Mindful of the stogie in his hand he held his arm out away from my body while wrapping the other around my waist. The warmth of his breathe heated my flesh as he buried his face in the crook of my neck.

"Thot attire?"

I wiggled against him, prompting him to lift his head from my shoulder as I twisted at the waist and looked him square in the eyes. "You know damn well grey sweats are to women what tight pants are to men. And who the hell wears shorts in April anyway?"

"Somebody who checked the forecast before gettin dressed. But that's funny as hell comin from a person wearin. . ." he removed his hand from my waist and slid it down my bare thigh, "booty shorts and a tank top." He finished his sentence with a firm squeeze to my right breast.

Hit with a sudden feeling of déjà vu I giggled while shaking off the tiny tremor his touch sent through my body. "I'm in the house dude. I ain't going outside in this shit."

"You bet not." He placed his hand on my leg again and inched it back up my thigh.

"Whateva. Just tell me you ain't been rockin this shit all day."

A mischievous grin eased across his face as his hand glided further up my leg. Gingerly spreading my thighs apart, he used the tip of his thumb to softly caress me over the top of my shorts. "What's wrong wit my shorts Miss Banks?"

"First, they're shor—"

"You do know it's seventy-five degrees outside today?" he asked, cutting me off while increasing pressure on my clit.

I attempted to smack my lips but was overruled by an involuntary moan. "An. . . and? It was just sixty-four degrees yesterday."

"Your point?"

"Don't expect me to take care of yo hardheaded ass when you get sick, that's my point," I sassed, while jumping out of his lap and standing next to him.

"You'll do it and love it. Where you goin?" He pulled from his cigar as one of his bushy brows climbed up his forehead.

"Away from yo ass. And for the record, all of you. . ." I dipped my eyes toward his crotch, "is on display in those damn shorts," I finished, sliding my hooded mahoganies up to his face.

"That's only because I'm rocking a semi-chub thanks to yo ass in those hot shorts," he reasoned, as smoke spilled from his parted lips.

I cut my eyes at him before bending down and grabbing my glass off the table. Careful not to spill my drink I sat down in my original spot then pulled the hose toward me, balancing it in my opposite hand. "Nice try but that anaconda you call a penis greeted me at the door, flaccid and all. So back to my original question, where all you been in those damn shorts?"

A boisterous chortle fell out of his mouth. "Nowhere baby. After the gym I showered and changed clothes before comin over here. I ain't even stop for gas." He reached onto the table and put out his cigar, exchanging it for his glass.

"Hmmm."

"So, the whole grey sweatpants shit is really a thing?"

Inhaling the flavored tobacco, I nodded my head. "Hell yeah, and you ain't rockin a normal size dick either. So yo shit is real noticeable," I responded, exhaling smoke through my nostrils.

"Wow, women are just as perverted as men." He took a sip of his drink and angled his body toward mine, pulling one of his legs off the floor he tucked it underneath him. "That smells good. What flavors you put in there?"

I rested the hose in my lap as I looked at the hookah propped on my coffee table. "Strawberry, peach, and a pinch of mint. You wanna try it?" I picked up the pipe and extended it toward him.

Taking the hose out of my hand Dre placed the tip up to his lips and pulled. He dragged the cord away from his mouth and looked at me. Confusion marked his face as he blew out a tiny puff of smoke.

I chuckled as I removed the hose from his relaxed fingers and rested the tip against my bottom lip. "You have to pull baby. It's not a cigar, it's okay if you inhale." I sucked in a lungful of shisha and let the smoke stream out of my nose while passing the cord back to him.

His second attempt was better, but I could tell he still hadn't gotten the hang of it. I chuckled at the perplexed expression resting on his face as his eyes lowered to a squint. Holding the cord away from his mouth he studied it for a beat. A creased formed in the middle of his forehead like he was thinking, then he relaxed his face. He placed the tip back up to his lips and pulled from the coiled hose. Smirking at me he parted his lips and released a full stream of smoke.

Fuckin show off.

Giggling I sank back against the cushions. "So, what you think?"

"It's different but I like it. The combination of flavors you picked tastes good together." A fresh wave of smoke floated into the air as he passed the hose to me.

"I'm glad you like it. It took you long enough to figure out," I teased, taking a toke of the hookah.

Dre flipped me the bird and chugged down a hearty amount of his cocktail. A subtle grimace settled on his face as he drug his cup away from his mouth. "Goddamn Rocky, did you put any juice in this bitch?"

"Stop being a baby." I sat the coiled hose on the table and took a swig of my own drink while drifting my eyes down to his mouth.

"Oh, I got cha baby. I wanna hear you talkin that same shit when I'm balls deep in yo shit later."

Clamping my teeth down on the brim of my cup I clutched my thighs together before slowly bringing my eyes up to his. "Whatever crazy."

"So now it's whatever? Okay." He intimidated my classic eye roll before lifting his glass to his mouth again.

Damn that mouth. Umm. I can't wait to feel those lips on me.

"Anyway. So, are you ready for everything you got lined up this month?" I asked, purposely changing the topic to avoid jumping on him before I had a chance to pick his brain.

He flashed me a wide ass smile, exposing all his damn teeth. "I really don't have a choice. I'm just going to take it an event at a time. First thing first, my meeting with Royce next week. After that I'll focus on the draft then graduation."

I nodded my understanding. "I'm so proud of you. I still can't believe y'all are about to launch a freakin app."

Dre chuckled at the enthusiasm in my voice. "Honestly, me either. But truthfully, that's all your brother. He just took what we've been doing since high school to the next level."

"I'm so excited for y'all."

"We are definitely blessed. Who knew two lo-key nerds who started tutoring online for extra cash would be meeting with a major corporation to launch an app?"

"Yeah, that's dope as fuck." I bounced my eyes around his face while chugging back the last of my drink.

"Thanks baby. You gone miss me when I'm gone?"

I leaned forward, sitting my empty cup on the table. "Hell yeah. Why else you think I didn't want to go out tonight? I wanted my man all to myself."

"Is that why you've been givin me googly eyes since I walked through the door?"

My lips kissed my teeth. "Ain't nobody checkin for yo yellow ass,"

I lied, while pulling my legs off the floor and tucking them under my butt.

A boisterous chortle spilled out of his mouth. "Yeah okay."

Reflexively my eyes rolled up in my head. "Have you decided if you're gonna attend the draft or wait at home witcha family, so you can attend graduation?" Again, I deliberately shifted the conversation away from sex.

"We're goin. Imma book our room and flights when I get back from Atlanta. As far as graduation, I ain't trippin. They can mail my degree. Once I finish my finals my sole focus will be the draft. Well that and my baby's birthday of course."

Both my brows hiked in the air as my eyes bulged wide. "We?"

Dre gulped down the rest of his spirit and sat his glass next to mine. "Yes we. I know you didn't expect me to experience one of the biggest moments of my life without you?"

"Bae-bee," I squealed, while using every ounce of self-control I could muster not to jump into his lap.

"You're so damn dramatic." He flashed his pearly whites at me as specks of emerald flickered in his irises. "So, you ain't got shit to say about your birthday?"

I hunched a shoulder. "What's there to say? It just another day."

"Excuse me but can you please tell me where my lady went because I have no idea who this person sitting next to me is." Raking his eyes down my face he feigned disgust.

I chuckled at his horrible acting and melodramatic reaction. "Now who's being dramatic?"

"Certainly not the person I expected to be over the top and super excited."

"Excited for what? Gettin old? Yeah, I'll pass." I couldn't help the sarcasm in my tone as my eyes rolled up in my head.

"That's funny comin from someone who constantly complains about being carded almost every time they buy liquor. Pick a struggle witcha spoiled ass." The humor in his tone was annoyingly cute.

"Okay, I'll give you that because that shit does irk me. But twenty-eight Dre." I released a dramatic sigh. "I might as well start tellin people I'm thirty."

"Twenty-eight is not thirty Raquel."

"Well it damn sure ain't twenty-two. I'm knockin on thirty's door and yo ass won't be twenty-three until next month." Poking out my bottom lip I dropped my eyes to my hands.

"Oh okay, so we gone skip the dramatics and go straight into baby mode? Now I get it. So, I should take your gifts back and get you a binky to go wit that pout?"

My eyes sprang up from my lap as a huge smile spilled onto my lips. "You already got me something?"

A wide ass smile stretched across Dre's face. "Aah. There she goes. Your spoiled highness has returned. Of course, I got your gifts already. There is a certain amount of planning and preparation that goes into shopping for someone of your caliber."

I lifted a hand out of my lap, held it in the air and flicked my middle finger in his face. "I don't know why you clownin me when you know you love it."

Grabbing my finger, he placed it up to his puckered lips and winked before letting my hand go. "Every spoiled, bratty, dramatic part that makes up Raquel Marie Banks. You damn right."

"Anyway, back to your graduation, you're not going?" I asked, not bothering to hide the blush that crept on my cheeks.

"No ma'am. I talked to my pops about it and he's good with me not going so I'm good. Besides, if I get drafted, I won't be using my degree any time soon anyway."

"This is true."

He swiped his tongue across his lips, making it hard for me to concentrate on anything else. "Glad that's settled. Now what else you wanna know? Cuz I'm ready to take these. . ." he placed his hand on the hem of my shorts, "off yo ass." Shifting his head forward he grabbed the hose off the table and placed the tip in his mouth, drawing in a mouthful of shisha.

I watched the rings of smoke ascend into the air as I contemplated how to ask my next question. Although Dre and his mom had been talking regularly since their meeting, I knew that it was still a touchy subject. I didn't want to ruin the feel-good vibe we had going but I really wanted to know. Blowing a gush of air out my mouth I dropped my eyes to my hands resting in my lap.

"Sooooo, about draft day." I tried to keep my tone leveled as I shifted my gaze back up to his face.

"What about it?" Using the tips of his fingers he traced circles on my inner thigh.

Extemporaneously my lids clamped shut as I melted underneath his touch. Tiny spikes of pleasure prickled at the nape of neck, slid down my torso, and brushed across my nipples before scaling over my belly and taking residence in my groin. Without warning a soft moan seeped through my lips, prompting me to flutter my eyes open and look over at him. A perceptive smirk was splayed across his face as his gaze dipped down to his hand. Trailing his nimble digits further up my thigh he continued teasing me. He littered my skin with feather soft touches while dragging his eyes back up to mine. I was quickly losing my resolve. Placing my hand on top of his I halted his movements.

"Baby I can't talk with you, fuck—"

He wiggled his fingers underneath my hand. "Ain't nobody stoppin you from talkin. Say what you need to say so I can handle this." His eyes lowered, zeroing in on my pussy.

Releasing an exaggerated sigh, I flicked his hand off my thigh and snapped my legs close. Dre's eyes shot up to my face, smirking he nodded his head.

"Okay, you win for now. What you wanna talk about Miss Banks?" He slid the hose off the table and took a quick toke from the hookah then sat the coiled tube back on the table.

"Back to the draft. Will your family be there? Are you gonna invite Alex?"

He released a mouthful of smoke as his eyes settled on me. "My parents and Maddy are comin—" His words trailed off while his eyes shifted toward the ceiling.

"So, no Alex?"

"Honestly, I don't know. I've been going back and forth about it ever since I decided I was actually going."

"I get it, trust me I do. I just thought it would be nice for her to be there instead of off in the cut watching from afar like she's done your whole life. You know what I mean?"

His eyes were back on mine and thankfully a smile adorned his handsome face. "Yeah, I've been leaning toward inviting her for that reason alone."

"So, why the hesitation?"

A V formed between his brows. "Truthfully, I don't wanna offend Shalonda."

"That's understandable but based on what you've told me I don't think she'll mind. Didn't you say they met before?"

"Yeah. Alex said my pops introduced them after he proposed to Shalonda."

"Wow, that's some grown man shit right there. Did she do the same before she got married?" I knew I was asking a lot of questions, but I was truly fascinated by the made for TV dynamics of his family.

Dre shook his head. "Nah. Apparently her marriage didn't last long. Besides, she said my pops wanted them to meet because Shalonda was gonna help raise me. Since I didn't have contact with Alex there was no need for my pops to meet her husband."

My mouth formed an O. "Gotcha. This shit is so interesting to me. I hope I'm not stirring up any negative feelings by asking so many questions."

"Not at all. I don't mind talking about it, especially with you. I know you're not asking to be nosy but to understand."

"Good." My voice was higher than normal, triggering an embarrassed chuckle to spill out my mouth. "Um, do you have a picture of her? I wanna put a face to the name."

Snickering Dre looked around the couch for his phone. A few minutes later he held it in his hand. He clicked on a few buttons and turned the phone around, holding it up to my face.

"Oh wow."

"What?" Dre flipped the phone toward him, peeking at the illuminated screen before turning the phone back around to me.

"Um. . . I've seen her before," I admitted, staring at the image of the woman who resembled the man I loved.

"How? When?" He dropped his phone in his lap and stared at me, waiting for me to respond.

"It was my sophomore maybe junior year of undergrad. I was home visiting the twins and Miss Brenda when I spotted them outside your house. She and your dad were her standing in front of what I assumed was her car. She was crying, and your dad appeared to be comforting her."

"Damn. This shit gets deeper and deeper."

I stared him directly in his wide stretched eyes. "Baby I'm sorry I'm not—"

"Stop." He held up his hand, cutting me off before I could finish. "I mean, it fits the timeline. Maybe it was the day she met him and Shalonda. I'll have to ask."

"That makes sense. Back then I thought he was creepin," I admitted, slightly embarrassed now that I had more information.

"Yeah right. Shalonda ain't neva been one for the bullshit." Chuckling his eyes glossed over like he was remembering something.

I stretched out my arm, placing my hand on his face I gingerly swiped it down his jawline. "Okay, I'm done for now. But I really hope you invite her to the draft. I want to meet the woman responsible for bringing such an amazing man into the world."

"It's about time. Now about these. . ." his hand found its way to my thigh again, skating up to my shorts, "itty bitty ass shorts. Can I take em off now?" he growled.

And just like that the only thing on my mind was him. My body naturally responded, sending a powerful jolt of pleasure trickling down my spine every time my shirt brushed against my pebbled nipples. My heart rate accelerated, and the palms of my hands felt misty. The moisture between my legs reactivated as a fresh puddle formed in the bed of my shorts.

This shit was insane. I had never experienced this level of intimacy with anyone else before. Dre had the ability to rouse my senses without so much as laying a hand on me. It frustrated and trilled me at the same time. I was willing to bet his ass could make me cum without touching me.

Hmm, I might have to test that out.

I shook my head and glanced down at his hand then quickly shifted my eyes back up to his. A set of hooded emeralds stared back at me, trigger a lascivious grin to stretch across my parted lips. Easing off the couch I slid my head forward and leaned over the table to check the coal on top of the hookah. Satisfied that it was out I spun around and gazed down at him.

"Why you still sittin? I thought you were ready to take my shorts off." I barely finished my sentence before Dre was out of his seat and on me.

Dre wrapped his arms around my waist and slid his hands down to my ass, squeezing my cheeks he peered at me through his lashes. Instantly a chill shot down my spine while my heart thumbed wildly in my chest. Digging my toes into the carpet I tried to ignore the tingle radiating through my extremities as the scent of his cologne tickled the hairs of my nose. The woodsy aroma of his manly fragrance mixed with his natural redolence was intoxicating. Hit with a quick and unexpected bout of dizziness I dug my nails into the meat of his shoulder blades to keep from falling on my ass.

The corners of his mouth tugged upward forming a mischievous smile as his eyes bounced around my face then shifted to my hands still piercing his flesh. "You good Short Stuff?"

I loosened my grip while shaking my head. "Yeah, I'm. . . I'm good."

A light chortle spilled from his parted lips as his eyes settled back on mine. Playfully I shoved him in the shoulder in an attempt to create some space between us. An attempt that proved futile as he caught my hand before I could drop it down to my waist. He pulled me back into him. His hands returned to my ass while he stared down at me wearing the same roguish grin, the one that made my heart flutter and toes tingle.

Smirking I slid my hands up his biceps, draped them over his shoulders and stepped up on the tips of my toes then placed my mouth on his. A gruff moan seeped out of his mouth and tickled my lips as his grip tightened on my cheeks. Finally. I felt a small semblance of control. Nibbling on his bottom lip I ran a hand up the back of his neck into his hair while keeping my eyes focused on his. His exotic orbs glistened underneath the dimming light shining in from outside then disappeared as he clamped his lids close. Indolently I released his lip from between my teeth while gradually inching my eyes shut.

Running my tongue across his parted lips I glided it into his mouth, savoring the traces of cognac sprinkled with a hint of mint peppering his frenulum. I felt the evidence of his arousal pressed against my leg as his arms tightened around me. Possessively he pulled me deeper into his arduous frame. Holding onto a moan I coursed my fingers over his waves while slithering my tongue around his before slowly pulling back and suckling his bottom lip. He raked his hands up my back and underneath my shirt, dragging his hands up toward my shoulders he lifted my top away from my body. Listlessly I fluttered my lids open while unhurriedly disconnecting my mouth from his, allowing him to pull my shirt over my head. Tossing the tiny garment onto the floor he looked down at me.

"Fuckin beautiful," he breathed out in a low growl as his eyes traveled down my body then lazily returned to my face.

My mouth fell slack, but no words came out. Drawing in a mouthful of air I peered at the top of his head as he dropped down on his haunches, placed his hands on either side of my waist and yanked my shorts down to my feet. Caught off guard I stood frozen in place while bouncing my eyes over his crotched frame. The warmth of his breath dusted across my pelvis as he angled his head to look up at me.

"Lift your leg sexy." He slid a hand over my ankle, helping me step out of my shorts. "Now the other one," he instructed, smirking at me as I raised my other foot off the floor and out of the small material draped across my foot.

Dre remained stooped at my heels peering up at me with an intensity that made my breath hitch in the back of my throat. Slowly he glided a hand up my calf, using a little force he pushed my legs apart before continuing up the inside of my thigh. A knowing grin swept across his face, then quickly disappeared the moment his fingers glossed over the dank liquid dripping down my leg. A crinkle formed in the middle of his forehead as his brows furrowed, making him look deliciously sexy. Releasing a breath, I placed my hands in his hair and dropped my chin to my chest, watching him closely through the small slits of my lids.

The tip of his fingers brushed over my slippery fold before sliding inside and caressing me, creating a new wave of juices to ooze down his hand. "I think she's gonna miss me more than you."

"Umm." I fought to keep my eyes open as ripples of pleasure tingled in my toes, crept up my legs, fluttered in my belly, skirted up my neck, and prickled at the crown of my head. "Sh. . . she. . . she might."

The corners of his lips twitched into a subtle grin; one I would've missed if I wasn't paying attention to his every move. Pressing his thumb against my clit he swirled his fingers around my overly stimu-lated bud before gingerly easing out of my lubricated canal. His eyes remained fastened on mine as he drug his slick fingers up to his lips, slithered his tongue out of his mouth, and licked all traces of my arousal from his lengthy digits. I'd become accustomed to that shit. Hell, I even started expecting it every time he removed his fingers from my sex. But I'd be damned if it didn't turn me on every time, he did it. An appreciative groan tumbled out of his mouth as his hands returned to my heated flesh. Dropping my hands from his head I let them dangle at my sides as I continued to stare at him.

For the second time tonight, I couldn't ignore the uncanny sense of déjà vu as memories of our first time together flooded my brain. I remember vividly the exact moment I decided to stop fighting the undeniable attraction and insane chemistry between us. The moment I willingly gave myself to him. I could still see the look of shock on his handsome face and the noticeable tent in his jeans when my robe hit the floor. There was no doubt in my mind that he'd follow me back to my bedroom when I spun on my heels and left him standing in the middle of my entryway. What I didn't bank on, was him being one of the most selfless and passionate lovers I'd ever shared my body with. In hindsight I can honestly say, Dre had broken the walls of my heart long before knocking down the walls of my vagina.

The soft caress of his hand climbing back up my thigh snatched me out of my head, forcing me to focus my attention on him as he slowly hoisted my leg in the air and draped it over his globular shoulder. Thrown off balance I quickly adjusted my stance. I balanced my weight on the ball of my foot still planted on the floor and perched my ass against his hand. Dre helped hold me in place. He gripped my cheeks with one hand while the other rested firmly against the small of my back. Aligning his face with my pussy he breathed me in, growling low from the back of his throat he rubbed his nose across my skin. Instantly a jolt of electricity shot through my body, prompting an involuntary whimper to seep through my pursed lips. I was beyond aroused. My desire for Dre had surpassed anything I'd ever felt. I didn't just want him. I craved him, and the shit was driving me wild. I had reached the pinnacle of pleasure and was on the brink of an orgasm. But how? We hadn't even scratched the surface of foreplay.

What da fuck?

I was tired of thinking, exhausted from always trying to figure shit out while trying to predict the best outcome. I was done. I was ready to live in the moment. And at this very moment my body needed a release.

Staring down at the crown of Dre's head I slowly slid my eyes closed and exhaled. It started in my stomach with a tiny flutter then traveled to my pebbled nipples. Instinctively I brought my hands up to my small mounds. I kneaded my erect buds between my fingers as Dre planted feather soft kisses on the lower half of my body. His lips on my skin combined with the stimulation of my breast and my already roused state sent me over the edge. Clamping down on my bottom lip I willingly surrendered to the powerful tremors coursing through my body. A string of breathless moans toppled out of my mouth as my hands dropped from my tits and clamped down on Dre's shoulders. His grip tightened around my waist, allowing me the freedom to ride out my climax without falling on my ass.

"Damn Short Stuff."

A sheepish grin slid across my lips as my lids cracked open. "I don't know what hap—"

My words were silenced when his head dipped toward my sex and his tongue slithered over my slick lips. He teased me with soft deliberate strokes while meticulously gliding down my labia and settling at the apex of my ass. Releasing a muffled groan, he palmed my cheeks, spread them apart, and traced his tongue around my anus.

"Oh. My. Fuckin. . .Umm. Fuuuck." I slid my hands up his neck and buried them in his smoothly laid waves, desperately clinging to his soft tresses as his tongue lashed against my opening.

A soliloquy of breathless moans eased out of my mouth as Dre took me to new heights of pleasure. Taking his time, he grazed his tongue over my pulsating opening before sliding over my lips and rapidly swiping his tongue against the metal barbell sitting on my clit. Reflexively my grip tightened on his head as the walls of pussy started to quake. It was becoming harder and harder to keep my leg positioned on his shoulder. Dre must have sensed my struggle because he temporarily removed his mouth from my sex and carefully eased my shaking leg off his shoulder. Resting my foot on the floor he trailed soft wet kisses up my calf then rubbed his nose across the inside of my kneecap. I squirmed when he languorously dragged his tongue along the inseam of my thigh and was damn near shaking by the time, he made it back up to my pussy.

Staring up at me through the low slits of his eyes he ran his tongue across his top row of teeth. "You ready to cum again sexy?"

I shook my head.

He used his hand, one I hadn't realized he placed on my leg, to push them further apart. "Use your words Short Stuff." He kept his eyes stapled to mine. "Now, how do you want to cum this time?"

I opened my mouth to respond but quickly snapped it shut when the pads of his fingers glided up my thigh and across my clit. "Digital penetration? Or—" The corners of his lips tugged into a half smile before his face disappeared between my legs.

I felt his breath first followed by his soft lips then his tongue. Drawing in a mouthful of air I relished the feel of his tongue slithering over my clitoris, down one side of my lips and back up the other. I felt cheated when his mouth left my flesh and he slowly withdrew his face from between my thighs. "Orally?" He peered up at me waiting for an answer. "Which is it sexy?"

Dre had a way of snatching the fight out of my ass but not tonight. Tonight, I was revved up and ready to go. "I want you to taste me when I cum," I answered, holding his gaze.

"Say no more."

His head was back between my thighs before I had time to react. Covering my clit with his mouth he repeatedly swiped his tongue across it while suctioning his jaws like a vacuum. He created the most intense force of pleasure. My head dropped back on my neck and I stared up at the ceiling as my hands stilled on his head. Surges of elysium spiked in my nipples and trickled down my spine. I was on the brink of another explosive orgasm as Dre slipped his tongue into my folds while greedily slurping on my juices. He alternated his speed, increasing and decreasing based on the movements of my body and the sounds of my moans. Finally settling in a rhythm that had my knees weak he hummed from the back of his throat as he devoured me. I couldn't take it any longer. Filling the air with my unabashed moans I surrendered to the euphoria that swept over my body. Dre continued to lick and suck, gradually sweeping his tongue over my clit until my body stopped shaking.

Sluggishly he removed his face from between my legs and shifted his head to look up at me. "You good sexy?" He scrubbed a hand over his mouth, clearing away all evidence of my explosive climax.

I shook my head. "But I'll be better when you put your dick inside of me."

One of his full brows stretched up toward his hair. "Oh, is that right?"

The sound of Creed's collar jingling in the near distance stole our attention. We both shifted our heads in his direction to find Creed traipsing toward us. Stopping at my feet he rested his large head on Dre's knee.

"Put a pin in that. I think somebody needs to go out." Looking down at my beefy canine Dre brushed a hand over his head before slowly rising to his feet.

"I'll be right here waiting," I responded, leaning against the arm of the couch while watching him head toward the patio with Creed on his heels.

Digging my feet into the carpet, I readjusted my ass to fit more comfortably on my temporary resting place while keeping my eyes fastened on Dre. He'd just closed the door behind Creed and was making his own adjustments against the doorjamb while waiting for my dog to relieve himself and return to the door. He rested his right shoulder against the wooden frame and stretched his legs out in front of him, crossing them at the ankles before dragging his arms up from his side and folding them across his chest. His head faced the courtyard but the light shining in from outside allowed me to see the soft expression crest on his face.

Umm, I could stare at his ass all damn day.

I swiped my tongue across my lips and took my time dragging my eyes down his face, scaling them over his bulging biceps I grazed past his abdomen and settled on the large tent poking out of his sweat shorts. He was fully erect. His large appendage was trapped against his leg by the thin material of his cotton shorts.

"Aye, is it just me or is your dog takin forever to take shit?" His words slowly started to fade out as his head shifted away from the door and his eyes landed on mine. He caught me staring at his junk. I could tell by the crafty smile that played at the corners of his lips before he turned back toward the patio.

I didn't reply, instead I snickered underneath my breath while my eyes slid back down to his dick. Dre was right, Creed was taking an unusually long time. And his time outside was cutting into mine. I was still roused and judging by the size of Dre's erection so was he. It was time for me to handle that.

Pushing off the leg of the couch, I stood to my feet while sluggishly pulling my eyes away from his rod and dragging them back up to his face. I studied his reflection in the glass as I padded quietly toward him, stopping just a few feet away when he unhooked his arms and opened the door. The temperature had dropped substantially, sending a frosty breeze through the apartment. The hairs on my arms stood up and my nipples spiked on my small mounds, but I didn't let that stop me. Shaking off the tiny shiver from the temperature change I took the few remaining steps to reach him. Dre wasn't expecting me. His head was dipped toward the floor, watching Creed as he took his time ambling inside. He closed the door behind my leaden canine and damn near jumped out of his skin when my hand brushed across his back. I chuckled under my breath at his startled reaction but wasted no time ridding him of his shirt. He had on way too many clothes and I wanted him naked ten minutes ago.

Dropping his shirt on the floor I pressed my breast up against his back, hooked my right arm underneath his and laid my hand over his heart. I closed my eyes for a split second, lost in the melody of his heartbeat while synching my breathing with his. Slowly my lids fluttered open as my left hand rested in the waistband of his shorts. I stood there longer than I planned, just breathing him in. It wasn't until his head shifted over his shoulder to look at me that I remembered my reason for being in his space. A slick smile tugged at the corners of my lips as my hand inched down the inside of his shorts, over top of his boxers I caressed his stiff member.

A mouthful of air escaped through his parted lips. "Ugh. . . umm." That shit came out part grunt and part moan. "Why da hell you in front of. . ." his lids crept closed as I continued stroking him while planting soft kisses across his back, "this window and you butt. . ." a repressed groan tumbled out of his mouth, "ass naked?" He finally finished his sentence as his eyes cracked open.

Standing on the tips of my toes I trailed a string of kisses down his spine before removing my mouth from his buttery soft skin to answer him. "Becuz I don't give a fuck bout nothin goin on out there." I locked my eyes on his while tightening my grip around him. "What I want is right here and I was tired of waitin for it," I responded, letting go of his dick and maneuvering my hand inside his boxers.

He responded immediately. Quickly grabbing my hand, he stilled my movements. Slowly he pulled my hand out of his underwear, held me by the wrist and spun around to face me. Staring down at me through the cracks of his lowered lids his bushy brows scrunched up, damn near meeting in the middle of his forehead. "You are so fuckn hardheaded sometimes."

I couldn't help the defiant smirk that spilled onto my face as I watched the annoyance ease from his. In its place was a look that sent heat coursing throughout my entire body as his hooded orbs traveled indolently down my naked frame. When his eyes returned to mine, they were filled with pure unadulterated lust. And I be damned if that shit didn't excite me even more.

Ignoring the dewy mist gathered in the middle of my thighs I slid my arm out of his grasp and stepped forward, closing the tiny gap between us. Dre's hands immediately went to my waist and without warning he hoisted me into the air. The shriek that tumbled out of my mouth was loud and unexpected. Reflexively my hand flew up to my mouth while my other arm draped loosely over his shoulder as he settled me in place against his torso. Wrapping my legs around his toned waist, I dropped my hand from my mouth and rested it at the base of his neck, locking my fingers together to give myself a better grip. Silence clung in the air between us as Dre's eyes bounced around my face. He lingered at my pursed lips before returning his eyes to mine. Mesmerized by his penetrating stare I held his gaze while anxiously awaiting his next move.

I didn't have to wait long, removing one of his hands from under my ass he placed it at the base of my ponytail and tugged my face away from his. My chin stretched toward the ceiling, leaving my neck completely exposed. He mumbled something underneath his breath before his lips connected with my flesh. Soft warm kisses started at the base of my chin, sending a blaze of heat coursing all over my body. Clamping my eyes shut I bit down on my bottom lip when his kisses transitioned into an open mouth exploration of my neck. His teeth nipped my skin while his lips and tongue glossed over his bite. The skillful combination alleviated the sting while simultaneously delivering pleasure. A muffled moan slid out of my mouth as he glided his tongue into the crook of my neck. He took his time teasing me. He bit, sucked, and licked my most sensitive spot, triggering a string of stuttered whimpers as I wiggled against him.

Fluttering my lids open I dug my nails into his skin. "Baaaby."

Dre ignored my cries. Instead, he tightened his grip on my hair and dived into the other side of my neck. He repeated the same oral amalgamation. Licking, biting and sucking until I begged for him to stop. I was losing my mind. I didn't want or need any more foreplay, I just needed him. Pulling his face out of my neck he let go of my ponytail while quickly shifting his feet and switching our positions. I felt the coolness of the night's air on my back as he pressed me against the glass patio door.

He didn't speak right away, just stared across at me with a hard grimace crest on his face. "You drive me fuckin crazy. You know that?" I could see a semblance of a smile underneath his scowl before his mouth came crashing into mine.

He swiped his tongue over my bottom lip then slithered it into my mouth. Instinctively my eyes slid shut as I welcomed him. His mustache held traces of my scent while hints of my essence were peppered on his tongue. He was passionate in his pursuit, greedily rolling his tongue around my mouth while his hands moved busily below my waist. Fervently lashing my tongue against his I unclasped my fingers and positioned my elbows on his shoulders. I rested my hands in his hair, wildly running them over his waves while grinding against him. Dre placed his hands on my hips and carefully guided my movements. My lids fluttered open and a surprised shriek spilled into his mouth as the head of his dick slid inside of me. Peeking at me through his lashes he traced my swollen lips with his tongue before pulling his face back and languidly raking his gaze down my face.

"Is this—" he lowered me further down his rod, "what you—" An involuntary purr slipped from my mouth as I gyrated my hips on top of his rigid muscle. "Oh yeah, this is exactly what you were waitin for," he taunted, dipping his hips and matching my slow rhythm as he glided the rest of his dick inside of me.

My sex lubricated around his monstrous appendage, reducing the initial sting as my body acclimated to his girth. Dropping my head back against the glass I continued winding my hips while steadily increasing my pace. Dre's grip tightened on my waist and his face found its way to the crux of my neck. Clamping down on my collar bone he released a muffled groan. That shit turned me on. I placed my hands on either side of his face and drug his head away from neck, littering him with sloppy kisses.

"Dreee. Umm, baaaby," I breathed out in between pecks.

Scooting his mouth next to my ear he placed his hands on the sliding glass door, just slightly above my head. "What sexy?" He pummeled into me and stopped, just barely rocking his hips. "You need something?" He grounded deeper into me before slowly easing out and slamming back in.

My loud uninhibited cries reverberated around the quiet room as I found myself lost in ecstasy. Temporarily unable to move I let him do all the work. I felt like a little ragdoll as he fucked me slow and hard. My tiny body bouncing wildly against the glass every time he thrashed back into me.

This shit feels too damn good. Fuck!

"I think your neighbor can see us," he growled, pulling his face away from mine and looking me dead in the eyes.

"What?" I raised my head off the door and turned to the side. I couldn't see shit from that angle. "Why you say that?" I asked, swiveling my face back around to look at him.

He opened his mouth to respond but no words came out. Instead, he stared at me while slowly bringing his movements to a halt. *Oh, hell nah.* It was too late for the games; I was beyond the point of no return. Onlooker or not, I wasn't about to stop. Positioning my hands on his shoulders, I pressed into his dewy flesh while slowly bouncing up and down his dick, gradually increasing my speed each time I slid back down his lengthy rod. Dre removed his hands from the door and placed them on my hips. He didn't attempt to stop me, but I could tell he didn't know what to make of his newfound discovery. Me on the other hand, I could give ten shits who was on the other side of the door.

"You want to stop?" I slid up his engorged member until the head of his dick brushed against my piercing, then slammed back down.

"Arggh, shit!" His eyes squeezed shut then quickly fluttered back open.

Again, I scaled up his rod and back down, grinding my hips against his pelvis once he was all the way inside of me. "Ain't nobody pressed about Paige. I've seen her engaged in her own sordid activities on more than one occasion." I spoke those words in a matter of fact tone.

Dre's eyes stretched wide but the shit I was giving didn't allow them to stay that way for long. "Oh, word? So, what y'all just some damn exhibitionist out here?" he questioned, as his eyes rolled in the back of his head then settled on me again.

I couldn't help the chuckle that spilled out of my mouth. "I wouldn't say all that."

Squinting, he looked over my head peering out the door. "Oh yeah, she can definitely see us."

Another snicker passed through my lips as I worked overtime to take his mind off my neighbor. "I don't doubt it. But the way I see it, we got two options. Move from in front of this door or give her a show but none of those options involve stoppin. You pick."

When his hold tightened on my waist and his hips started moving again, I knew which option he'd chose. Happy that he was back in the moment with me I brushed my lips across his before quickly dipping my tongue inside of his mouth as my eye eased shut. He willingly accepted my slickened muscle as his tongue rolled smoothly over mine. Dre was deftly skilled in the art of kissing as he was love making. The aggressive yet yielding manner in which he lashed his tongue against mine sparked new levels of pleasure in my core as he strategically glided in and out of my slick canal, rubbing against my clit with each thrust. Tiny stars flashed behind my closed lids as I breathed him in. I savored his natural redolence while fighting to catch the impish whimper, the one that crept up from the back of my throat and seeped into his mouth. Dre acknowledged my unbridled cry by kissing me until I struggled to breathe. Panting I dragged his bottom lip down toward his chin as I lazily peeled my lips away from his.

The fluttering inside my belly paired with the involuntary constriction of stretched walls alerted me of my impending climax. Rolling my head back onto my shoulders I cracked my lids as my hips took on a life of their own, bucking heedlessly against Dre's body before abruptly coming to a complete stop. I was experiencing sensory overload— the kind where pleasure turned to pain then somehow morphed into unexplainable euphoria. Sliding my elbows down his dew-covered shoulders I dug my French tips into the meat of his neck, relishing the warmth that washed over my bare skin as the walls of the vagina quivered uncontrollably.

My head jerked forward at the feel of his breath against my misted flesh. Dre sprinkled a litany of kisses across my clavicle before shifting his face up to mine. "Yes, cum for me sexy," he coaxed, using his hands that were positioned under my ass to slide my stilled body up and down the full length of him.

A plethora of curses tumbled out of my mouth as my body shuddered on top of him. My nipples were beyond rock hard as fresh warm liquid spurted down his dick and slid out of my opening, drizzling slothfully down my legs. With his eyes fastened to my face Dre watched me through the small cracks of his lids, gradually slowing his strokes while patiently waiting for me to ride out my orgasm.

"I fuckin love watchin you cum." Carefully sliding out of me he lowered me to my feet. Confusion etched across my face as my brows descended toward my nose. "New position sexy. Don't worry, Imma get mine," he replied, damn near reading my mind.

He rested his hands on my waist again, turning me toward the sliding glass door. Yep, he was right, Paige was posted up on the low balcony wall sipping a glass of wine and staring directly into my apartment. It was dark outside but the faint light from the muted TV inside my living room combined with the light from the courtyard gave her a decent view of the libidinous activity going on between me and Dre.

"I told you homegirl was watching us." Pulling me a few inches away from the door he slid a hand up the middle of my back and gingerly pushed me down.

I assumed the position. I dropped my hands to the floor while simultaneously arching my back. "Well I suggest you finish strong and give her something to masturbate to later tonight," I declared, winking at him over my shoulder while making my cheeks clap.

His hearty chortle resonated from behind me as one of his hands came down on my ass. I yelped from the sting and surprise of the blow as I slid my head back toward the patio. Staring out the glass door my regard went across the courtyard to my voyeuristic neighbor. I scaled my eyes down her voluptuous frame as Dre teasingly rubbed the head of his dick against my creamy opening. He coated his erection with my natural juices before leisurely entering me.

"Fuck Raquel." I felt the full weight of his body on my back as his lips pressed against my ear. "Hold on, this is gonna be hard and quick. I'm ready to explode."

His raspy tenor tickled my eardrums and his words turned me on. Squeezing the muscles of my pussy I shifted my head to look at him. "I'm ready baby. You earned this shit." A lascivious grin tugged at the corners of my full lips before I swiveled my head back toward the door.

Standing upright he rattled off a string of expletives as he stroked me from behind. True to his warning he fucked me hard and fast. Listlessly he glided out of my slick opening and slammed back in, filling me to the hilt each time. The friction from his massive rod stretching me wide and his heavy sac brushing over my jewelry made my eyes roll in the back of my head.

The things this man does to my body is sinful.

He slinked his hands up to my shoulders and rested the weight of his upper body against my back again. "I fuckin. . ." he pivoted his hips up and grinded, "love yo. . ." he rounded his hips, stirring against my sensitive nub, "lil ass." His loud grunt filled my ears as he emptied himself inside of me.

"I love you too baby," I rasped breathless, as he lifted himself off my back and dragged me up with him.

He wrapped his arms around my waist and buried his face on the side of neck while carefully easing out of me. Satiated and damn near boneless I rested against his stout frame as my attention went back across the yard. Paige was still sitting out on her patio watching us. A crafty smile doned her full face as she sat her glass on the wall and extended her hands up in front of her face. Slow and dramatic, she gave us a congratulatory round of applause. I couldn't help the smirk that etched across my face as I dipped my head in her direction, subtly acknowledging her unsolicited approval.

"Fuckin exhibitionist," he huffed, while removing his arms from around my waist and smacking me on the ass before turning and sauntering out the room.

That made me laugh. A hearty chortle that rumbled up from the pit of my belly and spilled unapologetically out of my mouth kind of laugh. Paying my nosy neighbor one last glance I reached up and pulled the vertical blinds closed. *Oh, our next late night meet up is gonna be interesting.* My smile turned pernicious as I spun on my heels and headed in the same direction Dre had just traveled. Clicking off the TV as I passed by the coffee table, I exited the living room.

Feeling light on my feet and a little sore I trekked down the dark hallway with Creed trailing on my heels. The sound of Dre's light snore spilled out of my bedroom and resonated in the air around us. Creed stopped in his tracks and growled at the strange noise, charging toward the open door, ready to attack. Snickering to myself I watched as my protector slowed his strides while sweeping his head side to side, examining the scene. Gradually quieting himself he plopped down at edge of the door and I proceeded to the bathroom. I needed a bath or else my ass wasn't going to be able to walk in the morning.

CHAPTER TWENTY-ONE

*H*is large hands clawed up the back of my neck and rested in my saturated hair. He restricted my movements while forcing me further down his inflated rod. His choppy groans echoed around the modest sized bathroom, turning me on as I slithered my tongue around his lengthy shaft. Suctioning my jaws, I slowly dragged my mouth back up his dick while moaning from the back of my throat to create a vibrating sensation that I knew drove him crazy. Tepid water streamed from the shower head above us, cascading down my crotched frame. Dre's grip tightened on my head while his dick pulsated against my tongue. He was on the verge of an orgasm, spurring my fervent movements. Wrapping both hands around the base of his dick I moved them in opposite directions of each other, sliding them up and down his rigid member while rapidly bobbing my head in the same direction of my hands.

"Fuck Raaqueel," he grunted out the last part of my name as his large appendage jutted in mouth, filling it with his warm liquid.

I relaxed the muscles in my throat, gently suckling his sensitive flesh while swallowing his salty yet sweet semen. "Umm." Carefully withdrawing him from my mouth I swiped my tongue across his mushroom shaped head and lapped up the remainder of his cum.

I stood to my feet and wiped the droplets of water from my face before fluttering my lids open and peering up at him. A set of hooded hazels stared down at me as a contented grin settled on his face. Ignoring the obvious drop in temperature from the flowing water Dre enfolded me in his brawny arms. His chin rested on top of my damp mane while his nimble digits raked up and down my back. I melted in his arms, relishing the feel of his delicate touch as cold water rained down over us.

"Now what exactly did I do to deserve that?" His breathing was still strained, making his usually raspy tenor appear even deeper. Reaching behind me he shut off the water.

"Aside from, just being you?" I asked, reluctantly peeling myself out of his strong hold and stepping out of the shower.

I heard him chuckle behind me. "Yeah, besides that."

I peeked at him over my shoulder as I reached for my towel. "Just doing my part to help ease your stress. Did it work?" I hiked a brow as I waited for his response.

"Oh yeah. I feel like the weight of the world has been lifted off my shoulders." I could hear the sincerity hidden behind the humor in his tone. "Thank you."

"No thanks necessary." I dried myself off then wrapped the towel around my body as I made my way to the mirror. "What time are you meeting with your dad and coach?" I studied my reflection while surveying the damage my impromptu shower activity had caused my hair.

"In an hour. You want to do brunch after?"

I stared at him from the mirror, slowing raking my eyes down his naked frame before bringing them back up to his face. As much as I wanted to take him up on his offer, I knew we were pressed for time. Every minute of this day was accounted for. Today was draft day and Dre had several meetings lined up before the actual draft this evening. Although I knew his invitation was genuine, I also knew he didn't have the time to spare.

I shifted my attention back to my reflection while grabbing my paddle brush off the counter. "We don't have time babe. Today is about you. Don't worry about me. I'll grab something to eat before my hair appointment," I answered, peeking at him again while running the brush through my tangled locks.

I watched him through the glass as he ambled cooling over to me. His soft hazels glistened as they scaled down my body before indolently traveling back up to my face, meeting my curious gaze. Grateful for the small space I was sure he purposely left between us I studied his reflection in the mirror. His posture was confident, his smile contagious, but behind those colorful orbs was a hint of nervousness and doubt.

I stopped messing with my hair, sitting the brush on the counter I turned around and faced him. "I have absolutely no doubt in my mind that you will be drafted tonight but please know, that no matter what happens it doesn't in no way diminish your skills or define who you are as Andre Michael Cameron. Understood?"

"Thank you. I needed to hear that." Leaning into me he placed his lips on my forehead, lingering there before slowly pulling away.

I acknowledged his words with a wink before turning back toward the sink and picking up the brush. I resumed the task of detangling my hair, stealing quick glances of Dre, who to my surprise was still standing behind me. Flashing me a cinematic smile he placed his hand on top of mine and gingerly removed the brush from my hand.

A thousand thoughts ran through my mind as I watched him patiently comb though my tangled tresses. I still couldn't believe it had been damn near a year since we agreed to explore a friendship outside of her personal relationships with the twins. Who knew that in addition to building a strong friendship I'd fall in love with my new best friend? Dre was everything I could ask for in my first boyfriend and yet, nothing of what I expected from someone five years my junior. I had no idea what the future held for us, especially considering the likelihood he'd be a professional athlete after today. But I was here, and I was ready to see where our love would take us.

"All done Short Stuff." His raspy tenor pulled me from my musing as I looked into the mirror, meeting his gaze. Dre had detangled my hair and brushed it back into a neat bun, settled at the back of my head. "You sure you don't need anything before I leave?"

I shook my head while trying to contain the face splitting smile that threatened to spill onto my face. "I'm good. Go handle your business and I'll meet you back here when you're done."

Forty-five minutes later I was alone, stretched across the king-sized bed in nothing but my panties and bra. My stomach growled, reminding me I hadn't ate. Unfortunately, my nerves were fried, making me feel kind of queasy. Opting again to wait to pick something up before my hair appointment I rolled onto my side and sat up.

Running my hands over my damp ponytail I shook my head, partly because I couldn't believe Dre had fixed it for me but more so because I was going to let a complete stranger work on my unruly mane. That was new for me, considering that Carmen had been doing my hair for as long as I could remember. But according to her, I needed to wait to the day of to get my shit busted. So here I was, in a strange city with a scheduled hair appointment with someone recommended by Naomi, Carmen's homegirl whose shop she worked in when back in Columbus. The only consolation was my trust in my best friend and the respect I had for Naomi's skills and the value I placed on her professional opinion. Homegirl was cold and well connected, so when she called her friend here in Chicago to schedule my appointment, I graciously accepted it.

Lord please let this lady know what she's doing. I can't be looking crazy, not tonight.

Scooping my phone off the bed I lifted it to my face and checked the time. With a little over an hour and some change until my scheduled hair appointment I decided to call and check on my mother. It had been a little more than two months since her hospital spell and I'd been driving her crazy ever since, calling multiple times a week to make sure she was taking her meds and following her doctor's orders. But the purpose of today's call was a little different. I had some things I wanted to kick it with her about. After tonight the dynamics of me and Dre's relationship would change. I wanted to know how my mother handled my father's notoriety and see what advice she could offer me regarding dating a professional athlete. A damn celebrity, nonetheless. This was uncharted territory for me and although I didn't understand the dynamics of my parent's relationship, I was confident my mother could provide me with some useful insight on the situation.

I placed the phone on speaker and propped it on my knee. By the fourth ring my mother answered sounding unusually cheery and energetic as she spoke my name from the other end of the line.

"Hey beautiful, are you busy?" I questioned, excited by the exuberance in her tone.

My mother made a tsking sound and if I was in front of her, I was willing to bet it was followed by a wave of her tiny hand. "I'm never too busy for my darling daughter. How is Chicago?"

"Cold but I guess that's not really different from home and definitely no different from Cincinnati."

"This is true. So, what's going on, did you call to hassle me again? Because I thought we covered that earlier this week." Her tone was light but underneath the humor there was a slight annoyance mixed with appreciation.

It was my turn to release a noise from my mouth, smacking my lips my eyes instinctively rolled up in my head. "Nah, you get a pass today. I actually want to talk to you about something else. You got a minute?"

"Oh, sounds serious. Is everything okay?"

"Yes, everything is fine." I chuckled at the shift in her tone. Concern now overshadowed her lighthearted cheer.

My mother let go of a dramatic breath before speaking again. "Well spill it dear, what do you need?"

"Soooooo, you know tonight is the draft—" My words trailed off as I felt myself becoming emotional.

"And you want to know how I handled your father during his years in the NBA?" she reasoned, picking up on the purpose of my call.

"Um hmmm." That was all I could muster as my nerves fluttered in my belly, triggering my recent feelings of nausea.

"What took you so long?"

Pulling in a lungful of air I swallowed the excess saliva that had gathered in my mouth. I repeated that three more times before I felt comfortable that I wasn't going to hurl. "Come again. What do you mean what took me so long?"

My mother chuckled, and I couldn't tell if it was her nerves or because she found my ignorance amusing. "I've been waiting on this call since the day your father found out about the two of you."

I was completely lost but that came secondary to the shitty feeling that washed over me. In addition to feeling nauseous I now felt light-headed. *Fuck, I can't get sick today.* Hoping water would help I grabbed my phone off my lap and slid off the bed. I trekked across the room toward the mini fridge while concentrating on controlling my breathing. I told myself that would also help keep the contents of my stomach from spilling out my mouth.

"What does that mean mommy?" I flung the door open and grabbed one of the courtesy bottles of water, twisting off the cap I chugged back a hefty portion of the ice-cold beverage before I made it back to the bed.

"As a parent you make decisions that may not make sense to others, but you make them based on what you feel is best for your child and your family. I understand now, more than ever how the decisions I made for my family have impacted the one person I love more than life itself." She paused for a brief moment, signing audibly.

"I said all that to say, now that you've finally opened yourself up to love I know you must have questions regarding the choices I made in my marriage with your father."

I swallowed the fresh dollop of water I'd just took in, feeling a little more at ease about broaching this subject with my mother. "Well that wasn't exactly why I was calling but it is part of it. I mean, I'm not questioning your decisions I just want to understand them in hopes it will help me in my own relationship. And most importantly, I want to know how you handled being with someone in the spotlight."

"Well in order to answer that I think it's important that I start from the beginning. Everything that you think you know about me and your father is probably only partly true."

Suddenly I wished I felt better, for some reason it felt like this conversation would've been easier to digest after a drink or ten. Something I could've easily accomplished at the hotel bar located just outside the lobby. Unfortunately for me my stomach still hadn't settled so I had to tackle this subject sober.

"Um, okay."

Please don't let her tell me my daddy ain't my daddy. I can handle damn near anything but that.

The soft sound of my mother snickering pulled me out of my thoughts. "Get out your head dear. It's not like I'm going to tell you your father is an old boyfriend I was with before JB. Because Jonathan Wesley Banks is most certainly your father and he has the paternity results to prove it," she supplied, as if she could read my mind.

I wiped imaginary sweat from my brow. "Swoosh, you had me worried for a minute." I tried sounding playful despite the accelerated pace of my heart beating against my chest.

"Don't get me wrong, the things I'm about to share with you will be surprising and I'm sure hard to hear but it's time."

I chugged back the last of my water and tossed the empty bottle on the bed. My emotions were all over the damn place. "Well hell Vivika, just when I thought I'd calmed down you say that. Now I'm over here spazzing again," I admitted, wondering if I should've made this call at another time.

My mother's light airy chuckle seeped through the speaker and resonated through the modest size room. "I swear you are so damn dramatic." She made that damn tsking sound again before speaking. "I'm simply saying the dynamics surrounding the love triangle I've called a marriage for the past twenty-five years is deeper than you or your brothers know."

Oh! This is gonna be good. I could count on one hand the number of times I've heard my mother acknowledge my brothers' existence.

"Yeah, you've alluded to that."

"Such a smart ass." She spoke more to herself than me. "Any who, I'll spare you all the details. I'll give you the abbreviated version but will be sure to hit the important points. Is that okay with you little girl?"

It was my turn to giggle. I had rattled my mother's nerves, but she quickly recovered while putting me in my place in her own snooty way. "Yes mommy. And I appreciate the cliff notes seeing how I still have a hair appointment to get to."

"Well I'm happy I have the princess's approval." There was humor in her mocking tone.

"You do, you do. Now continue queen Vivika." I tapped an imaginary watch on my wrist as if she could see me.

"What time is your hair appointment? Are you sure you have time or even want to get into this right now?"

"I said I had the time. Now stop stalling woman and tell me what I need to know so I don't F this up with Dre."

A goofy snort slipped out of her mouth as her natural laugh boomed through the speaker. The one she only revealed when in the company of those she trusted, when she wasn't putting on an air. I wasn't sure what I said that had her cracking up, but her mirth was contagious. Before I knew it, I was laughing my ass off along with her.

There was something different about her. Her aura was calm and carefree, like the unspoken sadness she tried to mask had somehow been eradicated from her core. I could feel her light and cheerful energy through the phone, but I couldn't pinpoint the source. I made a mental note to ask her about it later as I sobered from my laughing spell.

My mother calmed down shortly after I did. Clearing her throat, I heard her speak to Gigi before turning her attention back to the phone. "I'm sorry dear. Where were we?"

"You were about to give me the deets on you and daddy," I answered, holding onto a giggle.

"Oh, of course. Now are you sure you want to get into this right now?"

"Mommy," I whined. "Please stop—"

"You stop it. Whining really isn't becoming dear."

"MOMMY!"

"I'm sorry baby but you really do make it easy. You're such a brat. That's your father's fault but I digress." She paused to chuckle at her own joke.

I looked at my phone and took note of the time. I wished I had more time to dig into my mother's happy disposition. I wasn't used to her being so silly.

The sound of my mother's voice brought my attention back to the phone. "As you know your father and I met at a popular sports bar in Atlanta when he was playing for the Hawks. The attraction between us was instant, and our chemistry was intense. Our relationship was casual. No titles, expectations, or commitment, just two adults enjoying each other's time until—" her tone softened, making it damn near impossible to hear her.

"Until what?" I found myself subconsciously mimicking her low pitch.

"Until six months into our. . . to use your term situationship, I discovered I was pregnant. It was then that the dynamics of our relationship changed."

"How?" I didn't mean for it to come out. I wanted her to tell her story at her own pace but before I knew it my thoughts spilled out my mouth.

"Like I said before, we weren't exactly a couple and the last thing your father wanted from a woman he was casually sleeping with was to find out she was pregnant with his child."

Now the paternity comment made sense. I rolled with it earlier, hoping it would be explained at some point in her story. And now, here we were. Of course, my father would want a paternity test if he and my mother weren't exclusive at the time of my conception. He was a celebrity for Christ sake, he had a reputation and a fortune to protect.

Wow, I couldn't picture my mother in a situationship.

"After the initial shock wore off, he agreed to be there for me throughout the pregnancy but not before delivering a blow of his own. He told me he had a girlfriend back home in Ohio and they'd been together since college. He said if you were in fact his child, he would be there as a father but our situationship was over. I was hurt by his deceit but respected his decision. I mean, it wasn't like we were in an actual relationship when I got pregnant."

"The woman, his girlfriend, who was it?"

Somehow, I already knew the answer before the question left my mouth but because I'd never fully agreed with my father having a whole other family, I never bothered asking either one of them how they met. But as long as I could remember Miss Brenda had always been a part of my father's life even before the twins were born. A thousand unspoken questions bounced around in my head as I tried to wrap my mind around my mother being the other woman.

"Brenda dear. It was and has always been Brenda." She confirmed my suspicions in a tone I wasn't used to hearing from her when mentioning my father's "mistress." There was no anger, sadness or bitterness. She just uttered a plainly stated a fact.

"Oh. Mommy I'm so sorry."

"Don't feel sorry for me sweetheart, I made my choices. What's done is done. I'm over being bitter and fighting to hold on to someone who doesn't love me." Again, there was no sorrow or disdain in her voice.

"Mommy daddy loves you. Don't say that," I pleaded, feeling sorry for her.

"Of course, he does sweetheart, but your father has never been in love with me. You see, after a photo of him and I leaving a doctor's appointment leaked he was forced to tell Brenda about me and the baby. She broke things off and two months later he came to me asking if we could give us a try, as an official couple. I was pregnant and hormonal, so I agreed. If I'm being honest, I hoped that the pregnancy would bring us closer. And it did. Your father and I developed a strong friendship that quickly turned into love for me." She snickered mockingly like she was laughing at what I'm sure she considered her stupidity.

I didn't know what to say so I waited for her continue.

"When you were born your father fell held over heels in love with you. It was my suggestion to establish paternity in order to secure your future in case things didn't work out between us."

"Seriously?"

"Yes ma'am. Being completely transparent, I did that for her not him."

"I don't understand. For Miss Brenda?"

"Un hun. Although I didn't think your father was still seeing her, I knew he still loved her. I also knew with him being a celebrity word would travel and she would know that you were in fact his biological child. It was my way of twisting the knife. I'm not proud of it, but it's my truth."

I formed an O with my mouth as I gazed out the floor to ceiling window across from the bed. My mother was right, this shit was deeper than I knew.

"I'm sorry, I'm dragging this out. Fast forward two years. Your father and were still going strong. I'd moved in with him and we'd built a happy life together. Later that year your father injured himself in the league. After months of hospital visits and physical therapy he finally relented, following the doctor's order to retire from the NBA. With no family aside from me and you he wanted to return to Ohio, but he refused to go without you, and I refused to go as his girlfriend. I've never regretted my decision to have you but forcing your father to marry me has been one of my biggest regrets."

"Mommy he had a choice. You didn't make hi—"

"That's what I told myself too, but he really didn't. He wasn't going to leave you," she reasoned, cutting me off.

"Wow, this is a lot to take in," I admitted, feeling a ton of unexplained emotions.

"I know dear, but it needed to be said. I'm almost done. We were married before we left Atlanta and lived a seemingly perfect life until about a year in when I got sick."

"That's when you were diagnosed with MS?"

"Yes. In the beginning I was really sick. Some days I couldn't get out the bed and it was very hard to care for you when I could barely take care of myself. It took time for my doctors to find the right medicine regime for me." For the first time since she started her story, she sounded defeated.

"I'm glad those days are over."

"Me too." Her tone had shifted back to her upbeat pitch. "I believe that was around the time your father reached out to Brenda again. It is my understanding that he asked for her help with caring for you during the day when he was work. I have no idea why she agreed but she did. JB said initially they were just friends but after a while temptation became too much and one thing led to another and bam. . . she was pregnant with your brothers."

My mouth dropped as tears formed in the corners of my eyes. I couldn't imagine my husband cheating on me let alone having a baby with another woman. The reality of my parent's lives had always been too much but hearing it in detail from my mother's perspective hurt. I wasn't mad at my father, I'd worked through that a long time ago, but I'd be lying if I said I wasn't disappointed.

"Why'd you stay?" I always wanted to know the answer to that question but never had the nerve to ask before today.

"That's simple dear, I stayed for you. Well at least that's the answer I told myself, my family and my friends." She damn near whispered the last part of her sentence.

"I don't get it."

"I don't expect you to sweetheart because you're not a mother yet but when you have children you'll understand. Growing up it was me, your three aunties, and your grandmother. My mother had four daughters by two deadbeat ass men. I swore that would never be me. So, when I found out about your father's infidelity, I made the decision to stay in my marriage in order to keep my family together."

I dabbed at the corners of my eyes, catching the tears before they had a chance to run down my cheeks. "You didn't have to stay in a loveless marriage for me. You already said daddy wouldn't leave me in Atlanta so why would he stop taking care of me if y'all divorced?"

A devious chortle crept through the line, drawing my misted orbs to the phone in my hand. "Before your father told me about Brenda and the twins, I had suffered two miscarriages in the span of six of months of each other. Because of my MS and the effects pregnancy could have on my condition my doctor recommended I stop trying and have a tubal ligation. So, I had my tubes tided three months before JB told me he fathered children with another woman. I was hurt and mad. Oh, I was so damn mad. She was having the babies I was supposed to have and never would. She already had his heart, so I refused to give her my man," my mother admitted.

"I spent twenty-five years telling the world while trying to convince myself that the reason I stayed with your father was because of you but the truth of the matter is, I was a bitter and an evil ass woman who was hurt and I wanted to hurt the two people I held responsible for my pain. It's not pretty but it's the truth. My ugly truth."

"I. . . I don't know what to say. Do I think I would've taken the same route, no. But by no means am I judging your decisions. I can't imagine that kind of pain and betrayal."

"Yeah but I didn't make it any better. If I would've let your father go when he showed me his heart was with Brenda, I would've spared all of us years of pain. Not to mention, the horrible example I displayed for the one person I told myself I was doing it for."

"Me?" I mumbled.

"Yes, you. The shambles of what I called a marriage and your father's outside life left you jaded. We—"

"I am not jaded," I countered, before she could finish her sentence.

"It took you twenty-seven years to commit to a relationship dear. You were jaded. But it's not your fault, that blame falls on me and JB. We didn't do a good job setting an example for you. And for that I'm truly sorry."

"Don't apologize. I had a good life and although you may not have set the example you wanted, I'm thankful for my upbringing." It wasn't until that very moment that I realized how much my made-for-tv upbringing taught me, good and bad.

"I tried, so it makes me happy to hear you say that despite everything I've shared with you."

"I meant what I said Vivika, there is no judgement here. Just a newfound appreciate for the woman I have the pleasure to call my mother. I do have a question though."

My mother chuckled, a sound that seemed to disappear the moment she went back in time to tell me her truth. "Yes, what is it dear?"

"If you could do it all over again what would you do differently?"

The line went silent, I assumed she was thinking about her answer. After a moment I opened my mouth but quickly snapped it shut when I heard her speak. "Nothing. I wouldn't change a single thing because despite everything I've been through I've learned some valuable lessons."

Now that's maturity for yo ass. My respect for this woman is at an all-time high.

"Like I said I can honestly say I stayed to hurt your father and Brenda, but it wasn't the only reason. I did love JB and I wanted my marriage to work. The bitterness came later, after years of trying to get him to love me like he did her. But that's water under the bridge now. Although JB and I have been through a hell of a time together it wasn't all bad. Your father was and still is one of my best friends. I will always love him because he gave me you. Not to mention he cared for me when I couldn't take care of myself. Life is too short for regrets. All I can do is move forward and learn from my mistakes. I just never wanted my faults to spill over into your life. Does that make sense sweetheart?"

I nodded my head as if she could see me. "It does. It makes perfect sense." I glanced at my phone. My mother and I had been on the phone for an hour now. As much as I hated to cut our conversation short, I needed to get dressed in order to make it to my hair appointment on time. "Thank you, mommy."

"No thanks necessary. I'm here whenever you need me. I take it you need to go?"

"I do." I stood up from the bed and walked over to the closet where Dre had unpacked and hung up our clothes.

"I understand. But let me leave you with this, you are not me and Dre is not your father. You are not doomed to repeat our mistakes. And regardless of Dre's upcoming celebrity status he is a man with values, and I don't believe he will compromise those values or risk losing you. I'm not saying he's perfect nor am I saying the temptation won't be there but as long as you two remain committed to the things that allowed you guys to fall in love with one another I have faith that things will work out."

I ran a hand down my tummy, surprised I hadn't shaken whatever was causing me to feel nauseous. "Thank you, mommy. I needed to hear that."

"You're welcome dear. Now go and get beautiful so you can support your honey. Call me when you get back to Cincinnati."

Snickering I held my thumb over the button to disconnect our call. "I love you Vivika."

"I love you more Raquel."

The line went dead with me staring at my phone with a goofy smile plastered on my face. My conversation with my mother was enlightening but it also left me so much to think about. My mother was right, I didn't know the half when it came to her marriage, but I was glad she shared her story with me. I just wished I had more time to process it. *Oh well, I'll deal with that when I get back home.* Sitting my phone on one of the built-in shelves inside the closet I yanked my all black Nike sweat suit off the hanger and held it out in front of me.

This will work, nothing to pull over my head after I get back from the salon.

Snatching my phone off the shelf I draped the jogging suit over my right arm and exited the closet. The next ten minutes were spent with me flying through the room, digging through drawers and throwing on my clothes before plopping down on the bed to schedule an Uber. I used Google maps yesterday to determine the distance from the hotel to the hair salon. If I left within the next ten minutes, I'd arrive fifteen minutes before my scheduled appointment. Unfortunately, that didn't leave me any time to eat but the way my stomach felt I didn't necessarily mind skipping a meal.

Glancing down at my phone I used my thumb to unlock it then immediately opened the Uber app to check the ETA of my driver, he was less than five minutes away. Slowly standing from the bed I plucked my purse off the chair by the door and headed out, walking toward the elevators at the end of the long hall. I pressed the button to summon the large car and went into my texting app.

Me: I hope your meetings are going well. Just wanted to let u know u were on mind. Love u <kissy face emoji>

My phone chimed at the same time as the elevator, stepping inside I lifted my phone to my face and read his response.

Dre: Swear, I just picked up my phone to check on u. Everything is going great. Can't wait to tell u about it. See u when u get back. I love you too. Oh, I got u a lil something something <winking face emoji>

CHAPTER TWENTY-TWO

*T*he rise of my cheeks caused my eyes to lower to a squint as I stared down at my wrist admiring the gold David Yurman Solari bracelet with eighteen caret gold and red enamel beads on each side. It was beautiful and paired perfectly with the sleek black gown and classy Decollete 554 Christian Louboutin stilettoes I was wearing, all of which were compliments of the man sitting to the right of me.

"I'm glad you like it." His raspy chords vibrated on the side of me, prompting me to shift my eyes up from my arm to find a set of hooded hazels staring at me.

"Huh?"

The corners of his lips twitched into a delicious smile as his gaze slid down to my wrist. "Your bracelet silly," he responded, lifting my arm out of my lap and grazing his thumb over my wrist.

I glanced down at his hand before slowly dragging my eyes back up to his face. Again, I found Dre staring at me. "I love it, but you don't have to buy me expensive gifts to express your love." I still couldn't believe he bought me more lavish gifts especially after gifting me a rose gold Cartier Love bracelet for my birthday just last week.

Lifting his hand off my arm he brushed his thumb across his nose.

"I know the difference between want and need, Short Suff. Maybe you should get more acclimated with them for yourself."

Smacking my lips, I rolled my eyes up in my head while simultaneously nudging him with my elbow. "Whatever smart ass."

He chuckled as he slid an arm behind me and wrapped his large hand around my hip, pulling me up against him. "How you gonna talk shit when you snuck behind my back and booked us a seven-day, six-night all-inclusive vacation to the Dominican Republic? I know that shit wasn't cheap." His neatly laid brows stretched high on his forehead.

I cut my eyes at him before sweeping them around the back of the car, checking to see if anyone was watching us. "That's different, it's your graduation gift."

"Well the Love bracelet was a birthday gift and this. . ." he ran his fingers over the gold bangle, "is a thank you gift."

"Thank you?"

Lowering his mouth to my ear I could smell the spearmint on his breathe. "Yes, a thank you for helpin reduce my stress this mornin in the shower."

"Oh, so we givin gifts for sexual favors now?" I turned and looked at him as a mischievous smirk slid across my pursed lips. "Then I believe you got some catchin up to do bruh."

A deep chortle flew out of his mouth as his grip tightened around my waist. "I'm playin. I just really wanted to get you somethin to show you how much I appreciate you."

"Ahh, thank you baby. I appreciate you too." I tried to hide the blush I felt creeping onto my cheeks by shifting my head away from his face.

His mouth was back at my ear. "But for the record, thank you and love can be expressed in various ways. And I plan to express the hell out of how much I love you and appreciate my graduation gift every day we are in the DR."

I felt the walls of my pussy throb in response to his licentious words as the tiny material of my satin G-string rode up the crack of my ass. "Dreee." I couldn't help the squeal in my voice as I peered at him over my shoulder.

"Don't act shy now. You ain't give no fucks when your neighbor was watchin us a few weeks ago," he teased, before kissing me on my exposed shoulder.

Crossing my leg over my knee I felt the warmth of my arousal in the pit of my panties as I shifted my head forward and darted my eyes around the car again. Thankfully everyone was too preoccupied to concern themselves with us. Madison sat opposite her father on the long leather bench all by herself. A pair of Apple Beats were neatly rested on top of her head. I'm sure strategically placed in a way not to mess up her pretty little hairdo. Her tiny legs were folded underneath her, elbows propped up on her knees, and her hands were stretched out in front of her face holding an iPad. She was oblivious to everything going on around her as she watched one of her little shows.

Dre's father stared at the top of Madison's head while chatting quietly on the phone. Every now and again he would look over at his wife. Shalonda was seated next to him engaged in what appeared to be a very animated conversation with Alex. The two woman seemed to be getting along as Alex listened intently about stories of Dre when he was a kid. The entire scene made me smile, almost making me forget that just minutes ago I was ready to jump in Dre's lap.

"Oh, so now you ain't got nothin to say?" His voice brought my attention back to him.

"Only because Maddy is here," I joked, referring to his previous comment while keeping my tone low so no one else heard us.

Dre pinched my side as his minted breath heated my cheeks. "Damn freak."

Smirking I opened my mouth to respond but quickly snapped it shut when I noticed Dre's father motioning for him with his cellphone. Dr shifted behind me before stretching out his long arm and accepting the phone from Tony's hand. He held it up to his ear and settled back against the seat while pulling me back against his arduous frame. The playfulness he used to address me just seconds ago was gone, in its place was a seriousness I wasn't accustomed to hearing from him.

Reasoning that the call was business related I directed my attention elsewhere, raking my eyes around the car until they landed on the group of people sitting directly across from us. Every member of Dre's immediate family was present. There was no fake airs or hidden animosity floating in the background as they conversed with each other. Egos and pride were left at home. Today they were just a blended family unit gathered to support Dre. Sliding my eyes over to Maddy I thought about what that must've meant to Dre. To me, it spoke volumes about their love for him.

I shifted against the rock-solid body posted behind me and reflected on my own family dynamics. Dre's story definitely didn't mirror mine, but I'd like to believe that our non-traditional upbringings played a part in our understanding of one another. It also made me wonder if my mother and Miss Brenda would ever come to an amicable understanding of their own, one that would allow my family to convene in one room together. I would like to think that after my conversation with my mother earlier that she had evolved. She sounded like she found peace. I just hoped that with that peace came under-standing.

"From your lips to God's ears," I breathed out quietly, as I slid my hand off the seat and placed it on Dre's knee. Instinctively he rested his hand on top of mine as he turned to look at me.

"Everything okay?" I twisted my neck to look at him as his eyes whisked over my face. "You look a lil flush."

I shook my head, afraid that if I opened my mouth to respond I would hurl. The only thing I ate today was a bag of mixed nuts followed by a bottle of 7UP, both of which helped settle my stomach. Unfortunately, that wore off approximately five minutes ago. Now I was forced to fight off the urge to expel the damn near to non-existent contents of my stomach.

Dre ran his thumb over the back of my hand while studying me. He squinted his lids and slowly raked them down my face before shifting them back up to my face. Holding his gaze, I mustered up all the strength I had to curl the corners of my lips into a soft smile in hopes it would diminish the worry present in his eyes. Gradually the muscles in his face relaxed. Relieved, my smile widened as Dre swung his head forward and called his father's name while easing to the edge of his seat with his arm hoisted out in front of his face. Tony responded immediately, meeting Dre's outstretched arm he accepted his phone and slipped back against the bench, resting his hand on Shalonda's knee.

Dre remained perched on the edge of the bench with his eyes stapled to his parents, discreetly swiping them between Tony and Shalonda before sweeping his low hazels over to Alex. I couldn't identify the look in his eyes as he continued to stare at his mother, but if I had to guess I'd say it was appreciation and maybe understanding. There was a peace surrounding him. The edgy uneasiness he tried to mask earlier had all but dissipated. He seemed relaxed and comfortable in her presence, something that I couldn't say twenty minutes ago when we all filed inside the back of the limo that Alex had rented as a graduation gift for her son. Comforted by his calm energy I peeled my eyes away from his face. I looked across at Alex just as she flashed Dre a bashful smile. Busted. Dre attempted to hide his smirk by covering his mouth with his hand while directing his attention my way.

Glancing at me out of the corner of his eye he slid back against the seat and stretched his long legs out in front of him, crossing them at the ankle. My regard quickly shifted from his feet to his face where I found a set of blazing sepias peering at me. "Why are you looking at me like that?"

"Two reasons." He slid his eyes down my face then slowly dragged them back up to meet my curious gaze. He didn't bother elaborating on his statement, he left it clinging in the air as he swiped his tongue across his bottom lip.

Reflexively I zoned in on his mouth before indolently sliding my eyes back up to his as I pivoted my head to one side. "Which are?"

He swatted me on the hip, reminding me that his hand was still on my body. "I'm waiting for you to sit back. I miss your body against mine." He paused, bouncing his sexy colored orbs around my face again. "But most importantly, I'm trying to figure out if you're really okay."

I nodded my head, feeling a twinge of guilt knowing I was sharing a half truth. But tonight, was his night and I didn't want him worried about me especially over something as small as a damn bug. Ignoring the heat, I felt from his penetrating stare I shifted my head away from him and snatched my clutch off the seat next to me. I could still feel his eyes on me as I hurriedly dug inside my bag and pulled out a mint. I unwrapped the small piece of candy and popped it in my mouth. I tried being discreet as I aggressively sucked on the minty treat, hoping the menthol would ease my current bout of nausea.

"Yeah okay, something is definitely off witcha ass but if you're gonna insist that you're good I'll drop it for now. But just know, after this ceremony I'm on yo ass," he spoke in my ear, scaring the shit out of me.

Cutting my eyes at him I smacked my lips while dropping my bag back on the seat. "You promise?"

"Promise?" he parroted, as one of his brows hiked up on his forehead.

"Do you swear to leave me be and let us celebrate you until after the draft?" I circled my head fully around to look him dead in the eyes.

Dre didn't answer me, instead the corners of his lips twisted up into a mischievous sneer as he eased back in his seat again. Giggling to myself I waited for his movements to still before inching back in my original spot and snuggling up against his hard yet welcoming frame. His hand returned to my hip and just like before he tugged, as if it were possible for me to get any closer to him. Happy that I was able to assuage his concerns even if it was just temporarily, I rested my head against his chest without a single thought given about my bountiful curls.

Finally, I was able to relax. My stomach had settled to a point where I no longer felt the need to vomit, making it easier for me to truly be in the moment with him. Smiling, I allowed my lids to drift shut as Dre hummed a song I couldn't identify, softly in my ear. His fingers drummed against my hip to the beat of his melodic tune, then casually switched to a smooth vocal rendition of Donnell Jones' "Where I Wanna Be". The syrupy bravado of his chords damn near serenaded me to sleep when I realized we were no longer moving. Fluttering my lids open I lifted my head off his chest and peeked at him out of the corner of my eye.

Dre winked at me as he reached inside his jacket pocket and pulled out his cellphone. "We're here but I wanna take a few pics before we get out. You up for that?"

I shook my head while leaning forward and craning my neck to the side. I continued watching him as he shimmed his arm from behind me and rested it on his capacious thigh.

A jolt of electricity shot down my spine when he pressed his chest against my back. "Aye pops."

Tony raised his face out of the crook of Shalonda's neck and shifted his head forward to look at Dre. "What's up son?"

Dre carefully maneuvered around me, making me aware of the fact that I was still pressed up against him. After unlocking his phone he held it out in front of him. "Can you take a few pictures for me?"

"Of course." Tony reached forward, grabbing the small device from Dre's proffered hand.

Chuckling I shook my head as Dre tapped me on the knee. "C'mon Short Stuff. You already know how we do."

Dre and I quickly fell into our usual routine, posing in various positions as Tony snapped away. We took several serious and semi-sexy photos before switching it up and taking a handful of funny pictures.

"Alright pops I just wanna take one more. Give me a quick minute tho." Dre turned and looked at me, his soft hazels scaling down my face.

Reading the concern in his eyes I flashed him a bright smile. "I'm good baby, I promise."

Dre nodded his head. "Coo. Stretch your legs out but make sure you prop your feet up on your heels, so the bottom of your shoes are showin. Got it?"

"Yep." I scooted toward the edge of the bench, placed my hands behind me on the seat and did exactly as Dre instructed.

Dre mimicked my movements. He inched to the ledge of the bench and stretched his legs out in front of him, propping them on the heels he ensured the bottom of his Mika Sky Christian Louboutin's were showing. "Okay pops, we're ready."

"I see you superstar," Tony teased, as he clicked away on Dre's phone.

"Thanks, old man." Dre extended his arm out in front of him, taking his phone back from his dad.

"Anything for my boy." Tony couldn't contain his beam as he bounced his eyes between me and Dre.

Dre saluted his father with a head nod before zoning out. He clicked on his photo app and scrolled through the plethora of pictures we'd just taken. I leaned into him interested to see how our mini photo shoot turned out when the door of the limousine swung open. Dre and I looked up at the same time just as Alex was being helped out of the car by the chauffeur. Shalonda followed behind her while Tony helped Madison, holding her little hand as she shuffled behind her mom.

"You ready son?" Tony asked, looking over at Dre who had returned his attention to his phone.

"Ready as I'll ever be. I'm almost done. Go ahead, I'll be right behind you," Dre answered, not bothering to look up from whatever he was fiddling with on his phone.

I chuckled at Tony as he nodded his head while shuffling out the car. Grabbing my clutch off the bench I eased forward, prepared to follow behind him but stopped when Dre placed his hand on my arm. "Hold up Short Stuff."

Sitting back down I rested my purse in my lap while turning my head to face him. I didn't speak, instead I stared at the top of his head waiting for him to look up at me.

"Look." A sheepish grin donned his handsome face as he handed me his phone.

"Oh, wow." I looked up at him. "Baby this is dope," I supplied, returning my attention to the image he had created and posted on his Instagram account

I stared at the last picture his father had taken with both of us sitting on the edge of our seats with our feet stretched out in front of us exposing the red soles on the bottom of our shoes. Dre had used an app that faded out the background, blurring our faces and emphasizing the color on the underside of our shoes. The caption below the image read, "Stepping into the next phase of my life with my best friend and love of my life #NFLDraft #RedBottoms #BlurredLines #RockysLove." Lifting my misted eyes, I shifted them toward Dre, who to my surprise was staring at me. I slid him the phone as I tried to control my emotions.

"You like it?"

I shook my head as a soft smile spread across my face. "I love it."

"Perfect." He glanced at our picture one final time before tucking his phone inside his pocket.

With my purse tucked underneath my arm I reached for his hand while scooting off my seat. "C'mon baby, your family is waiting."

Dre willingly followed behind me, holding tightly onto my hand as we exited the limo. His family stood underneath an oval enclave near a set of double doors waiting on us. Madison appeared antsy as she skipped around her mother's legs while Tony waved a hand at us, prompting me to pick up the pace. However, my steps were halted by Dre's firm grip on my arm.

I turned toward him, craning my neck up to look him in the eyes. "What's wrong baby?"

Dre didn't speak, instead he peered down at me. His burning sepias danced over my face before his lips crashed against mine. Purring I melted into his arduous frame as he sprinkled my lips with a litany of soft passionate kisses.

"Seriously? Boy if you don't get yo ass over here," Tony yelled out from behind us.

A gruff chortle spilled onto my lips before Dre pulled his face away from mine. "After you beautiful."

I pivoted on my heels and resumed walking. Dre strolled beside me, matching my assiduous steps. He kept me close, tucked at his side as we navigated through the crowd. People were everywhere. Sweeping my eyes from side to side I took in the family members, event staff, camera crews, coaches and their staff. I even caught a glimpse of a few celebrity athletes, and then of course there were the eligible draft picks. Suddenly I was nervous. This was it. We were here and in a few short hours Dre would be part of an NFL team. Swiveling my head to the side I squeezed his hand. Instantly his soft hazels were on me. My smile was so wide I thought my cheeks were going to split as I mouthed, "I'm so proud of you".

Dre leaned into me, placing his mouth next to my ear. "Thank you sexy I really appreciate that. And I really appreciate you holdin me down even tho I know yo ass don't feel good."

Once again, I found myself ignoring him while attempting to placate his worries with a bright smile. I made sure to flash both my dimples in order to sell the façade. With his eyes still stapled to my face he straightened to his full height. I shook my head and ignored his heated gaze while facing forward as we approached another mass of people. Unhurriedly Dre peeled his hand out of mine. He placed it on the small of back and carefully steered me through the maze of people swarming toward the door. I had lost sight of Dre's family amongst the large crowd, forcing me to rely solely on him to guide us to our destination. Lucky for me we didn't have a long journey. We reached the proud group in a few quick but measured steps. Tony separated himself from his family, making his way toward us. Easing out of the way I stood next to Alex as Madison walked over to me and grabbed my hand.

Tony stepped in front of his son and clasped a hand over Dre's shoulder. "You ready young king?"

Running a hand down the front of his suit jacket Dre looked his father square in the eyes. "I was born ready."

"That's what I wanted to hear." Tony dropped his hand from Dre's shoulder, pulling him into a quick hug before releasing Dre and running his soft ambers down his face. "Tonight, everything you have worked for will be acknowledged. You did it son and I'm so proud of you. This next level will come with its own set of tests, but I'm confident in the man I raised, and I know you will knock them out the park just like you've been doing. Remember to keep God first and everything else will fall into place."

"Thanks pops. You did a hella of job raising me and preparing me for this moment. I'm honored to share it with you and. . ." Dre looked over his shoulder, sweeping his eyes over each of us before settling them on Alex and slowly turning back toward his father, "my family. I love you, old man."

"Old my ass." Tony chuckled while resting his hand on Dre's shoulder again. "C'mon son."

Dre nodded his head then placed a hand up against his forehead, saluting his father. Watching the two of them made my heart swell. Tony was an awesome father and because of that he raised an amazing son. I couldn't help my face splitting smile as I watched father and son stroll back over to us. Dre stood next to me on the opposite side of Madison. He smiled down at his little sister while placing a hand around my waist.

We quickly fell in line with the crowd of people headed to the door, a few moments later we entered Auditorium Theatre. As soon as we stepped inside a middle-aged woman approached us and asked to speak with Dre. Excusing himself with the promise to return soon he left, trekking behind the short petite woman with dirty blonde hair. Not really sure what to do in his absence I took in the scenery. I admired the Romanesque style architecture while staying close to Dre's family as they continued navigating through the crowded lobby.

"I gotta pee," Madison whined, while tugging at my hand.

Looking down at her I smiled. "Me too. Let me tell your mom where we're going, and we can look for the restroom. Cool?"

Madison shook her little head as I stepped up to Shalonda and tapped her on the shoulder. After notifying of her of the plan and ensuring her I didn't mind, Madison and I shuffled through the plethora of people. I stopped a slender black woman wearing a vest and name tag identifying her as event staff and asked where the restrooms were located. Following her directions to a tee Madison and I made it to the other side of the lobby where the women's restroom was located without getting lost.

This shit is far as hell. I hope I don't need to use the restroom again before we leave.

Madison let go of my hand and bolted through the door as I held it open for her. Giggling I followed behind her and almost lost my footing when I was hit with a sudden bout of dizziness. I attempted to shake it off as I trekked toward an empty stall.

"Maddy, you okay in there by yourself?"

"Yes, I wiped the seat down and lined it with toilet paper," she called out behind one of the closed doors of a bathroom stall.

Swinging the door open next to where I heard her voice I carefully trekked inside and closed the door behind myself. "Okay, just let me know if you need my help."

I heard her smack her little lips. "Rocky I'm a big girl. Big girls don't need help using the bathroom."

"Okay big girl. Wait for me by the sink when you're done." I chuckled to myself as I pressed my back up against the door of my stall.

"Okay."

Slinking my lids closed I concentrated on my breathing while trying to keep myself upright. For the life of me I couldn't figure out the culprit behind my symptoms. I hadn't coughed or sneezed all day. My nose was dry as a damn desert and I didn't have a fever, but something was definitely wrong. My eyes sprang open as I drew in a lungful of air. Once again, I found myself focused on my breathing. Carefully pushing off the door I stood in front of the toilet. Using every ounce of strength, I had in my tiny body I managed to complete the task of relieving my bladder without falling square on my face.

"Maddy," I called out, as I let my gown fall back down to the floor.

"I'm here. I'm waiting on you like you said. Are you okay? You been in there for a long time." I could actually hear the concern in her little voice.

I walked out the stall and was surprised to see a line had formed. Women were lined up along the wall all the way back to the door. Cutting through the group of women waiting their turn to use the facilities I headed to the sink where Madison stood next to one of the hand dryers, waiting on me.

"I'm sorry baby. I didn't mean to take so long. I'm not feeling too good," I stated, looking Madison in the eyes. Eyes that reminded me of her brother.

"I'm sorry. You want me to call Cam Cam?" Lifting her arm in front of her face she stared at the blank screen of her smart watch.

"No baby, I'll be fine." I tossed my purse on the counter before pumping a dollop of soap into the palm of my hand. "You can make calls from that?" I glanced down at her wrist then shifted my head forward, cleaning my hands underneath the running water.

"Yep. Cam Cam got it for me for my birthday. He programmed his number, mommy, daddy, and my grandparent's numbers in it. You sure you don't want me to call him?"

I snickered as I opted to skip the hand dryer and plucked a few paper towels from the dispenser instead. "I'm sure. You ready?"

Madison's little head cocked to the side, letting me know I had asked a stupid question. *This lil girl is too smart for her own damn good.* Holding out my hand I watched as she linked hers inside of mine then followed behind her since it seemed she was leading me versus me guiding her. Feeling slightly relieved to have the support of her tiny body I fell in place behind her as she gracefully navigated us through the overcrowded bathroom and out the door.

Just outside the door I let go of Madison's hand. My arms flailed away from my body as my head shifted from side to side. "Shit!"

"Rocky."

Dropping down on my haunches I balanced myself on my heels while looking Madison in her eyes. "I'm so sorry baby, I didn't mean to curse. I forgot my bag in the bathroom, we gotta go back."

"ROCKY. ROCKY."

Fluttering my lids my eyes stretched wide as I stared at a frightened Madison. "What's wrong, why are you yelling?" I asked, trying like hell to concentrate on her little face.

"Rocky you're scaring me. You kinda blacked out. I'm going to call Cam Ca—"

"No. I clasped a hand over her wrist. I promise I'm o—" I couldn't finish my sentence, everything around me went black and I could no longer keep myself on my feet.

"ROC—" That was the last thing I heard as my body crashed against the floor and I lost consciousness.

***

*W*hat the hell is beeping and why da fuck is my head so sore? Oh shit! You passed out.

Slowly I peeled my eyes open while digging my elbows into a mattress. . . *where da hell am I?*

"Lay back down Raquel." There was a hint of sleep mixed in his raspy tenor.

Falling back against the mattress I slid my tired eyes in the direction of where I heard his voice. Dre stood from a couch located on the right side of the dimly lit room, aligned against the wall on the other side of a TV. I watched as he tried to mask the concern etched on his face with a soft smile as he approached the bed.

"How do you feel?" he asked, placing a hand on my arm and drawing my attention to the IV piercing my flesh.

I looked at the tiny clear tube responsible for filtering fluid into my body before settling my eyes on him. "I'm confused," I answered honestly, while attempting to sit up again.

Dre removed his hand from my arm and placed it on my shoulder, gently pushing me back onto the bed. "Stop trynna get up. Baby please relax." I glanced at the IV again before returning my eyes to his face. "It's just fluid. You were dehydrated when you got here."

"Dehydrated?" That came out louder than I intended.

Dre shook his head. "Yes, dehydrated Short Stuff. Would you relax. Please."

"How can I relax when I have no idea what's going on. Why the hell am I in a hospital? What happened?"

Dre opened his mouth to respond but quickly snapped it shut as a short black woman wearing all blue scrubs came bouncing through the door. "Miss Banks you're up." She strolled over to the bed, standing on the opposite side of Dre. "How are you feeling? You took a pretty nasty tumble. Does your head hurt? I can give you something for the pain." I remained silent as she grabbed my arm off the mattress and placed two fingers on my wrist, checking my pulse.

Gently placing my arm back on the bed, she moved on to checking my IV and reading my chart. "Well Miss Banks everything looks good here. I'll let the doctor know you're awake and he should be able to get you out of here soon. Do you have any questions for me?" She stopped moving and looked down at me.

I nodded my head before shooting my eyes over to Dre. "Okay, well you have a good evening and congratulations."

Congratulations. How did she know my baby had been drafted? Wait. . . Fuck, I missed the draft.

Hiking a brow, I waited until I heard the door to my room close before speaking. "Oh. My. God. Baby I'm sooo sorry that I missed everything. What team drafted my man?"

A meek smile played at the corners of Dre's lips as he ran a hand over my head. "Does your head hurt?" he asked, ignoring my question.

"No," I lied, anxious to hear his response.

One side of his lips twisted up in disbelief. "Then why are you flinching Raquel?"

"Okay, it's a lil sore but I'll live." I used my arm, the one not attached to the IV to swat his hand away from my head.

Dre snickered as she grabbed a nearby chair and pulled it up to the bed, plopping down in it he rested his hand on my arm again. "You know you scared the shit out of Maddy. I knew yo ass didn't feel good. Why didn't you tell me it was that bad?"

"Oh shit, Maddy. Is she okay?" I rolled my head to the other side of my pillow.

"She's fine. I FaceTimed her after I spoke to the doctor. She said to tell you she hopes you feel better soon."

"That was sweet of her. I didn't mean to scare her. Make sure you tell her I said thank you."

"I know you didn't, but can you please tell me why you didn't tell me how bad you were feeling?"

I shifted my head back toward him but focused my eyes on the wall behind his head. "I thought I could shake it off and I didn't want you worried about me. Tonight, was supposed to be about you but I guess I ruined that." I slid my eyes off the wall and looked at him.

For the first time since I opened my eyes, he flashed me a genuine smile. "You didn't ruin anything. Stop being dramatic."

"Dramatic? I missed your moment Andre. A moment you were adamant you wanted me present for."

"Welp, neither of us were there so it's not like I experienced it without you."

Tears formed in the corners of my eyes. "I'm sorry. You should've stayed," I whispered, as the tears cascaded down my cheeks.

Pushing his chair back as he stood, he placed a hand on my face and gingerly swiping my tears away. "You got serious issues if you think that draft meant more to me than you. I just wished you would've told me how you were feeling."

"What would that have changed? It's not like you could've stopped me from fainting."

"Not the point hard head. You could've really hurt yourself or worse—" His words trailed off as he took his seat again.

"I'm sorry. I guess I underestimated how bad it really was. But I don't want to talk about that anymore. Not right now anyway. The nurse said congratulations, so tell me who my man will be playing for this fall?" I hoped the excitement in my voice masked the worry lying dormant in the back of my head.

Dre's eyes lit up while a Kool-aid size grin etched across his face. "Your man won't be too far from home. I was drafted number one by the Akron Avengers. But Samantha wasn't congratulating me. Well, not directly."

"Congratulations That is so freaking exciting. How do you feel? How'd you find out? What did your par—" I fired off question after question until something dawned on me. "Who the hell is Samantha?" I asked, finding the button that allowed me to raise the bed into a sitting position.

Dre chuckled as he raised my arm off the mattress. Dragging his hand down to mine he intertwined our fingers. "Samantha is your nurse silly."

"Why in the hell would she be congratulating me?"

Dre stared at me but didn't speak. Slowly his smile faded as an unreadable expression settled on his face. His eyes dropped down to my hand and lingered there for what felt like an eternity before easing back up to my face. "You're pregnant Raquel, we're having a baby."

TO BE CONTINUED...

ACKNOWLEDGMENTS

Beta Readers

E. Aekins, E. Franklin, N. Hanks, T.Harlin, H. Price, M. Tuff

Thank you for your time, support, and honest feedback. I appreciate each and every one of you. You took this journey with me, some of you one slow chapter at a time, you helped give me the push I needed to see this project through. Your encouragement and desire to see me win has been invaluable. Thank you for believing in me and helping me see past my fears.

Editor - *Amber Williams of Align Editorial*

Your professionalism, dedication to my project, and attention to detail helped transform my manuscript into a novel. Not only did you correct my errors, but you took the time along the way to teach me and help me become better at my craft. Thank you for being available to meet my needy ways. If ever you were frustrated with my millions of questions you never let it show. I truly appreciate you and look forward to working with you again in the future.

Aquarius Creative Agency - *MT Dixon*

There are no words to describe what you've done for me. You tackle so much and yet you've extended yourself to me beyond your professional services. Thank you for being available and for answering my gazillion questions without ever showing your frustration. Thank you for taking time away from your millions of projects to just be you. Your energy is amazing, and I am so glad I found you. Your desire to see everyone have a seat at the table while knowing it won't affect your plate is refreshing. I cannot say it enough, THANK YOU. And my cover. OMG, it is phenomenal. You took what I had in my head and brought it to life. Your professionalism and dedication to your craft is reflected in your work. I can't wait to see what you do with my next project.

Photographer - *Robin Bowling*

You are truly a sweetheart. Thank you so much for extending yourself to me, especially last minute. Your spirit and energy are everything. There are no words to express how much I appreciate you.

Special Thanks:

Ebony Aekins (Twin)

I know I already mentioned you, but I don't think you truly understand how much your support means to me. I honestly don't think there would be a book if it weren't for you. I never thought I'd have bigger cheerleaders than my parents, Boog, and my hubs but you have now been added to that list. Twin your energy is everything. You don't know how many times I was ready to scrap this whole project, and not because I didn't believe in my story but because I let fear paralyze me. It was in those times I would receive a random text from you about something I wrote or asking where I was in the process. Something that may seem small to you was major in helping me push through. You truly are heaven sent. Thank you for believing in me and my pen.

Honesty Price

I felt compelled to list you here because you have been absolutely incredible. As a new author trying to navigate through the self-publishing world it can be overwhelming. So, to find someone willing to share information, their experiences, and resources has been invaluable. Not to mention your encouragement and support. Your quick wit, infectious humor, and honest feedback helped quiet that little voice of doubt in the back of my head. You're a true gem. Thank you for holding me accountable and pushing me. I appreciate you.

Karla Harlin

Thank you so much for being the face of Rocky. You helped bring my words to life. I appreciate your willingness to do whatever it took for us to capture her. Thank you for your support, words of encouragement, and for believing in my gift. I love you to pieces.

L. Belvin, M.T. Dixon, S. Holmes, C. C. Jones, D. Little

Thank you so much for taking time away from your craft to answer my questions.

Readers

Thank you for taking this journey with me. I hope you enjoyed this story and will continue down this path with me as I bring you more stories celebrating black love and families. Thank you for taking a chance on a new author.

To the Most High

Everything I do is made possible because of you. Thank you for giving me each day to get this thing we call life right. I will continue to live my life for you while giving you all the praise and glory.

Lastly

To anyone I may have forgotten, please charge to my head and not my heart.

ABOUT THE AUTHOR

Born and raised in Columbus, Ohio Tereesa L. Tuff attended school at the University of Cincinnati. Graduating with a bachelor's degree in criminal justice and a minor in psychology she has worked in the social service field for the past eighteen years. In her spare time Tereesa enjoys reading, writing, spending time with her family, and catching up on her favorite shows. An avid reader and supporter of stories highlighting black love and families Tereesa has transitioned from reader into author, penning her debut novel in 2020.

Where you can find Tereesa L. Tuff:
www.instagram.com/tereesaltuff
www.facebook.com/tereesaltuff
Website coming soon.

Made in the USA
Monee, IL
31 March 2020